Mary Brock Jones lives in New Zealand but loves nothing more than to escape into the other worlds in her head, to write science fiction and historical romances. For many years, she was a sedate office worker by day and a frantic scribbler by night.

Her parents introduced her to libraries and gave her a farm to play on, where trees became rocket ships and rocky outcrops were ancient fortresses. She grew up writing, filling pages of notebooks and filling her head with stories but took a number of detours on the pathway to her dream job. After raising four sons, a career as a government veterinarian and more than one house renovated, her wish came true.

To keep up to date with her latest news and releases, sign up to her newsletter here:
www.marybrockjones.com/

Or find Mary here:
http://www.marybrockjones.com/
https://www.facebook.com/MaryBrockJonesAuthor
https://twitter.com/MaryBrockJones

By Mary Brock Jones:

NZ Historical Romances

A Heart Divided
Swift Runs the Heart

Hathe Series

Resistance: Hathe Book One
Pay the Piper: Hathe Book Two
Toil and Strife: Hathe Book One and Two
Aftermath: Hathe Book Three

Arcadia Series

Torn
Taken
Exiled

EXILED

Arcadia Book Three

Mary Brock Jones

Mary Brock Jones

Auckland, New Zealand

Author: Mary Brock Jones
Published by Mary Brock Jones
RD 1,
Warkworth, New Zealand 0981
www.marybrockjones.com

Book Layout © 2017 BookDesignTemplates.com

Cover design by Amygdala Design. www.amygdaladesign.net

Exiled/ Mary Brock Jones
ISBN: 978-0-473-63417-9

CONTENTS

CHARACTER LIST AND GUIDE TO PRONUNCIATION

Mountainer region names describe a person's closest family connections. The emphasis is usually on the first syllable, but this can vary.

Mountain Language Sounds:
- 'ch at the end of a word - like the Scottish ch.
- 'h in the pronunciation guide indicates a degree of aspiration in the sound.
- a further, slight aspiration is shown by an apostrophe just before the letter in the pronunciation version (italicized - stress syllable shown in bold)

CHARACTER LIST

MAIN CHARACTERS

Seolta mar Bram an Scathach den Coille: Second brother, generally held to be the cleverest (or most cunning) of the den Coilles.

*See-**ole**-tar mar Bram an **'Ska**-thar'ch den Coyle.*

Seolta son of Bram (father) and Scathach (mother), of the family Coille.

Anyara a Prithand2: A biome scientist from the Surned system, based on Kevand Station.

Name in mountainer style:

Anyara ingh Gevard an Hrefne (no family name as the Surned naming convention doesn't use surnames. Prithand2 is Anyara's habitat of origin).

*An-**Yar**-ar ine **Gev**-ard an **'Href**-nay*

Anyara, daughter of Gevard (father) and Hrefne (mother).

DEN COILLE FAMILY

Bram mar Gliocas duine Scathach den Coille: Father and head of den Coille.

*Bram mar **Glee**-o-cas d'win **'Skar**-thar'kh den Coyle*

Bram, son of Gliocas, husband to Scathach, of the family Coille.

Scathach ingh Coibhneas bean Bram den Coille: Mother and doctor. Head of Manascraoch Hospital.

*'**Ska**-thar'k ine **Coy'**-nee-ars bee-**arn** Bram den Coyle.*

Scathach, daughter of Coibhneas, wife of Bram, of the family Coille

Samhchair ingh Bram an Scathach den Coille: Eldest sister and doctor.

Sarm-**'hair** ine Bram an **'Ska**-thar'ch den Coyle

Samhchair, daughter of Bram (father) and Scathach (mother), of the family Coille.

Cumchdach mar Bram duine Anna den Coille: Second child and eldest den Coille brother. Heir to the head of Den Coille. Married to Anna ingh Eolas bean Cumchdarch den Coille.

Coo-'var'kh mar Bram d'win Anna den Coyle

Cumchdach son of Bram, husband to Anna, of the family Coille.

Anna ingh Eolas bean Cumchdarch den Coille: wife of Cumchdach duine Anna den Coille.

*Ann-ar ine **Ee-o-larss** bee-**arn Coo**-'var'kh den Coyle.*

Birth name: **Anna ingh Eolas an Sumhneas den Falasch.** (Anna, daughter of Eolas and Sumhneas, of the house of Falasch).

*Ann-ah ine **Ee**-oh-lars an **Soov**-nee-ars den **Far**-lash.*

Seolta mar Bram an Scathach den Coille: Second brother, involved in systems and trade policy.

See-**ole**-tar mar Bram an **'Ska**-thar'ch den Coyle.

Ceart mar Bram an Scathach den Coille: Third, largest and quietest brother.

Kee-'airt mar Bram arn **'Ska**-thar'ch den Coyle.

Fioruisghe ingh Bram bean Caleb den Winter: younger den Coille daughter. An ecoengineer with the Survey and head of the Mountain zone survey team. Married to Caleb Winter.

Fee-or-**'hrish**-gay ine Bram bee-**arn Kay**-leb den Winter. Fioruisghe, daughter of Bram, wife of Caleb, of the family Winter.

Aigherach mar Bram an Scathach den Coille: The youngest den Coille.

Aye-ger-ar'kh mar Bram an **'Ska**-thar'kh den Coyle.

Den Coille: name of the festia pollen company owned by the den Coille family. Wealthy food company in the central continental zone, Protos.

WINTER FAMILY

Sol Winter: father and head of Winter Solaris.

Helena Bascombe Winter: mother.

Caleb Winter: Eco-engineer with the Survey. Married to Fioruisghe (Fee) den Coille Winter.

Ethan Winter: middle brother. Deputy head of Solaris.

Sarwenna Beren Winter (Sar): Eldest daughter of the Beren family and married to Ethan Winter. Union Representative for the Sulwith solar field workers.

Silas Winter (Si): youngest brother. Systems programming genius.

Winter Solaris: the solar energy company owned by the Winter family, usually shortened to Solaris. The dominant supplier of solar sourced energy on Protos and owner of the Sulwith solar field.

OTHERS

Marshal Marco an Fallon: Supreme Field Commander of the Federal Marshals of Arcadia, the planetary police force.

Deputy Malgrave: A past deputy to the Alliance representative on Arcadia.

Hilmar a Kevand3: representative of the off-world company Kevand3 from the planet Surned.

Captain Siebez: Captain of a free trader space ship.

Commander Talav: Captain of the Alliance Cruiser *Best Order*.

Administrator Sephtax: Alliance Patrol official and interrogator.

Jinke Wago: Social organiser in the Arcadian embassy on Alliance Central.

Zrah M'Senti: the senior marshal attached to the Arcadian embassy on Alliance Central.

Larena: biome student at the Alliance Academy.

Menta: biome student at the Alliance Academy.

Binku Vydayun: an Alliance official in the Biotics Department.

Ambassador Dysun: Arcadian ambassador to Alliance Central.

Advisor Broder: An Arcadian biome specialist in the Ecological Survey head office.

Eolas den Falasch: The head of a Mountainer export company. Father to Anna bean Cumchdach den Coille.

Meth Varkan: A major Alliance banking consortium.

Fongma Consortium: A major Alliance chemical company.

Esteemed Scholar Tularin Nanko: Senior liaison officer with the Alliance Academy.

Councillor Kamesh: The senior Alliance councillor in charge of both the Security and InterAlliance Cooperation agencies.

Messera Yarma: Secretary-General of the Alliance Council.

OTHER TERMS

Upper House: The upper house of the Arcadian government. Members are titled Representatives (eg Representative Joe Gibb).

Lower House: The Federal Assembly of Arcadia. Members are Councillors.

Regional House: Local government body, governing a particular region eg Protos Central, which includes the Plains, Mountainer country and Deadlands zone.

Moons: Jacopus is the dominant and most functional moon. The other, small asteroid like moons are only visible to the naked eye in certain geographic locations, depending on the coordinates and a clear sky eg the Deadlands beyond Sulwith.

Protos: main (eastern) continent.

Deuteron: second (western) continent.

Feldwesten: third (southern) continent.

Mountainer Country: The west coast and western slopes of the Western Ranges of the central zone of Protos. Home region to the den Coille family.

Deadlands: the desert region of the eastern part of Protos central.

Nieten: native grazing animal farmed for meat and hides.

Wernet: small bloodsucking animal (like hornet equivalent).

Dridust: The largest town on the Plains. Site of the Solaris head office and the main hospital for the Plains region.

Manascraoch: home city of the den Coilles. A fabled Mountainer city, built entirely in the branches of enormous baullnia trees.

Festia: A swamp loving tree and source of the edible pollen sold by the Den Coille company.

Brakka: A derogatory slang word. (Also means a small, ground dwelling pest animal).

Rakter: A vicious, ground predator of the Plains desert. Cunning and devious. A smile like a rakter bite means one that is untrustworthy and dangerous.

Glitchit: A small, ant-like bug which stores water in an underground communal nest.

Falk: The flying predator of the plains.

Foxllar: A Plains ground predator which hunts nieten.

Chapper: A ground dwelling animal used for food.

Smak: Teenage slang for awesome, great, good.

Dask: The equivalent of coffee and the main stimulant drink used on Arcadia.

Nanoglit: A very small amount.

Ganda: a small, ground dwelling animal of the plains which hides in burrows from avian predators.

Fricha: a popular strategy game, the Alliance equivalent of chess.

MEASUREMENTS

Arcadia uses decimal based, Standard Galactic units for distance, time, mass etc. They have been expressed here in current day terms i.e. second, hour, day etc. However, that is only a current day translation. The Standard Galactic units used throughout the Alliance, irrespective of planetary or deep space location, are based on Natural Units of measurement i.e. on universal physical constants independent of planet or spatial location. On Arcadia, they are roughly equivalent to the following current Earth measurements.

DISTANCE

1 Standard galactic metre is roughly equivalent to 1.5 metres or 5 feet.

Standard galactic kilometre (generally referred to as Kays) = 1000 SG metres.

TIME

Standard second is equivalent to 5 metric seconds.

Standard minute = 10 standard seconds.

Standard hour = 100 standard minutes, and is equivalent in usage to an hour, but in time is almost 1.5 hours

CHAPTER ONE

The planet Arcadia receded below him, a patchwork of blue and green fading into the dark. The trip on the shuttle to the space hub had been bad enough, but now he was on board an interplanetary ship and watching his world slowly and inexorably disappear from sight, taking with it everything he'd known for certain since birth. Even his name. He was plain Seolta den Coille on the passenger list. Seolta mar Bram an Scathach den Coille was banished with him. Seolta, son of Bram and Scathach, of the house of Coille. A man with a family, a home, a land like nowhere else.

A family and a home that he had thrown away in a singular act of stupidity. Out his porthole window, the sharply defined outlines of mountains, plains and sea dwindled to splotches of colour, then to a sphere glowing in the dark, then nothing as his ship twisted away from the planet and headed into the void of space.

All he had left was his assigned duty. Marshal an Fallon's order had been clear and unequivocal.

"Find out who's behind the plots against us."

Find out and report back, that meant. Don't do anything else. Don't make things worse than you already have.

We don't trust you, it meant.

Only the debt he owed to an Fallon had kept him quiet. The man had led those who broke him out of prison and saved his life, a debt he could never repay. He hadn't even tried to, embarking instead on a stupid quest for revenge that had cost him everything he valued from those who mattered most to him.

You betrayed us once. We will not let it happen again.

His family had farewelled him with pity and closed mouths. His older sister had tried to say he could return one day, but he knew the truth. A sentence of exile was forever.

He shut his eyes to banish the blackness out the view port and heard with relief the signal for translation. He'd flown in space once before and remembered the stark warnings to all passengers. He wasn't ready to die yet, whatever he might face, and dutifully settled into his floating pod. Escape came as the hiss of the drug infusions at last gave him oblivion.

When he woke, days later, he had a headache, a dry mouth, and the knowledge that he was worlds away from home. Below floated the station hub where he must change ships.

His route had been carefully mapped out by the Galactic Ministry offices on Arcadia, along with exhaustive instructions on whom to talk to and whom to absolutely avoid.

Top of the second list: Deputy Malgrave of the Alliance and Hilmar a Kevand3 of the planet Surned—the two offworlders who had led him into this hell in the first place. He'd thought himself so clever, but all the time they'd been the ones laughing. He'd been such a fool.

A com chime warned him to prepare for landing and he turned in relief to readying for disembarking. Too soon he was part of a crowd of passengers following station guidelines and waiting for clearance into the hub. A sharp odour of disinfectants and machinery stung his nose, and the underlying mechanical hum of the station systems throbbed through his feet. Missing was the constant motion of the living branches of home as rigid metal engulfed him. This was no planet. He remembered the strangeness from his one other off-world trip, the uncertain bounce to his stride from the lighter gravity of a standard space habitat, but that time it had been part of the collected memorabilia of a tourist soon to return to the normality of home.

Now, it must become his normal.

"Messer den Coille? If you will follow me, please." The dry voice spoke in Standard, using the common off-world form of address instead of Ser den Coille, but Seolta recognised with relief the trace of an Arcadian accent. The Galactic Ministry had not totally abandoned him. That they only wanted to ensure he didn't cause trouble and completed his mission didn't matter. Right now, he was grateful for their help. He nodded at the man and reached out the wrist bearing his com patch to confirm his identity.

"Not necessary, Messer. The system has already scanned and registered you."

He should have expected it, he supposed. The Ministry wasn't about to let him roam free to cause trouble. He plastered a concealing smile on his face but had no doubt the agent saw through it, saw the reality of a man with his pretensions shattered beyond repair. He dutifully picked up his personal bag and followed his guide out into the station.

The crowds thronging the thoroughfare matched the worst of Urbis in carnival time. He fended off one more elbow in his side and winced at a jab to his foot. A hand touched his arm and his guide pushed him into a gap and towards a nearby lounge.

"Your next ship departs at station standard, five point seven hours. No one will come in here. You should be safe till then."

"Thank you, Ser…"

"Messer is enough." No name to use against the man. "I will be back in time to see you to your ship."

The small room held all he would need but no more. Seolta roamed the space, feeling the walls crowd in. He checked his timer. Still hours to go. He'd been certain more time had passed. This room was too much like his never-to-be forgotten prison cell.

He couldn't stay in here. Not if he wanted to stay sane. He tried the door, found it locked, then placed his com against it. The work of only a few moments had the lock disengaged. His Ministry file must be missing a few salient facts. He grinned. The room's sensors would soon alert the agent, but he'd be gone by then. Pulling up the collar of his tunic and adopting a slouch far from his usual posture, he eased his way out of the room and soon mingled with the crowds filling the public walkways. Interim HubFourX was a major hub point, with connections to Alliance Central, capital of the Alliance, and three other major planetary routes. The owners of the station were rumoured to number among the wealthiest in the Alliance. In another time, he would have followed that interesting fact to a useful conclusion, but right now he had other concerns.

There was one place in the Alliance they had barred him from visiting.

"Do not, under any circumstances, go anywhere near Surned or Hilmar a Kevand3," had said Marshal an Fallon at the end of that excruciating last interview. "He is no longer your concern and you can only cause more harm than you have already."

They were wrong. He'd already hurt his planet and his family as much as it was possible and someone had to pay for that. Seolta had unfinished business on Surned and that was something he never tolerated.

He made his way to the main boards, easing into a niche where he could watch the travellers accessing various ticketing and route schedules while keeping an eye out for his guide. The Ministry might have decided where he should go, but Seolta had different plans.

"Hey, stop!"

A woman's screech and a frantic, "Thief! Stop him," split the concourse.

He'd learned early to listen closely to those around him, and the one man he'd met from the planet Surned had a unique accent. Dry, uncaring, metallic. An accent his dealings with Hilmar a Kevand3 had taught him to loathe. In this woman's mouth, though, the accent sounded none of those things. A flurry of movement, then she came into view. Small, more his height than most here, and shoving hard against the mob of people threatening to overwhelm her. "Stop! Thief!" rang through the room. "Who you calling thief?" equally rabid voices shouted back. Within minutes, the walkway erupted into a full-scale brawl with the innocent victim trapped in the middle. She floundered under the weight of the crowd and her cries became screams of fear. She was losing the battle. Her head turned this way and that, desperate for help. Then her eyes caught his, and before Seolta could think, he was moving out of his refuge and into the fight.

A lifetime growing up in trees and surviving his large family had taught him more than a few handy tricks. Duck under a flailing arm, sidestep, then elbow a pathway clear, and in no time, he had reached the woman just as she floundered wildly and fell backwards.

His arm reached out and snatched her close.

"Let me go."

"If I do, you'll be trampled by the crowd." He had no time to argue. The crowd had forgotten what began the fight and brawled now for sheer enjoyment. Nothing for it. He lifted her bodily and held her tight. "You're safe now."

No time for a proper introduction. He carried her into a nearby alleyway, blessedly free of brawlers. He was glad she'd had the sense to stay quiet in his arms as he twisted through the crowd. He could have put her down as soon as they reached the alley but found he didn't want to. Apart from the utterly feminine curves of her body, the feel of her settled something inside him. It wasn't until she began to struggle that he loosened his arms and helped her to stand.

"Are you hurt?"

"No, I'm fine, thanks to you." She'd have a few bruises, no doubt, but she dismissed them. "Thank you for your help, Messer." She stepped back.

He felt the corner of his mouth twitching but let her disengage. "Let me introduce myself so we are no longer strangers." He gave her the formal bow of his homeland. "Ser Seolta mar Bram an Scathach den Coille, at your service. If you need further assistance, please do not hesitate to ask. The request of a beautiful woman is always a pleasure to grant."

She made an attempt at copying his bow, a hesitant smile on her face. She didn't trust him, but this time it was no insult. To her, he was a just a stranger, not a disgraced exile. He offered his arm to help steady her, as he would one of his aunts, while she pulled her clothes back into order.

"Are you transiting to your home?" he asked. "Surned is a long way from here. I am of a mind to go there. We may even meet again on the voyage."

She stopped her tidying and a frown crossed those firm lips. "How did you know where I come from?"

"I had the pleasure of meeting a gentleman from there once. The accent gives you away."

It was a mistake. Fear suddenly sharpened her face. "My family are expecting me," she muttered and almost ran as she hurried down the alley and away from him. He could have caught her but she'd taken the route away from the still full-bodied melee and he had no reason to stop her. No sensible reason. He did follow—to make sure she was safe, he told himself. The street she emerged in was quiet and she seemed to know where she was going.

At the far corner, she stopped in the shelter of a doorway and looked back. He'd stopped at the alley entrance and was caught by her eyes. Clear crystalline grey, sharp and questioning, they challenged him. Then she fled.

For a rare moment in time, Seolta wished it could have been different then mentally shook himself. He couldn't afford any soft emotion. The woman came from the one place he'd been warned against and so the one place he meant to go. The rage inside him demanded revenge. Could he use her, or would she betray him? That's all he must consider, and he refused to acknowledge that foreign kernel of regret.

The Alliance Deputy was out of reach, protected by the powerful levels of Alliance Central bureaucracy, but not his other enemy. Seolta was going to Surned, and for that he needed a plan and a good cover story. There was no hiding his identity once he got there, not given his past history with Hilmar. The man had used Seolta's anger to manipulate him once before, and he trusted no one. Which meant Seolta needed to find out a tragging lot more about Surned and Hilmar a Kevand3's position there. He'd done some research before stupidly agreeing to help the man, but it had focussed mostly on Hilmar's Alliance-wide business. All he really knew about the man's home was that Surned was a habitat world and Hilmar a Kevand3 was its most prominent businessman.

He made his way to the central booking hub. Here, the voices and sounds of myriad worlds hit him full force, leaving him as stunned as any first-time newcomer. If he wanted to stay free and safe, he'd better figure out this place smartly. He could deal with the likes of the petty thief. His kind infested any transport hub, but the Arcadian Galactic Ministry would have sent word of him to their operatives across the Alliance and he couldn't discount the Alliance doing the same. He'd conspired with an Alliance official and a major player in the interplanetary business world. The ramifications of that reached too far and was too dangerous. Look at how well they'd buried his story so that not a trace had touched the public news feeds.

Had he also helped create an opportunity for the greedy to plunder his world? The thought had hovered in his head ever since the attack on Ethan Winter and his wife, but now, on this far off metal canister hovering in the black death of space, he must confront it head-on. What if he'd opened a way for the destruction of his home world as he knew it? If the environmental challenges his little sister kept shoving down his throat didn't end settlement on Arcadia, maybe the political changes he'd set in play would. He'd hadn't believed the threat from the Alliance before. De-populating an entire planet for failing to protect its environment? The other planets wouldn't stand for it.

Or would they?

The thought chilled him enough to keep the stunned look on his face and the wary tone in his voice as he set his com to full security mode. Hopefully none of those watching out for him could hack into his com stream. He'd designed it himself. You had to fully understand how his mind worked to break through it, and that was one thing Seolta den Coille had kept close all his life. Only his parents, and maybe his youngest sister, had a true idea of what he was capable, but none of them was here.

He refused to let the thought depress him.

Here by your own actions, remember.

He still put out a covering program. No point letting his watchers speculate about com activity they couldn't hack into. All he had to do now was figure out a way to escape his watchdogs. An image came instantly to mind. Eyes a crystalline wash of grey above a tipped up nose and a tightly plaited crown of auburn hair, her chin stubbornly thrust out as she refused his help.

What could be more natural than that he call on the Surned Sera to check she was all right after her ordeal?

He found a busy eatery and took a seat in a back corner, near the door to the kitchens for an easy escape route and from where he could see the whole room. Some habits stuck hard. Prison did that to you, and he shared this one with his brothers and Ethan Winter.

With a tankard in front of him and a large plate of something that looked as if it had been rehydrated too many times, he set up his com in hidden mode and quickly hacked into the station systems. It was surprisingly easy. Maybe he should hire out as a security consultant. Cogs began to turn in his head as he scanned the reservation records for anyone from Surned.

He almost missed her. She'd put her home base down as a satellite hub and it was only the broader solar system of origin that pulled it into his search. Her name? Anyara a Prithand2.

Anyara. A pretty name and one he'd not heard before. A name that suited that strong face and startling eyes. He scanned the system to find the exact location of her home base, then grinned. Just above Kevand3, the largest city habitat on Surned.

Occupation – Biome Manager, notification level one.

That explained the occupation question on the border form if not all the other overly intrusive ones. In a space station where all life depended on the artificial habitat's clean air and food, knowing there was a visiting biome expert was potentially lifesaving in an emergency.

He began to explore more files. First the outward-bound bookings. He had no trouble pulling up the passenger lists of all the docked transporters yet found no trace of her. He turned to the private vessels, and came up empty as well. Not that they listed passengers, but they did all have port of origin and destination. Surned was off the known routes and he'd already discovered that the first available commercial ship didn't leave for another two standard days. A private ship was leaving tomorrow, though, listed as under contract to Kevand Station. It had to be hers. It was listed as in station mode, refuelling and restocking for transit, which meant the majority of the crew and any passengers would be stationside, so she needed a hotel room.

It was surprisingly easy to log into the station admin records and find her details, right down to room number. A curt anger flared up in him at the carelessness of the hotel, and he swiftly erased her room details from all except hotel employees. It was only good manners, he told himself, and nothing to do with his reaction when her eyes had met his, pleading for help. His answer had been automatic, the least he could do for any fellow traveller in trouble.

You tell yourself that.

He ignored the annoying voice that increasingly sounded in his head. He'd been alone too long.

Now to create an excuse to call on her that wouldn't make her wary of him. A few more searches and he had it. He rose and marched out, keeping open the station map and his target zone on a screen in hidden mode in front of him, and refused to consider whether he was being an idiot. Soon he'd left the main transit area and entered a zone the station leaders no doubt hoped no visitor would venture near, stopping to buy a blaster and some other aids in a shop that asked no questions, then walked on. The area became even seedier. He set his com to full guard mode and sent out the small nanobots he'd bought. Completely illegal and highly effective trackers and alarms.

He was nearly too confident. A slight shuffle to one side and a body barrelled into him. Only the zap of his protective field flinging the man back kept him from being beaten before he'd begun. He pulled his blaster. The scar on the man's face—a nasty puckering over his left eye, probably earned in a street brawl—identified him as the petty thief he sought.

"You've got something I want," Seolta said, in no mood to waste time listening to threats or stupid blusterings. "You can either give it to me now and I'll pay you double the credits you'd get for it elsewhere, or I send the recording of this meeting through to the station police."

The man stared at him as if he'd lost his mind. Seolta shot out the bulkhead just above him.

"Hey, that's a bit close."

"The next one will be closer. Maybe too close, depending on your answer."

"You're a mad 'un."

"No, I'm on a timetable. Return the lady's bag to me now, contents intact." The man's fingers twitched towards his wrist. "Don't bother. I've inactivated your com access." That was real, unlike his threat to shoot the man. Seolta had never killed anyone and wasn't about to start now. Hopefully the man didn't realise it.

The man pulled his hand back from his wrist. "Three-fifty credits, and the bag's yours," he said in a sullen voice.

"Two hundred, and that's still generous. She will have already set off the trackers in it."

"She's a tourist. They don't carry no trackers."

"You sure of that?"

"I reckon you're just sweet on her." The man was blustering now, chin thrust forward and eyes narrowing. Seolta stared back, waiting.

Nothing moved.

He gave the man another blast, one close enough to singe his hair.

"You really are mad!"

Behind him, Seolta could hear a soft scraping. He had to end this, and soon. He held the gun rock steady and the man's eyes were trapped in his stare.

Finally, not a moment too soon, the man jerked. "Take it then. Nothing much in it anyway." His hand reached inside his filthy and voluminous coat, Seolta's blaster following every movement, and flung out the small orange pack. Then his hand moved back and Seolta quickly shot. A paralysing blast only but it would keep the man quiet and immobile long enough for Seolta to escape. He swung around and sprayed the far side of the street with another searing blast, and the scraping sounds from the shadows stopped immediately. Moving briskly, he walked off, eyes and blaster ready. The watchers stayed silent, but he didn't fool himself they were gone. He was thoroughly relieved to finally leave the lower streets and return to the safety of the transit zone.

Only then did he let the shiver of nerves surface. A momentary surrender before he hurried off to find the hotel sheltering Anyara a Prithand2.

The desk clerk was about as helpful as expected, going out of his way to misunderstand Seolta, but it was an old problem, easily dealt with. A discreet bribe worked as well on a station hub as it did in an Arcadian hotel.

"Don't worry, I know my way," he said to the porter and allowed himself a cheerful smile. Something was finally going his way. It wasn't until he reached her door that he suffered a reality check. Her face appeared on the outer screen, polite and with eyes widening in recognition, but her smile was forced.

"My apologies for intruding, Messera. I heard you give the paramedics your direction and wanted to make sure you took no serious hurt in that unfortunate fracas," he pulled out the pack from behind his back, "and to restore your possessions."

That shook her. What kind of world did she come from? "Thank you," she said with a gasp. "I'd assumed it was lost." A small frown creased those beautiful brows, then she disengaged the door locks and let it open.

He'd forgotten the effect of her. His heart lodged in his throat and he lost his voice for a full moment. Clutching the pack, he gave her a formal head bow.

"My pleasure, Messera."

That was unvarnished truth, a truth he didn't begin to understand. He enjoyed the company of women, but to go out of his way as he had for this woman? He held out the pack and her hand touched his as she took it. A soft blush covered her cheeks, and he wished he dared do more. The quick withdrawal of her hand warned against it. She stepped back awkwardly, but not far enough to be an invitation to enter.

"How did you manage it?" she asked.

He let a grin slip into place, the self-deprecating one that had disarmed many past women. "A word to the stationmaster and a reminder of the effect on business if the station became known as a risky stopover."

A slight adjustment of the truth, but the stationmaster probably would have been amenable to such an approach if Seolta had cared to give him the time and financial incentive. His com searches showed the man was knee deep in local scams.

She clung to the bag and her hand reached for the door controls. "Thank you. It was very good of you to take the trouble. If there is any way I can show my appreciation…"

His old charming tricks had only made her more nervous. Seolta quickly revised his tactics, wiping off the practised smile. For once, he must negotiate with a face devoid of tricks. He hoped he knew how. "There was a favour I'd hoped to ask you," he said. Honesty was usually his last refuge, but this woman demanded it of him. He was stunned to hear himself say: "Forget I said anything. It would be imposing too much on your good will. I trust you weren't hurt too badly in the attack."

"Just some bruising. Nothing that won't be fine in a few days."

They had hurt her. He felt the rage threatening to erupt inside him and had to clamp down hard on it. He lifted a hand towards her face, then saw her flinch and dropped it. "You are safe now," he said, and didn't know if he said the words to reassure her or himself.

The stranger who had rescued her stood at her door. Anyara might still have the security screen on, but something had impelled her to open the physical door. Alarm bells should be clanging loudly in her head. That they weren't had Anyara even more on edge. How had this man broken through her defences? She kept a distance from others for very good reasons. In the concourse, though, this man had shattered her self-imposed walls in an instant. Wiry and lightly built as he was, she'd had no reason to believe he could save her, but there had been strength in his arms and a promise in those dark eyes.

He made her feel something in that alley. Doing it again now set off a very different kind of alarm.

"How do I know you're not in league with the ones who stole my pack and started that brawl?"

His eyes widened. Then it was as if a mask slid across his face and he slipped on that smile again. The kind she'd seen her uncle adopt too often. She stepped back.

"What is it about you?" he muttered, as if to himself, and the practiced smile vanished. He gave that short bow again, the kind that seemed to come from some ancient vidcast. "My apologies, Messera. I'll leave you in peace."

He went to leave and she put out a hand without thinking, reaching through the door screen to touch his arm.

"You said you had a favour to ask of me, Messer."

"I did, but it wasn't right."

"Let me decide that." She threw all caution aside and tugged him inside her room.

He was a lot stronger than he looked. He stood still against her. "No, Messera. You know nothing about me."

"You came to my aid when no one else would. That's enough."

He planted his feet more firmly. "As you said, how do you know I'm not one of them?"

"Are you?"

Her eyes caught and held his, and it was as if the room and corridor disappeared. "Are you?" she whispered.

"No, Messera, but I will not put you at risk."

"You want to get to my home world," she suddenly guessed, "and preferably without the checks on a commercial ship."

He nodded slowly, as if reluctant to admit it.

"Are you a criminal?"

"Not … technically. But I have made mistakes."

Anyara had lived her whole life taking care what she did, whom she talked to, whom she aligned with. What was this sudden urge to discard everything life had taught her?

"Are you going to Surned to hurt me?"

"No!" he said emphatically.

"Or my family?"

A slight smile, self-deprecating and thoroughly charming, but this one didn't look as engineered as the other. "I don't know your family, Messera. I didn't know you existed until today."

Why did she believe him? "So you might hurt my family and friends?"

He dropped his hand, eyes wide with shock. "Yes, Messera, I might." He went to step back.

She reached for him again, grabbing at his arm to hold him in place. "If I help you, will you promise to leave my family and friends alone, promise to bring them no harm?"

His eyes darkened. "No, Messera, I cannot do that."

"Why? What are your reasons? Money, power?"

"Not … solely," he said, as if dragged from his depths.

"It's family then. Family and friends."

He was silent. Then gave that abrupt bow of his head. "I'm sorry to have disturbed you, Messera. Please, take care for the rest of your stay." He stepped back and turned away from her.

She watched him until he was halfway down the hallway. Then she began to run. "Wait. That favour you wanted. The answer is yes." He kept walking. She reached him and grabbed at his arm, using the skills taught by her defensive trainer to swing him back to face her.

"Come into my room now so we can talk unheard. I believe we can make a deal."

CHAPTER TWO

Had she finally taken leave of her senses? She should have pushed the man out of her room immediately instead of inviting him in. He even refused to promise he wouldn't hurt her family or friends. Stars knew she'd long wanted to escape the clutches of the only family she had left, and her closest friends were the plants and animals in her biome, but he wasn't to know that. Or that she couldn't trust anyone around her, not knowing who was an agent for her uncle, put there to watch her.

The stranger seated himself with the inbuilt grace she'd noticed when he came to her rescue. He moved like a dancer but she doubted that was his profession. Not with that practised smile and his ability to track down her pack and her room.

"You've taken a lot of trouble to find me," she said. "Why?"

Those sharp features stiffened and his eyes shuttered, as if assessing his options and her possible reactions. "I have my reasons."

"Then why are you so interested in taking a private vessel to Surned? To avoid being tracked?"

A ghost of a smile passed over his face at that, one that looked real, and she hoped it meant he'd given up trying to hide what he was thinking. She'd been followed and controlled for too many years by people hiding behind smiles. Why did this smile make her trust him? For that, she had no logical answer.

She did know it was a question she should have asked before agreeing to give him a berth on her ship.

A day later and facing the second translation for Surned, she lay in her travel pod and told herself she was all kinds of an idiot. There had been little enough time between the first and second translations to question her passenger, but they now had some days to go before their final translation point.

She had let a total stranger join her on a private family vessel. Her security had been near to apoplectic but could do nothing when she refused to listen to their demands. They were watching him closely but, beyond that, security had agreed to back off. Not unless he acted first, she'd ordered.

She would have to find out his reasons for going to Surned before her security's patience ran out.

Coming out of translation, she groaned at the thought. In a fit of what she knew to be sheer cowardice, she kept to her own quarters as long as possible, sending a message to ask the stranger if he would join her for dinner in her lounge.

Politeness alone demanded the invitation, she told herself. The crew and security had made it more than clear that the man wasn't welcome in their mess, the place she usually ate when on a trip, and the only other place for him to eat was his cabin. The captain might have preferred locking him in for the duration of the trip, but that was no help to her. Not with those shadows lurking in his eyes. Seolta den Coille wasn't a man to release his secrets easily, and she'd got the feeling what little he'd told her had surprised him as much as her.

She took extra care with her dressing then checked out her holo-image.

Good one. How better to set off his warning systems than turning up groomed to the utmost and looking like a woman on the prowl.

She ruthlessly tugged out the elaborate twists of her hair, letting it fall simply about her shoulders and catching a few strands back at her temples.

To keep it out of her eyes, she told herself, refusing to notice that the simple style suited her mad coils better than the overly complicated twists. She also discarded the gown she'd first ordered up and selected instead a simple sheath in her favourite soft sage. The kind she'd wear to a private dinner at home—as long as her uncle wasn't there.

She nearly rushed out again when Seolta entered the lounge. Tasteful, exactly right for the occasion and perfectly judged, the man had evening dressing down to a fine art. He also looked absolutely gorgeous with the elegant line of silver tracery on his tunic highlighting the lean face, the fine cheekbones, and the strong shape of those determined lips.

He gave her that semi bow of his and came up slowly, his eyes taking her in from feet to head. Then he smiled, with no trace of artifice she could see, and a shiver rippled through her.

"Good evening, Messera. I trust the journey has been pleasant so far."

She nodded stupidly. "Yes, thank you." Then finally got her brain working, wishing she was better at these social manoeuvres. "Please, take a seat."

An untrustworthy gleam flickered over his face and he sat opposite. She had thought hard about the seating arrangements and knew now she'd been right to put the width of the table between them. He flashed a thoroughly charming smile and focussed his attention on her. "You look very beautiful this evening, Messera."

She blushed, actually blushed, and took herself firmly to task. She was no Messera fresh out of higher school to be taken in by easy words and a silken voice. "I didn't ask you here to fish for empty compliments, Messer den Coille."

"Seolta, please. A private dinner shipboard is scarcely the place for strict formality."

Unfortunately, she couldn't think of a suitable reason to refuse. Her home world worked on a first name basis, and this man was the kind to have studied her world's conventions.

"Messer Seolta, then," she said, hopelessly attempting to catch hold of the conversation.

He inclined his head gracefully. He did everything gracefully. Part of her was starting to seriously resent it—the part that wasn't entranced by it.

"When we arrive," she said primly, "we will be docking at Kevand Station. It's where I live, not on the planet. The captain wants to know whether you want us to arrange for a shuttle to take you down to the surface."

He shook his head. "That would be imposing on your kindness too much. I can catch a regular shuttle."

"I'm afraid you will have to stay on station for a few days. We don't have sufficient traffic to afford daily shuttles. Is your business on Surned urgent?"

A flash of something dark lit his eyes, gone as quickly as glimpsed, and he put on a charming smile again. Only this one wasn't quite the same as the smile when he'd sat down. This one looked *practised* and it sent a shock of anger through her.

"Is someone waiting for you on Surned?" she asked, more sharply than she'd intended. "Someone who doesn't know you're coming?" Then cursed to herself as his face closed over. "Don't play me, Messer Seolta. I'm not completely stupid and you need my help."

"To get to Surned, or close to it. For which I am very grateful," he said, his lips beginning to curve. She glared at him, and the false smile disappeared. "I made you no promises. Not about my intentions."

He hadn't, and she'd been under no illusions either. He was no innocent. So why had she trusted him to come on board? She never trusted anyone. "I find I need more before I let you run free on my home station, Messer Seolta."

His face lost all trace of artificial charm, those dark eyes with their shadows staring into hers as if she were a puzzle he didn't know how to solve. Or was that only her fancy, a mirror of how she thought about him.

"A bit of honesty, please, Messer. Is that too much to ask?"

A flash of anger sparked those dark eyes, one he made no attempt to hide, and something inside her crowed in triumph.

"It's asking a lot, as you fully understand. If you don't like what I say, anything could happen to me."

"I agreed to take you with me to the end of my voyage, and I am not one to break an agreement, whatever may be the custom where you come from."

"It is the custom in my home too—or mostly." A trace of bitterness coated his voice. "You know I have a purpose in coming to Surned. I don't plan to damage your home but cannot promise more than that."

"So any harm will be merely accidental as you do what's necessary to fulfil your purpose?"

He stared back, refusing to offer even a hint of an apology with his face or body.

She'd asked for honesty and he gave her that at least. "You have a strange sense of honour, Messer Seolta. A truce then. You do what you need to and I will protect what I value. It seems to be the best we can agree on," she finished wryly.

Suddenly, like that, the tension vanished. "I will do my very best to ensure my actions bring no harm to you," he said, this time with that that truly charming smile. The one that felt real.

She sighed and leaned back. "I must be three kinds of a fool. I don't know who you are, what your background is, and a man with the unmistakable look of a government official tried to stop you boarding my ship. My parents would have thought I'd taken leave of my senses."

"The man wasn't from the Alliance. And your parents 'would have'?"

That was what he'd picked up on? "They died the year I started Higher School," she found herself telling him. She never talked about her family history.

"I'm sorry," he said. His hand reached out, the firm fingers taking hold of hers. Even stranger, she clung to them. "I hope whoever had the raising of you was kind."

"My uncle inherited that duty." The tight clench of his fingers said she needed to say no more. "What about your family," she asked to distract him, hating any hint of pity. The sudden darkening of his eyes made her wish she hadn't.

"Both my parents are very much alive. Along with two sisters, three brothers and two in-laws."

Her mouth gaped. "So many."

"It's allowed on my world," he said.

"But the habitat size needed. The resources…"

"My home world is more fertile than Surned. We don't have restricted habitats."

Her jaw dropped fully open. "You can't be… You're talking about an EA world." Earth Analogue worlds were the rarest kind of planet known. Only a handful existed, and they were zealously guarded by the Alliance and their governments. "*No one* moves away from an EA world."

He shrugged. "I had little choice in the matter."

"Oh." Then reason hit. "You mean a habitable world. Bigger than Surned and able to be bioengineered. Sorry for being so dense."

A flush hit his face and his hands picked up his glass, turning it round and round. "No, it's a full EA world. There was some bioengineering at settlement, but that was only to maximise its fit for settlers. We have an atmosphere, seas and plant-covered lands."

"And you left *that* to come here."

He flushed harder, the colour of his skin changing from its usual tan to a deep burnt red. "Not voluntarily. I'd been a fool."

"Nothing hit the intergalactic newscasts." A man sentenced to exile from an EA planet would have been top of the 'casts on every world in the Alliance.

"It was kept quiet. My family…" He shifted back in his seat. "Politics," he said as if in explanation.

What had she got herself into? She'd dreamed of visiting such a world since she was a small child, poring over any vid she could find. "Your world. Does it have trees?"

He smiled. "Yes." A look of longing covered his face. "All kinds of trees, and each one as beautiful as the next. My family home is built in a tree."

Now he was telling stories. That was impossible.

A knock on her com stopped her demanding the truth. The captain requested entry. She'd told him she wanted a private meeting and there had been nothing spoken of here to alarm her uncle's spies. Then the captain added the emergency code. She slammed a hand on the release pad for the door.

The man thrust in. "We've got a problem in the command systems."

"Can't our systems officer fix it?"

"Yes, given time and a feedback link to Surned Central."

"And…?" She was getting a bad feeling.

"Whatever the problem, it's also blocked the air controls. Unless we can unlock it, we've only got the air in circulation now."

She'd travelled on many ships and grew up on habitat worlds. "How long?"

"Four standard hours at minimised protocols."

That didn't sound long enough, not if they needed to receive a link from Surned.

A chair scraped the floor behind her. Her guest. The least of her worries at the moment. "I'm sorry, Messer Seolta, we will have to finish our dinner at a later date. Please return to your cabin. The required protocol will be sent to your com."

He stood up. "Maybe I can help. I have some expertise in systems."

He did? How convenient. "A space-going vessel is somewhat different from a planetary flyer."

"Not from upper altitude flyers, and the risks are the same if no one fixes it. I have no desire to terminate my journey quite so permanently."

He had a point. Did she trust him? "You could have a backup escape planned."

"I could," he agreed tersely, "but I don't, and we are wasting time."

She wished she knew what was going on behind that too clever face.

The captain looked as happy as she felt. "If he really can help, Messera…"

Or is prepared to fix whatever trouble he has caused.

They really had no choice.

"Thank you, Messer Seolta, for your offer. We would be pleased to accept. The captain here will assign one of our people to assist you." She flicked a discreet hand signal to the captain at the same time, one she hoped their passenger didn't know. He must be followed and monitored at all times, especially when he entered their critical control systems.

Seolta waited impatiently as the ship's com tech entered the required codes to let an outsider—him—into their ship systems. He had no doubt the woman had also activated every security alarm protocol available. Luckily, she didn't know he'd been blocking things like that since he was a child in first school. No point making this crew more suspicious than they were already. He had no doubt that if they'd had any other option, they'd have locked him up in whatever passed for a brig instead.

The woman finally motioned him to enter his credentials into the database and add his thumb trace. He'd never been so thankful at deciding to keep his own identity. He'd done it mostly out of pride but, right now, he wanted to keep living, and the only way to do that seemed to be fixing whatever had gone wrong here. A fake ID would have swiftly put paid to that.

He found the problem easily enough. He'd worried that off-planet vessels might use a different coding template than he was used to, but the basic principles were much the same. There were only so many ways to efficiently arrange a command system for a vessel, and the requirements were universal when it came down to it. Keep the engines going, keep good quality air circulating, keep the anti-grav system smooth. Keep out the bad stuff.

It was the last bit that had failed. He came to the glitch in the air supply soon after accessing it. He glanced at the tech woman beside him, following what he was doing step by step, and tried to work out if she really hadn't seen it, or was waiting for him to spot it.

Was this sabotage or a trap for an unwelcome passenger?

He locked the glitch to prevent more damage then side-stepped it to check the rest of the system. One obvious problem didn't mean other, more subtle and dangerous traps hadn't also been laid, and it gave him time to consider.

A standard hour later, he leaned back. "That's the lot. Do you want me to go ahead and re-code them correctly?" He'd found all of them some time ago, and fixed the worst but had no desire to let this ship know the full scale of his abilities. The com tech had noted the coding aberrations, he was sure, but he'd told her he was isolating them to stop damage and she'd agreed to let him do that much. But no more, had said the grim set of her mouth. The worst of the changes had been very subtle and his coding tweaks so minor that he'd managed to make them look like part of his checks.

They wouldn't have let him into their systems if their own crew had the training to repair these kinds of errors. Or so he hoped, and had a feeling his future wellbeing depended on it.

The woman turned away and clicked through to the captain and to Anyara. The Messera, it turned out, was the principal of the ship, the one who'd had the deciding say that let him on board in the first place. Not for the first time, he cursed not having made more enquiries into her background before he targeted her. He couldn't do it here, not with the crew monitoring his com transmissions so closely. He hoped he hadn't made another colossal mistake. Anger had got him into this mess in the first place, exiling him from the home and work he loved, and now that anger and the allure of a pretty woman looked to have landed him in another mess.

No, pretty was too mundane a word. The woman stunned him every time he saw her. But that wasn't why he'd targeted her. It was her ship. Her *private* ship heading to the Surned system.

You tell yourself that.

I need to get to Surned, and she can get me there with less scrutiny than on a commercial vessel.

Look where seeking revenge got you last time.

Just once, he wished he could win an argument with that tragging inner voice. Hilmar a Kevand3 owed him after what he'd done on Arcadia, and Seolta meant to call in the debt. It was as good a way as any to start making something out of this exile.

He'd planned to arrive inconspicuously enough to be able to scope out the planet and where Hilmar fit into the power system. He already knew the businessman had a galactic presence big enough to attract a crooked Alliance official. That meant he had money, prestige and connections. Alliance-wide connections.

Seolta had also read the gossip. The man was dirty through and through—unscrupulous, amoral, and bent only on his own enrichment. He'd found little hard evidence of shady dealings, but the man had managed to acquire a majority holding in his family company without a single complaint registered. Seolta suspected that the rest of the family only held onto their shares because Hilmar needed them as a smokescreen to shield him from Alliance regulators. He'd be very surprised if they received any of the healthy income generated by Kevand3.

Given how some of that income was generated, maybe they were only too happy to keep their hands off it.

Those family members let Hilmar keep going, so Seolta had little sympathy for them. If just one of them had called in the Alliance before the man set his greedy eyes on Arcadia, Seolta wouldn't be in his present predicament.

Don't blame Hilmar. You knew exactly the kind you were dealing with when you hooked up with him and Malgrave to exploit Arcadia's problems.

He'd been so sure he had control of the situation, so sure he could use them to retaliate against all those who'd tried to bring down his family and his company.

He'd been so stupid.

A sudden power surge brought him back to sharp reality. He hastily backtracked and fixed the coding bungle.

Get your head in the game.

Did he want to die here with a pack of strangers?

He ran one more check, then held his breath as he switched the changes to live and waited for the call of an alarm siren.

Nothing. He breathed out slowly and waited long moments more, eyes on the vessel status figures.

They held. He took another breath then released his link into the system and stepped back. "That should hold it until we make port and someone with better equipment can give the system a full audit."

"Captain?" said Anyara. She'd been standing silently against the back wall the whole time. Maybe she thought he wouldn't be aware of her there so wouldn't disturb him, but he was discovering that he never lost awareness of her. Not if she was in the same room.

She pushed herself off the wall.

The captain and techs in the room were busy running a full systems audit, their eyes as intent as his on the status figures. Finally, they looked up.

"It looks good," said the senior engineer. "Thank you, Messer."

The man didn't sound very grateful. More like downright suspicious. Any freedom he'd had on this trip was about to be seriously curtailed.

The captain gave him a curt nod. "Thank you for your assistance, Messer. It was lucky for us you were on board to fix it."

"Yes, it was," said Anyara sharply, and a small glow sprang to life in his chest. Not that she should trust him, no matter how innocent he was this time.

"I'll leave you to it, then," he said in his most humble voice. Not something he'd practiced enough, by the looks the captain and engineer shot him, but at least they let him leave. He made straight for his cabin and stayed there to avoid stirring up more suspicion, and wished he didn't so regret missing the rest of his dinner with Anyara a Prithand2.

He had a couple of days more of the trip to survive and needed to fill it. Searching her history was now even more out of the question. His position here was marginal at best, but he could enlarge his knowledge of her world. He started out with basic geography—the main habitats on Surned and their associated station hubs—starting with a simple list and mapping of the world, then fact-finding on the major locations. It meant he had to put Kevand3 first. The biggest, richest and most powerful habitat on Surned, he came away with a definite impression that it was far from the most desirable place to live. It suited Hilmar a Kevand3 perfectly.

He'd found early on that Surned names were taken from their place of birth or main residence, but Hilmar *was* Kevand3 in all meanings of the word. Chief executive of the Kevand3 corporation which owned and ran the Kevand3 habitat, he was also absolute ruler and controller of all the wealth in the place, thanks to holding forty-nine percent of the company shares, the maximum allowed to any individual under Alliance law.

The rest of the shares seemed to be owned by various minor associates and blind companies. He strongly suspected that Hilmar owned the majority share in these holdings as well. Only the Alliance rule that no one entity could own a controlling share of any human habitat stopped him openly owning them. The man looked to be following the old business practice of spreading out his assets to avoid detection. Hiding grains of sand in plain sight, it was called back home on Arcadia, where the desert crept silently over the Plains grasslands ever more each year. One blind company seemed different from all the others. It held fifteen percent of the shares, far more than any of the other individual companies. A company for which he couldn't find an owner. It wasn't Hilmar, though it did vote as he dictated.

Enough of Hilmar. The man was too powerful to risk lingering over. Not if his searches were to be dismissed as normal for a businessman looking for an opportunity on Surned. He turned to the next habitat on his list before the systems techs notified the captain and Anyara of his interest.

He had to break for the requisite sleep period and it wasn't till well into the next day of his lonely cabin vigil that he came to Prithand2, birth home of his true target. No one had come near him in the interim, and when he risked stepping out of his cabin, a security guard instantly appeared to shadow him.

The numbers in Surned cities bothered him at first. There was nothing third-rate about Kevand3, clearly the dominant population centre of its region, unlike Kevand1 and Kevand2. He might know that they were numbered in founding order, but his brain insisted on treating the numbers as ranks.

When it came to Prithand2, though, it really was a second-rate place. Set in an area with little natural resources and sited purely as a convenient staging post for transiting freight vessels, everything about it felt temporary. No major centre of learning, the shops only the minimum needed and the business premises confined to the practical. How did it give rise to a woman as complex and hard to fathom as Anyara?

Or create the wealth that must back her, given the level of education needed for her position as a biome manager and control of a space-going vessel.

He began with the ruling groups in hopes of working his way down the social hierarchy and wasn't surprised to find a link to Hilmar at the very first step. The man had fingers in every habitat he'd checked so far. He ran the routine bio for all the current upper tier, the kind of checks any hopeful trader or migrant would make, wondering what else to try that wouldn't arouse suspicion.

Then he noticed an anomaly. All the current upper-level administrator's histories went back to one single date. Before that, nothing. No history, no bio information, not even the normal economic data.

He quickly switched to the tax data, as if bored with his findings and wanting to find another angle to exploit. Anomalies and gaps meant an event, one that had been covered up. An event dating back to the childhood of Anyara a Prithand2. His gut instincts twitched into life.

Anyara a Prithand2 said she'd lost her parents as a child. Had something happened at Prithand2 that left her an orphan and gave Hilmar control of this seemingly unimportant secondary habitat?

He took a break for a snack, then logged back in, going to Prithand1, the nexus of freight for the region, and followed the same searches as all the other ones. He had to appear routine, bored, hungry for power and wealth, not fascinated by one intriguing woman. This time, he concentrated on the freight operatives, which ones might best reward an off-world investor.

Which ones might hide a subtle clue to what had happened all those years ago on Prithand2?

He discovered an entry while trawling through an old freight list. Many years ago, a single item appeared in the manifest of a freighter from Prithand2. Cargo type: ten human children. Destination: Kevand3.

Then the alarm sounded for translation. Lock down now or take the consequences.

He shut down his com.

CHAPTER THREE

Anyara walked past the locked door of the guest cabin one more time, unable to keep her eyes from the door or the guilt from her heart. The man had fixed a complicated systems glitch that had defeated all her crew. How likely was it they'd picked up such a passenger by chance? That's what the captain, the engineer and her senior com tech said. What common sense told her. Nor could she deny the man had deliberately sought her out.

No, sought out a ship heading for Surned.

The problem was, she liked Seolta den Coille. Liked him too much for a man with secrets in his eyes and a glib touch with his tongue.

Everything pointed against him being innocent. Had life taught her nothing?

"Messera, translation beginning in twenty standards. Time to lock down."

"Thank you, Captain."

The man didn't move, staring at the cabin door behind her.

"We have no proof against him," she heard herself say.

"Nor for him," said the captain, before adding a polite, "Messera," and stalking off. Her own cabin sat right next door to that of their problematic guest. She set her hands on her door pad then changed her mind. She did not want to meet their guest too soon after coming out of translation, when she was still in a haze. As principal of the vessel, she had a designated pod on the bridge. She didn't normally like to remind the captain she outranked him, but today felt different. He gave her an icy look when she walked onto the bridge and took her seat, but he said nothing.

He wanted to, that was plain, as were the shocked looks of the rest of the bridge crew. With good reason. What place did a comatose civilian have on a bridge during the rigours of translation? As she locked down and felt the fuzz of phase drugs take her under, her last view was of the bridge crew in translation lenses and gear. No wonder she came out many standard hours later with alarming images of alien invaders and an unnamed threat hovering just out of view.

Seolta waited till the customary haze of translation had fully cleared from his system before rising from his pod. He checked the door. It was locked but back under his control. Which meant only that the crew was fully operational again and ready to act against him if he made any move to seize the command systems of the ship.

He checked his com. Seven standard hours until docking, so still a long wait. He took his time over cleansing and chose an outfit with care. One that scared no one. A trader intent on making a fortune, with some capital behind him but needing more. Only when he was sure of his presentation and all fog had cleared from his head did he try the door again.

It opened, and he breathed carefully out then turned and headed for the main lounge area, looking for a meal.

The room was empty of all except Anyara, and by the lack of a plate in front of her, she had only just taken her seat. She looked up as he entered. "Messer den Coille. A safe translation?"

"The usual, Messera. An unpleasant sensation, but normal enough."

So polite, the pair of them. He took his seat and pulled up the prepper selections. They hadn't improved since the last time he'd checked them. He chose the least offensive option he could find and hoped his impression of enjoying the gluggy mess looked convincing. "We arrive soon on your home station. You will be pleased to be back," he said, taking refuge in the conventional.

"Yes," she murmured, but he was surprised at her pinched mouth, and even more at the flare of anger inside him.

"Do you manage the biome yourself, or is that the work of others?" he said, to banish that trace of misery from her mouth. Her smile was so beautiful, and it bloomed into life now.

"We have a team, Messer. You obviously have had little to do with habitat biomes. My organisms like a personal touch."

"You speak as if they're sentient."

"And you tell me your home is in a tree and surrounded by more trees."

He was pleased to see the tightness of her mouth disappear, replaced by a breathy astonishment.

"You don't believe me," he teased.

A lift of her shoulders. "You don't think plants have their own life."

"Oh, they have that all right." Now it was his turn to chuckle. "The number of times I've come home at night to find our tree has dropped a bundle of slippery leaves on the doorstep…"

She looked puzzled.

"Dead leaves mixed with water are lethal. Add in a good night at the bar and my backside made contact with the ground too often," he said with what he hoped was a self-deprecating smile.

It didn't work. She still looked puzzled.

She was a trained biome specialist.

"Trees shed their leaves," he reminded her, dragging up what he remembered from his school science classes. "Baullnia are evergreen, always shedding some dying leaves and growing new ones, although they tend to shed more heavily in adverse times or during low sunshine periods. Younger leaves are more efficient at photosynthesis, so they drop the oldest and go through a sprouting."

She waved a hand in dismissal. Of course she knew this. "We usually recycle them before that stage. To let them go through to a dead leaf phase…" She made it sound like all her dreams come true. "And the water?"

"Rain, mist, whatever. There's always water in our air," he said, as surprised as she looked. "I live in a temperate forest." Then could have cursed himself. "You've never seen rain?"

She shook her head. "Once. A long time ago. A treat from my parents. I was little and they dialled up a rainstorm for my birthday. I got very wet." Her face was caught between wonder, laughter, and a deep sadness.

He didn't know what to say. Then she shook it off, as if shedding an unwanted skin, and he wondered how often she'd had to do that to make it so automatic.

"Tell me more about your forest," she said.

When the call came to prepare for landing, he looked at his com in shock. Time had passed so quickly. He'd found himself telling her things he hadn't told family, let alone an outsider. He'd deliberately set out to banish the wash of sadness from her eyes, and told her stories of his childhood that made him look a crass fool, but her bell song of laughter made it worthwhile.

"I'm surprised your brothers didn't beat you up more often," she said after one of his more outrageous memories.

Cumchdach came close to it that time, in truth, and he couldn't blame him. At the time, he'd thought his actions perfectly reasonable and logical. He just hadn't realised he was spoiling a much longed-for day for Cumchdach.

"That was my first and last visit to the annual Den Coille meeting until I was the proper age to attend. My mother sat down afterwards with me and tried to explain why Cumchdach was so mad at me. It didn't do much good," he had to admit. "I just plagued him worse than ever until he gave in and let me play with him again. Ceart threatened to beat me up as well, and he was only tiny then."

She shook her head with an exasperated gasp. "I'm losing track. Such names, and so many of you."

He opened his com and sketched out a family diagram. "I'm third oldest and second brother."

"And you all still live in the same habitat. None of you had to leave?"

"Only Fiorusghe, but that was her husband's fault. The man is no tree lover. As for the rest of us, I doubt our mother would allow it, but we each have our own apartments in the main house."

Her face cleared. "By house, you mean a block building ... and your city is a kind of habitat."

He was torn between teasing her and the truth. "Yes, a habitat made of living branches and too loud people. Have you never been on an EA planet?"

He could have cursed his careless mouth. Of course she hadn't. Arcadia was cutthroat at restricting entry, as were the other EA worlds. None wanted to be overrun with tourists, or take the risk of letting habitat dwellers know what they were missing out on.

"Maybe one day I can take you there," he said, then remembered too late. "If they let me back again.

The door opened and Seolta was relieved at the sight of the crewman, even with his scowling face. "The Messer needs to return to his cabin for docking procedures," the man said stiff-lipped.

Her face froze, and Seolta had no answer to that. She was right not to trust him, though they'd spent their time together talking of himself, not her. For a few precious standards he had banished the sadness from her eyes and that, he found, was its own reward. He stood and bent his head and shoulders in the formal mountain bow to a revered and precious host. "Thank you for a pleasant morning, Messera, and for your hospitality. I hope to repay it one day."

She stood as well, awkwardly reaching out a hand, and he wished he knew the local customs of her home. He took it gently and brought it to his lips, just touching her fingertips. An instant in time only, one he wasn't likely to get the chance to repeat, but one he would treasure, and she should know it.

She didn't immediately pull back, and his heart glowed. Then the crewman coughed and she hastily shoved her hand to her side and gave him a brisk nod. "Thank you, Messer."

The crewman escorted him back to his cabin. "Please do not leave your room while docking procedures are in progress, Messer," said the man. "A com signal will notify you when to secure yourself in your pod."

The crew were too busy to watch what he was up to, Seolta guessed that meant. Nor was he surprised to hear the lock engage once he closed his door, but he was when he found he could only access his personal com files. They had shut down his external linkages.

Now that was a nuisance.

What would they do if they knew about your activities back on Arcadia?

Maybe he shouldn't have told her he'd been kicked off his home world, but found he couldn't regret it. After the damage he'd caused, he had no desire to lie to anyone important again. For some reason, that included Anyara.

You lied to your own family.

Yes, and look where that had got him. Samhchair always said one day his tricks would come back and bite him.

Not that she'd dreamed he'd end up in prison, let alone the whole family. Never could he forget the stark cells of the dark building and what he and his family had endured. They hadn't deserved that.

He'd been so angry, blind to sense, when the marshals had finally rescued them. All his family and half the Winter family locked up and facing execution because a greedy pack of bureaucrats wanted to steal the families' companies. Not surprising that he'd latched onto any scheme that promised revenge and enough power to never be locked away again.

Or not surprising if you were Seolta, the so clever, never-before-thwarted son of den Coille. For what he'd done, there was no forgiveness. Not for himself, and not for the offworlders who had used his anger to further their greed.

When he found them…

All very well, but first, he had to survive Kevand Station and make it safely to Surned. Once released from his pod, packing his gear didn't take long. His baggage had been stowed away securely at the start of the trip with only a light carrier kept out for his transit gear. Fortunately, the signs of landing—the clanking of the ship and the abrupt changes in gravity and light that told of arrival—suddenly stopped and the 'Station secured' call came through.

Good manners demanded he thank Anyara for her assistance, a good excuse to see her once more, but when he finally heard the release of his door lock and completed all the tedious procedures required to gain entry to a station hub, she had already left the ship. He was left with a dubious promise from the ship clerk escorting him off to pass on his thanks to the Messera.

Nor did his arrival pass as freely as he'd hoped. No one here knew who he was, so it should have been a simple matter of requesting a short-term stay. It began with his name.

"A man oss cray otch?" The man reading his entry form glared at him. "You trying something on here? Never heard of such a place."

"It's a city on my home world, a long way from here."

"Interim HubfourX ain't so far away. That's where you claim to been living before coming here. Why don't you put that down. Not some made up place no honest traveller can pronounce." Like most habitat and hubs, the people here spoke the common version of Standard. Simple, clipped sounds, spelling based on phonetics, and a smattering of local slang thrown in to further confuse someone brought up on the classic Standard that was the lingua franca of Arcadia, a world with multiple local languages and dialects. Seolta painstakingly spoke out the syllables of his name, before giving up.

"Just make it Manas. It's a common short form," he said, unable to bear the mangled version any longer.

The official wrote it down. "Could have said that at the start," he grumbled. The endless questions continued, increasingly less tolerant of his answers.

Was everyone in this system born suspicious?

"Yes, I'm aware that my decision to come here was sudden. I am a businessman seeking new opportunities. On the last station, I heard much about the Surned companies and their wealth. It piqued my interest."

"Knowing nothing more than that?"

He looked the annoying official up and down. "Of course not. My first plan was to go to Alliance Central, but the rumours on station had me looking up the Surned databases. There are credits to be made here."

The man clearly had no intention of helping him do that. But Seolta had long learned to know whom he could push and how far. He locked down his growing irritation and waited for the next question.

"Your training?"

He flashed his qualifications and awards, all from Arcadia's finest higher institutes, but he doubted the names meant anything here. The only one the man registered was Seolta's systems accreditation. Not surprising. Someone with his kind of training was rare. They would either welcome him with open arms or immediately march him to the brig until they could ship him out, depending on their level of paranoia and whether they had any resident specialists able to understand Seolta's capabilities.

This time, he got the welcome, but no open arms. More a grudging acknowledgment.

"The station master will want to talk to you," the man said curtly. "Make sure you input your credentials as soon as you log in to your accommodation. And do not move from the one you have entered here without permission."

Since even a cursory check on the station infodocs showed no other place as offering any kind of reasonable service, Seolta had no intention of moving from its hopefully civilised rooms.

"Understood," he said with a smile. The kind you'd bestow on a pet. The man glared as he snapped off his com link. "Enter, Messer," and gestured sharply to the hotel courier waiting to escort him through the station's main hatch.

The first thing he noticed about the hub was the smell. Or rather, the trace of a smell whispering under the mechanical odours he'd had to become used to since leaving home: the smells of spaceships, station hubs and human-made creations. Here, teasing his nose and near to bringing tears to his eyes, played the smell of greenery and the precious odour of dirt and mulch. Somewhere nearby, living plants fought back against the artificial world, and he stared round, eager for a sight of leaf or branch. Then he walked through the tunnel leading from the station entry and stopped in stunned shock.

Above him was no true sky, and outside the station lurked the endless black of space, but here he walked into a garden. A tame world, with plants marshalled into well behaved clusters unlike his wild forest home, but they were real. They lived, grew, no doubt seeded and died, to be replaced by another generation. Life cycled here. He'd been told of the greenery stations needed for a healthy atmosphere, but in the transit hub and other ships, the precious biota had been locked well away from careless human assault.

Here, people walked on the fragrant groundcover, a little girl ran laughing to her mother to present her with a bright yellow flower, and small AI bodies gambolled with children on a flat expanse of bright green lawn. Slowly, he began to walk forward.

"Is it always like this?"

The woman from his hostel laughed, a smug smile on her face. "Welcome to Kevand Station."

"But… How?" He was never lost for words but this took his breath away.

"It's all thanks to our biome tech. She promised to give us an EA world."

"The money it must cost…" was all he could say, sudden grief for what he had lost lodging in his throat.

The woman laughed. "They said you were interested in business prospects. Our service rates are no more than those down on the surface. Messera Anyara promised that too, and she should know about surface costs."

The name shoved back the darkness with a gleam of promised data. "You know the Messera?"

The woman turned a disbelieving look on him. "Mingle with a strata level that high. Not in my brightest dreams, Messer."

He let her keep talking all through the trip to his lodging, but all he gathered was that Messera Anyara came from a powerful and wealthy family. He'd guessed that from the first, so he was no wiser. He had to wait impatiently through check-in, through more impudent interrogations, even a skin scan to confirm his DNA and health status then, finally, the door of his room closed behind him and he was alone again.

It was much like any room in a hostel for business travellers back in Urbis, the capital of Arcadia, if somewhat smaller and more spartan. It did have a secure com port, one needing little tweaking to make it truly secure. He set to learning what he could about the mysterious Messera Anyara a Prithand2.

Caution made him start again with a typical business search, despite his security add-ons. Given what he knew of Hilmar a Kevand3 and the attitude of the border official, he couldn't rule out hacking of his feed. He began by tracking down the station's administrative class. Who ran it, who was in charge of trade, research, the maintenance functions? All the areas an investor needed to know about. What can I buy, who do I talk to about it and will this place stay safe? It wasn't till the end that he added in the hub's unique biome, almost as an afterthought. Who made the stunning gardens and who worked them? A natural enough question for any incoming tourist. He pulled the staff list, scrolling up the names till he came to the one he wanted. Not at the top as expected, but on a side branch of the organisation. She was listed as a specialist consultant, yet his courier had talked like Anyara ran this place. Suddenly, his screen disappeared and a 'Content blocked' warning came up.

Just who was Anyara a Prithand2 and why did her name cause a block that overrode his own, highly sophisticated systems? Time to go hunting.

He glared at the space where his screen should glow, as if annoyed at its failure. He tapped fingers, as if trying to rejig his com and break through, then gave a frustrated scowl, thumping the sides of the chair. Another glare for good measure, before striding to the cleansing unit, as if hoping a full cycle would relieve his temper. He discreetly switched on his com unit, using his own security mode. It worked again, thankfully.

Stepping into the cleanser, he first set it to a full pummelling massage before letting it slow down to a diffuse cooling mist. He pulled up a screen. His com was the best available on Arcadia, and he'd added his own modifications. Most coms were obscured by mist but his screen came up clear and shining. He set it to explore the current social calendar.

Where would an interested tourist be most likely to run into the fascinating Messera Anyara?

Days later, he was starting to wonder if he'd lost all his vaunted smarts. He'd become the latest toy of the establishment, using every thread of diplomacy and flattery he possessed. He knew all the tricks from working to make his family's company wealthier and more powerful. Power and greed had the same smell in any collection of humans, as did a restless need for flattery and entertainment.

He gave them what they wanted, smiling falsely at all the beautiful women and men, and talked and listened endlessly. Not one of the glittering social gatherings included an auburn-haired woman with skin of river pearl, glowing with the brilliance of sun striking the upper side of a storm cloud and made for him to touch.

Time to change tactics. He spent the next day poring through the economic data sites and analysing his findings. Or that's what his com log showed. It was what a businessman would do as a newcomer to the station and hungry for profits. He also wandered through the station's social pages and read what the ordinary people of this artificial island in space worried about.

The next day he looked out his window and saw the artificial light already touching the gardens and walkways below. He rubbed his stomach, as if a man who'd spent too much time at banquet tables, and pulled on the new clothes he'd purchased. The ones that were the best he could tolerate of what passed for current fashion here. Hopefully, they were of a kind to let him blend in rather than scare anyone off.

"Holiday time," he announced for the benefit of those listening in on surveillance. "I'll be out until this evening," he added to the room service bots.

Today, he chose to explore the walkways, the markets, and the ordinary streets of the station. First, he wandered through the gardens. Neat and tidy, with flowers and plants designed to please. He ached for something wilder. Something big and overwhelming.

"Pretty, but not much good to eat," grumbled a man beside him.

"Didn't they teach you anything in first school, Minas?" said the woman with him. His wife of many years, by the pained look the man gave her, before tucking her arm into his as her face bloomed with the joy of the flowers smiling up at them.

His father and mother had those small moments. A secret instant of something that had grown over years and children, the small and large trials and joys of busy family life. He hadn't noticed them much growing up. They were just part of life, but now he would give anything for the sound of his father's gruff advice or the gentle touch of his mother's hand. She'd always come into their rooms and touched each of her children when she returned home, no matter the hour. Her patients often needed her until late but, every night, he remembered that small touch, surfacing from sleep then drifting back again, knowing he was safe and loved.

She still loved him, that he didn't doubt, but whether she approved of or liked him was currently in doubt. He moved brusquely on. Somewhere must have plants that broke the ordered existence of the station.

Hours later, he stopped at a sidewalk bar opposite a field of what looked to be root vegetables. A shimmer of light surrounding it told of a strong security field keeping trespassers out, but inside the barrier, service bots moved carefully between the rows with scanners busy dropping in what he assumed to be water or fertiliser from time to time. That level of detail told him more than anything else about the hub. This was a world where every single plant was monitored and cared for.

As were the insects. He'd learned that when he'd gone to slap at an annoying bug buzzing around his head and heard a shocked gasp from a bystander. His hand froze then gently waved away the trespasser. Even that looked to be wrong, from the young woman's glare. He dredged up what he remembered from ecology classes.

Bugs must be used to assist plant growth here, for fertilisation, pest control and all the rest. No bots were as good, and he could see the efficiency of it. That didn't make him like bugs buzzing around his head, and he moved on from the cloud of hungry pests. "Go do what you're supposed to and leave me alone," he muttered balefully.

By the end of the day, he'd learned a lot more than in any of the dry reports. The biome of this place was woven right into the fabric of daily life. Every plant, bug, small creature, and fungus had a role to play in the maintenance of the hub—the air he breathed, the water he drank and the food he ate. He suspected the place was far more self-sufficient than the online databanks suggested. His sister Fiorusghe would be in her element, except for the lack of trees. Or storms, rain, and real weather. Fioruishge may be a trained ecological engineer and work for the cursed Survey, but she was born a Mountainer like him.

Yet somewhere on this hub lurked a mind directing all this. From their comments, the people of the hub were proud of their home and spoke openly of its special character. And all used one name: Anyara.

Anyara a Prithand2 might keep a low profile, but her people saw her in every smiling flower and healthy, glowing leaf. Anyara ran this hub, whatever any ranking chart said.

CHAPTER FOUR

Anyara dug her trowel into the dirt of the planting beds in the nursery. The rich smell rose up and welcomed her home and, around her, the only sounds penetrating her hidden sanctuary were the gentle hiss of the mister on baby plants and the odd trill of a cricket coming in an open window.

She remembered the long arguments before bringing in the crickets. They were a useful food source, she'd said. They helped control the more abundant plant species and brought balance to the ecosystem. Every scientifically sound platitude she could dream up.

The truth was, their call made her happy and she had long ago learned to grab tight to that precious commodity … ever since she'd said goodnight to her parents, not knowing it would be goodbye.

Her com buzzed sharply. Only one person used that signal. She hastily brushed off her hands and stepped away from the garden bed before signalling to answer.

"Good morning, Uncle Hilmar," she said in her best, deferential-niece voice. The one she'd spent years mastering.

"Anyara. What do you think you're doing in the planting rooms? You have labourers for that."

"I enjoy it, Uncle. It helps me plan out my work schedule."

He gave his usual bad-tempered harrumph, with the thin-faced glare she'd learned meant he was even less pleased than usual with her.

"How may I assist you, Uncle?" she said.

"Don't mollycoddle me, girl. You've been meddling."

She had? Alarm flared inside her.

"On your last trip off station."

"Yes, Uncle? I was attending a conference. You were sent the details of the attendees."

He lifted a hand as if in dismissal. "Not that. On your way home, you had a passenger."

"We often do, Uncle. You have always encouraged it," she said with every particle of humility she could summon. "The fee brings down the costs of my travel."

Another harrumph. "This one was from Arcadia."

Her mouth dropped and her heart sank. Seolta had been telling the truth, but Arcadia… "He didn't say that." It was true, to a point. With her uncle it was best to stick to the truth, but only as much as he directly asked for.

"What was the origin on his departure submission?"

"Interim HubfourX, en route to Alliance Central."

Hilmar looked about to strangle her and she stopped breathing for a moment. "That's a transit hub. The man's from Arcadia and had his fingers in a very juicy game I had in play there. Now he gets a lift to my system with *my* niece. Thank you, Anyara."

She had only one option. She fell to her knees, bowed her head, and used her most abject voice. "My deepest apologies, Uncle. I should have asked more questions. He said he was seeking investment opportunities, and Surned system is always looking for investors."

"Yes, yes, he's a smooth rogue. Seolta den Coille has been conning business rivals since childhood." There went her hope he had the wrong man. "You have landed me in a rare pickle, girl. Not to mention the man's knack with com systems."

Now Anyara had another fear. "What's he done?" Could Seolta have blindly wreaked havoc on her hub systems?

A crack of laughter. "Your precious station is safe. He's good, but not that good. We are watching him."

Did she detect a note of admiration? Suddenly the floor beneath her feet seemed sticky and unstable. "What do you want me to do?" she said. Her chest was tight with tension.

"Do? Smile, girl, that's all. And wear something better than those rags. My birthday gala is in two day-cycles, and this year you are attending the station celebrations. Looking like my niece, not a low-level worker."

She usually had to attend the gala planet-side. Her uncle's annual confirmation to Alliance officials that he hadn't killed her yet. He gave her the twisted sneer which was the closest Hilmar a Kevand3 came to smiling. "You're going to attend, and you will re-acquaint yourself with Messer Seolta den Coille. Then, my dear niece, you are going to find out what that slippery piece of ship leavings is up to."

The night of the gala, Anyara pulled up a full holo self-image and circled it, studying it intently. Was this what her uncle wanted? Her gown was spectacular enough: a soft shimmer of silver, sculpted in intricate pleats moulding to breast and waist, then falling in a cloud of light to settle on the ground. She frowned, scrutinising the fit. She could breathe, just, but was grateful for her daily workouts. The dress forgave no human frailty.

The looks on the faces of the officials waiting to welcome her was some reassurance. The light in their eyes before quickly shuttering anything personal gave her a boost and she planted on her best high-strata manners to receive their greetings.

"Messera Anyara. A pleasure to welcome you. So kind of your uncle to spare you to us on this happy occasion." The station master ended the fulsome words with a deep bow, reminding her disastrously of Seolta den Coille and his effortlessly graceful bows. Would he come?

"Thank you. I am pleased to join you," she said, keeping tight control of her face.

"It's a wonderful surprise to be able to welcome you here this year," said the chief operations officer with a fake smile.

"My uncle wanted me to personally assure the hub of his continued interest and support for Kevand Station."

Which was true enough, if not the reason for her presence. Her hub served not only as an important transit post for Surned, it also provided a significant share of the fresh foods for the surface habitats.

Unfortunately, her appearance meant she was forced to host the receiving line, greeting those chosen to be invited and those who'd wrangled an invitation for their own ends. The ones who cared nothing for her uncle but didn't dare offend him, and those desperate for advancement or to hold onto a sinecure position.

She could have told them that dealing with her uncle was very straightforward. Say yes to whatever he demanded and keep making him money. And don't ever criticise him, in public or private. His surveillance system was infamously good.

It wasn't until her face felt frozen from smiling and her fingers crushed by the overly enthusiastic grasps of the scared and eager that *he* joined the line. Outsiders came last, even ones splashing credits around with promises to invest. She'd heard plenty during these last days of the doings of their latest visitor.

"Messera Anyara, may I present Messer Seolta a Manas, currently visiting us on a tour of possible investment sites," said the station master. "Messer Seolta, the niece of the esteemed Hilmar a Kevand3, Messera Anyara a Prithand2."

She saw the shock of that hit Seolta's face, followed by something she couldn't interpret. Something dark and wretched. Then his smile came back, that practised smile she'd rejected the first time he'd used it on her.

"The Messera and I are acquainted, thank you, Station Master," said Seolta den Coille. "She was kind enough to give me a place on her ship on the way here."

Did no one else see through his masks? She swallowed then let him take her fingers.

He paused as if considering them. Then his head bowed elegantly and his lips touched her fingertips.

She had no escape. Those warm lips breathed against her skin. His head rose and those haunting dark eyes locked with hers. "Messera, a delight to meet you again. I hope to have a chance to further our acquaintance later in the evening."

It was as false as the chief operation officer's greeting, but more subtle. She daren't speak, not yet, refusing to let the quaver in her voice betray her. She gave him a slow head bow matching the formality of his own as she gathered her courage and regained control.

"If possible, Messer. I have a full evening in front of me."

A twinkle lit those untrustworthy eyes. "I will find you," he murmured, then moved on as the next in the endless line stepped impatiently forward to take his place.

By the end of the line, she felt like screaming.

She was finally released only to be swallowed by a morass of supplicants grasping for her attention. It was worse than being at the gala down on Surned. At least there, the greedy had direct access to her uncle and were well aware she had nil influence with him. Too many in this crowd imagined Hilmar cared what his niece wanted.

All she wanted was to be left alone, to stay alive and surround herself with her living, breathing flora and fauna. But her uncle had given her a task to complete, and the thought of it chewed up any courage left to her. Somehow, she had to bring herself to talk to Seolta again. When her smile felt like splitting her face in two and her innards churned so tight she was about to be sick, she gave in and slipped into the corridor leading to the ladies' withdrawing rooms.

No one followed her, thankfully, and she slipped out with a crowd of giggling young ones, excited to be at their first big party. They bustled off, nearly running to get back to the manic gaiety of the main hall, leaving her behind.

Not ready to face the crowd, she slipped into a side alcove and leaned against the wall, eyes shut.

"Who are you avoiding, Messera? A beautiful and *highborn* lady need fear no one."

She swung round in alarm. He stood half in shadow at the back of the alcove, graceful even in profile.

"Were you waiting for me?"

"I did promise to meet you later, and I *always* keep my promises."

"But you hedge them," she said, remembering what he'd said on board ship. "Are you here to harm my world or my uncle?"

"We're old friends, he and I. Why would I want to harm him?"

For the same reason she didn't trust the slick silkiness of his voice. A smooth rogue, her uncle had named him, a man who 'had been conning business rivals since childhood.'

She'd been avoiding his kind for years. "You tell me," she said.

He stepped forward, showing her his face, and her heart sank. On board ship, she had thought him easy to talk to and begun to wonder. She had enjoyed being with him. The glitter in his eyes tonight killed that.

Her uncle had insinuated that Seolta had helped ruin one of his schemes, not something her uncle was likely to forget or forgive.

"We have nothing to say to each other."

"Oh, I think we do, Anyara a Prithand2, niece of Hilmar a Kevand3."

"If you wish to speak to my uncle, you will have to approach him directly. He doesn't let mere nieces dictate his actions."

"Nieces who are the guest of honour at his birthday gala and warrant the use of a private ship for a holiday trip."

"I was attending a conference." One at which she had been invited to speak, but had declined. Her uncle would not be pleased if she became well known. Letting her attend was a big enough concession.

"And you suddenly decide to stay on the hub for his gala instead of attending the one down on Kevand3, which I've learned is your usual practice. Did your uncle ask you to do that?"

Her heart thumped. This was getting too close to truth. Her uncle's ears could reach into this small alcove.

"You are imagining things, Messer. After so recently returning home, it was more convenient to stay on station. It's not the first time."

"But the first for many years. Ever since you passed from girlhood into a beautiful woman. The kind that turns the head of any man your uncle wants something from."

Like him, he meant.

Yet under the taunts was a brittle edge, as if she had somehow hurt him. No, that path was dangerous. Time to end it. Except she couldn't, not with her uncle's instructions ringing in her ears. "Are you such a man?" she asked, "Or is it the other way around? You know a lot about me, yet I know little of you other than your claim to be seeking investments here. I have met too many this evening thinking to use me to get to my uncle."

"Oh, I fully intend to approach your uncle—when I'm ready."

Anyara flinched, glancing nervously up. Was he trying to get himself killed?

"What is it?" he said, in a suddenly changed voice. "Has he threatened you?"

"No, no, of course not"

Then he stepped closer, and did the one thing she hadn't expected. He took her hand and pulled her closer still. "Come with me," he murmured into her ear, so low she could have imagined it. "I know a place we're safe from surveillance."

She shook her head frantically and tugged her hand free before the warmth of his hold persuaded her. There was no such place. "It's been nice speaking to you, Messer Seolta. I hope you enjoy the remainder of your stay with us."

Then she took to her heels and fled back to the main hall. Safe from his beguiling eyes and stunning touch.

Safe in one way, but not safe from harm. As safe as she could hope for. She smiled desperately through the rest of the gala, relieved to find that their disturbing offworlder had disappeared, and she escaped as soon as she could to the earthy smells and living peace of her plant nursery.

She would have to meet him again; her uncle had ordered it. But not yet, not till she had conquered whatever it was about this man that unsettled her so much. She breathed in deeply of the earthy smells and gave no thought at all to the dirt latching onto the sweeping skirts of her fairy-tale gown.

Seolta watched her go and didn't know what he felt more: the anger that had swamped him when he'd heard her name and position, or fear for her. That had been real terror in her eyes. He couldn't stay and keep smiling. He possessed just enough control to put on his charming self as he made his excuses to the station master, dropping it as soon as he exited the building.

It was long past time to track down his real enemy. He needed to get to Hilmar's home.

Who's running now?

His evening boots clattered on the hard plascrete pavement and the scent of the multitude of flowering plants gracing each side of the footpath assaulted his nose. None of them belonged here any more than he did.

And none could go home, none could sink their roots into the honest soil of their home planet any more than he could.

In a churned-up mix of emotions, he found and organised his passage. The first light of the day-cycle seeping across the artificial sky greeted him as he marched into the shuttle port and took his place for the trip to Surned surface.

Hilmar would know he was coming.

And afterwards?

Hilmar wasn't a fool. He'd know Seolta was under constant surveillance by a number of parties. He'd be allowed to land, but after that, only his wits would help him.

They hadn't helped him last night. She'd been set onto him by Hilmar.

And the terror in her eyes? What would happen to her if she'd failed whatever instructions Hilmar had issued? Anger still warred with fear inside him.

She'd betrayed him.

She was terrified.

He stared out at the approaching world, abruptly wishing he could turn the shuttle around and take back the entire evening. Hilmar wasn't a fool, but Seolta could make no such claim.

The Surned border staff at landing didn't help, grilling him with a list of questions far exceeding what any sane person would regard as sensible.

Why did they need his shoe size, by all the seeds?

At the end, he had to sign a declaration preventing him making any call upon the resources and wealth of any Surned habitat.

If we fleece you or hurt you, that's your problem.

Then he was in. He plastered on a triumphant smile, despite the prickle on the back of his neck, and pulled up his com to order whatever passed for a skimmer here to take him to the main commercial sector of the hub. His baggage capsule had already been sent on to his hotel, or rather, the authorities had insisted he consign it to them for transfer, along with his access codes, before he was allowed to enter the habitat. As if he were stupid enough to leave anything of importance in a luggage capsule. He quickly found the pickup area shown on his com and stood waiting for what they termed a *skitter.* Then he looked around at his new home.

No, not a home. Not with the sights and smells that assailed him. Metal, hurrying people, colours of harsh grey and muted primaries, an overpowering sense of the mechanical and inorganic. The saving whisper of plants and dirt that graced Kevand Station hadn't made it down to the main city planetside. There must be a biome somewhere to maintain the atmosphere and other services, but his nose and eyes said it was locked well away from lesser mortals.

They didn't like greenery and dirt, or were they were too precious to risk damage by this stern-faced populace?

A box shape slid into the gap beside him. "Seolta a Manas to sector X3," said a tinny voice from its interior.

He stared at it in consternation. Maybe he was supposed to sit on top of the thing.

"Get a move on there," said a gruff voice behind him.

He would if he knew how.

"Put your hand on the panel," said an impatient woman. "You never seen a skitter?"

"No, Messera. We don't use them at home."

"Spare us. Another dirtminer come to the big city. It's simple enough."

The woman pushed his hand onto the stippled pad on the side and showed him how to open the contraption. A flap collapsed into the side facing him and she gestured him to take the spartan seat inside. "It'll stop and open automatically when you reach your programmed destination. You have twenty seconds to exit before it leaves for its next pickup."

He climbed in and immediately the hatch clanged shut and the vehicle jerked into motion. No window allowed a view of the exterior. Instead, a steady stream of adcasts streamed across all four walls. Blatant demands to buy, buy, buy, interspersed with quotations and praise of the esteemed senior executive of the habitat, Messer Hilmar a Kevand.

No number after his name. Unusual. There were four Kevand habitats. Did the man have a home in each?

More questions and too few answers. Maybe the streets would tell him more. A lot later than he'd expected—he'd checked the distance from the port to his destination—the box jerked to a halt and the hatch opened, disgorging him onto the main street of the commercial hub.

To a man used to the streets of Urbis, Arcadia's capital, the place seemed almost deserted.

It's only a habitat and the population of the planet Surned is a fraction that of Arcadia.

Maybe, but Surned was a world driven by credits and his research said this was the centre of it. So where did the trades, the negotiation, the general wrangling and dealing take place?

He had the names and location of all the major corporates loaded to his com files but ignored them for now. Instead, he chose to walk, to breathe in the feel of the place and find out what the carefully sculpted reports and publicity 'casts left out.

His first thought: it was clean, ferociously so, just as the publicity promised. Clean to the point of being intimidating. Probably the purpose of it. He observed a bot briskly sweeping away a piece of trash dropped by a skinny youth. The boy's face saw it and suddenly drained of colour. He frantically patted his tunic over and over as if making sure no other litter strayed from his protection.

Seolta had never before encountered a teenage boy concerned with tidiness.

A flashing sign advertised a bar and, below, a group of what looked to be typical mid-level business types walked through the door. He followed them, expecting to find the hubbub of voices found in any Arcadian bar.

Dead silence greeted him. Heads clustered together, patrons sat at scrubbed tables and stared at com screens with mouths moving but no sound escaping. Each group must be huddled inside their own privacy bubble. Drinks came by a slot on the table, as at home, but no wait staff wove through the room with cheery smiles and rapid quips. Nothing about the place smacked of cheer. Instead, it reeked of fear and secrets hardily kept. He stayed for a while to avoid notice by the bar staff, ordering a drink bearing the same name as his favourite on Arcadia. The stuff served up no more resembled that smooth ale than this place felt like a proper bar. He added counterfeiting to normal practice on this world. No wonder Hilmar had so many credits to flash around. Honesty was as lightly held on Surned as its weak gravity.

He pulled up the local newscast, appearing to browse it as he drank. He took careful note of the other patrons, and soon realised that solo drinkers were common, all intent on their com feeds, all set to privacy mode. This was a place for seeking refuge in plain sight.

Could Hilmar's surveillance reach into personal feeds? He'd previously have said it was impossible, but he was no longer so sure. He'd picked up a tracer the last time he'd tried snooping into the Surned systems and had pulled out quickly. So far, his own feeds were secure, but he was forced to recall Marshal an Fallon's warning back on Arcadia. 'Stay well away from Surned,' an Fallon had said.

Maybe the man wasn't just trying to stop Seolta causing an Alliance-sized diplomatic disaster.

He wandered idly through the newsfeeds, pausing on the local business and social sites. Then checked out a few of the more expensive-looking ad feeds. The kind of activity expected of an investor, even if Hilmar knew well he was here for something quite different.

The man owed him.

And look what happened the last time you went after revenge.

He'd thought he was using Hilmar and it turned out the opposite was true. He'd underestimated the sheer capacity of the man's greed. Not a mistake he'd make twice. He just had to find a suitable bait, one big enough to overcome the man's distrust of him.

An article caught his eye. A report on the birthday gala celebrations, with a subtly worded note on the absence this year of the Executive's niece, Anyara a Prithand2. It was covered by the effusive praise for the Executive in arranging for his niece to attend the gala on her home hub, but that didn't hide the underlying questions.

Why had Anyara felt it necessary to stay away from the surface celebrations this year?

He read it through a number of times, checking out the message under the words. It wasn't his imagination. Something had changed between Hilmar and his niece, or rather, in his niece's importance. Whatever it was, Hilmar would be the one to gain. Power, or wealth, they were the same thing here.

Accompanying it were reassuring vids of the 'beautiful and stunning niece of our esteemed Executive' dancing with a man he recognised as the Kevand Station master, looking smug and holding her far too tightly. A sudden, alien clench of his gut and a strange impulse to jump into the vidcast and pull her away from the man was made worse by the look on her face and the rigid set of her body. Anyara had no enjoyment in the dance. He switched abruptly away from the report. He was here for a purpose, and Anyara a Prithand2 was a means to that only.

Thankfully, his inner voice stayed silent. It didn't help.

You have a purpose. Keep to it. He read on, roaming wider over the social pages, from the most serious to the utterly frivolous. All shared the same care in presentation and a nervous obsequiousness to Hilmar a Kevand.

This place was terrified of his target. If the ordinary citizen took such care not to raise his anger or suspicion, what about his niece? Did Anyara live in fear of her uncle, or was she feared by the public also?

The woman he'd glimpsed so briefly on their voyage, then studied obliquely in his time on her hub? Not from the way the ordinary citizens of her station talked of her. Horror coiled inside him. Had he made a terrible mistake?

He'd given into his anger once before and it had nearly caused the death of an honourable man he should have called friend. That same rage had swamped him when he discovered who she was, when he thought she had spent time with him only because her uncle had asked it. Asked it, or forced her to it?

Nothing in his browsing implicated her in her uncle's schemes. Seolta had spent years studying his business opponents and working to expand the power of his family's company. The Den Coille wealth was built on the highly nutritious pollen harvested from the festia trees that thrived in the swampy conditions of his western mountain home, and Seolta had revelled in seeking out new ways to maximise its use and expand their markets across the Alliance. That was how he first met Hilmar a Kevand3 and Alliance Deputy Malgrave.

Those new markets hadn't saved him from prison cells and death warrants. The memory of that courtroom still ate at him. Nor had they saved him from the fury after his release that had driven him to collude with the kind of gutter-dwelling parasites he should have cut down immediately. A fury that still drove him, bucking his hardest attempts to control it and leaving him questioning everything.

He slammed shut his com. Enough time-wasting. He had a man to track down and revenge to plan.

One that must not hurt Anyara a Prithand2. What lay between Hilmar and him was between them only. No others must be affected, and particularly not Anyara.

Why, he refused to answer.

He strode out the door and down the street fast enough to block out the faces around him. All people whose lives must change if Seolta succeeded in destroying Hilmar.

That was what he intended, regardless of his instructions from the Arcadian federal marshals. He'd been told to gather information, not take matters into his own hands. An order made to be broken, he decided, unless Arcadia's Galactic Ministry agents managed to track him down in time to stop him. Before that, what he did was his own affair. Hilmar and the Alliance deputy had come near to destroying his and his family's lives. He meant to repay the favour.

By the end of the day, he'd learned little more and driven his frustration levels to maximum. Everything about this habitat was controlled by Hilmar's security services, closing down the citizens, any outsiders and, most particularly, he guessed, blocking any scrutiny by Seolta. Twice today, they had stopped him and put him through a full interrogation that would have broken a plethora of laws at home on Arcadia. Here, by the bored looks of passersby and their sudden veering aside to avoid him, interrogations were routine. They'd let him go, each time with the kind of warning that should have had him taking the first flight off world.

Interesting.

He arrived late in the day-cycle at the utilitarian hostelry that passed for the habitat's best visitor accommodation. His room held little more than a sleeper, a desk with the room's only chair, and a minimal cleansing unit. A ping on his com, and finally some good news. An invitation to attend a dinner the following evening. One hosted by Hilmar a Kevand3. There was no possibility of refusing, of course, but he still checked it out on the social pages before sending to confirm.

A routine gathering of the habitat's senior staff, major business managers, and some smaller company heads. He did a background check, wondering at the inclusion of the smaller companies, and quickly discovered the reason.

All were owned or controlled by Hilmar a Kevand3. Not publicly, but Seolta was good at tracking company ownership. He used the oldest rule in business: follow the credits. Of those owned by connections, none appeared to have any say in the running of Kevand3, or showed any sign of the wealth their shares should bring. That went to Hilmar, covered by private agreements that he doubted even an Alliance court would be able to prove.

He roamed wider and discovered the reason behind the lack of a number on that earlier vidcast. Hilmar controlled all four Kevand habitats. Kevand3 was the largest, so presumably why he chose it for a base, but the others were all highly profitable.

The Galactic Ministry briefings back on Arcadia had warned him about Hilmar's reputation. A shark of the first order, the type who sucked up whatever he could then moved on to the next victim, but he'd read that in the man when Hilmar first contacted him back on Arcadia.

Known and ignored it, telling himself he could use the man for his own ends and escape untouched afterwards. But mud sticks, and fouled mud left stains you couldn't remove.

That evening, he pulled on a tunic similar to the local style but different enough to hint at off-world wealth. The kind looking to expand into other profitable areas. Hilmar had met his family and knew of the generations of power in the western mountains that lay behind him. He'd also recognised Seolta's determination to be part of that history. Seolta couldn't deny he enjoyed power, not after what he'd done, and only the strong-minded care of the rest of his family had checked his youthful greed. Anyone from a family as large as Seolta's learned early to fight for their place in the hierarchy, to use their strengths and cover their weaknesses.

His family knew his weaknesses and still loved him.

He was welcomed into the hall by a man introduced as Chief Operations Officer of Kevand3. The man who ran the day-to-day affairs of the habitat, he guessed that meant.

"Messer Seolta, a pleasure to welcome you to our small gathering. We trust you will have a profitable and enjoyable stay on our humble world. Please let me or one of my officers know if we can assist you with any introductions."

Hilmar himself sat on a massive chair set on an elevated dais at the far end of the hall. He made no sign of having seen Seolta, but Seolta wasn't fool enough to think that meant he wasn't aware of his presence, not a man who played the kind of power games in place tonight. Hilmar was waiting for Seolta to come to him. Seolta began his journey to satisfy that wish.

"That's kind of you, Messer," he said to the operations manager. "Maybe you can suggest any who might be interested in some minor cooperation to both parties' mutual benefit."

The man gave a rapacious smile and soon Seolta had a sheath of names. By mid-evening, his place on Kevand3 was cemented, and he had been accepted into a circle of potential partners. Time for the next step.

"You have all been most helpful. Would it be possible to meet the esteemed Executive and pass on my thanks for his kindness in inviting me here tonight?"

A nervous titter ran through the group, but none looked scared or surprised. They wouldn't have talked to him in the first place if it hadn't been cleared with Hilmar's staff, and he'd just assured them he understood the way of business here.

It took longer than he'd expected to organise, but finally the major domo beckoned him forward and he walked up to the chair where Hilmar waited. Seolta plastered on his coolest smile, one designed to placate the locals but still ensure Hilmar knew Seolta had forgotten nothing of what happened back on Arcadia.

Seolta wasn't in the mood to waste time on games.

It didn't change Hilmar's attitude. "Messer Seolta mar Bram an Scathach den Coille," he said with arms stretched wide as if granting a blessing to a supplicant. "Welcome to our home."

"Thank you, Messer. Seolta a Manas is sufficient. I defer to local customs. It leads to fewer … misunderstandings."

Hilmar gave a beneficent bow of his head. "You're a long way from home."

And Hilmar was a big cause of that.

"Circumstances have changed since your time on my home world, Messer. It became expedient to look for prospects elsewhere, with my family's backing of course."

I am not alone in my exile, whatever you may assume, Messer a Kevand3. You attack me at your peril.

The man's sudden widening of eyes said he got the message. "Our humble habitat has much to recommend it, but nothing like your usual interests, Messer Seolta. I would be surprised if you find anything worthy of your particular bent here."

"You forget, Messer, my family has a range of interests, and my own area of expertise lies more in com systems."

By the clenching of Hilmar's hand on his chair, Seolta thought he may have ventured too far, but then the man's fist relaxed, he threw his head back and laughed out loud, turning to their audience. "Our esteemed visitor tried to meddle in our minor checks on his systems when he first arrived."

The wave of nervous laughter echoed the naiveté of such an attempt. Kevand3 may lack some of the amenities of larger places, but its com systems were as well developed as any. Better than Arcadia's in some ways, when it came to security, but Seolta had been following Alliance-wide com news for years. He'd hoped his tricks were hidden from their spying eyes, but hadn't counted on it.

He planted his feet square on the glossy faux marble floor and smiled back at Hilmar. "Since last we met, Messer, I've learned to make sure of the field before entering a new contest. Thank you for the much needed lesson."

The man's hand tightened on the chair again. "What have you done with those lessons, Messer den Coille? That is what concerns us today."

"Learned what is important, I hope," said Seolta. "Learned to work only with those whose interests also serve mine."

"Ah. And your home world? Do you have any plans to return there?"

Seolta let his mouth stretch into a half smile. "Only when I have achieved a healthy level of success in my travels."

"And the past?"

"Is no longer relevant, I've discovered. Best to learn its lessons and move on."

"Ah," said the man in the chair, but in quite a different voice this time. He'd given Hilmar the answer he wanted. Seolta could feel the relaxation in the room as Hilmar leaned forward, a decided gleam in his eyes. "And would this success of yours include a financial parameter, Messer den Coille?"

Seolta clasped his hands loosely together. "Most decidedly, Messer a Kevand3."

"Then it seems we have something to discuss after all." He turned his head towards the man beside him. "Make an appointment for the Messer. In the green office."

A gasp went around the room and the usher directed Seolta to step back, leading him away from the front of the hall. It was only later that he found a chance to ask about that gasp.

"The green room?" echoed a man in his current group. "I heard he'd asked you there but didn't believe it."

"It's true enough," said another man in the circle. "I heard it myself."

A shuffling of feet and the distance between him and the rest discreetly increased. "What is the green room?" he asked. "I haven't been able to find a reference to it in this habitat."

"Oh, it's not in Kevand3," said the one who'd already heard of his meeting. "You need official permission to travel to Kevand1."

"It's the Executive's private office. The one he uses when he wants to talk to you unrecorded."

"Only his closest allies meet with him there," said a third, a touch of awe in his voice.

Closest allies, or enemies? What had he got himself into?

Getting the required permission was the first item on his next day's agenda. Or rather, finding where and how to get it. He did the obvious: ask the coordinator at his hostel. All that achieved was frightening the man silly.

"Why do you want to go there? No commercial centres at Kevand1. It's mostly old factories and high-up's retreats, and they don't let just anybody visit them."

A quick com search confirmed the man's words. It changed nothing. Hilmar had been quite clear on the place for his meeting. Fortunately, he had the connections he'd made last night and had taken note of the places they talked of meeting. Mid-day-cycle found him strolling down the most fashionable street of the habitat, best day tunic on and looking his most urbane. An off-world tourist seeking a suitable place to dine and watch the world pass by.

It quickly became obvious which was the favoured establishment, but Seolta still made a show of wandering past them all, before finding a congenial seat by a sad-looking shrub. It's very rarity in the habitat made it stand out, and he doubted any here would recognise the washed-out leaves as a plea for better care. Not unless they'd visited Kevand Station where Anyara ensured all her plants were loved and flourished

No economic reason for it, one had told him when he mentioned it. Why visit such a place except to pass through when boarding a ship?

Seolta pulled up his com and booked a seat at the prime eatery, pleased to see that they offered a chance to join a group table. A much more congenial establishment than the bar he'd endured yesterday. This place was designed for deal-making and exploring possibilities.

He was given a table exactly suited to his purposes. One of the other guests was an acquaintance from the previous night and happened to drop into the conversation early on the story of Seolta's audience with the Executive.

"You've met Messer a Kevand3 before, I think you said." The man leaned forward, keen to bask in the shared glory of knowing someone with an entrée into the rarefied circle.

"I worked with him for a period last yearly cycle on an off-world project." After Anyara's reaction to his being from an EA world, Seolta was reluctant to reveal his true home.

"An off-world project?"

"In a nearby world?" said one anxious voice.

Seolta quickly shook his head. "Three space translations away, and it didn't work out as we'd hoped." Disbelief met that last comment. Hilmar achieved everything he tried here, apparently. "I misread the situation. The world wasn't suited to the project after all."

"Aah."

Much as it rankled taking the blame for the debacle, it did restore the equilibrium at the table.

"You wouldn't be a favourite with the Executive now." The woman barely kept the gloating out of her voice. "He doesn't fail often. Never, actually."

Seolta leaned back, arms loose on the chair. "He's a businessman. To make credits, you have to try a few dead ends. Nothing about it would affect Surned, so he had little to lose."

An alert registered on his com. He brought up the sender, then sucked in his breath. "Excuse me, I have to take this." They all lifted a hand in permission and he brought up the message in privacy mode.

Then chuckled silently. Hilmar was up to his usual tricks. It was an invitation to the promised meeting. In the green office for mid-morning cycle. The permit was attached but no other details to help him. He switched off the message and looked up.

"Good news, Messer?" asked his acquaintance of last night.

"Of a kind," he agreed, "but it has left me in need of urgent assistance. How do I get to Kevand1 by tomorrow morning and where exactly is Messer Hilmar's green office?"

Their mouths dropped open and they all shuffled. Soon afterwards, all found a reason to finish their meal early, many leaving with a decided glare in his direction, including the gloating woman. The last to go was his acquaintance of the previous night. "Shuttles leave twice daily. You'll need to use the overnight one. Anyone at Kevand1 can show you to the green office," he muttered quietly, before giving him a curt head bob and hurrying out of the restaurant. Immediately the wait bots scurried around his table, removing food and implements, including his own, and his com advised him his bill had been actioned. Seolta looked at the manager's booth, and sent an arrogant smile back to the man glowering at him there. He helped himself to one last savoury from the bot's busy arms, then rose slowly and sauntered out of the eatery.

Next on the agenda. The required ticket for the overnight shuttle. After that, he planned to take a tour of Kevand3, preferably without the accompaniment of Hilmar's intrusive surveillance. What about this habitat was Hilmar so keen he not see?

CHAPTER FIVE

The tickets proved easy, thanks to Hilmar's com note. Not that Hilmar was doing him much of a favour. The shuttle proved to be basic and uncomfortable and his chances of getting any sleep the night before the crucial meeting looked slim to impossible. It didn't make him rue having spent the afternoon exploring rather than sleeping. What he'd seen in the lower level areas of Kevand3 had him reviewing every interaction he'd had with Hilmar a Kevand3.

And you had him down as a good man when you first worked with him?

He shoved away the annoying inner voice and shuffled on the hard seat trying to find a way to get some sleep. He still didn't regret how he'd spent the afternoon and, since no one had stopped him boarding the shuttle, he had to hope Hilmar's agents hadn't figured out what he'd been up to. He'd managed to find a back door into their surveillance systems and discovered a tiny flaw. One that let him insert a feedback loop simulating him resting sensibly in his hostel room after lunch while he instead made his escape, trusting the flaw was real and not a trap. The hostel's back corridors were as closely monitored as the front exits, but he'd hacked into the building's plans and found a disused entrance with an easily broken lock and some used worker's coveralls. Head down, pacing wearily, he followed a full bin of refuse trundling down the alley and made sure it was loaded correctly onto the recycling unit, then activated it and walked around the other side to cling on as it made its way down the street. The unit was fully automated to follow its collection schedule and hopefully would carry on for many streets without supervision.

Around the corner, a quick slip into another alley and, many blocks later, he breathed a sigh of relief.

The rest of the day he'd walked or ridden the low-level worker transits, stopping at grimy bars and wandering past utilitarian living blocks, with square factories and schools butted side by side, as if emphasising to the pinch-faced children of the sector the only aspiration available to them. By the end of his explorations, he couldn't say which rode him harder: anger or depression. This might have been Arcadia if Hilmar's schemes had succeeded.

And you would have helped him.

As he squirmed on the hard shuttle seat, he couldn't shove his inner voice away so easily. It was true. Hilmar couldn't have done anything without Seolta's help. He'd introduced Hilmar and Malgrave to Arcadia and all those Arcadian corporate heads intent on holding onto their power and wealth.

What fools they'd been. Hopefully, his brother Cumchdach's digging discovered the names involved and put a stop to any such future plans. Seolta had never known which ones joined the conspiracy. Hilmar was too canny for that.

No, not Hilmar. Alliance Deputy Malgrave. A woman the citizens of Arcadia should have been able to trust.

His next target after Hilmar.

He pulled up the exterior view on his com, hoping for distraction. Surned had a natural day length many times longer than Arcadia's. Right now it was full day out on the surface, despite the habitat's artificial day length, and would be for months yet. The harsh sunlight striking the endless dirt and rocks of the lifeless planetary surface only reminded him of his exile. This couldn't be his lot for the rest of his life. He'd always known of his home world's strict laws. Immigrants were rarely allowed, and only if of overwhelming use to the planet. It had never meant much to him, not until he'd heard the shock in Anyara's voice at anyone leaving an EA world. He did a quick search on the laws of other EA worlds and reality hit home. If Arcadians failed to restore the environmental balance of their planet, a home on a habitat like the ones he'd seen today was all they could expect.

How would they survive? Would they?

Images of his little sister as a child shot through his mind, bouncing in the branches and cheekily challenging him to a race as she scaled madly through ever higher and more fragile branches. The same Fiorusghe who as an adult had saved the family from prison and threat of execution and now worked tirelessly to meet the Alliance's environmental demands.

While he, the so-called cleverest of the den Coille brood, had put them all at risk and brought the whole family under continuous Federal scrutiny, had put his entire world at risk.

He shifted in his seat, uselessly trying to find a better position. Why didn't the tragging vehicle offer sleeper cabins?

Because anyone of consequence would have hired a private shuttle, barred to an off-worlder like him. Few others travelled between habitats on the dead world, the cost prohibitive and too demanding of restricted resources.

He'd questioned the 'reason for this trip' box on the ticket request form, to be met with a shocked gasp by the hostel coordinator assisting him. He put down 'meeting with the Executive' and was relieved to see the box disappear.

Arriving at Kevand1 early the next morning, he slapped off the restraints and stood up to stretch the instant his com signalled the all clear. He had just enough time to take up the hostel room he'd booked and catch a short break before his meeting. Outside his window, the habitat walkways gave off a dull sheen, and the buildings had an air of faded splendour. It was the first habitat on Surned, and the place looked it. His hostel had the same feel, but his room was clean and held a sleeper and a cleansing unit. He flopped back on the sleeper in relief and set his com to wake him in time to find this 'green office'.

For the first time on this hellish trip, that proved to be no problem.

"The skitter will take you there," said the hostel coordinator. "You can't miss it. A real wonder, it is."

He discovered the meaning of that as soon as he stepped out of the skitter, to face a building covered with rustling green plants and the achingly familiar scent of leaf and flower.

He must not break down, not in public and not before this meeting. He'd known Hilmar was a brakka of the first order, but his choice of meeting place confirmed it. He didn't think for an instant it was done to make him feel at home. The man knew exactly the effect that living wall would have on Seolta. The taunting smell of it followed him into the building and right into the main office. Hilmar hadn't bothered with layers of minions or extraneous proof of his supremacy. That plant wall had been enough, and the unctuous smile on the man's face when Seolta signalled his arrival and strode into his office reaffirmed it. He'd even set the ventilation to bring in swirling currents filled with the taste of bruised leaves and budding plants.

If the man thought a blatantly engineered yearning for past delights would bring down a son of the mountains, he hadn't spent long enough on Arcadia. Seolta set his mouth to a matching smirk.

"Morning, Hilmar. A private meeting. I'm honoured."

A twitch at the side of the man's mouth was the only reaction to Seolta's deliberate insolence. "It seemed best, given your past associations and the delicacy of your position here. I am surprised you chose to come to Surned, though. You never struck me as a man to take stupid risks."

"We have unfinished business, and I am not a man who likes that."

"Aah." Hilmar propped his arms on the desk edge and arched his fingers together, eyes narrow. "So you've come asking for help since your misbegotten planet has seen fit to throw you out. Or are you now an agent for your cursed Federals?"

The words might be insulting, but the question was real enough. "I'm on my own," he said, "and you owe me."

A bray of laughter greeted that. "What, for offering you a chance to get back at that pack of miserable ingrates ruling your backwoods world? None of them truly value your abilities, boy, and you know it."

"You think so?"

"Give it a few cycles, and you'll thank me."

Seolta doubted it but kept the thought to himself. "No reason to yet," he said and waited. He might have grossly misread the man and would be shortly paying for that misjudgement. But he didn't think so.

"You expect me to compensate you? No one forced you to work with us. I seem to remember you doing a pile of talking to persuade us to invest in the cursed affair."

That's all it was to Hilmar, a failed investment.

"I lost all my future profits on Arcadia. You merely lost a minor side gamble."

Hilmar glared at him. "So you came here to collect. Do you have a death wish, boy?"

Seolta shrugged. "My own government already tried to execute me. I haven't forgiven that either."

"If you're trying to blackmail me, Messer den Coille, you've forgotten one important element. You hold nothing against me. You proved it when you pulled that disappearing act yesterday." That sneer again. "You registered as silent as soon as you set that loop into action and were picked up on the first skitter you took. What did you find of such interest in our commercial hub?"

That had been the third skitter he'd taken, late in the afternoon when he'd returned to the business sector, and the first on which he'd let his com loosen his blocks so they could see the loop he'd used. Hilmar knew nothing of his hours in the backstreets. "I told you. I need credits and this world seemed a good place to acquire them."

He set his jaw forward as if sulking and frowned at his target. The words and attitude helped, but Hilmar still looked at him like a bug he'd walked on.

"Take a seat." ordered Hilmar, waving to the basic plas chair in front of his desk and seating himself in the padded monstrosity behind the desk—a chair that sat much higher and had Seolta tilting his head upwards to meet the man's eyes.

The simple ploy amused rather than quashed him. Mountainers were not big people, and Seolta had been unsettling rivals much taller than himself since he'd first taken a major role in the family company. His father would have laughed outright at the man, before skewering him in a deal that wrung everything from his opponent.

Hilmar set his hands together. "I'd have thought this the last place you'd choose after what you did on Arcadia. If you hadn't interfered, Ethan Winter would have given in and we'd all have been sitting securely in control of our first Arcadian company."

Seolta sat up. "After you'd killed him for his 'generosity'. I shared a cell with Ethan Winter. I joined that scheme to keep Arcadia safe for my family and friends, not kill them off."

"If we'd chosen a different victim, you'd have let matters take their course?"

Seolta lifted both hands. "There are few allies in business." The man really was despicable. "The benefits to be gained by all of us seemed sufficient to guarantee loyalty."

A choked guffaw answered him. "I always liked you, young den Coille. A heart to match that miserable region you come from. Do your family know what they harboured?"

"They do now," he said shortly. "We're wasting time. You have a proposition for me?"

"That's blunt for a man famed for his subtlety."

"We've worked together before. No point trying to fool you."

Another bark of laughter. "None at all." Hilmar leaned back, blunt-fingered hand laid across the arm of the enormous chair. "To business then. You've seen enough of our habitat by now to decide if there's anything of use to you here."

Seolta nodded in agreement. "You produce mainly metals and raw ingots. Cheapest form for shipping off world. And you have good markets for all of them."

Greed was Hilmar's driving force, and this time, Seolta would use it better than he had on Arcadia.

"A fair summary. There's little potential for an independent trader unless you already have good contacts and can promise our companies a better deal than they already have. You already knew that before you came here." The man's eyes narrowed in suspicion.

Seolta thrust his head up. "I'm not a fan of being told what to do."

"Your Federal security forces barred you from here?"

"Them, and their Alliance contacts."

The man's mouth tightened. "You've brought that scum down on our heads?"

Seolta shook his head. "I gave them the slip back at the first translation point. It's why I hitched a ride with your niece."

"You expect me to believe that's possible."

"No, but they were already here anyway." Hilmar didn't disagree. "My coming here gives them something to focus on other than your own activities."

"A point," Hilmar conceded. "A point."

The man sat in silence, studying Seolta like some caged lab creature. Seolta had no idea what came next. He'd gone over all the possible outcomes of this meeting, his despatch and accidental death chief among them, but now the hairs on the back of his neck stirred.

"It could still work," finally muttered the man, setting his back against the rear of his chair. "You enjoyed your trip here with my niece?"

Seolta lifted his shoulders. "It was much as any other trip."

"And my niece?"

His inner alarm, already shrieking, went up a notch. "An attractive woman, but sadly I didn't see much of her. I spent most of the trip in my cabin."

"Aah yes, the incident with the breakdown." The way he said the word 'incident' had Seolta on full alert. "So my niece is aware of your particular talents."

"Some," he said cautiously.

"And wouldn't be surprised if you gave up on finding opportunities groundside and went back to a world with more to offer, one dependent on correctly functioning systems."

"As are all the habitats on Surned," Seolta pointed out.

Hilmar waved the objection aside. "We have the best systems available here. Her hub doesn't produce the same level of income as a full habitat. Your system talents would be of considerable use up there. You can help me tidy up some loose ends." He fell silent again, maybe rethinking whatever outlandish scheme festered in his mind. "You can go on a survey tour of the other Surned habitats first to check out their systems before transferring back up there. That will provide a decent cover."

For what? He had a nasty idea of the answer, one that included no good ending for Seolta—or Anyara. "Why would the station agree to that?"

"Because I have ordered it."

That confirmed it then. Hilmar didn't just run the Kevand habitats, he ran the whole tragging planet. When he left here, *if* he was allowed to leave here, Seolta was going to make the Alliance do a thorough audit of this man's dealings. Inter-Alliance law allowed no man control of an entire world, not when it put the lives of so many inhabitants at risk, and Seolta remembered well the pinch-faced children of the previous day's wanderings.

There seemed little more to say, apart from the all important matter of payment. "You will be well rewarded. Anything else would look suspicious," said Hilmar. He brought up a screen and a clerical figure materialised in a holo-vid. "Send the contract to Messer den Coille," Hilmar ordered the woman.

Seolta brought up the contract in restricted mode on his com as he checked it over. His own systems had already found the knots in the deal, but none looked to be unusual or problematic and the remuneration was as generous as promised. The nature of his specific task was left vague. Services rendered, it said, and he had a bad feeling what that meant. Tidying up loose ends. He quickly skimmed the rest, then lifted his head.

"It seems fair enough. A few matters need clarification."

"Talk them over with my assistant later. This is a take it or leave it offer."

"If I refuse?"

"That would not be a good idea, Messer a Manas*craoch*." The man rose and the meeting was over. "Good day, Messer. I'm sure we can rely on you to be as discreet and efficient as you were on your home world. And as loyal to those who pay you."

A warning and a confirmation, but he still had to check. Seolta inclined his head and stepped back. "The Messera your niece will be in good hands."

"That is not what you are contracted for," came the harsh reply. Seolta met the man's eyes squarely. He hadn't mistaken the man's meaning. A chill rippled up his back.

"I never forget who pays me," he said. "Your niece's fate is settled. Her shares will soon no longer be a problem," and Hilmar relaxed again giving him a wave towards his door.

"Enjoy your tour," he added with a private crack of laughter as Seolta turned.

Nor did Seolta breathe easier until he'd marched out, taking the fastest down tubes and heard the whoosh of closing doors behind him as he exited the building. He felt no cleaner. He'd suspected Hilmar might use him against Anyara, but not this. Hilmar had just contracted him to get rid of his niece.

He arrived back at his hostel to find that Hilmar's office had already sent through an itinerary. No need to go back to Kevand3, the coordinator airily informed him as if conferring a major treat. He scanned through the list. It took him all over the small world, to places offering potential for trade and others he could see no point in visiting. Hilmar's revenge, he guessed sourly, offering only boredom and wasted time.

Or opportunities to kill him. He'd never doubted at any stage that was Hilmar's first choice, removing Anyara a bonus if he failed to eliminate Seolta. The man just had to find a way to do it without stirring up the kind of scrutiny he couldn't survive. Accidents weren't unknown when travelling habitat worlds, while the suspicious death of a member of a prominent EA business family would bring Alliance investigators down on him fast.

He studied the itinerary again, looking for possible threats. One place was noticeably absent from the list: Prithand2, the birthplace of the esteemed Executive's only relative and the habitat that had sent ten children to Kevand3 all those years ago.

We'll see about that.

He used the rest of the day for a cursory tour of Kevand1 before setting out the next morning. As expected, there was little of note here. Hilmar wouldn't have given him access if there were. A few tired offices and living blocks in the commercial hub, but the residential streets held mostly closed-off gates guarding the private retreats of the favoured few. The publicity casts for the habitat gave the visitor stunning glimpses of highly engineered and madly artistic homes surrounded by gardens featuring a montage of plants from all over the Alliance, but the discordant mix of species and signs of distress in what he could see of the plantings gave the lie to the glowing voice over. Plants chosen for their rarity and expense only, he guessed. No real gardener would come up with these horror shows.

The first stop on his audit tour turned out to be on the exact opposite side of the planet. Did Hilmar hope to unsettle him right from the start? On a proper EA world like Arcadia, this new place would be in a different time and calendar zone. But on EA worlds, people lived in the open air and had to adapt to the planet's cycles, unlike this dead world with its long day/night cycle and even longer yearly transit. Habitat dwellers never looked at the outer world unless their job demanded it. He wondered if many of them had even seen the fascinating play of light and dirt playing on the exterior view screens.

Seolta wasn't so easily caught out. Even if Hilmar made an unexpected change to his schedule, Seolta had memorised enough of the planet's systems to be able to calculate the arrival time. Getting his mental clock to cope with it was proving a bit harder, but he told his head very sternly this was not another trip from Manascraoch to the plains. This trip went from one side of a place as treacherous as Urbis to the other, and his subconscious better stay alert.

As it turned out, the changes to his schedule became so routine that even the most resistant part of his brain gave up expecting any kind of orderly routine, going with whatever time and conditions he found on arrival at each new habitat. His sleep patterns were completely shattered and so were his expectations. He grabbed what he could whenever possible, and his body learned to live with it. It had to.

As for his brain, he'd long learned to take what was thrown at him and subvert it for his own ends. What he thought of as Hilmar's dirty secrets file grew at an exponential rate, as did his knowledge of how to expose it when the time came. He'd been forced to realise, though, that destroying Hilmar on Surned was no longer enough. It might make Seolta feel better but it didn't save Arcadia. The man's downfall had to be part of the wider mission the Arcadian Feds had set him.

Two more scheduled stops and he'd be done with the whole charade. What the tour had shown was much as he'd expected: Hilmar's grasping hands buried deep into all the enterprises on the planet. The convoluted connections that had won the man control weren't always clear, but he'd need a forensic accountant for that, one skilled in habitat systems. He added that to the 'what do I need to get him' file. Also abundant were the signs of inequality and the lies keeping the settlers compliant. The planet was infested with the age-old pattern of a few living well at the expense of ordinary citizens powerless to do anything about it. Their jobs, their very lives, depended utterly on the functioning of their home habitat, and the top strata made sure the lower levels never had access to any external means of changing that. The Alliance wasn't going to hear about it from an ordinary worker, not one from Surned. Maybe from a visitor on his way to Alliance Central?

If he survived that long.

He read through the file on the next stop on the tour, quickly scanning for economic pointers and other important conditions, then noticed something else about the upcoming habitat.

Haverner4 was the nearest stop to another minor habitat nestled in a sheltered plain a few hours shuttle away. Prithand2.

Had Hilmar made a mistake or was this a test? He'd checked out the other stops on the tour, pulling up a holo-map of the planet. If he wanted to go to Prithand2, Haverner4 was his only option.

So how to do it? And what would Hilmar's agents do about it?

He found out not long after his arrival at Haverner4.

"You have friends working in solar power I'm told, Messer," said the supervisor at the manufacturing plant. "Is it an area of interest to you?"

"Anything that makes credits is of interest to me, Messer. And yes, the Winter family of Solaris solar energy are connected to me by marriage and counted as friends," he added, stretching the truth. Ethan Winter had never been so stupid, and Caleb still reserved judgement on his wife's family.

"Perhaps you would like a tour of our habitat's solar field. The supervisor is about to set off on his daily inspection and would be only too pleased to take you with him."

Seolta didn't know whether to pump a fist in glee or check for the assassin. It was all too convenient.

He'd have no other chance.

In the loading bay, the supervisor waited for him in a transit flyer, one large enough to carry them all the way to Prithand2. The man was friendly enough as he took him through the required safety procedures for surface excursions and showed him where the emergency kits were stowed. All matched the standard protocols laid out in Alliance habitat rules. Seolta had memorised them before leaving Arcadia, reviewed them again before landing on Surned, and revised them every single night he stayed on this forsaken world. So far, what the man said matched the ones he'd memorised.

Of course they did. The checks had to go into the official habitat record.

Despite the nerves pulled tight in his gut, a sigh of pleasure left him as the outer dome doors opened and they flew out over the plain surrounding Haverner4. Above him was real sky, around the flyer flowed a real atmosphere, and at the edge of the plain stood actual mountains with achingly familiar, sharp-edged ridges. The air might be toxic in seconds if he tried to breathe it, but it was *real.*

Hilmar couldn't change it, not the atmosphere of a whole tragging planet.

He leaned forward, eager to see more. "Your world has extraordinary colours in its rocks."

The pilot looked startled. "Most folks can't wait to get back inside. You *like* it out here?"

"A few trees would improve it," he said with a grin, "but yes, I do."

The man's mouth gaped. "You seen real trees? They said you had good credits, not that you were a Central mega-rich boy."

"They had some near my home city." What would the man say if he told him his home was built in a tree? "This has its own beauty," he added, pointing to where the sun struck a pile of rocks in a cascade of red, gold, and brightest orange sparkles.

The man beside him shook his head, but there was something in his gaze. As if reconsidering. "The solar field lies fifty klicks ahead. Might as well relax and take in the view, Messer," he said in a decidedly neutral voice.

Seolta calculated. Given their current heading, the solar field had to lie near the border between Haverner4 and Prithand2 territories. He doubted it was a coincidence. Relax? Not a chance.

He nodded genially at his appointed assassin and went back to staring out the window. He'd given the craft a quick once over when he climbed on board and identified any potential weapons. The man's concealed blaster sat on his right hip, according to Seolta's highly illegal scan. He hoped that was the only one he had to worry about.

A whirligig spewed up a cloud of dust from below and the flyer bucked sideways. Seolta grabbed at the side of his chair. The pilot was the one who grinned now.

"Welcome to Surned, Messer." He corrected the sideways drift. "Don't worry, it's just her way of saying 'Hello'."

"Some welcome. Does that happen often?"

"Round these ways, yes. It's the shape of them hills. They put Haverner4 here for the local resources, not the views or comfort. Our outer shield looks like a battle-scarred hub cover."

Something in the words caught Seolta. "You a veteran?" War hadn't been known in the Alliance for centuries but local skirmishes between worlds still flared to life on occasion.

"First Patrol Regimental Sergeant," the man said, puffing his chest out.

"The Alliance Patrol? Is this your home world then? I heard the post-service benefits kept a soldier in comfort for life."

Now the man's face closed in as he glanced up at the right side panel. "My wife's. All her family's here," he said gruffly.

"She must be a special woman," Seolta said to cover the awkward gap.

"The best." The pilot had that same softness in his eye as Seolta's father when he looked at his mother.

"Your children are lucky, Messer."

The man glowed and agreed. "A fine pair they be too, and now we've got the grandchildren arriving. Family, it's something special."

Seolta had grown up in a family based on that kind of love. Family he had betrayed. He made a vow then. Whatever the outcome of this trip, the pilot would not be put at risk. Seolta would escape, but the pilot and his family must be kept safe.

The solar field was much as the older type Ethan Winter railed against back home, closely overlapping sheets, tuned to follow the sun's slow path and suffocate any possible life below. Not that it was a problem here.

Ethan had been niggling his father to update Solaris' fields for years. He'd nearly got himself killed because of it, but he was sitting pretty now. Boss of Solaris with a woman beside him prepared to take on anyone who said otherwise.

No thanks to Seolta and his fellow conspirators. Worse, if his fellow conspirators hadn't decided to use Sarwenna Beren as a weapon against the man who loved her so deeply, would Seolta have ditched the conspiracy? In the end, he'd saved Ethan and Sarwenna's lives.

Would he have let Ethan die if his wife hadn't been threatened? He went into the plot knowing full well what his fellow conspirators were like and what they planned for Arcadia.

He hoped he'd have saved Ethan, but did he know for certain? No.

One day, he might come to terms with that, but not yet. Not while Hilmar a Kevand3 sat triumphantly on his oversized throne of purported munificence, lording it over his world, and others waited to gorge on Arcadia's bones.

It won't change what you did.

Nothing would, and he must live with that until the day he died.

"I've got a few checks to make surface side," said the pilot. "Do you want to come along or stay here."

Seolta had to think about that. Out on the solar field was the most obvious site for an ambush, but the man wasn't pushing it. He wished he could read the pilot better, but his face was screened too well by the shimmer of the flyer's controlling com field, blocking any study of the deeply scored and lined face.

Trag it, the ambush was coming whatever he did. "I'll come with you. I've never seen a habitat field up close before."

Wrong answer, said the sudden stillness of the man beside him. "You passed open planet procedures?"

"Yes, last updated first quartile of this standard year." No need to mention it was part of the hasty training regime the Feds had put him through just before his exile. Today would be his first time venturing onto the open surface of a dead planet like Surned.

The pilot set down on a flat pad of plascrete on the edge of the field and adjacent to a small building. The flyer had one cabin only, with limited space in it. He had to don the outside gear under the close and watchful eye of the pilot.

"You haven't done this often," he said, tightening Seolta's fittings and scrutinising the finished suit.

Seolta didn't deny it. "Little call for it on my home world."

"Yeah, guessed you were from one of them Central worlds. I seen Alliance Central once. That's a weird place." The man gave him a quick pat down, then did the same to himself. "Never forget this bit, lad. Fingers tell things no equipment can match." Given the way the suit squeezed every part of his anatomy, he guessed the man meant any telltale loosening indicated a leak in the suit's shielding. "Bring up your face screen."

Seolta did as ordered, running through the pre-exit checks. The man held out his wrist and Seolta dutifully linked him into the checks.

"Good. You downloaded the local specs as well. Most newbies leave out those last two checks." The gruff voice clearly showed his opinion on that. "You've got good bones, lad. Keep by me and you'll be fine."

A warning? One Seolta meant to follow. For an assassin, there was something trustworthy about this man.

Outside, the suit adapted quickly to the planet's low gravity, and his breathing came in easily enough, apart from a couple of panicked gasps. All those hours with the marshals were paying off. They may have regarded him as a miserable thing that should be crushed underfoot, but the Arcadian Federal Marshals prided themselves on putting duty first. Seolta had been sentenced to exile not death, and they were going to make sure he had the best chance of surviving it.

Watching him closely as he crossed the field, the pilot gave him an approving thumbs up just before they ducked under the first sheets. He'd visited a Solaris field with his older brother and Ethan when they were first released from prison as part of the agreed process to create bridges between their two companies after years of jostling for dominance of their home regions. Seolta had plastered on a smile while they were in sensing range of reporters but wiped it as soon as the solar sheets gave them cover. Not that his smile had looked genuine, going by the scowl on Cumchdach's face. His brother had cuffed him on the shoulder as soon as the sheets hid them. "Try harder when we emerge, little brother," he'd ordered. Ethan had said nothing. He'd never been fooled by Seolta.

The Solaris fields used box-like carts to travel under the sheets, but here they had to crouch down and crab-walk their way through it. A piece of pointless miserliness. Well resourced sites always produced better, in his experience.

After an hour of this and with an aching back, the pilot suggested Seolta take a break back at the control building. At first, that warning sounded in his mind and Seolta shook his head. After another hour, he'd have agreed to anything to be able to stand upright again. How the older man managed, he had no idea. His woman, his children and those coming grandchildren, he guessed.

"It's a straight line, right down that way," said the pilot, sitting down and rubbing his back. "I've just got a bit more this way to go, then I'll head back and join you. You should be fine till I get there, and you can push the emergency codes on that local program if you run into trouble."

It sounded too much like a rehearsed speech. The ambush was coming whatever he did, he guessed. Hilmar would have given the man a number of options. It made no difference. Too much more of this crabbing around and Seolta would seize up, unable to deal with any kind of attack.

Might as well get it over with. He nodded his thanks to the man and put out his hand. "Thank you for the tour."

The man took it reluctantly. "You'd have made a good soldier," he said. "Follow the line of sheets. You can't go wrong if you follow my instructions."

Another warning? A sudden brief change in his tone then the man turned back to his work, leaving Seolta to head back the way they'd come. He kept checking his com as he intermittently crawled and crouch-walked, taking frequent stops when his back screamed in outrage. The return was taking a lot longer than their trip out. At this rate, the older man would beat him back to the flyer. He sat and checked his com, aligning his march route with the straight path to the flyer pad. Right on course.

A sudden whoosh overhead and he shot up, hitting his head on the flapping sheets. Uncaring now, he thrust aside the billowing flaps, tearing them to shreds, but he no longer cared. He pushed his head up between the last sheets and saw confirmed what his ears had told him. The unmistakable shape of the flyer, disappearing back towards Haverner4. His ride had just deserted him.

The man had warned him. For a long moment he cursed in every word he remembered as he checked his air supply. Enough for a day. It would take more than that to walk all those klicks to Haverner4, even if his energy supplies maintained his suit's dynamics that long.

He wasn't beaten yet. He lifted his wrist, switching to his own programs, then swung sharply around looking for the control building.

Over there, near to a quarter circle away from his previous heading. They'd fed him a doctored program and he'd missed it completely. So much for his vaunted system skills.

He locked onto the building and crouched down again. Half of him was tempted to crash straight through the remaining sheets to his goal and only the reflection that doing so would likely shred his protective suit and end in an abrupt death stopped him.

After more back-breaking slog, he wasn't so sure about avoiding that abrupt death.

His sister Samhchair's last words stopped him this time. "You come back to us alive," she'd ordered, tears streaming down her face.

Finally, finally he broke out and stretched up to his full height, back and knees screaming in protest. He wasn't off by much, a half klick away from the control hut with its welcoming protective shield.

It will be locked to you.

His com wasn't that useless. He ran through the start-up stretches his childhood trainers had drilled into him, carefully easing his body into full order again and checked his suit's status.

Ninety percent. A small stabbing puncture, readily repaired. Probably done when he'd shoved up so precipitately through the sheets and discovered he'd been abandoned.

Then he noticed the warning mark beside the readout. Thirty percent also at risk. Any more stupid acrobatics and he'd be dead. He could set the repair modes to reinforce them but it would cut down his energy supplies. He ran the scans. A third of the faults only needed one more stumble to make them unstable. He set the systems to repair them and had to live in hope for the others.

If he got inside that building, he could repair the rest. A sabotaged control hut was impossible to hide from the Alliance investigation Hilmar must know would be triggered by his death. It had to look like an accident. A lost newbie tourist who failed to follow simple directions and had downloaded the wrong program before leaving. A solar field was a big area to get lost in and he could have wandered out of it anywhere. How could Haverner4 or their pilot be blamed for that? He'd checked Seolta's gear and made sure he knew how to carry out all the required checks. Not his fault if his passenger's geoprogramming was out of date or his com would refuse to answer his calls. Right now, the pilot was no doubt logged in as heading back for a search party.

Yes, and how long would that take to arrive? Just long enough for Seolta to slowly lose energy, air, and heat protection, panicking and lost on the hostile surface of Surned.

Seolta refused to go down in the records as a loser. He set out for the hut.

Walking in the open had seemed a minor matter when he first landed on the planet, but alone, knowing any tear in his suit could end his life, and watching the energy and air readings shrink with each step was a different matter.

Slow your breathing, you idiot.

Tell my heart that. It beat a staccato in his chest, the adrenalin surging. He dragged up every mindfulness lesson his parents had put him through in childhood when his urge to just *do* had jumped too far past his young body's abilities and come near to breaking his bones.

Cumchdach used to grumpily accuse him of dabbling in dark magic. "You're charmed by evil sprites," he muttered once, laid up in a sleeper while Seolta merrily escaped with nothing but a few scrapes and bruises. A totally irrational claim, as Seolta had pointed out at the time, but he hoped really hard now that his charmed protections hadn't deserted him.

More tired than he thought possible after a walk across a flat plain, he reached the dome covering the hut. He walked around it, looking for an entry hatch. Nothing. The dull black exterior surface showed no markings, no cavities, nothing for a stranded human needing help. He pulled up the emergency com program and wasn't surprised to find that the hut failed to register on it. Only an older, rickety-looking halfway shelter. He set his com to examine the dome, seeking an airlock as he walked slowly around it again as the rising wind plucked fretfully at his suit. The only out-of-place object was a pile of rocks on the south side. He kicked at the stones and watched in satisfaction as they rolled away.

Then he saw something underneath them. A scrap of packaging apparently dropped there from a carelessly handled freight package, one with words scratched on it. Heart beating too hard, he bent and picked it up.

It was short, almost too brief to be understood. Words in Standard painfully scribed as if straight out of a first school writing lesson. A code, followed by a short sentence.

Prithand2 closer. Pick up in territory. Right back hatch.

He entered the code into his com and transmitted it on a general beam, then waited. Slowly, dust drifting in a cloud towards him, a shape appeared on the side of the hut, an extrusion reaching out into the plain. He lifted a hand to the control panel that appeared on the door, entered the code again, and the hatch magically cycled open.

He shoved the scrap into an outer pocket and moments later was through into the inner hatch, testing the atmosphere then pulling off his helmet and breathing in blessedly normal air. He was safe.

CHAPTER SIX

The inside of the hut offered little comfort. A workbench took up one whole side, a bare table and bench seats stood in the middle, and a food prep system next to a bank of hard cots lay on the other side. The door at the back opened to the service units. Not a hut to be trapped in for long with a crowd of others, but right now it looked better than the most luxurious holiday resort on the Feldwesten Islands.

The workbench held various scanners and equipment of unknown function, presumably used by the solar field's technicians. It also held a com station for enhanced transmissions. He plugged in his com and was more than relieved to find it worked. Sabotaging it would have looked too suspicious, he guessed. He used it to check the distances to the nearest habitats against the data loaded onto his com. Prithand2 was marginally closer, but when he signalled them, all he got back was an automated voice advising him to signal Haverner4.

"You are in the Haverner4 Search and Rescue zone according to 35.362 Interhabitat Protocols."

He knew better than to argue with a drone citing legal specifications. It explained the second part of the warning. If he wanted to get out of this mess, he had to get into Prithand2's zone. He brought up the hut's holo-map.

Walking across the line into the Prithand2 zone looked possible, but he'd be cutting it fine with his suit's remaining supplies. Nor did the hut's suit charging and repair unit have his suit type in its database so couldn't service it, and no amount of tinkering convinced the unit to try a makeshift job. That was a breach of its programming parameters, it advised him sternly. The inadequate list of suit types was unusual, but not illegal in a minor service building like this one. Nothing to bring the Alliance down on a resource-tight habitat.

He breathed in deeply and made the call to Haverner4's emergency service. A service bot accepted his call and gave him a priority status.

"Rescue scheduled for first quarter, next day-cycle. Priority level two."

Priority two sounded good, but he suspected anything lower than priority one was treated as routine. It shouldn't be a problem. The hut's supplies must be sufficient to last till the scheduled pick up.

So what else made that unlikely? He pulled up the food prepper's stores. Plenty of food and water in there. He then began to comb the hut and its records to find the flaw. Energy enough for ten day-cycles with four people; similarly the air supply, with an added backup oxygen conversion unit.

Finally he ran a series of scans of the area, checking for unstable geology, solar fluxes, and expected weather patterns.

That's when he found it. He'd grown up in an area with wild weather. Only recently, a torrent of mud had come near to destroying a large part of his home city. He watched the cloud patterns to the north of the field, watched the shapes of them coalescing and swirling, then pulled up the weather forecast.

Wind speed lifting, occasionally to gale force, expected temperatures rising to something approaching normal freezing temperatures, but nothing else noted. There was no water on the surface of this world to cause problems, but something he couldn't dismiss kept him on edge.

He studied the surrounding land masses, and in particular the pass between the wide valley holding this field and the narrower one of Prithand2 on the other side of the hills.

His eyes narrowed as he brought up all the predictions, then pulled up the specifications on Surned from his own, protected files. Next, he checked the hut's specifications and the ground readings for this location from the com feed. More specifically, the energy needed to withstand the kind of weather coming at him.

The hut would survive, the prime objective of its controlling program but, to maintain the protective fields against the weather, it had to shut down all other energy-draining systems. Long before morning, the air in this place would be gone, along with temperature regulation and gravity. Only his suit would keep him alive, a not uncommon expectation on a non-EA world. Except that after his battle to get here through the solar field and with the repairs needed to the damaged portion, his suit only had enough reserves to last till daylight.

Would the Haverner4 team arrive by then? He doubted it. He put through another emergency call, but every time he tried, it told him that his call had been recorded and scheduled. He could find no way to change the priority status. No doubt the locals knew what to do when circumstances changed, knowledge so ingrained into every habitat citizen that no one thought he needed to be told, nor could he find it in any guide to this cursed world on his com.

Staying wasn't an option.

His eyes narrowed. If his reading of the weather estimates was correct, in a matter of hours any attempt to walk through that pass and down the valley to Prithand2 would leave him a shredded and very dead mess. His only hope of surviving? Get to that border line and rescue by the Prithand2 SAR team within four standard hours.

What was the last bit of the pilot's note?

Right back hatch.

There were no hatches in the hut. He'd had his com search it thoroughly, including all the schematics on file. Or did the man mean another exit on the outside of the dome? He put his helmet back on, checked the functioning of his suit just in case, added a few more food and water sachets to his reserve chutes, then stepped out the door again, walking all around the hut with his com set on the highest search protocol.

It wasn't until the third circuit that it registered anything. A faint trace, there by the right back wall of the hub. A circular shape set into the ground. Too small for any flyer or large cargo, but just right for one person to crawl through. It had to be what the pilot had meant.

He set his com against the circle and entered the code from the note. A small opening cycled back, and he crawled into the space below, discovering it disappeared into a narrow tunnel. One so small he would have to slither through on his belly. He looked at the ground, at his suit, then mentally shrugged. The surface was smooth enough and the pilot's note hadn't put him wrong so far. He took a deep breath, brought up the light in his helmet, then ordered his com to shut the hatch behind him and crawled forward.

Not long into the tunnel, he discovered its real purpose. Pipes appeared beside him, all labelled, and warm to the touch in the increasingly chill atmosphere. He was in a plumbing service hatch of all places. Not long after that, the smallest of seepages confirmed it. He carefully avoided the frozen brown patch.

His arms were tiring by the time the pipes dived down into the substrate, to presumably disgorge their noisome contents into the processing tanks buried far enough below the surface to have a temperature where the processing biome could survive. He was relieved to find that his tunnel began to angle upwards, which he hoped meant a second exit on the outer surface.

The sight of a short ladder and a battered airlock door at the top had him grinning in relief. He still had to get to Prithand2 in one piece, but he'd trusted the pilot thus far.

And if it was just another convoluted plot?

Hilmar was callous enough to do it, but he was dead if he stayed in the hut.

He opened the hatch cautiously, letting his com scan the land outside before he wriggled through and pulled himself upright. He'd come out behind a small hillock at the back of the hut. He leaned back against the rock and took stock of his surroundings.

Over there, barely discernible in the bulwark of the surrounding hills, lay the entrance to the pass into Prithand2 territory. The actual border lay halfway through, but he doubted he'd get good com transmission until right through it.

It's not that far, he told himself. He set back his shoulders and took a step.

His foot struck metal in the dirt below. He looked down, angling his helmet light onto the ground by his boot then began digging in excitement.

A skimmer, just like the small, one-man crafts they used at home for short hops. A fully enclosed, and according to his com, fully operational skimmer. One that would fly low enough to avoid any surveillance of Haverner4 airspace.

He linked his com into the controls then, when nothing happened, added in the code from the note. The sand shifted. He stepped back and waited, and soon the snub lines of a battered, much used skimmer rose before him.

He turned off the olfactory sensors on his suit as soon as he stepped inside. The stench announced its purpose and usual pilots. Another tool of the plumbers servicing this hut.

Beggars can't be choosy. As a child, he'd said that to his brothers on more occasions than he cared to remember when he had yet again connived to beat them to a prize they all wanted. Wouldn't Cumchdach and Ceart laugh now? He buckled into the pilot seat and carefully lifted just far enough off the surface to keep the propulsion units clear of backdraught debris.

Hugging the ground, he headed towards the hills, keeping close to their cover as he set course for the pass opening and freedom. He'd kept the pilot's note safely tucked inside his suit and planned to dispose of it as soon as he passed into Prithand2 territory.

You're assuming Prithand2 is not under Hilmar's thumb.

He had to hope.

The wind began to build not long after he set out, and soon he had to fight to keep his course against the buffeting squalls. It was almost like being back in his own mountains. His parents had made sure all their offspring learned to pilot a flyer in the worst of the mountain airs. They hadn't been so happy when their children turned it into yet another competitive game. Surprisingly, it was Ceart, the quietest in the family, who routinely beat them all, including Fiorusghe and Seolta, the biggest risk-takers of their brood.

Now he thanked the roots for all those battles with Fioruishge as they fought for second place against Ceart, pushing their flyers into ever more outrageous feats. Their mother had forced them to promise not to try to beat Ceart. It was the one thing he excelled at, she'd told them. Not true, they'd chimed back, thinking of all the times Ceart's stubborn silence had won an argument for him, but their father's threat to remove their flying permits had been what stopped them. Not that they could have beaten Ceart.

"That boy was born with wings in his blood," their father had muttered. Mind you, he'd also banned Ceart from piloting any flyer holding anyone else, and definitely none of his family unless it was an emergency.

Stop thinking of family. They're not coming for you, and you can't go back there.

He wouldn't be going anywhere unless he made it out of today. A gust caught him side-on and he furiously worked the controls, bringing his craft out just in time to avoid crashing into the hard rock of the mountainside.

Farther out on the plains might be safer—if no covert surveillance followed him, plotting to have him meet a fatal accident. He slammed open the controls and linked directly into the command systems so he could skim as closely as possible to the ground and rocks. Who knew what a primitive flyer like this would do to him in a direct mind mesh with its controls, but he had no other option. Without that level of control, he was dead.

Finally he made it to the pass opening, the trickiest bit so far. He brought the flyer to a hover in the shelter of a gravel slide to one side and studied the wind patterns whistling through the narrow gap.

Tricky but doable. That's what the flyer's programmed routes promised, with a warning that a high-altitude passage was the preferred route between the two habitats and an addendum clearing the flyer's manufacturer of blame if he failed to make it.

It's the same as slipping between branches in a storm—and these rocks aren't moving.

Easy? Unlikely. He watched the currents, watched the swirls of rushing air on his simulator.

There was a pattern to it, unstable, complicated, but a pattern as long as the winds kept blowing from the same direction. He set in the calculations. Doable, yes—if the timing was exactly right.

No time to overthink it. He slammed the little flyer into high speed and grabbed at the airstream powering him straight in and through that treacherous gap. The skimmer's warning alarms roared into full alert.

"I know, I know," he muttered. "Alarms off," he ordered the system. The shocked silence and the glowering red shades obstinately colouring his screens felt almost human. His humble plumber's skimmer was not happy.

He didn't blame it. Neither was he.

A sudden screeched warning, louder than before, and he was through and heading straight for the first curving wall of rock in this excuse for a mountain pass. He switched direction and just missed the jutting wall.

The winds were still bad in here, but not yet up to the warned-about levels. His small craft rocked and ricocheted across the tortuous passage. Nothing stayed the same, not the base or the sides of the ravine, as if millennia ago angry torrents of liquid had scoured and gouged at the rocks here, each fresh flood carving its own passage through the looming mountains on either side—adding to the battering winds and shattering temperature changes.

He wasn't even halfway through and he was exhausted. Now the battle against the winds rocketed to a new phase, each surge battering his flyer closer and closer to submission. A clip on the side, and he jerked up, wrenching the small craft back from the boulders piled up in front of him and slipping through the tiny gap left by a thundering rock fall.

Not only bad winds but unstable rockfaces. Tragging wonderful. He ran a quick scan, hunting for the smoothest route.

None offered. High and low, the winds raced and jeered at him, twisting around rock buttresses, hurling down broken off slabs of cliff face, then swooping down to pluck at this puny vessel seeking to invade the wind's domain. He must fight the elements and, ever more, his own body.

A direct mind mesh wasn't meant to last this long, not at this level of concentration.

He jerked himself back from threatening sleep once more, as another smashing sound told of a collision.

"Damage to starboard pillars," warned his systems.

One more to add to the growing list of damages. He blinked hard and shook his head to better see the ship's view of the terrain. The training texts all said auto worked better in a space this confined, given the microsecond adjustments needed, but adding in the turbulent air currents and unstable ground made it less certain. Experience had taught his people that the unconscious, intuitive adjustments of a human pilot won more in a complex hostile situation.

Or did when the pilot was fresh and knew the terrain and weather patterns. He was getting dangerously close to becoming a liability. The air here was thin, dry, and cold, really cold, and behaved in ways he didn't expect. Another smash on the upper carapace and he gave in. He switched to auto and sealed his suit while he was still conscious. From here on he'd have to rely on the ship's reflexes to get him safely through.

On a beaten-up service skimmer never intended for use in a place like this?

The inevitable happened not long afterwards. The skimmer crashed with a loud bang into the side of the pass. Crashed and came to a shuddering halt, tilting crazily on a knob of rock and wedged tight between two buttress-shaped outcroppings. Seolta clung to his seat, held in place by his webbing and trying not to breathe too harshly from his remaining air supply. The controls spluttered then died, and his com warned of catastrophic damage to the hull integrity.

The skimmer was holed underneath. The air in the cabin rushed out, mingling with the toxic mix of gases from outside. He checked on the holo-map. Just a minute's flying time to the Prithand2 border and a bit over one klick to the end of the pass. He'd nearly made it. He still could, even with clambering over and through the messy rockfalls and against the scouring winds roaring through the pass.

He checked his seat was secure, set the emergency backup systems into play to block any dangerous circuit or energy pack leaks, was relieved to hear the completed signal come through his com audio, then eased off the webbing straps and went to stand.

"Aaaaargh."

He flopped back into the seat, gasping loudly as pain throbbed through his body. "Com, full body scan," he gasped out, beyond a mind mesh even to his own unit. "Display screen front."

The holo-image formed, sparking and shadowed. Then the red layers of damage began to colour it and he ran down the list in his head. Cracked ribs, three on the right and one on the left. They were the only bone breaks at least. Badly bruised muscles all over his torso and shoulders from the sudden snapping tight of the webbed harness. Standard, and not life-threatening.

Head safe, spine safe. The seat and webbing had done their job despite the old bucket's dilapidated appearance. One knee was badly wrenched as was the shoulder on the opposing side. Nothing permanent, nothing that would be a problem to a good medic rescue team.

A major problem, though, when rescue was coming only from someone over the border in Prithand2, even if he could get a clear transmission through.

He tried anyway, and the result was much as expected. No clear signal available.

What kind of world had hazardous zones out of reach of com transmissions?

"Suit, full compression," he ordered, and slowly leaned forward, setting his boots against the floor and using his good arm to lever himself upwards. "Tragging stupid world." He knew a lot of words his mother hated, street fodder from his student days, and he mouthed every single one of them as he forced himself to stand up, clutching hard to the flyer's battered frame.

He peered downwards at the ragged hole torn through the flyer's base. "Com, flyer hatch status."

The flyer's schematic appeared. The main hatch was out. The secondary hatch through the upper carapace remained fully operational, as long as he could manhandle himself up the ladder and onto the flyer's roof. The only problem: above it sat a sheer rock outcrop, blocking the exit.

Or he could fall through the gaping hole in the floor of the flyer, trusting in his suit and pure luck to survive the landing and tumble down the edge of the rocks below. "Com, locate medical kit."

At last a piece of luck. The kit lay in the locker closest to the pilot's seat and easily reached by stretching out his arm. It was on the injured side, so he had to painfully swivel his body around and manoeuvre the locker open with his other hand, but with a last grab he pulled the kit free, wrenching the top off. There, just where he hoped. A pile of painkiller infusers, local and full body.

He set the infusers into the suit's med-portals, linking its controls with his com to send the local ones to his shoulder and knee and the general at the highest allowed dosage to his bruised and battered torso, sagging in relief as the effects hit home. Then peered down at the hole in the floor again.

No avoiding it, but before moving, he took the pilot's note and shoved it into the destruct unit and waited until the controls signalled it had been reduced to a mere swirl of anonymous molecules. Only then did he grab hold of the side of the chair, leaning against it as he used his good side to reach the next handhold and made his tortuous way back to the emergency lockers. The evac backpack was still intact, as it should be. He thrust it on, shoved some more food bars and water packets into the outer pockets of his suit, then pulled himself back to the hole. It wasn't far to fall. The rock face below was like enough to the ones he'd slid down as a child.

Except you're now a grown man, one in less than full working order and you've learned that people don't bounce.

He ran the scans above the flyer again, just to make sure. Nothing had changed.

In other words, options—one. That hole in the floor.

He sized up the ground, looking for the slope with the smoothest surface, tucked his injured shoulder tight against his body, then let himself tumble out.

He hit the rock face then felt himself sliding. He leaned back, trying to give in to the slope, trying to ignore the rattling and banging setting off waves of pain despite the heavy-duty treatments.

His bad leg hit a knob of rock and his body jerked before he could stop it. That was it. No more sliding, no controlled fall. Just a mad plummeting down the last bit to slam onto the hard ground below.

Then nothing.

He came to, groggy as all bogs and wondering what poked at his back, then tried to sit up.

Not a good idea. He lay gasping until his brain worked fully again and he could figure out where he was and what was wrong.

Then it all came horrifyingly back and he checked the timer on his com. He'd just lost half a standard hour. Time he couldn't spare. He checked his suit's readings. That rubbing against the rocks had damaged more areas. Forty percent now at risk. The end reading was the one that mattered: Integrity still intact.

Of course it is. You'd be dead otherwise.

He felt near enough to it. He took in deep, slow breaths, the kind to clear his head, then eased himself cautiously up to sitting.

He could still do that, but not much else looked any better. He'd fallen into a gap between the two rock outcroppings holding his flyer tight above him. The knob in his back was his emergency pack. A quick scan of the contents. All still intact. What else did he have?

Outside his small hollow, the winds kicked up dust, but his own hideaway was safe. He tried again to get a signal on his com.

Nothing. No one knew he was here. He contemplated the route ahead and groaned.

Don't think too hard.

What was in the pack? He opened it carefully, using his body to keep it away from any winds that might snatch at the contents, then pulled them out one by one. Some were much like those in the evac packs back on his home mountains, but others he couldn't fathom. There was a stick of some kind, and that might be the most useful, as a crutch. After packing up the kit bag again, he tried putting weight on the banged up knee, and nearly collapsed, grabbing onto the rocks to hold him up. The stick was of a weird kind with a pointed knob at one end and a ribbed hand hold at the other. The pack called it a clamp stick, but he couldn't see any kind of clamping mechanism. He tried it out, leaning heavily on it as he took one step then another.

It held his weight and he could walk. Point one for him.

How far he had to walk to cross the border line and get to an area with com coverage, he refused to think about. One step after another. His father had tried to teach him years ago that was the best way to solve a problem. Seolta had ignored him, intent on his end goal and dismissing any damage he caused on the way.

Somebody had clearly decided it was time he pay for that.

Why are you wasting time and energy?

He wished his inner voice would shut up. It was worse than Cumchdach and Samhchair combined after one of his stupider escapades.

Not stupid; that was the problem. Just selfish.

As he'd already said…

Get on with it!

Only one way to turn off the voice. He put another step forward and dragged his leg with the bad knee after it.

It's not broken.

He knew that, but the agony each time he put weight on the wrenched and torn knee drained too much of his precious energy reserves. He pumped up the suit pressure on that leg, using the suit as a splint. It helped a bit and he put another foot forward. This time, by deliberately zoning out the pain and setting his knee carefully down, he managed to use the leg and after a while settled into a crazy kind of pattern. Stick, good knee, drag leg and carefully place bad knee.

Then he emerged from the shelter of his rocks and into the main passage with its roaring, swirling and twisting winds, tugging and tearing at his suit and his pack, digging into them and seeking any weakness. He clutched the stick tightly and hugged close to the side walls, desperate for any kind of shelter. The terrain didn't improve either, and he soon had to scramble over broken rocks and lean against the rugged sides of the wall or hold his breath as he scrambled over gravel-strewn washes where the walls crumbled down when touched. Too soon, his breathing set off his suit's alarm.

To think he'd always prided himself on his fitness levels.

Now, every breath brought a stab of pain, and his back muscles cried out for relief from the constant tension of acting as a support for the battered muscles of his front.

His com pinged. He'd crossed the border into Prithand2 territory.

He felt like crying. He slumped down on a lumpy rock just out of the wind and set off his emergency beacon.

Nothing. No signal, said the callous auto message. He was still out of range.

"Come back alive." His sister's voice rang so loudly in his head she could be standing beside him. He scowled, but there was no ignoring Samhchair, never had been. He levered himself slowly up, digging the point of the strange stick into the ground.

If only he knew what was blocking the signal here, he might be able to figure out how far he had to go yet to be in range. Back home, it was strange rock types with weird chemical mixes that caused an erratic local magnetic effect. What it was here, he didn't know, and nothing on his com helped. Maybe it was just the reality of a habitat planet where the worth of every resource had to be tallied and justified. He remembered all those times he and Fioruisghe had argued about what was more important, the natural world or his precious systems and man-made constructs.

Stop thinking of family.

He set off again. Time became a blur of agony, exhaustion, and fear. He constantly watched his suit readings, searching for the smallest advantage of terrain or wind, head down and battering his way forward. Everything on this nightmare journey began to merge into a hell of desperation.

"Come back alive."

I don't think I can. I'm sorry, sister.

If only…

Anyara.

He would have liked to see her one more time.

A chatter of static hit his comms link. One word made it through.

"Report."

Source of message, Prithand2 rescue brigade.

Against all the odds, his beacon call had made it. "Medical emergency. I've crashed in the pass," he sent.

No reply. The signal had gone again.

He set his com to keep sending out the emergency signal. Periodically a chatter came through, a too brief smattering of words. Had they heard him? He had to keep hoping, but no smooth transmission came through, nothing of substance. As the hellish time dragged on, he knew the hope was an illusion. No one was coming. Not unless he made it out of this endless excuse for a mountain pass.

There was no end. Not to this torment.

One more stumble, and a clarion call hit his eardrums. "Suit breach."

He looked down, seeing the razor-edged rock at his foot, dislodged by his dragging leg. Then the tear, small and lethal if not fixed urgently. He could feel the suit valves clamping tight around his upper thigh as it sealed off the cut, and watched as the suit readings plummeted. He stopped breathing, moving anything, while his suit's systems worked urgently to repair the hole.

He didn't have enough reserves for this. Not when the suit's systems were already supporting a battered and torn body and using more oxygen and energy than usual.

The screech shut off. The cut was sealed for now. He kept walking, or crawling, or stumbling blindly, only knowing which way he must go. Then another alarm, louder, more urgent, more lethal.

Oxygen reserves red-lined. He reset the emergency beacon, fingers madly working in his com field to send out a call to anyone who would hear. "Help, help. I'm dying."

This time it wasn't an act. Wasn't part of some clever scheme to get attention, a win, a meaningless advantage over some imagined rival.

He tried to breath slower, tried to walk on a smidgeon of breath, tried to push on. The light dimmed, darkened, became grey, then clouded over.

Then he knew nothing.

It was voices that brought him out. Strange, robotic voices, mouthing words he couldn't understand. Then they changed to the kind of voices heard when visiting his mother at work in her hospital, and the smells kissing his nose were the ones that lingered in her hair and skin when she arrived home. He relaxed and let his mind close again.

Someone shook him. "Messer, your name."

"Doctor Scathach's son," he said to the stupid man.

"Check his head again."

His head was fine. That wasn't what hurt, the only part of him that didn't. He opened his eyes, and saw a strange uniform and a face he'd never seen before. "Where am I?"

The face was joined by another. "Prithand2 emergency ward. The medics brought you in from the pass." The two faces shared a look. "You got caught in a storm and suffered a suit breach."

Memory returned, and the fear. "Prithand2? My com message?"

The other face leaned in again. "We got a report of a garbled message from the Haverner Pass. Our medics checked it out and found you. Your flyer is a tangled mess a klick back from that."

Seolta struggled up, but a hand forced him back. "Hold up, Messer. Time enough for that."

"I'm at Prithand2?" he had to ask again, barely believing it. "I made it?"

The first face returned. "Yes, Messer. You made it through. To try the pass in weather like that?" A shake of the head. "But you're safe now."

Seolta lay back and began to laugh, hugging tight to his ribs to stop the pain but unable to stop the howls of mirth. The faces above him disappeared and he could hear concerned muttering.

"Are you sure that brain scan is normal?"

Seolta's sense of self-preservation finally managed to conquer the manic laughs. He stretched out and wrestled a sane look onto his face. "I'm sorry. A reaction to finding I'm still on the side of the living."

"Aah, of course." The man didn't look convinced. More like someone trying to humour a delicate patient. "As it happens Messer, you are only just on the right side. Your body has taken quite a battering. You'll be staying with us a bit longer yet."

And after that? wondered Seolta. Then decided to worry about it later. The medics did more checks, set yet more of their indecipherable scanners into action, and left him with a cross-faced nurse who yanked at his sleeper's cover and shoved him ruthlessly back down when he made a feeble attempt to sit up.

"You're lucky to be alive. Don't waste the efforts of the rescue squad and doctors who made that possible."

The woman wasn't as old as his mother, but her eyes looked years older. Waste was a curse word here, said that prim twist of her mouth.

"Yes, Messera," he said meekly. Not even that brought the touch of a smile to her face. Nor could anything he tried in the days following as his body recovered from the ordeal. He came to calling her Messera Grim in his mind, but the woman was the one who answered the calls in the long darks of the night cycle when the smells and suffocation of the pass came back to torment him.

"It's just a bad dream, Messer." The stern voice of reason brought him out of nightmares many times a night. She might resent him, something to do with that waste word, but she would not desert him. Duty was to her as honourable a word as waste was filthy. She was the one who answered his questions about what was to happen next, and her answer was the one he believed.

"They're sending you up to Kevand Station as soon as you're fit to move." He didn't ask who *they* were, but had a good idea.

"You should have gone days ago," she added with a growl.

He put on his most humble face. "My apologies for using up your resources."

The rigid mouth and refusal to meet his eye told their own story. "Prithand2 has enough for its needs," she said stiffly, but he'd put a wager on it that 'bare needs' and 'best case' were klicks apart in this habitat. Then caught himself. Klick? He was starting to use local slang.

"Why the station?" he asked, and saw a faint twist of that straight mouth.

"It's all those pretty plants they have up there. More like your home habitat, they told our medics." A sniff said what she thought of such frippery. "They've decided you'll recuperate better up there."

The nurse slapped his chest, disengaging the mobile cleansing unit she'd been using on him, including places he'd never thought to be shy of exposing. He'd swear he'd shrivelled under that severe gaze.

He'd assumed at first her disgust for any escape of biota from their assigned growing sheds was due to her austere personality, but chatting to the few other staff who came to his room produced the same attitude. He had to use all his diplomatic charm to get them to say anything, but even the one who came nearest to having a bubbly nature, a very junior nurse left to tidy up after Messera Grim had finished, shared the older nurse's attitude towards the station's biota. "What do they need to be cluttering up the place with plants 'n' stuff. Keep them in the biome units where they can do their job properly."

Yet Anyara still claimed Prithand2 as her home of origin, despite their attitude. What about a place that scorned the living things she clearly loved had earned that kind of loyalty?

And what was Hilmar a Kevand's position here. He'd given up the numbering in the man's name. All the Kevand habitats belonged to him, as well as a marked chunk of Surned, as proved by what happened to him at Haverner4.

He needed out of this medical ward and onto the streets if he was going to get any answers.

Security arrived the next day with a long list of questions that left him exhausted. Too many must have come directly from whatever head office they answered to, one he'd bet was set in Kevand3.

"The Haverner4 supervisor abandoned you to the field. Not a worthy action."

"There's limited com coverage in that area, and he made sure I was correctly equipped before heading out to the surface. My own fault. I insisted on going out," he added with a deprecating lift of his hand. "I'd never been on the surface of a full habitat world."

The man clearly had no idea what he meant by that. The look on his face said 'rich Central Alliance brat', and Seolta made no attempt to tell him the truth.

"Since you'd veered off in an unknown direction, he'd need help finding you," agreed the man now. "As for you, Messer, a sensible man would have waited for the return of the Haverner4 search party."

Seolta gave an apologetic grimace. "Once I made it to the control building, I looked at the holo-maps. Prithand2 looked an easy distance away. It seemed quicker to go here myself."

The man considered him. "The supervisor has my sympathy."

Seolta hoped that would be the end of it, especially when security left him alone afterwards. He'd have to be careful with how he found out more about this habitat, though. He mentioned Hilmar's name to the bubbly junior one morning, only to get an incoherent rambling and a look of sheer terror. Nurse Grim wasn't an option either, and the doctors refused to discuss anything with him outside blood readings, muscle perfusion levels and bone recalcification. The words alone were enough to stop his questions. There was a reason he'd followed his father into business instead of becoming a doctor like his mother. Medical talk left him cold, and the fascination of his mother and older sister with the workings of an injured body was beyond comprehension. He knew enough to get by, enough to get him out of a scrape, and that was plenty.

Twisted plotting against business rivals and subverting a new com system on the other hand … pure bliss.

Yeah, and look where it got you.

That had been anger, pure and simple. Anger he was paying for.

As soon as he could sit up, he began trying to get out of his sleeper and explore. A medic suddenly erupted into the room, took one look at Seolta standing defiantly by the sleeper and his white-knuckled grip on the side frame, and spoke into his com. "Patient is ready for transfer."

Before he knew it, he'd been loaded onto a stretcher and whipped into a shuttle, headed for the Kevand Station Hub. All chance gone to explore Prithand2.

His interest ratcheted up a triplet of notches. Just what had happened here?

CHAPTER SEVEN

Anyara breathed in the smells of dirt and plants in her nursery and wished she could make the quiet last forever. Seolta was coming back, but why? The message had been simple enough. He'd been in an accident and the off-worlder needed a place to recuperate that was more like his home world.

Like Arcadia? The fabled earth analogue world had always hung like a crystal globe in a fairytale landscape. A place of myth, ever desired and impossible to reach. Then her uncle told her he'd met their visitor there. More, her uncle had been involved in a scheme on Arcadia, one involving Seolta a Manascraoch. A scheme that had failed. Her uncle shouldn't have been allowed entry to the planet.

His use of the off-worlder's name should have been enough to warn her. Her uncle's rendering was harsh and ugly. In Seolta's mouth, the sound of it flowed, with the crackle of twigs and the sweep of wind and water. She must ask if he had any holovids of his home.

No, she must keep her distance from him. Must not forget her uncle sent him back to her station. Surned may be restricted in resources, deliberately so, she often suspected, but it had perfectly respectable medical facilities in all its habitats, including Prithand2.

Why had Seolta gone there at all? She had memories and images of her early home, ones she kept tightly locked deep inside, but why did he go there?

Do not trust him.

Yet she was standing at the outer lock when his shuttle arrived, after using all the power of her uncle's name to wrangle a position by the front of the reception group. The shuttle door opened and Seolta walked out first. His white face and hesitant step, one hand clinging tight to the hatch railing, set alight the anger at her uncle she kept deep inside.

"A stretcher, now," she snapped at the station medic. Seolta didn't argue, and the tight line of his mouth showed what he thought of needing it even as he collapsed back into its depths. "Thank you, and greetings, Messera. This is not how I had hoped to meet you again."

His voice might lack its usual strength, but his smile was the practised one she hated so much. She gave him one as false back. Then caught the look in his eyes, and there was nothing false there.

"I expect a full report to my com as soon as the Messer has been assessed."

"Certainly, Messera Anyara." The medic looked as disgusted as she felt. "Our facilities here will have Messer Seolta restored to normal in no time."

Prithand2 had similar facilities.

"Thank you, Messers," said Seolta. "It is good to be back." He breathed in deeply and this time, the smile was real. Maybe the medics had been right to transfer him back here. Groundside habitats had a strict opinion of the proper place for the flora and fauna that fed their living systems, keeping them firmly under control and out of sight in biome rooms. She always took down a small pot of herbs for comfort on her periodic command visits to her uncle.

She refused to trail pathetically after Seolta as the stretcher bore him off to the main wards, but she did set a microbot to follow. It confirmed that they gave him the single room she'd ordered, the one with a view over the main boulevard and the central gardens lining both sides and blooming into glory in the central plaza. "Leave the windows open," she'd also ordered, much to the horror of the chief medic. Where any contaminating microbes were to come from, she couldn't think, but controlling the air in a patient's room must be an unbreakable part of their training.

That deep breath told her she'd been right. His deep intake of the smells of living plants and biota.

She forced herself to wait until the next morning to see him, despite a curt call from her uncle.

"Has he told you anything yet?"

She studied her uncle in the holofield. The hair was as dark as usual, as carefully set in place, and the garments as rich and tailored, but was that a touch of a line around his eyes, a hint of nerves in the finger tapping on the table? "He has been confined to the wards for assessment since arrival. To interrupt that would raise questions."

"Hmph. The man came to Surned for a reason, and I will know what it is."

"He's in no state to be questioned at the moment, uncle. The medics are only admitting necessary personnel." Hopefully, they'd back that up if asked. No, *when* asked. Her uncle didn't leave anything to chance.

"He was fit enough to avoid a straight answer to my people's questions groundside. The man delights in thwarting me." A scowl crossed her uncle's face and her heart faltered. "Don't ever work with the Alliance, girl. They play a deep game," he said, before abruptly signing off.

Could he have meant what she thought. She discreetly checked the hospital's security status. A squad covered the ward holding Seolta, but nothing else. You were expecting a record?

She approached the wards the next morning with care.

His smile as she entered was its own reward, his eyes meeting hers then noticing the flowers she held in her fist. She'd done a search on EA world customs. These blooms were near to completion and wouldn't deplete the cycling supply, but cutting them purely to bring pleasure had still felt wrong. Then his smile widened, and she discovered nothing else mattered.

"Thank you," he said.

"I have a container for them, to keep them alive a little longer." She held it up, feeling a flush of warmth coat her cheeks. "I understand this is appropriate on your home world." She filled the container with water and added the flowers, taking her time to arrange them to the look their best before putting them down on the windowsill, then marshalled her courage to turn back to him. "Is that correct?"

"Exactly," he said. But it wasn't the flowers he was staring at.

She stayed only a bit longer that day, leaving when his eyes drooped and he put out an arm to keep himself upright.

"You will be back?"

"When I can," she promised.

By her third visit, he sat in a chair in the corner of the room and managed to stand briefly as she entered. She quickly crossed to help him, then saw the tightening of hurt pride on his mouth and stopped. He gave her that archaic bend of head and neck. "Greetings, Messera. I trust you are well this fine morning."

His hand discreetly reached for the support of the wall, and she sat down quickly, relieved to see him copy her. "I can't stay long, I'm sorry. We're bedding out the new seedlings in the production rooms this morning."

He looked blankly at her.

"Vegetables, herbs, food crops in general," she said. We have three rooms in the production centre, each set to a different Earth-type season."

"Hence the appetising food I've been given since returning here. It makes a welcome change from shipboard and habitat offerings."

She twitched her nose. "We can't do much about shipboard rations, but the habitats all have perfectly capable production rooms and we ship our surplus groundside. It's our second most important income, after the space ports."

He looked over in surprise. "You supply the freight port as well?"

Surned had a second port for the major freight lines at another station in sync orbit with Kevand Station.

"Yes. It's cheaper than hauling it up from the surface."

"And planted gardens there as well?"

She had to blush. "My uncle calls them a waste of space, but the spacers complained when he mentioned ripping them out. He put up the docking fees instead."

He laughed. "That sounds like Hilmar. Thank the stars you don't take after your uncle, Messera."

And the light in his eyes had her blushing harder than ever.

It would have been easy to forget she'd been ordered to cultivate his friendship and the reason. She couldn't, though, not when her uncle called each morning, demanding to know what progress she had made.

"That boy is up to something. Don't let that 'I'm nobody important' façade of his gull you. Thanks to his cursed family and home world, the Alliance would certainly notice if he suddenly disappeared without reason."

When the day came that Seolta was fit to take a walk with her, she made sure the cycle was set to sunshine and steered them out into the gentle morning light. She'd also checked his room controls to find the temperature range he preferred and tweaked the local settings to suit. She couldn't set it cool enough without damaging some of her babies, but there was a touch of a chill in the air, and the moisture setting had passing locals giving her disgruntled glares.

He walked carefully, his injured leg supported by a med field, but otherwise showed few effects of his adventure. Once through the doors, he made for the grassed area, stopped still, then bent his head back and shut his eyes for a long moment. His hand reached out and she took hold of it.

"Thank you, Messera."

It was enough for today. She had questions to ask, her uncle's and her own, but first he had to heal. Each day, she returned when she could and walked with him in her gardens.

"Would you like to see the plant nurseries?" she asked one day when the weather cycle must be set for a day too warm and dry for his comfort. He'd taken refuge in the shade of a pergola she'd had built to support some plants she'd seen in an online catalogue and yearned to try. Strawberries, edralme fruits and other food plants trailed from the struts and roof beams, sending enticing smells wafting between the filtered beams of light, but her pride and joy surged up against each corner post. Roses, they were called. The old texts she'd unearthed contained enough uses for the extract of the post-season hips and the flower petals to justify their import, but it was the heady smell and the glorious flowers she craved, and these four plants had lived up to their promise. A brilliant yellow one with a smell as powerful, a softest white one with petals delicate as newly formed leaves, one a pale blush of pink perfumed with a subtle wash of tenderness, and lastly, her favourite: deepest, velvety red with a scent that lingered in the air long after the sun cycle had faded and the night bugs fluttered in the air.

He touched the red petals, then followed her. She signalled her com to open the doors of her nursery and stood aside to let him enter. Then waited.

He stopped in the doorway and breathed in. Once, twice, then again, before walking in as if in a dream. He stopped at the end of the second aisle and his finger reached out to touch the stringy stalk of a baby plant. In time, side shoots would sprout from the central stem, reaching out until it filled in all the space she'd allotted to it.

"A sapling." His voice caught on the word. "How tall will it grow?"

She held out her hand to shoulder level. "It's one of our food bushes. The berries and leaves are both useful."

His fingers caught hold of the thin stalk. She put out a hand to stop him, and his hand released it as quickly, with no signs of damage. He very gently stroked the young leaf. "Beautiful," he whispered.

"You have ones like it at home?"

"Not this species, but similar? Yes, in the undergrowth on the forest floor. Shrubs and tree saplings, waiting for a gap in the canopy." His finger lingered, then slowly withdrew as if reluctant to leave the shrub. "Thank you," he whispered.

She considered a moment, then came to a decision and sent a signal to her com. "There is no surveillance here."

It was as if she'd shattered into nothing the moment of introspection. The angles of his face sharpened, he straightened and those shadowed eyes studied her. "Are you sure?"

"I've blocked the sensors. We have a bit of time before they pick it up and restart them."

He pulled up his com and scanned the room, then his fingers played in the control field. "That should make it look like a malfunction. I've learned to be wary of your uncle's methods." A bench sat at the far end of the row of plants. He walked over and sat down, his arm inviting her to take a seat beside him. It was a very short bench. She pulled over a small potting table beside it and propped herself on that, safe from his touch. A gleam sparked in his eyes, but he said nothing.

She took a breath. "Your accident. How did it happen? You don't strike me as a man who loses his way easily."

A quirk of those deceptive lips. "Not usually."

He leaned back, eyes wide open. Why did she suddenly realise he was about to lie. She shoved up a hand. "Don't bother. I've read the official report. It leaves out a lot, but I would rather use *my* imagination to fill the gaps than yours."

For an instant, his mouth dropped open, barely perceptible, but she was watching him closely. He sat up and gave her that professional smile she hated. Deliberately, to provoke her she felt sure, seeing the small tug of a twitch at the corner of his lips. "Tell me what happened then," he said.

She refused to smile back or treat it as a game. His adventure touched too close to her reality and that manufactured smile, so calculated to charm, was also meant to hide what he thought.

"You have no reason to trust me. I understand that." She shot up. "When you decide otherwise, we can talk again. In the meantime, Messer, I have work to do."

She was about to walk out when a cough at the other door on the far side of the room interrupted them. Anyara recognised the youth, a trainee in the horticulture section. She gestured him forward. "Mathis, how can I help you?"

The boy shuffled. "I've been sent with a message, Messera." He blushed bright red when she held out her com arm. "No, for the off-world Messer. From the station master's office."

Seolta stood up beside her, replacing the hated smile with one of gentle charm. "Give me the link, Messer." He reached out his wrist, and the boy touched it with his com. Seolta's face blanked out as he began to listen in private mode, then he opened the link to her as well, excluding the boy. "A request from the station master for assistance with a systems glitch."

"My uncle has contracted you," she guessed.

"I'm to audit your station systems. It's why I was on that tour of Surned."

"I take it you have some useful qualifications behind you." She wasn't surprised, not after his work on her ship on the way here.

"Some," he said. "I'm on my way," he sent to the station master, then turned to her. "Do you often have malfunctions in your retail sector?"

She shook her head "It's too critical for social wellbeing." The sector was filled with cafes, bars, storefronts displaying goods, even direct-to-customer shops holding a wide range of both locally crafted and high-end luxury wares that shoppers refused to buy without trying them first.

She began to follow him.

"There's no need."

He used his com to pull up a map of the station.

"The staff know me. It will help if I come with you."

He shook his head in denial, but she still insisted on coming. Something about this smelled off.

He was right enough about there being no need for her presence, though. The retail staff greeted her warmly, but Seolta's assured manner in dealing with the store systems had him swiftly included in their welcome.

"The Executive said you would be the best to sort the problem out," said the maintenance manager. "Our own staff are good at the day-to-day stuff, but for anything like this we usually have to wait for someone to come up from Surned."

"What about the station's engineering branch. They must have system techs."

"Too busy keeping us all alive, they say. This isn't life threatening, just credit threatening. We'd have had to shut down for two full day-cycles without you."

The shopkeepers huddled miserably around them, watching intently. Not surprising. Their margins were tight and they'd take a big profit hit if this wasn't fixed quickly. She sent a message to the station master and he hustled the crowd out of the room.

"The Messer doesn't need to see your gloomy faces while he works," said the man gruffly.

At first, Seolta explored the system in public mode, then suddenly set it to private and sat studying it for long moments, a frown twitching at his lips.

"Don't worry if it's beyond your area of expertise. I'm sure the maintenance systems of a station hub are of little interest to a businessman such as yourself," she said.

"I've been playing in housing and work place systems since I was a first schooler. That's not the problem."

Her heart began to thud. "What is?"

He turned to check the door, then back to the station master. "I wonder if I can trouble you for a drink, Messer."

As soon as the man exited, Seolta's fingers played in his control field. He'd kept it in private mode so neither she nor any sensor could read his actions.

He moved closer to her, as if showing her the results on his screen. "That should mangle any snooping sensors. How much do you know about the incident on your ship on the way here?"

"The captain gave me a breakdown afterwards."

"And you have the training to follow it?"

"Enough." She'd known it was sabotage straight away. "Can you fix this?"

"I can. It's not so complicated, but there's a nasty trap in it. One that will backfire on the fixer's com if not disarmed first. This was more than a quick way to prove my skills to the station." He switched his attention back to his screen, then to her, and now she did feel nervous. "The question is, who's he trying to warn? Me or you?"

She didn't make the mistake of asking who he was talking about. The thought had been in her head since the ship incident. "He can't afford to lose me. Not yet. Not here."

"Not at the hands of a disgruntled off-worlder come to exact payment for the mess he landed me in back home?"

"Mess?" The breath whooshed out of her and she had to sit down. She'd always believed the Alliance would ask too many questions if anything happened to her uncle's last relative. More, she'd counted on it, and made sure she gave her uncle no reason to decide otherwise. The station ran smoothly, she made the correct noises on the rare occasions he required her presence on Surned, and asked no public questions of him.

If that was no longer enough, what was left to her? "What mess?" she demanded again.

"Later."

She didn't have a later. Maybe Seolta was wrong and this incident was simply her uncle wanting the off-worlder to look good in the eyes of the station hub administration. But they'd had no problem accepting his expertise in systems. Her uncle had endorsed him after all.

It didn't make Seolta a Manas any less a potential spy.

Nor did it take away her danger. The incident on her ship wasn't the first such mishap, but so far none had been lethal. Whether by luck or design she'd never been certain. This time might be another warning, but what about the next?

Then there was the look in Seolta eyes. She understood anger like that, had been intimately acquainted with it for years. The man hated her uncle almost as much as she did. So who was this warning for: herself or Seolta?

The man glanced up as her mouth opened, and his hand covered her lips. "Later," he repeated, then removed his privacy and blocking screens and the supervisor nearly fell into the room.

Anyara gave into a rare fit of frustration and stomped on their esteemed guest's foot. His smothered gasp made her feel better, but the laughing gleam in his eyes sent her senses spiralling. She turned away to greet the supervisor.

"We appear to have found the problem, Messer," she said smoothly, keeping her back very firmly to Seolta.

"Is it fixed?" he said.

"It is now," said the annoying voice beside her.

In the relieved ruckus that followed, she couldn't get a moment alone with Seolta, and he was soon swept off to receive the cheer and thanks of the retailers. She was included as well, but managed to plaster on a tight smile and excuse herself on the grounds of work that couldn't wait. They were used to her saying that, and none of them tried to make her stay. She walked away feeling more lonely than ever.

The next day she hid in her nursery, but not even the baby leaves reaching up to her loving hands or the stout walls and strict training of her staff kept her safe from hearing of the off-worlder's progress. A few days more and he'd have the entire station in his palm.

She called in her security the following morning. "Messer Seolta. Who is watching him?"

"He has a detail assigned from the Station Patrol."

"The routine one for off-worlders?"

The man kept a dead straight face and stared at a point just above her head. "The Trade Bureau suggested a higher level coverage."

"And what did the Alliance Embassy suggest?"

"I've had no official communication with the Embassy regarding Messer Seolta a Manas."

Which only confirmed their involvement. "Make sure he is kept safe. We don't need an inter-Alliance incident."

"Yes, Messera." He clicked his heels, then hesitated. "The off-worlder said the same about you to his security detail, Messera Anyara."

The man was marching out the door before she could close her mouth.

That evening, she let it be known she planned to eat out. Where, she didn't say. The whole station knew her favourite restaurant was the one overlooking the central reservoir lake. It played an important role in the passive regulation of air temperature and humidity as well as being the main store for non-potable water, but it was Anyara who'd insisted on planting its banks. Weeping grasses trailed the water's edge, bushes delighted the eye with flowers or berries, and floating plants dotted the surface giving shelter to the fish playing happily between them. They too were part of the hub's food cycle, but that wasn't why Anyara had ordered them. The Senior Biome Manager had insisted she provide proper technical reasons for the purchase, but they had worked together long enough to easily make the forms meet all the official requirements.

She took her usual seat by her favourite bush, a silver-leafed shrub with a small nondescript flower hidden under the leaves and a soft perfume that wafted over her table. It was a cousin of the famed chaullnia, the perfumed bush from her off-worlder's home world. She'd once smelled a small vial of extract from the chaullnia flower and spent months afterwards trying to get a license to import the bush to her station. Arcadia had blocked every move. Then she remembered the name on the blocking orders and wished she'd remembered it earlier. Den Coille, the same the man had first introduced himself by. She wished she dared pull up her com to find out what lay behind the name. Who had he been on his home world?

Word of her arrival soon swept the restaurant, and a procession of stationers began to stop by her table and pass on any gossip they thought might win them favour with her uncle. The one man she'd hoped to see made no appearance. She'd nearly given up on Seolta a Manas and had lifted her com wrist to signal the wait bot she was leaving when one more group wandered over.

Seolta hung in the back, letting the chief engineer, the local vidcast researcher and the hub's hydrologist greet her first. An interesting collection of acquaintances he'd picked. She made sure to watch his face as he came near and was privately pleased with his quickly hidden twitch as he caught the scent of the bush.

Since the others had spoken to her, he was forced to as well. "Evening, Messera. A beautiful place to enjoy this surprising world." His eyes never strayed to the bush, but she'd seen his hand reach toward the small flowers and then clench tight as he quickly shoved it behind his back.

"The head gardener was very pleased with how the landscaping turned out." A slight twitch of those unreliable lips said he knew very well who had chosen and planned this place. She decided to push it further and let her own hand lift and waft in the scent from the bush, taking a long breath and smiling. "You are no doubt familiar with the more famous relative of our *Miratio elumbis?*"

"Chaullnia? I've seen a bush," he said to shocked gasps and a chorus of questions from those around him.

She leaned forward. "I would love to hear about it."

Eyes hooded, he studied her face then turned with that charming smile and gave his apologies to those with him. "I have a feeling the Messera and I are about to become embroiled in plant talk. I'm sure she will excuse you, Messers. You must have heard similar many times before."

She blushed, before turning an equally practiced smile on the others. "The Messer has seen a plant I have always wanted to study. He can tell me so much about it."

The graceless man gave a chuckle. "I doubt it, Messera. It was just a plant to me. Its only interest lay in the astounding number of credits it made for its owners."

She was very tempted to expose him as one of those probable owners but she was in enough trouble already. The others made their farewells with barely covered looks of relief, and Seolta took the proffered chair, deliberately turning it so that his back was to the room and facing out to the lake. The practised smile stayed fixed on his face, but there was nothing soft about his eyes. "Who told you?"

"The name of your home world?" He nodded. "My uncle. I still can't believe he got landing permission for it."

"I arranged it. Not something I'm proud of."

"You had a good reason, I assume. "She set her lips into the nearest to an amused smile she could manage but suspected it looked more like a grimace.

"He was vouched for by a contact I thought I could trust."

"From your home world?"

A shake of his head. "Alliance Central. They were working together."

Anyara's smile vanished as the shock of that hit her. What had her uncle been thinking? You didn't play with the Alliance, not when you ran a world by breaking inter-Alliance laws.

Then the real consequence hit her. With an Alliance ally, he no longer had to preserve her ownership of her share listings. He no longer had to keep her alive.

"What is it," demanded Seolta.

She turned away from him. He was part of her uncle's scheming. Then she felt his hand closing over hers and, without thought, her fingers linked tightly to his.

She could not trust him.

He leaned closer and brought up a screen, as if discussing the restaurant's offerings. "What's frightened you?"

She shook her head and glanced at her wrist. "I'm sorry, Messer. My com has reminded me I have other duties calling for my attention. Your bushes will have to wait for another day." She shoved back her chair, sending it flying. She didn't care. She needed away from here, away from the man she had believed in for no reason except that her body called to his.

Running was out of the question—too suspicious—but she walked briskly, glancing repeatedly at her com as if checking on data inputs. In truth, she saw nothing, and her feet carried her by memory alone to the door of her nursery. Not until the outer and inner doors whooshed closed behind her did her heartbeat begin to slow.

Then she heard another whoosh. Someone had followed her. A towering vine wrapped around a nearby support pillar, the nearest thing to a real tree she'd managed to grow. Masses of bright green and purple covered it and reached up to touch the high ceiling of the room.

She backed into the screening curtain of leaves, hands on the trunk as if for protection. A man stood silhouetted by the light pouring in from the exterior.

"I have work to do, Messer Seolta. You will have to excuse me."

He lifted his com wrist and did his magic trick. "No one can hear or see us. I'm feeding in a doctored version."

"I'm not a fool, Messer."

He stepped closer and the door behind him closed. "I never thought you were. What about the Alliance frightens you?"

"You have no right to question me. I would like you to leave."

He took another step closer. "What is the Alliance to you? What happened at Prithand2."

"When you tell me your history, Messer Seolta, I'll consider telling you some of mine." She had no intention of ever doing any such thing. Her last memory of her home, her real home at Prithand2, had been of a dust-covered local lifting her into the rescue shuttle with a whispered order from a desperate man.

Live, Messera. For all of us, live.

She went to step back but the trunk of the vine stopped her and his mouth twisted.

"My story is not a pretty one." He studied her face, stared at her hands as they disappeared into the foliage and held tightly to the trunk. He lifted his hands, fingers spread wide, as if promising not to touch her, then stepped back. "Is there a more comfortable place to talk."

She shook her head. She wasn't moving until he left.

He sighed, then seemed to come to a decision. "What have you heard about my world? About the EA planet Arcadia?"

CHAPTER EIGHT

He'd said it. The name of his home, of his true origin. A world she'd known only in dreams.

"It's beautiful, a full EA world that needed only minor modifications for settlement. And it admits very few visitors."

His face twisted. "The last bit's true enough. Official planetary representatives or trade delegates only. As for the rest…" He looked up to the ceiling, taking in the full height of the vine she clung to. "Why don't you bring up a vid of it. I'm sending you the link to the official tourist one, the fuller version available to approved travellers. The images are real enough. Set it to full immersion."

She'd seen snippets of his world, but had never been able to access a full sim of it. Arcadia controlled its privacy too tightly. She didn't tell him that, though, didn't let him see what this meant to her. He threatened her peace enough already.

Within moments, the vine and room disappeared and they were coming into land at a space port. Urbis, capital of the planet Arcadia, according to the audio track. The vid took her through a city filled with architectural wonders and built around and over what appeared to be an actual river. A torrent of water, branching and spreading across the landscape until it spilled into a vast body of water that stretched as far as she could see.

"That's a sea!" She'd heard of such a thing, seen it in some vids, but this was bigger, wider, lighter and more … alive.

"Our northern sea," he said. "If you give me sole control, I can show you my home region south of here."

She was too stunned to refuse and found herself travelling over what appeared to be an ordered array of crops and grasslands.

"The northern coastlands around Urbis. Our most productive soils are found there."

Then they soared upwards. She held her breath as the controlled landscapes disappeared. Lands of the kind she understood, ones growing pasture and food crops similar to the ones in the station hub, were left far behind as they flew higher and higher, following the rising ground below.

She gasped. "Are those trees?" Lines of dark plants, reaching up towards them in every hollow.

"Yes, the lower slopes of the northern ranges are covered with a variety of trees at the base, but they disappear quickly."

She reached out. "Can we go down to them, please?"

He smiled. "Wait. These are nothing." His hands moved and they wrenched farther upwards, climbing steeply with the sudden change in the land. Now they were high above the world and it lay before her like a holo image.

"The northern ranges are our highest. That's why the trees fade into upland plant types so quickly. Above that, it's just rock, ice and snow."

"Snow," she breathed. "That comes from the sky too?"

He chuckled, but it wasn't a warm sound. As if she'd surprised it out of him. He turned them west and stayed high, hovering over a break in the mountains then slowly drifting southwards, talking all the way.

"This is the main pass between the northern lands and the central continental zone. Flyers can go over the mountains, but it's risky with the weather patterns. It's safer and more energy efficient to use the pass." They broke through the surrounding hills and he turned east again. She gasped. Below lay golden yellow grasslands as far as she could see, broken only by shimmering arrays of artificial sheets.

"Solar energy production?" They resembled the arrays covering the outer surface of the station.

"That's right. It rarely rains on the plains so they have very high sunlight hours. The solar fields get more frequent as we head east. The biggest is at the start of the Deadlands. It's too hot and windy east of that for them. Solaris is the company controlling solar production in this region. I understand they tried building a field in the heart of the Deadlands but the sheet life was too short to be economical. They were scoured out in no time."

The land had changed again. She gasped once more, staring at rolling banks of golden sand. "It's so beautiful."

He chuckled properly this time. "If that's what you like. It gets hot like you wouldn't believe."

Now he turned back west, zipping over the plains and coming to a hover over another mountain range at the edge of the grasslands.

"Are those more trees?" She stared hungrily at a dapple-leaved giant with branches spreading out and a thick trunk holding it all up. Delicate, stunning and as tall as her nursery wall.

"Beith," he said. "They prefer this side of the ranges where it's drier and sunnier." He tilted upwards and they climbed the slopes, soaring over more trees. She could have reached out and touched them if she'd dared disturb anything so precious."

Then he said, "Shut your eyes."

"You do know this is a simulation."

"It works better if you shut your eyes."

"Are there more trees?"

His smile this time was strained and his voice gruffer. "Yes, I promise you."

He had told her once what he could not promise, and that had been true. She shut her eyes.

She could feel them climbing higher, up and up. Then they stopped, buffeted by something on the outside, but she wasn't afraid.

Of course not. It's only a simulation.

Only that wasn't it. Seolta controlled the vid and he would not let her be hurt.

"Open your eyes."

She obeyed and her mouth dropped. Below lay rank upon rank of trees. Dark greens, mid greens, reaching up to the sky. Ones like she'd never seen. Above them, dark shapes filled the air, moving swiftly over the forest. Yes, that was the word. A forest was a collection of trees.

So many trees. "They're moving," she whispered in wonder.

"It's the wind. We get a lot of it this side of the mountains."

"And the sky? Those dark shapes?" They kept changing, hurtling in front of her and billowing over the land below, then darkening and blocking her view. Wispy tufts of grey and white clung to the tops. Then it all disappeared and all she could see was a grey haze. "What's happened? Is the program malfunctioning. I'll call up maintenance."

This time, he laughed out loud and put a hand on her arm. "We're in the clouds. This is what it feels like to arrive in Mountainer country."

It meant something. She glanced at him. His face was a strange mixture of taut control and soft yearning.

"My home region," he said in a voice that stopped her asking more.

He made another change and she could see the shape of a flyer all around them.

"You've added to the program."

"No, or not much. The shuttle on the original was boring. This is my own flyer. Much more comfortable and it can use my family's landing pad."

"It's a simulation," she reminded him again.

"Not even a simulation can break local law. No one lands on my family pad except those we allow. Luckily, they didn't take away my sim rights," he added with a touch of bitterness.

"They?"

"Later," he said.

He said that to her too often.

At that moment, they broke through the haze and buckets of water hit the front screen of the flyer. "Is that rain?"

"Of a kind. A full-scale mountain storm."

A sudden flash to her left had her jumping. "We're under attack. This is supposed to be an official sim."

"Relax. It's lightning. A natural electrical discharge."

"This world of yours has a number of surprises."

He grinned. "Wait."

They sank lower and the torrents of water became a soft mist. A drizzle, he told her it was called. Below them lay rank upon rank of trees, all the same type and packed more closely together than she'd thought possible. These were a deep green, with leaves glistening in the constant fall of water.

"Festia. The main source of my family's wealth."

"But I thought… I tried to order a chaullnia bush once and the rejection notice was countersigned as Den Coille."

He nodded. "My family name, and the name of our company. The chaullnia extract is a useful sideline."

"*Useful?* I've seen the cost of those perfumes."

He chuckled. "A *very* useful sideline. But it's not as lucrative as the festia. Its pollen is a carbohydrate base for many of our processed foods."

"Festin," she suddenly realised. "Spacers swear by it. We import a heap of it. It's lightweight and nutritionally dense.

He nodded again.

"That's your company?"

"My family's. My father is still the senior manager."

"And you?"

That grim twist returned to his face. "Used to be in charge of our com systems and policy. I did whatever Da found useful."

"You loved it," she suddenly realised.

He lifted a hand as if it didn't matter, but she could see the lie in his body. Rigid and too carefully held.

"Bring us down," she said.

"It's not relevant to what I need to tell you."

"It's relevant to me, and you were going to do it before I asked about the business."

"I hadn't realised…"

He stopped, mouth clamped and refusing to put into words what returning to his home meant. If she was kinder, she'd stop now but that would tell her nothing about him. "Put us down."

He stared at her for long moments as the flyer was buffeted by the unseen air currents. Wind, another phenomenon she'd never experienced. Her uncle never let her go out on the surface of Surned in any but the safest of local weathers and in a shuttle massive enough to withstand anything thrown at it. She suspected he used it as an excuse to keep her confined to Kevand3 or the station hub.

"On your head be it, Messera."

They began to descend, moving south and west until the tree types changed again. These were darker in colour, deep velvety green with branches reaching right up to the sky. "They're enormous," she breathed.

"The baullnia tree. The tensile strength of its branches is equal to the best structural plascrete."

They came to a hover over the highest leaves. The only break in the tree cover was a raw scar on the slopes above.

"What's that?"

He barely glanced at it, as if reluctant to remember. "The scar of a mudslide. The hillside gave way in a storm there. We nearly lost half the city that day."

There was a grim look on his face. He looked again and his face tightened. "We nearly lost my sister as well. She was trying to warn us and we didn't believe her."

There was more to it than that, but he'd already given her more than he'd wanted, she'd guess. Shadows clung to his eyes. More of that history that weighed him down.

She wasn't going to add to it. Why it happened was another matter. She'd read some of the history of this place, but he didn't need her telling him the probable causes of the hillside giving way. Whether he was ready to accept it was another matter, but his guilt told her enough. She turned her face to look at the rest of their surrounds.

The slip was the only break. She looked north and south. Trees covered the mountain slopes, broken only by occasional outcrops of cold grey rocks. To the west, the light sparked off something, but it didn't look like a landing field.

"That's the ocean," he said.

Ocean: a very large sea. Incomprehensibly large. She shook her head, unable to take it in right now, and looked down at the solid banks of green.

"Where do we land?"

"Wait," he said, as if about to produce a magic trick from his bag.

Suddenly a platform rose up.

They sank down, falling into the leaves. The flyer settled down on the platform and struts locked them into place. Then the platform sank within the tree canopy.

He stood and the hatch opened. He lifted out a hand to her. "Messera?"

Bemused, she took his hand and walked with him out onto the flimsy surface. It swayed under her feet and she clutched at his arm with her other hand. "How high are we?"

"Don't worry, you're safe with me."

She still held tightly to him as he walked over the unstable, treacherous pad. No wonder the man looked like he was dancing if this was the kind of place he called home.

A door opened in the thick wall in front of them. "Welcome to Manascraoch," said the voice over. "Renowned city in the trees of the Mountainer region of Arcadia."

She stopped dead, unable to believe what she saw.

"Come on," he said. "It's only a sim. Nothing can hurt you."

Maybe, but she'd never been in a sim quite like this one. Cautiously she followed in his footsteps as he led the way across the platform and through the station door. Desk scans checked her credentials and took her through landing procedures that were both the same as and different from usual. No habitat port had large beams of living wood growing through the office and a counter sprouting leaves. Real ones, from the scent when crushed.

Or spoke in the liquid language of this reception counter, translated afterwards into Standard by the com program. Beside her, Seolta answered in the same tongue, then took her hand. "Welcome to my home," he said as he tugged her through the opening door.

After that there was no plascrete-lined walkway, no moving floor. Just a surface unlike any she'd seen before. Worn smooth, but her heart recognised it, even as her brain rejected the possibility. She touched her toe to the mottled surface. "Is this the bark of a tree?"

He stopped tugging at her hand, and looked down as if only now noticing the material. "Yes, of course."

"You pave your floors with material from a tree?" She was shocked. Such a precious material, used for mere flooring.

"There is no shortage of trees around us," he said amused, "and it's not paved. You're walking on a living tree. Didn't you hear the introduction to the city?"

"'A city in the trees.' A nice slogan for tourists."

He looked to be throttling back laughter. "No, it's the actual truth. You're standing on the upper branches of a baullnia tree. I told you they have an amazing tensile strength. The ground around here is too boggy to build on. All our homes, offices, parks, everything we need is built in and on the branches of the baullnia trees."

Her mouth gaped wide open. "Not possible." She'd thought this was an elevated habitat, like the ones she'd read about on other worlds with dangerous ground strata, but to build on a tree...

"Possible, and is, beautiful Sera Anyara. That's the normal form of address here. I don't know your full mountain name."

"Full name?" It seemed safer.

"Mountainers like to know exactly who they're dealing with. My correct name is Seolta mar Bram an Scathach den Coille. Seolta son of Bram and Scathach, of the family Coille.'"

Something changed in him as he said it. It was as if he grew taller and a brightness came into his eyes. It lasted only a moment before the shadows returned, secrets filling the dark eyes again.

"What are your father and mother's names?" he asked.

She shook her head, horrified. "They died, a long time ago. Their names are no longer mentioned." Had he forgotten they were still in her nursery on a Kevand station hub? Even the best com's program couldn't be trusted against her uncle's surveillance. "Show me your home."

The spark in his eyes said he wouldn't forget, but he let it drop. For now, she guessed. He took her hand and strode across a walkway into a new passage. "Give me a moment and I'll take us direct."

"No," she protested. "The full passage." She didn't want to miss one step of this extraordinary place.

He checked his com.

"We have plenty of time," she said. Not true, she really did have duties calling her, but she didn't want this sim to end too soon.

After that, he took her by passageways she couldn't have imagined. Up actual stairs, around corners, stepping over *living* branches of the giant tree. At one point, they stepped out onto an open walkway and rain drenched her through to the skin as the wind dragged at her arms and pulled her dangerously close to the flimsy barrier at the edge.

"Shield," snapped Seolta.

The wind roared in as if personally challenged, tearing at her clothes and hair. He grabbed her arm and pulled her back into the safety of the passage they'd just left, slamming the door shut behind them.

"I forgot. Our weather shielding technology is copyrighted to Den Coille. We'll have to take a back way." She didn't care how they went, as long as it was free of the torrents drowning her. He took her by plainer tunnels and she was relieved to find she was quickly restored to a dry version by the program's systems. After more circling, they came to a large doorway that opened as they approached.

"Private family quarters beyond. I can show you my own quarters but everything else must be blanked out. Are you all right with that?"

She nodded, unsure what she'd agreed to. Then she discovered, walking from the living branch onto the grey plascrete of the nursery floor as the sim field vanished. She could have cried.

"A few more steps and it'll let us back," he said, an echo of her grief in his own voice, and she remembered what this place was to him.

Her foot found living bark again and ahead lay a doorway, old-fashioned in look. Beside it rose up a massive wall, rough-faced and curving slightly. Seolta touched it, as if greeting an old friend.

"The central trunk. I prefer sleeping next to the tree's heart, whereas my younger sister's rooms were always at the end of the safest branch. I'm told her husband loathes the feel of it." She looked up at the wry laugh in his voice. "He's a Plainsman. Hates being too far above the ground at the best of times, while Fioruisghe was born dancing on the smallest boughs. She says they have more spring. It leads to some interesting moments."

"Yours sounds to be an unnerving family to join."

He laughed out loud then. "That's one way of putting it." He put his hand on the door and pushed. It swung open, just like the old doors of myths, and he stood back for her to go first, that wry smile still colouring his face. For some reason, she liked this smile best. There was nothing soft about it, nothing kind, but it was real and told of the complexities lying beneath his controlled exterior.

The man had a very dry sense of humour.

Then she entered his room. No, rooms. This was a living space only. The sleep room and service room must be through the doors opposite. Her mouth dropped open again. She seemed to be doing a lot of that in this simulation. This one room was bigger than her entire apartment.

If she thought the building had been beautiful so far, this was more so. One entire wall was formed by the rough-faced wall of the tree's massive trunk, and the support beams appeared to be outshoots of the tree. Living plants, their roots clinging to the parent tree or set into pots in notches, mingled with stunning works of art. She didn't recognise most of them, but it didn't take a knowledge of art to react to these. Sculptures, living screens, and even one old-fashioned fixed-medium piece. The furniture in the room, if you could call it that, appeared to be formed from the tree, and whether twisted in growth or carved into shape, she couldn't decide.

Seolta walked in beside her, and breathed in deeply. Then, all of a sudden, his face closed over and his jaw clamped tight, white lines spreading from the corners of his mouth.

"What's the matter?"

"Nothing," he said curtly.

There was a lot more than *nothing* wrong.

She could almost see the effort he used to relax that jaw. "My apologies. Please, check out the rest of the room."

Then she realised. That was grief scoring his face. She'd have liked to explore his rooms further, but this had to be enough. "Thank you for showing me your home," she said, "but I really do have other duties to attend to, and you still haven't told me why you left this world." She swept her eyes around the amazing space then saw the holoimages decorating a work desk on the far wall. People laughing, holding each other close. People who looked very similar to the man beside her. She walked over, feeling more an outsider than ever, and her hand reached out, one finger touching a holo with a group of people flanking a smiling couple. Family, this was his family. All those brothers and sisters he had mentioned.

"That's all of us, the last time we were together just before Cumchdach's wedding. My father and mother in the middle, Samhchair and Cumchdach standing either side of our parents, Ceart and I in the middle on each side, and Aigherach and Fiorusghe on the outside. They're the youngest."

He spoke in a dream-like voice, his hand hovering over each in turn. The hologram Seolta had a slightly exasperated look on his face and, beside him, Fioruisghe grinned with some secret delight. She had a feeling this sister was one of the few to best Seolta den Coille and tried not to smile. Then she saw his face in the instant before he wiped a hand across it.

She'd had a family once. Tears sprang to her eyes. "Why leave them?"

His hand crashed against the com on his wrist and suddenly the room disappeared and they were back in the flyer, high above the city. "I was sent into exile. It was my own fault."

He'd hinted at it before but the plain words, clear, simple, their meaning unmistakable, smashed into her. "You're a criminal."

He shook his head, his face stark and bleached in the blue light of the sim. "There was no trial."

"But if there had been, you would have been convicted," she said flatly.

"Yes."

"What saved you? Good connections?"

He shook his head. "It would have caused a security nightmare and an almighty scandal. Arcadia doesn't need that kind of strife right now, not given my family's position and our recent history. Instead, they quietly got rid of me."

"Why?" she demanded again. If she lived on such a world, she would spend every day thanking all the deities worshipped by humans and making sure nothing ever spoiled this paradise.

"We need to go higher again." He moved his hand in the control field and stared straight ahead, refusing to meet her eyes. "Look down."

It was like seeing a vast holo-map, but this was a living, breathing world. She could see the slight curvature of the horizon, telling her just how big this world was in comparison to Surned.

"Watch the vegetation and cloud changes as we track from west to east." He spoke in the disembodied voice of a bot tutor, voice stripped of anything that might reveal what he felt. But she had seen the pain in his face as he walked into his home and looked at the holos of his family. He wasn't going to talk about it, though. Not ever, she suspected, if he remained barred from his home. She gave in for now and studied the land below. In the west, dark green trees cloaked his mountainside home region. Not the extraordinary trees supporting his home, but just as beautiful.

Then she realised there were no splotches of colour, no interweaving of species echoing the shapes that made up the land below. Mixing the biota and a careful transition between species types was something she always considered when creating vegetation beds throughout the station. She'd tried to get the same principle adopted on Kevand3, but the biome manager there had scoffed at her. Inefficient, he called it.

He was wrong. She'd felt it herself and saw it in the faces of the hub residents as they wandered through the station's gardens. Their irregularity and lack of precise mathematical shapes mimicked the landscape of EA worlds. Or as near as she could get from the images they released. Too many worlds were like Arcadia, restricting access and knowledge from habitat worlds.

The mountains below were covered with uniformly coloured and spaced trees. "That's a man-made plantation."

"Yes. Festia trees. We plant them over as much of the mountains as possible."

"All those slopes can't be equally suited to one tree type." She saw hollows and ridges, streams, and rock faces. Different sun exposures, varied drainage and soil types.

His mouth twisted. "My sister Fioruisghe would fall on your neck with joy to hear you say that."

She wasn't sure how to answer that and waited silently.

"Festia like wet, boggy ground, so we gave it to them."

"With no repercussions?" This was a natural environment. She remembered that from her training. You always had to account for effect and counter effect when engineering them.

He took them a bit higher. "Look at the cloud cover over the peaks."

At first, she didn't know what she was supposed to be looking at. Clouds were such an amazing thing to her. Then she saw it. A single line, right along the top of the mountains. "There's no transition zone between the storm clouds on the western side and the clear skies on the east. It's as if the clouds slam into a wall at the top of the mountains."

"Yes." He took them farther east, flying now under bright cloudless skies. The vegetation changed dramatically.

"Those are dry habitat plants down there."

He nodded, his mouth grim. "Look at the solar fields."

Below them now, between the waving fields of grass and smaller shrubs, wide fields of shining sheets stretched out over vast tracts of land. As they travelled east, more and more of the land was covered.

"Winter Solaris's main source of income. They own the plains financially, as Den Coille dominates the western side of the ranges. And solar fields love clear skies and low rainfall.

It suddenly hit her. She looked back at that unnatural line dividing wet mountainside from dry plains "Where does your weather come from?" She knew about air flow patterns. The station carefully graded its artificial weather patterns to conserve energy, with graded transition zones to keep them stable.

"From the west," he said.

From that vast western ocean. Clouds absorbed huge amounts of water and released it as they hit the land mass, according to the few lessons she'd shared with ecological engineers. The hot air rising from the plains must hit the moist, cold air flowing up the mountains in a catastrophic clash. No wonder the west had such storms with the turbulence it would cause. As for the east, it had to be in a downward spiral into ever more desiccated lands. She'd seen a glimpse of desert when they first flew over. A few more cycles would expand that till she would see more than a glimpse of it.

"They need to modify the vegetation on your side of the mountains and cut back the solar fields on those eastern plains."

"So we've been told," he said.

"And will you?"

"We have to. The Planetary Council ordered it. This isn't the only problem region. According to my sister, our settlers have driven the natural resources of Arcadia to maximise profit, creating too many imbalances for the planet to cope with.

He stopped, took a breath. "She works for the Ecological Survey."

"Your bioengineering agency? They shouldn't have too much work on an EA world."

"That's what we all assumed. Turns out they'd been working in secret to protect us from our own greed for years. But then…"

He stopped again and it was as if something froze his tongue.

"And then…" she prompted.

He swallowed. "The Survey acquired new managers, ones more aligned with the commercial trends on Arcadia. They saw an opportunity and took it."

"Aahhh." Her uncle was the prime example of a man who did that, and all his senior managers copied him. It was one way her uncle bought their loyalty. He only punished excessive greed; the small scams, he positively encouraged.

"What kind of opportunity?" she had to ask.

"The Council had warned my family we had to change the way we grew festia. Or rather, Fioruisghe had warned us. At the time, Den Coille was at odds with the Winters, the family who own the Solaris solar company on the eastern plains. Both our families wanted control of the central zone.

"And you? What was your position?"

"I was one of the worst. It was I who suggested taking action to settle it. Fioruisghe was partnered with Caleb Winter by the Survey. I thought he was holding her by force over on the plains rather than at home where she should be. We couldn't allow that."

He might be talking of another person, another family, his voice a mechanical recitation.

"We kidnapped her and took her back home. Caleb came for her and ended up having to rescue half the city from the mudslide." He waved aside her horrified gasp. "Everyone got out. The important thing was, in abducting Fioruisghe, we gave the Survey management an excuse to take action against us."

His hands clenched at his sides. "I can't talk about this here."

Suddenly the whole simulation vanished and she was back in the foyer of her nursery. She cried aloud at the loss, then clamped her mouth shut at the blank-eyed agony on his face.

"What action did they take?"

"They locked us up. All of us, my whole family except Fioruisghe; and they tried to do the same to the Winters. Two of their sons managed to escape, Caleb, the eldest, and the youngest, Silas, but Ethan Winter was thrown into the cells with us. My elder sister and both sets of parents were held in a standard prison. The Council had control of them.

"But you and the rest?"

"Were held by Survey troopers." He stopped again. "It wasn't pleasant."

He strode away from her. Not far, just enough to avoid any chance of her touching him, and propped himself against a post, staring at the ground.

"We were tried in common court. Tried, found guilty, and sentenced to death."

Someone gasped. It was her, she realised. "You didn't die."

His hands locked together. "Fioruisghe and Caleb raised the rank and file of the Survey against the corrupt managers and mobilised our local politicians to help. That exposed the managers' plots and we were all released. But after that…"

She held her breath. Then he raised his head.

"I was so angry, Messera Anyara. They'd tried to take away everything I loved, tried to kill my family just to satisfy their greed, and the Council stood by and let them." His hands gripped the wall, knuckles white. "No one was going to do that to me or mine again. When the Alliance deputy approached me to join in her schemes, I was a gandy ripe for the plucking. Then Ethan Winter got involved, and they nearly killed him for his pains."

He'd break his fingers soon unless he loosed his grip on the post. She didn't dare tell him to stop.

He dropped his head again and she had to strive to hear him. "In prison, Ethan stood up for Aigherach. For *my* baby brother. And they made him pay for it. He still suffers the aftereffects of that. And I helped the people who tried to kill him." He looked up again, and this time he met her eyes fully. "I am not a good man, Messera."

CHAPTER NINE

He believed it, and maybe he was right. She'd never met a truly good man, and suspected they would be something of a trial.

"You said my uncle and this Alliance deputy tried to kill Ethan Winter. What stopped them?"

He flushed. "I did." He pushed his shoulders hard back against the wall. "For what he did for my brother in prison, my family will always be in his debt. Revenge can't justify betraying that."

"But it does allow taking action against my uncle."

His face hardened. "It's more than revenge now. He has to go."

"Regardless of who else it hurts?"

Now she saw the anger he'd talked about. "Don't tell me getting rid of your uncle will hurt Surned. I've seen the habitats down there."

"You think it's all fear?" She braced herself against the vine and shoved up her chin as he stepped closer. "Surned's systems work, and my uncle is an integral part of that. Remove him, and you leave a void to be filled by the next greedy dictator."

"Not with Alliance supervision."

"You trust them? Despite telling me an Alliance Deputy is involved?" It all made sense. The change she'd sensed in her uncle.

"He's going to use her. Blackmail her to ignore *anything* he does here." A band of fear snapped tight around her throat, choking the life out of her. She sagged back against the vine as spots danced in front of her eyes.

A man's hand grasped her face and strong arms held her tight. "Anyara. Sweetheart. You're safe."

No she wasn't. "My uncle sent you back here. Why?"

It was a word she rarely used with others, too fearful of exposing herself. But now she *had* to have answers.

He looked around him. "Not here," he said softly. "Is there somewhere cooler till you recover," he said in a louder voice. "The heat in here would make anyone collapse."

This room was one of the higher humidity spaces, but Anyara had worked in it many times before with no ill effects. "The engineering plant for the nursery. It's a bit noisy but climate cooled. The machines need to be kept at a precise temperature."

The noise and emissions from the machinery interfered with any auditory surveillance, although it still gave shaky visuals. Security monitored it by data instead. He gave her that grim smile and picked her up. She'd thought the man lightly built, not much taller than herself, but she discovered he was a lot stronger than he looked. Once there, he sat her on a workman's table and stood close, ostensibly checking her pulse and helping her to stay upright. His face was too close for any sensor to read their words.

"What did he ask you to do?" she said. He held her arms and her heart began to beat louder. "You're here to kill me."

"He didn't say it outright," said the man sent as an assassin, "but that's what he expects. After which, my own lifespan would be decidedly short, but it was anyway."

Will you, was what she should ask. Would an assassin admit to it? "What happened down on Surned," she said instead and his eyes widened.

"I have no intention of following your uncle's wishes, and that is a promise."

"But he thinks you will."

He gave the slightest of nods. "It's a matter of length of lifespan and potentials. There is a chance I could escape from here. Small, but a chance, and your uncle knows I'm good at figuring the odds."

"On Surned?" she jogged him again.

His hand tightened on her arm. She leaned in closer. "What happened, Messer?"

A twitch touched those firm lips. "On my tour of the other habitats, one place took me close to Prithand2. We could have easily called in there as well, but it wasn't on the list. I have a dislike of others dictating what I do."

"So you went anyway?"

"Yes, and met an accident for my pains. Why did I go? Because you still use it as your place of origin and something happened there many years ago. The records go back only to around the time you came into your uncle's care. I dislike mysteries as much as I dislike being manipulated."

"You think you weren't on this occasion. This accident?"

That cool smile, one that said he knew exactly what had happened. "I miscalculated, but so did your uncle. I'm still here."

"But killing you? It puts him at risk. Someone on your world will ask questions."

"An accident. That's all it was. Just like whatever happened to you back on Prithand2."

She gasped, and fell silent.

"Another useful accident, wasn't it? One that took both your parents and left you in your uncle's control. You and your fifteen percent share in his company."

She slapped a hand on his mouth. Those words were too dangerous. He shook his head then leaned in closer.

"Give me a personal link, Anyara."

She gulped. That wasn't all he asked. Not by the glitter in his eyes, and she licked her lips. His eyes followed, then he leaned closer still and his lips touched hers. "Please. Give me your trust in this."

Then his lips took hers and his arms came round her, their wrists touching. She could barely concentrate, too taken by the shock of his lips on hers. They sought permission, and she opened her mouth to him as she opened a link. This was like no kiss she'd had before.

So beautiful, said a murmur in her head.

Yes, he was. A thought, not one she dared put into words. Not that she could formulate many at the moment. She fell into the kiss, and only vaguely became aware of someone talking to her through the com link. He still held her close, his lips caressing hers, but they had gentled enough to make thought possible.

"I will not kill you," promised the man she had learned kept his promises, "but something has frightened you badly. Has your uncle tried to kill you before?"

She had to force the words to form in her head and send them across the link. "Not that I could prove," she managed. His kiss took her under again, a violent pulse of fury in the strength he barely held contained, till finally he released her lips and drew back, his breathing as changed as hers.

"Why now?" said his voice through the link as his other hand ran a different message up and down her back. One that said she mattered. She marshalled her words.

"Your Alliance Deputy must have allies. With that backing, he can risk owning more than the legal forty-nine percent."

"Not openly. No corrupt official will stand by him if he tries that. Too risky." His hand kept up the firm strokes, promising her she wasn't alone.

"They will. He'll blackmail them into it," she sent bitterly. "With someone from the Alliance making it look good, he can twist the share ownership forms to suit. Your Deputy has given him that someone."

"And getting rid of me?"

"Removes a threat. You think he trusts you?"

A dry chuckle rippled through her body from his. "He's not stupid."

"So you're still after him."

"I told you. He owes me."

"More than your life?"

Those dangerous lips had twisted. "Not if I can help it, but if I can't…"

She pulled back hard. "No," she said aloud, and hoped any watcher thought she meant the kiss. "He's not worth it," she sent through the link.

"Nor am I," he sent back, and abruptly broke the connection. "My apologies, Messera," he said stiffly. "Your beauty overcame me. I have taken up enough of your valuable time. I will leave you to your duties."

"Think nothing of it," she muttered in a rasping voice, gripping the bench to hold herself upright. She had to act as well as he did. Their lives depended on it, on saying words the opposite of the ones that clawed at her throat.

He stood and gave her that strange half bow of his, this one a fraction deeper than usual, and she wished she knew what it meant.

Then he swung around and marched out of her building, out of her domain. She clung to the memory of his last words as he rose from the sinuous bow. "Keep safe," his lips had formed swiftly, barely seen by her or any sensors.

He had said them.

Seolta felt like smashing something. He may have regretted his past actions, but never before had he wished to be a better man. In no mood to talk to anyone, he ordered up a skitter, one with windows and a retractable top, and set it for a round tour of the station the next morning.

He needed to get out of the central hub area, away from growing plants, from managers, from the controllers of this massive station. From what he felt for Anyara a Prithand2. He hadn't yet seen the rest of the station, he told himself. It would take a full day cycle to circumnavigate it, and he set off the next morning with relief. A full day to think without interruption.

After the first hour of introspection…

Sulking.

That's what juveniles did. Seolta was thrown off balance, taken aback, struggling to figure out what had happened. Anyara and their kiss had done all of that. Nor had he found out about her past. He just knew it wasn't good, and that she feared for her life.

Another hour and he cooled down enough to start looking around him rather than letting the skitter choose the quickest route. He rolled back the roof and checked his timer against the light.

They didn't match. Then reality struck. Back home, they used standard hours when dealing with off-planet entities, but he was used to setting his com to adjust for Arcadia's own circadian rhythm and had done it this morning out of habit. That wasn't needed here—because he was in a metal hub stuck in orbit around a dead world with all living systems artificially regulated.

Everyone here was one hull breach away from extermination.

The reality of that sharpened when his skitter gave him a warning. "Intermittent moisture in air for the next section. Close roof."

It was going to rain? He pulled the skitter cover shut and climbed out, waiting. Then felt his hair, his hands and clothes beading with moisture. The fine mist came from all directions; up, sideways, and down, swirling in regular patterns through the nearby buildings and gardens, as if following a pre-set pathway.

No, that's exactly what was happening. This moisture release was no more rain than the precisely controlled garden beds resembled any natural world.

He looked around to see the station residents' reactions and discovered that the streets had suddenly emptied of people. Station residents weren't about to get wet. He tilted up his face regardless, the damp air whispering to him in a heart-breaking hint of his forest home. Not enough to heal the gaping wound of loss inside him but a help to forget it, at least momentarily.

That kiss had made him forget too. He'd had to yank hard at his self-control to form the words to tell her what he needed. Then he'd walked away and left her. She'd been as lost in that kiss as he, maybe as thrown by it, and he'd left her standing. He had to. She was safer that way, and that was becoming important to him. He'd destroyed his life; he mustn't destroy hers. This was her home. He was just a passing drifter of Alliance space.

He checked the station map and found the nearest viewing port to the exterior. It took the skitter only moments to get there, and luckily the security screens accepted his com ID.

No luck in it. Hilmar would have made sure of it, lest he forgot where he was or why he was here. Despite that, he activated the screen to remove the opaque covers and let him see the reality of what lay outside the station.

Stars, wheeling in time with the revolution of the station's core and, below them, at the centre of the spiral, the red-gold surface of Surned. A faint haze circled the planet, the only sign of the toxic atmosphere, and far off beyond it sat the alien sun that gave this system life. Caleb or Ethan could have told him the meaning of the spectrum types. All he knew was that it wasn't his own sun. Wrong colour, wrong place.

Wrong everything.

He wrenched away from the portal, refusing to blank it as screeched at him by the systems. "Do it yourself," he muttered at the bot's voice.

Back in the skitter, he ratcheted it up to its full, excruciatingly slow speed, and returned to his self-imposed circuit. He refused to stop for a lunch break, collecting a bland ration pack from a service centre and clambering back into the box.

Right now, he didn't trust himself to talk to any of the locals.

A ping on his com of an incoming message, then the more urgent sound of the *answer now* command. He checked the sender.

Hilmar. Just what he needed. He pulled over into the shade of the nearest greenery, climbed out to let the scent of crushed leaves fill his nose, then hit *Answer.*

"Hilmar, how may I help you on this delightful day?"

"Don't give me the charm routine. I know what you're capable of, Seolta den Coille."

"Nice to see you too." He sharpened his own image, improving the glamour quotient and enhancing the green of the background. Then eyed Hilmar. The man's com image had a decided edge to it.

He could be described as looking flustered. His own com would never have allowed such an image unless specifically ordered by him. But then, his own com had unique modifications.

"What do you want?" he said, dropping all pretence at civility.

"My niece. You were reported kissing her. You better not be trying to double cross me there. Her shares aren't transferable to non-citizens—and any application you make for that will be blocked, by me."

"I have no interest in a share in this world. I'm exiled, not impoverished." What kind of family did the man think he came from?

"Maybe, but keep my niece out of it. We had an agreement."

"And to fulfil it, I need to get close to your niece. After that, any accident will be as you require. I don't make false promises, Messer."

"Nor do I, *Ser* Seolta mar Bram. Fail me, and you will never see your own world again."

A glitter of truth lit the man's eyes. Then his holo-image snapped out, leaving Seolta staring angrily at a blank space.

The man had no say in his exile. No one had said it was permanent.

But no one had said it had an end either, and Hilmar a Kevand has contacts in the Alliance.

Or there was that other way to get rid of him that was even more permanent.

Deputy Malgrave had already made it plain she viewed the den Coille and Winter families as nothing more than obstacles to getting what she wanted. A profitable toehold on Arcadia. She'd nearly done it too.

It was the reason an Fallon had won him exile without imprisonment. Find out who else was connected with Malgrave's schemes. How high did the rot in the Alliance go? Instead, he'd selfishly chosen revenge against Hilmar.

"Surned is off limits," Marshal an Fallon had told him. Didn't the man know that would make it the first place he'd go? A thought he'd had more than once, and destroying Hilmar was a way to finding those connections. Or that's what he'd told himself, ignoring the huge flaw in his reasoning. Going after revenge on the Arcadian government had got him into this mess in the first place. Why had he thought going after revenge on Hilmar would turn out any better? Anyara's words came back to haunt him. Could he act against Hilmar and ignore the turmoil it would cause for the entire Surned system?

He thumped the acceleration control. Nothing happened, the skitter merely sending out a warning for attempted misuse and reciting the compulsory fine now debited against his account.

Great. Now he had an infringement record as well. Hilmar would smirk when that came across his desk. He needed a drink.

Bars weren't common here, and none he passed were of the seedy kind best suited to the miserable and unwanted. He pulled over at the first place that looked like it might be vaguely hospitable and stomped through the door. At least the lighting was dim enough for him to fall into a corner seat, order up the strongest drink on their list, and slouch back into the shadows, gulping down the noxious brew and wishing he could make the last few years disappear.

Be again the youth who thought the whole world existed for his pleasure.

Then a pair of men approached him. There was something unmistakeable about government officials, no matter which world they came from. The pair didn't wait for an invitation, and he didn't bother trying to tell them to go elsewhere, not when they flipped him their IDs. The Alliance Patrol. The galaxy's diplomats and police, all in one smooth and unforgiving package.

"What do you want?" he growled.

They took a seat and ordered up something that looked much tamer than his—no doubt putting it on his account.

"This system wasn't on your original route plan, Messer den Coille. Any reason you decided to detour here?"

"I felt like it."

"Nothing personal in that, we trust," said the taller one.

"Or contractual," said the broad and squat one, leaning forward.

"Did Hilmar a Kevand3 invite me here? Hardly. Not after the incident back on Arcadia."

"Yet he has done nothing to harm you."

Not quite true, but Seolta gave a non-committal lift of his shoulders. He had no proof connecting Hilmar with the pass incident anyway.

"So why did he send you back to the station? Back to his niece."

Seolta wished the two agents would drop their pass-the-ball interrogation game, but knew better than to try making them. Nothing bullies liked better than an admission they were getting to you.

The taller one leaned forward. "Your government would be very concerned to hear you'd become entangled with Messer Hilmar a Kevand3 again."

"And certainly if they learned you've become another of the assassins the Messer has sent after Anyara a Prithand2."

Seolta jerked up. "Assassins? Plural?"

"You didn't imagine you were the only one. He's waited a very long time for a chance to get rid of her."

Seolta reached over and grabbed at the man's arm. He'd have liked it to be his neck, but he needed information. "If anything happens to her, it will make public his shareholding in Surned and force the Alliance to act against him."

"Ah, but that seems to be no longer a problem. And we suspect you know why."

"Malgrave," Seolta spat out. Then suddenly jerked back and eyed the two in front of him.

"We're not with her," said the taller coldly, "but we might have been."

The squat one said nothing and Seolta felt an icy breeze snake up his back. He used to be called the clever den Coille. Right now, he was the confused one with no idea what was going on.

"There's a ship leaving in two days for Central," said the squat one.

"And you want me on it? Give me a good reason," said Seolta. He was bluffing, but hoped they didn't realise it.

"Your friend will appreciate it if you are on board. Messera Anyara has been dealing with her uncle's plots for many years."

He couldn't decide if they were threatening Anyara or merely speaking truth. "And if he succeeds this time? Remember Alliance law. The one prohibiting one man owning more than forty-nine percent of any human habitation."

The man's face didn't change. "The planet Surned is functioning acceptably. The Alliance would be loath to upset that."

So Anyara was expendable. He'd not expected that. Seolta's heart beat faster and he had to lock down all the muscles on his face to hide his reaction. "It sets a troublesome precedent for other habitat worlds. The kind that can lead to political ructions. Violent ones. The Alliance doesn't need that."

"Only if word of what happened here becomes widely known."

Nothing changed in the man's face, but Seolta found his hand reaching automatically for the small weapon he kept concealed in his boot. "You're playing a dangerous game, Messers." He stood up, slammed down on his com to pay the bill. "If you will excuse me, I have things to see to."

"Nothing of concern to our bosses, we hope."

"Nothing of any *business* of your bosses," he replied and marched out before he lost control and sank the small knife into the man's neck.

He'd never resorted to violence before. Been tempted? Oh, yes, many times in that hell of a prison, but he'd had no weapon there and prided himself on his tongue and brain being worth more than any weapon.

Surned had stripped away all his comfortable delusions. He thrust himself into the skitter and shoved it to full, ignoring all warnings as he used his com to override the speed restrictions built into the thing's programs and extract a touch more urgency out of it.

Nothing would get him back to Anyara as fast as he needed. Other assassins. Multiple other assassins, circling unseen and unexpected.

Come on, you stupid excuse for a transporter. He set the skitter to auto—no point risking it all for that drop of pure poison in his veins—and ordered it to use the fastest thoroughfare. He hunched back and shut his eyes, refusing to take in the artificial streets, the bland sky that wasn't one, the uniformly planted shrubberies.

And she called him out on the Den Coille festia plantations?

They're on an EA world. This isn't.

He wondered briefly if there was a cure for annoying voices in your head.

The skitter began to slow and he cracked open an eye. Too soon to be back at the central zone, nor could he see any congestion or obstacles. Must be some kind of maintenance in this sector.

Then the skitter pulled over and stopped, and he opened both eyes with all senses alert. The door opened and he reached for that hidden knife.

"I wouldn't, Ser den Coille," said the woman stepping into the vehicle and using an accent that could only belong to an Arcadian. She proved it by flashing her ID. Martis Katarvat of the Arcadian Galactic Ministry, on secondment from the Federal Marshals. He fought against the pull of that accent and the automatic sense of trust it brought.

"Sera Katarvat, how *nice* to meet you."

"I'm no more thrilled than you, Ser den Coille." She settled into the second seat in the skitter and set it to move again, using the automatic under supervision mode. So she wanted to talk, but didn't trust the Surned controls any more than he should have. Likely she hadn't just knocked back a full order of the station's worst either.

"What do you want?" he asked, and didn't care if his voice sounded as sulky to her as it did to him. "I've already told your friends in the Patrol everything I intend to tell nosy officials today."

The woman suddenly sat up straight. "Which friends would that be?"

"So not friends of Arcadia. I did wonder."

"And acted upon it, I hope."

He shrugged. "They already knew everything that mattered. I'm getting very tired of being warned off."

"Given your recent actions," she said, "we make no apology for assuming you are unaware of the ramifications of your stunts."

He didn't bother defending himself. Just smiled at her.

"Don't give me that either," she said. "Not after what you've done to Arcadia."

The woman had been talking to Marshal an Fallon. Her lack of sympathy made him feel right at home.

"I don't suppose you recorded your meeting with them?"

"I don't have a death wish … but I do have a holo-print of them." He sent her the file from the hidden annexes of his com.

She nodded. "Good. How did you get the DNA scan?"

"They felt it necessary to take a seat at my table. If they want to stick their prints over surfaces close to me, then they should expect my scan to receive the data and deal with it. It's very sensitive to encroaching organics."

She ignored everything but the basic facts. "We'll run them, though I doubt we can link them to Malgrave."

"Who else you can link them to is more interesting, unless you imagine Malgrave is working alone."

She looked over at him. "In your interviews with the Marshal, you gave no indication she had other partners in her Arcadian scheme."

"Not that I knew of then, and I didn't trust anyone at that stage."

"And you do now?"

He gave a lift of his shoulders. "It depends."

She studied his face, then let the remark pass. So he couldn't trust her either.

"What makes you think she has partners?" she said.

"Hilmar. His actions suggest he's got wider Alliance backing."

"The attempt on you and the assassination contract on his niece?"

"Yes, those," he said with a snap. His and Anyara's lives were more than items on a list of troublesome details. "I sometimes wonder why the marshals asked me to help. You know everything already."

"We had hoped that a man of your abilities might see fit to use them to help Arcadia rather than just yourself."

"I'm in exile. Isn't that enough?

"After what you did on Arcadia, helping us is the least you can do. Instead, you have indulged in a private campaign against the ruler of Surned. Not solely for revenge, it's hoped."

He felt the heat burn his cheeks. He might be having second thoughts about coming to Surned but he wasn't about to tell that to this woman. "The man needs to be stopped, and exposing him also exposes anyone else working with him."

She pushed the skitter speed up, and he sourly wished he knew the trick of it.

"More likely to make them take cover," she said, "as you should have realised."

He thought about arguing the point, then gave up. "So your plan is to leave him alone despite what he tried on Arcadia? Actions that would be taken as aggression by another planet, if you class him as ruler of this world."

"If the Alliance accepts his position, Arcadia isn't about to go interfering with another planet's affairs. We have enough problems of our own."

"The environment thing."

"Yes, Ser den Coille. The *environment thing,* if you mean the excessive development of natural resources by companies such as Den Coille."

The old anger stirred again, and Seolta was back on that day he walked out of prison. "My father is fully cooperating with the Federal authorities."

"Your father, yes. He is still the real brains of Den Coille."

Seolta slammed his hands against the front panel. "You had a message to deliver. It's done. My sentence is also set. It's exile, nothing more. I don't need to sit here listening to insults." He reached for the controls and she slapped his hand back.

"When you decided to sidestep your assigned mission and interfere in a matter the Galactic Ministry has been working quietly on for months, you lost the right not to be insulted. You were specifically ordered to stay away from Surned."

"And Marshal an Fallon knows me as well as anyone in your organisation."

She slammed the skitter to a halt and shoved open the hatch. They were at the space port, he suddenly realised. "Out," she ordered. You're on the next flight to Central. You will not be coming back to Surned in any near future."

A sudden shove in the back, and the skitter left him stranded. She couldn't be serious. He stared after the departing box, then noticed the pair standing in the shadows. They approached him, a man and a woman in middle age, looking like a harmless and settled couple on holiday.

He knew better than to trust that. Each took one of his arms as if greeting an old friend and flashed their IDs on a private band.

Arcadian Galactic Ministry, Security Service.

"You can't do anything to me here, not in full public view. It's called assault."

"The ship has full medical facilities," said the woman. The grips on his arm tightened. They began walking to the departure gate.

"I have contracts outstanding here," he tried next.

"The kind best forgotten," said the man, throwing an apparently amiable arm around Seolta's shoulders. He had muscles upon muscles and Seolta reached not much higher than his chin. The man also had military training by his bearing, and he suspected the same of the woman.

"And Messera Anyara?" Seolta asked.

"Our information says she will not be a problem much longer. She was never the concern of any Arcadian."

Seolta's heart thudded. "She has been of considerable help to me."

"Don't even think of claiming you owe her a debt of honour, Ser den Coille."

The grips hardened and the pair picked up their pace. They'd have him running at this rate.

"What about my gear?"

"It's been packed and forwarded to the ship."

"Mind if I check?"

For a moment, he thought they'd refuse. Then the man looked at the woman and she gave a slight nod. So she was the senior agent. Not that it helped him much. The woman looked at him with more loathing than the man did and neither seemed the kind to listen once given orders.

They pulled him over to the side and shoved him into a corner of a wall, with no chance of escape. Solid plascrete walls at his back and human walls in front. He pulled back his sleeve slowly and held his wrist with the com patch in clear view.

"A public screen, Ser."

He scowled but did as ordered. Fortunately their scanners didn't pick up his hidden second screen. He used it to patch into the Surned system and order the bots to offload his luggage capsule, sending it to Anyara's apartment.

His public screen showed the boarding invoice for his luggage. He closed it down before the system could say otherwise and scowled at the agents.

"I trust no damage was done to my gear."

"All designer-made, is it?" sneered the woman.

He looked down his nose at her, though had to tilt back his head to manage it. "Of course." He glanced down at himself and frowned. "Nor am I ready to set out on a voyage. I do trust you will allow me to tidy up first." The man gave a jeering laugh. "You can follow me into the service unit of course."

Again the man looked to the woman, who sized up Seolta as he stood beside the male agent. Then gave another nod. "Cuff him first."

Before he could do anything about it, the man slapped on a short cuff to tie them together. Then he dragged Seolta with him into the nearest service unit.

It was a standard public unit. Cleanser, a bank of toilet, hygiene and grooming units, and changing lockers. He couldn't access his luggage but he could smarten his appearance. He made for a toilet unit.

"It's been a long day and your colleague caught me coming out of a bar."

The man made a show of inspecting the unit, even banging on the back wall. Did he think Seolta would plan anything as obvious as blowing open the wall. He had no idea what was behind it.

"I'll be just out here."

"Not going to come in with me?" He lifted his wrist with the cuff on it.

The man touched the release, attaching the cuff to the unit's control box, then lifted the corner of his tunic to show the blaster stowed there. "In case you're planning anything."

Of course he was, but a blaster wasn't part of it. Seolta slammed the unit door shut and set it to full privacy mode. Then pulled up his com screen and accessed his hidden and highly illegal annexes. These agents were more naïve than they realised.

As standard in most space port toilets, it also included a grooming and hygiene unit. The agent outside would be scanning him, but his own com blocked it and sent through a covering scan track. He used the groomer to make a quick change to his hair style.

A shade lighter and dead straight, with cheeks plumped to minimise his sharp features.

Not much, just enough to confuse a scan.

"Hurry up, Ser," said the gruff call from outside.

He groaned. "In a moment."

He waited, then groaned louder. Then a high-pitched cry, and he doubled over in apparent agony, releasing his control of their scan to let the image of his collapse show through. He choked and gurgled.

"Help," he called in a strangled voice.

The unit door flew open, to show him gasping on the floor.

"The drink. A street bar," he gasped. "Rotgut. Poisoned." Then lay on the floor twitching.

"In here, quickly," called the man.

The woman rushed in and pulled out a med kit. "Go get help," she called, hauling out a med probe. The man stood still, unsure about leaving her alone. Seolta gave another croak, and doubled over on the ground, clutching at his stomach and adding gagging sounds for good measure.

The man turned and began running, quickly disappearing from sight. Seolta doubled over harder, hands reaching to clutch his knees, then lower, bringing up his knife in one smooth move and thrusting it against the woman's throat as he grabbed at her neck. One small drop of blood welled up.

She reached for her blaster.

He pushed the knife a fraction deeper. "Stop right there."

She froze.

"Pull that blaster carefully and throw it out the door."

She glared her hatred but did as ordered. He could feel her muscles bunching and thrust back hard on her, shoving her into the wall. In the instant before she recovered, he jumped up and slammed the door of the unit closed on her, bringing up his com to release the cuff and setting the lock on the unit to open at his command only.

They'd have to cut her out of there.

He threw the blaster into a locker and slammed it shut. He didn't need to add to his troubles by carrying an illegal weapon on a station hub. He ran out the door even as the sirens began screaming.

He checked his com and saw in relief the target was the old image of himself. The agent hadn't had time to register his facial changes.

He rounded the corner and slowed to a brisk walk. Behind him, the security doors slammed shut on the space port.

He'd made it.

CHAPTER TEN

Anyara had had a restless night followed by an aggravating day, and the memory of his kiss chased her through it all. His kiss, and those last words. 'Keep safe.' She returned to her rooms that night with a fog of anxiety hanging over her and a sense of being cast adrift from all that was familiar. As soon as the door clicked shut, she set the highest privacy lock. Even the plants filling any spare space looked to be waiting for something. She wandered around the room, stroking each one and noting their soil readings, at the end filling a jug with water. The pots they were in could have done it, but she needed the feel of nurturing them, the sight of the water darkening each pot of dirt to exactly the right colour and density.

Out her window, the shadow of the night-cycle approached. A welcome refuge. Even so, she stood to one side of the window, on edge and with a feeling she couldn't shake of being watched. She'd had the station engineer install an anti-snoop program in her room. It wouldn't block all her uncle's surveillance, but it gave her an illusion of safety and, tonight, she badly needed one place that felt safe. Before climbing into her sleeper, she went around the room once more, checking all the locks and security systems were in place and running one last scan.

She doubted even Seolta a Manas could break in.

No, that was another Surned corruption. After last night, she owed him his full name. Seolta a Manascraoch, a name fit for his extraordinary home and honouring the pain on his face as he'd walked its paths.

He lived in a tree.

After hours of failed attempts to sleep, she gave up and input a request to her food prepper. Maybe a hot drink and snack would do the trick. She gave up on the sleeper as well, shifting to her one piece of furniture bought for sheer self-indulgence: a squashy sofa with big fluffy cushions and a deep back and arms perfect for curling up in. It had taken her months of saving her small personal stipend to afford it but it was worth it. Everything else in her life was bought and ruled on by her uncle but this was hers alone.

"Vidcast on."

Flicking through everything from serious newscasts to the lightest of frothy storycasts was as useless as her attempts to sleep.

Finally, she pulled up her com and set it to full security. She hadn't dared take the risk before but now, her need to know overwhelmed her caution. She input a search for Seolta den Coille.

Instantly, a mass of news vids began to scroll across her feed. She stopped on the one with his face that looked the most real: tight-lipped and eyes flashing, his mouth open and shouting. Luckily she'd blocked sound transmission. From the straining cords on his neck, his shouts would have set off her security sensors.

She realised with a shock it was a courtroom scene. Beside him stood a woman, one with a mouth as tense as Seolta's. An older woman with lighter hair and a squarer shape. Elegant, but lacking Seolta's mobile grace. Not a relative, then, but from the anger on her face a kindred spirit.

She checked the accompanying notes. A trial for 'misleading commerce', whatever that meant.

He was so angry in the holo. Head up, eyes wide, he flung his accusations at the court. She pulled up the outcome. Guilty. He'd told her that. She checked the sentence and chuckled. The size of his fine was truly astronomical. From the curses he flung at the judges, the fine must have taken a sizable chunk of his realisable assets.

Next, she checked the details of the woman standing beside him. Helena Winter, wife of Sol Winter and a senior shareholder in Winter Solaris. So the matriarch of the other family Seolta had told her about, the ones living on the plains and owning all those solar fields.

Two rich and powerful people in the dock, being stripped of their wealth. No wonder the case had raised little sympathy but plenty of avid interest.

There was a further annex at the end, barely seen and hidden below all the lurid vidcaster reports. A second trial, one held in a closed court with no outside reporters. The charge this time was sedition. This must be the consequence he'd meant from kidnapping his sister, the one who worked for their bioengineering department. They had kidnapped a government official. The trial had evidence from the prosecution only, a guilty finding with sentence passed immediately, and no accused allowed in court.

The sentence: death.

Anyara took note of every single lawyer and judge present. Not hard, there were only two lawyers, both supplied by the Ecological Survey under the planet's legal assistance fund, and one adjudicating judge. A sham trial by any Alliance standard.

She checked the dates. Not much more than a standard year ago.

She needed to know more.

At the end, she leaned back and blew out a breath in exhausted shock. His story had it all. Wealth, politics, and subterfuge, with him caught right in the middle. That image from the first trial had been more accurate than she'd realised, an echo of the sheer rage he'd said drove him after he'd been rescued from prison, mere days away from execution.

It echoed the kernel of fury buried deep inside her. Her parents had been killed and her life shattered, all by the treacherous actions of others. Only in her case, it had been family who betrayed her.

Family who threatened her still. She snapped shut the vids before her uncle's snoops caught on. Anyara had promised years ago to live. A promise she would not break.

She pulled up a drink, selecting the strongest brew on her list. Anything to hide from the information battering her. Seolta a Manascraoch had flaws, many flaws, and too much eating him up inside, but it changed nothing. She'd flicked through so many images of him. In anger, in laughter, in deepest intrigue and coolest pride, his face sharp-edged in calculation and softened with delight. Every single one fascinated her.

What to do about that, she had no idea.

She leaned back and shut her eyes but still that courtroom face danced in her head, until a call from her door broke in.

Who could be calling on her at this time? She pulled on an overrobe and checked her com for any warnings from her biomes as she hurried to the door. She looked in the view screen. A man stood outlined in the light. She'd flicked open the lock before she had time to think, and he hurried inside.

She slammed the door shut. "Messer Seolta. It's late for a visit."

Then she took in his face and clothes. She'd never seen him like this, with all his elegance gone: hair tousled and with a twig caught in it, clothes with definite signs of dirt on them, and his knees showing two dark patches.

"What's wrong?"

His head swivelled in a long, comprehensive scan of her room. "You're alone?"

"Of course. It's late."

"My apologies," he said in a voice that held no such thought. "I had a package delivered here earlier."

A surprise package lurking in her home?

"My luggage carrier. I sent it to your wardrobe."

"Why would you do such a thing?"

"To escape detection," he said, as if explaining to a small child. "I've ordered your wardrobe to pack your gear too. You'll need to make sure it included all your essentials."

"My gear?" She peered at him, taking a discreet sniff. "Have you been drinking?"

"We're leaving the station tonight, both of us."

"No, I'm not," she said, quite definite in that. "I have responsibilities here."

"Set your programming to look after them until your replacement arrives."

"Why should I?"

"Because your uncle is plotting to have you killed, and it's going to happen soon."

Did he think to shock her? "You already told me he contracted you to do it."

He nodded grimly with no sign of discomfort. "I wasn't the only one."

She lifted a hand, dismissing that. "I never thought you were. Yet you want me to go with you and leave all the systems I have in place to keep me safe."

"Systems under your uncle's control." He reached up and dragged a hand through his hair, making it look even more dishevelled. "You have to believe me. This time, he will do it, and soon."

It was that fraught tug at his hair more than his words that convinced her. "Why now? What's changed."

"The Alliance," he said, and this time her arms locked so tightly around her she had to gasp for breath. He took two quick steps and gently untangled her. "Please, sweetheart, you have to believe me." He told her of his meeting with the off-world agents and the mission his own government had set him. "We need to be out of this room and off the station tonight," he said at the end.

"Because of your crooked Alliance official?"

He nodded. "It looks like she wasn't the only one. He has enough Alliance backing now."

All her fears of the previous day rushed back in. Could she trust this man?

Did she have a choice? "He's going to have you killed too," she said in a flat voice.

It wasn't a question but he nodded confirmation. "We need to leave."

She tried to think of an argument against it. He could be planning to use her as a hostage for his own safety, a thought she wanted to thrust into the dusty recesses of her mind but couldn't afford to.

It changed nothing. All he said matched those warning prickles plaguing her all day. Her uncle had waited so long for a chance to eliminate her.

"You have a plan?" she asked, hoping she wasn't being a fool.

"Thank you," he said softly.

He did, of course. After sending their luggage to her nursery buildings for consignment with the next freight despatch, they crept slowly through the silent work zone, one ear on his com's scanner all the way. He said his com had a blocking program, but she knew her uncle's expertise.

By the time they arrived at their destination, her hair and knees were as abused as his. He crept up to the shade of a wall beside the docking bay, picked up a backpack he'd stowed there, then eased up against the wall and pointed triumphantly.

All she could see was a freight container filled with plants and ground-dwelling animals, set for pick-up to the space port and shipping out on the next freighter.

"What?" she asked, inching up to stand beside him.

"You have your override codes?"

"Of course." Then it hit her. "You can't mean to leave in the container? It's a week's trip to the next hub."

"We'll be fine."

He'd taken leave of his senses. "You're planning for both of us to travel in a freight bin?"

"Why not? It's oxygenated, pressurised, and no one would expect it."

"Because it's a crazy idea."

"The container is outside any passenger scanning, and we're similar in body size and bio needs to a container of animals being transported. All we have to do is alter the manifesto and we're away free."

It sounded too easy. She had to admit it also sounded feasible … just.

"My codes and your com's hidden attributes," she said dryly. "With that combination, how can we fail?"

He chuckled and tugged her hand, slithering over to the far side of the container and the backup hatch. The one away from the bay's sensors.

A degree of smuggling had always been tolerated on the hub. As long as it didn't alter the biome balance, she'd never seen any reason to stop it. Not given her uncle's tacit approval and probable involvement.

She gave a dry laugh. 'Thank you, Uncle,' she said to herself and set her com against the hatch to enter the code. Inside, the container was exactly as she'd expected. Banks of living plant shoots, embryonic sprouts waiting for a new home, and a row of caged gripholons, a browsing animal about the size of a small child, popular for their ability to produce a prized fibre and their appealing nature. Not very bright, but extremely lovable. Their positive effect on the mood of habitat dwellers was as valued as their fibre.

"Sorry, little ones," she whispered as they unloaded two cage loads of animals into the loading bay stalls and put the empty cages back into the shipping unit. She peered into them. They might be comfortable for gripholons but she wasn't too sure about humans. Bare floors, a soft sleeping platform, and she knew they had a self-cleaning function that didn't damage the occupants … but spending any time in one was only for the desperate.

Like her and Seolta.

Each cage had a stasis field that Seolta was doing something to, from the way his fingers worked his hidden screen. Then he pulled two kits bags from his backpack, slung one into each cage, looked up at her and grinned.

"Left or right?"

At least he didn't plan for them to share one. They could probably fit together, but not for a week. "What time does this get picked up?"

"Climb in. The trucks are on their way."

"Nothing like cutting it fine," she muttered. She scrambled into her cage and activated the stasis field as he climbed into the one beside it. Each had a perforated, clear plas viewing window on either side facing the next-door cage. Gripholons were strongly social animals and needed the smell, sight and sound of their herd mates. She still sent him a grimace.

"You could have given me a warning about this."

She sat in her cage and waited nervously. Soon a clank of sprockets and a lifting sensation told her they were on their way.

"Keep the light levels low and no com use until we're out of system range," said Seolta from the cage beside her.

She clung to the sides of her cage and hoped the stasis fields were as good as the shippers claimed. She sat sideways and braced her feet against the far wall in case. The container's light dimmed and the nervous chitter of the gripholons subsided.

She held her breath until she realised what she was doing. Breathe normally, she told herself. The air in here is sanitised. *Maybe, but there was a definite odour, and whether from her own fear or the gripholon's reaction to their trip, she refused to think.*

She risked a glance into the next-door cage, and caught the grin on Seolta's face. She'd like to tell him what she thought of that grin, then shut her mouth. If he could treat this adventure so lightly, she could too.

Or die trying, said the black humour forcing its way to the top of her churning emotions. She glared at him.

He planted a kiss on his fingertips and blew it towards her. She had to chuckle inside at it and sent him a leery grin in reply. Then the lights dimmed further and she could barely see more than the outline of his face.

They were being loaded onto the carrier bot. She frantically rifled through her memory. She'd signed off on this consignment, but on which vessel?

Then she remembered. The freighter X-Intrepid, with a crew of three and headed for the nearest hub, Station S-NED. A station hub still under Surned influence if not control.

Her uncle's tentacles stretched there. Even if they made it, they weren't out of trouble. She hoped her fellow escapee still had access to that astronomical wealth of his.

He's in exile. Who would send a near criminal off with funds of that magnitude?

She may have just made one of the worst mistakes of her life. But what choice did she have, when Seolta's warning matched so closely her own fears? *Live*, she'd silently promised that long-ago man, and this gave her a chance, no matter how slim. She settled back into the cage's supports and let the stasis field hold her firm. Not long afterwards, more sounds from outside warned they had arrived at the space port, with all its pre-departure checks.

Who had she assigned to supervise this load out? It was a routine task for her juniors, but which one? One hungry for advancement, who would carry out every single check with relish, or one of the few with connections that made them free of such worries? Please let it be one of the latter.

Moments of horror later, moments filled with the sounds of tapping and the intrusive touch of a scanner probing her vital signs telling her it was one of the hungry juniors, she told herself off. What in life had made her expect a lucky break? Then she heard more sounds from outside. Talk she had to strain to hear and unusual scrapings.

Surely they wouldn't dare break the biome department seal on the container. She watched as a small line of light appeared around the door frame, automatically scrunching right back to the rear of her cage and darting a glance at Seolta den Coille.

He'd copied her and stretched out a hand to the shared plas panel with its piercings. By touching a finger to the same hole, she could imagine touching his finger. It shouldn't help, but it did.

Around her she could hear the chitterings of suddenly roused gripholons, as nervous as she. Their vital signs must also be rocketing up. Hopefully they would stop her rising heart rate showing up as an anomaly. She waited, watching that growing band of light.

Then a call from outside. No, a bellow in guttural Standard, and thanks to the slight opening in the door, she could hear every word.

"Hey, what you think you're doing, brakka?"

"There's something a bit odd about the readings from this pod," said a small and whiny voice she recognised too well. The latest recruit to her intern group, the young man had been plaguing her since his arrival with questions seemingly designed to catch her out in a mistake and make him look better. She'd checked into finding a way to get rid of him, but he came from a Surned habitat family on the upswing. The kind that would be sure to spread discontent if their offspring's career hopes were dashed too early.

Someday, the youth would no doubt be a useful addition to a habitat biome department. He knew his stuff, but she'd yet to see a sign he cared as much for his living charges as he did for his own prestige.

Heavy footsteps came closer. "Show me," said the gruff voice.

Quiet, a pause, and she could only torture herself with images of what they must be looking at.

Then: "Nothing more than transport variations. Them critters is scared silly in there. You're a biomer. You should know that, and they're not as scared as you'll be if you have to explain to the captain why you've broken that biome seal to check out a boy's nervous wobbles. You'll make us miss our leaving window."

A slam and, to her relief, the bar of light disappeared. The pod began to move again with all the clanks expected as it was loaded into the freighter's storage bays. More clangs, and not long afterwards, the quality of the blackness changed, becoming darker than ever. Live freight were always loaded last to minimise stress, and the ship was now readying to leave.

She was actually leaving home? Her fingers clenched on the plas screen and she looked instinctively towards where Seolta den Coille sat in the next cage. A touch in the holes, just a touch, and she felt his fingers probe the gaps. Then she tucked her fingers back as the stasis field took firm hold. The ship lifted from the docking bay and left the station's gravity field.

They shot into space.

The first day wasn't too bad. The gravity well was restored once they cleared the station, and their cages had a built-in light schedule, designed to match the gripholons' normal day and night. Seolta also found a way to make that very tricksy com of his cut a small hole in the plas screens between the two cages. Only the size of a fist, but they could touch and that, she found, mattered.

"I thought you ordered com silence," she said to cover her ridiculous relief.

"I've put a block in place. Although we'll still need to minimise talk and transmissions.

She didn't care. Not after the hours of fraught silence. Spending a week like that was unimaginable. And there was still the problem of ablutions.

"The cages do have full hygiene systems," Seolta said after watching her squirm.

Did he really think she was going to relieve herself in front of him?

With a huge grin, he pointed to the portion of the cage set aside for the gripholons' deposits. Fortunately, these animals were nearly as particular as humans in this matter, an attribute that had been bred into them to make them space-station friendly. Then Seolta switched his cage light to dim, replaced the plas square and turned his back.

She stared at his cage, then gave an annoyed huff, driven by necessity to make use of his discretion. Had he thought through every part of this escape? He'd even included a sanitising unit in the kit he'd shoved into each of their cages, and the rations in it were the spacer emergency pod variety. Maximum nutrition, minimal residues. The bare minimum needed to maintain body function.

"Thank you," she said when she had finished and turned her cage light back on, refusing to show any sign of her embarrassment.

After two more days, she was heartily sick of the rations and longed for a big, crunchy, leafy salad. Also to be able to stretch out properly, use a full hygiene unit and change out of her stupid, supposedly self-cleaning coverall. She would also like very much to talk freely, shout, sing, dig in the dirt, or any other normal activity of a healthy human adult.

A blush rose to her cheeks at the last thought. Yes, including doing something about the effect of spending hours in close proximity to a young, healthy, very attractive human male that she had already spent too much time thinking about before this incarceration. One night, she woke up unable to sleep and looked over at him. It was never quite dark in the pod. The gripholons came from a triple moon world where there was always a glimmer of night light and they tended to panic in complete darkness. The light outlined his body, curled on his back to meet the confines of the sleeping area but otherwise at ease. Relaxed in a way he rarely did when awake, he breathed with the even rhythm of a man deep in slumber and free of worry. A man confident in the safety of his surrounds. She hadn't slept like that since childhood. Around her, a constant huffing, puffing, and chirruping of sleeping gripholons filled the pod with a continuous thrum, but the sound of his breathing broke through it. She drew it in, filling her lungs with the scent of human male, the musk of a man cloaking her in a comforting blanket. Slowly, her eyes drooped and sleep came to her.

Each morning of their confinement, she lay still on waking, seeking the sound and smell of him to tell her he was still there and she was safe. She also became increasingly and frustratingly aware of each line and sharp edge of his body. The only thing that helped was finding she wasn't the only one suffering after Seolta abruptly snapped his cage light off one night and turned away with a brusque, "Good night, Sera."

She'd been attempting the stretches taught by her trainer for use in an emergency escape pod, arching her back as she coiled up from a kneeling crouch and bending her head and shoulders back as far as she could, thrusting out her chest towards him.

No, her *breasts* towards him, she realised, and a tingle shot through them.

That miserable square of broken plas screen was too small to do anything about it and making it bigger risked triggering the ship's sensors. She dimmed her lighting and finished the stretches, on edge and dissatisfied. Only when she'd moved up to the sleeping pad did Seolta turn back, taking in her sudden stillness and the shadows around her.

"You think that makes a difference?" he said.

"We've been stuck in these boxes for three days now, this coverall is well past its change date, and my hair looks a mess."

"You could be wearing a box and your hair shaved off completely and you'd still be the most beautiful woman I've ever seen."

He didn't sound happy about it.

"That's nonsense."

"I wish it was," he said with a glare.

They weren't even halfway to their destination. Maybe talking about something else would help. "I know why my uncle wants to kill me; why does he want to kill you? Whatever happened on Arcadia isn't public knowledge, so he doesn't need to warn any others against crossing him."

"I told you."

"The bare bones. Give me the full story."

For a long moment, she thought he'd refuse, his shoulders set in rigid denial and his hand set square on the cage floor. Then she heard him pull in a deep breath. "I'll tell you, if you tell me what happened at Prithand2. The crew haven't marched in here and opened up that pod door, which means we're safe from eavesdropping sensors."

Maybe, but he kept his voice low as he told it all, from the degradation of the prison cell, the terror of the death sentence, and the furious rage driving him when he was released. He told her of the bravery of his sister and her husband, who had won the help of senior politicians and their Federal Marshals under the leadership of the marshal who had wrangled him into this exile, the courage of his brothers, and the self-sacrifice of Ethan Winter and the price he'd paid for protecting Seolta's little brother. Then Seolta told her what he'd done after his imprisonment, in words blunt and starkly honest. Seolta den Coille had actively worked to stop those who were trying to save his world from environmental decay, betraying his home planet and letting her uncle and others come close to stealing control of it. She should be horrified but nothing could make her forget the look on his face as he stared at his family's holo-images in that sim. He didn't speak of that, of what losing his family had cost him.

"You wanted someone else to pay as well?"

"Yes, and your uncle knew it." He let his hands lie loose on his knees and stared at the floor, refusing to meet her eyes. "Your turn now," he said in a voice so low she could barely hear it. "What happened to your family and home?"

She had promised and could see no way out of the telling of it. Not when he'd stripped his soul bare for her. When she tried, all that came out was a croak. He lifted a hand to that small opening and she grabbed hold and clung to it. Then told him, flat and stripped of details.

"My parents were teachers. Prithand2 used to have a Higher School, with a specialisation in mathematics."

"Not usually a hot bed of rebellion."

"No." She swallowed. "They were statisticians. Both of them. I don't take after them."

He had gone still. "What kind of statisticians?"

"The kind who collect data, and then publish it."

"Ah."

Yes, publishing. That was the rub. "My uncle. He's my mother's brother. She thought that made her safe."

His fingers held hers and his thumb began a slow stroking on her palm.

"What kind of data?"

"My father… He used to laugh all the time. I can remember he and my mother dancing in the kitchen and laughing." She concentrated on that slow stroking. "They found something. I'm not sure what, but something to do with credits, I know that much."

"You never looked?" His voice was low and slow, steadying her and urging her on.

"Afterwards?" she said in an equally soft sound. "No." Her other hand fisted in her lap. "But I can guess. You've seen the habitats."

Yes, he'd seen the habitats, he said. Had walked the streets her uncle never let her explore. She'd occasionally had students who made it out of there and chose to work in the biome buildings with her babies. They said little of their childhoods, but it wasn't hard to fill in the rest. A curse from Seolta, one she'd never heard before but had no doubt of the meaning. She couldn't help her blush.

"My apologies, Messera."

"Do you ever mean your apologies?"

He looked up, startled. "Sometimes." She raised a brow. "All right, rarely. But this time, I should. You think your parents were studying income disparities and their correlations?"

All lightness left her. "Something like that," she muttered.

"And...?"

This was the bit she never said out loud. His stroking thumb stopped and his hand gripped hers tightly, holding her safe. "No one can hear you here."

She looked up into that sharp-angled, untrustworthy face and those dark, dark eyes, and found her courage again. "There was an explosion in the school's hall. My parents were attending a dinner after a seminar. I see them still, walking out the door dressed so smartly. My mother was beautiful and my father so tall and handsome. It was the last time I saw them." She drew in a breath. "I woke to a strange face telling me of an accident and packing my gear. Next thing, I was with a group of children being handed up into a freight shuttle. My uncle's assistant met me at the other end."

"The other children?"

"I've made no attempt to contact them since, nor have they sought me."

"There is no Higher School in Prithand2 now?"

"No. All the senior academics were at the dinner and the rest left. They pulled the habitat shields back from the school grounds. It's all dead now, all gone." Then she told him of the man who'd lifted her into the freight shuttle and given her that last whispered message. "'Live', he told me. And that's what I've done since."

"No, there's living, and there is existing. That's what you chose," he said in an angry voice.

It was true, and the shame of it struck her hard.

Then his hand reached farther through the hole until the edges blocked him. He reached for her cheek and cupped it gently. "I'm sorry, *mo Graidh*, and this time I do mean it. I was angry for you, not at you. You survived, and that takes a special kind of courage. You survived, and now you will *live*. That I promise you."

She choked. "In here?" she said, torn between tears and hysterics.

He grinned at her, his mouth half twisted. "I said *will*. When we get out of here."

CHAPTER ELEVEN

Seolta wasn't sure which had shaken him more, confirmation of what had happened to her parents or his words. *Mo Graidh.* He'd heard his father say those words to his mother so many times.

She still had that shocked and terrified look on her face, but in the dim light he made out the shape of her body, shoulders back and head up. Her uncle hadn't defeated her in all the years since devastating her world, and he wouldn't defeat her now.

She didn't say it was her uncle behind the explosion.

She didn't have to.

He reluctantly pulled back his hand. He needed very badly to feel that soft skin, give her whatever illusion of strength he possessed. If she believed in it, that's all that mattered.

She gave a quick shake of those shoulders as if consigning the story to the vault in her head that let her survive. One day he would make her laugh and dance with him in joy.

"Those words you said. I haven't heard them before."

He felt the heat steal up his cheeks. "Just a local term from my home. A relic from the original roots of our language."

"Oh. What does it mean?"

"It's just words," he said. "Just something we say to others."

"Oh." When she said nothing more, he breathed a silent sigh of relief. She was talking for the sake of it, to cover her grief.

How could he tell her what those words meant? My heart, the core of me, my strength and my centre. My love. He'd never said those words before, never thought to say them to anyone. Yet they'd come out now without thinking, as if a truth had thrust up from inside him.

Truth, another thing he'd never thought to worry about; but now he must, if they were both to survive, and he shoved the memory of how right those words had felt down deep into the recesses of his soul where he kept all such inconveniences.

All the things that matter, you mean.

He really did need a conscience transplant. Exile might have made him a loner, but it was no excuse.

"So your uncle saved you and made sure the families of those lost were kept safe?" he said.

"He had to. More than one convenient 'accident' would raise questions."

"The Alliance investigated?"

She shook her head, her voice barely audible. "I don't know. I did ask about it once, but not again."

"I'm still here" he murmured, and was relieved to see her eyes come back from that far-off gaze.

"The first attempt was after that," she said.

"To kill you?"

She nodded, short and terse.

"How old were you."

He could hear her swallow, hear the throttling down of terror. "Fifteen standards," she said. "I never asked again."

"And ever since, you've worked hard, studied hard, kept your mouth shut and acted the compliant niece."

Her head dropped, and that hurt.

"You survived. Never forget it." She had so much courage, and he reached again through the broken pane seeking her cheek. "For how long is of course the question now," he added, daring her to spark back at him. "We have two more days until we land at S-NED. We need a plan."

He pulled back his hand and plastered on a smile when she glared at him. Right now, she needed to find her courage on her own. He could only give her his presence.

"You do know S-NED's main client port is the Surned system," she said. "Most of our imports come through there."

He shrugged, and grinned when it made her eyes spark brighter. "I was short on time and it was the only destination on offer if we wanted to get out alive."

"So do you have any brilliant ideas about how to avoid my uncle's agents when we land at S-NED?"

"Some."

She stared at him with narrow eyes, then burst into laughter. "You're making this up as you go along."

He couldn't deny it. "You know this system better than I do. Any ideas?"

'Not yet' was the unspoken truth, but then she wasn't the one who'd thought it perfectly reasonable to stuff them both into these tragging cages.

"We need facts."

That night she told him all she remembered of the workings of a station and what would happen to this container once they docked. "They'll have to offload the gripholons. They need a rest period before transiting farther," she said. She went through the protocols but those only revealed more problems. All they had by the end of the night period was a very tight window of time when any escape might go unnoticed.

She frowned. "We'll upset the station's bio-loading."

"No, they're expecting our equivalent in organic loading from the gripholons."

"Humans might have an equivalent loading; they are not the same biome-wise," she shot back, "and don't tell me that com of yours—that must-be-highly-illegal com of yours—will fix it. You don't even know what needs fixing."

"But you do," he said. Quite rationally, he thought. At which point she huffed, switched the light in her cage to deepest dark, and shifted back to the sleeping platform.

"I need sleep," she said, "before I find myself agreeing to any more of your schemes."

The next day, he gave in and asked her to teach him the escape-pod stretches. His body groaned in dismay as she put him through contortions and knots. He'd have new aches next sleep cycle for sure. She scoffed at his complaints.

"Do you want to be ready for action when we get out of here or not?"

"Action, yes. A hospital sleeper, no." He gave an exaggerated moan as she took him through another bend, one he'd swear twisted his back in half. The stretches were working, his body relieved to move again in this too small space, but he wasn't ready to tell her that yet. Her near chuckle as he moaned again was reward enough. It didn't stop him eyeing the door greedily. They couldn't risk leaving their cages to reach up to full height in the narrow space between the cages and the plant boxes. Anyara had warned that might set off the pod sensors and bring the crew in here.

That evening, he watched Anyara playing with the gripholons on her other side. At first the creatures had huddled away from both of them, but within a day they'd become accustomed to their strange new herd mates. The ones on his side mostly ignored him, and he awarded them the same service, but Anyara had from the first set out to make friends with the animals, and now they regularly came to her plas screen to check on her wellbeing. Or that's what she said the snufflings and nose touchings meant. She had made him try the same with his neighbours. He'd done it, feeling all kinds of fool, but after a series of huffles and puffs through the screen holes, the creatures had calmed down if he moved and mostly ignored him. Their previous chitterings if he came too close to their plas screen had become a worry, especially when they began to set off the rest of the gripholons. They didn't need the crew coming in here to check on signs of excessive stress in their cargo.

He personally doubted they would. What would this crew know, or care, about animal stressors, but Anyara had said it was part of their contract. Or at least, that they must contact the nearest biome manager if they had problems. Now, the gripholons all accepted the two humans as part of this strange new home of theirs.

Or was it just that the humans had come to smell like gripholons? He needed a cleansing unit as soon as they got out of this tragging box.

Anyara woke with a start. What had disturbed her? Around her she heard only the soft chitterings of sleeping gripholons or the odd sound of one waking and helping itself to the food pellets. Next door, Seolta's soft breaths said he still slept. She'd never slept all night through with a man before, never trusted a man in her rooms when she'd made herself vulnerable by sleeping. Now, she'd spent a number of sleep cycles listening to Seolta's breathing, watching him and listening to his occasional mutterings.

Dreams plagued him often, and by his agitated twitchings, they weren't easy ones. Once, she'd held her breath as he jerked up, then cursed and fell back down again. Not for anything would she have let him know she was witness to his nightmares.

Tonight, though, his breaths were untroubled. That wasn't what had woken her. She stretched out her scrutiny, listening to the pod ventilation, the barely audible shooshing of air in and out, then to the ship itself and, finally, heard what had changed.

The ship was slowing. It would be some hours yet before they docked at S-NED but liberation lay ahead—as long as Seolta's crazy scheme to evade detection worked.

He woke as she listened, going straight from dead sleep to full alertness in that disconcerting way of his.

"We're docking soon?"

"A few hours yet, but we've begun braking."

"Good."

That was all. No 'do you remember what to do' or last minute plan changes. He wasn't a man for second-guessing his decisions. Once set on a course, he put aside worry and went for it.

What if they were expected at S-NED? They had sent their luggage on as well, but by a circuitous route. It should be waiting for them, thanks to the slow speed of this ship, but Seolta had assured her they couldn't be tracked. Together, they'd talked through all the possible problems, including premature discovery or waiting agents.

"They'll be there," Seolta had said. "It's our most likely destination, though hopefully they don't have this ship's name."

"They'll be checking all incoming ones and this is the first ship to leave my station that night."

"Our window is still clear." He said it firmly, convincingly.

She just wished he had a way of knowing that for fact, and cursed yet again their enforced com silence. She spent the remaining hours in small, trivial actions. Tidying up the cage as if apologising for the lost gripholons, checking her coverall for stains or spots; there were so many, and blotting them with the drinking water did nothing.

"All you'll do is drench it," said Seolta with a chuckle. He had propped himself against the cage side, hands behind his head. She'd have sworn his eyes were closed.

She plucked the wet patch away from her stomach then looked up, just catching his eyes on her hand movements. She sat back and crossed her arms. This fascination, hers as bad as his she admitted with a huff, was just from enforced togetherness. He'd forget her as soon as he got back to his own kind.

She would lose him, and then she'd be alone, no credits and friendless. Terror struck her.

"What are your plans? We still have to get off S-NED." she blurted out.

"It depends."

"On what?"

He chuckled, and she could have slapped him. "Don't panic, my dear Messera. I need to check what credits I can access without stirring up our buzzing pursuers. Then it's either a first class ticket or we find a working transport ship."

The *we* had her letting go a whoosh of relief. He wasn't going to abandon her on the first station.

He shot up as if reading her mind. "You can't have thought that..."

"You're not responsible for me."

"If that were true, I would have left you back on your station and found a tragging sight more comfortable escape route. You helped me when I needed it, Messera."

An unpaid debt. That's all she was. She felt smaller and more unwanted than ever. "Thank you. I won't bother you any longer than necessary."

His curses this time went on the longest yet, and in words she'd never heard before. She hugged her arms tightly around herself, wishing she could see him more clearly, see those dark eyes of his. He was good at putting on a face to suit, but a shade of truth lingered in his eyes if you looked close and hard enough.

"You're no bother, Messera. Nor will you ever be. ..." Then he stopped, as if going to add something more before catching it back. "Take me through the arrival procedures again."

They'd been over them so many times, but after studying that shadowed face, she recited them once more. "They are Alliance-enforced protocols for reception of live materials from other worlds. The station wouldn't dare make any changes. They're all in place for sound biosecurity reasons."

Only a station with a death wish would ignore the protocols, yet Seolta questioned that, astonishing her. Despite growing up in what seemed to her a biological paradise, Seolta's interests, she'd discovered, lay in the workings of people and com systems. He knew enough about biology to understand economic or political ramifications, but that innate love of the living world for its own sake had passed him by. Or so he claimed, but she had walked with him through a sim of his living home.

"The only risk is whether your com will do all you claim," she said now to stop his questions.

"It will."

There was no more to be said. He lay back again and she copied him. So close to freedom, silence was more critical than ever. She couldn't even fill the waiting time with talk, exploring this unusual man in what might be her last chance to understand him.

She'd had days to do that and was still no nearer. All she'd learned was that her fascination with him was real; and she could tell him things in a way she'd not known since her parents died. That scared her more than anything else.

Finally the gradual braking came to a grinding pause, then they began to move slowly again. The gravity well disappeared and the lights flicked off as the ship went into docking mode. Around her the gripholons chittered anxiously and her own heart raced. Not long now, she thought at the creatures.

They heard clankings, grindings, and the sudden return of a light gravity well told that the ship had stopped. It was time. She held her breath then released it slowly. Living cargo might have priority, but that didn't mean unloading was immediate. They had more waiting to endure.

She hoped it wasn't too long as the odour of many disturbed gripholons releasing their anxieties overwhelmed the pod's hygiene capacity. Finally, a crack of light and she heard the grinding of the door opening. Immediately Seolta lifted his wrist and signalled towards the cage doors. She crawled over, pushed open the door and crawled out. Finally, she could stretch upright, feeling every creak of disused muscles as she did. A blurring and dizzying faint threatened. She grabbed hold of the cage and breathed in deeply to banish it, forcing her body to answer her command. A touch on her wrist and she lifted a hand to let Seolta know she was all right, relieved to see he also had to grasp hold of the cage side. It had been so long since they could stand fully vertical.

There was no time to waste. Carefully, they slid between the plant pallets and around to the door of the pod. She kept forgetting to breathe, waiting for his com to fail. At the doors, they slid into the shadows at either side, and waited as the light bar widened. Thankfully, the docking bay used lower light intensity for unloading live cargo shipments.

Seolta had promised he could manipulate the customs bots. The door was fully open now and the stubby body of the bot nosed its way forward. She waited, but it didn't change track, heading straight for the first of the plant pallets.

A cargo carrier arrived outside the door and they slipped out into its cover. The only risk here came from the bay of windows set high above the loading dock. Seolta's com may be able to twist the readings from all manner of·tech but not even he could make them invisible to a human looking through those windows. They must play an old-fashioned game of hide and seek. Her shoulder blades twitched as they jumped from carrier, to freight stack to pile of discarded strappings, and at last to the bay door.

He set his com to the controls and she held her breath, torn between their need to escape and her engrained training. This bay was locked under quarantine conditions for very good reasons. No living thing should be allowed out of here without full checks and quarantine clearances.

They'd been in that pod for long enough for any disease or disturbance to have made itself obvious but she'd still made him agree to leave in place the sterilising field as they passed through the lock from the inner to the outer door. It had to be enough.

At the inner door, he paused and scanned the other side, then put up a hand. More waiting. Just as she was sure she'd reached her limits of endurance, he lifted his hand again and opened the door, hurrying through it. She copied his moves exactly, switching into a new corridor at the first turning as Seolta used his com to divert any bot guards.

He pulled up a screen, then pointed to the left branch of the next turning. After that, it was a nightmare of scurrying between and along deserted corridors as they hurried through the backways of the cargo dock. Then they were out, safely on station and hiding behind whatever offered cover in the busy walkways.

Suddenly Seolta grabbed her arm, pulled her sideways, then dragged her into the door of what looked to be the seediest premises she'd ever seen. He slung an arm familiarly around her shoulders, then leaned in and gave her a sloppy kiss that was so far removed from his others that she started to pull back.

"There's an agent sitting at a table across the street. One of the Alliance's," he hissed at her. She risked a glance then swiftly copied his sozzled grin as they lurched together towards the bar.

"Best of the house," he demanded, banging his fist on the bench.

The bot behind the bar looked grubbier than them. It pointed towards a table. 'Chips in the slot," it said. "There's beer and rotgut. Take your pick." Then gave a metallic cackle at the pre-programmed joke. It came out more creepy warning than welcoming.

Seolta jostled her across to a far table. One just by the bar's less than pristine amenities. He nearly toppled over as they went to sit, leaning over to grab at her to stop himself falling. "The back door will be through the amenity corridor."

Then "Faugh" he said aloud. "You need a cleanser." He sniffed dramatically, then shoved her up and towards the service door. Then sniffed at his own armpit. "So do I," he decided drunkenly. Shoving her first and lurching after her, they both headed towards their exit, to the odd chuckle from nearby tables but little notice from the rest. Dirty, newly arrived spacers were nothing new in this place.

Anyara had to breathe lightly through her mouth until they stumbled out the rear door into an alleyway only marginally cleaner. And she'd thought she was noisome enough after a week stuck in that revolting cage. Or maybe she had just become immune to her own odour, she realised when a woman passed and crossed to the far side to get past them. "We need to find a place to recover," she said to Seolta. "I have no desire to stay like this a moment longer."

He smothered his grin and beckoned her to follow, leading her into another alley as revolting as the one they'd just left. He was heading deep into the transient area of the station. Home to all those who'd washed up here at one time in their lives and never seemed to find the means to move on, living in makeshift units built from the leftovers of the rest of the station and tolerated by the registered inhabitants as long as they agreed to take on all the lowest paid work and kept within the strict resource limits set aside for them.

A miserable existence all around and one she'd done her best to snuff out on her own station. She hadn't been able to stop it completely; the cheap labour of the transients was too useful for the station's bosses and, through them, her uncle.

A place where it was dangerous to linger if you weren't one of those cursed to exist here. Right now, they must look like they belonged as no one had challenged them, but her eyes continuously swept their surrounds as they walked, as did Seolta's.

He finally brought them to a halt outside a ragged collection of discarded ship sheeting and pathway railings, with a ramshackle door through which he tugged her. They stopped at a makeshift counter behind which sprawled a huge woman with a coverall only a step above Anyara's for awfulness.

"Room. Two hours," he said in the lowest of gutter Standard, completely unlike his usual polished speech.

"Incoming spacers?"

"Yeah," growled Seolta back. "Room?" he demanded again.

"Two credits an hour and one extra if you want a cleansing unit."

"Robbery," muttered Seolta, pulling out a card. One that had to hold black market, unlinked credits.

"Where'd you get that," she hissed as soon as they were out of hearing of the woman.

"Home, of course. It's small change only, but comes in handy."

"You had that with you the whole time and never told me?"

He raised an eyebrow and tugged her on, shoving open the door of a room smaller than her clothes unit back home. He looked as disgusted as she felt. So he wasn't prepared for everything. She poked him in the back.

"I can see the cleansing unit. You may wait downstairs."

"You want to be left alone in a tragging dive like this? Not happening, Messera."

He was right again, trag it. "You can sit on the sleeper and wait then. I'm going first."

There was a suspicious gleam in his eyes but he opened the door of the cleanser and bowed her in. Then took in the primitive box. "She charged for this? You sure you want to risk it?"

Her unit in the Academy dorm hadn't been much bigger, though indisputably cleaner, and she had loved every moment of her year there. The Academy had nabbed her for their research programs after her grades in biomes were published and her uncle could do nothing to alter the official record. Not without setting off too many questions about his other interferences with official data.

He had saddled her with a bodyguard, of course. More watcher than protector, but she had revelled in the freedom she'd managed to leach from the year.

"Go find out if that clothing slot works," she said in answer to the gleam in his eyes and wrested the door back from his control. Was there no romance in Messer Seolta from the unpronounceable paradise? Or had those days of enforced closeness been as hard on him as on her? The thought restored her mood, and she happily stripped and stepped into the unit's warm beams.

"Your clothes are out here," said his voice as she regretfully switched the unit off. She eased open the door and reached out, hand searching.

"Looking for something?" said a teasing voice.

"Just hand them to me, then I'll switch with you."

Before she could stop him, the door swung open. She had the brief pleasure of seeing his jaw drop before she grabbed her coveralls out of his hand and slammed it shut again. Then collapsed against her side of it throttling down the laughter. Burn, Messer, burn.

Unfortunately, her own body burned as well, but if he thought she was going to make love to him in a disgusting room in a seedy dump, he didn't know nearly as much about women as she suspected he thought. She hoped he was a quick learner, for she was definitely planning to make love to him. Just not *here*. She shimmied into the coveralls, opened the door, stepped out and demurely beckoned him to take her place.

He glared at her, but then the twitch at the corner of his mouth won. "Witch. And you're right," he added with a quick grimace at the space. "My apologies, but you, Messera, are a trial for any man."

He slammed the door behind him and she gave in to another fit of giggles then stood and surveyed the small space. She wasn't even going to sit on that sleeper, let alone do anything else on it, and she waited impatiently for him to come out. Fortunately he didn't take long, making clear what he thought of that primitive excuse for a cleanser and fully agreeing with her that they leave this place as quickly as possible.

She just wished they could leave this whole quarter as quickly. "How can a station board let any of their inhabitants live like this?" Across the road, a scrawny child carefully inspected the treasure in its hands, a dirt-covered, leftover ration pack. It eyed it, sniffed it, carefully licked the noisome lump, then shoved it whole into its mouth and chewed with a face of pure bliss.

Not surprising. By the hollows and angles, she doubted the child saw too many meals. Where were its parents?

That was soon answered. A bellow, a squawk of fear from the child, and a woman showing the same signs of scarcity as the child hustled out from a side door and snatched at the child's arm, shoving it back inside the hovel with a stream of angry curses. Anyara couldn't decide which had angered the woman more, the risks to the child on the streets or the child's failure to share the disgusting scrap of rations.

Seolta glanced over. "It's no worse than any habitat on Surned or the back streets of Urbis."

"Yes, it is."

"You have led a protected life, Messera."

She hadn't, and wished she could swipe away his smile. His face stilled. "How long have you been a prisoner of your world?"

She blushed, hating the truth in his accusation, and refused to answer. She'd attended conferences but always kept a low profile and her full identity hidden. Her uncle's guards made sure of it.

"One day…" he muttered.

Why did she know without asking it was her uncle he was angry with?

They began to walk faster, slipping into the main street of the station and melding with the rest of the hurrying footsteps, all set on a purpose, with little time or thought to spare for another lost drifter adding to the throng of the miserable.

"Breakfast," he said, and pulled her out of the stream to stop at a small diner. It had a doctored health clearance logo in the header, the lettering smudged, but otherwise looked as safe as any other place.

"Are you sure we can't go up to the legal levels?" she said wistfully. He rightly ignored her, taking the least filthy table and pulling out that unlisted credit token again. "Have you much left on that?"

"Enough," he said, as if that was sufficient answer.

"Sometimes, you remind me of my uncle."

A purple flush suffused his face. "In what way, Messera?"

"I am not a piece of baggage to be commandeered and ordered about. I've had a lifetime of that."

"And you think you can survive these streets alone?"

"Of course not." It wasn't the point. Right now, though, he looked every bit the man who had betrayed his own family and colluded with her uncle, that sharp-nosed face retreating behind a mask of pride. "Order breakfast then, but please keep a record of my costs. I'll pay you back when I've secured my own funds."

"With the credits your uncle has made for you," he said as if shot.

"Biome managers are sought after in many parts of the Alliance." A thought struck her. "You blame me for what my uncle does with my shares? You think I dare vote against him in the Assembly?"

"Surned's so-called ruling body," he said, lips curling. "How long would you survive if you tried?"

"Exactly," she said, and turned to the menu scrolling across the grubby table. Hadn't this place heard of cleaning bots?

She selected the least obnoxious choice, then folded her hands and waited, refusing to meet his eyes. He stabbed in his own choices and crossed his arms.

Stars, were they going to play who blinks first! "This is ridiculous. How about you apologise for being so highhanded, I promise to keep your secrets from our *mutual* enemies, and we get back to the business of getting off this horrid station."

He turned an alarming shade of dark purple at that. Seolta a Manascraoch may not be in the habit of openly losing his temper but he clearly had one. Hadn't he admitted as much to her, more than once. A giggle bubbled up inside her, and she hurried to bury it, stunned at her daring. She'd spent so many years terrified of setting off her uncle's bad moods.

"You're laughing at me," he said accusingly. Then his mouth twitched. "You must meet my sisters one day. Samhchair would approve of you," and that real smile bloomed on his face. He bowed his head graciously. "My apologies, honoured Sera. Pass me your com and I will transmit the token details to you."

"Thank you." She accepted it and read the amount, more than enough to keep them until he could access his full funds, as he told her, though sadly not to pay for a full fare to Central. Regardless, that stupendous amount on the vid casts began to seem more and more real. She picked up her fork and shoved the unappetising mush in front of her into her mouth. It tasted as bad as it looked, but the nutritional value hadn't been faked—not by much—and she soon felt much better. Enough to demand of him, "What's next in your plan?"

Just then, his eyes fastened on something behind her. She swivelled, and saw a crackling holo field on the far wall, showing the latest Alliance vid casts. This was of an angry crowd shouting in unison. Must be a food riot on one of the marginal worlds. She turned back to Seolta to tell him to ignore it, but he shot up and thrust his card into the slot.

"We're leaving."

He grabbed her arm, and before she knew what had happened, they were out the door and striding down the street as he pulled up the newsfeed on his com.

"The port's this way."

He hurried on, tugging her in his wake, and she quickly discarded any thought of reminding him what she'd said about being a piece of baggage. "It was just a food riot. They happen all the time on the marginal worlds when the shipping gets interrupted."

"No, it wasn't."

They were walking too quickly now for her to demand more. Not till they neared the port did he slow down.

"What was on that vidcast?" she said as soon as she caught her breath.

He jerked as if she'd hit him. "Arcadia. My home world. It wasn't a food riot, but it was a riot."

"Trouble in your paradise?"

His mouth thinned. "Seems so. That was a street scene in Urbis, the capital. They were workers who'd lost their homes thanks to flooding in the city. Lost their homes, their jobs, and any hope for the future. The vidcast said they weren't the first."

CHAPTER TWELVE

He couldn't get the sounds of that vidcast out of his head. He had to get off this world, had to get to Central and start fixing the mess he'd made

"Go to Alliance Central and find out who else is involved," Marshal an Fallon had said.

A simple enough instruction, and he'd ignored it like a spoiled child, as he'd ignored everything since that prison cell outside his single-minded pursuit of revenge.

"You can't do anything about it," said Anyara, "and right now, we have more urgent business. Those people don't have someone trying to kill them."

"Yes, they do." Maybe not physically, but if the Alliance followed through on their threats, it would be Arcadian voices in the seedy dives and backstreet hovels of the offcasts of the Alliance. Arcadians who watched their children grow up short of food and with no future. That vidcast had proved it.

He'd scoffed at his sister's and the Survey's talk of the Alliance threats if Arcadia failed to protect its environment, but that vid had shaken him to the core. It didn't even matter if there was a real crisis on Arcadia; enough believed there was. The back streets of Surned and this station was what happened in worlds when the powerful played their games and seized power without restriction. It's what he'd allowed to infect his home world when he'd invited in the likes of Hilmar a Kevand and agreed to work with a predator like Alliance Deputy Malgrave.

"I *can* do something about it," he said to Anyara now. "It's what I was supposed to be doing."

"You have a new plan," she said, her eyes threatening sparks.

He did, for what it was worth. He'd had it down as a possible option, but now it was the only one. "You don't have to come with me. A biome manager is welcomed anywhere, and your uncle controls only Surned space. We can find a ship to a safe port for you." He'd also contact his family to help her.

"I'm coming with you."

"No. I can't promise to keep you safe."

"You have up till now. Safer than I've been for too long."

It was the fear in her eyes that made him stop. He'd dragged her out of her familiar home and now threatened to send her off on her own. He couldn't do it. He gave in.

And Hilmar? Or have you finally seen sense?

I haven't forgotten him.

Now he was arguing with his conscience and even to him, his riposte sounded childish. He hadn't forgotten Hilmar, but Anyara and Arcadia came first.

Anyara stared in horror at the ship he'd finally settled on. "That thing's not safe, let alone sensible."

"Yes, it is, Messera," said a woman emerging from the depths of the hatch. The woman looked as beaten up and worn out as the ship. Hair cut close and showing signs of greying, a face with more wrinkles than the holos of Anyara's grandparents just before their passing, and a handclasp that felt like raw iron filings. "Captain Siebez at your service, and this old darling will get you anywhere you choose to go, Messera. For a fee."

"We have negotiated that already. It's in the com contract we agreed on," said Seolta. The captain glared at him then conceded.

"So we have, laddie. So we have. Can't blame a lady for trying, though. Welcome on board. We leave soon as you're stowed."

Seolta began to follow the woman inside, then realised Anyara hadn't moved. He grabbed her arm and towed her with him, leaving her no choice unless she wanted to make a scene. Unfortunately, she couldn't miss the ship's logo and certificate as they entered and her eyes filled with fury. "This is a free trader."

"You want off?" he said. "She'll take us where we want, no questions asked, and knows how to get past the port officials."

"And probably kill us both as soon as we get into deep space."

"Not if she wants the second half of her payment," said Seolta, "and that won't happen till we arrive in Alliance Central."

"Quarters through there," said the captain. "Biome rooms are to the left, engineering's to the right. Settle in to your cabins and I'll send my second down to show you your duties."

Anyara stopped dead this time, swivelling round on him. "What part of *paid passage* includes working our way."

"The kind that gets us out of here." He hustled her towards their cabins and wondered how to get her to agree. He'd seen enough trouble already in life; he had no desire to end it on some miserable excuse of a station hub. "You said yourself this place is under Surned influence," he reminder her softly. "We can't stay here, and any agents are likely to be watching passenger lists, not a tramp freighter's crew."

"They still have to register a bioscan of all crew."

"Taken care of, Missy," said the captain, coming up behind him. "You told me you both wanted a berth and a job," she said. "You two even what you claim?"

Anyara bristled at that. "First class graduate of the Alliance Academy, and this piece of junk hasn't had a decent biome manager on it for a long time, from the smells of the air in here."

Seolta held his breath, wondering if he was going to have to fight their way off the ship. He'd done plenty of training for it since his imprisonment, but whether he'd stand up to the dirty tricks of a tramp freighter crew he very much doubted.

The captain's face turned bright red, then a guffaw of laughter exploded from her mouth. "We stink, do we, Missy? You've got some spirit." The captain turned to Seolta again. "She can stay. As for you, we'll have to see how that goes."

"We're both staying, and the fee stays the same. You won't know this ship when we get off."

"That's what I'm worried about laddie," she said. "Now get going. Our leaving window is closing and we're out of here, unless you've a liking for this world and want to stay on a bit."

Most definitely not. He tipped a hand to the captain, gave Anyara a small prod in the back, and was relieved when she moved on to their cabins, shoulders set rigid but her mouth shut tight. Hopefully, she stayed that way until they were out of Surned space. At least they'd been allocated separate cabins. He hadn't been sure of that on a junk freighter, nor how he felt about it. Those days on the gripholons' pod had been very long days and he had visually explored far more of Anyara's body than was healthy when he couldn't do anything about it. He liked her mind fine, was coming to think it might be more than liking, but what her body did to him… That, he was still coming to terms with.

He let Anyara take the bigger cabin and turned to set his gear into the smaller one next to it, only to feel a sharp tug on his tunic. Anyara had yanked hold of it and now dragged him into her cabin. Surprise had him going with her, and watching as she slammed the door after him.

"You have some explaining to do, Messer. You *paid* to sign on as crew of this ... thing?"

"*We* paid for our berths in credit and work. It was the best option at the time. Or would you rather march up to the customs port, announce our names and see how long we survive?" He'd seen the agents skulking around the port area and knew they were looking for the both of them. Hilmar knew his abilities and the kind of information he'd have collected too well to let him live.

She had no reasonable answer to any of that. She had plenty to say about it, though, and he was told in no uncertain terms why making one-sided, autocratic and catastrophic changes to their plans without discussing it or even telling her about it was plain wrong. He could almost be at home again, getting a scolding from his mother or Samhchair. They at least made sense when they let loose on him.

"I'm trying to save our lives," he said, deliberately using his most haughty voice. The one he employed when dealing with recalcitrant staff of a subsidiary business. In this case, it had her balling her fists, to the point where he was sure her nails must be biting into her palms, and swinging away from him to stand silent and rigid, staring at a blank wall. "Or maybe that doesn't matter to you anymore." He grabbed her by the shoulders and twisted her around to face him again, refusing to be beaten by a temper tantrum ... then discovered how wrong he was.

Pale-faced with mouth set tight, the silent drop of a tear gathered at the corner of one eye. She brushed angrily at it, as if embarrassed to be caught out in a weakness.

"You think I don't know when my life is threatened?" she said in a too quiet voice. "Or threatened more than usual?"

He lifted his hand to that small tear, trembling below eyes brimming with a sea of them. "Did you ever cry for your parents?" he asked softly.

Her one short shake of negation ground a dagger into his guts. "I'm sorry, *mo Graidh*. I was wrong, and you were right. But … it's been a long time since I answered to anyone," he said. "I'm used to organising things to suit myself."

That was putting it mildly. He didn't just organise things his way. He manipulated anyone and anything standing in his way, and told himself all kinds of lies to justify it. The company needed it, his family had to be kept safe, *no one* was going to throw them in a prison cell again or threaten their lives. He and the Den Coille company would be so powerful no one would dare, and that included all those interfering Councillors and Alliance officials demanding they change their entire business model. Fioruisghe had been drumming her arguments into his ears for ages and he'd refused to listen, even when a catastrophic mud slide took out half of his beloved home city thanks to the growing rainfalls and a disastrous festia planting scheme.

"This is our only option," he finally said, tired beyond reason. "We need to live, or *they* win."

Was it that echo of the last words she'd heard in Prithand2, or that he was right. Anyara didn't know anymore, didn't know too many things anymore. Or was it that sad and lost tone in his last words. The voice of a small, clever, and overly eager boy always fighting for his place in a big, busy family and missing them badly. She would never forget his face as he'd looked at that image in his room.

She gulped, wished she could rub her face clear and start again. Wished hard he'd told her about this before boarding rather than taking her by surprise.

"Next time you have a bright idea, tell me about it first. I don't handle shocks well."

His face as serious as she'd ever seen it, he gave her that formal head bow. "My promise, Messera."

She believed him, although everything she'd learned from her past told her not to be a fool. "Just remember that promise next time you're about to dump us into who knows what." She even managed a watery chuckle at the end.

He leaned down, touched her cheeks with his lips, then moved and traced her lips with his, lingering there just … not quite long enough. Then he looked down at her and his fingers followed the lines of her jaw. "You are so beautiful and so strong."

Then he stepped back and it was as if the strange interlude was no more. "Shall we tell the captain we're ready to get off this tragging station, Messera?"

She had little to stow. They had reclaimed their baggage from the freighting service on their way, and it was already locked into the wardrobe. Seolta also overrode the ship's systems to put them under his own security lock and sent her a private link to it. Once set, they strode back to the main room of the ship, as directed by the ship's system, and locked down in the crew chairs marked to them.

They were in the main dining area, she'd guess, in chairs that doubled for dining, easy seating, and anything else needed. Also in the room was a man who introduced himself as chief cook cum supplier of everything, so presumably the ship's operations officer, and a grubby-faced urchin who claimed to be ship's engineer. Jobbo, the youth introduced himself. Whether the name was a title or a legal name, he didn't say. He was too busy finding out which of them was to work with the ship's control systems. He and Seolta were soon engrossed in discussion and flinging around technical words that might as well be in a foreign language to her. Only the sudden jolt of the change in ship's gravity stopped the flow of technobabble.

"You've found a friend." She watched in amusement the fastidious man and the scruffy youth with heads together and twitching fingers playing in their com interfaces. Seolta looked up in surprise. "The boy knows what he's doing," he said, as if that covered everything, and was soon lost in discussion again.

The captain soon came into the room. They stood, but she waved them down with a bark of laughter and took a seat beside them at the table. The cook and Jobbo hadn't moved, and the youth didn't pause for breath.

"He's met our Jobbo then," the captain said to Anyara. Met, and passed muster, Anyara had a sense she meant. "You'll be wanting to see the biome room," the captain said next. "Preppo, take her down."

Anyara looked around wildly for another crew mate, but it was the cook cum ops manager who stood up. The man was in charge of the biome room too? No wonder the air smelled so stale.

"This way," he mumbled. At least that's what she thought he said, and followed the gruff jerk of his head rather than his words. Seolta began to rise, his face suddenly sharp.

"Sit down, Commo. She'll be fine. Preppo's too relieved to be rid of that room to do anything to jeopardise her."

She doubted anyone had called Seolta such a name before. The look on his face was priceless. She'd be Bio, she supposed. At least it was respectable. No one called the captain, 'Cappo', she noticed, and hurried to follow the cook, torn between laughter and dread of their new home. All she could hope was that the biome rooms weren't too inadequate and the supplies she needed were on board.

"I'll see you back here, Bomo, with a full breakdown of what that biome room needs," said the captain's voice, and this time it was Seolta's mouth twitching and hers stiffening.

Bomo! Not respectable at all.

The biome room was every bit as bad as expected. She was sure the plants lifted their drooping leaves in supplication when they entered, then flopped again as the hard bootsteps of the cook followed her. She hurried forward, tenderly stroking the leaves of the first tray.

"There, there, sweethearts. We'll get you fixed in no time."

She looked at the arrays. Someone had known what they were doing when they set up the room, but these babies had been neglected a long time.

"Where are the control banks?"

"Over there. It's all set up like the last bomo left them." The cook hunched his shoulders. "I ain't no biome expert. Only done it to get us going again."

She gulped down all she'd like to say to him.

The man is the source of your food and supplies. Be nice.

"How long have you been running the room?"

"Couple of trips now."

Looking at these poor, abused babies in front of her, it was lucky any of them were still alive. "The bomos before me, what happened to them?"

The man shrugged. "Had a row with the captain. Most weren't no proper bomos anyway."

"Lied to get a berth, did they?"

"Yeah," grunted the man. Like you, she could hear him thinking.

"Hmmph." She turned around, taking in the full expanse of the room. No live animals. The protein came from vats, as was common on a ship this size. But the equipment was adequate and the arrangement of plants and vats done properly.

"The first bomo, the one who set this up. Did they leave a manual?"

"Set in the first screen on the panel." Thank the stars. "Follow it to the letter unless you want spaced," growled the man, then rushed out before she could ask anything else.

He couldn't be serious. The ship had to be trading in the shadier side of interplanetary routes, but spacing someone…! The captain didn't look that bad.

The captain, who none on board dared cross, gave no crew member their own name, just faceless and demeaning job titles. She walked over to the controls with a new wariness. Then told herself not to be an idiot. She'd run habitats and a full station biome. A small junk ship setup was nothing in comparison.

An hour later, she wasn't so sure. She'd reset all the supportive levels to restore the biota to the closest possible to operational, but when she input a request for missing supplies from the store, she got a big, fat negative.

One urgent and harried call to the preppo, and she was no better off.

"What do you mean, you don't carry that kind of luxury good. I'm talking basic biome needs here. You have to have them on board or you'd never be allowed to ship out of any properly regulated port."

"Exactly, Missy," said the surly voice of the cook, before slamming closed their link and leaving her fuming. Cut her off, would he? She'd been fighting tougher than him for years now. She went back over her selections, rechecked her adjustments, and set out a list for the captain. Before she left the rooms, she made a point of running a hand softly above every single abused plant in the trays, fleeting, barely registerable, but every single one of these plants needed to know someone was prepared to fight for them.

Tracking down the captain turned out to be harder than she'd expected on a small ship heading out from one system towards its first translation point. They may be a day away from it yet, given the cumbersome speed Anyara expected from this kind of ship, but the captain should still be near the bridge or main systems centre.

The woman had her own cabin somewhere, no doubt, but Anyara was at a loss to discover where. She stomped back and touched the pad on Seolta's cabin. It was annoyingly empty too.

"My cabin, next standard section," suddenly snapped the captain's voice in her ear. "And when you come, you can explain why my cook is currently slapping some mush together instead of tending to the menu he promised me before you stirred him up."

Anyara seized up, heart racing, remembering the preppo's threat. '*Spacing*', he'd said. Impossible, surely

She'd lived with the threat of death too long. Anything was possible, and she slapped open her com and snapped onto one link she'd promised herself never to use. The one Seolta had added to her com when they first escaped.

The panic link.

She clung to the wall, and waited. A skid of boots behind her, then a warm scent surrounded her and strong arms rocked her close.

"You're safe. I'm here," said Seolta a Manascraoch.

Magic words, words that helped her breathe again.

"What is it?" he asked softly.

"The captain. I've messed up."

"No you haven't. Can't you smell the air. The crew notice it too."

She shook her head, and played him the captain's message. "I can't find her anywhere."

His arms tightened. "The cook is as bad-tempered as his food is good, according to Jobbo." He tilted up her head, smoothing a hand across the lines on her face. "The captain is not your uncle. You are safe, and in a few hours, we'll be through translation and out of Surned's jurisdiction."

She shook hard and clung tightly, burrowing her head into his shoulder. "Preppo said … she spaces you if you fail," she finally managed to stutter. A hull breech was the worst fear of any habitat dweller and to be deliberately spaced, the stuff of nightmares.

"Come with me."

He pulled up his com, then took her hand and led her down a corridor she hadn't noticed. It was hidden behind the bridge's second entry door. A number of doors opened off it, but the controls showed those rooms as empty. At the far end, a more imposing door showed a number of scratches and what looked like an old burn mark. She clamped down on Seolta's hand.

"Chin up," he said softly. "She'll eat you for dinner if you let her, but you know what you're doing, and she needs you as much as we need this ride." His eyes held hers. "You have more courage than anyone I know, the kind that can endure for years. Just think of her as a crustier version of your station master."

Anyara gave a fraught burst of laughter at that. The captain had more sense in her little finger than the station master had ever shown.

"Draw a moustache on her mouth. It always worked for me when dealing with the worst of my aunts," he added just before pressing on the entry pad.

"In," said the rough voice of the captain, and the door opened.

They marched in and stood side by side. Seolta stayed within touching distance, as if sending a message. To the captain as well as to her, she realised at the heavy silence in the room. The steely set of the captain's face as she studied Seolta said it was received. As for herself, she'd had plenty of practice at these kinds of interviews, and she was *not* going to imagine this woman wearing a moustache, or anything even vaguely clownish. They were in enough trouble already.

"I don't remember ordering your presence here," the captain said to Seolta.

"It seemed necessary."

"Don't take that tone with me, Seolta mar Bram an Scathach den Coille."

She felt his sudden stillness. "You do your homework well."

"Of course," said the captain. "When a well spoken drifter offers me a large sum in untraceables, I'd better ask questions if I want to stay alive."

"And yet you took us on board," Seolta said. "The remaining credits are a sizeable amount. Or is the Alliance offering more?"

The captain grinned and Anyara knew real terror. The woman's smile was worse than her uncle's. "No denial?"

"You clearly want us to know all you've found out. So what comes next?"

The captain sneered. "Didn't take much digging. The news of the loss of a biome manager from Kevand Hub is all over the sector, and who else went missing with her. You're very good at your job, Missy."

Anyara froze.

"And your uncle is very eager to get you back—or at least, to have news of your fate, good or bad."

Seolta thrust forward. "How much did he offer you?"

"Almost as much as your total, and you've already paid me half of that. So many interesting possibilities." This time, the smile was real and the laughter that hearty bray. "My sources had you down as the tricksy one of your family. Doesn't say much for the rest of them."

Seolta gave her a smile back, one as false and lethal. "I'm used to dealing with the predators of the business world. Not in your league, it appears."

That brought laughter again. "A compliment. Well done, young man." Then her face was wiped clean. "You're safe from me, for now. Luckily for you, my need of a good bomo and commo outweigh the risk of taking you on board." She leaned back in her chair. "But that doesn't mean I will tolerate you upsetting critical staff."

They had met only two other crew, and Anyara didn't believe there were more. Seolta would have found out by now. She remembered the dreary defeat of the biome room and used it to bolster her courage. "Preppo has no idea how to run a biome unit. It's more than just following old protocols. They are *living* plants and microbes, not chemicals you just mix together."

"You can do better?"

This time it was Anyara who thrust forward. "You know I can. Take a sniff of your air and look at your crew's energy levels. This ship was close to stasis when we came on board."

"Then maybe you'll explain that to our cook. Crew need to eat as well as breathe."

"Breathing comes first, and the cook needs reminding of that," put in Seolta dryly. "We are a one-journey package, but we'll leave your ship able to survive the next few routes without serious mishap. From my early assessment of your onboard systems, that was unlikely before."

Anyara watched the battle of wills. Seolta had drawn the captain's attention away from her, shoving himself into the firing line. Why, she didn't know. She knew he was attracted to her, thanks to their days in close confinement, but attraction didn't give rise to a death wish. Both sets of eyes locked together, the captain's old and wily sea blue challenging the dark glint of Seolta's deep brown. It was Seolta who finally broke it by taking another step forward. The captain's hand immediately shot out of sight and Anyara's breath seized. Seolta put up both hands.

"I have no doubt you can out gun and out muscle me, but you let us on board, so I'm guessing you were desperate."

"That biome room is badly in need of care," Anyara said.

"And the com systems are a mess."

The woman shot forward in her seat. "Don't push your luck. Right now, you two are useful. Now get back to work. I expect you in your cabins for translation and all systems to be in working order before then. Dismissed."

She slapped up a screen and deliberately turned away from them. Seolta gave her a look of pure irritation, then swung around and marched out with no word of farewell. Anyara stared after him, then looked back at the captain. She drew in a deep breath and forced herself to think of those drooping babies.

"I'm sending you a list of missing critical inputs for the biome room. Preppo claims we have none on board. You want a properly operating biome room, I need those stores." Then she walked as quickly as she could after Seolta, too scared to look back. As soon as they exited, the door slapped shut behind them, closing with a fierce whoosh and a loud clunk of the locks engaging.

The captain trusted them no more than they did her.

"Now what?" she said as they marched back down that corridor of deserted rooms.

"You heard her. We get this ship running correctly so we have some chance of making it through translation."

"That's not what she said."

"No, but it's what she meant," he said grimly. "The systems on this heap of junk are scrambled to beggary and will fail if anything goes wrong."

She gasped. "The biome room isn't that bad. It was set up properly and no one has managed to destroy that completely yet.

"But the atmospherics will support a major stress and crew failures?"

"Well, no."

"Can you get it up to stress level?"

"Without the supplies I need?" Supplies she couldn't get until they next landed somewhere. "It's a toss-up."

CHAPTER THIRTEEN

Seolta cursed as one more hidden trap nearly snagged his efforts to restore the ship's systems to full working order. The previous commo really had taken against this ship and crew. Fortunately, Seolta's father had made sure all his children could survive if stripped of resources, a necessary skill in a place as prone to storms and wild weather as his home.

Seolta knew flyer systems inside out, and the basic principles of a ship like this were similar enough. Or should be.

"Idiot brakka. He could have left the critical systems alone."

Jobbo drifted into view, a tool shoved behind one ear and yet another swipe of grease coating his cheek. "You got them all yet?"

"What did your captain do to the brakka who did this?" He screwed up his mouth and held his breath as he reset the trigger code. Then listened.

No sirens, no sudden loss of vital systems. He was still breathing and gravity still mostly held them to the deck, with only periodic glitches. He'd have to get Jobbo's help to fix that next.

"Good?"

"Yeah good, Jobbo. Any luck on those parts?"

The youth shrugged, as if a critical lack of components was nothing out of the way. The boy had a refreshing view on life. Problems were just another source of entertainment. You might fix them; you might not.

"All set for translation?" Seolta asked now.

Jobbo shrugged. Seolta felt the prickles rising on the back of his neck. He had quickly learned to be wary of Jobbo's shrugs.

"What do you need?"

The sprite pointed at the com interface. "Can you fix that in time?"

"Yes," he said, making himself sound more competent than he felt. He might be good at systems, but he was still no ship specialist. "As long as your engines do their job."

"Yeah, should do."

"If…"

Jobbo pulled out the tool and began to fiddle with it. "Systems will need to be flexible. Switch between engines if needed. Nav's good, but propulsion needs some touches."

Seolta had a sudden vision of being stuck halfway through translation. He'd heard stories of what that did to a living body.

"Nah, nothing like that," said Jobbo at the sight of his face. "She's always got through before.

"Get back to work and tell Preppo what you need. I'll make him deliver." He would too, or else. "Let me get these systems working," he added with a growl.

He could feel himself sweating as the ship's timer ticked over the countdown to translation. He'd tested the systems again and again and could only hope they held. If only he knew what in tragging stars Jobbo meant by 'propulsion needs some touches'. He'd always hated running blind. Homework, good research and putting backups in place kept you safe.

Relying on others, on half-baked systems and unknowns—relying on luck—never worked well. Look where it had got him. He had to get to Alliance Central, had to find out all those things he should have learned before going into a deal with scum like Hilmar a Kevand and Alliance Deputy Malgrave.

Had to get Anyara safely through this nightmare and out the other end. He'd *promised* her he would keep her safe.

His com pinged to warn of an incoming call. The captain on ship lines. "We ready for translation?"

This is a junk ship. Different standards.

"Should be."

The woman's voice hardened. "We safe?"

"Safer than your last translation." That was truth at least, and the captain let out a harsh bark of laughter. The woman had a seriously skewed sense of humour.

"Let's hope you're as good as your girlfriend at your job. She's done all right."

"This isn't my primary skill set." She already knew that, so there was no danger in admitting it, and he liked her calling Anyara his girlfriend, he discovered. Too much to enlighten her. "I know enough to get us through."

"Would an easier hop work better?"

He wasn't surprised at the question—any free trader would have to be flexible—but still breathed in a sigh of relief. He brought up the stored local routes on his com in a shared screen. "Yes, but the exit points aren't too friendly on the best option."

"You know, Commo, I'm beginning to like you. 'Not too friendly', huh?" Another cackle. "Hellhole nests of scumbag pirates is what that first exit point is."

"You got allies there?"

"Not as you'd notice."

So that route was out. He brought up the next-ranked options. One looked obscure enough. "What about this one?"

The woman switched to visual and her face had a real grin on it. "I'm starting to believe the stories about you, Commo. No one's going to believe that lump of religious bigots would let us anywhere near their precious sanctuary."

"Nor will they," Seolta felt impelled to point out, "but their defences are basic and we need only a short transit stay before going back in."

"Re-routing a translation point? That will take some kind of piloting."

He said nothing and the woman gave him that cackle again. "Thanks for the compliment. 'Course I can do it, but it ain't legal."

"Leave the log to me."

"Been fudging com systems since you were a nipper I suppose?"

"Something like." Not on this level, but he should be able to ensure their travel wasn't blocked by Alliance patrols. Or hoped he could, remembering the astute gaze of Marshal an Fallon. The Alliance Fleet could give even that committed law officer a run-off.

"It's a plan," the woman said, suddenly turning serious. "Feed the route into the systems and get ready. We go into translation in fifty standards."

He didn't know where the captain had learned her craft, but she must have been kicked out of a serious fleet somewhere. He hadn't flown with her before, but there was something tragging *competent* about her that couldn't be faked. His gut said she could do this.

His gut hadn't always been right.

He had to see Anyara before translation.

The captain's voice cracked to life on the all ship channel. "Translation will be in the bridge pods. We're coming out active. No moaning about headaches either. Take what you need."

"Yee hah," said Jobbo, locking down the last of his repairs. "Come on."

"Coming out active?"

"Yes, full in and out."

"You mean, she wants the whole crew coming out of translation fully operational?" Seolta couldn't believe it.

"Yeah," said Jobbo, hurrying out of the room. "Must be expecting trouble. Come *on*."

Trouble didn't usually bring on that kind of unholy glee. "Where were you born?" Seolta muttered.

"Here of course."

"You mean the captain…?"

"Me mam? Yeah," said Jobbo just before disappearing from sight.

He should have known. Anyara appeared out of another side corridor and he forgot all about Jobbo.

"Your babies all safely locked down?"

She nodded. "Preppo *managed* to find some of my supplies. What's going on? Are we expecting difficulties?"

She looked tense but in control, and he realised again the kind of courage it took to survive a lifetime of being threatened.

"Maybe," he said, taking her hand and hurrying with her to the bridge. On the way, he gave her a quick rundown on what the captain planned.

"She's expecting the locals to have a welcoming party when we come out?"

"More making sure she's ready for one, just in case."

"What can she do?"

"If you're asking have I seen any sign of weaponry on board, the answer's no. Do I think she's got some surprise hidden somewhere? Oh, yes, certainly."

"Well that's good, I suppose," said Anyara, and he gave her hand one hard squeeze.

"If this doesn't work out, I'm sorry."

"It will," she said, and squeezed his hand back. "You and the captain will make sure it does."

He stopped, shocked into surprise. "Even after the idiocy of those cages?"

"We're free. Whatever comes next, you gave me that. Now, come on."

They emerged onto the bridge and he could say nothing more.

"About time, you two. Your pods are over there."

The captain had settled into the command pod and the other two were already locked down, Preppo in one at the back of the room and Jobbo in the one next to his mother. That still surprised him. There was little resemblance, apart from a shared disregard of normal space rules, and the captain showed no maternal care. But Jobbo sat close to the woman.

"Commo, what you taking for translation?" she snapped at him now.

He told her.

"Not enough. Jobbo, pass over a sim tab."

He looked askance at the infusion capsule Jobbo passed over. "What's in this?"

"You don't want to know. Now, take it. I'm going to need your too-smooth-by-half ways when we come out of this."

He hoped that was true. Anyara put out a hand as his gaze locked on hers, and he slapped the tablet against his neck, feeling it dissolve instantly into his system.

He hoped he hadn't just made a huge mistake.

He jerked awake to the sound of a proximity siren blaring wildly. What in tragging roots! Then clutched his head hard. He was awake—too much so—and his head complained madly. Then he remembered why he was so tragging awake coming out of translation. He sat up, checked the boards, and discovered the reason for that racket of an alarm. A scarred battle cruiser faced them, nose on. Seolta quailed and quickly brought up the ship's systems board.

"That's big."

The captain stared at it, but otherwise showed no sign of concern. "It's also years out of date, and if all the patches on the side are any indication, it's badly in need of maintenance. We can beat it no problem."

Seolta wished he shared her confidence. Then he lost control of his board. "Hey."

"Sorry, farm boy. I need your system and that fancy com of yours."

Seolta swore as he saw the attempted intrusions into his com web. He blocked them out then realised an entire, previously unknown system had appeared on the boards.

"I knew you'd have a weapons cache but leave my com out of it."

"With all its fancy tricks? You want to live, farm boy? Then give me first level access."

He stared at that beaten-up hulk in front of him, more particularly, the blast ports opening in that beaten-up hulk that dwarfed this equally beaten-up hulk. "As long as I'm in control," he heard himself say, barely able to believe he was doing this.

"You ever fired a gun for real?"

He had to shake his head. On a practice range, he was generally counted a top shot, but in a real, beat 'em up, battle? "You can have superficial first only," he said and hoped he didn't come to regret it.

The captain didn't bother thanking him, and the sight of those opening ports stopped any complaints. He had no idea how to control a board in battle.

He soon got a short, sharp lesson from the aging harridan in charge of them, and at one point knew a small knob of sympathy for the ship pitted against her. The first direct hit on their shields banished that. Old, not as well manned, the battlecruiser still outgunned and out teched their smaller vessel. The captain's quips and taunts at her opponent got wilder and more outrageous. He said nothing about that either, not when he saw the sneakiness of her attacks ramping up. Whatever got her going worked for him.

He turned around to check on Anyara. She was bolted into her pod at the back, face still and showing nothing. As if she'd withdrawn into a protective shell. He wished he could get out of his seat to go to her.

Remove his com from the fight? Not an option. Part of him revelled in what the wily captain did with his system, boosting her and helping out where he could, but the rest of him hadn't been so scared since the day they told him he was scheduled for execution. He studied the schematics of the battlecruiser downloaded from the captain's scanning probes. A completely illegal scan and one for which he was heartily grateful. Seolta had never been a fan of rules anyway, particularly stupid or self-damaging ones.

He was surprised at how much he did understand. He followed the trend of the captain's attacks and quickly figured out what she was up to. Find any weakness and exploit it. He just hoped her battered and outdated heap would stand up long enough.

He ran down a mental checklist of what should be in the opposing battlecruiser. The heavy stuff was all there. Infrastructure, frame, life support systems. What it lacked, he suddenly realised, was the more recent updates to increase the efficiency of those basics. In particular the energy systems, the ones that drove life support and gravity, had a great big hole in them that was an open invitation for anyone with sneaky fingers to walk in and take over.

"Captain, I'm taking back partial control." He did it before she could argue, and heard a stream of impressive curses burning his ears. He ignored them, concentrating on the other ship. "Just about there. Be ready to negotiate with their captain." He zeroed in on the system points he wanted. Nothing life-threatening, not yet, but enough to scare the roots out of any reasonable captain. "Done." He looked up to see Preppo out of his seat and facing him with blasters drawn. "Take me out and you lose my com. You can't afford that."

The captain glared at him. "He's right, Preppo. Stand ready but don't touch him. Not yet. And Commo, you pull a trick like that again and Preppo's trigger finger goes into full kill mode before you can so much as think a goodbye to your pretty girlfriend."

A threat that chilled Seolta fully. "Just wait."

He gave the captain back control and a silence fell on the bridge, the kind that made it hard to breathe. Finally, a ping of an incoming hail. He waited with body tensed to move.

"Captain Righteous Order of the Battlecruiser Blessed of the Gods. We need to talk."

When the man said he needed to talk, he meant it. Seolta was beginning to wonder if he took a breath between words. Captain Siebez looked as fed up with the prolonged stalemate and had more than once given Seolta a private message to find a way out. He wished he could, but short of hexing new parts and a modern control system out of empty space, nothing jumped out at him. They were stuck here, two old ships in a worn out standoff. The battle cruiser couldn't fire on them for fear of what Seolta could do to their life support systems, and their own ship lacked sufficient weaponry or speed to give the bigger ship the slip.

Captain Siebez jabbed a pointy finger at the battle cruiser's captain, her eyes as hard as plasteel. "You got anything else to add …" the other captain opened his mouth to do just that, "you can shove it back inside that thick skull of yours where it belongs. We are passing through in legal transit. You got no place *impeding our passage.*"

Seolta guessed she'd taken that last bit straight out of Alliance transit laws, both from the sarcastic slant to her voice and the blossoming flush on the Righteous Captain's face.

"Now wait here a minute, *Messera Captain.*"

Suddenly, Jobbo prodded his mother and the captain glanced down. "That two-timing piece of space debris. No wonder he's been jabbering on forever. We should've blocked their transmissions."

Seolta pulled up Jobbo's board, and his heart sank. A new ship had appeared in the blackness of space just outside their cover sphere. A ship that was sleek, capable, and marked with a familiar logo. The Righteous Captain had called in the Alliance Fleet. Captain Siebez looked as unhappy as Seolta.

A new face came on the holo screen, one both captains greeted grimly.

"Commander Talav. Well met," said the Blessed of the Gods' captain, his face twisted.

"Commander," said Captain Siebez.

The cruiser captain stared back, lean-faced, dark-eyed, with shadows lurking behind him.

'Quiet, Commo," ordered the captain on her com line. "Don't jerk this one around."

"An explanation, captains," said the Commander. "Both of you, my common room, immediately. And bring the full registrations of your ship's complements. Crew, cargo and any other hangers-on."

Both captains signalled agreement and Seolta's heart quailed. As soon as the holo image shut down, he turned to Captain Siebez. "What are you going to tell him?"

"The truth, boy, every single drop of it if that man demands. Ain't you heard of Talav and the *Best Order*. Sharpest ship in this sector, and the commander don't tolerate anything upsetting the good running of his region. And, boy, the man has *no* sense of humour. You deal with him straight, or you get the kind of trouble that lasts."

"So he's local?"

The woman looked about to brain him. "He takes his orders directly from Alliance Fleet Central. You got a problem with that, you take it off my ship." She stomped out. "Preppo, you're acting. Make sure I've got a ship and crew on point when I get back."

As soon as the captain left the bridge, Anyara shot the catch on her strapping and hurried over to Seolta. He sat grimly, with hands for once still and clenched by his sides. She'd watched him working the boards with the captain, looking more at ease than she'd have thought possible for a man from a supposedly respectable planet-bound family. "What have you done?"

"Not me, Messera. Blame that pompous windbag from the other junk heap."

"You two want a fight, take it out of here," snarled Preppo, and terror shot through Anyara. What had possessed the captain to leave that man in charge?

"Get back to work, the pair of you," Preppo ordered. "Bomo, get the biomes in best working order. Jobbo, you know what to do, and Commo, you're in charge of the system boards, stars help us."

Jobbo was the only one smiling. "What's he mean?" Anyara asked him as they both hurried from the bridge. She caught Seolta's harried glance but was too stewed up to respond.

"The ship has to be ready to move, and fast, as soon as the captain sets foot back on board. That Commander Talav is scary if you cross him."

"And the captain has before?"

"Not outright, but enough to get a warning."

She wished she could be as unconcerned as Jobbo. He left her at the door of her biome, whistling and with an eager grin on his face. May he never have to learn the truth behind all the power games and what happens if you lose. She closed the door of the biome room with a sigh of relief, sending a shaky smile to her babies. Already the plants looked perkier and the vats glowed with vigour. "We have work to do, my darlings," she said, and thrust anything else to the back of her mind.

Soon afterwards, she gave up. What was Seolta doing up there on the bridge? What were they facing? She always fell in love with her biota babies, but right now she badly needed to know what was happening on the bridge, and on that ship with the scary commander. She strode out of the room.

On the bridge, Preppo sat in a corner glowering. Couldn't he take the captain's chair like he was supposed to as acting captain?

"Get back to your room, girl."

"The biota are all in place and working well. They don't need me."

"Nor does the bridge, unless you've suddenly turned into a weapons master."

She shook her head. She'd been trained in fighting, both that ordered by her uncle and the extra classes she'd arranged to keep safe from his goons, but personal self-defence lessons were no preparation for taking on an Alliance Fleet cruiser. She didn't know what was, except a glib tongue, and she wasn't the one with that. She ignored Preppo and leaned in close to Seolta. He didn't protest, moving slightly to accommodate her. "How's it going over there?"

He shook his head. "They're blocking me from everything except the captain's audio stream, and she doesn't sound happy."

"You wouldn't be either if Talav had you in his sights," Preppo was only too eager to tell them.

"Got a temper?" asked Seolta.

"Not as you'd notice. Wish he did. Cold, that's our Commander Talav."

"He's crooked then," said Seolta.

Preppo's mouth tightened. "If only." He pointed a bony finger at them. "Get this ship ready."

Then, in much less time than she'd expected, the captain was back on board. Preppo had ordered the ship's engines fired up and they were ready to go when she marched onto the bridge. "Belay that, Preppo. You two," she swivelled round, "the Commander 'asks for the pleasure of your company'. Get going."

Anyara's mouth dropped.

Seolta looked grimmer than ever. "We're not going anywhere. We had a deal with you."

"You do, and it's done. Get going."

"If we don't?"

"You really don't want to ask. Last time I had a run-in with that frigid excuse for a human, he marched his squad right onto my bridge and took it over. This is my ship and I ain't about to lose it for a pair of no-bit drifters." A blaster appeared in her hand. "You're going out that hatch, and it's nothing to me if you step onto that cruiser or into black space. Move!"

She could see the fury in Seolta's eyes but barely heard his growled concession over the banging of her heart. "Why does the commander want us?"

Seolta touched her arm. "It will be all right, Messera."

He didn't promise it, though, not this time, and she could see no other choice. At the hatch door, she stopped and turned to the captain. "The biome room's set and should run smoothly until your next port. Don't let Preppo anywhere near it."

Something flickered in the woman's eyes. "Will do," she said gruffly. Then she gestured with that blaster. It looked well used. Anyara started walking. She reached for Seolta's hand, briefly clasping it as they passed through the lock onto the Alliance Fleet ship.

The air of this ship smelled perfect, precisely as expected with a well managed biome system. Smartly uniformed guards closed around them and snapped their weapons into place. The biota in this place wouldn't dare underperform, she decided sourly, her heart hammering louder than ever. She wished she dared reach for Seolta's hand again.

They stopped at a door, one without a trace of dust or grease marring the control pad, and the guard in the front lifted a hand for them to halt. None of the guards had spoken a word since they surrounded them. The pad lit green and the door whooshed open.

The guard gestured with his weapon for them to walk inside then all three guards followed them in, weapons trained.

Commander Talav sat at the desk, bigger and more threatening in person than in the holovid despite doing nothing more ominous than looking at a hidden screen. He looked up with no change in expression on the blank mask of his face.

"Section one, dismissed. This is a discussion only."

She heard an indrawn breath behind her, but the commander put up a hand before the soldiers said anything. "Visual and full recording will remain in place. Audio is off—to be released after my review. Section Leader Omaris is aware. Squad dismissed."

No mutterings of discontent came from the trio, but Anyara didn't mistake the crisp tread of their boots. It changed nothing in the commander's demeanour. This was a man with unquestioned control of his ship. "Sit," he ordered them, as he finished reviewing that hidden screen.

She had to quell the urge to fidget as he kept reading. How Seolta managed his air of ease, she had no idea. He'd either been subject to situations like this before or had nerves of anchrium. She was beginning to suspect it was a combination of both. His history hadn't broken him.

Nor has yours, she sternly reminded herself.

Then the commander settled back and looked directly at them both, and her heart shot up into panic mode.

"Anyara a Prithand2 of the Surned system, Seolta mar Bram an Scathach den Coille of Arcadia. You present my superiors with an interesting dilemma. I am sure you have very good reasons for shipping on board a notorious free trader under smudged identities."

He waited. She didn't know what to say and Seolta showed no sign of talking.

The commander tented his hands and set his screen to public display. Scrolling over it were Seolta's images and his full court history, including his official sentences and the unofficial one of exile. It also showed his file as a senior manager for Den Coille, and an approximation of his net worth. It was even more than she'd guessed. "Your home planet is eager for you to be located. They have lodged a seek and constrain order for you, Messer den Coille." The edge to his voice made it quite plain that no considerations of wellbeing were included in that constraint as far as the commander was concerned. "As for you, Messera Anyara, it appears there are two official requests in place for you. One is from the Surned system, a rescue and succour request due to your kidnapping by a known criminal." Here he glanced sharply at Seolta, who finally jerked up, hands clenched tight on the chair arms.

"I did not kidnap her. She was in danger."

"And the criminal charge?"

Seolta lifted a hand as if in dismissal. "I was found innocent of the official charges and there was no legal filing on the matters leading to my exile. You have the records and Hilmar was as much a part of that mess as I was."

The commander managed to convey what he thought of the *mess* in one indolent glance. Anyara didn't know how Seolta managed to hold the officer's eyes but she recognised the anger in his rigid hand on the chair.

"And the second request?" she said.

"Ah, now that is where the problem lies, Messera Anyara. It is for the Esteemed Scholar Anyara a Prithand2 from the Alliance Central Academy. They are concerned that the Esteemed Scholar has failed to acknowledge normal requests for contact. Alliance Central have required that you be conveyed to a place of safety until your status is clarified."

Seolta swung on her. "Esteemed Scholar?"

Did he expect her to apologise? "I use the title only in academic settings."

"And you never thought to mention it? Not once in all those days stuck in that box?"

"It never came up."

He looked as if she'd struck him, and now it was her turn to be insulted. How dare he judge her. "It's not as if you told me everything you've ever done."

He flushed bright red at that, and it wasn't just in anger. "I've told you all that mattered, and I did warn you."

He had, and she'd known she was a fool for ignoring it but, for the first time, she thought she'd found someone who accepted her as she was.

"It doesn't matter now," she said, and turned back to the commander. Childish squabbles from supposedly mature adults were nothing to him, apparently. "What will you do, Commander, given your two issues?

"As ordered by Fleet Central, of course," the man said. "You will be transported to the Academy, Esteemed Scholar, as per their request.

"And my uncle?"

"Surned will be advised that Alliance priorities require you to be transferred to the Academy. He has been told for many cycles that the Academy wants you returned to them. Now it is required."

Her mouth dropped open. "He has?"

"Alliance Central had allowed his concern for you to keep you in the Surned system; but it seems you're no longer safe there, so Central have decided you are to be transferred back to the Academy.

"How?" Seolta leaned forward, face urgent.

The commander's eyes widened, the first tiny sign he had shown, "On board this ship, of course, Messer den Coille."

"The Fleet won't let you leave this sector."

"I think you will find, Messer den Coille, that the Fleet is capable of a lot more than you consider possible." The commander activated an order on his com and the doors snapped open. Two guards entered, both women. "Convey the Messera to a guest suite." He turned towards her. "Please accept our hospitality for the rest of your stay with us, Esteemed Scholar. The Chief Steward will be waiting at your suite. Tell him what you need." The Commander flicked an eye at her cheap outfit.

She didn't stand. "And Messer den Coille?"

The very slightest of smiles. "Will be accommodated also."

"In a guest suite?"

"He will come to no harm."

They were going to lock him up. She reached out a hand and he took it. "Go with them, *mo Graidh*."

"Where are you taking the Messer?" she said to the commander, undeterred.

He refused to answer. "Your escort is waiting, Esteemed Scholar."

A touch of his hand again and Seolta spoke in the voice she hated most. "It's called the brig, Messera, but don't worry. Fleet brigs are clean, dry, and run to regulations. I've been in worse."

A very slight twitch of the commander's mouth at this one, and a brief nod. "As the Messer says."

"I will hold you to that, Commander," she said, making her voice as stern as she could. He'd better keep Seolta safe. She held his gaze as long as she could, then walked out between the two women, head held high.

He had to be safe.

Her suite turned out to be just as the rest of the ship, as fine as on any commercial ship and better than the one on Kevand's private ship that she usually used. Pristine, everything in place, everything standard. Nothing to welcome her. The chief steward was waiting for her as the commander had said and introduced her to her personal steward. In a short time, she had everything she might need. It was a relief to feel clean again and dressed in clothes better than the ship suit she'd been wearing on arrival. It didn't stop her worrying about Seolta. The steward was all kindness, and couldn't have been more helpful.

"Your luggage carrier has been conveyed to your wardrobe, Esteemed Scholar," she said with a twinkle in her eyes.

"It has?" She had thought Captain Siebez would have taken it.

"That old cockroach knows better than to mess around with the commander," the woman said with a chuckle.

"And Messer Seolta's gear?"

"Has also been conveyed on board," the woman said, the twinkle banished and a grim set to her mouth.

"He did not kidnap me. He rescued me."

"The commander will sort it out."

How could she make the woman believe her. The steward gave a long scrutiny of her room. "If there is anything else my section can do for you, please call us immediately. Someone will be on call at all times. I have ordered dinner and sent the entertainment links to your com."

"Do I have full com access?"

"The public com links are open, Messera. Please let us know if there are any personal links you need to access."

"And secured channels?"

"As appropriate, Messera. You will be able to receive more public links than on Surned though."

A bow and the woman left. The door closed. She tried the lock and wasn't surprised to find she couldn't open it. The suite may be the finest available, but it was no less a prison than wherever they'd taken Seolta.

But she was assured of better treatment.

Seolta heard the door clank shut and the lock engage, and he fought back the panic threatening to overwhelm him. These guards were Alliance Fleet. They obeyed Alliance laws.

Anyara was safe. The Academy kept a close eye on its Esteemed Scholars, a title he was still coming to terms with. Esteemed Scholars were the best in their fields, carefully protected and highly valued. If the Academy chose to make it public, any harm to her would set off a vidcast storm. She was safe.

Was it wrong to wish he could say the same for himself? He was locked in a cell with no idea what came next, and that situation was all too familiar. He felt the rage growing inside, alongside that other feeling he refused to let out.

You mean fear. Call it what it is.

If he did that, it would overwhelm him. The rage kept it back. He banged on the door and yelled out his outrage. On an Alliance cruiser like this, the brig would be fully automated, but someone should be monitoring the vids. He banged again, then had to pull his hand away before he damaged it. He was going to get out of here but not to a hospital ward. That would be humiliating.

Seolta mar Bram an Scathach den Coille did not use children's tricks to get his way. Subtlety and complexity were his marks. Unfortunately, there was nothing subtle or complex about a prison cell. Four square walls, no decorations, a utilitarian service unit and a locked door. Basic but effective. At least they hadn't taken away his com, but who knew what an Alliance Fleet coms specialist could hack into, and his com held secrets he'd rather keep hidden if he was ever to talk himself out of this mess.

They can't execute you on a Fleet ship. Not without a notified trial, and Marshal an Fallon had promised to keep track of him. He'd know already that Seolta had been caught again. Maybe he should have given in to the Arcadian and Alliance agents tracking him back on Surned.

Maybe, but he had a serious aversion to having his hand forced. He'd cooperate with Arcadian and Alliance officialdom when it suited him.

Now might be a very good time. Preferably before they solve the problem of you permanently.

He hated that inner voice. If only Anyara were here. She kept it away.

What were they doing to her?

Esteemed Scholar, remember. She's untouchable and safe.

The Academy on Alliance Central had links to the highest levels of the Alliance Council and they named few members as Esteemed Scholars. Anyara's work must have been something special to be awarded such a qualification.

And you're surprised. After seeing what she'd made of Kevand Station?

He'd known all along she was beyond him. Had told himself that Hilmar a Kevand's niece was no partner for a den Coille, not after what Seolta and Hilmar had nearly done to Arcadia. She was blameless and as much a victim as Arcadia. He should resist her.

She is so beautiful

And an Esteemed Scholar. She truly is beyond you.

Maybe, but he had to make sure she was safe.

Worry about yourself first.

How did you shut off uninvited voices? He paced around the cell, checking every surface and using his com in short bursts to scan for sensors. Hopefully by varying the bands, he could stop the ship invading his systems. He gave no thought to making a complaint if they did. For all he knew, deep scanning of a suspect was legal on a Fleet ship. Their first priority was defence of the Alliance against threats.

He sat down abruptly on the sleeper. Threats like himself, and anyone involved in his conspiracy. Was Arcadia even in biological danger?

He'd checked out the claims of course, but not thoroughly. Not as he should have done. He'd just sat and stewed as Fioruisghe had ranted at him and his mother had said something about balance and illness. His mother had always made everything right for her family. Samhchair was like her, always trying to fix things for everyone else, no matter what happened in her own life. His big sister had tried so hard to have his sentence of exile changed. His parents too. Few outsiders would have guessed how his son's messed up life was tearing apart Bram mar Gliocas duine Scathach den Coille. He'd only spoken of it once to Seolta. A brief moment before heading into one more meeting with officials.

"Why?" he'd said. "What did you think to achieve?"

My life back, Seolta might have said if he were more honest. Wiping out those months in prison, the terror and the fury. Obliterating the memory of the smirks on the guards' faces as they inflicted one more humiliation, one more petty blow on prisoners unable to fight back. Not without risking yet more agony for their baby brother. Aigherach had been shot in the leg when he was captured and every time one of the brothers looked like stepping out of line, the guards forced their baby brother to walk on it until the tears leaked from his face.

He had courage, his baby brother, but the rest soon learned not to step out of line. Including Ethan Winter, but the guards never believed a Winter would care about what happened to a den Coille. Ethan wore their worst punishments. It was why Seolta had betrayed the conspirators and exposed their plots. There was something so *decent* about the middle Winter brother, despite the man being as adept in business as Seolta. No, be fair, Ethan Winter raced ahead of him, spreading his investments widely outside Winter Solaris. Seolta put all his funds, all his tricks, all his business savvy, back into Den Coille—a business that had always fascinated him: the games of strategy, the power plays, and the challenges.

His father ran it with a sophisticated guile that still awed Seolta, but even he had missed his younger daughter's undercover work, hadn't realised what Fioruisghe was up to in her work for the cursed Survey. Seolta's lip curled at the reminder of the hated department. His sister might be one of the good ones but, for Seolta, the Survey would always stand for the crooked managers who had imprisoned and mistreated him. Who had threatened his life, his family's lives and the company to which he'd given everything.

Had now deprived him of family and home.

No, you did that.

Shut up, voice.

CHAPTER FOURTEEN

Seolta woke to yet another morning shut in a box. There had been too many mornings like this in his life. This box might have a different name, but a ship's brig was still a prison. No control, no way out, no *humanity*. And no news except what your captors gave you.

He also woke aching with wanting her.

You're a man. It's normal in the morning.

Not like this, and not the need for one particular body, one special woman.

His breakfast arrived in the slot at the precise time it had every other day on this ship. It was the same tasteless sludge as in all his prior prisons. He forced it down and followed up with the exercises Anyara had showed him. He had some of his own that he and his brothers had developed in prison, but he kept those till after Anyara's. The memory of her flexing body helped drive out the other memories.

By midday, they'd come crowding back, along with the hidden fear in her face as they were separated.

Alone. He'd left her alone and defenceless.

She's stronger than you. She's survived her uncle since she was twelve standards.

Stupid voice. It didn't change what he'd done.

He stared at the slim sliver on his wrist. They hadn't taken his com, but he had no doubt they had scanned it thoroughly and tried to break its shielding. Good luck to them on that one. He was good at what he did.

As good as a Fleet technician?

Maybe not. He forced his hand away from the com's activation zone and stood up, abruptly swinging into a brisk march, back and forth across the cell. On the tenth crossing, he banged his head on the far wall thanks to staring at his com sliver. Roots alive! He gave up and went back to the sleeper, propping himself against the wall, and slapped his hand on the zone to bring up a personal screen and initiate a direct brain link.

Show me the ship schematics, he ordered.

He started at his brig. Right in the bowels of the ship, of course, and the closest living quarters to the engines. It stopped any enemy hoping to rescue captured prisoners from blowing up the ship's main units. No point doing that if you blew up the people you were trying to free. It was decades since the last inter-Alliance flare-up, but the Fleet was seriously paranoid.

Out of habit, he started to run an escape route search. Then stopped it. A ship like this wasn't going to tolerate his snooping. His first priority was to find Anyara.

Trace live organism Anyara a Prithand2 since boarding.

At the end, he sat back in disgust. Worried about her, was he? Dinner with the commander, a meeting with the ship's officers in their mess, and a tour of the biome rooms. They were treating her like a visiting VIP. He zoomed onto her face but could read nothing. Her smile was as false as the one he used in meetings with business competitors. More polite than his but no less insincere.

At night? No. What was the point of torturing himself. She was safe and treated well while he rotted in a cell. He snapped the com off with an oath, then slammed it on again.

Night schedule for target.

He scanned through the results, checking again and again for anything he might have missed. She was in a suite. The best one on the ship, and every night she stayed in that room, in that large sleeper, and tossed the night away. Alone.

He shouldn't be so relieved to see that.

He checked the locks, and then counter-checked for any fiddling with the ship's log. It was risky, but he couldn't help himself.

Alone. Every night. Locked in by the ship's security system. Anyara a Prithand2 was as much a prisoner as he was.

He reset his privacy seals and slammed shut his com. Just in time, the quick march of boots outside warned him he'd reached the ship's tolerance limit. Moments later, a shimmer of a force screen appeared over his cell door and it slammed open.

They'd sent a full squad. He was less impressed at the weapons pointing straight at him. He sat back on the sleeper, refusing to stand or show any sign of nerves. The leader's weapon gestured unmistakeably.

"Come this way, Messer." It wasn't a request.

Regardless, he gave a formal bow and sauntered to the door. "Where are we going?"

No one answered and he followed them out, trying not to look cowed. He wasn't surprised when they stopped and a plain door opened. Interrogation rooms all looked the same. They also had the same smell. Stale sweat and starch. He had no doubt his own sweat was adding to it, feeling a first rivulet forming between his shoulder blades. He shoved up his head and took the seat indicated. The guards formed a semicircle behind him as another man walked in the door and took the seat opposite.

"I do apologise for this inconvenience, Messer den Coille, but there are a few points we need to clear up." The man's voice was quiet, polite and had the polished tones of one educated in a Central higher school. The smile was the same as that of all his other interrogators.

"I understand completely," said Seolta, plastering his own slippery smile onto his face and making sure the man knew he understood exactly the situation here.

The man sat up and relaxed, his smile real. "It's always so much easier when dealing with a professional."

"I wouldn't say I'm that," Seolta demurred. "A simple businessman is all I am."

"And one with a sense of humour. Even better. We should be able to conclude matters in no time. Now, if you would, please place your com on the reader, Messer."

Seolta dropped the smile. "For what reason?"

The other's smile got more oily and less friendly. "As I said, there are a few points we need to clear up."

"I will open up the public files, of course, but as I'm sure you are aware, the personal files of an Alliance citizen are private. Unless, of course, you have a court order to show me."

The man hadn't, of course, but it made little difference. "A Fleet vessel does have some leeway if they suspect any security concerns."

Seolta wished he'd taken the time to pull up the interplanetary security laws instead of stewing in his cell. "My personal com files contain nothing of significance to this vessel."

The man permitted himself an amused twitch. "You just hacked the log of a Fleet cruiser. How you did that is very significant to us."

"Only the external files covering the Fleet's treatment of Messera Anyara. She is my responsibility and I am concerned for her wellbeing."

"How so?"

"My actions may have contributed to her current need to leave her home. That makes me responsible for her. It's the code we live by where I come from."

"And you are a staunch and upright adherent to that code?" The man brought up a scroll. It was the record of the Federal Marshal's investigation. He paused on the summary and conclusions. Seolta could have told him not to bother. He could recite every word from memory.

The man looked up, all traces of humour banished. "By rights, you should be sitting in a high security cell in your planet's main prison serving a life sentence. Yet here you are, wandering the Alliance on board a known free trader, dragging with you a woman who just happens to be a foremost scholar in an area critical for the survival of any habitat or space vessel and the niece of a senior planetary official. That makes you and your *personal* com files of the utmost interest to the Fleet."

Seolta felt the jolt of it in his gut. They would have sensory readers in here and he fought to keep his heart rate smooth. From the expectant air on the man's face, he failed.

The man leaned forward and reached out his hand. "Your com, Messer."

Seolta shook his head. "You have no right to ask that."

The man lifted a hand and next moment a weapon dug sharply into the side of Seolta's skull. "We have every right, Messer."

Another guard moved into position and held his wrist. Seolta sent a quick message to his com before his brain link also abruptly cut out.

"Don't try that again, Messer," said the interrogator coldly.

Seolta lifted his lip in a curl and locked onto the man's eyes. Then gave free rein to all the fury locked tight inside him as another guard ran a scanner over his wrist and gave a sign to the interrogator.

"Release your com to us, Messer, or we will kill you."

"You wouldn't dare."

"Because you are the son of an important company family on an EA world? One for which the status, I would remind you, is currently in suspension by the Alliance for environmental neglect. There are many citizens of the Alliance only too willing to live on and respect an EA world if the current inhabitants fail to do so."

Seolta's blood chilled. Find how far the Alliance conspiracy extends, had ordered Marshal an Fallon. Did he have an extension right here in front of him?

The commander is straight, had said the free trader, with no reason to lie to him. But what about his crew?

Still holding the man's eyes, he wriggled his other hand and waited till the guard freed it. A weapon dug tightly into the side of his head and he carefully input the required code then laid his hand flat on the table. The guard immediately snapped one end of a cuff on it as another guard used a tool to peel off his com and place it in a security box.

"I want that back afterwards," he said to the interrogator. "Undamaged and complete."

The man ignored him. He rose and walked out after a quick order to the guards. The one holding his com disappeared, and the weapon at his head dug in again as he was dragged up, the cuff attached to his other hand and frogmarched back to his cell.

Good one, hero. Look where your tricks have got you now.

Shut up voice, he said wearily.

Without a com, he had no way of keeping track of time except by the periodic deliveries of food. His stomach said they stayed the same, so he could at least keep track of the days. They'd been through a translation since the interrogation. Not comfortable, not for prisoners like him. The narrow sleeper doubled as a translation pod, with strapping that left marks on his shoulders and only the most basic of meds available. The minimum required by Alliance statute, he'd guess. Two more standard days had passed and still no news. The frustration ate at him.

What was happening? Where were they going? What had they found on his com? Was the interrogator a traitor to the Alliance or just a man greedy for something better than the artificial worlds of ship or habitat. A man with a hunger for dirt under his feet and the wind on his face.

He knew what that felt like. In his case, it was the feel of a tree moving under his feet and storm-driven rain slashing his face.

Home.

And what was happening to Anyara? His earlier hack showed they locked her in every night. Had what they found on his com made her more safe or less? Questions, rocketing around his brain and burning holes in all his feeble attempts at control. He was stuck in a prison cell on an Alliance Fleet ship with a suspect security officer overseeing the pillaging of his com. Of his memories, his researches, his ideas, and his fears.

Too many questions.

At last, his door opened again. He sat up expectantly. It was the same squad of goons, but this time they stood well back as they held those weapons on him. No sign of the interrogator this time and the squad leader wore a scowl.

"The commander wants to see you."

Against all the advice of his security staff, from the growl in the man's voice. Captain Siebez had said the commander was straight, and she was no fan of the Fleet. They frog-marched him into line, hauling him to a halt at a shiny door in a corridor stripped of traffic.

"Don't try anything," said the squad leader. "There will be eyes on you at all times."

Seolta didn't doubt it. These were the commander's troops, and they would protect the man from anything, including himself.

"Enter," came the commander's voice from the door panel. His door slid open and Seolta was dragged into the room, set on a chair at a distance from the commander, and his cuffs secured to the chair. The Commander took as much notice of him this time as he had the last, but as soon as he was in place, he waved a hand and the guards retreated from the room.

"You want a private conversation?" said Seolta, fear making him insolent. It was a habit that had got him into trouble so many times, but he couldn't stop the impulse to strike first before the thunder exploded.

The commander studied him as before, but this time let an annoyed twitch play at the corners of his mouth. "You're good. At what, we haven't quite decided, but that com of yours is a clever piece of programming."

He shrugged, breathing an inner sigh of relief. They hadn't broken into his hidden files.

"I don't suppose you would voluntarily open the rest of it to us."

Seolta stared back. "I value my privacy. Nor is there anything in there of interest to the *Best Order* or your Fleet bosses."

The commander's face stayed unmoved. "Lying to a Fleet Commander is unwise."

"So is hacking the files of a private citizen. It can blow up in the Fleet's face."

For a moment, the commander went still. Then he leaned back and his face split into a grin. It did nothing to diminish the aura of power surrounding the man. "You are either a brave man, or a very foolish one. Threatening a Fleet officer is a remarkable challenge. Now you have me wondering exactly what it is you have hidden in those files."

What was he going to tell the man? He did not want the Fleet delving into his personal files. He doubted they would be able to break the link to an Fallon's orders. Not even the Fleet should be able to break an Arcadian Council lock, but did he want him to discover the lock's existence?

It might help him.

Or the man could wonder if the charges against Seolta were even worse than in the file in his possession already. That it happened to be true made it worse. The investigation had been held under a security blanket and only the barest details recorded in the public register. That had been done so discreetly that none of the vidcasters had picked up a whisper. The commander would have a fuller file, but not all the details. An Fallon was as good at his job as this Fleet Commander was at his.

Even more than that, though, Seolta did not want Fleet officials pawing through his personal files. All the family memories, the reminders of home, messages from his brothers and sisters when he was away at higher school, the short notes from his mother that he cherished, the stern warnings from his father when he'd done something stupid.

All the precious pieces that made up a family's history. They were his and not this man's to delve into and scrutinise for hidden clues. As for that slimy interrogator, Seolta was not about to let such a man defile the honour of his family.

"The files are mine, they are personal, and the Fleet has no business reviewing them."

Maybe he was a fool, but in this, he had lost too much already. The commander studied him, that deceptive quirk lingering at the corner of his mouth. Seolta had no doubt it was deliberate. This man patrolled a sector containing the likes of Captain Siebez, a sector where the Alliance's laws were enforced only if the lawbreakers threatened the wider Alliance. A sector where the injustices of Surned and stations like S-Ned were allowed to continue on the basis that they worked. The commander struck him as a man without a naïve bone in his body and who'd been here long enough to know what kind of region he patrolled. His crew were certainly honed and ready for action. Yet Siebez had called this man straight, meaning the commander hadn't been bought. The whole sector would have known if he had.

This was a man who followed orders from Fleet Central first, last and always.

The man frowned. "I have orders to release you from the brig."

Seolta let out a muffled breath. "Thank you."

The man lifted a hand in dismissal. "It wasn't Fleet's decision. You will be transferred to a general passenger suite for the trip. I trust you will not abuse the privilege."

Seolta got the warning clear and loud. He nodded his understanding. "And Messera Anyara? Will it be acceptable to call on her?"

The commander gave that suspect twitch again, as if amused that Seolta understood his freedom had limits. "Under supervision, Messer den Coille."

Seolta gave a formal head bow and the door opened to his guards again.

"The Messer has been granted Alliance Interest passenger status. The steward's department has his new room assignment." The Commander turned back to him. "That will be all for now, Messer den Coille. I trust we will have no occasion for more such discussions during your voyage."

"As do I, Commander," said Seolta, and set his own dubious quirk on his mouth before turning to follow his guard. He caught the trace of a muffled laugh from the commander.

His 'suite' turned out to be a single room, but it did have a decent service unit attached and included a food prepper unit, eating area and comfortable chair. The sleeper doubled as the translation pod, but this one looked more comfortable, and he hoped it had better meds. Best of all, his com sliver lay on the table. He snatched it up in relief, snapping it back onto his wrist as if a long lost part of him had returned. The squad leader gave a cursory glance around the room, before standing to attention.

"The steward's department can be reached from the service hatch or your com hail. They will explain any required ship rules to you and attend to any concerns."

The squad leader snapped a salute then departed, leaving Seolta alone once more. He heard the unmissable sound of a lock being engaged.

He gave a silent laugh. At least his guards made their position clear. *You have freedom, of a kind, but it's still a prison. Obey the rules, don't cause trouble, and you may have some limited privileges. You will make it to Alliance Central, but only because we have been ordered to take you there.*

We are watching you always.

He spent the rest of the day shift exploring his room. To his surprise, he discovered his own luggage carrier had been installed in the room's wardrobe, still intact. His possessions would no doubt have been carefully inspected, but they were all there. He used the cleansing unit as soon as he'd finished checking out the security of the room. To be properly clean again and dressed in his own clothes restored him more than he'd thought possible. He peered in the holo-mirror and put on the smile he preferred when a client was being recalcitrant. What Fioruisghe grumpily called his 'evil smile'. It looked nearly as effective as usual.

Wait till our next session, slimy interrogator.

You're being childish.

Maybe, but it felt good. His evening meal was brought by a real person. "You requested a visit with Messera Anyara. She has agreed to see you tomorrow afternoon."

Suddenly, all his bravado crumpled. A night and most of a day shift away. Why wait so long?

Did she too believe what they said about him? He wished he dared hack their log again, but hadn't yet lost his mind. One more attempt and he'd be back in the brig until they arrived at Alliance Central.

He supposed he got some sleep that night. The next morning, disgruntled and hating it, he decided to test the limits of his new freedom. He signalled the door to unlock and wasn't surprised when nothing happened. A while later, though, it opened and a woman wearing the logo of the steward's department stood in the doorway, with a soldier on guard behind her. An older woman with a tightly knotted hairstyle, drawn sharply back from the taut planes of her face, she was thought too old to be charmed by a wayward reprobate, he guessed sourly. As if he would stoop to such tactics.

Of course you would if it got you what you needed.

When he made it home again, he was going to book himself in for a full psych evaluation. He was *not* going to live with a smart-mouthed conscience the rest of his life.

If you make it home.

"You need something, Messer?" said the woman coldly.

"I was hoping to take a walk to the library or the viewing deck," he said politely. "Maybe there is a gallery. I would like to stretch my legs."

The woman scowled. "There's a viewing gallery on the near deck. The soldier will escort you there. We have your word you will not talk to anyone or make any com recording?"

"Agreed."

He'd have agreed to much more for a taste of freedom and hoped they didn't find that out. He was becoming seriously averse to being locked in by the same walls for too long. Many more prison cells and he'd be as badly phobic as Ethan Winter about enclosed spaces with no way out.

The woman stared at him, sweeping him from head to foot, then turned to the guard. They spoke but he couldn't hear, so they had to be using the ship's band. Then she walked out and the soldier lifted his weapon, pointing it at him.

"You really going to keep that weapon trained on me the entire time? You best me by at least a third again in body weight and many times the experience in martial tactics."

"That is correct," said the soldier in a flat tone and kept his weapon pointed. "Do you wish to leave your room?"

He had no choice, it seemed. They walked down grey tunnels until they came to a long gallery and Seolta stared out the windows lining one side. The port on Kevand Station was minuscule in comparison.

"Are they holos?" he asked breathlessly.

The soldier behind him grunted. "That's what's outside the ports."

Seolta put a palm against the plas of the window. It had to be layers thick; even so, he felt a chill. He quickly touched the wall beside it then back to the plas glass. Definitely colder. He stared, spellbound at the intensity of the blackness and the brilliance of the myriad sparkling points of light.

"Space. We're really out there."

"Yes, and if you try to walk into it, it really is a vacuum, and the temperature will kill you in nanoseconds even if the lack of air doesn't," said the soldier in a bored voice.

The soldier was a man who lived in space routinely and to whom the risks and the reality were the norm. Up till now, Seolta had known he was on a spaceship, had read the schematics of both this ship and the others he'd been on, but the reality of it suddenly hit hard. Even more than when looking out the port on Anyara's station. It had living plants and the smell of dirt inside to reassure him. Here, he couldn't avoid the truth. Not with that cold biting into his palm. Outside was empty space and inside this metal cylinder was his only hope of survival. If anything happened to that precarious shell surrounding them all, they were gone.

He clutched the port's frame.

"Seen enough?" said the soldier.

"Yes, more than enough," he said and meekly followed the man back to his rooms. There, he buried himself in his com again, checking on all his crypto traps and seeking the trackers he was sure the ship's techs had inserted into his com systems. It was painstaking, meticulous work, and almost banished that view from the gallery.

He was in space, on a ship, crewed by people who mistrusted him completely.

A knock on his door. He looked up in surprise. Lunch already? But when he opened the door, it was to a man wearing a medic's logo and with the inevitable brawny soldier standing beside him.

"May we come in," said the man.

As if Seolta had any choice. He stepped aside. The man walked in and took a chair. The soldier wasn't so trusting, waiting till Seolta moved back from the entrance way. Not a man to turn his back on a suspect prisoner. Seolta warily took the other chair by the small table.

"How may I help you, Messer? Your systems scanned me as I boarded. I am fit and well."

"Physically, yes, despite your recent adventures," agreed the man with a pleasant smile—the kind you used when you wanted to set at ease a reluctant client. Seolta's inner alarms started ticking. "You have admirable fitness and reflexes." The man eased back. "Must be from you EA origins. We see few such onboard. How are you finding being on a ship instead of your home world?"

Seolta shot up. "You're monitoring my biologicals."

"Well, yes, of course. It's standard protocol with persons of note."

With suspect persons of note, he guessed that meant. "And you saw something of concern?"

The man shrugged. "It may be nothing. This isn't your first trip in space after all."

Seolta grunted a yes. "A few trips a while back, then this one."

"And how often had you visited a habitat world before?"

"Once, before Surned."

The man hummed, clearly noting something on his com.

"You're recording?" asked Seolta.

"Well, of course, Messer den Coille. Or may I call you Seolta?"

"The correct form for non-family in my home region is Seolta mar Bram an Scathach den Coille."

The man's eyes widened. "Quite a mouthful."

"Messer den Coille is fine."

"Aah."

"What's this about?" asked Seolta, frustrated and wanting whatever this was out in the open.

The medic watched him a bit longer, as if studying a subject in a lab, then seemed to come to a decision. "Have you heard of Artificial Habitat Reality Overload syndrome?"

"I'm no medic," said Seolta impatiently.

"But you are a highly skilled negotiator with impressive academic results in business. You must have studied the applicable behavioural syndromes."

Seolta inclined his head, his inner alarms flaring wildly.

The man's voice gentled, and his alarms went mad.

"This morning, in the port gallery, your readings registered a spike."

They had him under that level of scrutiny?

"What were you doing?" asked the medic.

"Looking out the ports."

"And…"

"Space is bigger than I'd imagined," Seolta conceded.

"Bigger, yes, and inhospitable. You never realised that before?"

Seolta could feel the sweat beading at his hairline. "Not as clearly," he said. "It's not a problem."

"Ah, but it can be. Your reactions are not unusual, you see." The man could be talking to a first schooler. "EA or Habitable World residents commonly react to being in an enclosed habitat, and it's not always on first exposure. Sometimes, the reaction can be problematic. For the ship's security, all EA or HW passengers have to be monitored and evaluated if needed."

"You don't seriously think there's a risk I'll freak out and attack someone."

"Not quite how we would put it," said the other with that false chuckle medics used.

So it was what he meant. Seolta swallowed. A full psych evaluation from a Fleet medic? Not a good idea.

"What can I do to assure the commander I am no risk to his crew or ship?"

The man smiled as if praising a child. "Don't worry. Nothing too strenuous. I will be coming to your cabin daily for a chat. Now that doesn't sound too scary, does it."

Seolta plastered on his 'I've got you' smile, the one he used when a target looked about to back out of an agreed deal. The medic's patronising smirk faltered as Seolta agreed that no, it didn't sound scary at all.

"Good. I'll see you at the same time tomorrow then." At least the man had the good sense to know when not to push his luck. Then a thought struck Seolta.

"This syndrome. Is there an equivalent for habitat dwellers visiting an EA or HW world?"

"Yes, of course. The lack of a shield can be terrifying for some."

"Have you ever visited such a world."

"Not in person, no."

Did the man know of his tell, the slight twitch at the corner of his eye that told Seolta everything he needed to know about what the man thought of venturing out beyond the protection of shield or ship without a suit?

Then the man's eyes opened wide. "Do you want me to discuss this with Messera Anyara?"

"No, no. Not yet." Seolta desperately retreated behind his most bland of masks.

Tell Anyara a Prithand2 she may never be able to visit an EA world?

His EA world?

The man's eyes settled on the pulse Seolta could feel beating against the large lump suddenly lodging in his throat. "Until tomorrow, Messer den Coille," he said as he bowed himself out of the room.

CHAPTER FIFTEEN

Anyara waited nervously. The steward had told her to expect a visitor today but refused to tell her who. Please let it be Seolta. She'd asked about him repeatedly when they first put her in here, but not in the last few days. The steward she least liked was on duty today. A stiff-necked woman. What made Anyara mistrust her most was the faint trace of a Surned accent. The woman never admitted coming from her home region, but Anyara wasn't fooled and was grateful she rarely served her. The steward's awkward silences echoed with the same resonances as Anyara's clipped exchanges with her uncle's staff. Today, she picked at the beautifully prepared lunch the woman had brought her. The ship's gardens were first-rate and her visit there with the ship biome specialist had been one of her few enjoyable times since boarding. For a brief interlude, she was herself again, breathing in the gifts of plants and other organisms, sharing tips and theories with a fellow biomer. The ship specialist had even attended her own department at the Academy, although some years before her, and they laughed together over tutors they had shared. She had asked to be allowed to visit again, and the woman had prevaricated.

Letting a highly qualified but suspect biome manager into the heart of the ship's biome system needed security's permission. She was still waiting for the second visit.

She stood up, shoved back her plate and marched over to the table beside the lounger. One plant sat there, a spiky-leafed little beauty. The species did have some use in restoring oxygen levels, but its main value lay in the tiny but exquisite flowers. The ship biomer had showed her this plant's parents as if revealing a precious secret.

"My little treasures," she had called them. "The stewards complained about the waste of resources, but the commander said everyone needed a hobby." The woman had carefully stroked a finger just above a newly emerging leaf, and a few days later, a thoroughly stick-faced steward had deposited this darling on Anyara's table. A small bud lay hidden in the folds of the plant's middle leaves and a day later it opened into a bright yellow jewel of a flower. Yellow flowers had always made her smile, the colour rich with the promise of new life and laughing children.

Now she stared at the tiny flower as she waited for the signal to tell her that Seolta den Coille had come. That he was still alive.

At last the door pinged and he stood there. She gasped. She'd forgotten what he looked like when not hiding from authority. Had forgotten the effect of those fine cheekbones, the distinctive way he carried himself, his hair springing to vibrant life and, most compelling, those deep, dark eyes meeting hers.

He gave a full courtly bow that could have come straight from a vidcast.

"Messera Anyara, I hope I find you well."

She hadn't forgotten how easily they understood each other. The stock phrase wasn't an empty nothingness. It was a real question and one for which he badly needed an answer. She smiled in welcome and gave him her own version of a formal head nod.

"As you can see, I have been more than adequately cared for."

He gave a quick and dismissive glance around the room, as if he already knew of the quality of her suite. It wasn't possible, of course. No one could hack a Fleet vessel.

"And you," she said. "Have you been keeping gainfully occupied?" He gave the smile she loved best, the one she thoroughly mistrusted with its hints at mischief. "What have you been up to?"

"Nothing of note. The commander and I have come to an understanding."

How she wished she dared ask him outright what outrageous scheme he'd put into action this time, but that air of assurance said at least he was no longer in their brig. The steward beckoned them both to the table and called in a service bot that began unloading multiple dishes.

They sat, staring at the plates full of food she did not want, nor did he from his rigid stance. Then he looked up, muttered something and put out both hands to take hers, discreetly setting his com in contact with hers. "It is *very* good to see you safe and well, Messera," he said as she felt the link to his com through her own, as velvety smooth as his spoken voice.

They can read our coms. Be careful.

She gave a discreet nod. Then asked about his room.

"Not quite as elegant as yours, Messera Esteemed Scholar," the teasing twitch at the corner of his mouth drew an answering quirk from her own mouth, "but perfectly comfortable, thank you."

This steward has the trace of a Surned accent, she sent him.

A faint clasp of his fingers said he understood. *Message me if you need me. Otherwise, com silence.*

"You are a rare sight for a man's eyes, Messera. Now, tell me everything you have been up to. I have no doubt the commander has already had you check out his biome rooms and tried to plug in to your expertise."

She grinned, feeling an out-of-place bubble of joy swell up inside her. No one else teased her. "Very well run rooms they are," she said primly.

His smile widened and she had to gulp back an impulse to giggle. She hadn't giggled since … she didn't know when.

After that, talking came easy, despite the constraint of having listeners; it was so easy to tell him of her days and hint at her fears. With him, understanding didn't need words.

"You have your luggage back," she said, leaning back to take in his tunic.

He gave a laugh and straightened his shoulders. Preening for her. "I'm glad you realise there's a difference between Fleet discards and proper tailoring."

"Yes, most definitely." The warmth in his eyes reflected the heat in her body as she drank in the sight of him. If only they could be alone and free from scrutiny.

Too soon, it was time for him to leave. The attending steward coughed discreetly and he had to stand.

"I hope I will be permitted to visit you again soon, Messera," he said, looking at her, although it was the steward who replied.

Tomorrow, she heard. If the commander and security approved, that meant. If there was nothing in what they had said to set off ship alarms. If, if … so many conditions lay under a tiny word.

She chose to ignore them for now, giving him her hand in farewell and blushing madly when he raised it to his lips and kissed the tips of her fingers. Nothing that the steward could object to.

For all she knew, it was a normal courtesy from Seolta's home world.

There was nothing usual about those lips or the swift caress of his tongue on her fingertips. Laughter lit his eyes.

"Until tomorrow, hopefully, Messera." Then he was gone and her room felt emptier than ever.

The days passed. Seolta had come as promised, but the visit had been so fleeting and they were watched so closely, all she had from it was that he was alive and whole. One more translation and now they neared the locus for the last one to Alliance Central. She hadn't been there since her Academy days and tried nervously to imagine this return.

Who would they see? Esteemed Scholar Anyara a Prithand2, or the runaway rebel niece of a habitat-world tyrant, begging for refuge.

Or a marked outcast, linked to a known EA criminal exile. Part of her hoped so. At least that way she stayed with Seolta. Despite all logic, being with him still felt safest to her. To be with a man who saw *her*, or live in comfort as the empty avatar of a privileged nobody.

She was allowed to visit the biome rooms again, accompanied by a silent security guard. The biome manager took one look at the woman soldier and stepped back to let them both enter, a slight tic in one eye. The guard was no simple soldier, obviously, and Anyara immediately banished the relaxation she usually felt in a biome room. This one was the life support biome of a military-class vessel.

She could still enjoy the biota and talk technicalities with its guardian. The biome specialist shared her own love of her living charges and, despite the watchers, she spent a few happy hours seeing what they did here and sharing her studies and recent work she'd read. The woman behind them wandered along, saying nothing, but the biome specialist looked to her occasionally as if expecting an answer. Did the soldier know more than she let on about biomes? Both women were enlisted Fleet officers.

A day before translation, a siren sounded and a warning code came over the systems. *Lock down. Orange status in place.* She'd lived her life on a habitat station and automatically went into prep mode. Wardrobe, loose items, her precious baby plant, all locked down and secured against sudden violent movements or worse. Then she suited and strapped down in the translation pod, breathing mask ready.

The steward's voice came across her com systems. "Military action in progress. We have encountered a known pirate vessel under a detain and search order. Minimal disruption to ship's voyage expected. Emergency protocols stat two engaged. Please follow all orders as required."

A document opened and she scanned down it. It was much the same as the drills she routinely had to take part in back on Kevand Station and she'd already done everything on the list. She leaned back, opened an entertainment file, and kept another screen open to the ship's comm links. This was real, though, and pirates had weapons.

As did a Fleet cruiser, much bigger and more lethal than any pirate's. She was safe enough here.

The first shockwave running through the ship had her switching to an even fluffier entertainment file. Right now, she needed to lose herself and forget what was going on outside her cabin. She hoped this 'minimal disruption' didn't take too long.

It felt like a long time. Her timer said mere minutes were passing, but lying here, unable to act, it felt like hours. Long enough for questions to stab at her. Why would any pirate be stupid enough to stay near a fully manned Fleet battle cruiser?

The next wave buffeted the ship. The pirate was throwing everything it had at the cruiser. It should have retreated as soon as its sensors picked up the Fleet vessel's presence, she thought crossly. Not only was it desperate, its captain was very stupid.

She wriggled in her seat and wished she could log into the ship's comms. Not possible, of course. The Fleet kept non-combatants out for very good reasons. The last thing they wanted in a conflict was some untrained civilian disrupting the precision of their systems.

She lay still again. Was the room warmer?

She checked her com. No, exactly as before, to a micro degree. They hadn't taken a damaging hit and the Fleet had the best heat dispersal systems of any ships. They had to.

Stop imaging the worst. She found herself wishing for Seolta den Coille. The touch of him made her feel safer, for no logical reason. He'd got her into this mess.

No, he had got her out of the mess back on her home station. She'd been watching her uncle for too many years to be mistaken. If she had stayed, she'd be dead now.

Another buffeting wave, this one stronger and longer, and she clung to the edge of her pod.

"Get it over with!"

Suddenly she heard a sound at the door. Her heart seized as the lock disengaged. Had they been breached? She checked her com for a warning. Status still orange. Not even a tinge of red. Then the door opened and Seolta den Coille rushed in. He ran to her pod and began tugging at her straps.

"We're getting out of here."

She grabbed his wrist. "Stop. Get back to your pod."

Another shockwave and he was thrown across the room and into her lounger, coming up with blood blooming on his forehead.

She thrust off the straps and rushed to him.

"It's nothing," he said, pushing himself up, "but you need to come with me. We can't stay on this ship."

"Where do you plan to go?" They were on a ship in deep space, in the middle of a skirmish.

"There's a life raft down this corridor. We can take that while the two ships are busy."

"No, we can't."

He refused to listen to her, dragging her madly from the room and into the corridor.

"Can you even pilot a deep space ship?"

"I'm a class one flyer pilot."

"A dirtsider flyer is nothing like a deep space ship—and you know nothing about taking one through translation."

"There's bound to be a planet nearby."

"Nearby!" She just about choked on that one. She thrust her elbow into his gut, forcing him to come to a halt. "What's got into you?"

"We're under attack. Do you know how thin the membrane of this ship is? That's space out there, nothing. If they hole it, we'll die."

"And you think we're safer in a life raft with an unqualified pilot? This is just like all the drills." She glared at him, then took him in fully. "You haven't even put on your suit!"

"Drills?" He was pulling them along. "It's not safe here. No one will see a life raft slipping away, and we will be in charge of it."

A clatter of boots and a troop of marines arrived with a medic just behind. Seolta tried to run, still tugging her along, but she dug her heels into the floor. The soldiers grabbed Seolta and threw him down, while one prised his fingers off her and helped her away.

"It's all right, Messera. We have him. Let me help you back to your cabin pod."

On the floor, the medic took out an infuser and shoved it against Seolta's neck as he struggled furiously.

"Wait, what are you doing to him?"

Seolta slumped to the deck as the sedative took effect. "To the med ward, security pod," ordered the medic, before turning to Anyara. "He's quite safe, Messera. We should have secured him before the skirmish, but we didn't think it would take long enough to worry about."

She watched in horror as the marines flung him over their shoulders and marched him off. "Secured him?" Seolta den Coille was one of the most knowing people she'd met and had faced all their adventures with a cool calculation that awed her. What was going on?

The medic shook his arm where Seolta had clamped hold of him. "It's not an uncommon reaction in an EA dirtsider."

"What do you mean? He's been travelling on board ships for months now."

"Sometimes, the reality of space habitats affects them. It doesn't happen to all EA-worlders, and not always on their first flight, but it hit him a few days ago. Then he gets dumped in the middle of a skirmish where there's a real risk of an outer shell breach. You grew up in habitats and space stations; you've had a lifetime's trust in outer skins and you know we have procedures for breaches. He's used to skies with layers of atmosphere between him and deep space."

"Oh."

"Don't worry. We're trained to manage it. He'll be fine, and the all clear will sound soon." The medic turned to follow the marines, then stopped. "Usually all dirtsiders think of is saving themselves when they lose it. Yet he took the time to save you as well. He's a tough one."

Leaving her with that last enigmatic comment, the medic walked off.

The marine holding her arm tugged her gently. "Come along, Messera. You'll feel much better once you're safely back in your own pod. Don't worry, we will make sure Messer den Coille doesn't bother you again."

That brought her to a jolting stop. "No, I need to see him as soon as he's settled. He's no bother to me. Quite the opposite." He thought he was saving her, and it had been a long time since anyone cared enough to do that. Not since that long ago evening when she said goodnight to her parents for the last time.

She was still locked in her room after the all clear had sounded. Pacing its parameters didn't help. Where was Seolta? What had they done to him?

Would he recover? That last thought was the worst. She hadn't realised quite how much she'd come to depend on him and his *outrageous* schemes. So far, he had kept her safe, if not always comfortable, but she was still alive, and that mattered to her very much.

Now, it was she who must keep them both safe.

To distract herself, she tried pulling up a sim of Arcadia and was surprised to be granted access to one. The last time she'd tried, she'd received a curt message that it was blocked to all but acknowledged parties of interest. Maybe it was a Fleet privilege. She didn't ask any more questions, and zoomed down onto the mountain region.

Seolta's homeland. The sim still had restrictions, and all she got was the official advice version, the flat and toneless one for those without visitor permits, and she had to land on the public flyer platform. A 'blocked' warning came up whenever she tried to reach his family platform or home quarters. All she was allowed was the public areas of his city and a zoom over the surrounding forests.

Why a mindless vidcast felt like a rejection, she refused to think, and swung back up into the high-atmosphere view then dived at random down to various places, swinging the world around and shutting her eyes before she chose a spot.

So many were empty of human settlement. The habitats on Surned might be scattered but not like this. All of Surned offered mineral resources to the first colonisers, and most parts of it showed some mark of the presence of people. Arcadia was another matter. Bigger, more complicated, so much of it covered by that mass of water known as ocean. The western continent, Deuteron, was scarcely settled, huge tracts of it still cloaked in untouched native vegetation. She changed her search filters and chose only those landing places within a useful distance from settlement. Slowly, she explored the entire world and, as she did so, began to see patterns.

Not good ones. Seolta had told her what he'd done, but now she saw revealed what he might have cost his world by helping those eager to prey on its starved carcass. Exile? The commander had been right. He was lucky not to be rotting in a prison cell for the rest of his life.

Everywhere were the signs of a world out of balance. She checked the date of the vidcast. Only a few months old, so after the Alliance had given Arcadia the ultimatum. There were signs of change, but not enough.

She'd always had an ability to see the overall picture of a habitat or station, to recognise the multitude of interactions needed to make a biome work, some so small that an outsider would think she was wasting time worrying about them. It was the work that had won her the Esteemed Scholar status. As she looked at the planet, she forced herself to look past her wonder and look at it as a single habitat. A very large and complicated one, admittedly, but some rules were universal. This habitat was in trouble.

There were signs of recent corrections. New plantings in the mountains were starting to break up the solid banks of festia trees. Whoever planned them knew what they were doing, she thought. In the adjacent plains, the solar fields were being modified and in the fertile land of the upper river reaches leading to the main city of Urbis, protection of the riverbeds had started. She swung southward again, past the central region of Seolta's home, over another mighty mountain range and into the equatorial regions with their mass of tropical orchards and cropping lands, interspersed within clearings of dense jungle. Then farther south to beaches of a beauty that took her breath away. Too many were stacked with holiday homes and towers of summer apartments. Bigger than the units on her own station, but all the same, all brightly coloured. The voice-over gushed about the fun to be had here. She preferred the occasional empty stretches the tourists had not yet found. Then across again to the western continent with its volatile volcanic region in the south, and north to farmland and a barely touched plateau region of scrubland and grasses, then north again to another wild tropical jungle. She couldn't resist a side trip into the scientific studies on the area and gasped when she realised the volume and complexity of the biome. Man-made stations and habitats paled in comparison.

So many trees on this world. She stared at them with a hunger that had no answer. Right at the start of the travelcast had been a warning. Access to Arcadia was closely controlled and allowed only by agreement of the Arcadian government. Usually, a visitor required sponsorship by a citizen to be granted access.

The only Arcadian citizen she knew was Seolta, and he'd been banished from his home world. Banished, and still dealing with the effect of that. She put another call through to the medic ward, and got the same answer as every time before.

The patient was not yet ready for visitors. She asked to speak to the main medic in charge of Messer den Coille. A woman came on screen.

"You aren't the medic who took Messer Seolta to the ward."

"His care has been transferred to my section, Messera. We will let you know as soon as he is ready for a visitor."

"He's in isolation then?"

The woman must have seen the horror in her eyes. "Oh, no, Messera. He is surrounded by our staff and under constant care."

"So he is up to meeting people."

"Medical staff are not visitors, Messera. They are there to care for the patient. Now, if you will excuse me…"

The woman cut the link. She was getting a bad feeling about this. She was also losing patience. She tried the medic ward one more time and, after getting the same answer, eyed her locked door.

Given the quality of her suite, the commander must have been ordered to treat her as a valued passenger. Which meant he would have to see to her needs within reason.

She marched to the door, input her com codes and waited.

When nothing happened, she changed the code and this time, waited with her heart beating. In no time at all, the door lock released and a marine barged in.

"What's wrong, Messera?" He looked frantically around the room. She sat serenely on the lounger.

"What's wrong is that my request to visit with Messer Seolta is being blocked for no valid reason. Has the Messer been charged with any breach of ship regulations that necessitates keeping him imprisoned?"

The marine blustered. Of course Seolta hadn't.

"Then take me to see the commander, immediately."

The commander?" The man's eyes goggled. "I can't do that. He's busy."

"Take me to see him or I invoke the unlawful detention statute."

The man's eyes just about popped out of his head at that one. She just hoped he didn't demand she recite it in full. She had a rough idea of the wording but that was all.

He tapped his com and began a frantic conversation with whoever was on the other side. Soon, another marine arrived. More senior this time, the woman broke into a flurry of protestations regarding her request. She continued sitting on the lounger, hands folded, and waited for her to finish. The tactic had always worked with her station manager whenever she'd requisitioned more plants and the man had objected to the use of credits.

"You have any further objections?" she asked in her sweetest voice at the end, then flattened it as the woman shook her head helplessly. "Will you please escort me to the commander's office?"

The woman made another of those harried com calls before finally nodding her head. "Please come this way, Messera."

They stopped at the door to an office suite and waited as the woman requested entry. Then Anyara was touching the pad on the commander's door.

It opened on a very exasperated man. "How can I help you, Messera?" he said from his desk, his face dark with annoyance.

She took a seat in front of the desk, ignoring the lack of an invitation. "My request to see Messer den Coille is being blocked. I would like that rescinded."

"Not possible." He glanced at the clerk standing in the doorway. "Now, if you will excuse me, I am busy. My assistant will see you out."

"I am sorry, Commander, but I must insist," she said, staying seated and folding her hands in her lap.

"Messera, in case you hadn't noticed, we have just been engaged with a rogue vessel far too close to Alliance Central space that has only just been taken under control and locked down until another Fleet ship can take it into port. We don't know whether any other threats are still around, and we are also preparing for translation. Ship's status has been maintained at yellow for a very good reason."

Yellow meant normal duties but at alert status. All staff wore breathers and carried emergency suit skins. She had dutifully buckled on her own kit before she left her suite, so couldn't plead ignorance. "Regardless, Commander, I feel the medic staff may be under a misunderstanding in regard to Messer den Coille and, as my companion, he is my responsibility."

The commander flicked a hand at the assistant, who gave up the pretence of courtesy and grabbed at her arm, hauling her out of her chair.

"Gently, Sergeant. The Messera is a respected Esteemed Scholar from the Academy."

What happened next was the commander's own fault. After all, it was his words that gave her the idea, and she was desperate. She shoved at the annoying guard.

"That will be quite enough." She sat back down, slapped at her wrist and opened up a com call. Next moment, the insignia of the Academy materialised and she set the screen to public, hoping against hope that the Academy valued her as much as this man had told her. A woman answered.

"Esteemed Scholar Anyara a Prithand2. The registrar will be very pleased to hear from you. Please wait while I forward your call."

In moments, the familiar voice of the registrar filled the room and the commander's hand chopped down an order to the man holding on to Anyara. She was released and switched off the public audio feed to talk to the woman in charge of the most revered academic institution in the Alliance. She might be small in stature with grey, flyaway hair and an eternally crumpled appearance, but no one messed with the registrar. The woman had been ordering the Alliance Council around as long as Anyara could remember, and no Council member dared risk her displeasure.

"Messera Anyara, we have been looking for you," the woman said bluntly.

"I am safe aboard a Fleet vessel, as you can see, and will be in Alliance Central after our next translation."

"Yes, we are aware," the woman said dryly. "Is there a problem?"

"Possibly," said Anyara. "The commander seems to be under a misconception regarding the status of my companion."

"Companion? You can't mean that idiot hothead from Arcadia?"

Anyara winced. She hoped Seolta never heard this. "If you mean Seolta den Coille, a son of a prominent Arcadian business family, yes."

"Prominent, hah. Power hungry despots, is what they are." The registrar had little time for the power of anyone other than herself.

"Nevertheless, the family is well respected on an EA planet at an interesting environmental juncture. His viewpoint has been very helpful to me."

The registrar's face perked up. "What are you proposing, Esteemed Scholar?"

"You are aware of my work. I would like to see if it also applies to EA or habitable worlds."

"Mmm." Anyara could just about see the wheels turning in the registrar's head. Or rather the research credits pinging into the Academy's accounts. "It's an interesting notion. Let me consider it. In the meantime, put on this commander."

Obediently, Anyara restored the audio mode and added the commander's link to the screen.

"Commander," said the registrar in full authoritarian mode, "the Academy requires that the Esteemed Scholar's companion be restored to her. He is part of an important Academy project and we would be most distressed if any impediment to that project was created by the Fleet."

The commander looked furious. "You have to understand, Messera Registrar, that the man acted in a way that could have been seriously detrimental to my ship."

Anyara had a feeling the wording came directly from Fleet law.

"Are you telling me that a Fleet cruiser is unable to contain one errant businessman?"

The commander flushed. "He is being held at present in the medic wards under the care of Fleet medical staff."

"If he's under Fleet control, there is no risk to his receiving a visit from the Esteemed Scholar. Arrange it promptly. This matter has taken up enough of my time. I am sure I will have a happier report from the Academy's Esteemed Scholar in the very near future. For now, Commander, Messera, that will be all."

Her image blanked out and the logo of the Academy shone briefly before also vanishing as the connection was cut. Anyara sat in her seat and waited for the commander's orders. Part of her felt sorry for him. He was just trying to do his duty.

She had other priorities.

With a growl, the man shoved back his chair. "Sergeant, escort the *Esteemed Scholar* to the medical ward. I will send them an order that she is to have full access to Messer den Coille." He gave an abrupt and very military bob of his head. "Your servant, Messera. Please let me know if there is any other way I can be of assistance. Now, if you will excuse me."

The man stood very erect, and very stiff. She might have gained his cooperation but she had lost his good will. It doesn't matter, she told herself, and wished she could believe it.

CHAPTER SIXTEEN

Seolta tried to lift his head and a painful hammering exploded inside his skull. One like a herd of galloping nietens at full pace. Then a woman hustled into the room and shoved his favourite breakfast in front of him. The smell of it assaulted him, turning his stomach and leaving him wanting to gag.

"Feeling better, Messer?" she said in a disgustingly cheerful voice.

The cool filter of an infuser touched his arm. Moments later, the hammering subsided, his stomach settled and the room came into focus. Light-coloured walls, smooth blocks of soft colours and a distinctive smell.

He was in a hospital ward. But where, and why?

The drug finished clearing the fog in his head and he suddenly remembered everything in appalling detail. He groaned and the annoyingly cheerful woman bustled up and ran a scanner over him.

"Where does it hurt?"

Everywhere, but none of it was physical. "I'm fine," he said gruffly. He elbowed himself up and discovered they'd also set a restraining field on him. Enough to let him sit up, but that was all.

Worse, a large and grim-faced man stood by the door, watching his every movement, and wearing the uniform of a Fleet marine.

He flopped back. No point hiding his self-disgust from these people. They'd seen him at his worst. He was too scared to ask the next question but had to.

"Messera Anyara? Is she all right?"

"Of course she is, Messer. She is safely in her suite and her needs have been attended to."

"May I see her?" Better to get the apology over with. After his crass attack, she probably wanted nothing more to do with him, but he badly needed to hear it from her mouth. To know he had no hope.

"That isn't possible at present, Messer. The ship is still at yellow alert and the Messera is safe in her present setting."

She didn't want to see him. Or they were keeping her away. "If we were at green status?"

"We'll see," the woman said. "Now, your meal has arrived and the psych med is waiting to talk to you."

Ah, so that was the problem. "Why don't I go to his office now and get it over with."

The man at the door came to attention and the woman paled. "No, no, Messer, he can come here. It's no problem for him."

That restraining field wasn't being lifted anytime soon then. Not for a passenger with suspect reactions on a Fleet ship at yellow alert. He put out a hand to shove the food away. "I'm not hungry."

The woman medic looked unimpressed. She pulled out another infuser, larger this time, and set it against his throat. He thought about struggling but took one look at the guard and decided there was no point.

It couldn't get much worse.

This infusion was slower, but just as inexorable, and at the end, he admitted he felt better. His stomach had stopped growling and he felt more able to deal with whatever awaited him.

Anyara didn't come, not at any time in the slow hours that followed. Who did was the psych med who'd talked to him before he made a fool of himself.

"Messer den Coille, I hope I find you better today."

Seolta scowled. "Will I attack you, you mean? Don't worry, Messer, you're quite safe today." He slammed his hand angrily against the field margin.

"Our apologies, Messer, but the commander deemed it necessary. AH syndrome can be quite a shock for a patient. It's for your own protection."

The man had actually resorted to the most trite of a medic's platitudes. Seolta usually scorned needing to resort to violence to gain a win. His wit and tactics had done the job much better for him in the past, but right now, he wished for some of the guard's brawn and training.

"Just fix it, will you. There must be some drug regime you can use."

The man plastered on a reassuring smirk. It was probably meant to be a smile, but it looked like a smirk. "We can give you something to help, Messer, but talking through your fears, along with training in habitat and ship protection procedures is more effective. It takes longer, but the fix is more lasting."

Seolta opened his mouth to say something, but luckily his brain caught up in time, and he snapped it shut, counted silently, then opened his mouth again. "So when do we begin?" he asked instead of the really stupid retort he'd had been about to throw at a Fleet medic on this very large ship where the commander's word was absolute.

They would be at Alliance Central in a few days and he mustn't give them any reason to hold him once they got there.

"We can start now," said the medic. "I'll send a link through to your com with the anti-breach procedures for this ship for you to review, but for now we'll just talk. How about you tell me what happened earlier and how you felt about it. What frightened you, Messer?"

"Nothing much. We were being shot at. Nothing at all to worry about," he added sarcastically.

The man grinned, and this time it was genuine amusement. It still felt patronising.

"Read through the files I'm sending you. It's not that easy to breach the hull of a Fleet cruiser. Or of any ship, if it comes to that, but we're tougher than most. Even if there is a breach, there are protective procedures to follow. All ship and habitat children are drilled in them from childhood." The man pointed to a bag at his waist. "This is an emergency breathing mask and space suit. All crew carry them at all times while in yellow status. At red, we fully suit up. Your own yellow stat kit is beside you." He pointed to a similar pouch attached to the side of Seolta's sleeper that he had previously thought to be something medical. "Clip it onto you now, Messer."

The medic waited until Seolta had done as ordered, and Seolta had to admit it made him feel safer. It didn't take away the flutter lodged deep in his gut, but it did dampen it. He doubted it would go completely until he'd seen Anyara and knew she was safe.

No, until he had got them both groundside, preferably in a world without those cursed outer domes, but that would have to wait. The main government and residential areas of Alliance Central were all domed.

The medic checked his readings and gave a pleased hmm. "Better, getting there," he muttered. "Now, Messer, what else frightened you? Most AH reactions have an underlying secondary cause. What happened to you in the past?"

"Nothing, nothing at all." Seolta snapped his mouth shut to keep any careless words firmly inside, refusing to answer more of the medic's questions. It was all in his file anyway. At last the man gave up and left.

What else had happened to him? Nothing much, apart from being thrown in prison by conniving usurpers, threatened with execution, taken in by a devious wannabe and thrown off his home world. Nothing much at all. He flopped back onto the sleeper and resigned himself to wait. If only he could feel the sunshine of Anyara's smile or the touch of her hand making everything right again ... but he'd forfeited any hope of that.

Not after what he'd done.

Then the guard at the door stiffened, the door whooshed open, and the force field around him dropped away. Anyara marched in the door looking like a general coming to liberate him.

"*Mo graidh*. It is very good to see you," he said before his head took charge of his mouth.

"I'm sorry I didn't come sooner. There were ... complications."

That set off his alarms. "What have they done to you?"

She hurried forward and her hand touched his arm. He felt it in every part of his body, but it took her "Nothing," to soothe the tight knots in his throat. "The commander needed persuading, that's all," she added.

"How did you do that?" The commander didn't look to be *persuadable* by anyone, not when his ship's safety was concerned.

A glint of mischief lit her eyes. "I made a call through to the Academy."

That just about knocked the breath out of him. "It worked?"

"Yes, it did," she said, sounding as stunned as he felt.

He had to get hold of her thesis records. For as long as he'd known her, Anyara a Prithand2 had been minimising her public profile, yet she had used the premier academic institute in the whole tragging Alliance to blackmail a Fleet Commander.

"Now, tell me why they are keeping you in here. No one will give me any information."

"Aah." He could feel the flush rising in his cheeks and wished he knew of a way to hide it. He could see no answer but the truth. "There is a known syndrome affecting EA residents, it seems."

She looked puzzled. "What kind of syndrome."

He breathed in deep. "The kind that sets off behaviour that risks the safety of a ship."

"Well, yes, but we're no longer under attack, and about that…" She blushed this time, and on her it was utterly charming. "I want to thank you."

His mouth dropped open.

"You thought you were saving my life," she said as if awestruck.

"It's been pointed out to me rather forcefully that there was no real threat," he said, feeling all kinds of an ignorant idiot. Then a thought struck. "Have you ever felt safe, at any time since you turned twelve?"

She thrust up her chin and her eyes flared. "Yes. I made sure of it."

That meant he was right. She hadn't felt fully safe since her parents died, and yet she functioned. Better than functioned, she'd made a place for herself, produced the kind of work that had the Academy prepared to challenge the Fleet on her behalf, and had become someone in her own right. That took a kind of courage he could only marvel at.

While he…

All those wasted months of self-pity mocked him. Bitter months seeking a pointless revenge instead of helping to fix his world. That stopped, now.

"Time's up, Messera," said the guard behind them. "Permission has been granted for another visit after translation is complete."

Her hand didn't leave his arm. "The Messer?"

The woman medic moved forward now, scans running madly on her infernal reader. "Is perfectly safe under our care, Messera."

Anyara had no recourse but to leave. He watched her go and felt the emptiness growing again.

She stopped in the doorway. "I will be back after translation. Keep safe," she said. Then that warm light touched her eyes again. "And please, no more attempts at bravery."

"Not till after translation," he promised, "as long as they keep you safe."

She left and the emptiness came back. The hollow emptiness that had hit him as he watched his home world disappear from sight. She'd taken that emptiness away and until now, he'd been too busy to realise it.

Hah. Too busy falling in love.

He had no rejoinder, not this time. All he knew was that Anyara had left the room and the hollow in his chest was back.

The medic hustled forward again. "There is a spare pod in this room. I will be locking down here to supervise your translation, Messer." She pointed to an alcove in the corner he had assumed was a cupboard holding supplies but saw, now that the door had opened, a pod."

"And the guard?"

"Will be just outside. There's a pod unit there, and they are trained to go into translation with less restraint or assistance than most."

He glared at the marine. He hated the fuzzy lethargy invading his body when he came out of translation.

"Training," grunted the man. "You wouldn't survive it."

Nothing like confirming what the man thought of him. "You'd be surprised what I can survive, Messer Marine."

"Strap him down for translation," growled the guard.

The medic sighed and touched the field restraints. "Are you going to cause more trouble?"

He stared belligerently at the marine while answering her. "For you, Messera, no."

"He moves, he's dead," said the marine.

You're an idiot.

He didn't deny it, but the exchange had driven that hollow feeling back to the depths of his gut.

The woman cautiously lifted the pod restraints and Seolta lay completely still. That marine didn't make empty threats. One twitch and he was likely to be gracing a stretcher in the morgue. The medic placed the translation restraints and locked them down, then set an infuser against his arm and soon the familiar haze began to descend. She'd hit him with a heavier dose of translation meds was his last thought.

He woke to a growling stomach and pounding head. Post-translation recovery was uncomfortable with meds at the usual rates. A woman's face bent over him and he reared up to tell her exactly what he thought of her treatment.

Only he failed completely. That cursed field snapped him back onto the sleeper as soon as he tried it. "Let me go," he said, furious.

"When you are fully recovered, Messer," she said in what she probably considered a soothing tone.

"Give me the antidote, now."

"No need for that. You'll be fine in a few moments."

Did she think he was a schoolboy? He shut his eyes to get rid of the sight of her. A loud thump came from the doorway.

"He out yet?" It was the marine again. Why did both of them sound so alert when he felt like he'd been hit by a falling log?

"He will be soon. Give him time."

"Shoot him with a stim. The psych med wants to talk to him."

"The psych med will have to wait. I'm not giving someone a stim after the dose he had—and you can tell your boss that too. Security doesn't run everything on this ship."

"Get him ready. He can't stay in the wards forever."

Seolta couldn't make out the medic's answer but it was no compliment. Then the chill of an infuser hit his arm again.

He came to head-blasting awareness with a barrage inside his head that dwarfed the previous poundings. "What in all the roots…"

"Sorry, Messer." She didn't sound sorry. "Security insisted. The head will settle down soon." He saw her turn to the guard. "Tell the psych he can see him in ten."

Seolta shut his eyes again. Ten minutes of peace before his next ordeal. The woman prodded at him and demanded to know if he was all right. He kept his eyes and mouth firmly shut and was relieved when she left him alone.

Then the time was up and the smarmy psych med was back.

Cooperate or be stuck here.

He *was* cooperating. Didn't mean he had to enjoy it.

"Messer den Coille. You'll be pleased to know you are now only a few days from your destination," said the mealy voice of the psych med. "Better still, the commander has agreed to release you from the wards as soon as I can confirm you are stable and no risk to the ship."

Seolta snapped open his eyes and stared in disbelief at the man. "Stable?" What did the Fleet think was wrong with him? "One small bout of temper and the commander thinks I'm ready for a permanent place in a psych ward?"

"It was the nature of the outburst, Messer," the man said carefully.

For the umpteenth time that day, Seolta wished he was still at home. He never had 'outbursts' there.

You did, when it suited you.

That voice had to go. Except he was coming to realise it spoke truth. Maybe it was an indication he was becoming more *self-aware*. That would make Samhchair happy at least.

The medic coughed loudly. He was going to ask him something awkward.

"Your outburst, Messer. Was there anything else behind it?"

"Of course not," lied Seolta, looking the man straight in the eye. "You told me my reaction was not uncommon in EA-worlders."

"I also said it usually happens on the first trip into space. That is not the case for you."

Seolta struggled to sit up. The medic signalled to the marine, who eased back the field limits to let him sit straight. Thank the roots. He was not going to have a discussion like this lying flat on his back.

"What else bothered you that day, Messer?"

"I was concerned for the safety of Messera Anyara. She is my responsibility."

A patronising smile met that attempt. "She is something more than that to you, I would venture, Messer. But that wasn't it, was it?"

Seolta shrugged. "I'm sure you've read my file. My past is all on record. You work it out."

"It shows the *events* of your past, including the events leading up to your exile, not how you felt about them." The man's face looked open and inviting but Seolta didn't miss the sneer on the marine's face. He refused to let it bother him.

"You are a proud man, Messer."

"I'm a den Coille and a Mountainer."

"While I am a gutter brat from a minor habitat," said the psych in a flat voice that didn't fool Seolta. "The kind who will never see a world like the one you threw away."

"I didn't throw it away. I was trying to protect my home and family from the scavengers up in Urbis."

"So you gave it to scavengers from off-world instead," the psych med said in a dry voice. "Your file said that prior to the recent events you had a reputation for focussing on the advancement of your family company to the exclusion of all else. You were also said to be the cleverest of your siblings."

He'd also been called less complimentary things. Slippery, a trickster, too clever for his own good. That last one was proving spot on.

"Yet despite that, Messer, you fell for a venal conspiracy by grasping off-worlders who you must surely have realised could hurt your family?"

"I thought I had it under control." The man's questions scraped him raw but he was tragged if he would admit it. "Their greed should have been sufficient to make them target the right people."

"Ah, yes," the psych med pulled up his notes on a private screen so Seolta couldn't read them. "Your rival company, Solaris, I assume."

Seolta shot upright. "No."

The man raised his brows. "No?"

"Ethan Winter of Solaris stood up for my brother in prison. He was supposed to be merely warned off."

"He's a friend of yours?"

Seolta thought of claiming that, but gave up. "He's a close friend of my eldest brother."

"You don't like him?"

How had the man picked that up? "We're too different. It didn't mean I intended for him to come to serious harm. He's an ally."

"So out of bounds." The man made it sound as if he was slotting a puzzle piece into place. "Who were your preferred targets?"

Seolta could feel the old anger boiling up and fought to quell it. "Urbis officials," he said, as offhandedly as possible. "The ones who turned a blind eye to what was happening to my family."

"You resented them?"

Seolta shook his head. "Den Coille can't afford to let enemies threaten us with no consequences," he said, trying to make his actions sound like cold-blooded strategy."

"Your involvement in the conspiracy was purely a business decision?"

"Yes, it was." Tell this wernet of the shameful fear buried deep inside him? Not going to happen. Not today, not ever if he could help it.

The psych med studied him again. Did the man think him a specimen in his lab? He kept quiet, though. He wanted out of this interview in one piece, not sliced open and exposed to view. Or worse, locked in the brig until they landed on Alliance Central, to be transferred into a retraining institution. He'd had more than enough contact with psych meds on Arcadia after being freed from prison.

His thoughts were his own and would remain so.

The psych med let the silence between them deepen. Seolta leaned back in his chair and shut his eyes, as if bored with the whole charade.

He heard the scrape of a chair and opened them again.

"I will see you again tomorrow, Messer. Oh, and Messera Anyara wishes to see you again. As an honoured and highly valued guest of the ship, you will understand that's not possible unless the commander can be assured the Messera will be safe."

What the… Had the man just threatened him? Seolta shot up, shoving back his chair violently and taking a step forward. Only the sharp crack of the weapon slapping into the guard's hands stopped him. He glared at the psych med.

"Messera Anyara is always safe with me. I would never do anything to harm her."

"Oh." The man stopped and turned. Gone was the genial expression. "You've been doing a good imitation of it throughout this interview."

"You really are Fleet!"

The man gave him a mirthless smile. "Yes, Messer, I am. Now, if you will excuse me, I have others to talk to who value my assistance. Till tomorrow, Messer."

The man walked out and the door swished shut again, leaving him in the ward with the guard. Seolta stared after him, scarcely able to believe it. Had that man really just told him that unless he gave him all the answers he needed, Anyara wouldn't be allowed anywhere near him? That he'd have to leave her alone and unprotected among this shipload of folklars? The main predator of the mountain forests, the folklar was cunning, sneaky and a born killer. Fleet crew gave them a real run for their credits.

He stewed it over all night long but when the tragging psych med walked in the next morning had found no way out.

"What do you want to know?" he snapped at the man before he even sat down.

"Everything," said the man. "Starting with why you were so angry after you were freed from prison."

Seolta's mouth dropped open. "It's obvious."

"Not to me. And not to your family." He pointed to his hidden screen. "The Fleet was granted access to your medical records following your release from prison."

"My rescue," Seolta corrected him sourly. "The imprisonment was found to be unwarranted and illegal. The perpetrators are all now serving long sentences in a remote facility on Arcadia."

The man's mouth twitched up. "And that pleases you."

"They deserved worse." Seolta growled, hating what was coming but seeing no way to stop it without abandoning Anyara, and that had become unthinkable. "It was the harshest sentence under our laws."

"Why is the reason for your anger obvious?"

Why do you ask such stupid questions? Seolta wished he could say it aloud, but this interview was bad enough without adding honesty. Or rather, honest insults. He had a sinking feeling another kind of honesty was unavoidable.

"I was illegally imprisoned, as were all my family. My family's company was stolen from us. The lowlifes for hire posing as prison guards treated my brothers, myself, and Ethan Winter appallingly. And to crown it off, we were all charged with betraying Arcadia, found guilty and sentenced to be executed in a farce of a trial. I think I had good reason to be angry."

"Yes," the psych med said.

Thank the roots, finally a victory for logical thought.

"But," the man continued, and Seolta braced, "your anger was of an exceptional order. Anger to such a degree that you acted in a way that created a threat to the family and company you claim to care for so deeply."

"A mistake in judgement. Even I can make those."

The man wasn't in the slightest put off by Seolta's sneering voice. Instead, it was as if it confirmed something he'd guessed.

"Have you ever lost control of your fate before, Messer den Coille?"

"What do you mean?" Seolta tried.

"Exactly that, Messer den Coille. According to your file, you are manipulative, conniving and totally focussed on achieving your goals. A control addict who is prepared to use any means necessary to achieve your goal."

Seolta flushed. "Please don't spare me."

"I am speaking as a professional, Messer den Coille. It is not a value judgement. Whether or not I approve of anything you may have done is irrelevant. I am merely setting out the personality traits dominant in your history."

The dispassionate judgement felt even more humiliating. "I've always tried to act in the best interests of my family and my company."

"As you see them."

Seolta shifted in his chair. He'd known today was going to be bad, but not how bad. There was too much truth in what the man said.

Truth he'd been forced to face in the long days of house arrest before he was sent into exile. Days when he was barred from company files, barred from all the heady power games that had been his lifeblood for so long. Barred from the trust of his family.

Days when his room became both prison and refuge.

The psych med leaned forward. "My comment about control was not meant to insult you. It was a straightforward question.

According to your files, you are a man who has always driven his own fate. Even as a child, you wanted to be part of the business so much, you blackmailed your family into letting you attend an important meeting despite being far too young."

Seolta nodded confirmation. He'd been excited to attend the annual general meeting and see first-hand the inner workings of the company that was his family's life. Unfortunately, it was supposed to have been his eldest brother's big day. The day Cumchdach was introduced as the first son of the next generation. Cumchdach refused to speak to him for weeks after that, and when Seolta finally complained to their mother, she sat him down and told him a few home truths. Mam did that so rarely, it shocked him to the core. Seolta had never forgotten the lesson. What he did affected others. Not only had he annoyed his brother, he had hurt him. Seolta swore to never hurt Cumchdach or any of his family again. Not that he was about to tell this psych med about that. It was private, his mother's lesson a family matter.

A lesson he'd ignored completely after prison.

"Take me over that last day in the cave system. The day you turned on your co-conspirators."

"It's all in the records you claim to have."

The psych med nodded. "Indulge me. I'd like to hear it directly from you."

All right. He'd done this before, repeatedly, in session after session. He could recite it in his sleep. He gave the man what he wanted, the whole story of that day, from walking in on the meeting of his co-conspirators with a captive Ethan to escaping the caves and contacting Marshal an Fallon to tell him what had happened. That he had to rescue Ethan Winter and the woman he loved, immediately, before the cruel incarceration sent Ethan permanently into shock from his claustrophobia, a nasty hangover from their prison days.

The psych med listened to it all and thanked him politely at the end. "But why did you return to the caves? Why keep trying to personally rescue Ethan Winter until Ethan himself urged you to leave. You were lucky they didn't decide to kill you as well."

Seolta swallowed. "I owed Ethan a debt. All the den Coilles did. He got that phobia trying to protect my youngest brother."

"Yes, family matters to you, I understand that."

"I'd caused the mess; the least I could do was try to clean it up."

The man nodded. "That's in your file too. An over-developed sense of responsibility for those who belong to you."

It was more that he belonged to his family, but this discussion was cutting too close already without trying to make the man understand subtle differences.

"Ethan made it clear my actions weren't helping and he wasn't leaving without his now wife. He finally managed to get through to me that the only way to save them was get out of there and bring in proper troops. The kind trained to deal with the criminals holding him."

"Which you accepted you were not. That must have been a shock to your self-image." Seolta flushed again. He'd be permanently scarlet after this interview. The psych med studied him. "It still sounds a dangerous and brave action."

He shrugged. "Maybe, but that doesn't make it the right one. Thankfully Marshal an Fallon did take the correct actions, just in time to save Ethan and his wife."

The man took a breath, then leaned back. "You weren't frightened?"

Seolta sat up straight. "Of course I was," he said in his rote learned response. "It was a volatile situation."

The psych med tented his hands together. "Let me see if I understand this all correctly. For months, you'd been consumed with anger, to the point of helping a conspiracy of off-worlders and major company heads to undermine attempts by the Arcadian government to meet the Alliance's ultimatum."

Seolta thrust forward. "You can't know about that. It hasn't been made public. Roots alive, most on Arcadia aren't sure what the truth of it is."

"There's enough in your file to make a good guess. Suffice it to say, you were hell bent on stopping any move by the Arcadian government to force you to into making changes to your business."

"They were making mountains out of hillocks. Putting together a bunch of hard-luck stories to create a crisis and scare the companies into submission." Or that's what he'd thought at the time. His little sister had beaten a mass of facts into his head since, and Anyara's response to the sim of Arcadia had backed it up. He wasn't yet convinced, but he was beginning to listen.

"So you thought the government was playing an underhanded game with your company."

"I wasn't the only one who thought that."

"Yes, these other companies you claim joined you. Yet you were unable to give any actual proof of that to the investigators."

Trag it, the man had read all of his file. "Deputy Malgrave kept names secret—for our protection, she said. They were real, though. I heard the talk in Urbis, heard the mutterings. I wasn't the only unhappy one."

"You went into the conspiracy without a complete set of facts? That doesn't sound like your usual mode of operation. The file also says you have a reputation for being almost obsessive about gathering information and keeping a finger on current trends. What happened this time, Messer den Coille?"

"I made a mistake. I already told you that."

"Because you were so angry. Consumed with it, in fact. Yet anger alone isn't usually enough to make us act so thoroughly against innate behaviours."

Seolta swallowed.

"What else drove you to betray your company, your home, your family, Messer den Coille? What happened to you in that prison when you lost control of your fate and nearly lost your life?"

Seolta snapped his mouth shut. Maybe, if he pinched his lips hard enough and clenched his jaws tight, he could keep it shut.

"What did losing control of your life do to you, Messer Seolta? Being locked up and waiting for others to decide your fate?"

He clenched his jaw tighter.

"Come, Messer Seolta. It's not hard to imagine. Messera Anyara is in a similar position right now, sitting in her very elegant suite behind a door locked by us, not by her. Yet she is not so filled with anger that she can't think rationally. Why would she? Her current position is little different from the threat she's been facing her whole life, according to our informers. Never knowing when her uncle will no longer need to keep her alive."

Seolta surged up, and was snapped back into place by the tragging force field. "Leave her alone. She's done nothing to hurt you or the Fleet. You can't touch her."

The psych med sat quiet. "No, Messer Seolta, we can't," he said in a quiet voice, studying his hidden screen again. "Don't worry, the Messera is safer now than she has been since early childhood. The Fleet is not about to allow anything to happen to an Esteemed Scholar of the Academy."

He touched his screens, letting one become visible. It was a scanner read out and Seolta had a nasty feeling it told the man everything. "Thank you, Messer. You have answered all my questions admirably."

The man rose, leaving Seolta in a stew of confusion and fury. The psych med touched the door pad but turned back before he opened it. "To be afraid is not a weakness, Messer den Coille. You faced execution at the hands of miserable scum. Fear is a natural response to that. Burying it as you have done ever since is harmful. Because of it, you have lost almost everything you value and you came close to losing yourself. Do not make the same mistake again."

The door opened and the man walked away, leaving Seolta's hidden scars exposed and bleeding. He glanced at the guard, and saw the contempt in the man's stony face.

The whole ship must know by now that Seolta den Coille was nothing but a fear-ridden, miserable excuse of a coward.

CHAPTER SEVENTEEN

Anyara had been demanding news of Seolta since they'd locked her in this room. Two days out of translation, only a few more days until landing, and still they refused to let her see him.

She couldn't lose him. Couldn't be stranded in that lonely void again.

The door opened and a steward came in, the woman she trusted the least of those who visited. The woman was more buttoned up than usual today, her chin pulled in tight to her corded neck and her mouth so straight you could use it to plumb a garden bed.

"The commander has said you may visit the Messer den Coille this afternoon. You needn't worry about your safety, Messera. A guard will be with you at all times."

"I'm not," said Anyara. "The guard isn't necessary."

"The commander has ordered it."

The woman didn't need to sound so pleased about it. Anyara gave a stiff bow of her head, and suspected the guard was set to watch her as much as Seolta. That trace of a Surned accent was a touch more pronounced in the woman today.

"What time will suit the commander?"

"The visit has been organised for the second hour of the afternoon shift."

Anyara inclined her head again. "I'll be ready."

Thankfully, the woman left immediately after that, locking the door securely behind her. Anyara spent the morning browsing through recent biome publications, and pacing up and down her room. What would Seolta say? What lay ahead for them?

They didn't dare try anything on a Fleet vessel, but after landing?

She used the cleansing unit just before the time of the visit, using the cover of the unit to slip her bio-scanner into her pocket. It was her own design and carried her most precious data. Not something to leave in her room on a ship where she wasn't sure whom to trust.

They gave her a full body scan before entering Seolta's room and demanded she empty her pockets.

"You'll have to leave that outside, Messera," said the marine, pointing at her scanner.

"Impossible," she said. "It was made to my personal design." A guard went to pick it up. "Do you have biome training? If not, do not touch that. You'll upset the programming and lose me years of data."

The man jerked back. The senior marine guard put out a hand. "Your gear is safe with us."

She put it back in her pocket. "It stays with me." Her final statement and she held her head high.

The man looked at the waiting medic, and the woman sent through a call. To security, she'd guess.

"They say it's harmless. She can keep it if it makes her happy."

Anyara somehow doubted that her happiness was the main concern here. More they didn't want trouble, not the kind which threatened to create a stir with outside parties. When the door opened, she wasn't surprised to see the warning shimmer of a force field around Seolta's sleeper. She could sit, talk, but no coming near him.

The shadows were back in his eyes.

She forced on a smile. "Messer Seolta. It is very good to see you again."

"And you, Messera," he said. "Very good."

The smile looked real enough, but so did those shadows. "I hope they have been treating you well," she said.

"Of course, Messera," said the woman medic. "You'll be glad to know Messer Seolta is much better and is cooperating fully with the ship's medical staff. Is that not so, Messer?"

"Oh, fully cooperating," said Seolta. The medic took it as his tone implied, genial and benign, but Anyara saw the tension in his hands. She doubted it made any dent on the scanners continuously monitoring him but his fingers had curved very slightly against the side of the sleeper.

No wonder the shadows were back.

"He's free to leave the wards then," she said brightly. "That is good news."

"No, no…" began the medic, but the senior guard stepped forward. "Yes, but only if he can be properly supervised. We would not like Messer den Coille to become agitated again as we dock. Alliance Central space becomes very busy on occasion."

"He can room with me," she said hastily. Seolta's sudden lurch upwards told her she'd fallen straight into their trap.

"That would not be appropriate for a lady of the Messera's standing," he said, face set.

"The suite can be modified, Messer," said the guard. "Her privacy and safety will be assured."

Anyara could guess how. Putting Seolta in her suite gave the ship every excuse to monitor both of them at all times. Not even the

Academy could object. "Thank you, Squad Senior and tell the Commander I would be very pleased to host the Messer in my suite. I assume that all normal rules of carriage will be followed?"

You stay out of my private areas. My cleansing unit and his are out of bounds and I will have the ship's log audited if I so much as suspect any off duty security is taking a peek at either of us.

The guard knew exactly what she implied and gave her a stiff-necked nod of agreement. The commander would be seriously annoyed, but she didn't care. The intimate areas of her suite were off limits.

"Good." She turned back to Seolta. "I look forward to having dinner with you this evening, Messer. Please let the steward's department know what you prefer and I will ensure the menu is adjusted accordingly." She gave him the formal half bow she had watched him give so beautifully on her station, and stepped back.

His voice stopped her.

"Are you sure about this, Anyara. I am … not all you think."

What had they done to him? She swung back and thrust forward her chin. "I have never been so sure of anything in my life."

She spent the rest of the afternoon alternating between reviewing her entire wardrobe for a suitable outfit and pacing the ostentatious elegance of her prison. More than once, she had to stop her hand from slapping her com with an order to call the Academy again. Wait till dinner. If he hadn't arrived when her meal arrived, the commander would hear from the Academy Registrar.

Or she hoped he would. She still found it hard to believe the woman had come through for her last time and had no intention of stretching her goodwill further. The woman would have called up every available file on Seolta den Coille and would have his whole sorry history by now.

None of it told the truth of him.

He had warned her he was not a good man, and she'd told him she didn't know any good men. Not quite true. There were plenty of good people on her station, people who cared for their families, did their work honestly and looked to her to keep their world safe and bountiful. None of them had stood up for her against her uncle. Seolta den Coille had done bad things and there was a strong streak of selfish determination in him, but he was there when she needed him.

She'd just about given up hope of his coming, her hand hovering over her com too often, when the door signalled. Her dinner had arrived. When she opened the door, he stood on the other side.

The steward hovered forbiddingly beside the dinner cart, and two guards stood behind Seolta. She ignored them all. "You came."

"Yes, Messera, I came. Complete with escort." He glanced at the crew with him. She didn't care. She hurried forward and took his hands, felt the shock of his skin on hers as she tugged him across the threshold and pulled him into the safety of her territory. He baulked, then gave way.

"That will be all. We can serve ourselves," she said in her haughtiest voice, holding her breath as the steward and guards frowned. The guards spoke something into their coms, sent the steward a look, and came to attention with a click of their heels.

"A guard will be posted outside if you need any assistance, Messera."

"The Messera will be quite safe," said Seolta. She felt the tension build in his arm and hurried to intervene, giving him a warning squeeze.

"Yes, quite safe," she said on a breath "Thank you for your help."

Still reluctant, the guards waited for the steward to leave then gave her a short salute and marched out. The door slid closed behind them and the now familiar sound of the lock snapped them shut inside.

Silence filled the room. She gestured to him to a seat and sat down beside him. Then she jumped up and hurried over to the dinner cart, checking one dish after another.

"I asked them to include something from Arcadia." She hoped her voice didn't sound as falsely bright to him as it did to her.

"Thank you, Messera. I am sure it will all be delicious." A smile tugged at his lips and the shadows retreated. They still hovered there, though, dulling the shine of his eyes.

She touched the cart to move it over to the small table she'd had set up in the alcove off the main living area. She'd even managed to wrangle one precious plant from the biome room for a centrepiece on the guise that she needed the feel of leaves to settle her nerves.

Seolta watched her clattering dishes together and talking madly, then stood with that light grace of his and walked over. He laid a hand on hers, gently stilling her as she pointlessly moved a dish from one place to another.

"Let me help you, *mo Graidh*. What have they sent us?"

He opened dish after dish, coming to a bowl filled with large, bread-like things she didn't recognise. He stared at it for a moment, then slammed the lid closed again and burst out laughing. "This will be the Arcadian dish. It's a popular street food in our main city. Personally, I can't stand it. All stodge and stinks of the streets. But you're welcome to try it."

She had caught a whiff as he opened the cover and was grateful when he closed it again.

"Here's a salad," he said. "Much more the thing to start with."

He pulled over a dish filled with a tantalising mix of greens, reds, orange, and something aromatic in yellow. Her smile burst out again as she handed him two plates.

"Definitely, Messer."

"The name's Seolta," he said softly. She raised her eyes to his and was caught in their soft, dark depths.

"Seolta," she whispered. She leaned closer, drawn inexorably to him, and lifted her mouth to his. He held her shoulders, held her eyes as if asking a question; she leaned closer in answer then his mouth claimed hers and she was home again.

He then held her close and she snuggled into his shoulder. "You must be hungry."

"Always," he said. One hand roamed over her shoulder, down her back, touching and tracing each bone in her spine as if mapping out a rare treasure. "I imagined you at night so many times in that tragging cage."

She chuckled, remembering those long nights. "There are two rooms here," she teased. "You're safe from temptation."

"You're not serious."

She lifted her chin and let a grin split her mouth. "As you so strongly pointed out, I have my reputation to consider."

His arm dropped and she was alone again. "We are watched. I'd almost forgotten."

She cursed silently. "You think the crew haven't classed us as a pair already?"

"Whatever happens between us is none of their affair. The first leaves know I've dreamed of making love to you, but it will not be under the prying eyes of Fleet security."

"As opposed to the prying eyes of Alliance Central or Academy security? They're not going to let us wander unmonitored around Central to cause who knows what havoc."

"It wouldn't be safe for you, anyway. Your uncle won't have cancelled those contracts on you."

It was too true to deny. "We're safe only in Alliance quarters or the Academy."

"Or the Arcadian embassy."

She felt the stillness in him at the new thought and reluctantly shook her head. "They won't take me. Not the niece of the man who tried to grab Arcadia's resources."

"That had nothing to do with you."

She prodded him lightly in the chest. "But it did you. Now you're hooked up with the man's niece. That will really look good."

"Hooked up?" He almost spat. "That's not…"

She put a finger over his mouth. "Maybe not, but looks matter."

He scowled, clearly hating what she implied. It didn't matter. "Let's eat," she said, suddenly hugely depressed.

"No," said Seolta. "Not yet." His eyes scanned her, face, breasts, body and down her legs, as if making a decision. "You, Anyara a Prithand2, are the most beautiful woman I have ever seen, and I have waited so long to show that to you." He pulled her back, gently, gradually. At any time, she could have stopped and tugged out of his grasp, but his words had set off an answering surge in her. She had waited too long too. A sigh of relief escaped her as his mouth found hers again and she quickly forgot about sensors, dinner, and locks. When he stood up and lifted her with that strength that always surprised, she didn't protest and pointed the way to her sleep room.

"My sleeper's bigger," she whispered and felt his laughter rumble against her.

He set her in the middle, then stepped back and just looked. She stared back, waiting, then began to release the seals on her gown. She had spent so long choosing it, and now was impatient to get out of it. A clank, a clatter, and she threw it aside then lay back, basking under his hot gaze. He stepped forward, eyes locked on her, and kicked his foot against the pocket of her gown.

"Ow. What, by all the roots, do you keep in your pockets, Messera?"

He stooped, swooping on her mini-scanner. "Oh-ho, what have we here?" He switched it on.

"Here, be careful with that. It's a bio-scanner, not some toy."

"Exactly, a scanner. And they can be made to do all sorts of interesting tricks. You are about to have your guaranteed private room, my dear Messera."

"I have important data on that."

"Don't worry, it's safe with me." His eyes shone with mischief as he opened his com and laid the scanner in its field, his fingers flying faster than she could follow. At the end, he lifted the scanner, slowly passed it around the room, then placed it back on the side table.

"That's it" he said. "I've got them all. You're safe now."

"You're sure," she said.

"Oh, yes. Now where were we, Messera? His hands lifted to the seams of his trousers and the hunger in his face had her lying back again, arms dropping away from her body. The smile on her face couldn't get wider.

She saw him fully, free of his clothes, for the first time and drew in a sharp breath. Finely boned he may be, but those bones were covered with honed muscles, and he prowled towards her with that dancer's grace that set off every pulse in her body. He set a knee on the sleeper and waited, watching her closely.

Is this what she wanted?

Oh, very much so.

Seolta watched her sleep beside him. She lay sprawled on his arm, one leg flung over his as if claiming him. He liked that. His own arm curled around her body, and the deep sweep of her lashes covered those stunning eyes. A sense of peace he hadn't known in a long time filled him, and he hardly dared breathe for fear of disturbing her or that fragile sense of rightness.

Slowly, her lashes lifted and those crystal clear eyes smiled in welcome, the light in them like the morning after a storm at home. "Hey, you," she murmured.

"Hey, you," he murmured back, lying still and wanting to make the moment last.

She lifted her head slowly, touched his lips, and lay back. "Worth the wait?" she said with a pert uplift of her nose.

"More than, Messera."

She blushed, and he delighted in it.

"How did you manage this?" he wanted to know next, lifting a lazy hand to the room and the touches that said this place belonged to Anyara a Prithand2 and no other.

"The same as any other woman, I imagine," she said, being deliberately obtuse and sending a sneaky hand tracing down his stomach muscles and lower still.

"Like no other woman," he said very firmly as she found her target, and his questions were forgotten.

Later still, he sat up, feeling younger than he had in years. "I don't know about you, but I'm famished. A man needs energy to keep working."

She giggled, and he stared, entranced. "Esteemed Scholars do not giggle," he told her firmly.

She did it again and he had to kiss her. This time, it was she who broke off. "You're right. We need food." She touched a control by the sleeper and the cart trundled towards them, empty plates still waiting. She struggled to sit up, then set the cart's top to hover over the sleeper in a makeshift table.

"Please, fix mine for me," he requested, curious to see what she would choose. At the end, he'd guessed right. She had selected all the dishes he preferred. He added a smudge more of the tangy sauce, causing her to wrinkle up her nose, then he watched as she picked at her own.

"You need more than that. "You've lost weight since we left Surned."

Her mouth dropped. "Only a bit. How would you notice something like that?"

"I notice everything about you, Messera, and this has not been easy for you."

"Pfft. I'm alive, and so are you."

For now, he thought privately to himself, and vowed to make sure she stayed that way. She also had a right to enjoy whatever her new life should bring. For now, that included some old-fashioned pampering and fun.

Which suited him very nicely.

The next morning, she had reverted to the reserved biome manager. Seolta watched in amusement as she dressed, banishing the playful partner of their night. She thanked the steward politely as the morning crew removed their dinner tray and sent in breakfast. He'd rather they had access to a food prepper, but that wasn't an option, and the chef on the ship was a rare talent.

"Is there anything else you require, Messera," said the stern-faced woman.

"No, that will be all, thank you. Messer den Coille, do you need anything?"

"No, I'm quite comfortable, thank you Messera," he said, smothering his laughter. The surly steward had refused to so much as glance in his direction since she walked into the room.

She left and the door closed after her. Seolta grinned. He was doing it a lot this morning. "That woman doesn't like me very much."

Anyara didn't smile. "No. I think she's from Surned."

Just like that, the peace of the moment vanished. He raised a questioning brow at Anyara. She lifted her shoulders. So was unsure, but wary.

He wished she didn't have to be, but the reminder was needed. Not even a Fleet vessel was safe. As the psych med reminded him, all crew were Fleet, and that included the Surned-voiced steward. Fleet should be loyal to the dictates of Alliance Central, but nothing in life was guaranteed, and this more than most. Especially when he'd been sent here to find out how deep the conspiracy went into the upper levels of Central's administration.

If a Deputy Ambassador had used her position to manipulate the crisis on Arcadia for her own gain, so could anyone in Central, including a lowly Fleet steward.

He moved over to the breakfast cart as if inspecting the morning's offerings and leaned down to brush her cheek with a kiss.

"You can trust me, and that is a promise," he said softly.

She jerked around and stared at him, those beautiful eyes darkened with worry. Then a small sparkle of light lit them from within. "I do," she said.

He wished they could have stayed in the sleeper, but the small alcove with its round table had its own kind of romance, and through breakfast he set himself to tell her some of the worst, most humiliating stories of his childhood. Stories that had her giggling continuously, lighting up her face enough to quell the anger inside him. Gifted, kind, passionate about the biomes in her care and the people depending on them, she was all that and more. Her life was a travesty of what it should have granted her, one built on a brittle shell of endurance and false docility. Yet within the limits her uncle allowed her, she had made a life and a career for herself, earning the highest academic accolade available and creating for herself a place on her station where she could practice the work she loved.

His arrival had precipitated the loss of it all.

Her hand stretched out. "What is it?"

He thrust off the guilt and set himself to bring the smile back to her face. Only because she allowed it, he guessed, and felt guiltier than ever. She had so much courage.

At the end, he began to clear the dishes away to keep busy. Anything to avoid inflicting himself on her.

Her hand stopped his as he picked up yet another dish. "Talk to me."

It was an order, not a request.

"I don't want that steward spending more time in here than necessary. We can leave the full cart by the door for her to remove."

She shook her head. "Something's changed for you." Then a shadow crossed her face and she stepped back. "Sorry, how stupid of me." She began to walk away and he discovered he couldn't let that happen.

"Stop, Anyara."

She did, but came no closer. "I'm sorry if I read more into last night than I should have. This…" her hand swept around the room, "is only for a few days. Then you can get back to your quest, and I will be safe in the Academy."

"What… No!" He dragged a hand through his hair. She couldn't think that. Last night had been a precious gift he would never forget. "It's me," he dragged up the courage to admit. "You shouldn't have anything to do with me. I've ruined your life, and here you are laughing at my pitiful stories."

Her mouth dropped open. "Ruined?" She shook her head. "How? When you stood up for me against my uncle's stooges? When you rescued me from almost certain death? When you endured those days in a *cage*, or that pirate ship? When you gave up whatever it was you came to Surned to do so you could help me."

"I came to Surned to destroy your uncle and anyone one he called family. Vengeance, that's what I was after. Nothing worthy about that. Instead, I put you in danger. Without me, you'd still be safe on your station, creating a biome second to none."

CHAPTER EIGHTEEN

Anyara stared in disbelief. "My uncle's been waiting for a chance to get rid of me for years. You didn't give him that. That Alliance Deputy would have contacted him long before you became involved."

"I invited them to Arcadia and gave them the opening they needed. Credits for the taking and a simple fool to make it all work."

There was too much truth in that.

"How angry were you?"

A twist of his mouth. "Enough that my family called in a psych med. We're not big on that kind of thing in the mountains."

"And you fully cooperated with them?"

He laughed at her dry tone. Short, brittle, but still a laugh. "I gave her all the answers she needed to leave me alone."

"And the same worked with the ship's psych med?"

He slumped down in a chair. "Of course not. He had better ammunition."

And was Fleet. It's why she was so careful with the steward. The woman might be crooked, she was sure of it in fact, but she was still a trained Fleet crew member. That made her dangerous. "What did he find out that your civilian one couldn't?"

For long moments, she thought he'd refuse to answer. When he did, she barely heard him and he looked steadily at the floor as he spoke.

"He learned I'm a coward."

"No you're not." The idea was ludicrous.

He looked up at that, his eyes briefly meeting hers before he dropped them again and she could have cried at their emptiness.

"That's why I gave into the anger. It kept the fear at bay."

She could understand that. She'd been fighting fear every moment of her life since that long-ago night. "What's wrong with that? If it worked, that's all that counts."

"I *hurt* people. I got exiled for a reason. Arcadia is being threatened, and I made it worse."

"And now you're going to help fix it," she said as firmly as she could.

He shook his head, and refused to look at her, pulling over his mug of dask. She hated the drink so refused to touch it, but in the cage, he'd cursed not remembering to pack some. It appeared to be the stimulant of choice on his home world. He took a slug of it now, his face twisting as the hot brew hit his tongue but he buried his nose in the mug and took another long mouthful then slumped back and stared at the simcast on the nearby wall. She'd set it to display her favourite view of her station.

She doubted he saw anything of it.

"The anger. It's real too," he muttered. "I told you I'm not a good person. I've been manipulating people all my life, and if you give me half a chance, I'll probably do the same to you."

"Will you hurt me?"

"No!" It burst from him … but then the shadow closed back over him. "I hope not. I don't know, that's the worst of it."

"Like you hurt me when you shoved me in that cage? When you wrangled a berth on a pirate ship?"

"They seemed the best options at the time, given the available information."

"Best options for whom? You could have shipped off-station at any time.

"Your uncle's people would have followed me."

"And if you'd called on your planet's backing?"

"I didn't have to," he mumbled.

That brought her to a grinding halt. "Excuse me?"

"They caught up with me that last day on the station. Arcadian and Alliance agents," he said. "They wanted to warn me about what your uncle planned. To get me away from him."

"So instead you ran from them and rescued me."

"They were going to let you die. I couldn't let that happen. Not when there were other solutions.'"

"Outrageous, way off-centre solutions—but they worked. I'm still alive, and you don't get to feel guilty about that."

He jerked up his head and she hoped that was a spark in his eyes.

"You have to stay safe, Messera. You could say you hold my life in your hands. I don't think I could live if anything happened to you."

"Don't. That's not even half funny."

"It wasn't meant to be, *mo Graidh*. It was fact."

"Then we're both in trouble." It was her turn for a feeble attempt at humour. "That steward won't try anything on board. Too risky for her. But once we land, my uncle's agents or your people's will be waiting."

"So will Fleet and Alliance military. You're travelling with a potentially dangerous criminal. I'd back the Fleet any day."

So would she.

He pulled the dask towards him again and added a sweetener. It had been put there for her morning chocostim but she hadn't felt like any thanks to their hearty dinner the night before. "You don't usually use that."

"Our dask isn't as bitter as this."

"You could always not drink it."

He gave her one of those looks. The kind that said she couldn't be serious.

"Addicted," she murmured and sent him a cheeky grin. His mouth twitched and he lifted his mug to salute her before taking a long, long draught.

Suddenly he clutched his throat and toppled forward, gasping loudly. A terrifying, gurgling sound.

She hit the panic mode on her com. "Medic. Emergency."

His lips began to swell and turn blue, and panic rocketed through her.

"No. You don't get to leave me. Breathe."

He was trying. Loud, desperate, grabbing for air.

The suite door smacked open, a medic raced through and slammed an infuser into his chest.

Anyara waited long, long moments.

Then a gasp. His eyelids fluttered and his chest heaved.

The medic spoke into her com. "Stretcher to suite one. Code red."

Anyara's heart seized again. "He's breathing," she said stupidly.

"For now, Messera." The medic kept working on Seolta.

He was breathing. Shallow gasps, but lifegiving air swelled and fell in his chest again. He would live.

The stretcher arrived with a phalanx of medic and security staff. She didn't care, watching intently as they loaded Seolta and attached a bunch of scary accessories she recognised as life preserving.

She'd nearly lost him.

They slammed down the stretcher cover and set off at a run. She went to follow. The guard on her suite shoved a hand into her chest and slapped up a weapon, pointing it directly at Anyara.

She flung up her hands, palms out. "I have to go with him."

"He will be quite safe with the medics, Messera. My orders are that you are not to leave the suite without protection, and none has been authorised."

"Then get it authorised." She stared after the stretcher as it disappeared into the nearest down shaft. Then it was gone and she panicked. "Get it now."

"I cannot leave. I have been assigned to secure this suite and all in it. The commander has issued orders that it is not to be left without cover."

Security had sensors in every surface allowed, but one look at the soldier's face was enough to discard any thought of breaking out. She began to pace, smacking uselessly at the walls.

"Calm down, Messera. Our medics are very good, and you're on a Fleet ship. He's quite safe."

"Don't tell me he's safe. He nearly died."

She smashed her hand against the door control, again and again, and only the first drop of blood brought her to her senses. The door showed no effect at all but her hand ached and she'd broken the skin on her fingers.

They would think she'd lost her mind.

They wouldn't be far wrong.

She needed Seolta here, now, telling her he had a plan. Asking her to do something so mad it was brilliant. Telling her nonsense like what a bad person he was, how terrible were the things he'd done.

She didn't care. He made her feel happy, safe, *noticed.* All the things she'd never felt in her adult life.

She kicked at the lounger's base and hurt her toes. So now she had a bleeding hand and bruised foot. Great. At this rate, she'd be the one needing the attention of the medics.

No, that is not a good plan. Do not go there.

She slumped on the couch, carefully stretching her toe and cradling her hand. *Please let him be all right.*

Then the door opened and a woman entered the room. "Messera Anyara?"

She leaped up. "Yes? Messer Seolta?"

"He's fine," the woman said. "Or will be in a short time, but the medics are no longer worried. Not about his current state."

That was when Anyara noticed the woman's uniform. She was from Security.

"What are they worried about?" she forced herself to ask.

The woman took the opposite chair. "Have you heard of anaphylactic shock?"

"Yes." It was a fundamental part of any biome course. Identifying risky foods or at-risk individuals potentially prone to allergic reactions was an essential to planning a biome. Anaphylactic shock was the extreme version.

"Is that what happened to Seolta?"

"Not … quite," said the woman. She signalled the door to open again and this time a senior medic walked in. One she hadn't met before, one wearing the logo of security as well as his medic uniform.

"Squad Medic Archeset is our military specialist medic."

All the medics on board were Fleet. That made them military.

The man took the other chair. "I spent time in our intelligence section," he said, and a tight knot began to form in her gut. "We've taken a blood and gut content sample. The Messer's physiological signs indicate anaphylactic shock. However, it wasn't natural. His tests showed a trace of a certain chemical that induces a mimicking reaction. We also took your breakfast trays. The same chemical was found in traces in his mug.

The man lifted a packet from the pouch on his side.

"That's Seolta's. He drank dask out of it this morning."

"He takes that every morning?"

"Morning, lunch, whenever he can," she said.

"So this morning was no different."

"No, he always has it. He did add sweetener—he said it was too bitter—but nothing else."

"Aahhh. Thank you, Messera. You have been a big help."

They both rose.

"Wait. You don't think…?"

They sat again. "What is it, Messera?"

"The sweetener," she said, her voice blunted with horror. "It was meant for me. I always use it with chocostim but decided against having any this morning."

Each looked at the other then leaned back as if settling in. Tell us more, she could hear them say in an oily voice. But this wasn't some cheap vidcast. This was real. "Are you quite sure of that, Messera?" said the man.

She nodded her head. "Seolta used it only because he said the dask was too bitter. Would I have reacted the same as he did?"

The man looked to be choosing his words carefully. "As I said, the chemical we found is one that mimics the effect of an anaphylactic cascade."

"Someone was trying to kill him? Or, no, trying to kill me." This was unbelievable. "Stars beyond, we're on a Fleet ship."

"Exactly, Messera. And we don't know who the target was. We have yet to test the dask itself."

"They set him up," she whispered.

"Not necessarily, Messera. Fleet dask is known to be … vigorous. We're used to it."

"Someone tried to kill one or maybe both of us, someone on this ship."

The medic leaned forward and all Anyara could see was that security logo on his chest. "Precisely, Messera. They tried and nearly succeeded, and on a Fleet ship."

"Does the commander know?"

"Oh, yes, Messera. Most definitely he does. Your guards have been doubled."

A sudden fear struck her. "Seolta. Can they get to him?"

The man's mouth tightened. "Security is all over the ward." He leaned forward, elbows on knees and hands tented. "Do you have any idea who may have done this?"

"Do we have any enemies, you mean?" A bitter choke of laughter escaped her flimsy control. "How long a list do you want?"

"Who's at the top?" he said patiently.

She shrugged. The Fleet probably knew it all anyway. "My uncle and Alliance Deputy Malgrave for Seolta. For me, anyone who thinks to profit by my death, which would include most of the senior hierarchy of the Surned habitats and stations. If they can make it look like natural causes or an accident, my uncle would be very grateful."

"What about the Alliance Deputy?"

"Is after Seolta. I doubt she knows of my existence."

That was the only name that interested him, not her uncle?

Of course it was. She was just collateral damage in a bigger political mess.

The man, senior medic Archeset, put out a hand and took hers. "You matter as well, Messera. The Academy is very protective of its Esteemed Scholars, and we are told that your work on biomes has the potential to make significant improvements to both habitat and ship biome systems. Believe me, a Fleet ship considers looking after you essential. Maybe you can even persuade our catering section to add more fresh produce."

The man was a trained interrogator, she reminded herself. That didn't just mean energy shocks and torture. "I have found the food on board to be of excellent quality," she said stiffly.

The woman beside the man grinned. "You get the extras, Messera. Serving crew get the optimal nutrition menu." A slight grimace said what she thought of that. Anyara had worked on a station long enough to know the woman probably spoke the truth. It had taken her months of arguments to get the station master to agree to let all levels of workers on her station have access to fresh produce. Only her promise that it would improve morale and thus productivity had persuaded him to agree. Luckily for her, she'd been right. He'd taken the credit of course, but it had kept her name out of the spotlight, despite being landed with this cumbersome title.

Don't complain. Esteemed Scholar Anyara has more hope of getting what she wants on a Fleet ship than humble Anyara nobody.

The man took the next question. "A veritable list of suspects indeed, but what we need, Messera, is any hint of trouble you've had on this ship."

"Apart from Messer den Coille being locked in your brig and attacked by your security?"

The faintest of creases appeared on the woman's brow but the man's smile only showed a slight twitch. "An unfortunate necessity, Messera. The risk to the ship overrode the rules of hospitality, and the Messer does have significant psychological scars from his recent history."

"None of us is free of those."

He lifted his shoulders, but his eyes suddenly shot her a keen glance. "You have a point, Messera," he said with a false chuckle. "However, his particular scars are of a well known kind and can result in real risk to a ship. The AH syndrome is too well documented to take chances. The commander had no choice."

"And now Messer Seolta is confined to your medic wards yet again with what you tell me is a case of deliberate poisoning."

"Maybe," the man said. "So there is no one on board you can think of who may be involved."

She hesitated. A feeling in her gut and a trace of an old accent weren't much to go on. "There is a steward. Her accent is now Central standard, but there's a trace of a Surned one. I think she may have grown up on my world, or her parents did."

The smile disappeared. "Her name?"

"I don't know it. She never introduced herself."

The woman grimaced. "Standard protocol to protect our crew from com intrusions. I'll bring up the holos of the suite's roster."

The grim steward wasn't there, and both her interrogators' faces sharpened. The woman spoke into her com. "Surveillance list of all persons entering the suite."

Again, there were no clear shots of the woman Anyara remembered all too well. She had never liked that steward and could bring her face easily to mind. Then one view came up. Not a full head shot, just a side-on one as if the woman knew exactly where all the room's sensors were. "That's her."

"She's not a regular steward," said the woman from Security. "She's one of the maintenance crew. She's only called on if the stewards are short and we haven't been advised that was the case."

"Was crew," said the man. If Anyara had any liking for the woman, she'd feel sorry for her and whoever had changed rosters with her, but Seolta lay on a sleeper in the medic ward and she still hadn't been allowed near him.

Both stood, and Anyara scrabbled up. "Thank you for your assistance," said the man. "Please don't hesitate to call if you think of anything else that may help."

"And Seolta? When can I see him?"

"I will organise a squad to escort you," said the woman, "as soon as we can be sure it is safe for you to leave the suite."

She was stuck here? "Make it soon." She heard the begging in her voice and didn't care.

"It will be, Messera," said the man.

The woman spoke into her com. As the door opened, Anyara saw that four more security stood outside, as well as the ones who entered the suite.

"You may still be in danger. This area is now status code red four," said the woman.

A curt nod and the woman withdrew, leaving a squad of four grouped around her room as the door shut firmly behind her.

So she had troops inside and outside her suite, and no doubt all the sensors were on full cover mode. No privacy at all. She hugged herself tight. Two of the troopers had taken up guard in the lounge, one by the door and one by the main controls. The other two prowled around, coms sweeping every particle of her space.

"Your com, please, Messera."

Did she have any choice? She didn't have the nerve to find out. She unlatched her com and laid it on the guard's scanner field. The man watched his readouts on a hidden screen then picked up the sliver and handed it back. She was more relieved than she ought to be to feel the cool material latching onto her wrist again and to see the shake of his head.

"No sign of any intrusions."

The pair went back to their scrutiny. She sat down on the lounger and brought up some biome data, trying to occupy herself and failing miserably. She fled instead to her memory of the night before. So short a time, so precious a time, and so quickly lost.

What was happening to Seolta?

She wasn't to find out till the next morning. A knock at her door and yet another squad stood outside her suite. Seolta stood in the middle, washed out, pale, and she suspected it was only his stubborn cussedness that kept him upright, but those dark eyes sank into hers and she forgot to breathe.

"We hadn't finished our discussion of the other night," he said with a definite tilt of those beautiful lips.

She blushed. "I'm looking forward to it," she heard herself saying and gave him her arm to bring him into her suite. He leaned too heavily on her, despite the tremble of muscles that told her he tried not to. He made a beeline for the lounger and sat heavily. Anyara stood protectively beside him, and caught the worried frown of the medic. She refused to ask the man if Seolta was ready for release. Seolta thought he was and that was good enough for her.

The medic checked a patch on the wrist opposite the one where Seolta wore his com. "I'll know the instant you try to remove this, Messer. It's here for your own good. Please, just take it easy and signal the moment anything feels wrong again."

"I'm fine," Seolta said, his voice carrying a definite edge. She'd long recognised he wasn't a man to let others run his life and resented it strongly if anyone tried. Unfortunately, when it came to his health, he had no choice, and she fully intended to point that out to him as soon as they were alone, or at least had the appearance of it—with all the sensors activated, being truly alone wasn't an option.

"I'll keep an eye on him," she promised the medic. The woman looked highly doubtful, but she shrugged and gave the patch one last tap.

"The moment you feel unwell again…" she warned him before stepping back. "Messera, the guards all have medic training. Please follow their orders if needed."

She promised solemnly to do so and had to avoid looking at Seolta as she did. She could almost feel him twitching with annoyance. Luckily, the woman had no choice but to accept Anyara's assurances and leave. As soon as she did, Anyara sat down beside him.

She took his hand, needing badly to feel him. "You're all right?"

He sent her a fixed smile. "I'm fine, *mo Graidh*. You can't get rid of me that easily."

"Don't." She felt the tears threaten and tried hard to stop them. "You came so close. I can't lose you."

His arm snaked around her and pulled her in close. "I'm here, sweetheart. I'm not going anywhere."

"You'd better not be." Her arms snagged his body, returning his clasp. "I want another night," she murmured. "One wasn't enough."

She felt his grin as his mouth captured hers. "I've no argument there, sweetheart, but maybe not quite at the moment," he added with a groan.

She let him go, touching his face and arms desperately.

"I'm all right. Just a bit tired."

One of the guards stepped forward, staring at a space just above them, and his face was a mask of stone. "The Messer woke only half an hour ago. He chose to discharge himself against the medic's advice."

It was as she'd thought. Anyara turned in exasperation to Seolta. "Of course you did."

"They wouldn't tell me what was happening to you, *mo Graidh*."

When he smiled at her like that, she would forgive him anything. "Put your feet up. I'll get you something to eat."

He began to shake his head, then stopped, clearly in pain.

"You need food," Anyara insisted. "Something solid, instead of whatever synthetic infusion they've been shoving into you."

She badly needed to care for him. Maybe that way she could convince herself he wasn't leaving her.

She ordered up a half meal, supplemented with everything the medics had prescribed, and waited while the guards scanned it, tested a sample and cleared it for use, then picked up a spoon to offer him a mouthful. He grabbed it from her, scowling.

"I'm not that useless. Not yet."

She had to force herself to watch as he slowly ate some of the meal. He couldn't hide the tremor in his hand but refused to acknowledge it. He'd barely touched more than a quarter of it before he shoved down the spoon and laid back.

"You need to be in the sleeper."

A faint twinkle lit his eyes. "Why, thank you for the invitation, but maybe not quite yet." His head tilted mischievously at the guards.

"To sleep, idiot."

"What a shame," he murmured. But he had to let his head fall back again. "Maybe you're right," he said grudgingly.

She looked to the guards. They lifted him up and she led them to her own room. This sleeper was more comfortable, she told herself.

The second room was just as well furnished as hers, but she needed him near her. They laid him down on the sleeper and pulled up the covers.

"Get some sleep," she whispered to him, leaning down for his kiss, as much for her own benefit as his.

"This is your room. Where will you sleep tonight?"

"Here. With you." She said it loudly enough for all the guards and the sensor listeners to hear. "Where I belong," she added for him, and saw something in him relax.

"Yes," he said, as his eyes began to close again.

She sat and held his hand until his breathing told her he was fully asleep then marched out to the main living area to confront the guards. One had gone into her room to watch Seolta; the rest still ranged about the other rooms. "I would like to contact his medics."

The senior one nodded. "They are waiting." At her look of surprise, he added: "The psych med said you'd ask."

"Oh." She wasn't used to anyone reading her so well. Her uncle had always said Fleet crew were tricky and she was learning why. If only she could trust them.

Both the medic who'd come with Seolta and the psych med of earlier came back. Anyara swallowed. Then gulped once. "I understand that Seolta left prior to being discharged."

The medic stepped up. "He insisted on it."

"He would," she said. "Can his recovery be managed in this suite?"

"Yes," said the woman grudgingly.

"Good. Then you will explain to me exactly what is needed to have him back to full strength as quickly as possible, and between us, we will make sure he follows it."

The psych med smothered a sound. One that sounded suspiciously like a laugh. She swung on him. He raised his hands in surrender.

"I wish you luck, Messera. I truly do."

"You doubt I can do it."

He studied her, then grinned again. "No, as it happens. If anyone can, it's you." Then he lost the grin. "You do know he won't willingly relinquish any control of his life?"

She lifted her shoulders. "Once the medic has finished detailing his treatments, then perhaps you can explain that to me more fully. Without all the sensors on record."

His mouth straight and grim, he looked at the guards and got a short com message back from the sudden other-place gaze in his eyes. "No record, but all will stay monitored. The security situation is too delicate."

She bet it was. "I have no doubt the commander is furious." Not as furious as she was, or as tense. She waved the two medics across to the table in the alcove. If she couldn't have privacy, at least she would have a facsimile of it.

The woman medic left first after a final check on Seolta and confirmation he was sleeping naturally and that that was what he needed most. It was a long time till the psych med left, and when he did, Anyara stayed in her chair staring at the swirling images playing on the vidcast beside her. Her mind saw none of it, lost in thought.

She had a lot to consider.

CHAPTER NINETEEN

Seolta woke in a strange sleeper filled with the scent of green leaves. Only the overlying tang of metal and synthetics told him he was still on board ship. He relaxed. His sleeper smelled of Anyara. He put out a hand to the pillow next to him.

It was untouched. He sat up, then lurched back down at the pounding in his head.

She rushed into the room. "You're awake."

Shadows bruised her eyes. "What have they done to you?" He had a faint memory of darkness and the shape of her sitting vigil beside him. He reached up to smooth away those dark smudges, but then had to drop his hand. He was as weak as a baby. He looked at the timer on his com.

"It's early night-cycle," she said, her voice sounding exhausted. "You've been asleep all day."

"Tragging stars. Are we safe?"

A lift of those small shoulders that carried so much weight. "For now. There's a guard in here and three more in the outer room."

He struggled to sit up and she hurried to help him.

"I'm supposed to be the one looking out for you."

"And you will. Just not right now."

She helped him up enough to see the burly figure standing with weapon palmed by the sleep room door. "Why are you here?" he demanded of the man.

"Commander's orders."

Were they trained to talk in soundbites only. "Am I under arrest again?"

Anyara answered. "Not this time. You were poisoned."

"On a *Fleet* ship."

She gave him a mirthless smile. "You can imagine what our friend the commander thought of it."

He fell back against the sleeper, wishing he could talk to her without the guard. Anyara looked as frustrated as he felt, and glared at a spot on the wall he'd mapped as a sensor on their first night.

"Active?"

She nodded.

Trag it. He thought furiously. The past day was a blur. The last thing he remembered was… "My dask!"

She shook her head. "The sweetener."

That had him shooting upright. "That was meant for you."

"Maybe."

He shot another look at the guard then raised a brow at her. Why he thought she'd understand, he couldn't say, but she did.

She shook her head.

So not officially sanctioned. No wonder the commander was furious. But the alternative, a rebel on a Fleet ship, was equally horrifying.

"I hope they lock them up."

"They will," she said. "When they prove who it is."

Meaning they weren't safe yet, not with unknown enemies loose on board. He needed answers. "Who let me sleep the day away?" Leaving Anyara open to all kinds of threats.

She squeezed his hand. "You needed it." The faint tremor in her grasp told him the truth of what this day had done to her. Anger welled up, but this time was different. Not the unthinking fury that had engulfed him after his imprisonment. This was cold, contained, *targeted.*

A hard squeeze on his hand brought him back, and he looked up in surprise. She'd squeezed hard enough to hurt.

"You left me. Don't give in to your demons, not again. This time, we're in it together and I need you."

He shoved the anger back down, back to the toolbox in his head where it belonged and from where he could bring it out when needed. "I wasn't lost to it, not this time, *mo Graidh*, thanks to you. Now, what do I have to do to get out of this sleeper—or to get you into it?"

He tried lurching for her but only made a fool of himself. She laughed. "The medic left me instructions, and that wasn't included. Not yet."

Only the promise in her eyes stopped him trying again. 'Soon,' those bright crystals said. Soon.

"At least sleep beside me."

"With pleasure, Messer." He had to be content, easing into her warmth as she lay with him after ordering the lights off. When the morning came, he discovered he could do much more.

An hour later the guard, supposedly slumbering in the chair, sat up and ordered the lights back on. His face stony, he told them to prepare for docking. "We'll be locked into berth by midday. A squad from Central Military will escort you both to a secured shuttle down to Alliance Central."

"Do you think he knew?" she said, a blush heating her cheeks.

"Yes, but I'm sure he's trained to be discreet," he murmured back. "Only the commander and all his officers will hear about it."

"What?" Then she poked his arm and leaned in for another kiss, with smothered laughter. "You will pay for that."

Her smile was a promise. One he treasured, and he added it to the pledge of their early morning loving. He was going to need them today.

Docking at the main station above Alliance Central began normally enough: a warning over the ship's com to lock down and the usual clankings and changes in engine sounds. He'd stopped noticing them during the voyage, but now the faint hum slowed then shut off and was replaced by hurrying steps outside the suite and a sense of busyness in the ship. The all clear of a successful docking released them from their pods. He helped Anyara out and sat to wait with her. Their door was still locked, according to the control pad.

A new sound battered the outside corridors, loud enough to have them both standing and waiting. It stopped outside their door, and she reached for his hand. The door unlocked, and a full troop of soldiers marched in.

He'd never seen anyone wearing the uniform before but recognised it. Everyone in the Alliance did. Anyara dropped his hand, but inched closer to him.

"Squadron Leader," she said to the woman in front. "A full troop of the Alliance Patrol? We are honoured."

Seolta wondered if the woman could detect the wariness in Anyara's voice. The soldiers' faces gave nothing away.

They came to attention with a clatter of boots, weapons palmed as if ready for action. "You will accompany us, please."

It wasn't as if they had a choice. Most of the troop surrounded them and four peeled off to clear the room, scanners checking every corner and inputting an order into their wardrobes. He hoped they got their gear back at some stage. He did prefer wearing his own clothes to begging for ill-fitting hand-me-downs. The troop marched them off into a deserted corridor and to a hatch he hadn't seen before—not the usual crew hatch or cargo hold door. This one was smooth-walled with no opening for any intruders to use.

All these weapons surrounding them must be getting to him. Why else would he be thinking of wars and invasion? He wished he could hold Anyara's hand again, but any sign of weakness could be used against them.

This was not how he'd pictured arriving at Alliance Central. They passed through the receiving station, customs and bio checks with barely a pause as they were hurried through. Then they were at a shuttle, one with no markings to give him any kind of information, locked down and heading away from the station and towards the planet's surface. He didn't even have a viewing window to see the planet below.

He suspected his feeling of disorientation and loss was quite deliberately given. To counter it, he reviewed what he'd learned about Alliance Central before leaving home. He was a firm believer in making sure of his facts before venturing into new territory.

One of the first habitable worlds, Alliance Central was a mix of domed habitat and open settlements. The latter were confined to the upper mountain regions where the atmosphere was thin enough for humans to breathe, unlike the heavy air of lowland regions where habitats ruled and most of the residents lived.

All the images he'd seen of the planet showed it wasn't a patch on Arcadia, but Central was better placed, right at the confluence of the main routes linking the major settled worlds. What had begun as a small habitat on a lowland plain had become a sprawling complex covering much of the world, with the giant dome of the Council habitat at the heart of it.

The planet supported a population many times that of Arcadia, yet when they landed, the only people in sight were fully armed patrollers and a single official wearing the logo of the Council. The bay was brilliant with light and had that same smooth appearance as the departure hatch on the Fleet vessel. It felt military, reminding him of the marshals' headquarters back on Arcadia. The same ruthless efficiency marked the shining walls and smooth floors.

A man stepped forward. "Messer den Coille, Messera Esteemed Scholar, welcome to Central. Please let me escort you to your new quarters."

"I had expected to lodge with the Arcadian embassy, and the Academy is awaiting the Messera's arrival."

The man gave a formal bow that would have won approval from his grandfather. "They have been informed that your arrival will be delayed. Please follow me."

The troop surrounding them began to move forward, with Seolta and Anyara set square in the middle with no option but to start walking or be trampled. He glanced at Anyara. Her face was set, giving nothing away, and she'd moved even closer. The feel of her arm brushing his helped contain the anger boiling inside him. He couldn't afford to lose his temper, not with these troops.

He wished he had when they arrived at their destination. Walking in the door felt exactly the same as walking in the door of the Survey prison building in Arcadia. A faceless façade, featureless black door, and no one speaking to them except for the occasional brusque order. The small official had disappeared as soon as they arrived and another officer took charge of them.

"This way," she said, without any explanation. He'd had enough of that and refused to move. He reached out and held tight to Anyara.

"Why?" he said. "What is this building and why are we being made to come here?"

"In due time," said the officer, without a hint of apology. She gave a swift nod to the guards immediately behind them, and the man thrust his weapon right into Anyara's back. She pulled away, held her breath and stood rigidly still.

"There's no need for that."

"Then come along."

The officer gave him back stare for stare and the soldier's hand on the weapon never wavered.

"Put it down. We're coming," said Seolta, memorising all the faces around him. They maybe under orders, but they had chosen to use terrorising Anyara to get their way, and he was tragging sure that wasn't in their orders. He kept a tight hold of her hand as they moved off again. Down endless, blank-walled corridors, up and down shafts, till he had no idea what level they were on. It was a technique his family also used and found highly effective at weakening a subject's defences. He wasn't about to let it work on him.

They finally arrived somewhere. At another blank-faced door with no markings, the squad ground to a halt and the leader lifted her com and sent a signal. The door opened, and she gestured them in.

It wasn't a prison cell and a part of him relaxed. He'd had more than his share of being locked up.

Not yet it isn't.

It was an office. He'd seen mid-level government officials' offices often enough as well, and this one had all the usual fittings. Standard, not especially comfortable, but sufficient for the occupier to do their work. It had two equally standard-issue chairs set in front of a plain desk, behind which sat yet another official.

The squad leader gestured them to sit. Anyara did as ordered; he wasn't as sanguine. He'd been locked down in similar chairs before.

"My office has no restraint facilities, Messer den Coille," said the woman behind the desk. Middle-aged, her face comfortable rather than striking, he suspected she cultivated the mediocre appearance on purpose.

He took the vacant seat.

No field wrapped around his ankles, no constriction bound his chest. That didn't make him relax. Two of the squad stood immediately behind their chairs and the rest marched out again. By the official's sense of ease, he suspected they'd taken up positions at the outer door.

Does she know she's facing two dangerous outcasts?

Not two. Messera Anyara is a refugee. You're the one kicked out by your world.

Thank you very much, voice. How about keeping your comments for when you're asked for them? I will tell the psych med about you.

He scowled at the woman behind the desk, and she rapidly altered the pleasant smile she'd been using to one more serious. "Messer Seolta, you have had a trying time of it. We understand that. Be assured that the Alliance wishes to do all it can to assist the both of you to a happier outcome."

Anyara's face had that bland look she wore when feeling especially threatened, the one he'd first seen at her uncle's birthday celebration when she was talking to the station master. "Thank you, Messera…?"

"Sephtax. Administrator Sephtax, I have been asked to facilitate your arrival procedures. Alliance Central has very strict requirements in place for all visitors."

He just bet they did, although he had a feeling they were less strict for welcome visitors than for problematic ones.

"And you work for…?" said Anyara in her polite and perfectly reasonable voice. The one even the most suspicious of interrogators would find it hard to take offence at.

"A minor administrative branch of the security services," said the woman. "We are often called on to assist our border staff when they're busy. It seems that all our subsidiary worlds have chosen this time to come seeking trade rulings." The woman gave a titter, so false she couldn't have believed they'd fall for it.

"Not surprising," said Seolta. "There are few other worlds more effective for finalising trade deals than Central, and we all like credits," he said in his most urbane of voices. I am here to make my fortune, not spying, he hoped it said.

"Yes, but it does make a lot of work for us poor backroom people," she said with another titter. He guessed that meant she wasn't fooled. "And the 'difficulties' you met on your way here do complicate matters."

"In what way?" he said, injecting ice into his voice this time. I may be a rejected nobody now, but I was born the son of a wealthy family. "Is it my precarious legal position or the Messera's relationship to the virtual ruler of the Surned system."

Anyara gasped, but the woman waved a hand and sat up with a real smile, dropping the dim-witted aunt pose. "A man who likes to get to the point of a negotiation. How refreshing."

"Yes, but what is the 'problem' you have been tasked with handling, Administrator? Or is it Patroller First Class?"

That pleased smile again. "Well done, young man. It's Patrol Captain, as it happens, although I really am an administrator."

"Captain in the security section, I assume."

The woman nodded and Anyara's face lost all colour. "My uncle asked for your help," she said. "That's what this is about."

"The Patrol works for the Alliance, Messera, not minor potentates." He heard Anyara drag in a breath and wished he could take her out of here.

"But…" he prompted.

The woman sighed. "The Surned system is a valued source of a number of chemicals that the Alliance would be loath to see cut off. The current nature of the government of the system may be irregular, but it works."

He leaned forward. "You mean Hilmar a Kevand's position as de facto ruler, and the injustices suffered by the ordinary inhabitants of the system. Only those at the top of Hilmar's administration live comfortably. Except for residents of the Messera's station, the rest of the working population merely survive, rather than thrive."

The woman shrugged. "They do survive, Messer den Coille, and that is the point. The system is stable, they live on a world where they know the risks and have security of income and resources. That is not to be underestimated."

"And the ones who don't accept that. Are they just casualties?"

"Yes, Messer, they are. Officially, the Alliance deplores such a situation, but reality is another matter. The Central administration must concern itself with the bigger picture, not individuals."

Anyara struck out a hand and grabbed at his, squeezing it tight. Her voice when she spoke was polite, but each clipped word betrayed her anger. "All individuals, or only those without influence. It's a dangerous position for an administration, Messera. Power is not always forever, and the top rank can very quickly become the bottom."

"True enough, Messera," said the patrol captain, still sounding unconcerned. "It changes nothing. It is today's reality we are dealing with, and what to do about your position."

Seolta squeezed Anyara's hand back, the only way to keep the lid on his temper. "Which is, in your estimation, Captain? We do appreciate frankness when it comes to our prospects of surviving the next few days."

Control, that is the secret of a successful deal. He'd read that in a business article many years ago and it had immediately resonated with him. Now, he had to fight hard to remember it.

The woman's face turned serious. "Without help? Fifty–fifty. We have detected a number of operatives interested in one or both of you and your presence here. The incident on board the AC *Best Order* is of particular concern. For the security of the whole Alliance, the Fleet must be wholly trusted and loyal to the Alliance, not to any regional interests. The *Best Order* has been stood down and all crew subjected to a full audit before it can be allowed to return to service."

Seolta was surprised she'd told them so much. "I'm sorry to hear it. The commander and the medical staff in particular were a great help to us. I hope it can be resolved quickly."

"As do we all," said the captain.

It was the only moment of unity in the whole nightmare interview. Having laid bare the main points against them, the woman set aside all pretence that this was anything but an interrogation. Her questioning technique was second to none, and avoiding a damaging answer became more and more difficult. Anyara looked exhausted, and still the woman continued.

"You have lived with your uncle's threats ever since your parents' death, yet you only now decide to flee from him. Why, Messera? Messer den Coille is undoubtedly a handsome man, but he is also a suspect one. Was it his charms, or did you have other reasons?"

Both of them flushed bright scarlet at that one.

"That is insulting to the Messera," rushed in Seolta before Anyara could answer.

Anyara smiled, the first time in all that hellish discussion. "You're right, Captain. He is *very* handsome, and tells a good story, but I ran away with Messer den Coille because I would have been killed if I'd stayed. I have become adept at reading my uncle's moods and there were too many hints of trouble. As for my being a problem for the Alliance, I fail to see why. I am here because the Academy asked me to come to Central."

The captain glanced at her com files. Seolta wished he could see them. The woman frowned. "Yes, we have the request, Messera."

"That is Esteemed Scholar," Anyara said gently.

The woman's mouth tightened and she bowed her head. Titles and rank mattered in the military. "As you say, Esteemed Scholar. I had understood you don't normally use the title."

"It seemed expedient on Surned. Here, there is no such need. I have earned the title and to deny it is to insult the Academy."

The woman's mouth tightened another fraction. "As you say."

She glared at Seolta. "So why are you here, Messer? You were sent into exile for trying to block your government's attempts to comply with the Alliance's environmental directive. That would appear to make you a risk to Central."

"Not at all, Captain. As you may be aware, I was exiled rather than charged with a crime because I chose to betray my co-conspirators rather than let them hurt Arcadians for their own financial gains."

"You helped save the lives of Ethan Winter and his wife. It doesn't change what else you did, or your risk to Arcadia. Do you really expect us to believe you are now reformed and wish only to further the interests of Arcadia and the Alliance?"

Seolta forced out a laugh. "More correct to say I wish to further my own interests, Messera. There's little chance they'll ever let me back onto Arcadia. I still have a healthy credit balance, and I need to find a *legitimate* way to use that to build a future for myself."

"You really expect us to believe that, when your first action upon leaving your home world was to head off to the home of one of your co-conspirators? Despite being explicitly warned against going to Surned?"

This time it was Seolta who lifted his shoulders. "A mistake, I agree, although I will always be grateful it gave me a chance to meet and assist the Esteemed Scholar. I went to Surned for the most venal of reasons. Revenge, Messera Captain, pure and simple. It does me no credit, but Hilmar a Kevand3 owes me. He caught me when I was vulnerable and came near to killing a man to whom I owe a debt of honour. In my culture, that is not acceptable."

"And you are such an honourable man, Messera den Coille."

Only the realisation that she was deliberately provoking him stopped him shooting out of his chair and doing something really stupid. He stared at her for a long moment with what he hoped was a superior smile.

She gave him back a smile that could have graced a rakter just before it pounced on its prey. The threat was perfect. Too perfect.

She's bluffing, he suddenly realised.

He stood up. "It's been interesting talking to you, Messera, but the Academy is keenly awaiting their Esteemed Scholar's arrival and I'm sure my embassy is aware of my location by now. Our agents are not that inept. Or am I mistaken? Are we, in fact, under arrest by the Patrol? In which case, please contact the Academy and my embassy to arrange for the required legal representation."

He pulled Anyara's hand, feeling the continuous tremor as she stood. This woman had really frightened her, and that was the most unacceptable part of this whole ordeal.

The captain scowled back. "I haven't finished with you."

"But we are finished here, Captain." He looked to Anyara, holding tight to her hand. "Isn't that right, Esteemed Scholar?"

Shadows smudged her eyes, but she forced her chin up. "Yes, quite finished." Together they walked to the door. Nothing happened. The door stayed fully closed. He turned back to the captain.

She grunted, and stabbed at her com. The door whooshed open. "There you go." Two guards stood in the corridor either side of the doorway. "Escort the Messers to their destinations," the captain said curtly.

Their mouths dropped open.

"The Arcadian Embassy and Academy are to be notified of their arrival," the captain added gracelessly.

The two saluted. "This way," the largest guard grunted.

Seolta kept a tight grip of Anyara's hand all down the maze of faceless corridors, uncaring whether it showed a weakness. Not while that faint tremor ran through her hand and fired every nerve in him. It only stopped when they escaped to the outside of the building. He wished there was open sky above, but then remembered what the psych med had told him. No, that was one shock she didn't need today.

He didn't even quibble at the windowless, black security vehicle that drew up. The captain had spoken a pile of lies and evasions, but the bit about people being after them? That had been all too true.

Neither of them dared risk walking the streets of Central alone.

CHAPTER TWENTY

The doors of the Academy closed firmly behind her and Anyara drew in a deep breath. The Dean of the Biome Department had come personally to welcome her and escort her to her new quarters. She was back home with her own kind.

She should feel safe. She stretched her fingers, feeling the emptiness around her. Seolta had been forced to say goodbye at the Academy's security office, and she'd felt his eyes on her as she walked away. The patrol's driver was taking him to the Arcadian Embassy, where he too would be safe. Safely separated from her. The satisfied smile on the Dean's face as he watched Seolta's skimmer disappear said it all. They had her back under their control and away from the disturbing influence of a known troublemaker.

He's not. He was just angry. What he had done was wrong, terribly so. But unforgivable?

She had lived every day of her life since twelve standard years under the control of a man who wanted her dead because he wanted her inheritance. Given the standards of her world, Seolta's crimes were minor and short term.

He could do it again. That was the constant message battering her, in the Dean's smile, that interrogator's focus, and the Fleet

Commander of the ship. Even in her uncle's scarcely concealed smears.

Yes, he could, but he would stop if she asked.

Not if you're threatened, her subconscious whispered.

Did a man prepared to break any law to protect her frighten her?

After my life till now? She sent her conscience a cackle of laughter, and heard the silent chuckle from inside.

She would survive this and see him again. They just had to make it happen.

"What were you saying, Dean?" she said to the bumptious man prattling on beside her.

He slowed, missed a shuffle, then began again with a steady beat of his feet. "Your lab is ready and waiting for you when you're ready." It was said with a bright smile and she waited for what came next. He coughed. "We were … ah … wondering, Esteemed Scholar. That is, we would be greatly honoured if you would consider taking on a few students. We've heard much of your internship program and would be very grateful for any mentoring you cared to offer."

"You have?" The Academy had monitored her more closely than she'd realised, though how did they get past her uncle's systems? "I don't know if you would call it an internship program, exactly. It's normal practice on a station to have trainees working with the techs. We can't afford to lose critical knowledge."

"Precisely, Esteemed Scholar. Your trainees who have come to us have been most impressive."

"Oh, good," was all she could manage. She'd suggested Academy training for a number of her juniors over the years, but her uncle had always said the cost of it was prohibitive.

"I'm still paying off your fees," he'd grumbled. "To fork out for more…" and she had quickly dropped it. She'd never seen the Academy fees for her studies to know whether it was true.

"The trust your uncle set up has been most successful," added the dean.

"Trust?" Her uncle wasn't given to charity.

"Yes." The man looked non-plussed. "The one using the fees from your research royalties. Since you chose not to touch it, and he couldn't without your consent, it's gone into a trust for Surned graduates. Those grants are very sought after." The man missed another step. "You were messaged about this. We sent reports every quarter, as we do for all such trusts."

She lifted a hand as if acknowledging it. "I leave such affairs to my uncle," she said hastily, trying to assemble her thoughts. Her uncle had used her earnings to train up more resources for Surned. Typical! He probably took a cut as well somewhere. An administration fee, he'd have called it.

All those trainees. Every time she found one who seemed to understand her and how she worked, her uncle had transferred them to another habitat. Or that's what he'd told her.

"Are any here at present? I would so enjoy catching up with them again."

"Not at present, Messera. They are too highly sought after by habitats, but they will be very pleased to have a chance to catch up with you when they are next at Central. Now, your lab is this way."

The dean appeared very eager to get her back to work again. "Thank you, but first, Dean, I would very much appreciate seeing my quarters. I've been looking forward to proper groundside amenities for weeks now."

The man blushed. "Of course. This way, Esteemed Scholar. We have put you in the researchers' wing. It seemed the most appropriate, but let us know *immediately* if anything is not to your liking."

She groaned inwardly. The researchers' wing was venerable and a rare badge of honour in the stratified world of the Academy. It was also old, draughty, and in need of upgrading. The only advantage: it was right in the middle of the Academy and impossible to breach by outsiders. She suspected that was the real reason they'd put her there. The Academy was taking no chances on any attempt to kidnap her—or on Seolta rescuing her.

Her room turned out to be exactly as she'd expected. Charmingly picturesque with furniture at least a century or more old and with real plants gracing the numerous shelves and benches. It opened onto the central gardens of the campus and had a real window she could open, though a shimmering line beneath it warned of a protective field. The room also held a sleeper that should have been traded in a decade ago, and the service amenities clanked when she tried the cleansing unit.

"We'll send in a serviceman," said the dean complacently. She thought of her old student quarters. Cramped and spartan, but the plumbing there had worked.

The student hostel was also right on the outer edges of the Academy hub, easily breached and with poor security. She might be cut off from Seolta, but here she was safe from all the others dogging her steps. After that interview with the patrol interrogator, she lumped the Alliance security forces in the same bog as her uncle's stooges. She trusted neither and had no desire to come under the control of any of them.

"This is delightful," she assured the dean and bowed him out with every assurance of meeting his students and inspecting her new lab as soon as she was rested and refreshed. "It was a long and tedious voyage. I am sure you will understand, Messer."

The man flushed. Clearly a break from his presence wasn't part of their agenda. "Certainly, Messera. I will return to escort you to your lab as soon as you are able. What time do you think will suit?"

"Thank you, Messer. You have been most courteous. I will com you." She tapped on the door control and bowed him out, leaving him no choice. For an instant before the door closed, the man let his genial mask slip and she had to smother a smile. The Academy was as full of predators as anywhere, and it paid to remember it.

She began to explore her new living quarters, scrutinising each square. She wished she had Seolta and his com with her. Its clever tricks would come in very handy at the moment. No, first priority, requisition a better standard of cleaning bot, she decided after the lurking dust under the aging fittings choked up her lungs and had her coughing madly.

'They are antique, not aging.' She could still hear the scolding of her old staff matron on the students' first visit to this venerable building, her voice heavily infused with a sense of offended awe.

They are old, decided Anyara, fingers feeling over the multiple scrapes and bumps time had brought to the antiques. She stopped at one scrawled line etched into the side of the shaky desk. Another thing for the serviceman to repair when he came. The list on her com was well over a few hours' patching work. Then she looked closer. She knew that name. Etric. She'd once had a trainee called that. She remembered him because he was in her first group, a bunch of suspicious, nervous conscripts who were all too aware they were there to further their family's position with her uncle rather than for any interest in biomes. It was just after her return from the Academy and she was only a year or two older than most, put in charge of them by her uncle.

She had to have a position and the Kevand station's biome was short of staff. Her uncle had named her as a consultant, but it was an empty title. 'The system needs some return from your skittering away your time on Central, and a niece of mine must have a decent position. Just don't interfere. The old techs know what they're doing.'

She'd accepted hastily before he'd changed his mind. Any chance to escape his daily scrutiny had seemed a lifeline to her at the time, and she had made a good home on the station, soon coming to an easy compromise with the elderly biome manager.

She and the trainees had butted heads a few times, but they'd eventually come to a kind of truce. She certainly remembered Etric. A solidly built boy, arms and legs too big for his body like an overgrown leggy plant, and with an attitude to match. He'd wanted to go into the security section, he'd told her once when she set him yet again to a penalty shift. Yet for all his sullenness, the plants under his care responded like magic. The boy could make any seedling thrive. She caught him once when he was alone, crooning softly to just emerged babies, tiny leaves barely poking above the dirt medium, and nearly cried in relief. Someone else who understood.

She hadn't interrupted him that day, but gently, cautiously, she had brought him into her own experiments. By the end of the first year, he'd become her recognised deputy. Even some of the old techs came to him for advice, and she saw the scowl on his face replaced by an astonished pride.

Then he had disappeared, along with all his family, and she had never heard of him again. It could be a coincidence, but she had long ago lost any belief in coincidence. Etric had been here, had lived in this room. One of her students was now an honoured member of the Academy.

Hope bloomed, and a determination to win free, just as Etric and his family must have done. She needed to be doing something, not hiding here in her tired old room. She activated her com before she could think twice and sent a message through to the dean. She was ready to see her lab and meet her students. Then she was going to get Seolta invited into this fortress sanctuary.

She needed his arms around her as she faced their enemies.

The dean arrived at her door so fast he must have been waiting in a nearby room.

"Are you ready to see your lab?" he asked, looking absurdly like a pet gripholon eager for a pat. After a week in the animals' company, she had no desire to spend more time with them.

"Yes, if you are free to show me," she managed to say politely.

The lab was every bit as excellent as expected. She walked around it, hands trailing over the shiny benches, the vats and seedling beds, exclaiming out loud when her fingers activated the controlling systems and discovered the huge range of variability available for programming.

"This is…" she slowly revolved, taking in the expanse of it, "it's stunning. This is all for me?"

"Does it meet your requirements?"

She smothered a snort. "Oh, yes, it will be quite adequate." With a lab like this, she could finally do the kind of work she'd dreamed of. "I will begin as soon as I meet the new students." She'd rather start right away. She had so many theories battering inside her head, experiments she had never been able to run, ideas clamouring for release. She then realised she'd forgotten one important factor. "And the budget, Messer Dean? What is my spending limit?"

"Oh, you don't have to worry about that, Messera. That is my problem."

She snatched her hand away from the shiny analyser she'd been caressing in delight. "A lab like this must have been funded by commercial interests. Who are they and what do they want of me?"

A real look of distress crossed his face. "Oh, no, Messera. Nothing like that. The Academy has sufficient funds to support your research. All we want you to do is continue the exciting work you began on your station."

"This is a blue sky lab? No strings, no set goals, just whatever I can come up with?"

His head nodded vigorously. "Exactly, Esteemed Scholar. With a talent like yours, the Academy long ago learned that it is best to give you free rein to explore as you will."

She had to sit down, falling into the nearest chair. "No one's waiting for me to deliver anything, no set parameters? You will warn me well before time if that changes and the finance boffins begin making noises. I can't guarantee any kind of result, not with that kind of uncertainty sitting over me."

"Would you rather we asked you to solve a set problem, Messera?" The man squinted at her, a hand rubbing at his neck.

"No, no. What you're offering is amazing." She was used to having to plot and manipulate her station master's staff for every single innovation she wanted, and always knew that the first complaint by a resident would mean the end of her attempt. There'd been plenty of those in her first years at the station, but she had since won popular approval and the station master had grudgingly given her more leeway to do as she wished.

What the dean offered here? Unimaginable—and unlikely, came the second thought. No one was ever given an unlimited budget or a lack of restraint.

Someone wanted her work, and wanted it very badly. She put on the charming smile she used to fool her uncle. It hadn't actually worked with him, but he'd allowed it to keep face. The dean fell for it completely.

"May I bring in your students now, Esteemed Scholar?" he said, eyes shining and hands clasped together over his portly belly as if clutching each other in relief.

She bowed her head and let out a breath as he walked out. She looked around the lab and felt the breath leave her again. The level of sophistication of the equipment was astounding. All this, built for her? Some serious credits had been laid out for this place. The kind of credits that could come only from the military or the Alliance Council.

A cold wave of goosebumps ran across her arms. She'd thought they would be safe here.

She began to review the lab's equipment and resources, needing desperately to bury her fears in action. A chattering surge of excitement broke through the dark thoughts and a crowd filled her lab.

"Messera Esteemed Scholar, your students," the dean said, beaming with delight and lifting his arms wide to take in the cluster surrounding him.

"I'll leave you to get acquainted," said the dean. "Until we meet again at dinner, Messera. It's not every day we welcome back an Esteemed Scholar. The faculty are very excited."

She quailed. Whatever anyone else in the Academy wanted of her, the dean was clearly thrilled to be able to grab the limelight for his department, and she loved her work too much to do anything to hurt another biomer. Tonight was going to be such fun! She sighed as he left, no doubt to spread word of the biome department's latest success. She turned to her students.

They were quite a collection, in both age and origin. If they were all mere students, she was a ship's pilot. They stared back as she assessed them. Some wary, some downright awed, and some with a look of calculation on their faces that was all too familiar.

"Let's take a seat and get to know each other," she said in as firm a voice as she could manage. "To start with, how about you introduce yourselves. Names, home worlds and general backgrounds," she added once they were all settled into their seats. Anything to break the uncomfortable silence. "I'll start first, shall I?"

A general titter ran through the group. "We know who you are," said one of the dewy-eyed younger ones.

"Yes. Who hasn't heard of Esteemed Scholar Anyara a Prithand2 of the Theory of Balanced Compatibilities," said the oldest in the group in a dry voice that came out as more an insult than anything else. "Your work is compulsory reading for any biomer wanting to secure his standing with the Academy."

Aah, one of those here for advancement. A sparkle lit her gut. "You don't agree with my assertions?" she responded. She hadn't been able to argue her findings for years.

"Not all," said the biomer.

"Then once we've made the introductions, you can tell me exactly what you think of my work. Who knows? You may be able to prove me wrong."

The man looked at her with astonishment. She grinned back and beckoned at him to start.

An hour later, she felt much better. The students came from all parts of the Alliance and all backgrounds. Some were experienced biomers wanting to step up, as she'd guessed. Some had hit a dead end in their current placements and some, to her shock, were greedy for the fame it appeared she'd gathered. She'd never been aware that anyone had heard of her outside of the higher academic world, but these were commercial biome managers—those dealing with the day-to-day pressures of keeping their home habitats safe.

Best of all, they argued about her work, criticised her, came up with alternatives, discussed possible ramifications. The kind of talk she'd dreamed of. After a while, they even relaxed enough to let her join in and make counter arguments.

A timer sounded and she looked up in shock. The afternoon was nearly gone and she had to dress for dinner soon or risk being late.

"Oh, dear. I have to go. Thank you, everyone, for an extraordinary afternoon. We can resume this tomorrow. I'll issue work assignments then. This has been a wonderful start."

"Until tomorrow, Esteemed Scholar," they all chorused as they left, still talking and arguing, even the youngest occasionally finding a voice.

She could do something with this group. She was sorry to see them go, she discovered. Another glance at the timer and she gasped again. She'd be late. Her place here wouldn't last long if she made that a habit. She hurried back to her room, wishing she had time to com Seolta.

No. Better to wait till after dinner and her first lab session. Make a place of strength then reach out. It had worked for her on her station. She had to hope it worked here. Not seeing him was not an option.

She just wished the Academy shared her viewpoint.

Seolta marched into the embassy with head held high. No point starting out a supplicant, though his fingers ached with emptiness and the memory of her last touch. He daren't risk any sign of weakness, not with a pair of Alliance Patrollers guarding his back and the fixed scrutiny of an Arcadian marshal watching him from the embassy hallway. In the middle, a stern-faced woman moved forward. "Ser den Coille," she said, "welcome to Alliance Central."

There wasn't much of a welcome in her face. She looked like she was being forced to receive an itinerant rakter into her fold.

"Marshal M'Senti, please escort the Ser to his quarters. Once he is settled, we will meet again in the second operations room."

Seolta plastered on his phoniest smile. "Thank you for your hospitality, Ambassador Dysun, I hope not to incommode you too long." They both knew he'd no choice in coming here and would be staying until the patrol agreed to another refuge. She gave him a tight-lipped grimace, then forced her lips into something resembling a folklar's threat face—the nearest she could manage to a smile, he guessed, when faced with a problem like him.

The woman must have been fully briefed by the marshals, but the secrecy surrounding his exile meant she had to treat him as he appeared, the travelling son of a wealthy and powerful family. No risk of his being excluded from the social life of the embassy, not if he asked publicly for it.

And gave her no warning.

As for meeting with an Esteemed Scholar of the Academy, she'd probably fall over backwards to go with him. The Academy had powerful tentacles in too many Alliance games to be ignored. What she thought about the identity of the Esteemed Scholar in question was another matter.

She did succeed in venting her opinion of him by her choice of the quarters he was assigned. His sleeper at home was bigger than this entire space. He forced on a genial smile to thank the steward beside him.

"Thank you, Sera, this will do very well."

The woman gave Seolta a bow that would have satisfied the most austere of Mountainer critics. "Two marshals will be stationed outside to ensure your safety, Ser. Marshal Zrah M'Senti here has been assigned to your protection and is your first contact for security matters." The marshal was an older man, with cool, flat eyes, grey hair and a no-nonsense air. Seolta suspected Marshal an Fallon had personally selected the man. "Please advise the chamberlain's office if there is anything else you require," added the steward.

A click of her heels and she marched out, leaving him free to explore his quarters. Not that it would take long. His luggage capsule had been unloaded into the wardrobe and the food prepper stocked with basics. He had to use his com to find out how the rest of the space worked. The sleeper packed away, revealing a table, a chair and a small lounger unfolding from the storage space underneath, and the wall display answered to basic inputs. He set it to a view of the forest from his sleep room at home, uncaring what any psych med attached to the embassy made of it.

It was too risky to send a com signal to Anyara, but after the last weeks he needed at least to see a tree. He left the artificial smell of the place intact to remind him of the reality of why he was here. One short scan of the room had been enough to show it was packed with sensors. He set his com to maximum privacy. There weren't too many with the skills to break his com's walls. Silas Winter maybe, and little Finn Beren when he was older, but neither had his particular mindset and he had to hope none here did either.

In an Arcadian embassy stacked with marshals and Galactic Ministry officials? The most devious pack of brakkas to be found on Arcadia. He took one more look around the room but saw nothing out of place. The sensors were well hidden, and there was nothing he could do about them. He shrugged and changed out of his shipboard travel gear into a suit more appropriate for a boardroom meeting then signalled the door to open. The delay before it responded told him it had been locked. He should be used to that by now, but it still grated.

Still ignited that small hidden ball of fear crouching deep in his gut.

The second operations room turned out to be as utilitarian as its name. Little to distract from the business at hand.

Him.

The ambassador, Marshal M'Senti and a phalanx of blandly dressed officials sat around a table. He took the only seat remaining, the one opposite all the stern faces at the other end.

"Ser den Coille." The ambassador gave a perfunctory head bow. "We had expected your arrival some time ago. You took some interesting side trips on your way here."

"I had business to attend to," he said, giving them a face filled with as much self-assurance as he could dredge up. Thankfully he was a good actor.

"On Surned?" said the marshal.

Seolta shrugged.

The ambassador's mouth tightened another turn. At this rate, she'd freeze her face into a permanent frown. "You were specifically warned against going to the home world of Hilmar a Kevand3."

"A warning is not an order. You shifted me off Arcadia to stop me causing trouble there. Now, I have to find a way to build a life off-planet."

"Not one that brings more risk to Arcadia. As you are surely aware now, Hilmar is the real head of the Surned system, and a number of powerful Alliance enterprises have significant stakes in the raw materials his system produces."

"I was always aware of it, though it's news to me that anyone on Arcadia is."

The ambassador hmphed. "They will be, after your antics. We're already receiving strongly worded protests about Arcadian interference in the operations of another world."

Seolta raised a brow. "How so? I have no official position, nor do my family."

"After their actions last cycle, your sister and brother-in-law do."

Seolta scowled. "That's all on Fioruisghe. I agree that since the revolt, our family's story has become vidcast fodder. Brothers abducting their sister makes great headlines. It doesn't mean what I do is official Arcadian policy."

"Don't be naïve, Ser den Coille. Your company's Festin is a valuable export from the planet, and you had a significant role in making that happen. When you interfere in the affairs of another planet, it gets noticed—and Arcadia gets blamed."

"My father started the export branch. I merely built on his work."

The ambassador's mouth twitched. "You undersell yourself, young man. The potential scandal wasn't the only reason your case was kept quiet. Our government had hoped you'd seen the error of your ways and would use your abilities to further our world's position."

That was one way of looking at it, he supposed.

"Instead," continued the ambassador, "you have created a major interplanetary incident. Kidnapping a planetary chief's only family member? What were you thinking?"

"The Academy is pleased to see the Messera, and it was not kidnapping, as you are well aware." Which of the faceless minions around her was really pulling the strings. "I *rescued* the Esteemed Scholar. Her uncle had put out multiple assassination contracts on her."

"You know that, how?" asked the marshal.

"I was one of those contracted."

The marshal would know it already, but the ambassador didn't, from the way her eyes widened. She glanced sideways at an older man seated to her left. A Galactic Ministry agent, he'd bet. The folklar in charge of this web.

"It seemed an unnecessary loss of a fine biome manager," he added.

"Nevertheless, it has put Arcadia in a difficult position with Alliance Central. We hadn't expected you to arrive with so much notoriety attached," said the ambassador, clearly trying to regain control of the discussion. He could have told her not to bother. He looked directly at the grey-haired man, fed up with subterfuge.

"A number of parties are currently out for my blood. Follow them and you'll find those working against us. I'm being targeted by Alliance troops. Why would they do that to the citizen of a cooperating and valued planet?"

"You're suggesting, den Coille…?" said the grey-haired man.

"All I'm trying to point out is that the situation isn't as simple as it appears."

"An Alliance Deputy is involved. Of course it's not."

It was the first time she'd been mentioned, and Seolta wasn't surprised. The woman had always felt more sinister than Hilmar, and her involvement raised too many questions. "Do you know where she is?" All his searches had brought up a dead blank. It was as if the woman had disappeared into the darkness of space.

"The Interplanetary Bureau are saying nothing and refused to respond to our queries."

He wasn't surprised. Her involvement was as sensitive as all roots. The Bureau was probably as on edge about what it meant as the Arcadians. He had set a watching bot on the boards to notify him of any mention of her, but he didn't expect any. Truth to tell, the woman had always scared him silly, and he wasn't looking forward to any confrontation. But she did owe him.

"Did you want us to make further enquiries?"

"I thought to leave it with the Ministry's officials. They are more experienced in dealing with the Bureau. I doubt they are any more happy with the implications than we are, not officially." It was the one positive he'd found in the whole thing. Malgrave had overstepped and embarrassed her bosses. Whether they were involved was another matter—some must have been—but they'd be very careful to keep their hands clean for the near future, and that was all Arcadia needed at the moment.

"It's a relief to hear you admit to some limitations," said the man from the Ministry.

Seolta gave him his smoothest smile back. "In diplomatic matters." The man's twitch was the first particle of enjoyment he'd found in this meeting. "On the business side, though, you need me."

The man studied him, his face inscrutable again. "You're offering yourself as bait?"

Seolta shrugged. "I'm bait anyway. It seems a waste not to use it."

"How?"

"Nothing more than what I planned to do in the first place. Seek out contacts and make business connections in Central, exactly as expected from a wealthy prospector looking for interesting propositions."

He kept his voice even and relaxed in tone and hoped they couldn't hear his heart hammering. They'd trapped him, his choices either a prison cell or freedom, isolation or Anyara.

"It matches the plan from head office," said Marshal M'Senti, "and the Ser is a skilled operative in the social sphere."

Why that sounded like an insult, Seolta wasn't sure. He only knew the words left him feeling soiled. "As you say, Marshal."

The ambassador still had that annoyed look on her face. "If anything happens to Ser den Coille, the Galactic Ministry will be held responsible."

"I'm planning to attend social functions, not take part in the Games," said Seolta, adding a cut-off chortle for good measure. The Central Games, the triennial competition between the best of the Alliance planets' militaries and anyone foolish enough to challenge them, were notorious for their injury rate. They would be starting soon and competitors already jammed the local training sites.

"You won't have to. Not with all the supporters filling the town," said M'Senti dryly. "The timing is ideal. The Games bring out all the carrion eager to exploit the simple and overexcited. An ideal cover for an attempt to lure Ser den Coille deeper into a conspiracy against us."

The ambassador still looked unhappy, opening her mouth then closing it again, clearly unable to counter the marshal's argument. A big part of Seolta wished she'd find a way.

"It's settled then," he said. "You arrange a discreet guard for me, and I'll scope out the most likely prospects. Ambassador, I'll need your social organiser's assistance. Someone with a finger on the pulse of the current movers in City Central. Not the obvious ones. I need the influencers and the puppet masters behind the scenes."

"I'll have her call on you as soon as she is available."

"Within the half hour," he said firmly. If he had to do this, he wanted to start as soon as possible, before his nerves gave out. He was discovering a new respect for his annoying baby sister. Fioruisghe had lived with this level of subterfuge for years and had the courage to stand up to the entire Arcadian government. He wished he were as brave. "In the meantime, I assume it is safe for me to take a walk in the Embassy gardens. It's a long time since I was able to walk among living plants and, for a Mountainer, that is not good."

"Yes, of course," said the ambassador, her smug look restored. Always leave an opponent feeling as if they've won, his father had told him. Revealing an apparent weakness was the best way to hide the underlying threat.

Or that's what he told himself. Right now, he really did need to walk in a place with real plants and the smell of mulch and wet soil, needed the touch of living things to push back the terror.

And outside these walls, he could try comming Anyara.

CHAPTER TWENTY-ONE

Like most planetary embassies, the Arcadian embassy sat in the main dome of Central city, close to the business district and safe from any environmental incursions. Alliance Central might be classed as a habitable planet, but that was being kind. The undomed areas were cheap to live in for a reason. Subject to sudden windstorms severe enough to cut communications and other interesting local effects, they were inhabited only by those who had to live there. As Seolta walked into the embassy's garden, he wished for a moment the embassy was built there too. The dome above was set today to a shining blue with gentle wisps of clouds chasing over the sky, and he wondered what they'd say if he asked them to change it to dark grey clouds and the lash of storm-driven rain. The squalls of his home region had never seemed so precious.

He strode away from the house, ignoring the guard hovering at his heel. Each footfall fell on the dead pad of plascrete pathways bound either side by groomed shrubberies protecting central wells of nodding flowers—a controlled and carefully artistic display of Arcadia's finest varieties. It was pretty enough, he supposed.

Was this what Anyara preferred?

He took in the surprisingly large area taken up by the embassy's private grounds.

"How did we manage to secure such a plot size?" he asked the guard.

The man wasn't happy at being acknowledged, his eyes continually raking the far margins of the embassy's land. "That's not in my brief, Ser."

He'd have to ask the social organiser, but it appeared that Arcadia was a more highly valued planet than he'd realised. The scarcity of EA worlds didn't figure much in Arcadian thought.

We've taken our world for granted for too long.

"Where is the less formal part of the gardens?" he asked the guard.

A twitch of the man's cheek, but he pointed down a small path to their left. "On the border of the protected zone."

Seolta ignored the man, relieved to feel the crunch of fine gravel under his feet. Not dirt or mud, but still a surface that moved under him. He walked faster, eager to find something wilder. Ahead lay a hedge broken by an archway. He brushed through it, welcoming the scent of bruised leaves, and entered a small shrubbery. Not real trees, but they still reached over his head. He saw a tell-tale patch of green that looked like the connich found growing on many mountain trees, and he angled off the path, pushing his way through the undergrowth in the careful way automatic to him from a childhood in forests, and finally felt his boot sink into real dirt, spongy with damp.

"Ser den Coille!" he heard the guard call urgently.

He signalled the man. "You have my com readings and I'm still in the embassy grounds. I'm perfectly safe."

Behind him came the sound of twigs snapping. He sighed and turned back to where the guard was bumbling through the bushes.

He stepped out from his leafy cover and stopped the man's destruction of the bush with a hard shove against his chest.

The guard's weapon slapped up.

"It's me. Stand down before you wreck the whole grove," he snapped. The man was supposed to be protecting him, not killing him.

"Do not leave my sight again, Ser den Coille," the guard said, his voice as hard as Seolta's.

Seolta breathed in once, twice, filling his lungs with the familiar scent of mud and leaf, then nodded agreement as he turned back to the gravel walkway. "Is this path acceptable?"

The man's eyes glinted, but he lowered his weapon. "As long as I have full visuals at all times."

"You mean stay in sight? There's nothing wrong with using plain Standard." Maybe he shouldn't needle the man, but he'd been in the nearest to woodland he'd found since leaving home, and the grief of that nearly choked him up.

The man merely lifted that weapon again and gestured for Seolta to walk in front of him.

"Can I at least com someone?"

"Yes."

"Will it be monitored?"

The weapon waved him forward. A stupid question, and if he tried to avoid their surveillance, a locked room waited him quick smart. But there was nothing wrong with checking on the welfare of an acquaintance. He sent out the signal.

Her face formed in front of him and he ground to a halt. For a moment, joy sparked in her brilliant eyes and the wonder of that made him blind to everything else.

The guard's footsteps scraped on the gravel, and her eyes turned wary.

"Messer den Coille. How nice to hear from you. Where are you? It looks like a garden."

He had to grin at her sudden understanding. "In the embassy grounds." No reason to hide that. Anyone eavesdropping would surely know to where he'd been delivered. "And you? I hope they're treating you as they should."

He held his breath. Could she tell how important her answer was to him?

A slight lift of her lips and her eyes softened. "I am being more than adequately cared for. You have no cause for concern," she said. She lifted her hand, stretched out towards him and he lifted his to meet it. Their fingers touched, the phantasm of hers in the holo-field sim touching the physical reality of his. He couldn't feel her, couldn't smell that unique fragrance of hers, but it was a promise, a renewal of hope.

"I hope you can spare time soon for a visit," she said.

"As do I," he said. He had to sign off. Already, spies would be tracking them down. Maybe the finger touch had been stupid, revealing too much, but he'd needed it as badly as she had. "I'll come to you as soon as my business here is sorted," he said. "I'm sure you must be busy with your work too."

Could she read the warning in his eyes. Don't try to find me. Don't put yourself at risk.

"Yes, very busy," she agreed, leaning forward with eyes wide open. "I hope we'll both find time soon."

"I have to go." He touched his hand to his lips, reached for hers. "Till we meet again." He switched off the holo-image. Then put out a hand to where her face had been.

Goodbye for now, mo Graidh.

Then he had to return to the house and to business. The social organiser was waiting for him as requested.

No, as you demanded.

Which meant they needed his help as badly as he needed theirs. Or he hoped they did, very conscious of his weak position.

Not that he let the woman in front of him know. Dressed in what must be the latest fashion in this city, she had her com open and ready for input. She'd done this before.

"Seolta mar Bram an Scathach den Coille," he said, giving her a semi-formal head bow.

"Sera Jinke Wago, Ser den Coille," she said with a curt head bob. Not from the mountains then. Her speech said she'd grown up in the middle levels of Urbis. That was when he realised how long it had been since he'd heard familiar accents, and he plastered on his most defensive smile. The one his brother said made him look like a rakter about to bite. Cumchdach had little tolerance for Seolta's tricks. Seolta wound back the smile to one he hoped said, 'I like you and want to get to know you better'

She gave him an equally congenial and false smile back. He had to laugh. "Let's get to work, shall we?"

Sera Wago turned out to be as professional as promised, and they soon had a planned schedule and campaign. At the end, he leaned back, well satisfied with the morning's work. First item on their joint agenda, a trawl through the local fashion sites to update his socialising outfits for maximum effectiveness among the Central elite he needed to use. No, to *connect* with. Thinking of it as using them would affect his approach. Far better they didn't see him coming.

"A most satisfying session, Sera Wago."

She closed off her com with a flourish of her hand. "Always pleasant to work with a man who understands matters." She stretched, arching her back as if to ease a kink, and let one hand trail through her hair. Her eyes looked straight at him as her hand wandered down her neck line. "Would you like to break for lunch then continue afterwards?"

An innocuous enough invitation, and she was a beautiful woman with warm, dusky skin, artfully swelling curves and a skilfully made up face. An experienced woman who would make a pleasant companion for a shared afternoon, but he had no interest. Nor did he have to wonder why.

"Sadly, I have other appointments today." He stood, keeping his hands firmly by his sides and gave her his semi-formal bow. "I look forward to sharing your company at our first scheduled event. Please contact my com if I need to know anything in the meantime."

She leaned back with a chuckle. "No harm in trying, Ser den Coille. You're a very attractive man."

He was startled into laughter. "Thank you, Sera. Working with you is a pleasure."

"But only work. I understand." She stood as well and stretched out her hand. "Until our first event. You are going to succeed brilliantly."

"That's the plan, Sera."

"And Ser den Coille…"

"Yes?" They had covered everything and she had accepted his refusal. What was left?

"She is a lucky woman."

Then she walked out, leaving him struck dumb. He wasn't usually so transparent. And the Sera was wrong. Anyara a Prithand2 didn't need the likes of him in her life, but he had no intention of letting that stop him. Yet he should.

Anyara settled quickly into the life of the Academy. It wasn't hard, or shouldn't have been. Her lab gave her resources she'd dreamed of having, her students met her every challenge with excitement and a unique blending of ideas, and nobody within the Academy was plotting to kill her as far as she could work out. Not that she left its safety, the guards dogging her steps a constant reminder of the dangers lurking outside the walls.

After his brief call, she didn't try to contact Seolta. His warning had been clear. Under her contented façade, though, lurked a prodding thorn. Was this to be her life, locked in an academic citadel communicating only through her ideas and published works? No human touch, no family of her own?

No Seolta?

They'd had a bare smattering of intimacy. In the dark spaces of her lonely nights, she began to wonder. Had that been all he'd wanted ? A momentary pull of attraction, easily sated? He'd delivered her here as required and could now carry on with his life with a clear conscience.

No, those days and nights had been real. He was still the man who had locked himself in an animal's cage for days to get her safely off station.

He owed you.

She tried shutting her ears, but still the doubts nagged at her. She was so alone here, despite the dean's protective hovering and her students' eager enthusiasm.

So what was different? She'd always been alone on her station, and it hadn't stopped her making a good life for herself. Her life might still have limits, but it was up to her what she did with them. She stabbed at the files in her com and set to work.

She was in her lab, selecting plant types by pulling up genomic sequences on her com. Behind her, a sudden spurt of giggles broke the silence. That could be only one girl. She glanced back, half her attention still on the com files.

Yes, she was right. It was the youngest, the prettiest, and to all appearances, the silliest of her students. Larena came from a wealthy world, one that had been making a sizable donation to the Academy for many years. Most thought that was why she'd been picked for Anyara's team but beneath the giggles and the astonishingly frequent changes in hairstyle lurked a canny brain. Not that Anyara managed to get the girl to drop her cover often, but she was ever hopeful.

Today, Larena was the glittering jewel at the centre of the leading crowd, as usual. The kind of group Anyara had never managed to make her way into.

Well, now you're the boss and you have to build a team here. She leaned over to see what held their attention.

Of course Larena had the latest in holo viewers, the kind with full sensory functions. An array of gorgeous people in ever more gorgeous clothes filled the field. A parade of some kind, blocking a street that must be right in the heart of the city by the looks of the stately, archaic buildings around it. As she approached, she could smell and feel as well as hear the crowd. Rich scents, a riot of singing and shouting voices, laughter and cheers.

"Look at that one in the middle," said one of the gaggle of young women. Anyara followed her pointing finger, curious at what had caught their attention among all those colours and sounds. Her mouth dropped.

It was Seolta. He marched in the centre of the crowd, laughing with the others, and dressed in what even she recognised as the latest of local fashion.

"He's new," said Menta, a girl who tried to copy Larena but always failed. Anyara could have told her not to bother. It took a special kind of self-belief to pull off Larena's charisma.

"I could eat him up," said Larena, zooming in closer. "He's delicious."

Anyara had to agree, drinking in the sight of him. And, unlike the silly young girls, she knew what lay under those expensive clothes.

"Who is he?" demanded another.

Larena did something with her com, then Anyara was shocked to see Seolta's biography. All the facts, all his family, all true and accurate. It ended with a doctored version of his leaving his home world, to 'explore and prospect for investment opportunities'. The kind of specious blather spread by a commercial publicist, one with the subject's full cooperation.

Did he want them to be found and killed? Then something about him made her look closer.

His eyes. She'd seen that dark haze before in workers in her uncle's factories, barely glimpsed on a rare excursion into the lower levels as he toured there. He'd had her accompany him that day. As a threat, she suspected. Behave or this is where you will end up. The despair in their bodies had shocked her.

Seolta was smiling manically, no despair in his face, but his eyes had that same blanked look. He was using. What, she couldn't say, but something had him in its thrall and she had no way of contacting him. She'd tried but her calls were blocked.

Anyara stepped forward, concreting a smile onto her face. "That looks a fun party. What's the occasion?"

A bright flush from Menta but Larena covered it with an artificial giggle. "Messera Esteemed Scholar, we didn't see you there. It's the triennial pre-Games street party. The biggest event on this year's calendar. All the celebs join in."

"All the biggest vidcaster stars take part," said Menta, recovering from her fright. "It's invitation only."

"You'll have to excuse my ignorance. The price of spending too many hours in labs. Are these all stars?" She lifted a hand at the holo-image.

"Nah," said Larena. "That's real money walking there. That one," she touched a braying, slick-haired man at the outside of the crowd, "he's a Meth Varkan."

Even Anyara knew that name. "The banking family?"

Larena nodded vigorously. "He may not be much to look at, but he's rumoured to be an inter-Alliance investing master. He's said to smell a potential prospect light years away. The woman in the front, she's the secret weapon of the Fongma consortium. A chemical genius."

Another name she knew. The consortium was a major buyer of Surned's minerals.

"And the one in the middle, the one walking next to the tall woman?" she asked in what she hoped sounded a casual tone.

A giggle from Larena. "Cute, isn't he. A newbie. He arrived in the city not long ago, my brother tells me. The woman beside him is his publicity manager. Must be a good one to get him into that crowd. Mind you, he needs credits to back it up. Not that it's a problem. According to my brother, the man is throwing them around.

Larena came from a major trading family. One that had a finger on all the business strands of the day.

"Who is he?" Anyara said.

"Messera Esteemed Scholar! Don't tell me you're interested too."

Anyara tried out a giggle. It sounded as fake as Menta's attempts. "He is very cute."

Menta pulled forward his bio again. "Seolta mar Bram an Scathach den Coille." It sounded nothing like Seolta had said it, had none of his music. "His family's in food ingredients."

"What a mouthful of a name," Anyara said. "Can you bring up where he's from?"

Menta pulled up the details, screwing up her nose at the strange name of his city of origin. The bio at least blocked his planet of origin, giving just his regional address.

"Rumour has him from an EA planet," said Larena. "That's what my brother claims, anyway, but he does like to sound like he knows it all. No one would leave an EA planet to look for investments elsewhere. Especially not if you're already rich."

"No," agreed Anyara, lost in the changing images and floored by that address. It was true, all of it, right down to each, damning detail. Did Seolta think his powerful friends would protect him or that her uncle's agents would forget what he did?

It even showed his current locality.

Was he trying to get himself killed?

Seolta woke yet again with a blinding headache and a growl of frustration. He'd given out enough hints and made himself more than available. When was someone going to make an open move? He dimmed the light from the window, squinting, and brought up his schedule.

Then reached for the glass of water he'd taken to leaving on his bedside table, the one he'd filled himself. All he'd won from his nights of over-rich food and excess drink was a permanently scorched throat and a blazing thirst. The way he was going, he had to find a contact soon or die trying.

She wouldn't like that.

Today, Anyara's face was hidden by hazy veils. He dragged himself out of the sleeper to prepare again for a day of fun, or the nearest to looking like it that he could manage. His chances of succeeding dimmed with each day.

Later, bright sunshine hit him square in the face as he lined up for a race with all the other rich young fools trying their hand at the nearest amateurs were allowed to the death-defying contests of the Games finalists. He'd checked out his flyer and had the embassy staff run a security scan on it as well.

"Are you sure about this?" said Marshal M'Senti. As per Games regulations, Seolta had his com but no armour or personal shield. The organisers had no stipulations about com extras, thankfully. He blinked, swallowed a drink from his water bottle, and manufactured a cocky grin for Zrah M'senti. From the marshal's face it wasn't his best attempt.

"I'll be fine. I grew up flying the Western Ranges. Central is a breeze after that."

The marshal looked dubious. "Just be careful."

An alarm sounded. 'All flyers take position', came the order over his com. He clapped Zrah on the shoulder, said "Get the drinks ready for me," and climbed into the flyer. How had he got himself into this?

You wanted to make yourself a target. Looks like you've succeeded brilliantly.

Maybe, but right now, he wished he had his brother Ceart's genius for reading air currents. He'd spent the previous evening devouring anything he could find about Central's air patterns and hazards. He had to hope it was enough.

The racers took off like a swarm of excited critchets. The flyer hatch in the outer dome wasn't as wide as he would have liked with this conglomeration of experienced flyers and novices eager to show off what skills they'd managed to acquire. Most of the novices headed straight for the opening, crowding together in a mad scramble for the exit. He held back a bit, as did the other more experienced flyers, and waited for the crush to even out. Only two novices scraped the sides, and three others were forced to pull up before they crashed. He doubted they would have given way but for the automatic overrides on their flyers from the race controllers. No one wanted a tragedy played out so close to the spectators.

Farther out on the course would be a different matter. He wondered again why he was here. In the past, he'd been able to extricate himself from such idiocies with ease. He shook his head, trying to battle the fuzz of the previous night. All he could remember was that his entry into the race had been accepted before he was barely aware of taking up the challenge.

A challenge. From whom?

No time to wonder now. He was through the hatch and into the open. That was when he discovered that charts and recordings of weather patterns were a poor replacement for the real thing. His flyer was hit by a sudden surge of air and he swore madly as he battled for control.

He pulled up the local terrain map. Below lay a wild tangle of sharp-edged spurs and sudden canyons. The whole region had once looked like this, and the only attraction Seolta could see for the first settlers was the continuous supply of water from the massive underground reserves lying under the tortured landscape.

It's not much different from your own mountain ridges, he told himself, and you've flown the northern ranges plenty of times. That's even worse.

Except that the airs over his home world's mountains weren't laced with caustic dust squalls and his body knew the gravity of his own planet better than this one. Central wasn't much larger than

Arcadia but that difference, combined with the different composition, was enough to throw off his judgement. He didn't usually have to rely consciously on his ship's systems, but now he listened intently to both ship and winds.

A proximity warning blared, and he barely avoided an incoming flyer swooping up from under and attempting to block him from rounding the first mark. It was the first of many challenges. The planet wasn't his only enemy in this race. You had to make it home intact to win. The vicious assaults should have scared him silly. Instead, his heart beat faster and a wild grin settled on his face.

Bring it on, brakkas. I'll show you what a Mountainer can do.

He might have succeeded too, if the other flyers had stuck to the race rules. A vain hope, of course, and he should have been ready for it, but that annoying fuzziness in his head worsened as the race progressed. A flyer swooped over him, then dipped suddenly. He just pulled himself out of the collision in time but too slowly. He shook his head again.

"System, full evasion level." His own responses were too sluggish. Another flyer challenged, he twisted away again, but they were all arrowing in on the next mark. The only approach was a narrow defile in the mountains, and his systems warned of a muddy swirl of currents in the approach.

He could miss the mark and forfeit the win, but he would finish. Or he could go for it full throttle and hope for the best.

He linked into his ship and thrust it to maximum. All around him, more cautious pilots took the slower but safe route over the top of the peaks, giving up the win, but a few followed Seolta's lead into the gorge. They began to catch up, but he was still in front, still free of interference.

Then his controls went dead. His ship began to plummet. An instant only in physical time felt like a lifetime of terror. He fought the fog clogging his head and called on all his com's tricks to bring his ship back online. The zigzagging spikes of the gorge's base waited hungrily.

Just in time, his com answered his alarm and the flyer lifted, right into the path of the other flyers crowding into the narrow opening. He tried to pull out, tried to avoid them.

Too late. The shielding of a black-striped flyer caught his outer wing edge and sent him spiralling through the defile and up, up into the open air in an uncontrolled whirlpool of horror. He reached the upper atmosphere, more alarms screaming, then began to fall back down. Below lay the greedy crags and gorge bottom. He fought for control.

Suddenly, he felt a dragging lift and his flyer began to even out. The race officials had followed them. He pulled up the schematics, and saw with relief the large shape of a ship hovering overhead.

Having a visiting trader crash and burn in an amateur race was not good politics, apparently. He'd never been so grateful for his family's wealth. Then he slumped against the console and knew no more.

He came to in a place with which he was becoming all too familiar. A sleeper in a medic ward. A face loomed over him and for an instant he felt the sharp dregs of disappointment. It was his social organiser, not Anyara.

No, she was safely locked away in the Academy. His mother used to tell them old fairy stories, and Samhchair's favourite told of a princess trapped in a tall tower. At the time, he used to groan out loud but now he understood. The uncomplaining rock of their family, Samhchair had always known her future.

Now, it was his Anyara locked away. Of course she wasn't here. She knew nothing of this latest fit of his, and that's how it must stay.

Jinke Wago's face had lost all resemblance to the woman who had tried to seduce him. Jaw tight, lips pinched, she stood over him with arms crossed. "Are you insane? Kephartin? What, by all the seas, induced you to use that filth?"

So that's what it was. He hadn't known a name to put to the fuzziness in his head, but nothing he'd tried had stopped it getting worse.

"If this gets out…" she said, voice snarling. "Don't you know it's banned on most worlds?"

Another face came into view. "How long?" said Zrah, and the cool grey eyes had none of the contempt of his social organiser. The narrowing said he was angry too, but not at him, Seolta thought.

"Not long after I arrived. The effects have been growing worse."

Jinke had begun to pace. "You could have been killed out there. What will I tell your family?"

"Perhaps you should draft a press release," suggested the marshal. "I will stay with the Ser."

"Can you stop him doing anything else outrageous until I get back?" Outrageous was Anyara's word for his more outlandish ideas. It sounded better from her.

"If needed, I will have the Ser strapped to the sleeper," said Zrah with a tilt of his lips

"Good idea." She flounced out, muttering phrases Seolta had no desire to hear.

Zrah took a seat beside his sleeper. "Any idea who's been feeding it to you?"

Seolta went to shake his head but stopped as the pounding ratcheted up to unbearable. "I've been eating outside the embassy when I can, and I ran a scanner over all the potential sources in my room. It has to be an insider, but whoever it is, they're good." He shut his eyes till the room stopped swirling then opened them again. "Did you see which craft clipped me?"

"Meth Varkan, but he pulled away immediately and looked genuinely upset. What caused your sudden drop? You were all but through that gap and clear to go. The winds get you?"

"Please," said Seolta, making a pained joke of it. "I'm a Mountainer. No, my flyer lost power. Have you checked it out?"

The man nodded. "Nothing. The log reads normal. No record of any power drop."

"It did happen. I'm not that lost to the stuff yet." Seolta struggled against the sleeper restraints, trying to sit up.

The marshal put a hand on his shoulder. "Easy, Ser. I believe you. Whoever it was, as you said, is good."

Seolta breathed in. He had to trust someone, and the marshals had saved his life once before. "We're up against it this time."

"Looks like it. Only the military have access to power blocks like that—or those few with the level of credits required."

The marshal gave a squeeze of his shoulder. "The next daily cycle will be bad. The medics can help, but there's a limit, and it will make recovery longer."

Seolta swallowed. "We can't afford that." If only he could.

The grey eyes softened, but the man nodded. "I'll stay."

Seolta shook his head. "You need to find out who was behind this. Starting with a full scouring of my room and anything I had with me."

The man looked about to refuse.

Seolta forced out a grimace. "I'd rather no one from back home saw me go through this. No one I have to meet later."

"You can't do it on your own."

He needed Anyara, but the thought of her seeing what he was about to be reduced to was unthinkable. "The medic staff are here.

As long as you make sure they do nothing to shorten the recovery time, they can do anything else needed."

The older man stared him down, regarding him critically. "You were sent into exile for political reasons, not to seek punishment."

Seolta's mouth dropped open. Then he pulled it shut again and tried a weak smile. "You did hear what I did?"

"I have the full file," the marshal said. "You still don't get to invent a bigger sentence."

Seolta gave a slight shrug. "We have to find out who's behind this. Lingering in hospital for longer than needed to recover from the incident will raise too many questions."

The marshal took a step back, a click of his heels, and he stood at full parade alert. Then he gave Seolta a military salute. "I will be back as soon as you are fit again, Ser den Coille, and the medics will be instructed as per your orders. I will see you soon."

A full head bow and the man marched out. The door whooshed closed and Seolta was alone. He wished, very badly, he could call the man back.

The next hours were as gruesome as he'd expected. The fuzziness grew worse. At one point he heard someone raving wildly, calling out for help, for a drink, for anyone to save him.

He heard a voice calling her name and realised it was his. He clamped his lips shut. Her name mustn't be soiled by this nightmare. He clung to his vow through all the long dark hours of torment. He would *not* call her name again.

There were other voices, but they barely intruded. At one point, a wave of peace stole over him. They were using a pain-smothering beam.

"Stop," he croaked out before his courage failed. "Finish this quick."

The pain came back, but not quite as bad. "This level of intervention won't change the timescale, Messer," said a cool voice. A voice of reason, a lifeline to cling to. He recognised the tone, the one medics used with stupid patients.

He wished he didn't care.

"Must finish quickly," he whispered.

"Yes, Messer, your instructions are on your file. We will make only interventions necessary to preserve your life."

The drop in pain left him hypersensitised to his surroundings. The hum of the ventilation. The tap of her shoes on the floor. The faint edge in her voice. The woman thought he'd chosen to take the drug. She would not let him die, but she would let him suffer. His instructions gave her that right.

It should not terrify him.

Then the cramping began. All his muscles firing against him as spasm after spasm of agony hit home. Legs, stomach, arms, back, neck, even the small muscles on his crown played sticks and stones with him, tapping and writhing madly. He clamped down hard on his jaw. Do not call out, do not call out.

His body won, and screams echoed through the room. Wordless, harrowing, racking bouts of tortuous horror. Not *her* name. It was all he could manage. Then blessed dark, and nothingness.

The respite was short as the pain broke through the medics' armoury.

Something cold touched his arm. He shook it off. "It's only an energy and fluid infusion, Messer," said the cool voice. He stopped fighting so much because he was no longer able.

Then it began again.

Her name, her name, her face. Please let the screams be inside his head.

Whose name?

CHAPTER TWENTY-TWO

Anyara felt as if a chaotic whirl of craziness had taken over Central in the lead-up to the Games. The hospitals might be full, but that didn't stop the elite of Central society. Periodically, the Alliance Guard stepped in when an important personage looked like doing serious damage to themselves, and by implication all those depending on them. Anyara could only wish Seolta was counted among this top tier, but the Guard seemed quite content to let him run wild. Better him than anyone important, she could hear an officer say.

She tried to avoid the vidcasts, but her students were avid followers of the spectacle, and the brazen exploits of the 'handsome newcomer to the social swirl' was centre front of the madness. Nor was she exempt from the heart-jolting drama of the Games Flight, the so-called crowning glory for amateurs of all the fevered excitement. It was the talk of the Academy, and too many insisted she watch it with them. She put them off by telling them her students had already claimed her for their viewing on a holo-screen set up in her lab. Unfortunately, her students really had organised a screening party and expected her to join them. She'd run out of reasons to refuse.

She entered the room and her heart sank. Bright banners lined the walls, and they'd set the holo-field to enhanced VR mode. The one that made the room part of the horde of onlookers lining the route in any kind of ship imaginable, avidly watching their favourites at close quarters and with enhanced sound effects as if the whole thing weren't taking place high in the Central atmosphere.

She could see, hear, know immediately everything that happened. Watch as his flyer set off with all the other hotheads, jostled for place and shot to the front.

Don't try to win, she stupidly willed him, knowing it for a false hope.

In front was safest in that crowd, but it made him a target. She watched as he made a straight run at a bare slit in a mountain wall, as he slowed and dropped, released her clenched fists as he recovered.

Then he clipped another flyer.

"What's he doing?" called a voice near her. Not her own. Not when she could barely breathe let alone cry out. She watched helplessly as his flyer tumbled over and over, closer and closer to the sharp-edged rocks reaching up for him.

She shut her eyes and slumped to the floor.

An arm reached around her. She tried to wrench away.

"It's all right, Messera. The stewards have got him. They don't allow deaths on this race. Not with the amateurs."

It was Larena, for once dropping the giggles.

"Are you sure?"

"Yes, Messera. He is safe."

Anyara dared to open her eyes. The view had changed. She searched in vain for the black stripes of his flyer.

Larena touched her com. "I'll take it back to the pickup point." A zooming, then stop, and she saw to her relief the large bulb-shaped ship hovering above the racecourse, then his black-striped ship, tumbling over and over till suddenly, it stopped.

"They caught it in a field and pulled him up," she said, as if unable to believe it.

"Yes, of course. That's what they're there for."

"Their hangar is usually full by the end of the race," said another. "The authorities can't risk the backlash if they let anything happen to the racers. It makes it looks serious instead of fun."

And it might make people realise how stupid this race was, thought Anyara furiously. She stared at his flyer being lifted up. Intact. Not smashed into pieces on the rocks.

"Turn it off," she snapped. "We have work to do." She scrambled up, legs shaky and raced towards her office, slammed the door pad and locked it then sat behind her desk and fought for control.

He was alive.

He wasn't her concern. She pulled up her latest projects and tried to bury herself in them. When she upended a vat of microbes she'd been carefully nurturing since arrival, she yanked her hands out of the control field and smacked them back down on the desk surface where they wouldn't do any harm.

She shoved back her chair. When that wasn't enough, she marched out of her room. They had the holo going again. She glared at it.

"I'll be in the gardens if anyone wants me."

Then ran from the room.

Not even pacing up pathways and across the calming scents of herbaceous lawns helped. She held out as long as possible. "Search function: Messer Seolta den Coille. Games Race contestant."

Her com answered immediately, as if waiting for her to ask the question.

'Medic ward on Guards Transport X756 en route to Central Hospital annex zone 45-D.' They were taking him to the nearest medic facility. That's what medics did when there was an emergency.

Or when there was a notified race and the medic system had put in place procedures for expected casualties.

She was in no mood for reassuring platitudes, even when they came from her own brain. Seolta den Coille might have blocked her communications and made it clear their association was over, but she had not agreed. She hurried to her room, changed into inconspicuous streetwear and set out for the hospital.

She got no farther than the Academy gatehouse.

"I'm sorry, Messera. Given the festivities in the city at present, it's not safe for Academy staff to wander unattended in the streets. Please wait for a suitable escort."

"When will one be available?" she forced herself to ask politely.

The gate system took a very long time to reply. Stars above. She stamped her foot. "You're a state-of-the art entrance security program. You can answer that in nanoseconds."

The system voice came out flat and metallic. "I'm sorry, Messera, but there are no available assets at present to meet your requirements. Please come back later."

"How much later," she asked suspiciously. Systems could not lie. Not outright.

"I am unable to determine a response to that at present."

Anyara had heard that kind of programmed answer too many times before. She'd be set free when those in charge of the system decided to let her go free, and that was likely a long time away.

She stomped back to her office and glared so hard at her students that none dared challenge her. Only Larena had the gall to give her a sympathetic wave, before turning back to gawk at the fleet of idiots still racketing around that wretched course.

She tried the gate house later in the day, and got the same answer. Then the next morning, the next afternoon, and last thing before night shift began. No doubt she'd get the same answer tomorrow, and the next day, and the next. If she wanted out of the Academy, she'd have to find her own way out.

Present location of Seolta den Coille, she sent grumpily to her com.

It had changed. Central Hospital Zone 004. The main building, a massive medic complex set near to the central administration offices. And all the embassies, she suddenly remembered.

So maybe it just meant he'd been taken to the medic wards closest to his current residential address.

"Room number. Show precise location."

Yet again she had to wait for a sophisticated com system to answer a simple question. Then it came back. "Information unable to be accessed at this present time."

Trag it.

She should be glad they were keeping him safe and secure. Except something nagged at her, a sense of urgency. She had to get to him.

"Show hospital schematics with last publicly available location for Seolta den Coille."

This time, there was no delay. That magic term 'publicly'. Nothing to alert security here, it said. She'd used it often enough in the past. It may not get you the data you needed, but came close enough to not matter. Now she saw the entrance they'd used and the readout for the building he'd entered. Her heart sank.

He was in the addiction recovery unit. She'd been right, and the knowledge jolted her as much as it had done when she'd seen those unmistakable eyes.

Seolta den Coille was not the kind to seek refuge in chemicals. Something about this was all wrong.

She had to get to him. But how?

The gardens were a possibility. She wandered slowly along the pathways, gradually nearing the wilder shrubberies. The ones that lined the outer wall protecting the Academy precinct.

Halfway along, she 'just happened' to meet a guard wandering towards her. "Evening, Messera. It's late to be out."

"I need to clear my head," she said. "Too many hours staring at a screen."

"Can't say I know the feeling, but plenty of the staff say the same. You're better off using the inner paths though," he added. "Lots of ground rubbish and hazards to trip you up in this section, and we prefer you don't use com lights this close to the wall. It sparks off the alarms and makes the head of security right tetchy. "

She forced out a chuckle. "Wouldn't want to trouble him. I'll head back to my room."

"Thank you, Messera. Much appreciated."

"And you? Won't your lights set off the alarm too?"

He shook his head amiably. "No, I'm keyed into the system. It knows my patterns and ignores them unless something's unusual."

"Oh, that's good." Was the man giving her a warning? "I'll say good night then."

Back in her room, she opened her holo-mirror and stared at her image. Where had they hidden the tracker. Her clothing was the easiest, all of it laundered by Academy systems.

There must be a way to escape. She had a spare burner com, one she'd had a teen set up for her years ago and carried in her baggage ever since. She slipped it on her other wrist. This time her wandering took the corridors closest to the service rooms. She met three more guards and took to muttering complex biome theorems as a cover. The next guard stepped to one side as she passed, shaking his head and wearing an amused smile. Academics pondering obscure problems while walking the halls clearly weren't new to him. She ended up in the laundry collection area and eyed the bins.

Everything came to this one room. Her chute in her room, the kitchens, the cleaning staff. All gathered together here in their separate bins. Was it possible?

She pulled off her outer smock, glared at it as if noticing a stain, then dumped it into the bin marked faculty, wandering past the others as she did. Her hand brushed over a used coverall. She walked on, careful to keep the purloined suit between her body and the bins. Surveillance monitored every other part of the precinct; she had to assume this room was covered too.

Around the corner to a service unit, a quick change, and she emerged minus her clothes and swathed in the new coverall. Luckily it was of the fully cloaking and heavy duty kind. Must be a gardener's outdoor one, she guessed. Another wander by the bins to discreetly drop her own clothing with its tracker into the return chute for academic staff, along with her com. She selected some gear from the workmen's collection bins and returned to the service unit.

At the end, she grimaced as she looked down at herself. Rough coveralls of the labourer's kind, a worn cloak with covering hood, clumpy boots and under it all, the irritation of a coarse bodysuit. Nothing of her own remained to give her away.

Had it been enough? She activated the burner unit and strode off down the hall, stopping at the garden workers' room as if leaving a tool there, and exited it by the outer door leading to the side gates—the ones the workers used to access the precinct. There was a guard on the entrance, but not one she'd met earlier, nor did the woman recognise her. She had a brief window to make her escape, she reckoned, before security became suspicious, and the knowledge made it hard to keep her steps to a slow trudge as she walked up to the gates. A casual wave at the guard as she set her com on the exit scanner then walked on through.

Nothing. No sirens screamed or overprotective guard hurried out to stop her. No constraining field suddenly fell on her. Why worry about a lowly gardener trudging home after a long shift? It was the unauthorised seeking entry the guards here worried about. No security concerns in someone leaving, not unless you carried something with the Academy's stamp on it, and dirty clothing didn't count.

She carried on down the road, waiting for a shout and call to halt. They must have found her empty room by now. Hopefully they'd search the garden walls first. Before they could try anywhere else, she slipped on board the first transit unit and shoved through to a seat in the centre, hidden by the crowd of passengers. Not that she felt safe yet. It took two more transit changes before she dared take a seat near the door and check for the best links to the hospital.

Her erratic jumps had taken her well away from the central hospital, and she used four more transit jumps to get back, slouching gruffly down the city streets as if wandering home from work. She slipped into an alleyway just across the square from the hospital and hid in the shadows as she figured out her next move.

The front door was out. Too many guards, too public, and she recognised a familiar face in the crowd on the sidewalk. Whether after her or Seolta, she didn't know, but she'd seen the man before on S-NED station. Nor would he be the only one hunting her, and

Seolta's room would be their main target. So how to get in, and soon. The feeling of urgency ate at her gut, driving her to action. He needed her.

She slithered out of the alley then wasted time taking a circuitous route around to the side and back exits. Using a disguise had worked once for her. Could it work again?

One look at the main service entrance ruled it out. The street outside and the doorways were packed with suspiciously fit-looking staff members. Growing up under her uncle's rule had given her an acute ability to pick security staff. They were waiting for her.

She checked all the other entrances to be sure, including ground-level windows and close balconies. All protected.

She was losing time. She had to get to him. Why, she didn't know, just that if she didn't, something terrible might happen.

She hunkered back down, back in the dark alley, and stared in frustration at the front entrance packed with guards. Did they really expect her to walk in under their noses? She'd be recognised as soon as she came into the open.

She glared at the undercover agents, no doubt thinking themselves clever with their pathetic ploys. A pair sitting in the café across the road and an older woman strolling by with a pet gaffin. Innocent enough if she didn't take the same route and pass by the same spots on a regular repeat as if on patrol. Then there was the crowd of hospital security on the steps and crowding the entrance way, far too many for a hospital unless it held someone important.

Admittedly, there were probably enough of those after that stupid race, and given the elite taking part, but Seolta hadn't been brought here first. Another hospital had been arranged to handle race casualties. All those extra guards, the ones that looked far too alert, too expert to be simple hospital guards, were here because of him—and her.

She kept watch, trying to find a flaw in the patterns. The longer she looked, the more impossible it seemed, and slowly, gradually, an idea came to her. One she might even term outrageous. Seolta had contaminated her. Carefully, she stood up, stretching out tense muscles and eased away from her shelter. Only when she was outside any possible security ring did she change her pace, walking briskly to the nearest fashion outlet.

Her current disguise wasn't at all suitable for this scheme. She accessed the booth and locked it behind her, then pulled up the shop's offerings.

No, not at all what she wanted.

It took three more auto-shops, and brought her dangerously close to an area of the city she'd rather avoid, to find an auto-shop with clothes that were halfway to credible. Stylish and well made, although closer examination would show they weren't from the more expensive shops. Those had real people staffing them. These fashions were good enough to pass for top end if you didn't know better. She dropped her workman's gear in a disposal chute and walked out with head high, as if she belonged there. Now to find the rest of what she needed.

It took a few hours before she was ready. She walked around her rented skimmer, eying the trimmings she'd added. Again, they wouldn't stand up to close scrutiny but hopefully were good enough. She stepped back to view her charade. Luxury-style skimmer complete with the insignia and flag of Surned, two guards planted either side wearing a mock-up of the uniform of the Surned planetary security staff, and her own suitably formal outfit. Now all she needed was a genuine official, and she bowed her head to the woman walking towards her.

"Messera Vydayun, thank you for coming."

The woman gave a brusque dip of her head. "I have received your file. Is there anything else I need to know?"

"No, no. I don't think so." Binku Vydayun had been recommended to her once by the only Alliance official Anyara had ever dealt with. The woman gets things done, had said the official, with a sneer of distaste. She'd banked on that meaning that Messera Vydayun was less interested in the means than she was in the end goal. In this case, a promise to introduce her to the biome experts in the Arcadian embassy. Anyara hoped the woman didn't realise until too late that Anyara's reputation was smashed to nothing by today's actions and that the Arcadians were more likely to have her locked up.

"You have the permit I need?"

The woman nodded, opening up a file in her com for public display. It was an official permit requiring the hospital to let her and the accompanying official meet up with Seolta den Coille immediately. It looked legal, undoubtedly was legal. She only had to hope that the guards on duty hadn't been told enough about Seolta den Coille to realise he'd know nothing about exotic biotic ephemera affecting nanobiomes or that a consultation on it wouldn't usually need a face to face meeting.

"Let's go." She slid into the skimmer, Messera Vydayun took the other side, and the guards took up position on the outside. This whole charade had used up a sizable chunk of her reserve funds. She had to hope it was worth it.

It is, said the fear gnawing a hole in her gut.

They drew up at the bottom of the ramp leading to the front entrance of the hospital. Immediately a phalanx of guards at full alert clattered down to surround them. Anyara stayed seated as Messera Vydayun stepped out and addressed the leader.

"The Esteemed Scholar, Messera a Prithand2, is here to consult with Messer Seolta den Coille regarding a prime objective matter. Please escort us to him immediately."

If Anyara hadn't been scared silly, she would have grinned in exultation. The woman had dry officialdom baked into her bones, the kind that flummoxed the soldiers. The leader studied the permit then spoke swiftly into his com. Anyara held her breath. Had her outrageous strategy worked? It depended on who commanded these troops.

Time seemed to stop for the longest moment. Finally the leader snapped off his com and bowed to Messera Vydayun. "Follow me."

The official leaned into the skimmer. "We are ready, Messera Esteemed Scholar."

Anyara gave an equally frigid head bow and stepped out of the skimmer, head held high and rejecting any kind of contact with the soldiers. Hopefully, she looked as if it was beneath her. In reality, she was terrified that if she had to talk to them directly she'd lose her nerve and confess everything. She followed Messera Vydayun up the ramp, keeping her gaze fixed on the back of the woman's head. In the lobby, a harried-looking clerk hurried up to stop them. Messera Vydayun waved the permit and the man fell back, glancing up at the sensors with a shrug as if to say he'd tried. The troop leader kept gabbling into his com on a private band. She could only guess at what was being said.

Nothing that made the man happy, by the scowl on his face. No doubt someone was poring over her permit trying to find a loophole.

Only a court can give you that, she felt like telling them. She kept walking, ignoring all protests. Down a corridor, up more shafts than she cared to count, around and through a veritable maze of passages.

This couldn't be the quickest route. She abruptly stopped and turned to the troop leader. All around her, their growing entourage ground to an undignified halt.

"You are prevaricating, Troop Leader," she said in the haughtiest voice she could manage. "Take us directly to Messer den Coille's room or I will be forced to lay a complaint."

"Not at all, Messera," the man tried.

She turned to Messera Vydayun. "Please advise the troop leader of the consequences of blocking us."

The official was a miracle worker. Her back ramrod straight, she read off a string of horrific-sounding penalties, complete with what sounded to be legal references. They appeared to work, the troop leader blanching and beginning a stammered apology.

"Enough. You have your orders," the woman snapped.

This time, there was no traipsing around obscure corridors. In a few minutes, she stood with her troop outside a doorway. "The Messer is in the second doorway off this ward entrance," the troop leader said. "Beyond here is controlled by Arcadian Security staff. You will have to convince them to let you through."

Vydayun's eyes widened in shock. Anyone working in the biome world knew the name of every EA planet.

"They will give me entrance," said Anyara, with no idea whether she could pull off the promise in her confident-sounding voice. "Open the door."

A whoosh, and she was confronted by another squad of troops, all at sudden attention and with a swoop of weapons raised to point directly at them. Stepping forward into the open area between the two squads was one of the bravest or more foolhardy things she'd ever done. What happened to her lifelong strategy of keeping a low profile and fading into the background? The one that had kept her alive until now.

"Messera Esteemed Scholar Anyara a Prithand2 to see Messer Seolta den Coille. I have a permit."

She waved Vydayun forward and, to her credit, the official didn't pause but turned her com screen to show the soldier.

His weapon stayed pointing straight at them. "That has no effect in this area. This ward is temporarily under off-world diplomatic control, as per the Alliance Interplanetary agreement." The man had practised that statement by his flat delivery. "Only our citizens and associated family members may enter, or those with sanctioned duties."

She was relieved to see that Seolta was so well guarded. On the other hand, this soldier was well aware Seolta knew nothing of biome academia. She took a deep breath.

"I am Seolta den Coille's agreed life partner." She had no idea what they called it on Arcadia. Hopefully the man would accept.

For the first time, a fraction of doubt touched the soldier's face and his free hand tugged at his ear. He lifted his com wrist and said something into it. She was getting very tired of soldiers using privacy screens to cover what they said.

A medic hurried up. The soldier gestured her to keep her distance. The woman skidded to a halt but turned to Anyara.

"You are the Messer's partner?"

Maybe her claim was stretching it, but they had shared life-threatening adventures and memorable nights. She nodded her head firmly.

"Let her through," the woman ordered.

Anyara gave a silent sigh of relief. Then saw the slight droop of Messera Vydayun's head, as if she'd been taken to the brink of a promised treat then denied at the last minute. "The Messera from the Biome Department accompanies me also."

"Will it assist the Messer's recovery?" said the medic dubiously.

"Yes," said Anyara firmly. She'd told enough lies, what was one more? "And will be of great assistance in furthering Messer den Coille's objectives."

The woman gestured them both to enter. "Hurry. He's peaking and we don't know if we can stop him."

"What does that mean?"

It didn't need garbled medical-speak to tell her. The bruising under the medic's eyes and the soft sympathy of her mouth said it all. Was she too late for Seolta? She scowled at her escort. "You want to save your citizen? Then let me through."

After a brief glance at the medic, the Arcadian soldiers reluctantly stood back. The Alliance troop leader frowned darkly. "I have notified the Academy that you are here, Messera Esteemed Scholar," he said loudly enough to be heard right down the hallway. "They are waiting to hear from you."

Which meant trouble, if she didn't report back soon. It may give her an easy way out, but she didn't count a return to the confinement of the Academy Precinct as a welcome escape.

First, she had to find Seolta. "The second door?" she said to the medic.

CHAPTER TWENTY-THREE

He was lost with no way home. Dark corridors lined with spikes yawned on every side. Corridors offering nothing but death or despair. No light, no joy, no hope.

There was something he had to find. No, someone. A name, a face.

He couldn't remember, but somewhere, a light marked his escape. He glared at all those dark corridors and refused to enter any. Then the walls of his temporary refuge began to cave in and the pain waves hit again, hurtling him towards those greedy dark hallways.

"Seolta, Seolta. Come back. It's me."

That voice, he knew it. He dug in his heels and refused the dark openings.

"Open your eyes, please, my love. You're safe. I'm here. I need you to come back to me."

Her voice. She suffered, and that was not allowable. He opened his eyes and a face hung before him, beautiful and precious.

Anyara.

She'd found him.

Then terror struck. "You can't be here. It's not safe."

She smiled at him, a shaky, tremulous smile, but more wonderful than any smile he'd ever seen. "I am, and it's too late to worry. Now, wake up properly. I need you."

The terror struck harder. He shook off the last vestiges of sleep and tried to sit up, but only fell back uselessly. "Why?"

She put a hand on his shoulder and it felt like someone had flung him an anchor. "Because I do."

Which made perfect sense. He felt the same about her.

"Wake up and get better. Then help us find out who did this to you," she said next, and he was so weak he could have wept. He had never cried; not when the prison guards beat him, not after those filthy courtrooms, nor when they read out his death sentence. Or later when the marshals rescued them and he knew he was safe. But now, he felt tears touch his lashes. He blinked them back. "How do you know it wasn't me?"

"Because you wouldn't be so stupid," she said with a grin. What it cost her to smile like that, he didn't want to know, but it was better than food or medicine. He lifted his hand and caught hold of hers, clinging to it, never wanting to let her go.

A medic bustled forward. "Are you ready yet for our help, Messer den Coille?" she said.

Then he remembered his instructions and the reasons for them. He cursed. "Within reason," he said. "Whatever gets me out of here the fastest."

"What do you mean, 'within reason'?" Anyara asked. "Are you doing that stupid hero thing again?"

His mouth dropped open. "I'm no hero," was his first thought. She couldn't believe that.

"So why do you want to get out of here so quickly? You're safe here."

"And someone out there is trying to kill the both of us and hurt my world."

"Arcadia owes you nothing. Didn't they wipe their hands of you?"

"It was nothing I didn't deserve. I've told you that."

She waved a hand as if dismissing it though the carefully rigid faces of the Arcadian troops at the door told her the truth of it.

"It was done, and you're trying to make amends. That doesn't mean you have to put yourself through hell to do it."

He shook his head in denial. She'd have none of it and turned to the medic. "What's he on and what does he need to break free of it."

He glared at the medic, but she ignored him.

"Kephartin, Messera," said the woman. "His recovery is proceeding satisfactorily, but he needs the symptoms suppressed if he wants to survive with his intelligence intact."

"She's exaggerating," Seolta tried.

"Are you?" Anyara had turned away from him and looked at the medic.

"No, Messera," said the woman.

"Then treat him," she said, and swung back to him, "and you are going to let them."

No one had talked to him like that since he started first school. He still remembered that teacher vividly. Sera Curaim had made it clear on their first meeting that her word was the final one, and Seolta had shockingly discovered his parents weren't the only people he couldn't manipulate. He had nodded meekly when the Sera told him to sit down. He felt the same now.

"I can't afford news of this to get out. I have to heal quickly."

His Anyara brushed that off. "You will take as long as needed to recover safely. The vidcasters can't know how badly you were hurt in that crash."

A weight lifted. "Yes, Messera," he said.

"Don't give me that smile either, Seolta den Coille. It might be irresistible, but you matter more."

She though him irresistible. The world began to turn right side up. He let his head fall back and stopped trying to fight his body. "You heard her, Sera Medic. I am to be treated."

The woman gave one of those 'about time' looks that a surprising number of people around him adopted, and moved purposefully in with her infuser. That was all he knew for too long. He woke to early morning light breaking through his hospital window and panicked.

She had been here. He couldn't feel her anymore.

A hand took hold of his and he clung tight to that preciously familiar shape. "You didn't leave me."

"No, my Seolta. I will not leave you."

He let sleep take him again. When next he woke, a hum of voices filled the room. He opened his eyes a crack. Anyara's hand still held his, but her head slumped back on her chair. He made no move. She needed her sleep, and a part of him regretted the worry he'd caused her; the rest of him sang in answer to her presence. He lay still and listened to the voices, separating out speaker and owner. Closest was the medic who had sent him under, the most dangerous to him. A disinterested patter as she read off data and rolled off a list of unknown words that had to be medical jargon. The others he had to concentrate hard to identify, people met too recently to be engrained in memory. The nervous one was Jinke Wago, the social organiser. She'd come to formulate a publicity screen, he guessed. The ambassador wasn't here of course, but the firm and untroubled voice was Marshal M'Senti. The man had a good head on his shoulders; he trusted him to keep the madness safely outside the door.

The fainter hum must be security forces outside his room. Friend or foe, he couldn't tell, and wasn't sure it made much difference. After this latest stunt, the Arcadian embassy troops had as little reason to be on his side as the Alliance ones.

The medic's voice sharpened and his peace was over. He opened his eyes fully and began to sit up. She hurried forward and shoved him back down again, waving that tragging scanner of hers over him.

"I'm fine." He looked pointedly at Anyara, struggling to open her eyes. The medic dropped her voice a fraction but didn't stop fussing.

Anyara jerked up her head. "You're awake."

"Shh, *mo Graidh*. It's only the medics with their infernal checks."

A red glow lit her cheeks. "You're better."

"Not yet, Messera," said the tragging medic, "but will be soon, if the Messer follows orders."

"He will, Messera. I promise you that." She reached out her other hand and leaned over. He couldn't resist, taking her precious face in his hands and returning her kiss with a much longer one. She had stayed with him.

A cough behind them, and he reluctantly lifted his mouth. It was Marshal M'Senti. "As soon as you are ready, Ser, there are officials waiting to talk to you."

He kept tight hold of Anyara's hand, but it didn't need the marshal's warning glance to put him on full alert. "Which officials?"

"Our embassy team first, then the Alliance Security Council."

"They've found the source?"

The marshal said nothing except a slight hooding of his eyes. It was that sensitive?

"Let me get cleaned up," he said.

This time, the medics merely warned he still had some distance to go. Not that he needed telling. The drug prodded at him still, along with an overwhelming need to sleep. No time for that.

Soon enough he'd been made presentable. He looked around the room. Anyara still sat in her chair, with the heavy bruising of a sleepless night under her eyes. Others included the team of medics, though he failed to see why he needed so many. There was enough equipment in here to monitor an entire hospital ward. Then there was the marshal and three more Arcadian troopers, two by the door and one on watch by his window, all in full defensive gear. The embassy social organiser had flopped into a chair in the corner, and another woman stood to one side. Dressed in mid-income auto-shop clothes, bland and designed to blend into a crowd and none of it organised in any way to enhance the wearer, she stood quietly watching everyone in the room. A backroom official, unless he was mistaken.

He pulled himself upright. "How'd you get here?" he asked sharply of Anyara

"I had help," she said.

Marshal M'Senti stepped forward. "The Sera's vehicle is parked in the front of the building, and her guards stand beside it."

A flush covered Anyara's face. "Oh, dear, I'd forgotten them. Please, tell them they are no longer needed." She looked around as if seeking something. "You're still here, Messera Vydayun?"

"You haven't yet dispensed with my services or completed our agreement," said the quiet woman, clearly not about to go anywhere.

"Oh, that's right." Anyara turned back to him. "Messera Vydayun is with the Alliance Biome Department. I had promised her an introduction to a counterpart in the Arcadian embassy. I couldn't have made it here without her."

The marshal looked as stiff-faced as he'd seen him. "Messera Vydayun issued a permit allowing Sera Anyara entrance to this wing."

Seolta grinned. "What an outrageously effective action, Messera Anyara," and he delighted in the pink flush staining her cheeks. "The Sera and I are heavily in her debt. Marshal. I do hope it will be possible for her to receive the promised introduction."

"I will take care of it personally," said the marshal. Seolta glanced at the woman and surprised a small glow on her face. Beside her, the embassy social organiser looked about to expire in shock. Since it was the woman's idea for him to enter that tragging race in the first place, Seolta had little sympathy, turning back with a smile to Anyara.

"And how did you plan to get back to the Academy?"

Anyara said nothing.

He did sit up this time, struggling against his own body and the growled efforts of the medic to stop him. "You don't have a plan? Can you get back?"

"Yes, if they escort me."

"When you get there, will you be free to visit me again?"

She shrugged her shoulders but ducked her chin. "Maybe."

No, he realised. "Who's stopping you?"

"The Academy has good security."

"So how did you escape it this time?"

She told him, and he could have crowed at her inventiveness, if his gut hadn't tied itself in knots. She'd been in danger because of him.

"Marshal, we need this room cleared."

No chance of that, the marshal's face said. "I will secure the room," was all he was prepared to promise.

In no time, the marshal had got rid of all but the two senior troopers, sent the official off with the irritating social organiser to be introduced to the biome experts in the embassy, and bluntly ordered the medics to leave the room until summoned back. One refused to budge. The marshal gave her an irritated glance as he put a call through to the embassy.

"I've called in the appropriate persons," he said at the end, whatever that meant.

"Who?" Seolta demanded.

The marshal flicked him a brief file, one that showed him only the officials' positions and truncated bio details.

"They're safe?"

The marshal's face gave nothing away. "Their attendance here is required."

The recalcitrant medic loomed up beside him again. "What did you do? The Messer's recovery is still fragile."

Seolta fought to control his heartbeat.

Fear is your enemy. He remembered someone telling him that a long time ago.

He'd since learned a new codicil: Fear can give you a fighting edge. Use it.

He'd never looked for a quote for when you feared for someone else. Could he trust the marshal to keep Anyara safe?

"I'm all right," he said, forcing a scrape of irritation into his voice as he waved the medic away.

She looked about to argue and he lifted his hand in a gesture straight from the streets. The twitch of laughter on Anyara's face was nearly worth the shock on the woman's.

The marshal put a hand on her arm and walked the medic inexorably toward the door. "This room is required for urgent diplomatic discussions. We will signal when the medical staff may return." The marshal's cool voice stopped all the medic's blusterings, and in no time he had her out the door and locked it after her. Then he turned back to face them.

"The troopers are mine. It's safe to talk in front of them. Who's after you, Sera, and what do they want?"

Seolta felt a tremor run through Anyara's hand. "Don't frighten her."

"She needs to be." The marshal turned to Anyara. "Is it your uncle's people, the Academy, or is it because of your relationship to the Ser?"

She looked confused.

"He means me," said Seolta, guilt assaulting him as not even his actions on Arcadia had done. "We use a shorter form of salutation on Arcadia. Ser and Sera for Messer and Messera."

She sat back in her chair, fingers gripping tight to his hand. "Someone trying to kill me to get to you?" Horror marred her face. "I don't know. It was Academy security who blocked my departure, but they may have been trying to protect me."

Seolta glanced again at the carefully still face of the marshal, then spoke softly to Anyara.

"What work are you doing there?"

She gulped, then squeezed his hands again as if for courage. "A continuation of my work on Kevand Station. Integration of biome imperatives." The marshal looked as blank as Seolta felt. "Transitions," she explained. "Blending everything together. Biota and people, social and physical needs."

He remembered her station and the jolt of finding an artificial habitat that felt a lot like home. "Ah. I understand now. You do know you're a genius, *mo Graidh.*" The marshal looked no more enlightened and Seolta doubted he could explain, despite his time on Central. The marshal knew he could go home at any time. "Marshal, can you bring up the Academy's financial records? In particular, their earnings from research projects."

Now the man looked interested. He bent to his com and within a few minutes, sent Seolta a link.

He scanned them quickly, stunned at what the marshal had delivered. He had no idea the embassy had this kind of access to private financial accounts, and made a private vow to check the security of his own accounts. Then he began to study the records more fully.

The pattern soon became clear. He got the marshal to pull up Hilmar's records as well.

"I don't suppose you can pull the same trick for Alliance tax data?"

"Not a chance, Ser den Coille." The marshal actually looked shocked at the request. The man had just messaged him highly confidential financial records. Seolta ignored him and took Anyara's hand.

"Tell me more about this lab the Academy set up for you."

"There's not much to tell. It's a biome research lab."

"So just an ordinary research facility How long to set up one like that?"

"Not that ordinary," she said. "It certainly held everything I needed."

"And setting it up?" he prompted again. "That would be easy enough?"

"Maybe," she conceded. "If you had the required supplies. Some of it is highly specialised."

"So longer than usual to set up."

"With selection and ordering, then setting up. Maybe a couple of standard months minimum."

"Before the Fleet carrier rescued us?"

"Yes," she said reluctantly.

The marshal sat up straighter. "The Sera is a useful source of income for the Academy?"

"You could say that," said Seolta. He singled out the external project fees, then isolated the ones he was fairly sure were for Anyara's work, the ones titled "Biome specialist ES." Then he highlighted the dates.

"At a guess, the Academy wasn't at all upset at your escape from Surned. These fees date back to well before your escape, although the recipient on the earlier bills isn't one I recognise."

He showed her a record, and she shook her head. Then paused. "There's a suburb in Kevand1 with a similar name." Her brows furrowed. "What are you thinking?"

"See that item?" He highlighted a fee on the invoice. It was more than a third of the total bill.

"A broker's fee?"

"Your uncle, at a guess. He knows the tricks of this kind of thing." He highlighted another fee, and heard her gasp.

"That's double my actual costs, including my living expenses—and I was always so careful with my costs for fear of annoying him."

"You still would have," he said dryly. "The man was making a fortune out of you."

"A pity he didn't work harder to keep me safe then."

Seolta agreed, but it also told him something about the man that he should have realised a long time ago. "To give up that kind of income means he values power more than wealth. Your death gives him full ownership of his company and nothing can stop him."

"I never could."

"The potential of it must have driven him muddy. You were gathering a following and influence on your station. What would happen if you turned that on Surned?"

She grunted as if to say 'not much chance of that', and he agreed. Anyara was not the type. Her biomes mattered far more to her than any power over a planet.

"You're saying then that the Sera's best course is to go back to the Academy," said the marshal. "At least we know she'd be safe there. The Academy will do nothing to stop you working, although they will control your life. It's an option."

"No."

Anyara said the word for him. Seolta swallowed. "It's an option you have to consider. It's the safest one."

"I'm staying here, with you." She shoved herself firmly back into the seat as if to emphasise it. Then her face clouded. "If you want me, of course."

There were some things he couldn't lie about. "Always," he said, holding her eyes.

The marshal coughed. "Which leaves the problem of who is trying to kill you, Ser den Coille."

"Ah."

That was more complicated. He sat and thought. "Hilmar's people, both for stealing Anyara and to stop me talking about our past dealings—the ones on Arcadia and the one to assassinate Anyara. He can't afford it getting around that you can break a contract with him and get away with it."

The marshal knew it all. He shouldn't be surprised. One day, he'd like to meet an Arcadian official without an agenda. "So you intended to honour all those contracts?" the man asked.

"We left Surned territory so I wouldn't have to."

"The one on Sera Anyara, yes. The Arcadian ones?"

How many times was he going to face this question? "Circumstances have changed. It's all in my files." The ones M'Senti would have read front to back.

"Then who else is after you?" Seolta had to fight hard to choke back his angry retort. Thoughtless rage had got him into this mess. It was time he learned to keep his mouth shut and think, not react.

What had he learned since leaving home? He glanced at Anyara and felt his heart soften. Love, first and foremost. Never to take it for granted. Not his family's love, and not what he felt for this extraordinary woman.

Anyara had also taught him something he'd never properly understood: the rarity and value of living on an EA world. That was the factor he'd failed to take into account with Hilmar and Malgrave. He hadn't understood the lure of the prize he offered them. Nor had it occurred to him at the time that others in the Alliance might be involved.

No, were definitely involved, given what had happened to him since leaving Arcadia.

"Who knew what I was sent to do in exile?" he said to M'Senti. The marshal was one of the few he trusted. Marshals had saved his life on Arcadia; a marshal had proposed this mission, and Marco an Fallon had given him no reason to doubt him.

"It was restricted on a need-to-know basis. Five in the marshals' office, the Head Councillor and the Galactic Affairs Minister, ten special branch operatives from the Galactic Ministry, your family, and Ethan Winter and his wife. In government departments, it was no secret you were sent into exile for crimes against Arcadia. It's on the file blocking your entry permits. They put in the severest of penalties for leaking it to a news outlet. I suppose someone may think the sentence inadequate."

"Thanks." Just what he needed. Some rogue vigilante sticking his nose into what was already a tangled mess.

The marshal's face stayed the same bland mask. The man must be a brilliant fricha player.

"Who else is a suspect?"

Seolta dragged his thoughts back to the problem. "Hilmar's the most obvious one behind the attack on the fleet ship. He wants both of us dead and Anyara recognised the Surned accent of the probable poisoner."

"Doesn't mean he ordered it and certainly he can't have been behind this latest stunt," said M'Senti. "It needs high level contacts to arrange a race attack."

Seolta thought harder. It could be so many. "I'd back Alliance-based agents first, either corrupt officials or businesses wanting a bite of Arcadia. Malgrave can't have been working on her own. This is my current list."

He sent the marshal a file, who received it with a raised eyebrow. "That long? You haven't narrowed it down more?"

Seolta shrugged. "There are a lot of hungry predators out there, and we're a prime target."

"What makes you so sure it's not someone from Arcadia."

"Because anyone thinking I got off too lightly is too angry for that. They want me to suffer, want me locked up and charged with my crimes, yes; killed, no."

Beside him, he heard a sudden gasp from Anyara, and he cursed silently. "Don't worry, *mo Graidh*, I'm safe here." A sudden warmth flooded his chest. She cared. No matter what, someone was left to mourn him.

No, his death would hurt her too badly.

"No one is killing me. Not today, not for many years," he promised her.

"Make sure of it, Seolta a Manascraoch."

He couldn't stop the grin. "You pronounced it properly."

She flushed. "I found a language program. I had to do something while I waited for you to wake up."

The marshal's cough from the background broke their entranced gaze at each other. "Are those the only options, Ser den Coille?"

Seolta gathered his wits and turned back to the grim-faced marshal. "Hilmar a Kevand3; corrupt Alliance interests; Arcadian agents, legit and rogue; legal Alliance forces; anyone with an imagined grievance against me or Arcadian business interests. That's not enough for you?"

Anyara gasped again. "What do you mean, legal Alliance forces? You've broken no Alliance law."

"Thank you, my Messera. You're probably the only one who thinks that though." It still sent another warm glow through him. But he had to turn to the marshal.

He studied M'Senti's face, wishing he could read the man, then took a deep breath. "I used to be against the Alliance's demands on principle, but now I'm starting to wonder. Who was it decided Arcadia was on the brink of environmental collapse?" His sister Fioruisghe had been adamant it was true, showing him evidence enough in the days before he was exiled. He'd let her rant, thinking it was her grief talking. Whether he believed in the threat had made no difference to what happened to him, so he hadn't stopped her. Anyara now had him reconsidering. "I don't mean that there isn't a problem, just questioning the severity of it. Are we really at the point that the Alliance needs to remove the entire settler population if we don't change within their timeframe?"

"You will have to ask the ambassador those questions," said M'Senti stiffly. "Internal Alliance Council deliberations are restricted."

"You've wondered too," Seolta realised, "and don't give me that restricted line. Marshals are tragging good at finding out stuff."

"What does that have to do with legal Alliance interests trying to kill you," said Anyara, doggedly sticking to her point.

"If the Council is using the environmental issue to get control of Arcadia and increase settlement there by people grateful to them, they won't want me stirring up public dirt. My going after your uncle played into their hands. They can dismiss me as a small-time scoundrel angry at losing out to a senior player like Hilmar. My involvement in your disappearance is another matter, and they don't want any vidcast reporter poking into that. They need you back on Kevand Station and me discreetly eliminated."

"By a public accident in an event long castigated for being foolishly risky," said M'Senti. "It's going to be interesting to see which officials the Alliance sends to investigate."

Yes, and he was stuck in a sleeper looking like a victim ready for plucking. "Get the medics to bring me my clothes. I mean my own clothes, not some fashion reject's cast-offs."

If he was going to face his enemies, he'd do it looking like a worthy opponent.

CHAPTER TWENTY-FOUR

They gave him a short rest time to marshal his pitiable strength but too soon afterwards, he sat in a boardroom in the hospital, flanked by Anyara on one side and the imposing figure of M'Senti on the other. He was barely fit for this but hoped he hid it better from the other side than he did from his watch dogs. M'Senti wore that bland look of a marshal at his most dangerous and Anyara's hand crushed the folds of her tunic under the table. The medic's injections made the pain from the flyer crash manageable, but nothing could hide the aftermath of the drug's ravages. His eyes staring back from his holo-mirror earlier had that sunken, haunted look of a recovering addict, and he'd slapped it off angrily.

Thankfully, the boardroom door signalled the arrival of the delegates. He took Anyara's hand under the shelter of the table, giving it a quick squeeze to banish the tightness around her eyes. She gave him a shaky smile, and squeezed back, then released him.

The ambassador and her team were the first to arrive. She'd brought three advisors: a scientist, a financial expert, and a diplomatic attaché. M'Senti went to stand, but the ambassador thankfully waved him back down so Seolta didn't have to use the edge of the table to lever himself painfully upright.

Surprisingly, they were followed in by Binky Vydayun, the Biota official who had helped Anyara. The woman was being handsomely rewarded for her services. That, or she had a much higher rank than she'd let on to Anyara. She walked to the far side of the table, taking a seat near the bottom and leaving room for the other Alliance officials. At least she made her allegiance clear.

Next the door pad signalled the arrival of the Alliance contingent. He waited to see who entered first.

It was a Council advisor, but what that meant, he'd have to wait to find out. Then came two officials from the Finance Bureau, and all his synapses went on alert. The Finance Bureau did much more than tot up credits. The Exoplanetary Research Ministry and the Biota Ministry followed, but he wasn't as concerned by them. The ERM and BM were the ones who'd advised the Council about Arcadia, but they didn't make the decisions. He gave a formal head bow to them all, and waited for the opening gambit.

Surprisingly, it came from the Arcadian ambassador. She half rose and gave a formal head bow. "Welcome, Messers all," she said, claiming the role of host.

Good on you, Sera.

The BM and ERM officials' mouths twitched with annoyance, but none of the rest showed how they felt. "You will excuse us from standing. As you are aware, Messer den Coille was recently involved in an unfortunate incident in the pre-Games race."

Not so good on you, Sera.

It might put the blame for the chaos on the racetrack squarely on the Alliance but it made him look weak, vulnerable, a victim. Not that he leaked any sign of his irritation. Not in this room of class-A predators. The thought perked him up. Nothing he liked better than a good boardroom wrangle.

The Council advisor smiled placidly. "Of course, Messera. No offence taken. After all, it is the series of incidents affecting Messer den Coille and Messera Anyara a Prithand2 that precipitated this meeting."

We begin with a draw.

It didn't stay that way, of course. First, the advisor invited the Arcadian delegation to set out their concerns, effectively stymieing them. Far better if the ambassador asked the Alliance what their investigations had revealed instead of shoving it back onto them. The Arcadians were in no position to accuse the Council or its Ministries of corruption or conspiracies against Arcadia, not without more concrete evidence. Mentioning the missing Deputy Malgrave would only warn off any favouring the unknown co-conspirators, which meant the Arcadians had to confine themselves to the Fleet and race incidents, not to anything prior. It gave the Alliance free rein to infer what they liked about Seolta's interactions with Anyara, no matter how much she denied anything illegal had happened.

"I was not kidnapped, Messers. I left the Surned system of my own free will."

"Why such a dangerous route, Messera Esteemed Scholar?" said the unctuous voice of the administrator from the Biota Ministry, a man Seolta had already marked down in the enemy column. He clearly wanted the current settlers out so he could get his grubby fingers on a planet rich with life. Did he already have his own patch of paradise staked out?

Anyara's fist clutched tight to the material of her tunic, and he wished he was free to take her hand, but her voice showed none of it as she coolly answered the BM wernet. "At the time, it seemed the safest option. My uncle was unlikely to allow my departure by regular transports."

The junior from the Finance Bureau looked sternly at her. "Not surprising, given the risks involved, Messera. You were doing sterling work on Kevand Station, exciting work that enhanced the reputation of the Academy and had real benefits for habitat dwellers. Why upset everything with these quixotic adventures?"

Did the man have shares in Hilmar's companies? He'd have to use double and triple blinds to hide them. Or would if the Alliance Council cared about conflicts of interest in their officials. Right now, he wasn't sure of anything, least of all that.

The woman from the Biota Ministry leaned forward. She was the scientist of the pair, one who actually knew something about living things. "The Messera no doubt had good reasons for her actions. Whatever they are, the internal politics of the Surned system are not the main concern of this meeting. The Academy was delighted that the Messera chose to return there, and did not question how she did it. As far as I am aware, there have been no proven attacks on the Messera, whereas there have on Messer Seolta."

Anyara had turned sharply towards the woman and was listening intently. Seolta shut his eyes a moment and concentrated on the woman's voice, dropping his head as if studying a related screen on his com. The accent, that was it. A slight trace of Anyara's. The woman was from the Surned system.

Not an ally of Hilmar, though. Not by her words—but not yet in the sympathetic column. He opened his eyes again to watch her. Her mouth was set in a grim line as she reminded the room of the situation on his home world.

"Arcadia is in trouble, but they are working to correct it."

"Not quickly enough," put in the scientist from the Exoplanetary Research Ministry. "Nor is that the issue here."

"It is exactly the issue," said the BM woman. "The Messer was sent from his home world because he had put at risk the planet's settlers' attempts to repair their damage. That surely is a sign that they are taking the problem seriously. The current settlers are those most familiar with the planet and with an emotional imperative to treat it better."

"Then why did they get into this mess in the first place?" said the ERM man. "How do we know this man wasn't sent to Central as a spy?"

The Council advisor raised an eyebrow, then turned away from the man. "As has been pointed out, the situation on Arcadia is not the topic of this meeting. Nor is it likely that any spy would have made as much of a splash as Messer den Coille has."

Seolta dipped his head in thanks. "It seemed as good a way as any of meeting the business contacts I needed, and Central is the trading hub of the Alliance."

"And that was all you were planning?" said the senior Finance Bureau advisor.

Now they were getting to it. "Of course," he said, injecting outrage into his voice.

"Hmmph," said the man, and turned towards the scientist from the Biota Ministry. "You had some questions, Messera?"

She did, none that Seolta could answer, and left the floor to the embassy's science advisor as he discreetly studied the senior Finance advisor. Why had the man withdrawn like that? He supposed the BM's technical questions were important to someone, but not to this discussion. All had the weary feel of questions and answers hashed out over many previous sessions, and the embassy's science advisor spoke as if reciting words from memory. At least the BM boffin showed no signs of irritation; for now, the woman was on their side.

By the time every single scientist in the room had also trotted out a litany of arguments and rebuttals, Seolta was less sympathetic. Too many old and hashed-out arguments, of little relevance that he could see. It gave him an insight into the crossed lines of the Council departments, but no real answers, and he'd had more than enough of that.

Why bother? They're not going to let you go home, no matter what you find.

Because he had to. His selfish quest for revenge had nearly got Ethan Winter killed and still threatened to destroy his home world. A wave of homesickness surged through him. Every other Arcadian here was going home when their tour of duty was over. Everyone except him.

And Anyara? Where was her home? He suddenly shoved up, ignoring the pain ratcheting through every muscle. Had he forced her into exile as well?

"What is it?" she murmured, sharpening his guilt.

"Later." He sent her a reassuring smile, feeling like the worst kind of double-crosser, and concentrated again on the discussion.

To his relief, the scientists sounded like they were running out of energy. By the watchful eyes of the Council advisor, it seemed he thought so too but wasn't yet prepared to let it stop. The man must be doing what Seolta should be: summing up the participants, their arguments, and what lay behind them.

So what did Seolta have? Of the ERM and BM officials, the BM scientist was opposed to the Council's deadline, the ERM scientist thought it justified, the ERM administrator was equivocal, and the BM administrator positively enthusiastic and probably corrupt. The junior Finance man was the same, but he couldn't yet read his senior or the Council advisor, and they were the two with real power here. All he had was a couple of possible strings to follow, but nothing concrete.

No, what he needed, and badly, was the seniors' take on it.

He twitched in his seat. Anyara swung around and grasped his arm, her mouth pinched with concern. He patted her hand, then shifted again in his seat and squinted, as if finding the light too bright.

"Are you all right, Messer," said the ambassador, a touch too smoothly.

He lifted a hand. "It's nothing," he said, and shifted his weight again. "It's been a long few days," he said, teeth gritted.

The Council advisor's hooded eyes watched him. "We can leave much of this discussion for another time, if you would prefer, Messer."

"No, no. It's my life on the line, after all. Or so I'm told." He shifted slightly as if trying to smother an attempt to find a more comfortable position. "But if we could stick to the essentials, I would much appreciate it." He leaned back, letting his head fall onto the backrest, then determinedly sat up again.

He caught a quirk of the advisor's lips. So the man could read him. Then it was high time he got to why he's here. He stared back at the man, and got the slightest of head tilts in reply.

So the advisor was still equivocal, but he was also a man with priorities Seolta thoroughly distrusted. He leaned forward, and saw a flash of alarm shoot over the ambassador's eyes. Trag it, if she'd done her job properly, he wouldn't have had to put his sorry hide out as a target. He stared straight at the advisor.

"I've come close to being killed twice since entering the Alliance Central area of control. A Fleet ship is meant to be the safest place in the whole of settled space, and what happened in that race was no accident. Someone tinkered with my flyer, which was under full security with the Council's people overseeing it. They had to, given the strategic importance of those involved." He switched his gaze to sweep over every single person on the other side of the table.

The only one who hadn't talked was Anyara's lowly BM official. The one who was so keen to learn about an EA planet. He let his gaze slide over her, but noted her stillness. The unnatural kind or the understandable reaction from an official who never expected to be in the same room as the others here?

The woman had come in with the ambassador's party. She knew exactly what kind of meeting she'd gate-crashed.

"Would anyone care to explain it to me?" he said.

"The why, or what we knew about it?" said the Council advisor, still with that untrustworthy quirk at the corner of his mouth. The man hadn't been involved, Seolta decided, but was as keenly interested as himself in finding out who had been.

"Are you suggesting that someone from this government deliberately sabotaged your flyer and corrupted a Fleet crew member?" said the outraged junior Finance man. The one he already knew was involved.

"That's exactly what I'm suggesting," said Seolta, "and like the Messer from the Council, I would very much like to know who and why so I can stop any more attacks on me, or on Messera Anyara."

No one else spoke, but he caught plenty of uncomfortable looks and shifting in seats. Good, because right now he was plenty uncomfortable.

"What you suggest is unconscionable," said the Council advisor, a tad too smoothly for Seolta's liking, as if challenging Seolta to the natural reply.

Seolta did not like being led, but in this instance, he had to allow it. "Then prove it, Messer," he said as smoothly. "I suggest a full review of the applicable departments."

"That is already under way for the Fleet, as is automatic following any such incident. However, the Council's understanding is that your poisoning there resulted from your interference in the internal politics of the Surned system."

"Do you mean by rescuing me from my uncle's assassination threats?" said Anyara hotly. "I'm alive today because of Messer den Coille, and am very grateful. Nor do we know whether the Fleet attack was aimed at Messer den Coille or at me—or at both of us."

"There's no proof of that, Messera, and you have only Messer den Coille's word for your uncle's threats," said the senior Finance man. He might be equivocal about Arcadia, but not Surned. Seolta wasn't surprised. Hilmar had too many lines of influence and profit, both official and underhanded. The Bureau didn't like anything that hurt the flow of credits.

He opened his mouth to answer the man in a way that wouldn't frighten him further, but Anyara beat him to it, fixing a furious glare on the man. "Messer Seolta's warning only added to others. I have been under my uncle's 'tender' care for a very long time now. I know when he's planning something against me. Messer Seolta gave me the escape route I'd been looking for."

Not quite true, but Seolta was grateful for her vote of confidence.

The BM administrator bent what he probably thought a kindly smile on her. "Your uncle has cared for you for a long time, as you say. You have never lacked for anything. We all see a healthy, well educated and well provided for young woman. An Esteemed Scholar of the famous Academy, no less. Yet you ask us to believe that the man who ensured you grew up wanting nothing now plots to kill you?"

"He made a healthy profit by it, I have recently discovered," said Anyara, throwing off Seolta's hand attempting to stop her. She mustn't put herself at more risk.

He put his hand firmly back on hers. "I checked out the Esteemed Scholar's financial profile and the record of proceeds from her services. Messer Hilmar a Kevand3 acted as her agent, as well as charging out all her costs to those using her services. Understandable possibly when she was a minor, but the Messera has long passed any legal definition of that. If more usual business practices had been followed, the Messera and the Academy would both be a lot richer now," he added before Anyara had a chance to put herself in more danger. "The records are all publicly available if you know where to look."

"And you would, Messer den Coille," said the junior from the Finance Bureau. "Weren't you in charge of ensuring your family's continued dominance of the Festin supply market?"

His voice implied something inherently grubby and underhanded. Seolta's fists clenched but he kept his hands well out of sight. "We control and dominate the market because the festia tree grows well only in our territory. We developed the product and created the market for Festin; we'd be fools to let that expenditure go to waste by throwing away control of the results."

"As is normal practice," agreed the man's senior, and the junior flushed deep red. "However, it is true that your own reputation, Messer den Coille, is somewhat *opaque*."

Seolta gave him a deep bow of his head. "Thank you, Messer. High praise indeed. Talking of 'opaque' reputations, and since the Finance Bureau has brought up the matter of my previous interactions with Messer Hilmar…"

"I don't think that's necessary," put in the embassy's finance advisor.

"Quite unnecessary," agreed the Senior Finance Bureau official sternly, glaring at Seolta. "I would have thought, Messer den Coille, that you would prefer to have your deplorable history forgotten, rather than rehashing it."

"I would," said Seolta, "if those involved would stop trying to kill me."

The junior from the Finance Bureau half rose. "You decided to insert yourself into the internal politics of another planetary system, out of some petty quest for revenge, it appears, and they took the obvious retaliation. These attacks are no more than that."

"A complicated retaliation, Messer," Seolta said, "and not in the Surned Messer's usual style. Luring me into a contract to kill his niece then having me killed for attacking a member of his family? That is his style. Duplicitous and efficient." He smiled at the man with all his teeth. "Subverting a Fleet crew member and tampering with a flyer in a race involving members of the Alliance's most illustrious families needs more heavy hitters than the Surned system can muster." The junior began to sweat. "No, Messer. Those attacks weren't simple retaliations."

"What, then?" said the man, who seemed incapable of learning.

"Whoever is behind them wants me dead to stop me talking about who else was involved in my, as you say, deplorable actions on Arcadia, and as a warning to anyone else who thinks to stop them. The attacks on me were by traitors to the Alliance."

A crash of silence hit the room. Seolta let it spin out, watching the faces opposite all the time. Then he leaned forward. "So let's talk about who else wants to steal Arcadian land and assets, and is doing it from right here in the heart of the Alliance. "

He let another silence spin out. Then stared straight at the science representatives from the ERM and BM, the departments that had set in progress this whole disaster.

"Esteemed Messers," he went on, "you are the experts, we're told. The ones who know what's wrong with my home world." It wasn't quite the truth. The original data that had precipitated everything came from the Arcadian Ecological Survey field staff, including from his little sister Fioruisghe, who had told him in no uncertain terms they were in trouble. But these officials had recommended how to use that data. He deliberately snared the eye of every technical expert in the room, ending with the equivocal tech from the Exoplanetary Research Ministry, who seemed not yet opposed to Arcadia, and understood exactly how rare his world was.

"How real is the disaster on Arcadia?" he said into the silence.

A chorus of voices erupted. 'How dare you,' crowed one loud and strident stream, to be battered by a rising tide of cross thrusts. 'Of course it is', 'Maybe it is', 'Who said it is?'… right down to, 'It's all made up' from the embassy finance officer, voiced very quietly, but an echo of it slithered across the BM junior's face as well. His words said differently though, the loudest of the 'how dare you' brigade. Definitely had his fingers in the muck, but not bright enough to conceal it. Seolta discreetly checked out the Council advisor, and saw him also watching the BM man with fingers held stiffly against the tabletop, as if stopping them curling up.

Where did the man from the Council really sit? More importantly, how much of the Council did he represent?

The ambassador discovered her backbone and broke up the shouting match by shoving back her chair loudly and standing up. She glared straight at the Council advisor. "The environmental crisis facing our planet? We were told it was proven beyond question and must be fixed immediately. What were the voting figures on that, Messer?"

"That is confidential information, Messera."

"So highly classified that you can't tell the representative of the planet you're threatening to destroy."

He hadn't thought the ambassador had so much courage.

"It is a matter of wider Alliance concerns," said the advisor sternly.

"And wrecking the economy and lives of the people of my planet doesn't matter? Arcadia has always paid its share of Alliance levies and is home to a number of Alliance-wide business entities." We're rich pickings, the ambassador was telling the advisor, and you're conniving with the pirates taking aim at us.

"Nonsense," the man spluttered.

Surprisingly, it was Anyara's lowly official from the Biota Ministry who broke the deadlock. The one sitting quietly throughout the meeting, the one he'd wondered why or how she'd been allowed to attend. She suddenly stood up and the Council advisor turned to her with what Seolta was sure was a look of relief.

He put an urgent message through to M'Senti. 'Who is this woman?'

"Messers all," said the woman, "there appears to be a simple solution to this discord. An outside expert must be sent to Arcadia, one trusted by all sides."

Seolta waited, suddenly on edge and, beside him, Anyara stiffened as the woman looked straight at her.

"We have with us an Esteemed Scholar from the Academy, one renowned for her studies in the integration of biota and human systems. I propose that Messera Anyara a Prithand2 be sent to Arcadia to evaluate the situation there and judge whether the current crisis is as portrayed."

Anyara gasped. "I've never even visited an EA planet, let alone studied one."

"Exactly," said the woman, no longer the self-effacing, anonymous bureaucrat.

"Out of the question," said the embassy Finance advisor, his hands smacking hard against the table. "She's the niece of the man who tried to swindle Arcadians out of their assets."

"He's been swindling the Messera for years and recently put out a contract against her life. She has no cause for loyalty to him," replied the Biota woman.

Seolta shot upright in his seat, all his aches forgotten. It didn't take M'Senti's sudden intake of breath to tell him. 'She's security?' Seolta asked via his com.

'Looks like it. I'm getting a blank under her image, but there is one older trace, a face in a crowd from many years ago. Her Academy degrees are real, according to her public profile, but the crowd scene was students leaving the Alliance political studies school. The one where they train their intelligence agents.'

Nor did the Council advisor tell her to sit down or stop talking. The woman had to be seriously high-ranked. What in all the roots was going on here?

The ambassador was still on her feet. She glared at the other side of the table, her mouth straightening furiously when she looked at Vydayun. "No enemy's niece decides the fate of Arcadia."

Then she sat, both hands gripping her chair arms and mouth firmly set.

Another deadlock, and beside him, Anyara looked ready to burst into tears. It wasn't obvious, but her hand under the table had reached for his and gripped hard enough to bruise.

He leaned forward. "There is no need for the Messera to go anywhere."

Just then, the outer door slammed open and his medic bustled in. "Messer den Coille has had enough. His readings are rising."

"No, I'm fine," he tried to say. He couldn't leave now. Who knew what they'd cudgel Anyara into? The tragging woman ignored him. He looked to the ambassador, pleading.

She rose, and he gave a silent cheer. "This meeting is over, Messers. Please forward any further proposals to the embassy for consideration." She turned and strode out, waiting at the door for him to be transferred to a carry chair, then blocked the entrance to allow him and Anyara to leave first.

"We will see you to your room, Ser den Coille," she said with no hint of compromise in her voice.

"And the Messera Anyara?"

"Will return to the embassy with us, if that is acceptable to the Messera."

"No, no. I can't ask that of you," said Anyara. "I'm sure it will be safe for me to return to the Academy."

"No, Messera," said M'Senti grimly.

"He is right," said another voice behind them. Seolta swung around, or as much as he could in the cursed confines of his chair. It was the suspect Biota woman.

"Who exactly are you, Messera?" he asked.

"I'll tell you when you're all safely in the Arcadian embassy," she said. "Ambassador, are your medical facilities adequate for Messer den Coille's recuperation?"

The ambassador looked as wary as Seolta felt. "We have the standard diplomatic setup."

Vydayun turned to the medic. "Will that be sufficient for the Messer's needs?"

"As long as their medic contacts us immediately if there's any deterioration. I can send through his medical file and required treatments, if that is acceptable to Messer den Coille."

Was he happy to have his personal file open to the embassy medics? Not really, but he couldn't see he had a choice. "It is," he said, "as long as Messera Anyara agrees to come with me."

He was forcing her, but right now he didn't care. Not if a high-ranking Alliance intelligence official thought the embassy the safest place for Anyara. Nor did he relax until they'd made it through the city streets and the embassy gates clanged shut behind them, especially when he saw the vehicle the ambassador had called up for their transport. A fully armoured city skimmer, large enough to take them all and accompanied by a pair of security skimmers with weapon docks ready. Vydayun rode in her own transport, an unmarked skimmer that looked even more menacing. The hairs on Seolta's neck twitched all the way through the streets, and Vydayun's skimmer followed them through the embassy's gates.

Once inside, he fought to hold on to his patience as the medic fussed over him, taking an interminable time to pass on a litany of instructions to the embassy's medic and inspect his quarters. His room had been upgraded, it appeared, and was large and comfortable. Fortunately, his new medic finally drew the clinic medic away and escorted her out of the room.

And out of the embassy, he hoped, never to return. The tragging woman thought he'd chosen to take that filthy drug. He waited until M'Senti returned.

"She gone?"

A slight twitch of the marshal's mouth. "Yes, Ser … for now." Then the twitch disappeared. "We also found the source of the drug. It was your personal canteen."

He shot up. "I didn't put it there."

The marshal waved him back down. "The inside had been coated with a lining. It released the drug in response to contact with water. You have many attributes, Ser, but the required expertise in pharmacology isn't one of them."

"I could have paid for it."

The marshal shrugged. "You also have a strong predilection for being in control of anything touching you. Surrendering to a drug like kephartin isn't in your personality profile."

"Thank you, I think." He'd come to like the marshal, but the man had entirely too much knowledge about him. "Has the canteen been destroyed?"

"It is being held by embassy security as evidence."

"Oh, good," he said, wishing it was good. The canteen was a present from Samhchair when he left Arcadia, and he would hate to lose it, but he did not want to risk any more of that filth in his system and didn't yet know when the canteen had been tampered with.

The embassy medic returned. He eyed her warily. Her lips lifted. "Yes, Ser den Coille. You need to rest. You are still far from well."

"After we find out what's going on."

Surprisingly, M'Senti supported him. "The Ser will rest after the meeting with the Alliance official is completed."

"And I've made sure Sera Anyara is properly looked after," Seolta added.

"She has been shown to her room," said M'Senti. "Then she is being escorted to the meeting room."

"We'd better join the rest then" said Seolta, taking hold of his chair controls and whizzing out of the room before the tragging medic said anything to stop him. M'Senti hurried after him. "Wrong way, Ser."

Seolta slammed on the controls and followed him the other way down the corridor.

They both arrived in the boardroom at the same time. Inside, the rest of the embassy staff and Vydayun were already waiting. The Council advisor had also arrived and sat in a chair on one side of Vydayun. Anyara sat across from her, looking no happier than when he'd last seen her.

They all stood when he entered and every hair in his body stood on end.

CHAPTER TWENTY-FIVE

Anyara watched as Seolta angled his chair into place beside her. If only they'd give him more time to recover after the transfer to the embassy. He hadn't told her everything he suspected about the crash, but she badly needed to see him walk freely into the room, that dubious smile lingering in the corner of his mouth as if amused at the lead-footedness of those around him.

He wasn't the only one here who liked to manipulate people. Messera Vydayun rose as he wheeled in his chair. The woman had used her, making Anyara feel all kinds of fool. Worse, she'd used Anyara to put Seolta at risk, and that was unforgivable.

"Are you up to continuing, Messer den Coille," the woman said now.

"Of course," he said although Anyara seriously doubted it. If the medic said Seolta's readings showed trouble, she meant it and his hands gripped the sides of the chair as if needing their support to keep going.

Whatever happened in this meeting had better happen quickly.

"You can start," said Seolta, "by telling us exactly who you are."

"Messera Binku Vydayun, second-degree advisor with the Biota Department."

"Who else?"

The woman's face creased in the nearest Anyara had seen to a smile. "I was seconded some years ago to the President's Attachment."

Was that gasp from her? She wasn't the only one. The President's Attachment was an arm of the security forces rarely mentioned, its activities so secret that the very existence of the unit was the merest of whispers. They did the Council president's work, monitored by a Council security panel.

Fear stalked the room.

"Which Council faction sent you?"

The ghost smile vanished and the woman crossed her hands. "You are aware of the current population dynamics in the Alliance, Messera Anyara."

Her uncle had tendrils everywhere. She nodded, terrified. "Almost evenly balanced between EA and habitat worlds. Last I checked, the EA representatives held the balance."

Vydayun nodded. "And still do, just."

The ambassador leaned forward. "What's that got to do with the Council's ultimatum to Arcadia?"

"As I said, the EA group holds the balance of power, but it fluctuates. They lost the Arcadian vote. Your planet is in real trouble, Messera, but there is disagreement about the solution."

The embassy scientist spoke up next. Anyara just wished he was a biome expert. "Show us the reports, Messera. The full ones given to the Council. We've never seen the justification for the tight deadline or the highly punitive penalty if we fail to comply adequately. Depopulating an entire world is exceedingly harsh and dangerous."

"The facts can support it," Vydayun said mildly. "Whether it is a dangerous response depends entirely on who replaces the current settlers."

"No one is better than the *current settlers*," snapped Seolta. "It's our home; we know it best."

"Then prove it, Messer," said Vydayun, all trace of humour gone.

She saw the tide of colour rise up in Seolta's face, saw him try to stand, then his jaw shut tight and he sank back into his chair with a thump that must have hurt. "How?" he said, voice flat, and Anyara tensed.

Vydayun leaned back and took in the whole room, including the Council advisor. "I've already told you. A full and independent audit of Arcadia's environmental state. The EA faction is winning at present, but it can't continue. The habitat populations are rising and their citizens are demanding lives that match those of the other Alliance citizens, in particular, those living in the EA paradises."

A harsh grunt of laughter from the embassy staff. It was an old joke. All the EA worlds were named by one of the old Terran language words for paradise. Some met the term better than others, Arcadia reputed to be the closest.

"And you, Messera Vydayun? What is your allegiance?" said the ambassador.

"I work for the Council, Messera."

"Your home planet?" said Seolta.

"Divaajin."

The least habitable of the EA worlds. A lower-water planet at the edge of Alliance space. The settlers there were fiercely independent.

"An EA planet," said Anyara.

"Yes," said Vydayun.

"You would sacrifice the habitat worlds?" she asked, feeling suddenly very alone in this room.

"No, Messera," said the woman, "but we all need each other. None of the habitat worlds can maintain a population anywhere close to an EA world, and the EA worlds provide resources that cannot be found on habitat worlds."

"Yet," said Anyara stubbornly.

The woman nodded. "You are one of the best biome techs of your generation, Messera. Given time, you can probably make even the most forbidding habitat bloom. But no artificial habitat can reproduce the complexity of an EA world, just as no EA world can afford to exploit the mineral or non-biotic wealth of their planet as the habitats can. We all need each other."

Anyara wasn't convinced. How did she know that what this woman wanted from her wouldn't harm her home world. "The children of Kevand Station deserve as many opportunities as any other children," she said stubbornly.

"Would they prefer to live on an EA world, Messera?"

Could she live without a protective shell over her head? "I have never visited an EA world, Messera," she conceded.

"Now is the perfect opportunity," said the woman.

"We'll agree to the environmental review but not her," said the ambassador flatly. "Not with her connections."

Anyara shrank inside. The ambassador was right, and nothing could change it. Or could it? An idea came to her.

"I need to talk to Messer Seolta. In private," she said.

The table erupted in a torrent of words and shouts, but finally they were given a room to one side, with a guard on the door. Whether to keep others out or to keep them in, she didn't like to ask. There were comfortable chairs by a window, but she was too nervous to sit. She paced up and down, then glanced at Seolta, waiting quietly by the window in that stupid motorised chair. He'd said nothing at all since entering.

She grasped her hands together, heaved in a breath, and turned to him, watching him brace himself against her.

"Will you be my life partner?" she said bluntly.

His face flashed red, then lost all colour. She suspected it was the last thing he'd thought she'd ask but all he said was, "Why?"

Wasn't it obvious? "It makes me a connection of an Arcadian. They can't deny me entry. Then I can do this audit they want." He sat still, saying nothing, studying her.

"I'll be neutral, belonging to both EA and habitat worlds. No one can argue with my report."

"You're not a planetary biome specialist," he said in that scarily controlled voice.

"No, but I am a recognised biome tech and understand habitat biomes. Habitat dwellers wouldn't trust an EA specialist; they all come from EA worlds."

"And if you find that the Council's first ruling was correct? That my home world must meet their deadline or face the consequences?"

She swallowed. Could she make him homeless? "It's for the Council to make the final ruling."

"Your report will decide it, though. Will it be the truth as you see it, regardless of the outcome?"

He'd never let her be less than she was capable of. For a craven moment, she wished he would. She gripped her hands tighter.

"It will be accurate. It has to be."

He never took his eyes off her, not for one moment. "Why?" he said again.

"I've told you."

"You've given me a list of reasons. All very rational and worthy. Is that all of them?"

"Of course. Only a neutral report can stop the plots and expose those trying to steal a place on Arcadia."

"But you can't promise to save my home world."

"No," she whispered, "but it's a chance."

"A chance for which you're prepared to sacrifice yourself. To become life partner to a man likely to be homeless if you're wrong."

She flung herself away from him, and marched to the far side of the room. "At least you'd be alive." When she turned back, he still watched her, those dark eyes never once leaving her face. She forced herself to meet his gaze.

He watched her feet shift restlessly, his body never moving. Then he slowly stood, using the chair to lever himself up.

"No," he said.

What did he mean? No, he wouldn't be alive?

"No, Messera Anyara a Prithand2. I will not marry you. Not for those reasons. Not to save my world, not to save my life. They're not enough."

"Marry?" She knew the word. It came from the old fairy tales.

"It's what we do on Arcadia when we find someone we love and want to be with them for life," he said gently.

She waved a hand. "I didn't… That's not what I asked you."

"No, *mo Graidh,* it's not. But you see, I do. Love you, I mean. Want to share my life, my corrupted wealth, my pathetic dreams with you. So the answer, my dearest Sera Anyara, is no. I will not become your *life partner* to force my world to accept you. I will not take part in such a travesty. No."

A loud thumping filled the room, then she realised it was her heart beating. "What do you mean?" she said stupidly. She groped for and found a chair, falling into it. "You can't."

"Love you? No. Presumptuous, I know. But I do have one precious dream, and that is that one day, I will ask you, and you will say yes to me, for all the right reasons. But that is not today."

Tears beat against her eyes. "You have to. I can't keep you safe any other way."

"And you, *mo Graidh*? It puts you in more danger. You're safe here in the Academy."

"That doesn't matter."

A twisted smile touched his face, one she'd never seen before. "But you see, my heart, it does to me. Very much so."

She stared at him, unable to believe her plan was in ashes. Lines gouged each side of his mouth and his hands gripped tightly on the chair. He loved her, he said. A dream, he said. Yes, an impossible one. Did she love him? It had been so long since she'd dared let herself like anyone, let alone love. Love was scary. Love left you open to loss. She'd learned that when her parents died. Never since had she dared to open herself up.

But barren places in a garden rarely stayed empty, and some of her most prized plants were those that had found their own homes, sprouting up to delight her in forgotten corners of the station gardens. Barren places like her heart. She'd refused to wonder why this man's life, this man's future mattered so much to her.

She lifted her chin. He put out a hand, as if trying to stop her. "No, *mo Graidh*."

"Yes, Messer Seolta. You do not control everything. You claim to love me, but you will not let me do this for you. That seems a poor kind of love to me."

His mouth tightened and she wished she could stop the words she had to speak. "Do I love you? I don't know, not yet. You grew up surrounded by love, but for me ... it is a difficult proposition."

"I know that," he said, sounding as if his voice was strangled.

She gripped her hands to stop them lifting towards him. "I am asking for a life partner. It is a legal construct. Whatever else it may mean is between us and is no one else's business. Nor does it bind you permanently, but it does let me do this for you and for your world. You have no better choice." She wrung her hands tighter. "Or will you betray them again?"

He dropped back into his chair as if she'd shot him with a full charge blaster.

"If I refuse, what will you do?" he said, tight-lipped.

She hadn't thought of a backup plan. She'd just assumed…

"I am going to Arcadia regardless. It is the best way to find the truth. To expose the conspirators and force the Council to decide on your world's fate on the basis of science, not political gain."

"They won't let you in."

"They will if the Council orders it."

Seolta's skin blanched completely. "Every disaffected idiot on Arcadia will be after you if they force us to let you in. The kind of changes we're facing don't make us hospitable."

"I'm sure the Council will provide me with a security guard and so will the Arcadian government."

"One that meets your uncle's approval? That will really keep you safe." A harsh drawl cut through the words. "Arcadia is not the world of the tourist vids."

"You think I don't know that? You're from there."

This time he did flush.

"I'm going, with your family's protection or without."

"That's blackmail."

"I know," she said sadly, "but I have no choice. Not if I want you to live."

The rest of the meeting didn't take long once they returned to the outer room. After the gasps and wrangles had died down, they all agreed. The ambassador and the Council advisor were the only ones looking satisfied at the end. The finance and tech embassy advisors grudgingly accepted and Vydayun gave no clue to her thoughts, but Anyara suspected she was also smugly satisfied. The woman probably had this in mind right from the start.

The ceremony didn't take long either. Seolta insisted on leaving it until he was well enough to stand and sign his agreement without faltering. He didn't look at her once during it, setting his thumb scan and skin trace to the agreement with a deadly precision. Nor did he talk to her afterwards, bowing scrupulously to her before returning to his room. It was the last she saw of him until she found herself standing on an interplanetary docking bay, waiting for a shuttle to their ship, baggage carefully packed, notes organised, Council warrant properly filed—and with her legally constituted life partner by her side.

Someday, Seolta might forgive her for the last part.

Not throughout the long trip to his home world. He was polite, attentive, played the new partner studiously, but at night he kept to his own room in their suite and his eyes never lost a hard sparkle.

She hated every moment of it, through all the smiles and pleasantries she returned him, each one adding to that cold glint. Yet there was one question she didn't think to ask herself. Did he love her still?

Of course. Why else was he so angry?

When they were above his home world, her gasp of wonder matched a tear standing in his eye.

"I didn't think I'd see it again," he whispered, gazing down on his world with hunger stark on his face. She reached out a hand, and this time he took it and gently squeezed it. "Thank you."

It was enough.

He kept hold of her hand all through the ordeal of border clearance, of greeting the incoming officials, of the barely concealed antagonism on the faces of the security staff checking their Council and Arcadian travel permits. She could feel the tension in him, the barely suppressed urgency to be done with it all and hurry on outside these bare rooms. She also saw the shock on his face when the first official had spoken, addressing him as *Ser den Coille*. He was home.

She wasn't.

When they finally finished all the regulation stuff, far more onerous than any she'd met before but what she'd been warned to expect on an EA world, they had a delegation from the Arcadian Galactic Ministry to navigate. Security stopped them as they went to take the doors to the outside and diverted them into a side room. Seolta took one look at the waiting group and dropped her hand, but kept close, a fingertip touch away. She needed it, and suspected he did too.

The leader bowed to her and introduced the team with him. "Arcadia is honoured at your visit, Esteemed Scholar." He gestured forward one woman, middle-aged and round-faced. "Sera Broder has been assigned to assist you during your stay. Please let her know of anything you need."

Seolta bristled beside her. The delegation had ignored him completely. "Thank you, Messers," she said hastily, then remembered she was on a new planet. "Sers and Seras. We will be taking a few days private leave first, to meet my new life partner's family. I'm sure you will understand. I will contact Sera Broder as soon as I am ready to begin my audit."

"Of course, Sera. A transport flyer is outside to take you to your hotel."

"My family flyer is waiting for us," said Seolta abruptly. He took Anyara by the arm and steered her briskly out the door and towards a side entrance she hadn't noticed till now. A troop of soldiers immediately split off from the Ministry group and hurried to follow them.

Seolta was having none of it. Before she knew what had happened, they were out of the hall and he'd dragged her into a huge open space. She hurried to keep up with him, eyes fixed on the ground to avoid tripping. He came to a lawn. A precious patch of living grass. He marched right to the middle of it, and she had to follow, trying to step as lightly as possible on the live plants. Then he stopped, threw back his head as if in worship and breathed in deeply.

"Sun. Air," he said. The smile on his face was one of pure happiness. "Feel it, *mo Graidh.*"

She looked up, felt the warmth, then saw where he looked. Up and up into…

Nothing. A light haze, a blue seen only in vids, wisps of … clouds? No shell protected her.

Anyara froze. She was out on a planet surface, without suit or breather, vehicle or protective shield. Exposed.

Seolta's arm came round her shoulders. "Beautiful, isn't it. But we need to move. My flyer is over this way. Come on, we need to get away from this port."

She shut her eyes and dug in her heels. She clutched his arm and clung tight. She tried opening her eyes. Colours, space, a wide-open emptiness looming over her. She hastily shut them again. "Please tell me this is a vidchamber."

Something finally got through to Seolta. He stopped trying to pull her. More feet clumped to a halt around her, and a woman's voice snapped at Seolta.

Messera Broder, that was her name.

"Is this her first time on an EA world?" demanded the woman.

"Yes," said Seolta.

"You idiot."

That was Messera Broder again. A strange pair of arms surrounded her and she felt the shock in Seolta's arms at the intrusion. "Messera," said the woman softly. "I'm going to put a vid shield on you. Then we will take you back inside and condition you properly to an EA world."

Next minute, the familiar feel of VA probes shrouded her head and she opened her eyes again.

"Take a minute," said the woman. Seolta's arms had dropped away but she could feel him brushing her close. Could feel the tension in him. "Now try."

The exterior view hadn't changed, but the slight shimmer at the edge of her vision was blessedly familiar. You're in an immersion vid, her brain told her. No need to panic. You're safe in a habitat.

It wasn't true, and her hand reached out and clung to Seolta's. "Don't leave me."

"Never, *mo Graidh*," he said, and his long, clever fingers linked with hers.

"The Sera will be safe with us," said the woman. Seolta gave her a look of sharp dislike.

"The Sera is promised to me. I'm not leaving her."

Anyara felt all kinds of stupid. "Your family are waiting," she said, guilt stepping in as the panic receded. "I'll be fine."

He shook his head and kept a tight hold on her hand as she followed Messera—no, *Sera* Broder to another building on the side of the port. A kernel of relieved warmth filled her as his crisp steps kept pace and his hand grasped hers.

Once inside, a medic came hurrying forward. "We have an habituation chamber waiting, Sera. Please, this way."

"What's that?" said Seolta suspiciously. "And who are you?"

Anyara wished she could disappear into the floor. This wasn't how she'd imagined coming to an EA world. "I'm sorry," she said. "You were right. This plan was never going to work. I didn't understand."

"Shh, *mo Graidh*."

How did he do that. Speak so gently to her while glaring so fiercely at the medics trying to order her away?

More bootsteps, and her embarrassment was complete. She recognised the uniform as the same worn by Marshal M'Senti in the Arcadian embassy. She tried releasing Seolta's hand. He didn't need to be arrested on top of being lumped with a feeble life partner.

"Marshal an Fallon."

She'd never heard that note in Seolta's voice before when addressing someone. Almost as if he trusted the man.

"You've been creating your usual strife, young Seolta?"

"Ever ready to oblige, Marshal," said Seolta. "You're here to save me again, I hope."

"From yourself, I hear. Nothing changes."

Seolta grinned, and Anyara stared at him. The marshal was more grim-faced than M'Senti. Older, lines of duty carved into his face and a sense of authority she doubted ever left him.

The man turned to her. "Esteemed Scholar, it is an honour, though I do question your judgement."

Seolta's mouth twisted as if enjoying a joke, although what it might be she didn't understand. The man had just insulted him.

"Messera Anyara a Prithand2, this is Marshal an Fallon, head of the Federal Marshals. He's had to save my sorry self more than once and, fortunately, hasn't yet decided it's not worth saving again."

"Hmmph," said the man. "Don't tempt me. I hadn't expected to have to deal with your unique brand of disturbance again. Didn't we exile you?"

Seolta shrugged. "The Alliance Council decided otherwise. They felt even an unworthy specimen like me deserved a conjugal trip. Don't worry. It's only temporary. Our permit runs out before the year's cycle is up."

A look of profound sympathy crossed the man's face. "Yes, I heard that too. You'd better not waste time then."

Anyara felt even more guilty. "Go," she said. "I'll be fine. I'll come later." She didn't add 'if I can' but thought it.

"Marshal, we need your help," said Seolta.

"No, you need a dose of sense, as usual, Ser den Coille. The Sera is right. She has to go into the chamber or risk damage from EA shock."

He looked at both their faces.

"Did no one warn you?"

Seolta flushed. "We didn't give them much chance."

Which wasn't quite the truth, and Anyara blamed Messera Vydayun, their so-called benefactor, most of all. The woman had always had her own agenda.

"No matter," said the marshal. "The Sera will need to spend a few days with the medics, and you can stay or go on to visit your family."

"I'm staying," said Seolta. That ended the argument.

Not that she got much chance to see him. She was bundled into a large chamber, complete with everything she could need, and was introduced to what the medics euphemistically called transition. What they really meant was claiming control of her life, her day carefully mapped out complete with medication. It was to habituate her, they said, but it left her feeling woolly-headed and dislocated. Seolta was allowed to see her for breakfast, and she couldn't miss his quickly controlled flinch when she fumbled her drink mug.

"You don't have to come," she said, wishing the drugs would let her cry. "Go home, see your family. Enjoy what time you have."

"I'm staying," he said stubbornly.

There was a window in the ceiling of her room. She'd wondered what it was there for until the second day when the cover was removed. A beam of sunshine angled down onto her floor and the medic encouraged her to dip her toe into the bright patch. She baulked at first, then gathered her courage, stretching one foot cautiously towards the bright spot.

"It's warm," she said in delight.

"Sunshine usually is," he said. "You're lucky. Urbis is notorious for its weather, but we're in for a fine spell."

What was he talking about? Then she remembered. Weather. Uncontrolled environmental conditions. She'd been out on the surface of Surned, but never in 'bad weather'. No one did that if they wanted to survive. A normal day on the Surned surface was murky, dull brown, with a surface temperature too high for humans without a protective suit. Their system's sun never pierced the thick cloud cover, and Kevand Station had few ports from which sun was visible. She had preferred to look at her gardens rather than the black deadness of outside space. On the station, sunlight was used for energy creation. Daylight for her biomes came from artificial light sources tailored to suit the biome sector's needs.

Random weather in a station? Unthinkable. She pulled her foot away.

"Try it again, Sera," said the soothing voice of today's medic. "We are monitoring your exposure. You're quite safe."

She thought back to the hunger on Seolta's face when they'd arrived above his home world. Did she have less courage than he did?

She stretched out her foot again.

"With your eyes open, Sera." There was a smile in the woman's voice, and Anyara grudgingly opened her eyes.

The next day, they asked her to stand in the light and look up. She managed two standard seconds on the first session, and they gushed fulsomely. She felt a fraud. By the end of the day, she had withstood the panic for a full half hour, and welcomed their praise. She'd earned it. By day four, she had graduated to a first venture outside into a courtyard garden, and they began to step back the drugs. Seolta's face wasn't as tightly schooled when he joined her that morning, and by day's end, she had begun to enjoy the smells and sounds of the abundance in the garden welcoming her. They stopped the medication on day five and, for the first time in far too long, he gave her the smile she loved most, a slight lift of his lips and an edge in his eyes. The smile that was real. She'd dreamed last night. She was walking in a forest, the one in Seolta's sim.

The medics woke her on day six. "Congratulations, Sera."

She sat up groggily. "What do you mean?"

"You're leaving us today. Well done. It usually takes first-time spacers a full week to habituate."

She blinked, then shook her head, shaking away the sleep-muddled fog. She'd dreamed again, and wondered now if that was their doing. Dreams of wind in branches, of green and brown. 'I'm not ready' she wanted to say.

"You'll be fine, Sera," said the woman.

They took her for a walk in the morning, out the main entrance and down what they called a street, though it was like none she'd seen before. Vegetation in abundance, buildings a strange hotchpotch of what must be apartment or office blocks and others looking abandoned. Why would anyone abandon a building without reclaiming the materials? She even managed to throw her head back and look up at the sky, as Seolta had done on his arrival on this world, and laughed as the medic pointed out shapes in the clouds. Faint twinges battered at her, demands to get out of here before she vanished in a caustic cloud or floated away, but she thrust them back and hoped the medic didn't see.

It was afternoon before Seolta arrived, an enormous smile on his face. He held out his hand and she walked out of the chamber.

"You ready to go home?"

She grinned and took his hand. "Yes, my dearest." She didn't voice her silent 'I hope.' Then noticed the shock on his face. She lifted his hand to her mouth and set her lips to his knuckles. "You've waited long enough. Thank you."

He pulled her close, ignoring the medics, and kissed her thoroughly. "You brought me this far. Now, I'm taking you home. I promised you trees once." Then he pulled out a package. "I got you this." He held it out, as if unsure whether she'd accept. "The medics said you might still have moments of panic. I thought this might help."

He'd never bought her anything before. Not personal. She smiled, feeling as if she had already been given the best present. He'd even had them wrap it in a proper presentation wrap. She carefully peeled it off and folded it up for preservation. Inside was a box made of real wood. She gasped.

"Wood's not that rare here. We use it for many things."

Maybe, but she'd never seen it used for anything like this. "It's beautiful." She stroked a hand over it, wondering at the smooth feel.

"Open it," he said. "There's a catch at the front.

There was. An old fashioned one, a hook fitting into a small loop, surrounded by small metal plates carved into intricate whirls. She lifted the hook and slowly opened the top. Then gasped again. Words left her. It was exquisite.

A small hair clip, not much larger than her smallest finger, a maze of tiny curling wires fashioned into an intricate flower design, each delicately edged with sparkling jewels she had an ominous feeling were both real and precious. She reached out a finger, too scared to touch.

He lifted it and set it just behind her ear. The clip fit neatly into the curve there as if made for her.

"The medics said having the feel of a vid piece might help. You can touch it whenever you feel the sky beginning to overwhelm you."

No vid piece looked like this. "Thank you," she said, stunned. She pulled up the holo-mirror in her com. Small and precious, the clip was the kind that could be worn any time. Discreet enough for everyday wear and special enough for the most formal occasion. "I was always told you were the cleverest in your family."

That lean face of his tightened and she wished she could take back the words. Then he gave her his rare smile. "I haven't shown much sign of it in recent times, but falling in love with you, *mo Graidh,* was the most intelligent thing I've ever done. Forgive me."

She didn't have to ask 'what for'. His silence on the ship here. "You had good reason."

"Few have crossed me before for my own good and succeeded. My mother is going to enjoy meeting you."

Anyara's heart plummeted again. "I haven't much experience with mothers."

"Don't worry. You'll love her. Everyone does."

"And your father?"

Now he laughed. "He's the one I take after."

"Oh."

CHAPTER TWENTY-SIX

All her poring over sim illusions hadn't prepared her for the reality. They flew over lands greater in scope than any she'd known. Neat squares of what Seolta called farms, edged with lines of trees and bushes. At each new vista, she asked to set down, and each time he laughed and shook his head.

"Another time, please. If we stop to look at every new plant or animal you spot, it'll take us months to get home." The buried yearning in his voice had her agreeing each time.

A while later, they left land that had at least some resemblance to the controlled biomes of her habitat homes and began to lift higher. She looked up ahead and squawked in fright.

Huge, jagged blocks of rock rose up from the controlled plains, reaching higher and higher. What did Seolta think he was doing?

Another chuckle from him. "Sorry, I couldn't resist the chance to feel the upwells from the mountains again. There's a pass up ahead." He angled to one side, and the terrifying cliffs faded to be replaced by a band of rolling hill country and more signs of settlement.

"You're going to die laughing at me by the time this trip's over."

His grin vanished. "I didn't mean to frighten you. I will not let this land hurt you."

She took a breath. "I know." She tugged at her straps to tighten them. "Give me a warning next time."

He nodded, and his face eased at something he saw on hers. "Your world is so … big," was all she could manage.

"Surned's not much smaller."

"A station is, and there are no more than a hundred habitats on the planet's surface. Here…" she swept her hand at the scene below, "we've been flying for ages and it's still habitable."

He smothered the grin that peeked out of the corner of his mouth. "Yes, Sera, it is."

Not long afterwards, the looming bulk of mountains on either side started to get smaller.

"There's an inn coming up. We can stop there for a break."

"You want to get home."

"Yes, but another hour or so isn't going to make a difference, and I'd hate you to first arrive at my home worn out and starving."

She shouldn't feel so relieved by the delay, but the closer they came to that home in the vids, to his family, the more her nerves jangled.

He set down in front of a building unlike any she'd seen. Two storeys only and plants bloomed everywhere—along both sides of the pathway leading to the large front door, in gardens batting up against it, and in shrubberies set in the wide, wide lawn, dotted with tables at which people sat as if to have such a large expanse of unproductive flora was nothing.

As if the only worth of the plants lay in the pleasure they gave. She'd heard of such places, read about them, knew they existed, but to visit one … She tugged at her strapping and jumped up as soon as she'd untangled the stupid thing. Seolta rose more slowly, a grin on his face. He pulled out a piece of fabric from the hatch beside him and took her hand as they walked down the hatch ramp. Whether to reassure her or stop her running up to each and every plant, she couldn't decide. A large woman bustled up.

"Ser, we haven't seen you for some time. Are your brothers and Ser Winter on their way too? I'll get your table ready."

"Not today, Sera, and," he looked at Anyara, one brow raised, "a table outside?"

"Ooh. Yes, please," she breathed out, touching her clip to centre herself. She must be dreaming.

He laughed again. "That one over by the centre flower bed will do nicely, Sera."

He walked her to a table set right beside a group of plants she'd never seen before, with a small, branching shrub set in the middle. Seolta gestured her to sit.

She couldn't. Too entranced. She touched the leaves of the bush, felt in wonder their glossy, crinkly surface. Then made a discovery. "It has flowers, hidden under the leaves." Small, tubular, and a stunning deep pink, each one tipped with creamy stamens peeking out from a petal-like skirt.

More flowers grew around the bush. Bright, crystalline blue leaves surrounding a fuzzball centre flower in a startling emerald green. She darted over and went to touch the gorgeous leaf. Seolta's hand snatched hers away.

"Not that one, *mo Graidh.* It's a native, and not a friendly one. Look down at the base."

She did, careful not to touch any part of the plant. There, to her horror, she saw a gelatinous shroud surrounding a small, insectoid creature. "It's carnivorous?"

Seolta nodded. "Those pretty leaves release poison-tipped spicules if you touch them. It won't kill you, but it leaves a nasty rash that itches like mad. It comes from a cold desert area and is designed to trap small browsing herbivores. They aren't leaves either. Those flowers are where the photosynthetic cells are found."

Her mouth dropped open, and he chuckled. "Come on, that's not what I stopped here to show you."

He tugged at her hand, and she followed him around the side of the building and to a hidden pathway between banks of even more shrubs. "These are safe?" she asked tentatively.

"Perfectly. Shut your eyes," he said with a mischievous edge in his voice.

Intrigued, she did as ordered and was immediately conscious of the scents surrounding her. Floral, earthy, herbaceous and sweet. They rounded another corner and a chill breeze caught at her sleeves, making her shiver but bringing even more intriguing scents. Sharp, slightly acidic, a smell that immediately made her think of the colour green. He dropped the fabric around her shoulders, and immediately she felt warmer. Her hand lifted and stroked the soft material.

"It's a mountain wrap. Wind-, water- and sun-proof. Our weather is subject to change without notice." He took her by the shoulders and angled her away from him. "Open your eyes," he said softly.

She did, and gasped. "It's a tree. A real tree." Tears touched her lashes. "It's so beautiful. The vids don't…"

The tree had the classic round shape. A tall, strong, central trunk with a maze of limbs branching off, tipped by leaves of a delicate stippled green.

"It moves."

"There's a bit of a breeze," he conceded.

"I can hear it," she said in delight. She moved forward as if in a dream, feeling the difference in temperature as she moved into the dappled shade of the canopy. She touched the trunk, running her hands gently over the rough surface: bumpy, and in a rainbow of shades from brown, to rust, to a deep cream. A flake came off and she grabbed back her hand.

"You haven't hurt it," said Seolta. "Beith trees shed patches of bark routinely. Do you like it?"

"It's…" She couldn't find a word, just shook her head and stared in wonder. "Beautiful, stunning, amazing. The words are not enough."

He dropped his head, and when he lifted it again, she was sure there was a touch of wetness on his lashes. "I thought you might like to see one," he said gruffly. "It's a clear day here and I wanted to show you a tree while we had good light."

She lifted one hand to his cheek, then her other and pulled his head down to hers. "Thank you," she said softly and set her lips to his.

He let her look her fill, then tugged her gently back towards their table. Drinks waited and a delicious baked flat bread with side dishes. She touched her hair clip as she sat, still feeling like she walked through a sim. Since seeing the tree, she hadn't had a moment of panic, too lost in delight.

Time flew, and soon they had to leave. The manager thrust a packet of the delicious bread onto them as they left, planting a smacking kiss on her cheeks. "It's good to see a proper smile back on this boy's face," she said. "It's been far too long. Come back soon, Sera."

There was a new tension in Seolta when they set off. She leaned forward as they lifted up from the inn and headed towards the mountains. For the first time, she began to wonder if this trip was a good idea.

"Let me know when we enter your home territory," she said to cover the taut silence.

"We already have. The first foothills to the south of the Junction Inn are the northern boundary of den Coille country."

She looked out the window. They had lifted high above the inn and headed towards the mountains, lifting higher still. "You own all this?"

He shook his head. "Not so simple. We're the dominant business here, but other mountain cities also have interests. It's why the older tree growth is still mixed types." In the sims she'd viewed of this region, the heavy preponderance of the festia tree species had rung a warning bell for her. The subject was too mixed up with Seolta's past to know what he thought, though. "We own a lot of it," he said, "but also contract out to other landowners. Closer to home, we own more but lease some too."

"Who's in charge of the region?" She hadn't yet worked out how the politics of this planet worked.

He gave her the dry answer, naming Council representatives and councillors, and local region executives. It was too pat and she opened her mouth to challenge him. He raised a hand from the control field with a grin. "All right. They're the elected officials, and handle most stuff, but Da is the power. Any of them try to cross Den Coille and they soon get voted out. Or that's how it's been most of my life."

They headed up and over the forbidding peaks of these western ranges, settling down on the far side. No more clear skies. Dark clouds and wicked air patterns hit their flyer and a spark of excitement filled Seolta's eyes. She tried to conceal her tight grip on the flyer's seat.

South and down they flew, hugging the western slopes of the mountains, and after a while she forgot her fears.

"Is it always like this?"

"Changeable or wild?" he asked.

"Both."

"If you're lucky." He laughed. "Some days, it's even more fun."

She groaned, but couldn't banish the prickle of excitement beginning to invade her. He was so *happy*. He'd taken them out over the sea, white waves churning madly below. He dipped down, then soared up again and hugged the mountain sides. South and south they flew, the trees growing denser. Then she saw her first of the giant baullnias, a massive specimen standing high on a bluff above a fearsome cliff face and the clawing seas below. Seolta took them as close as he dared in the tearing winds.

"It's huge," she said breathlessly. Maybe his talk of their tensile strength had some truth. "It shouldn't be possible for a plant to be that big."

He grinned, as if she'd given him a special present. "That's what the first engineers said when they came across them. This one is a special grandaddy. The last survivor of a city that used to stand here. There was a catastrophic collapse of that bluff many years ago. They lost much of the city and the rest of the inhabitants moved away."

He dipped the sides of the flyer as if in salute. "We always mark the place when we come by here."

Too soon they hovered over his city. Or he claimed they did. She remembered how well hidden it had been in the sims but for some reason hadn't expected it in reality. She peered through the swirling rain and mists.

"Wait," he said with a grin she suspected his mother had been only too familiar with when he was a small boy. He sent out his call sign.

"Den Coille five, clear to land."

They dropped down. Closer and closer to the forbidding wall of the tree canopy. She recognised the leaf type from her studies. Below them lay a small forest of the mighty baullnia, which meant that any mistake had them crashing into branches well above a safe falling distance from the ground.

'Wait,' he'd said, and she held her breath.

They touched down on … something. She dared to look out. It was a flyer platform, rising up from the canopy. Then it began to sink down into it and she had to shut her eyes, wishing hard for the reassuring shimmer of a sim.

They came to a stop, without any sounds of tearing or smashing. She dared to open her eyes, and looked right into his laughing dark ones. "Come on, Sera Anyara. We're home."

He took her hand and tugged her from her seat as soon as she'd managed to finally hit the button to release her strapping. She held tight to him, hit with a new fear.

"They will love you," he murmured. "You brought me home, after all."

For a too short visit, and would take him away again. Nor could they tell his family the real reason she was here. Only the marshals and senior planetary heads knew that. Then his words struck her. What would it be like to have a family like his, one he had no doubt would welcome him back?

Her only relative would rub his hands in glee at news of her accidental demise.

Outside the hatch, the landing pad looked much as the one in the vid. A flat plasmetal pad and a waiting office. She'd expected to face a deluge from the wild weather but thankfully there was a protective shield.

You haven't come to a primitive backwater, no matter how wild it looks. Best she not forget that.

Waiting in the arrival building stood a full contingent of people. "They're not all family, are they?" she muttered to Seolta.

"No, just the centre grouping. The rest are various officials and guards."

The centre grouping looked big enough, most clearly recognisable as the family in the holograph, all with the same dark hair, tan skin and dark eyes. He was lighter in build than his brothers, but they all looked as fit. In the back, behind the sister who looked most like him, stood an anomaly of a man. Tall, rangy in build and with sandy hair and fair skin. The Winter brother, partner to the sister with the unpronounceable name. She had memorised all their faces on that long trip, but nothing stopped the quaking in her gut as Seolta brought her to a halt in front of them, or prepared her for the tears in the eyes of his sisters and mother.

The formidable man in the middle spoke first.

"You're home, son," said Seolta's father, "and with a guest."

Seolta bowed low. "My life partner, Da. Messera Esteemed Scholar Anyara a Prithand2 of Kevand Station, let me make known to you my father, Ser Bram mar Gliocas duine Scathach den Coille of Manascraoch."

Nice, he'd combined the expected addresses of both their home worlds. The man bowed low to her and not so low to his son. "Welcome to our home, Messera Esteemed Scholar. May the trees shelter you and keep you safe during your stay."

"Thank you. May the waters of life sustain you always, Messer Bram mar Gliocas duine Scathach den Coille." She seemed to have got it right, or almost so. A slight twist of the man's lips but that was all, and it was probably at her atrocious pronunciation. Seolta's home language was a challenge she hadn't yet mastered. Thank the stars they all spoke Standard.

His mother came forward next, bowed low, and greeted her. "Thank you for bringing him home to us, Sera," she said, before finally giving in to the urge Anyara had seen in her eyes since her first sight of her son. She pulled Seolta into her arms and Anyara released his hand at the sight of the moisture tipping his lashes, then stepped back at the sound of his mother's sobbing. She'd read this woman's bio; the woman ran the main hospital here and had seen plenty of grief in her days.

"She's been walking the boards every night since we heard the news," said Bram den Coille with a fond crease around his eyes. "Thank you, Sera."

"You know it's only temporary," said Anyara.

Messer den Coille nodded. "We can talk about that later," he said firmly.

Only there was nothing to talk about. It was fixed, and one look at her face must have told him that. "Let me introduce you to the rest of the family."

He started on the right. From the elder sister, one of her hands reaching out to touch her brother, then next to the eldest brother. Samhchair and Cumchdach. Anyara managed to get out a version of their names. Both had the look of their mother, with a similarly steady gaze and feet squarely planted. Next was another brother, Ceart, the biggest and broadest of them all. The man gave her a short grunt in place of a greeting—his usual response, she gathered from the rest of the family. Next came the sister with the name she didn't even try to pronounce, the ecological engineer with their Survey. Smallest of all of them, with a dark mischievousness that echoed her brother's subtlety, she grinned widely at Anyara's stumbles.

"Call me Fee," she said, "and the big hulk here is my husband, Caleb."

Anyara couldn't stop the smile of relief. "An honour to meet you both," she said.

"Believe me, the honour is ours," she said. "You can help us beat some real science into these anachronistic fossils."

A chorus of complaints greeted that, and Anyara reddened, starting to step back again, only to meet the comforting support of Seolta, his arm snaking around her waist.

"Don't scare her off too soon, Fioruisghe. It was hard enough to persuade her to take me on." He may have added a chuckle, but there was an edge to his voice. This was the sister most like him, he'd once hinted, and she could see it. In both build and temperament. The glint in the dark eyes of both was identical.

The youngest thrust forward, despite a slight limp. "Give over, you two. Ignore them, Sera." He gave her a low bow, ending with a flourish, and a glarc at his sister and brother-in-law. "Caleb, can't you control her?" he said to the tall man behind Fee, who just chuckled.

"I'm not stupid enough to try. You are very welcome, Esteemed Scholar. I hope you can spare some time while you're here to visit the Survey headquarters in Urbis. Many there are eager to discuss your work with you."

"We'll see," she said, and doubted she had fooled the man. The Arcadian embassy had passed on an information pack from the Survey before she left Alliance Central and she'd made contact with their head office not long after her arrival. She had an appointment to meet with them at Survey headquarters once her audit was completed.

Seolta's arm tightened on her waist. "Maybe after our tour of the planet. She's never been on an EA world and I'm looking forward to showing it to her."

"You've only just got here," said their mother. "Not so soon."

"No, Mam. We've got a week here."

"Good."

Anyara watched in fascination as the woman pulled her control around her again. "Then we need to get you out of this weather and settled in. The kitchens have been working all day. There are so many wanting to see you. Come along everyone."

They all crowded back through the door, and Seolta edged closer to the sister Anyara thought he least liked. It turned out she knew nothing about how families worked.

"Is she talking about a full mountain feast?"

Fee turned a gleeful smile on him. "Yes, with all the trimmings and every relative to the nth degree. Welcome home, big brother."

Seolta groaned.

Anyara had some hint of what to expect from the sims of his home, but the reality was so much more. Sounds and smells hit with a new richness. The texture of leaf and branch, the air brushing her cheek or the dewing of moisture from the damp air on her lips. The route to their quarters was as much a maze as in the sim, but this time, there were no blanked-off areas. All of them lived in the same wing, with hallways made for lingering, seats and artwork in the spaces left by the living tree … and she saw all of his suite. The main area was as spacious as she remembered, but the service areas were nothing like the utilitarian cubes of a station apartment. These were made for indulgence, and the sleep rooms the same.

He had two, a guest room which now held her baggage carrier and his own room. He showed her both, then stood diffidently in the connecting doorway.

"It's up to you. The guest room, or if you'd prefer, I will arrange a guest suite for you? Or … he gestured towards his own room with a rare hesitation.

It didn't take a moment for her to step forward and take his hand. "You are my chosen partner, Seolta a Manascraoch."

He pulled her in tight, and held her close. "You will not regret it, *mo Graidh*."

Afterwards, he showed her the rest of the suite. She sat in a chair made of trained branches and human artifice, walked on real wood, kicked off her boots to dig her toes into the pile of a rug or onto the smooth shine of a glossed floor. The atmosphere was controlled as in any habitat home, but more subtly, so that she had to concentrate to sense the manipulations of temperature or humidity. Seolta had warned her to bring warm clothing, and she quickly discovered why. These Mountainers ran their homes in sympathy with the outside environment, including the routine temperature setting, and he laughingly ordered the settings to tropical when she began shivering then passed her one of the ubiquitous Mountainer wraps. Not long afterwards, his sister Samhchair signalled the door and bustled in, carrying a pile of the local clothing types.

"These should help, Sera," she said with her gentle smile.

Anyara glanced sharply at Seolta but he maintained an innocently blank face. She narrowed her eyes and he lifted his hands. "I just mentioned to Samhchair that your wardrobe wasn't designed for a Mountainer home."

She swallowed her chagrin and turned to thank his sister for her kindness. They were beautiful, and when she tried them on, she sighed in relief. Soft, silky to touch, the skimming clothes were deceptively tough and easy to move in—designed for a world where stepping on and over branches of trees was normal practice, as she discovered when Seolta took her exploring his home. She wore her own clothes to the night's dinner, though. She was not going to meet his family in borrowed gear.

The noise hit her first. Seolta had said it was an informal family dinner in the private dining room. She hated to think what they used for more public dinners. This room alone was bigger than her whole apartment on the station. Another item to add to the points of difference on an EA world. Space didn't matter here.

Then she took in the table. "You said it was just family," she hissed at him.

"It is." She might have believed the innocence of his voice if he didn't wear the smile he used to hide himself. Not quite the obviously fake business one. If you didn't know him better, this one looked genuine. His sisters all glared at him and he gave a curt head bow back. "Family is defined very loosely in Mountainer families," he told her. "It includes any available cousin, aunt, and uncle, and certainly all the members of the older generations still living. My grandparents are no longer with us—you would have loved my Granda, my mother's father—but all my father's aunts still live here. And we have a few honorary members as well."

She gulped in a breath and dredged up everything dealing with the people of her station had taught her. Fortunately, the same tactics worked here. Let the other person talk until you can figure out who they are and whether they have an angle. When all else fails, smile and nod knowingly. After dinner, they moved to what they euphemistically called a 'family parlour', another cavernous room with more of the stunning Mountainer furniture and twining plants. She stuck as closely as she could to Seolta, but too many wanted to claim his attention. She soon found herself stranded in an island of strange faces, but she was being watched. His sisters and mother rose, and she had seen the frequent glances of his father and eldest brother.

To her relief, it was the other outsider who arrived beside her first. Caleb Winter may be Arcadian, but physically he stood out among the den Coilles even more than she did—taller than anyone else in the room and with a dryness to his skin that reminded her of the miners back home, telling of exposure to unfriendly elements. Except that the miners' faces all showed the patches of goggles and breathing masks. She touched Seolta's clip, and saw him across the room trying to push his way through to her. She shook her head. He deserved this time. His eyes still held hers, and she forced the lines of her face back to calm, turning to smile at the man taking the seat beside her.

"Messer Caleb Winter, isn't it?"

He gave her an abbreviated bow, a half-hearted attempt at the Mountainer version. It clearly came no easier to him than to her. "I've been looking forward to meeting you, Sera. Your Academy thesis was outstanding. I know the specialists up in Urbis are eager to discuss it with you."

"Oh? That's nice," she said, quailing inside.

He chuckled. "Fee and I can come with you, if you want. They're not too bad a bunch, just a bit hyper-focused." He glanced at the rest of the room. "How are you surviving the den Coilles. They can be a bit overwhelming."

She tried to smile, but he wasn't fooled. "Want a breakdown?"

"Thank you, Messer." Then she remembered the correct word. "Ser Winter."

He waved off her slip. "You're partnered to the trickiest of the den Coilles. That's enough of a challenge for anyone."

Her back straightened. "I am quite happy with my choice."

Another laugh from the man. "Well said, Sera. You'll do fine here." He turned back to the room. "Now, the family. You know the basics, I assume?"

"I called up their files on our journey here."

"Good, so we don't have to waste talk on what they do. As for how accurate those files are, that's questionable. Sera Scathach, yes. Mother to a tribe of strong-headed individuals and manager of a major hospital, how she stays as calm and sympathetic as she mostly manages, I have no idea. Samhchair and Cumchdach take after her. They're the heart of the family in many ways."

"Not Ser Bram?"

He shook his head. "He's the brains and the leader of the business. Sera Strathach and Samhchair run the family. If you need a shoulder to lean on, Samhchair's the one."

Anyara's look sought out the elder sister. She had the same dark hair and lean build as the rest of the family, but she remembered the woman's eyes. Deep pools of stillness, as if a haven. "Who does she lean on?" she asked without thinking, and was surprised at the twist of Caleb's mouth.

"Fee says that's what worries her parents." He frowned at where Samhchair was bringing together a group of the older generation and simultaneously directing a steady stream of drinks and snacks in their direction. "She is one of the strongest women I know."

Anyara took in the effortless way the woman managed the demands of crotchety elders and service bots, all while maintaining an aura of calm attentiveness. "I wonder what made her so strong?"

Caleb gave her a shrewd look but shook his head in answer. She checked on Seolta and he threw her a harassed look. He also frowned at his brother-in-law. She smiled back to reassure him, and then laughed as he looked even more concerned. That relaxed him at least, and she turned back to Caleb.

"And Cumchdach? Is he as enthralled by business as Seolta?"

"No, but he's the natural heir." She looked up sharply. "Their people trust him in a way they will never trust your partner," Caleb said brutally. "Seolta is too slippery for his own good and has taken action against too many rivals." He met her look with no sign of apology. "You ought to know the truth of him."

She bristled, but had to acknowledge the man's sincerity. It didn't mean he had any right to expect her to agree with him. "According to Cumchdach's files, he's married. Where is his wife tonight?"

A grin then, lightening the mood. "She's expecting and having a foul time of it. All the old aunties are telling him what else did he expect when he waited so long to marry her."

His file said the wedding had taken place not long before the collapse of her uncle's schemes here. "Why did they wait?"

"Word is Anna had always refused him. They've been friends and part-time lovers for years, but she baulked at marriage."

"I wonder what changed her mind."

A chuckle. "You're not the only one. The gossip webs went crazy at the time. But Anna ingh Eolas an Sumhneas den Falasch is harder to read than your partner, when she sets her mind to it."

"Fallash?" she said, copying the sound of his pronunciation.

"Her family name. She's now properly called Anna ingh Eolas bean Cumchdach den Coille, of course." He sighed. "Mountainer names are a curse to pronounce and remember, but they act as if mortally insulted if you get them wrong."

She was only half listening. Fallash. She'd heard that word before. The files on record had used a Mountainer to pronounce all the strange names, liquid and beautiful sounding. She'd made herself memorise the sounds, but Caleb's version more nearly matched her mangled attempts to speak them.

Where had she heard it? She shoved it to the back of her mind, hoping her subconscious would work on it and give her an answer.

"What about the rest?" she said to distract Caleb.

He eyed her suspiciously but continued. "Ceart is the silent one. Rarely speaks but is one of the best flyers I've come across. A good man to have at your back if you're in trouble and one hundred percent loyal to his family and business. As for Aigherach, he's young but don't let that fool you. That limp was hard-earned."

She grimaced. "I read the file." More proof of her uncle's vile past.

Caleb touched her shoulder. "You're not your uncle."

"No, but I am his niece. How is Aigherach coping now?"

"Another strong one. Luckily, he's young enough still, and his father is keeping him busy."

"Leaving only your wife, Ser."

He put up a hand. "I am not giving you a run down on my own wife. Fee is a law unto herself. Talk to her and she'll tell you exactly what she thinks of your partner."

"They're close, she and Seolta?"

"No." Then his face split into a wide grin. "Too much alike for their own good, and don't ever tell her I said that. Both of them will go after what they want with a bullheadedness that can be downright scary. In Fee's defence, she's straighter and is usually trying to help others, not herself. But then, Seolta seems to have changed. Exile may have been the making of him."

He closed his mouth as if he'd said enough and was still waiting to be convinced of the latter. She could take offence but didn't see any advantage in it.

"You've been more than helpful, Ser Winter. Thank you. Now you can tell me about this amazing world of yours. I am still stunned by the small taste I've had of it."

Talking to others in the biome sphere had always delighted her, and the rest of the evening passed more quickly than she'd hoped. Fee den Winter joined them, as did Seolta, although a few moments of listening to their conversation had him grimacing. "Tech talk," he said, and reached for a glass from a passing bot.

Yet he stayed beside her, turning from time to time to talk to others as easily as he slipped into their talk. He may dismiss it as tech, but Seolta's own business interests made him more knowledgeable than she'd guessed. If it affected Den Coille's interests, he'd made himself familiar. For a man with his understanding of mathematics and systems, gaining a working ability in biome systems wasn't a major stretch.

She couldn't miss the wariness of the others though. His family may love him, would always welcome him back, but they did not trust him and, as the evening wore on, she saw what that did to him. His face sharpened and his words cut deeper. As if challenging them. He saw the worry on his mother's face and a constant awareness on his father's. Ser Bram was as closed as Seolta and Samhchair when he wanted to be. She was grateful when Seolta finally said it was time to leave. "We are still on Standard time, and Anyara hasn't yet adjusted to an EA world."

It wasn't until she had nearly fallen asleep that she remembered. "Fallash."

"What?" mumbled Seolta.

"Cumchdach's wife. Her family name." He struggled to sit up, looking vaguely affronted. "You mean *Falasch*."

"Yes." He said it correctly, as in the files. "Caleb said her name and he said it more like I did."

"Wrongly, you mean," he said with a scowl in his voice. He trusted his brother-in-law no more than the man did Seolta, it seemed.

"Yes, almost as *wrongly* as I did, but I'd heard it said that way before, and I've just remembered where. It was on a visit to my uncle. He had some people in his office when I approached. It meant nothing to me at the time, but the word was unusual."

"Your uncle was talking about Anna?" Seolta shot up and ordered the lights on.

"No, silly. Just someone with a name Fallash." She pulled herself up as well. "They had to be in business together, so that wouldn't be Cumchdach's wife. Isn't she a botanist attached to the Urbis university?" A woman she'd hoped to meet while she was here after reading an article in her file.

"Yes, but her father is head of a major Mountainer corporation. It's why there was so much pressure on them to marry. The Falasch family is primarily involved in shipping, including export from Arcadia. They are our major distributor. I wonder…"

"Could they have been working with my uncle?"

Seolta didn't answer at first, staring into the shadows at the far end of the room. Then he turned to her. "Not that he ever said. Eolas den Falasch has a lot of contacts and a good working relationship with the Alliance office. Was he likely to be involved in something underhanded with your uncle? It wouldn't surprise me. He's a greedy old brakka."

She moved closer, needing the feel of him. He turned over and kissed her, and problems were forgotten for a while as the force between them flared up again. She gave in to it, eager to escape the currents tugging them into danger. There was an edge to their love-making this evening, and she suspected Seolta felt as frazzled as she did.

Afterwards, they lay close, replete and safe again. His hands played a random pattern on her arm. "You'd better not be working out a new systems strategy," she said after a while as the pattern changed, becoming definite.

He stopped and pulled her closer, letting her head settle into the nest of his shoulder. "Guilty as charged, *mo Graidh.*"

She gave a sigh of resignation. "What was it?"

"The Falasch tree of contacts," he admitted. "On-planet and off. I wouldn't be surprised if the conspirators were using him."

"Talk to the marshals in the morning. That's their job."

"Yes, Messera Esteemed Scholar," he said with that laugh she loved in his voice. He so rarely let it out.

One day, she'd make it ring out all the time.

CHAPTER TWENTY-SEVEN

Seolta woke the next morning with Anyara nestled against him in a sleeper that felt so familiar he almost thought he was dreaming. He was home, with her beside him, and his family hadn't yet kicked him out. By some of the looks he'd got last night, they'd been tempted. Not his mother or Samhchair, but the rest…

His father had told him he wanted to talk to him this morning, making it very clear it was an order and he meant alone. Anyara was still on trial but, so far, they seemed more stunned by her presence.

"How did you get so lucky?" Fioruisghe may have been the only one to say it, but he saw it on the others' faces. Except Mam, of course. She would always think anyone more than blessed to have one of her children, but his father had given him a raised eyebrow after contriving a 'chat' with her last night.

How long his luck would last was another matter. This trip had always been a gamble, one he'd have refused if he'd had any say in it, and he had to plaster on a smile when Anyara woke. The small crease over her brow said she wasn't fooled, but she held on to the pretence. She was getting good at that.

She shouldn't have to. He'd been raised in a true marriage, one where his father and mother shared everything, bad news and good, for a very simple reason. Neither could hide worry from the other.

If he wanted to keep Anyara, and he very much did, he'd have to let her in. All the way in.

There was so much in him that wasn't good. Exile had shocked him into a self-examination long overdue and had shown him too many unpalatable truths, one of which was how easy it would be for him to repeat his old mistakes. He'd been born with a brain that loved to solve puzzles, both in systems and in people, and the lure of it would never leave him.

Could he make a life for himself by silencing much of who he was?

He'd have to, if he wanted to keep Anyara.

Just then, she lifted her hand and touched his mouth. "Put a call through to the marshals' office before your meeting with your father."

It wiped away his false smile. She'd read him as easily as his mother read his father. "I can't desert you on your first morning here. I promised to show you my home."

"And you will, after you've vanquished this morning's demons." She grimaced. "Your sisters have invited me to what they call a morning nibble. Is that as fearsome as it sounds?"

"Worse. Did they tell you how many to expect?"

"I assumed just the two of them. And hopefully Messera Anna as well. I've been looking forward to talking with her about her studies."

"Good idea. Keep it to tech talk and you may survive."

She laughed at that. Still reluctant to let her go, he put a call through to Fioruisghe. "Be careful with Anyara," he said to his sister. "She's not one of your Council targets."

"Don't worry, big brother." He felt no easier, not when she gave him that fake smile from when they were children and she was planning something particularly diabolical. Fioruisghe had spent hours off in the forest, and it was usually his job to find her. Mam said he knew how her mind worked. It wasn't a compliment, and Fioruisghe had quickly learned to set traps to slow him down. He still had a small scar on his left foot from one of them.

"I mean it, Fioruisghe ingh Bram. Sera Anyara doesn't deserve whatever it is you're planning. She's had more than enough trouble in her past without my family adding to it."

She grinned wickedly. "What are you going to do about it?"

"Whatever I have to," he said.

Fioruisghe looked surprised. "You mean that." A huge and genuine smile lit her face. "You really mean it. There's hope for you yet, brother. She's safe from me, and Samhchair is there to protect her."

He was relieved to hear it and had to hope. He added a small threat to make sure, but she laughed back at him before Samhchair and Mam came online.

"Your partner is safe with us, Seolta," said his mother, and he could finally relax. Mam would make it happen.

He hugged Anyara tight before he left her. "Walk out if it gets too much. They'll understand, and too bad if they don't."

She still looked like she was going to an execution. He walked her as far as the communal hallway and was relieved to see it was Samhchair waiting for her. She gave him a half bow and her steady smile, then took Anyara's arm.

"Come along, my dear. Anna and Fioruisghe are eager to see you. They are using words I never knew existed, but they assure me you will understand."

"Is that all who's there?" Seolta had to ask.

"Mam's coming a bit later, after she finishes her hospital rounds, but that's all," Samhchair assured him, the touch of a sparkle in her eyes the only sign she understood exactly what he meant. She gave another half bow, much deeper and more ironic this time, then they walked off. Anyara held herself tall and straight, her height a match for Samhchair, but Seolta wished she didn't remind him of his own march to the podium during his court trial.

He waited till they disappeared around the far corner. Then he turned and headed towards the room he used as an office to put through his call to the marshals.

He entered the direct code for Marshal an Fallon, but got a stranger. The woman stared down her nose at him, making it plain she knew exactly which den Coille brother was calling.

"Please state your business, Ser den Coille."

He was in no mood for games. "I understood this was a direct access link."

"The Senior Marshal is busy. Please give me your message and I will ensure the marshal is advised at the earliest opportunity."

Sent directly to the waste folder, that meant. "Put me through to an Fallon, security code X-1." The ambassador had assured him that would always get him through.

The woman pursed her lips. "You are through now, Ser den Coille. You will have to wait online until the marshal completes his current commitment."

"And how long will that take?"

She smiled too sweetly. "As long as needed." Then the annoying underling clicked off, leaving him in a holding pattern with nothing to do but stomp around his room. He didn't want to see any family members until he'd talked to the marshal.

So use the time better than by sulking.

He refused to answer that even by a thought. His subconscious was occasionally right.

Is always right.

I'm telling the psych meds about you.

Not that he had any intention of telling a psych med he'd fallen to threatening himself, but it made him feel better. He began to go back over the memories of his original crimes. An ideal subject in his current mood. For the first time, he didn't look for reasons to justify his actions, but instead noted down any comments or hints from his meetings with Hilmar and Malgrave that might be a clue to identify their co-conspirators.

He'd told the marshals some of it before, but not all. He was too churned up then, harbouring a toxic mix of guilt and anger that had him resenting all the world and dreading the future. Now, he was back, if only for a short time, and his travels had given him a new perspective on past incidents. And he'd found promise of a future he'd never dared dream of before.

A future that would be his only if he was worthy of it. Anyara deserved no less. He'd done everything they'd accused him of; now he needed to make reparations.

It was more than a standard hour before an Fallon came back to him, and by then Seolta had a full list of memories to share.

"Den Coille," said the spare voice of the head of the Marshals and most trusted man on Arcadia. Marcus an Fallon was approaching his middle years, but the only sign of it lay in the odd silver hair and the lines around his eyes. Seolta had probably put a few of them there.

"Marshal, thank you for accepting my call."

The man's eyes narrowed. "I assume this is more than a social call?"

What had he expected? Marshal an Fallon wasn't a man to waste time in small talk. "It relates to Ser Eolas den Falasch."

The marshal's eyes sharpened. "Ser Cumchdach's wife's father?"

Seolta nodded. "I'm sending you through the file." He waited till the man received it and began to scroll through it. "I'm also sending through some things I've remembered from before I left."

The man sat back and paused the com file. "You only just remembered them?"

Seolta grimaced. "I'm in a better frame of mind now. Some more facts came to mind."

"About time, Ser den Coille," said the Marshal, and Seolta cringed. "I do hope your list is complete this time."

"As much as possible. I'll let you know if I remember anything else."

"That would be very wise," said the Marshal and set to reading both files. At the end, he sat back with a grim twist to his mouth.

Seolta squirmed. "Is it possible Falasch is involved?"

"More than possible."

"And my other list?"

"Opens up a number of interesting lines of enquiry. I will get back to you if we need more information. You start on your tour of the planet next week?"

The marshal was one of the few on Arcardia who knew the truth of their tour.

"Yes. As agreed, after a look around den Coille lands, we're starting on the plains as that's the most obvious place for us to visit."

"You're calling on the Winters?"

"I don't think so," said Seolta dryly. He had no desire to subject Anyara to any more unpleasantness than necessary.

The marshals had a full route map of their planned trip. Starting on their own continent of Protos, after the plains they headed down to the southern coast, a brief visit to the smaller continent of Feldwesten, across to the sparsely populated western continent, Deuteron, then back to Protos, and the settled area north of the northern ranges, the most fertile and densely populated region on Arcadia, finishing in the capital city of Urbis.

The environmental experts from Arcadia and Alliance Central had argued for days over the agenda before they left Central. It had been a struggle to remind them that he and Anyara were human and needed occasional stops for food and sleep. "This is supposed to look like a romantic trip with my new life partner," he'd snapped one day in exasperation. The committee had made some concessions after that, but he still thought the trip made them look more like mad adventurers than a couple celebrating a new relationship.

"Call on the Winter homestead," said an Fallon now. "Ethan and his wife are there; that will provide you an excuse."

"Sol Winter is not a complete idiot and no longer has any power to cause trouble."

The marshal grunted. The man had never been one to leave loose strands untended. "You will not discuss this with anyone, including your family," he said at the end. The grim set of the marshal's face showed he was serious. "Understood, Ser den Coille?"

"Understood," said Seolta.

"Keep me informed of any progress."

"And a security detail?"

"You are under surveillance watch at all times. If you encounter trouble, that's your problem, not the government's."

Thanks for nothing, Seolta thought sourly as he signed out and opened up a channel to his old security detail. Thankfully the den Coille security section wasn't in the least surprised at his request. "Cumchdach notified us of your arrival, Ser. A detail has already been assigned."

"Full discretion required," Seolta warned.

A formal head bow. "Of course, Ser Seolta mar Bram."

The meeting with his father was no more enjoyable. "Congratulations, son," he said, "your chosen—life partner, is it?—appears to be an admirable woman."

"I am a fortunate man," he said.

"And marriage? That's the usual progression on our world."

"Not on hers" he said, and refused to explain further. He should have remembered his father was as stubborn as he and twice as wily.

"What are your plans then?"

He'd never been able to lie to his parents. He managed to finish without admitting the truth of his visit, but had no illusions he'd fooled his father, and by the end of the discussion he felt as wrung out as if at the end of a full circuit of the trees."

"Can you not stay?" his father finished with, making no attempt to hide a kernel of hope.

He shook his head. "This visit strained the good will of the Planetary Council enough. They agreed to it only under full supervision. The marshals have watched us since landing."

His father waved that away. "They watch us all and we'd assumed it would be stepped up with you here. As long as it won't be a problem for you."

He looked up in shock. "I don't make the same mistake twice."

"Good. As long as you're not planning to make a new one."

"No, father, I'm not." He shoved back his chair, feeling as if stabbed twice over, and went to walk out.

His father slammed locked the door controls. Seolta stopped and slowly turned back. "Nor do I like locked doors. I've had too many of them in recent times."

His father's gaze held him as he disengaged the door. "You're still my son. I will do whatever it takes to keep you safe, and I make no apology for that. Are you? Safe, I mean."

"I don't know, Da. I just don't know. But Anyara is mine, and I will keep her safe, whatever happens."

The strain on his father's face eased and Seolta blinked. What had he said?

The rest of the week passed all too quickly. His greatest joy was watching Anyara explore his home region. The awe on her face as she stood at the base of his family tree, scrambling all the way around the massive trunk, had him laughing, but her digging in the dirt surrounding the base was what made Fioruisghe her ally.

"She dug through the leaf litter and could name every single bug she found," said Fioruisghe later, a silly look on her face.

He showed her the festia and the pollen collecting, then took her to the secret dells where the chaullnia bushes flourished. None were in flower at this season, but the scent from the crushed leaves gave the area a pleasant aromatic fragrance. The ocean was the greatest wonder to her, though. He wanted her to discover his own coast first, the wild breakers smashing against forbidding rock cliffs and the precious coves hidden between sheer-faced headlands and reachable only by flyer or terrifyingly steep pathways down windlashed slopes. His coast was alive to him in a way the more popular beaches of the south could never be.

Then came the time to leave for their tour and they were standing on the landing pad. He hoped his face didn't show the same devastation as his mother's, but he felt it inside.

"We will see you all again before we leave Arcadia," said Anyara beside him. "Thank you very much for your hospitality."

He couldn't speak, and was grateful she did it for him. This time was almost worse than his first departure. Now he knew what he went to, how different it was from all he was losing. The round of hugs and back slaps from his family nearly finished him off, but he managed to keep a straight face. Then he came to Cumchdach.

"Be careful, little brother."

It was too much. Seolta gave his brother a brusque nod and bundled them both into his flyer before he made a complete fool of himself. "Auto," he ordered and sat staring at the city below as his flyer took them high into the air. Only the growing storm buffeting it brought him back, and he gratefully seized the control field to fight the air currents.

Their reception at the Winter homestead was no more pleasant. At least Ethan was away at the time.

"Ser den Coille," said the butler at the front door, exuding all the welcome of an arctic cold front. Plains courtesy wasn't as wired in as Mountainer manners, but luckily the butler wasn't under orders to refuse them. After that, the combination of Anyara's presence and Sera Helena Winter's pride stopped any outright aggression. Sol Winter was his usual overbearing self, but the bluster was more pronounced than usual. Not surprising since the man was definitely more windbag than power these days, thanks to Ethan's takeover of the family company.

His comments that evening at dinner explained the marshal's insistence on their making the Winter homestead a stop on their trip. 'Bitter' barely described Sol Winter's frame of mind. He should be grateful. Ethan had saved both the company and Sol Winter's reputation.

One to add to the suspect list, although it was hard to believe Sol Winter would betray his own sons, whatever he felt about his current position. Sera Winter was changed, though, her pride restored and the underlying anxiety he'd seen in her last time he'd been home diminished by Ethan's actions.

The evening light lingered on the plains in this season and Sera Winter took Anyara for a tour of the gardens. Anyara glanced at him, then hurried after the Sera with a gleam in her eyes. She'd gasped when they came in over the house on the way here.

"Look at the succession of plants," she'd sighed in wonder. "This was designed by a real gardener." She was even more excited when she returned from her walk, and Sera Helena had lost her frosty formality in a mutual love fest. "It's a miracle," Anyara told him. "Introduced and native plants, all blended together in a natural progression that benefits both. Science says it shouldn't work, but it does." She turned to Sera Winter. "You are a genius, Helena."

Helena Winter grinned back with the kind of smile Seolta had never seen from her before. "Sol's grandmother did most of the design. I just added to it."

"The Earth trees and plants, yes. Marvellously done, but the transition between exotic and native is the true delight."

Sol might glare at him more often than not, but between them, Anyara and Sera Helena managed to make the visit quicker than he'd hoped. Of course his luck didn't last. Ethan and Sarwenna arrived at the homestead just as they were about to leave.

"Seolta mar Bram. You're a long way from where I expected you to be," said the man whose death he had nearly caused.

"I'm showing my new life partner our planet. She's a biome manager and your homestead gardens are mentioned in every Plains travel guide," he said, unable to keep the coolness from his voice. Anyara caught it and hurried over.

"Anyara a Prithand2, meet Ethan Winter and his wife Sarwenna Beren." The plains used a deplorable casualness in their address, but right now the brevity suited his mood.

Ethan smiled at her in the way Seolta was only too familiar with. It was the one both of them used in business meetings with those not a threat. The look Ethan had turned on him was quite different.

"We'd heard of your visit, Sera. Arcadia is honoured to welcome an Esteemed Scholar of the Academy."

Anyara bowed her head, and extended a hand in the universal Alliance greeting. Ethan took her hand but Sera Sarwenna was more hesitant. A onetime union delegate, the Sera was as suspicious as her husband and hid it less well.

Seolta saw Anyara touch her hair clip and took her arm protectively.

"We would like to stay and talk, but Representative Gibbs is expecting us in Dridust. The Ser has invited us to stay the night and Anyara is keen to visit the Dridust gardens." The marshal had also ordered him to find out what the Representative for the Plains region knew about the local corporations.

Dridust was almost a repeat of the visit to the Winter homestead. The staff were polite enough, but they arrived too late to meet the Representative or his family and merely passed on their thanks before being shown to their rooms. Next day, the household had organised an official lunch. The botanists at the regional gardens almost fell over themselves in a fight to properly welcome Anyara, a handy cover for Seolta's cool reception from Gibbs.

"What are you up to, young den Coille," said Joe Gibbs. Seolta owed his freedom from that Survey prison in part to Gibbs' actions, and he would not forget the debt he owed to the gruff elder statesman. Gibbs might snipe at him, but Seolta was determined to be respectful back.

"I'm showing my new life partner our world."

"What else?" Gibbs came across as a bluff and crusty old bencher, but he was as tough and cunning as any politician, with plenty of political clout. "A woman of your partner's reputation doesn't visit an EA world for a holiday. The woman's been asking questions of any tech she gets close to."

That brought a real smile to Seolta's face. "I think you will find that is Sera Anyara's version of an ideal holiday. She tells me this world is all her dreams come true."

"Hmmph." Gibbs wasn't convinced. "As long as she gives Arcadia credit in her next article."

"Credit, or credits?" Seolta couldn't resist asking. "Good luck getting any real wealth out of the Academy."

That got a hoot of laughter from Gibbs. "You're learning, young man."

Fortunately, the Representative dropped the subject and moved on to discussing the business trends Seolta had seen in his travels and, from there, Seolta managed to lure him back to what had been happening in the economic world on Arcadia. It brought a speculative gleam to the representative's knowing eye, but the man refrained from delving further. Knowing Joe Gibbs, it probably meant the man had come to his own conclusions. Gibbs was experienced enough to do any further digging without stirring up trouble, and in the unlikely chance he did, it was an Fallon's' job to shut him down. He hadn't gained an ally—for Gibbs as for too many on his home world, Seolta would always be a traitor—but the man had never denied Seolta's skills. The evening improved more when Anyara stopped talking roots and wind patterns, and hurried over with the smile on her face that bloomed for him alone.

"The garden techs are organising an expedition out to the desert tomorrow and have asked me to come along. I've told them I can't go without you."

"When do we leave?" he said, and her smile widened.

First light, it turned out, by which the techs meant a full hour before there was even a hint of sunlight peeking over the horizon. They intended to be on the desert floor by actual first light. Normally, he wouldn't have chosen to spend any time on the desiccated eastern side of the continent, with barely a whisper of a leaf let alone any proper tree, but seeing it through Anyara's eyes turned out to be a rare gift. They took their own flyer, and at the end of the day when the hatch closed on the others, she turned to him with arms open wide and a kiss filled with the scents of dust, heat and a joyous excitement.

"There's so much *life* here!"

"So Arcadia is as perfect as you hoped?"

A shadow of trouble crossed her eyes. "No. The desert is extraordinary. A greedy and overwhelming beast. That's the problem. There are too many signs of change to ignore. The skeletons of old plants and animals from species that no longer belong here. This is new desert. The Survey were correct. It's creeping west, and something must be done to stop it before it swallows the plains."

"You said this to the techs?"

She shook her head, and her grin banished the shadow. "I was the perfect undercover auditor, if I say so myself. A thoroughly enthralled guest, listening avidly to all they said."

He had to kiss her again, seeing the mischief in her eyes. "They bought that? You're an Esteemed Scholar."

She shrugged. "My area of expertise is station biomes. Why would they think I would understand anything about EA biome systems."

They were her own words to the Alliance Council.

"But you do."

"Yes," she said, as serious as he. "Yes, I do."

The rest of the trip was a flash course in his planet's ecological systems. Seeing his world through the eyes of a habitat dweller was a revelation.

No, the gift was seeing it through Anyara's eyes. He watched her delight bloom with each new discovery. Saw her carefully touch a plant he'd seen so many times before. What he thought of as ordinary rendered her speechless as she traced each leaf, each tiny blend of colour. More, she explored how each fit into a whole, unravelled the strands that made his world work. Through Anyara's eyes, he journeyed into a version of his world he'd never known existed, despite the Planetary Council's decrees. He'd never been the kind to take anything at face value, always needing to pull apart a system and find out for himself how it worked.

Now Anyara pulled apart the strands of his world's systems, all in excruciatingly disastrous detail. From the multiplying holiday villas on the tropical beaches of southern Protos, across to the smothering of the sun-baked centre of Feldwesten with vast solar arrays, to the empty stretches of the western continent, she wondered, talked, delved, and cried. On Feldwesten, they met up with an old ally of Caleb's, now running a wildly profitable waterfront restaurant. Seolta lazed on the front deck, taking in the view, the volume of tourists and locals wandering along below, and enjoying the feel of sun on his face and the food on his plate. Maybe he would look into investing in the place.

"Why didn't you re-join the Survey after the troubles were sorted," Anyara asked their host.

The man shrugged. "I did for a while but…" he too looked at the foot traffic below. "Who's to say the same thing won't happen again. Nothing's really changed, not yet, and too many of the same players are still in the game. You can be kicked only so many times in life." He picked at the salad on his plate, moving pieces listlessly from one side to another. "A group of us keep in touch still. Nothing official but we help where we can."

They left not long afterwards, having arranged to meet a contact of his in the interior, but Anyara looked back down on the busy harbour and the smiling holiday makers. Her lovely face wore the shadow he was becoming too familiar with.

"If this were a station, I'd be talking to the management about evacuation for biome repair. But a station is easier to fix. Strip all the biome back and start again. You can't do that on a planet."

After a few days of hopping across Feldwesten, with nothing to counter that uneasy lump in her gut, they set off across the ocean again, and a few hours later, Anyara looked down on Deuteron, the westernmost and least populated of the continents on Arcadia. The bulk of the continent sat in the southern hemisphere of the planet and they were coming in over the bottom end, a region of ice and widespread thermal activity. She shivered and pulled up the holo-map that was becoming her constant companion on this trip, then looked ahead at the thin trail of smoke hovering above a conical mountain in the distance.

"I can see why this region has few settlers." Apart from the odd fishing settlement on the coast, the southern region was empty of habitation. "But why the rest of the continent?"

Deuteron had a simple design. In the north, a massive mountain range divided the heavily jungled northern tropical region from the rest, while the central zone was split into two regions. The eastern coast lands were largely made of broken and rocky scrublands with few natural sources of water and a number of threatening predators, but the land to the west was another matter. The cold steppes of the central plateau tended to slope west and gave birth to a number of rivers, draining from massive underground aquifers that gathered up the thousands of tiny rivulets and marsh outlets intersecting the plateau region then released them in a flurry of rushing torrents, sparkling waterfalls and cheeky bubbling streams as they fell down the steep escarpment dividing the plateau from the western downlands.

The western half, in contrast to the rather barren eastern side, was fertile, rich in water and biomes, a mixture of open forests and waving grasslands. Lands ideal for habitation, yet it was nearly empty by Alliance standards. Two small cities only, both sited near the coast, and a scattering of smaller settlements and isolated agricultural homesteads.

Seolta barely glanced at the map, then returned his concentration to the flyer's controls. They were in a bumpy air patch, like many they'd met between here and Feldwesten. "History mostly, with a helping hand from geography," he answered. "The first colonists settled the Urbis region. This area is good, but the Urbis estuarine and inland country is better, and the rest of Protos offered better options than Deuteron. No volcanic region, for a start," he added with a chuckle. "That put off plenty of colonists."

"That was hundreds of years ago. There's been plenty of time for spread to this continent."

He shrugged. "Building a new world is a hard job, believe it or not. Most were too busy to venture out, and those who did found plenty to explore on Protos and Feldwesten. Easier to get to, as well. The wind and tidal patterns aren't great for travel between Protos and Deuteron. You can set up business here, but the economic return has to be twice what it is for the other continents to cover the increased cost of freight."

She looked pointedly at his easy handling of the choppy winds. "Not now."

"Not as much," he conceded, "but believe it or not, the eco-engineers do have some say on this world, and by the time freighting from Deuteron became viable, the ecos had begun to crack down on biome change. Whether we like it or not, Alliance laws still apply here, especially if we want to keep trading with them, and we were nearing the cut-off point for the percentage of territory under development. We could either keep developing Protos further, or stagnate there and develop Deuteron. Guess who won that vote."

She laughed. Then frowned again. "So if you stuck to Alliance rules then, what happened? How did you get into this current mess?"

"*If* we're in one. That's what you're here for."

He couldn't be serious. "You've seen the same places as I have these last weeks. How can you doubt it?"

He frowned, a troubled, twisted frown. "I did before. Now, thanks to you… I may have been wrong." He checked the outside, altered a setting, then leaned back. "Before this, I looked at it from a business and politics angle. You may have noticed I'm not one to trust easily," she choked back a retort at the understatement, "especially the claims of politicians standing to gain a powerful say over my family's company. Believe it or not, in my world people lie. Shocking, I know."

"Yes, shocking," she said dryly, considering he was a prime offender when it suited him.

He laughed and a warm glow filled her. He rarely laughed openly, not a genuine laugh, and with only a few. His family and now her.

They were near the coast and he'd switched his focus to the view ahead. "Do you really need to see those volcanoes up close? The middle one is nearing alert levels."

She checked the readings he'd brought up. Surned had a small volcanic field, one the rest of the planet studiously avoided. "Unfortunately, I do. Just enough to confirm the data collected by the Survey. We can get air samples as we go, but I need a sample from a stream draining them." She studied the holo-map again, filtering it out for the parameters she needed and adding in the prevailing winds. At the moment, they blew south from the mountains.

"Can we go north of the mountain and come up on that marshy land draining it. I don't need to land, as long as we get close enough to scoop up a sample of dirt and water."

He gave her the grin that said he wasn't sure, but he'd do it. Sometimes she could have cursed that bullheadedness of his, but it had helped him survive this far and she trusted it to get them home.

A crackle on his com and the voice of his security squad leader boomed through the cabin. "Ser, you're heading into a zone of unreliable transmission and high hazards."

"But no one's trying to kill us. We'll be fine, Squad Leader. Keep your flyer back in case."

Anyara could just see the look of outrage on the man's face. "That is not possible, Ser."

"It is, Squad Leader, and that's an order. The marshals have us under surveillance if anything serious happens. Monitor the zone and meet us when we emerge. Den Coille out."

Seolta leaned over and switched off.

"Was that wise?" said Anyara.

"Maybe not, but it felt good. No one breathing down our necks." As they neared the field, she wasn't so sure about it. If only she had another way of corroborating the Survey data.

"You need these samples?" he asked.

"If possible," she said unhappily. "Volcanic activity on this scale can make major changes to climate patterns. The biome balance will tell me whether the level of output is stable or becoming dangerous. According to the Survey, the current level of activity isn't enough to explain the many local climate disruptions." She looked down. "Can you do it?"

He looked down as well. "Hope so," and began to glide sideways into the clouds of steam.

Maybe she was wrong. "It's too dangerous."

"I may not be Ceart, but I've been hugging the slopes of the mountains since I was a junior. Hold on tight, Sera."

She did as ordered, shutting her eyes and listening for the shriek of a siren. She opened them as the winds buffeted them and the interior of the flyer began to heat up. Then they were lifting up again and she breathed a sigh of relief.

"Got them," he told her with a grin as he levelled out and headed west towards the seashore, the quickest route away from the danger zone.

She began to plan the next leg.

Then the ship lurched and she clung to her seat.

"Buckle down," yelled Seolta.

"What's happening?"

"Wind shift. A cloud of volcanic dust is clogging the engine inlet."

Her heart thumped. "Can you do anything?" On her home world, flyers were only used if the conditions made it viable. They did everything they could to avoid an accident for good reasons; in Surned's atmosphere, the outcome was too often really bad.

Seolta had survived a flyer crash on Surned. Trust him.

The alarm screeching through the ship made that hard.

"The flyer's working overtime to expel the debris, but we're on limited fly time." His fingers flew over the control field. "Best option's a beach on the coast. Flat, hard and close enough if we have to do a glide finish."

She glanced out the window. They were horrifyingly close to the ground and none of it looked inviting. A bounce, and she clung to the sides of her chair, gasping as her crash harness suddenly tightened.

"We'll be fine," he said, "but it's going to be rough."

She pointed to a flat patch of ground between the twisting streams and jagged tongues of rock. "What about there?"

He shook his head. "Too fragile. The land here is mostly a thin crust over underground channels. The beach is safer."

After that, she dared not say anything more, too near to panic, and her hand gripped tight to her hair clip. Seolta glanced at her frequently but she blocked it out, fighting to keep from screaming. He needed her to stay calm, not add to his troubles.

After a while, she gave up fighting and shut her eyes, listening hard for the changing sounds of the engine.

"Nearly there," he said.

She opened her eyes again and looked down. They were coming in over a large sand dune beside a long rocky slope. She knew enough about landforms to recognise it—an old lava flow, spreading out to crash into a death maul with the cold waves of the sea. Beside it sat a small stretch of black sand.

"We'll be drowned."

"There's enough of a strip above the high tide mark. We should be safe until the flyer repairs any damage."

He sounded too soothing. "What aren't you telling me?"

He went to shake his head but she glared at him. "I'm not a business rival, Seolta a Manascraoch."

A smile twisted his mouth. "No, you're not." He looked out the window again, then took a breath.

"What do you know about volcanic debris."

"It's best avoided by any sensible flyer. This is my fault."

"No," he said. "Don't. After all I've done wrong in my life, I deserved that. All you did was try to do your duty. I've spent most of my life avoiding mine."

She was getting an ominous feeling. "Can we land?"

He eyed the beach. "We should, but our engines may not survive it. Volcanic debris can include tiny shards of glass spicules. I don't know if we can lift off afterwards, or if we'll have internal power. The temperature in these regions is brutal at night."

"Help will come." She counted on it, then saw his face. "It will come."

"Yes. I sent out a com signal and will keep transmitting as long as I can, but the signals in this area can be temperamental and the nearest rescue base is a good day's flight away."

It was her turn to take a deep breath. "Set us down, Seolta. We'll worry about the rest later."

CHAPTER TWENTY-EIGHT

Night had fallen by the time they'd finished 'setting up camp'. That's what Seolta called it. She tugged her wrap tightly around her shoulders as she eyed the temporary hut erected on the closest dune and the other shelter holding their baggage.

"You sure they're safe?"

He finished doing something to the doorway. "Trust me," he said with a grin, looking like a schoolboy facing a new adventure. He patted the frame. "These are straight out of den Coille design labs. They can stand up to hurricanes and blizzards."

She knew the technical definition of the words but had no real understanding of what they meant. "What about a dumping of volcanic ash?"

His smile slipped and she wished she hadn't asked. "We should be out of fallout range," he said.

"Oh." She shoved a smile onto her face and refrained from asking all the other questions that buzzed in her head. Was the flyer's engine repaired yet? Could it be fixed? Had he had an answer to his emergency transmission? Her own com was stubbornly silent, and she guessed all her other questions buzzed around in his head as testily as in her own. Her hand reached for hair clip again but she deliberately shoved it into the pocket of her jacket and huddled into its warmth.

"I've got the heating system set up now," he said. "Come inside."

Another gust of icy air tormented the bottom of her jacket. She hurried up the bank. "It's a lot colder here than in your home region."

"It's late winter here. We were at the end of summer on Protos."

He ducked into the hut after her. Inside was more than she'd expected. A bench and table, a basic heating unit with shelves holding survival packs of food, and a water cistern in the corner. She could even stand up.

"Everything we need," she said in surprise.

"Maybe not as fine as your rooms in the Academy, but it's enough for now." He had that pleased grin on his face again. "I haven't camped out for years. Take a seat and I'll get dinner sorted."

There was one thing missing though. "Where do we sleep?"

A wicked glint in his eyes this time. "Who says we're planning to sleep tonight?"

A warm shiver went over her, and this one had nothing to do with the dropping temperature outside. "Maybe, but we still need a sleeper," she said dryly. That boyish grin was irresistible.

He touched a pad and suddenly the table rearranged itself into a basic sleeper, complete with mat and thermal coverlet. He patted it invitingly. "All built in to the table's underside."

She stepped up, touching the support mat as outside the wind sent a rattle of warning over the roof. "Very clever," she said, and reached up for his mouth. She needed more than a simple peck on the cheek.

He pulled her close, deepening the kiss. "Shh, *mo Graidh*. It's nothing but sand and pebbles."

He pulled her down and laid her out on the strange sleeper. She reached for him hungrily. With the wind growling and the strange land a constant presence outside, she needed to feel him, to have him bury himself in her and forget the strangeness of the world. Make her a part of this place as she couldn't be on her own.

It was fully night by the time a rumbling stomach reminded her of the need for actual food. He pulled out a thick jacket and opened the hut's door.

"Come on. You can't know this planet until you've sat by a campfire at night."

He closed all the seams and handed her gloves and yet another wrap then tugged her outside.

They stood in the shelter of the hut, out of the battering of the night wind, and he set up a small thermal unit. In no time, the cheerful glow gave off a welcome warmth and had heated a ration pack each.

"Chairs?"

"You're camping outside. The grass is safe and the soil's too sandy to be damp. Take a seat, my dearest Esteemed Scholar."

He was laughing by the time she'd gingerly sat on the actual ground, after carefully pushing aside as many of the small and tough local grasses as she could.

"They're unkillable, Anyara, and abundant. Crushing a few isn't going to damage this region."

She still felt uncomfortable doing it. Sitting on a living plant, just because it felt good. Although it did, with the scents of plants, sea and sand mingling together in a unique blend she'd never smelled before. She finally settled and accepted her meal. Finished, she stared, entranced, at the rolling waves lapping the black sand below. They sat quietly, and after a while, she realised they were not alone here. Tiny creatures scuttled across the sands, in and out of the waters and digging below the damp patches. Other animals darted into the shallow water, grabbed at something and darted out again and, swooping down from above, came more small creatures, with wings and opening jaws that scooped up the sand then took it out to sea, swished it in the water, and gulped something down.

"Sifting out the sand." said Seolta softly. "We have a species similar to it on our beaches. They're after the smaller animals feeding on the microscopic biota in the tidal margins."

There was a sudden shriek and a larger flying creature swooped down, grabbed one of the smaller ones, swooped up again and disappeared. Only then did she realise the beach had been full of sound. Now only the swish of the lapping wavelets in a hypnotic rhythm remained. No splashing, no barely audible clicking on the sand. All the animals had gone silent, crouching down in hiding.

She peered up into the sky. That flying creature had been as big as her. "Will it come back?"

Seolta glanced up. "Maybe. Or another one will come, if it's anything like our folklar. It's unlikely to attack us though, not when there's so much easier and smaller prey around."

That didn't make her feel any better and she eyed the sky again. It was a strange colour, nothing like the multiple of greys and white of the skies over Seolta's home region or the splashes of light and crystalline blue in other areas, or the beautiful streaks of red and orange she'd seen on other evenings. This had a metallic sheen to it, and a faint brown tinge. Grey, black and burnt. Seolta glanced upwards as well, then froze, staring hard at the gloom.

"Is that normal for here?"

"I've never been to this region before," he said, his voice tense. He activated his com, pulling up an emergency channel, the one with extended reception. It was a degree less patchy than the others, but the last time they'd managed to link into it, nothing had showed up as out of the usual. This time, there was a bright red symbol showing. He linked into it, and they both gasped.

That volcano stewing away and puffing out smoke as they passed by had stepped up its activity level.

An evacuation warning. That's what that nasty red patch meant.

"How?" she said without expecting an answer. Seolta may be from this world, but he didn't have any more experience of this threat than she did. She pulled up her holo-map and searched anxiously. "Any chance you can get the flyer going?"

"To fly us out? No." He stared down at the bronzed hulk where it sat on the beach, taunting them. "Not in a volcanic warning. We're likely to get ourselves killed trying to fly through volcanic ash, even if the engines are ready." He stood up and began walking towards it.

"What are you planning?" Her voice squeaked in alarm as she hurried after him. He was looking out to sea. The huge body of water that went on and on … and, she remembered, had as many creatures living in it as there were on land, all the ranges of prey and predator. Some very big and scary-sounding predators. People were definitely within their prey range.

"It's a possibility. We can't stay here."

"We could take cover in the flyer."

He shook his head. "Too risky if there's a heavy ash fall."

He opened the hatch and activated the ship systems, busily muttering while his fingers flew through the control field. "All long-range flyers have a backup mode for seaborne travel in an emergency. The speed's not great and the range is limited, but it should be enough to get us to the next settlement up the coast and out of danger."

"Seaborne?" Something heavy and cold settled in her stomach. "You don't mean…" She pointed out to sea, struggling to say the words. "Float, on water?"

He turned to her, that eager boy grin on his face again. "Yes, like in boats and ships. People have been sailing vessels on the seas for millennia. It's better than being buried or burnt. You get the gear packed; I'll ready the flyer."

One more look at the sky and she didn't bother arguing but, oh, how she wished she could. Already the gloom had thickened and a chemical taste coated her tongue. Heart thumping, she hurried back up the dune and activated the packing sequence her com sent her, sending everything down on their floater pads once they were finished, and locking them into the baggage hold.

Then she scrambled on board the flyer and shut down the hatch. Inside, she heard a constant patter of pebbles beginning to beat on the outer shell.

"All locked down?"

She nodded, peering fearfully upwards.

He looked at her, and reached over. "Time to go." He threw her a dark-coloured strapping, matching the one around his chest. "Put this on. It's a flotation aid. Compulsory for sailing jaunts." He sent her a grin that was so deliberately faked she had to try to smile. He touched her cheek. "We're going to make it, you know."

"Yes," she said, and wished she could sound as fearless as he did.

A groan from the engines. She held her breath. More grinding, a high whine, then they lifted clear of the sand.

"We're free." She grinned. They were safe.

"I can't stay in this mode," he warned her. "The airside engines are already taking on debris. I'll keep it as low as I can, and it'll have to be fast to create a backlash to blast the sand away from us. Hold on."

Her heart plummeted again. For a blessed moment, she'd imagined them lifting off and flying away. He hit the Go signal and they rocketed forward. She was flung back against her seat with a whoomph of air, and clung tightly as he barrelled down the beach and hit the waves with a huge splash that sent water careering over the view screens. Then they settled and she felt the rocking of the sea under her for the first time. He switched off the airside engines and a faint hum sounded from under her feet.

"In seaborne mode and past the breakers. I'll take it farther out to sea before heading up the coast." He brought up a holoscan unlike any she'd seen before. "This is the seafloor in this region."

An ominous dark blob moved into view and wove around the sharp ridges of what he said was a reef reaching out from the headland.

"What's that blob?"

His fingers worked on the controls. "I'm putting out a defensive field to keep unwelcome visitors away. You're safe."

"It's dangerous?"

"Only if you were stupid enough to go for a swim." He grinned, then it disappeared. "Can you? Swim, I mean."

She shook her head. "On a station, water is too precious to be wasted like that."

He touched the strap around her chest. "This inflates in contact with water. Best advice is, don't fight it. It will keep you afloat in the unlikely event of anything happening to the flyer."

"Like crashing on a beach under a volcano."

"Yeah, like that."

She'd meant is as a joke, but there was nothing funny about it. Her hand reached for the hair clip just as they were hit by another heavy rattle of debris.

Seolta's hands never stopped moving in the control field. "You're the expert on air and water flow patterns. Can you check the maps and pull up the fastest route out of here?"

He didn't say it, but the words 'before it's too late' hovered in the space between them. She opened the holomaps and ran a prediction based on surface water flows and air patterns, adding in the volcano's current eruption pattern and pulling up any historical data she could access. The ship's external reception was shaky at best, and she wasn't sure how complete were the data trends she'd pulled in. Then she overlaid the red warning signals.

Right now, they were smack in the middle of the danger zone.

She studied the map again, searching and filtering for any other options. The currents here were treacherous thanks to the many lethal undersea rocky outcroppings from a long history of lava flows and other volcanic activity. The patterns were so complex, far more so than in the station shell she was used to, and she had to hope she was interpreting the data correctly. Not that she harassed Seolta with her fears. He was fully aware of the dangers lurking under the waves.

One in particular gave her a nasty jolt. An underground cairn of boulders sitting on a long underwater lava platform. Huge boulders that looked to have been flung there and piled up haphazardly by some ancient mythical giant creature.

Or thrown out by a viciously erupting volcano.

A jolt of the flyer and she shrieked out loud, then clamped her mouth shut. Seolta flung her a glance and she saw the worry in his dark eyes.

"We'll make it," he said.

"I know we will," she said, fighting to control her voice and putting out a hand to touch his arm, hoping it didn't tremble too much. "I'm sending you the best route I can find to clear the danger zone. It takes us northwest for a while to clear the rougher seabed, then straight north."

"Is it the shortest or quickest?"

"Shortest. The currents here are faster," she pointed out a location farther west, "but it takes us right through that large whirlpool between those islands."

He stared at the map, a crease in his brow, fingers feeding data into the ship systems. Then looked again at the volcanic spread.

"We need the quickest. That thing's on the verge of blowing. If I hit the correct entry point to the whirlpool, the flyer can make it through."

"The risk analysis?" She clutched the chair grips, fighting the need to tug on her hair clip or latch onto him.

"The risk of getting hit by a dumping of ash or boulders is high if we're still in the red zone. Getting the whirlpool wrong is not quite as high." He looked at her, eyes wide open and no trace of any artifice showing. "Our chances are negative either way."

She heaved in a deep breath. "You're asking me to trust you or brave a volcano's wrath. You give me little credit, Messer Seolta. A life partner may not mean much on your world, but in mine it is a solemn promise. Take us through the whirlpool."

His fingers worked the control panel and the flyer veered onto the quickest route but his eyes still clung to hers. "Your promise? Is that the only reason?"

It wasn't the simple question it sounded. He was asking her for everything. "We're possibly about to die and you want to know this?"

"What better time, *mo Graidh?*"

She gasped in a breath. He was right. If they didn't survive this, did she want to die without telling him … what?

Why was she even considering it? She'd known the answer for many months now. Flawed, erratic, driven—many would have told her Seolta den Coille was a poor choice of partner—but she had chosen him regardless, and not just to protect their worlds. The Arcadian embassy and Survey could have fabricated another reason for her trip here. Not as useful or as effective, and not with him, but good enough.

That wasn't why she had taken Seolta as her life partner. She took a breath.

"I love you, Messer Seolta a Manascraoch," she said, "and I trust you to do everything you can to bring us safely through. You have saved me before; you will do it again this time."

His hand reached out and clamped down on hers, a too bright sheen to his eyes. "My Anyara. The bravest woman I know. I will bring you safely through, *mo Graidh,* or die with you." He brought her hand to his mouth and touched it with his lips as if in solemn benediction. "I love you, *mo Graidh.* You will not regret this day."

She blinked, and he squeezed her hand again. "Now, let's get out of here."

The whirlpool looked as dangerous as she'd feared. A churning washpool of blue, grey and white, dark and ominous under the glowering skies. She stared at it in horror.

"I'll skim the surface and take us through on that leading edge. The thrusters should have enough life in them to make it if we get the line just right."

She nodded, clamping her lips shut. She'd told him she trusted him, and she did, but he couldn't beat everything. Life had already taught him that, and this looked fearsome.

"Shut your eyes, *mo Graidh.*"

And maybe lose her last sight of him? "No," she said.

That defiant grin and a laugh in his dark eyes. "The bravest woman," he said in a soft murmur. Then all humour vanished and he set his sights dead ahead, fingers working furiously and his face taking on that subtle distance of one syncing directly with machine systems.

They headed into the vortex.

She might not shut her eyes but she kept forgetting to breathe. She stared straight at the gap between the rocks. The flyer lifted, skimming the surface as he'd said. The roar of the airside thrusters joined the mechanical thrum of the marine drivers.

"Forward drive on full," he said. She rocked back against her seat. A fine spray covered the side ports. She pulled on her ear covers as the sounds of the whirlpool and the engines joined the constant pummelling on the roof from the volcano's fallout, and yet, above it all, she could still hear the thump, thump of her heart, echoing through her body.

She clenched her hands and watched Seolta. His face was set tight, but she focussed on his hands, fighting to keep the flyer to the ordained passage. They didn't waver.

He would get them through.

The buffeting of the flyer added to the cacophony of noise and sensation. Only her strapping kept her in her seat. The gap neared, then they were in it, huge slabs of grey rock looming on either side.

Then daylight beckoned and the sounds dropped. The flyer dropped with it, as the growl of the airside engines vanished.

"Thrusters gone," said Seolta, as if commenting on the time of day. "Water drivers fully engaged."

The swirling currents caught them and shoved them all the way through.

"We're out," he said now, still engaged with the flyer's systems.

We're alive? She blinked, not quite able to believe. "We made it."

He disconnected from the sync as they hit smoother water. "Did you doubt it?"

"No," she lied, not very convincingly, and his chuckle said he wasn't fooled.

He kept one eye on his controls as his head turned to hers. She couldn't reach his face, but she had his hand and rained kisses on it then threw caution to the winds and loosened her harness, reaching for him, taking his precious face in her hands.

"We are alive, and you made it possible. You are a genius, my beloved." He flushed a bright pink and she laughed. "You've been told you're a genius many times before," she told him.

"Yes, only there was always a *but* to it."

"I don't know why so many believe you to be bad," she said airily.

"Possibly because I deserved it," he said softly, eyes set on her for a long moment, before turning back to the dangerous waters. "I've told you I am not a good man."

She remembered too well. "Too many good men have let me down."

"I will never do that." His voice was soft, flat, and carefully stripped of emotion. As if he didn't yet trust her response. "I will keep you safe or die in the trying."

"I know you will," she said, equally solemn, putting all her heart into the words. It was time. "As long as you know the same works in reverse. You are my heart and soul. I will keep you safe, keep you loved, keep you whole, or die in the trying."

His eyes darkened and his lips took hers again. This time it was a kiss of promise, long and slow, a physical vow sealing their words, over in far too short a time as a wave hit them and he had to turn back to the controls with an oath.

"Just give me a patch of still water," he muttered.

She knew how he felt. Desire, strong and sharp, hung in the air. She needed him, needed to feel him in her. Needed to seal their promises.

It was hours later before he dared set the flyer's controls to automatic. They had turned north, and the constant rain of debris on the outer shell had died down to an occasional pattering. He could have turned off the outer sensors, giving them peace from the constant sense of threat, but she didn't ask him to do that.

She liked knowing the score against her.

Slowly, with each beaten wave, each rocking of the flyer, she began to believe they were going to win. She yawned, fighting off the tiredness that threatened to take her under. He would not fight alone this time, and she only wished her flyer expertise extended to nursing a battered vessel through the vastness that was a planetary ocean.

There were none on Surned, and if any had been present, the liquid they held would have been too caustic to risk taking any vessel out on it; but here, almost two thirds of the whole planet was covered by actual water: salty, minerally balanced, a ready home for the millions of creatures adapted to an aquatic life. She leaned back and stared out the view screen. Occasionally, a flying or diving creature broke the view, but mostly it was the splashing slosh of water and waves. She switched her com to scan the water beneath them. The first time she tried it, she gasped. So much life. She watched the shapes in fascination, then risked a short spurt of the high energy-program that brought the scan signals to fully synthesised and coloured life. Her jaw dropped. Small and large, vicious and panicked, the surface waters teemed with the constant interplay of myriad species. Her com told her also of the microscopic fauna spawning all this activity. Grazed by filter feeders, some little more than microscopic but one memorably enormous. She thumped Seolta on the arm to point at the huge shadow.

"It's all right. It knows we're here and has no more desire to meet us than we do it."

Maybe, but she was heartily relieved when the monster cruised out of range.

"It's so beautiful," she said.

A while later, he brought up the scans of the volcano. It had blown, as anticipated. She watched the violent outbursts from the core of the planet. If they'd been back on that beach…

They'd made it.

"Any reply to your signals?" she said idly. They were so far north, something must be on scan.

He was silent.

"What's wrong?"

"We should have heard from Mangolon station by now."

"The volcano's charge field still interfering?"

He shook his head. "We're far enough away for my com to bounce a signal off our low orbit sensors to local receivers." He frowned again at his com, fingers playing uselessly in the control field, then huffed in indignation. "The reception's not great but it's enough. Try yours."

She did as he said but didn't see what difference it would make. Her signal was patchy at best and not calibrated as finely for this world. Nor did it have the refinements she suspected he'd built into his. One day, she must have a serious talk with him about what was expected between life partners. His ingrained reticence about the ways he subverted the systems around him were of such long standing that hiding what his com could do was second nature to him.

Her com sprang to life. "Fishing vessel *Arch Lampton* responding. What's the emergency?"

Her mouth dropped. Seolta's face was as furious as she'd seen it, but he clenched his fists and she watched, fascinated, as he wrestled his anger down.

"Tell him we're a downed flyer, escaping the eruption, and transmit these coordinates and ship file." He linked through the details and she did as ordered.

"Received, Flyer. Do you need pick-up?"

She wished she could refuse, unsure about their rescuers, but Seolta shook his head. "I don't know how long we can keep going."

"Yes," she said to the ship.

Silence, and she began to fret again.

Her com crackled to life. "We'll be there in four standard hours. That soon enough?"

"Should be," she said back again, and made no attempt to hide the nerves in her voice.

"Right. We'll keep you on com. Signal again if the position changes. *Arch Lampton* out."

The transmission stopped. She turned to Seolta. "Is your com's send mode faulty?"

He shook his head, the fury back. "I ran a scan while you were linked. They were receiving my signal and the ID was clear."

"Did you use an emergency channel."

He nodded brusquely. "Not the extreme one; we're not there yet. The one for disaster needing assistance."

"They read your ID and chose not to help you."

"Exactly."

"I'll tell them we are fine. We don't need help after all."

"No." She could see the effort it took for him to say that. "Too risky. The sea mode is only ever meant to be temporary and we're reaching the end of the drivers' life cycle. They've been working double in these seas. We need help, and four hours is pushing it."

Hopefully we'll last that long.

He didn't say it but the thought hung in the air. He didn't need her fears to make it worse.

"What can we shut down to help ship's systems last?

He shook his head. "Plot the best course through these seas. Any route that gives us smoother waters."

She looked and gave him some minor course corrections, but they both knew they made little difference. The sea still chopped at them, each swell another hill to climb. Only heading back towards land offered any improvement, and there was nothing there but sharp-edged rocks and empty shores.

"We will make it," he said to her. Whether defying her fears or the elements of his world, it was hard to say. All she asked for was the sight of another vessel on this vast and unfriendly ocean. Seolta spoke little, but she could see the frown touching his face whenever he thought she wasn't looking.

She began to listen to the engine sounds with the same intensity as when following the sprouting of a new and precious plant in her nursery. So far, they held. Periodically, she unstrapped and moved back to the prepper area, bringing him food, a hot drink, anything he might need to stay awake and pilot them safely to rescue.

Then the sound of the drivers spluttered.

"They've gone?" she asked, unable to keep silent this time.

"Mostly. I've got just enough left in them to stop us drifting too far shorewards."

Onto all those sharp-edged shorelines she'd checked out earlier. Wicked cliffs lined with razor-edged bulwarks that promised only death and destruction. She pulled up the rescue ship's position. "They're not far away now."

"Let them know our status," he said. "Use this emergency code."

She looked at the list of codes, and her mouth dropped at the one he'd chosen. *Status imminent loss.* Was that as ominous as it sounded? "We'll make it," she muttered again, ignoring the growing rocking of the flyer in the surging seas. What she'd give for a properly programmed habitat. The environment didn't kill you in a habitat.

Grey waves splashed against the view screens. "Switching to reality view," said Seolta. "Power reserves low." The screens went blank, then slid back to show the plasglass ports. She was looking at actual waves now, not a screen view. No more pretending the outside view was a sim illusion. She gripped the hair clip tightly.

"You are not dying today, *mo Graidh.*" His fingers moved to a side panel on the control field. "Emergency evac procedures engaged." He turned to her. "Your support strap will keep you afloat if we get separated." She gasped in horror. "Head straight for land. I've sent your com the coordinates. Your support has an inbuilt guidance system."

"We will not get separated."

He gave her a trace of a smile. "I will try not to, my brave lady. But if we do…"

An alarm sounded from the com field. They both looked up. There, finally, a grey hulk showed up on the view screen. "It's here," she yelled.

"Not before time," muttered Seolta grimly as the skies opened and rain pelted them.

Soon, the beaten-up vessel hovered beside them. Seolta kept the grinders going as best he could while ship and flyer manoeuvred into place. At last, they were latched to its side.

The ship's captain came onto the comm screen. "You're too big for us to tow. You'll have to take off what you need and leave it for salvage. Use the emergency chute."

Seolta's face grew grimmer as he turned to her. "Pack what you need. Bare basics, to fit in one small baggage carrier."

"Can't they float our luggage up?"

"Not in these conditions. The ship won't be able to hold us long enough."

Seolta was already unbuckling and ordering his baggage selection. She copied him. The precious samples from the trip were already stowed carefully in their custom carrier. She just needed a case of her personal gear and she was ready.

"One case only," Seolta said.

"I need the samples."

"Only what you can carry in one hand. You'll have to leave the samples."

Impossible. Not after all the work it had taken to collect them. Seolta went first into the chute and she followed, holding tight to her carrier. He reached out for it at the top, setting it down on the rolling deck of the ship then hauled her up.

"You brought the sample carrier."

"We need it."

He said nothing, but the tight mask of his face snapped into place. He picked up the case, passed it to her as soon as she landed on board, then grabbed up his own.

A loud splash below them. She looked back.

"They've released the flyer," Seolta said in a flat voice. The flyer was his family's, with many of his personal innovations. He'd just lost his home again. He turned to the sailors surrounding them, back straight. "Thank you for your assistance."

"The captain's waiting inside."

He nodded curtly, and the seamen gestured to the inside cabin as abruptly. She hurried after him, drenched by sea spray and the rain pummelling down on them. Once inside, he took her sample case from her frozen fingers.

"Captain," he said, lifting a hand in greeting. "Seolta den Coille, and my life partner Anyara a Prithand2."

The captain was an old, grizzled seafarer, with a coarse beard and unfriendly eyes. "We got your file, Ser den Coille. You're a long way from home. What's a Protos boss doing out here."

"Showing my partner my world," he said, and she recognised the smile on his face. It was the one he used when manipulating a difficult prospect. He put his hand on her shoulder. "If you could show Sera Anyara to a cabin, she needs to change out of these wet clothes."

"Only females on board are the cook and navigator. She'll have to bunk in with them. Ain't heard of no life partner. You two married or what?"

"No," she said as she saw Seolta about to open his mouth. This married idea was too foreign to her to claim. His frown almost matched the captain's. "She'll have to stay there."

"She stays with me," said Seolta, his practised smile vanishing.

"Got news for you, Protos boss. On a ship, the captain's word is law, and we don't have no nonsense on my ship. Where's she even from? Don't recognise none of the places on her file and they ain't on the charts."

Seolta looked about to explode. "I'm an off-worlder," she said hurriedly. "From the planet Surned."

The captain's face suddenly changed. "Surned? Mmph. That's interesting. Don't suppose you know a Hilmar a Kevand3 from there?"

"Happens we do," said Seolta, his face and manner suddenly changing. He gave her a quick, discreet glance, one she hoped the captain couldn't read. "Why?"

The captain shrugged. "He was through here a while back. Understood he ran into a bit of trouble with those big necks in Urbis. You know him, Sera?"

Seolta gave a barely perceptible nod.

"He's my uncle," she said.

The man's eyes opened wide. "You don't say. How about that."

After that, everything changed on board. She was hustled off to a cabin with a big woman introduced as the finest cook this side of the western reefs, and stripped, exclaimed over, and bundled into a coverall and jacket that were far too big for her. Rolling up the sleeves and cuffs helped, but she felt like a walking puff ball. She was warm, and that mattered more.

"Leaving your own gear on board for a bunch of dirt and stuff," said the woman in disbelief when Anyara explained why she had no change of clothes. "You're no fisherwoman, that's for sure."

"No, Sera," she agreed ruefully. "I'm a scientist."

"Ah, that explains it then." She shook her head. "Come along. Even scientists have to eat."

She returned to the main cabin to find Seolta and the captain had reached a state of armed truce, but the captain's face eased at the sight of her. "You look like my daughter the first time I brought her out to sea. But she had proper sea legs. Take a seat, Sera, and Matty will get a plate of something hot into you."

She sat down beside Seolta. He had changed too, she saw, into his own gear with a fisherman's jacket thrown over the top to keep warm. Climate control for the living quarters was a low priority, apparently.

"Matty tells me you left your gear on board so you could bring that case of…" said the captain.

"Samples," she said helpfully. "There are so many fascinating kinds of biota on this world," she added in a gushing tone. She caught the strained look on Seolta's face and suspected he was trying not to laugh. Maybe she had laid it on a bit thick.

Not to a man who'd said she reminded him of his daughter it seemed. She reached for her plate of food and took a hungry mouthful, then lifted her spoon in appreciation. "This is delicious, Sera." A rich broth of something tasting of the sea. She wasn't lying this time.

Seolta pulled his plate towards him and took a spoonful, then stopped. "Yes, quite delicious," he said, in a tone she mistrusted. "My mother would love the recipe."

"Oh, just a bit of this and that," said the cook.

"Something in it tastes extra good."

"Oh, that will be the new stuff I got through your uncle. Adds real body to a dish."

"Ah, yes, that must be it. The Sera and I met off world and they have many interesting foods there." That had the captain peering suspiciously at Seolta, and he hurried on. "Do you think you could show it to me. My family's involved in the food ingredient business, and we're always eager to find new products. I'd like to contact the importer about a deal."

"You wouldn't cut him out?" Matty looked as suspicious as the captain. "That's what Protos folks generally do."

Seolta looked outraged. "Of course not. It's a waste of time and credits if the importer already has a system in place. We're suppliers, not importing agents."

"Well, if that's the way of it. Here." She brought up her pantry stores on her com and showed the applicable listing to Seolta. It looked harmless enough to Anyara, with no reason for the tension she could feel in Seolta's arms, but he showed none of it, merely asking permission to copy the listing, then turning the talk to other ingredients the woman used. Soon, they were both buried in talk of thickeners, protein additives, fresh versus processed, and a stew of other equally obscure subjects that appeared to be fascinating to both of them. At the end of it, Matty had acquired new recipes and Seolta a smug air of satisfaction that for some reason settled the captain's suspicions.

"Your uncle, how's he keeping?"

"In his usual spirits, last time I saw him," she said, quite truthfully. "We've been travelling, so it was a few cycles past, but I've heard nothing to the contrary from him." She hadn't heard from her uncle at all and would have all her senses on high alert if he did contact her, but the captain didn't need to know that.

It was an interesting evening but, frustratingly at the end of it, she was led to the woman's bunkroom and had no chance of a private word with Seolta. Nor did she in the days that followed as they chugged through the seas and back to port. The captain saw no reason to cut short his fishing trip. One day, Seolta told her the link to his security was back, and another day he swore furiously and claimed to have caught a spine of a fish on his hand. She couldn't see any sign of injury, and had to assume he had full global contact back, bringing with it an unwelcome link from the marshals. None had contacted her, and she bent back to sorting the catch into various bins, a frown on her face. Would he ever trust her? She scrubbed at her face with its threatening tear, then cursed as the smell of the catch assaulted her nostrils.

By the time they finally glimpsed the port city of Mangolon they were both intimately familiar with all the edible species on offer in the western seas. Far too familiar.

She leaned with him on what she'd learned to call the gunwale, staring out at the hive of activity in the port. "First priority, shopping," she said, sniffing cautiously at her sleeve. "I'm going to incinerate this lot." She still wore the coveralls given to her on boarding. She'd tried cleaning them overnight, but the ship's laundry system left much to be desired. Battered and cranky, it appeared to have the smell of seafood ingrained. Her clothes came out smelling as bad as when they'd gone in.

Seolta copied her, and grimaced. "It'll have to be at a storefront booth. No decent shop will let us in the door.

She suspected he'd kept at least one outfit untouched in his baggage carrier and said so. He grinned. "My carrier is top of the line for Arcadia," he said, "but it's not fish proof. That smell gets through anything."

She leaned farther over the edge, needing badly to ask too many questions, but he shook his head. "Later," he said softly.

Then they both caught sight of a familiar face. In full Den Coille uniform, their security squad had arrived, the look of strain on their faces matched only by the black fury in the squad leader's.

"Holiday time's over," said Seolta. She glanced pointedly at his hands. They were as scabbed and battered as her own.

He laughed, and waved to their security.

The squad surrounded them as soon as they disembarked, forming a tight quadrant around them despite their stench and glaring at any poor passerby who dared come close. Anyara had a marked dislike of being conspicuous after a childhood spent avoiding her uncle's attention and hated every step of the way to the hotel rooms the squad had procured for them. Not enough to forgo the needed visit to a storefront to buy new clothes, but she was thoroughly relieved to reach the privacy of their hotel room and see the door slam shut behind them. Seolta had ordered the squad to take the next door rooms and stand guard in the hallway. The leader had argued, spooked by their misadventures and wanting to station guards right in the room with them. Seolta was adamant and flatly ordered the troopers out, locking the door firmly after them.

He stalked into the cleansing suite and began throwing the hated clothing into the trash chute. "This cleanser is big enough for us both."

She'd made love with this man, had shared days on a flyer with him. The constraints of the fishing ship must have affected her. She began slowly to undress, thrusting her own smelly gear into the trash chute and hearing with relief the hotel's ventilation systems flushing out all trace of fish and sea. Then she turned and saw he watched her with a closed look on his face. She put her hands up as cover.

"Don't. Please," he said softly. "You are so beautiful, *mo Graidh*, and I have missed you very badly."

"You haven't told me what you learned on the ship yet. What was in that soup?"

"Later," he said. "You can also tell me what the captain told you of your uncle. But right now…" He held out a hand, and let his face fall open. She walked into the cleansing unit with him.

CHAPTER TWENTY-NINE

Seolta woke wondering what had happened to the swell of the ocean and the smell of fish then opened his eyes fully and saw daylight through large windows and grime-covered buildings across a walkway.

He was in a town, in a proper sleeper.

He panicked, twisting around. Beside him, Anyara snuffled softly, then settled back to rest. He hadn't lost her.

He watched as sleep took her under again. Lines of exhaustion covered her face, those endearing freckles standing out on skin as washed out as any lower level habitat dweller under the tan she'd begun to acquire in their travels. He lay as still as he could. She needed more sleep.

Her hair, those amazing twists of red, amber and gold, sprawled in a mad tangle on the pillow, one stray tendril stuck to her cheek. She complained about it sometimes, twisting it back ruthlessly into a single braid or dragging it into an untidy knot at the base of her neck. He'd asked her once why she didn't cut it short and she'd snorted in laughter. She'd tried that once, she said, and it stuck out like a fuzz bush from Celadon. The only way to tame it was to shear it all off.

He was heartily relieved she'd not done that. Her face was beautiful, with strong bones, a tough face that came to life when she laughed, but he loved the softness of her hair, breaking free of any constraints she put on it. He reached towards it now, tracing a finger just above the surface in case he disturbed her. The coverlet hid the rest of her, but he traced the lines under the sheet and saw her in his mind's eye. A strong body, small by her world's standards but just right for a Mountainer, compact and neat. She didn't have the kind of beauty that grabbed the lead in vidcast streams. Not tall enough, not dramatic, not voluptuous or sleekly slim.

No, she was the kind that brought a slight glance as your eyes passed by, only to come back and be caught, again and again. Firm, high breasts, a body honed by her constant activity, that sweet curve of her waist and a backside… His lips twitched. He was never going to tell her how much he appreciated that backside, running his hands over it in memory.

He could have lost her. In the steam, in the volcano, in the sea. He could have lost her forever.

The marshals watched them. They wouldn't come to his aid, but they'd never let anything happen to her as long as she was in com range. Not to an Esteemed Scholar of the Alliance Academy.

They'd been out of range when the volcano hit, and he wasn't going to let that happen again. He pulled up his com and searched again for the marshals' tracking link. It was subtle, too complicated for him to control.

Or was it?

Given time, anything was decipherable. He pulled up systems, explored, stopping carefully whenever he came to a ward code. The marshals were as suspicious as he was.

Finally he got control. He took a moment to review it, and to appreciate the wonder of the marshals' tracking systems. No wonder he trusted Marcus an Fallon. The man was in charge of an organisation as shifty as they came. For a while, he'd begun to doubt he could change their programs without setting off their warning systems, and he really didn't want to find out what that would bring down on him, but he'd beaten them on this one. He smiled then made his changes. If anyone removed her com, or if she was out of range of him for more than ten standard minutes, an alarm went off, signalling trouble to both him and the marshals.

When it came to her safety, he'd take whatever help he could get.

He lay back, watching her breathe, in and out, alive and so lovely. He lapsed back into sleep, and woke much later to the delight of her smile welcoming him back to daylight.

"Good morning, Messer Seolta."

"Good morning, Messera my heart," he said, and this time he need not keep his hands shy of her body.

"What do you think of your first EA world?" he said later, one finger playing with those fascinating curls. A small crease touched her brow. "Not the paradise you expected?" he asked cautiously.

The crease deepened and she stared at the ceiling. "Not quite." Then turned and grinned at him. "Neither is it very welcoming. It nearly killed us."

"And Surned won't?"

"Oh, yes, instantly, if you're fool enough to go outside a dome." She gave a twitch of those luscious lips. "But on a habitat or station or ship, it's simple. Inside the shell is safe; outside will kill you. Here, it's more … complicated."

He waited, and she threw him an exasperated scowl. "You know it is. In a habitat, we control everything inside. Water, temperature, atmosphere, even gravity if needed."

"Not everything," he protested. "They're still set on a planet."

She just looked at him. "Everything. That dome goes right around us, even under the substratum. Nothing gets in or out unless the inhabitants allow it."

She laughed at the horror on his face and he shut his mouth.

"And here?"

"It's like…" She was quiet again. "We don't belong here, you know."

"We do," he said, seriously alarmed. His arm circled her waist and reached down to prove it. The softening in her face and lifting of her hips had him grinning in triumph.

"Not *us*, silly. *People* don't belong on Arcadia."

His hand stopped, shocked. "Yes, they do."

"Now, maybe, but humans didn't evolve here. It shows up in lots of small ways. There are so many types, so many cultures, so many ways people have adapted to the planet, but I'm a biome specialist, and we are not from this world."

"This is my home," he said, becoming seriously disgruntled.

"It is now. But it's as if the settlers said that to the planet, and the planet said, 'Prove it. You want to stay here, you'll have to earn your place.' On a habitat, if we want to do something, we do it. The parameters are known, set in plascrete, but on Arcadia you have to open a negotiation with the planet every time you do anything. Adjust for temperature changes, landforms, seasonal differences. For violent fluctuations like droughts and floods, storms and blizzards … and volcanos."

"You have storms on Surned. I was caught out in one."

"Exactly. An EA mistake. We don't venture out in a storm and build habitats only in known safe regions. If anything changes drastically, we shift the habitat. Nothing changes for the citizens. On Arcadia, you have to live with change. It feels both scary and exhilarating and I'm not yet sure who is winning."

He didn't understand, but one important question stood out. "Could you live here?"

She smiled, a very special smile. "If you were here, yes. But we can't stay on this world," she added softly.

She'd said *we*. They had so little time left on Arcadia, less than twenty days. A part of him wanted to be on that ship now, wanted it over and done with, while the screaming lump inside him dreaded it. Leaving this time would be worse. This time, he knew exactly what he was losing.

But she was coming with him.

A blare on his com signals and a hammering on the outer door. The security squad had reached the limit of their patience. They sat down to breakfast a little later with two guards hovering by the door and another by the main window. Whether to stop him escaping or keep out the ravening hordes of Deuteronians walking in the streets outside, he wasn't sure. The guard at the window was glowering at the outside as if expecting a fully armed onslaught.

"Deuteronians are full citizens of Arcadia, Squad Leader," he said, unable to keep the amusement out of his voice.

"Yes, Ser." The man stood rigidly, then allowed himself a muttered, "Barely."

Den Coille had always fostered honesty and independent thinking in its security troops. Some days it had a definite downside. "We're here on holiday," he reminded the man. "I expect full discretion from your team."

"Yes, Ser," said the man even more stiffly. "As you order."

He sighed, and Anyara laughed. "We could have done with their help these last days. Which reminds me."

"The fishing boat?"

She nodded. "You found something?"

He had, but didn't want to involve her. She was at enough risk already.

She glared back. "We're *partners*, Seolta mar Bram an Scathach den Coille. Partners share." She glanced at the guards, then back to him. "Give me a private link." She stretched out her wrist.

The squad leader stepped forward.

"This is personal, Squad Leader," Seolta told him.

The man looked even less happy but had to stop. Seolta lifted his wrist and spoke into it. "Comms spec, put a transmission block on this room. Nothing in or out." Then he stretched out his wrist and made the link with Anyara.

'What was in that soup?' she demanded on the private link as soon as their coms synced.

'The cook called it Restin, but I know my family's product. It was Festin, straight from a festia tree. We've always had trouble getting distributors for Deuteron. It wasn't a problem; we had plenty of buyers off world. It's available here in only the largest city, and I know of no synthetic version that gets the taste right.' He showed her the list the cook had sent him, arrowing down on the production details. It showed an address on a station hub.

'That's a Surned associate. My uncle has a minor stake.'

'And the main owners are?'

She knew all her uncles' major associates. She'd made sure of it over the years, never wanting to be caught out by a surprise attack. Jongma, with backing from Meth Varkan.'

'Aah.'

His friends from the calamitous race at Alliance Central.

'Jongma could have synthesised it,' she said.

'I know Festin and this wasn't synthesised.' He frowned. 'We need a sample. Did you learn anything more from the captain? Such as what was your esteemed uncle doing nosing around Deuteron?'

She scowled. 'Causing trouble. The captain called him a fine gentleman who listened to what folk were telling him, not like those stick pikes in Urbis. I assume you know who the stick pikes are.'

'The Council, at a guess. Anything else?'

'He made them some promises of aid. With what, is the question. My uncle is no bank.'

'But he might have access to a major Alliance banking family with plans to expand, and Deuteron has been blocked from expanding for hundreds of years.'

He thought, but shook his head in frustration. 'It's not enough for the Council. We need to get out and talk to the locals.'

She glanced at the guards.

'Leave it to me,' he added, suddenly feeling a wicked thread of an idea. He'd played nice for too long. Mangolon was the third largest settlement on Deuteron. Talk here held weight but wouldn't hit any planetary vidcast. He needed information, and fast. First, though, he needed some of this tragging Restin. He'd been taste-testing Festin and its derivatives all his life; he knew the taste of the real thing, and that soup had used it.

"We're going for a walk," he announced to his security guards after they had finished eating. "I need to feel ground under my feet."

The guards didn't look happy at the prospect of their charges roaming free, but dutifully lined up ready to leave, uniformed and armed. Seolta took one look and gave them his most supercilious stare, head back and fully drawn up. "We're a new couple going for a stroll around a peaceful town, not the leaders of an armed assault team."

"A town you know nothing about. If there's trouble, you are both still recovering from your ordeal."

Seolta took Anyara's hand. "Are we invalids, my Sera? You feel weak, anxious?"

Anyara shot him a sharp glance. "Not that I am aware of."

"Thank you. Leader, we are neither decrepit nor timorous. You've been with me long enough to know our recent mishap won't hold me back, and I assure you that Sera Anyara is every bit as capable. We can survive for the split moments before you get to us, and I have every confidence in your abilities, whatever you are wearing."

He raked the leader and his team up and down, watching the slight shuffle of feet under his scrutiny with an inner smile. "Meet us at the entry foyer in local gear and follow us discreetly. This troop is among the best of Den Coille's. I take it you can stay unseen."

The Leader looked like he'd swallowed a ganda. "Certainly, Ser. As you order."

As soon as the team left them, Seolta grabbed Anyara's hand and hurried to the door controls.

"This way," he said, as soon as they were in the hallway. "There's a back entrance down to the left."

"Your troop won't let you out of their sight for a moment afterwards if you do this."

"Tough. We've got work to do," he retorted as he ran down the corridor then swung with her into the side door he'd found on the hotel plans. He opened his com and put in a block on the security's trackers. "Come *on*." He hadn't felt as alive since this whole, crazy time started, before his capture by the Survey. They erupted from an outer door to an angry shout from the hotel cleaning staff and into a back alley that smelled nearly as bad as that fishing boat.

A dark figure stood in the shadows. It watched them, but made no move, not yet.

"The marshals?"

He nodded. "They'll interfere only if you're in trouble."

That's what he hoped anyway. He grabbed her hand and dragged her on, forcing her to run until they were well away from the hotel, slowing only as they reached a deserted alley. Then he opened his com and disengaged the marshals' tracker, pulling them through the back door of a shop immediately afterwards.

It was a women's fashion store, and they rushed through to a chorus of shocked yells and angry battering from outraged attendants. He erupted from the store holding his hands over his head and choking with laughter, then into the next café on the street and back into another alleyway. After that, it was more rushing, more backtracking, more racing through a maze of shops, streets, shrubberies, and open parklands. He didn't slow until he was sure no more figures lurked, and he could only imagine the curses littering the marshals' headquarters.

"Stop, Seolta," she said, her voice a breathless mix of laughter and gasped panting. He let go her hand, grinning at her in triumph as she bent over, hands on hips and sucking in air. She straightened out in a short time, eyes sparkling. "You! I am an Esteemed Scholar of the Academy. I am *not* supposed to be dragged around the streets of a backwater town like some piece of stray baggage."

"No, *mo Graidh*, you are not." He seized her face with both hands and gave her a thorough if too brief kiss. "We lost them," he couldn't resist another kiss, "and you can now be as respectable as you please. We are going grocery shopping, Messera."

They'd been running so long that they were in the outer suburbs, behind a collection of shrubs in a small side street near a neighbourhood shopping cluster. He pulled off his jacket, then his under tunic, shivering as a chill breeze tripped around the corner. It might be nearly spring here, but they were still in the south of the continent and it was much colder than back on his home mountains.

"Put that jacket back on. You'll freeze."

"In a minute." He dipped the corner of it in a dirty puddle and dabbed it on her face.

"Hey." She put up a hand to fend him off.

He took hold of her chin and wiped off the careful enhancements from the hotel's grooming unit. "An ordinary backstreet woman has neither the time nor credits for that level of cosmetics."

She still put up her hands, blocking him from touching her nose and cheeks.

He carefully prised them away and kissed the tip of her nose and each little, entrancing brown dot. "You are more beautiful this way and I love your freckles, my heart. They make you look fallible," he added with a grin.

"That water better not carry anything contagious." Since she'd been inoculated against anything that might harm her on Arcadia before leaving Alliance Central, he ignored that, standing back at the end and studying her critically.

"Scuff your boots," he said, doing the same himself against the rough stones littering the ground. He rubbed his tunic against the nearest building to hide its newness and did the same to his jacket before he donned them again, then made her do the same.

At the end, they both stared into a nearby window, studying the mottled reflections. "We should pass," he said. '

"As long as we keep our mouths shut," she said dubiously. She was right. He could mimic an accent, within limits; her own sounded nothing like anyone from here.

"Nothing we can do about it." He'd learned long ago the trick to a ruse was to fix what you could and work with the rest. He reached for her hand.

The shopping cluster held only a few stores. Maybe he should have tried for a place where they would be less conspicuous, but it was also the last place anyone would be looking for them. He hadn't forgotten that the marshals and his security team were tracking them for a reason. The grocery market was as busy as he'd hoped, filled with locals checking the fresh greens and trying out all manner of free samples in a cheerful bustle. He soon found the ingredients display area, with the protein additives in one section. No Festin, as he'd expected, but the Restin interloper held a prime place and was surrounded by a bunch of eager shoppers. The cheerful voice of the bot seller was urging them to taste the dishes on offer.

"You'll never have to serve up bland slop again, and you know you're giving your family the nutrients they need."

He turned to one of the women. "I can't find any Festin. Where do they stock it?"

He made his voice as low and surly as possible, copying the captain's growl.

"You don't want that stuff. I hear they sell it up in them fancy spesh-ee-all-ity shops in Deesik. This is much better, and cheaper too."

"Oh, right, thanks. The boss is from up there and ordered us to find some," he grumbled and turned away before the woman could look twice at them, quickly ordering the Restin and stopping at the counter to pick up a package. The price of it was similar to what he'd expect Festin to sell for, even taking into account the cost of freight. They hurried on.

They wandered into the main shopping district after that, finding another busy market and strolling through the booths and crowds, listening all the time to the gossip. There was another Restin display here, with as eager an audience.

After a while Anyara said, "Let me do the talking this time. We need to find out what they think of outsiders."

She wandered over to a stand holding thick orange globes of the mattan root. He smiled. She had tried them at his home and been an eager fan since. This time, she picked over the vegetables, looking as knowledgeable as any homemaker. She picked up three of them, passing them over to the stall holder for pricing. The growers here sold their own produce, they had realised, and she entered into a volatile interrogation with the woman behind the counter. He kept silent and watched. Anyara held her own with no trouble, bargaining sharply with the woman, who appeared unconcerned with her accent, though wary. More concerned with the ping of her credits, Seolta guessed in amusement. At the end, the grower threw up her hands, then smacked them together and held out the globes.

Anyara reached for them. The woman grabbed hold of her hands. "You just come off a fishing boat," she said, examining the scars and lines still marking Anyara's hands, and the wary glint in her eyes faded. "No wonder you sound funny. You're not from here."

"No," agreed, Anyara with a sour look. "Signed on for a full trip and that lousy captain pushed us off here. Reckons business not good enough. You know of any work around here."

"Sorry, Sera. You're not the only one asking that. Fishing's been bad for a couple years. Word is them Protos types been messing with stuff."

Anyara put on a puzzled look. "Must be other work. Spring planting's due soon."

"Yeah," said the woman sourly. "Or would be, if the groundwater had recovered from the last drought. I'm planting only half as much this year. Can't afford to waste good seed on dry ground."

Seolta had stood back, looking as sullen as possible, and watched fascinated as Anyara's shoulders drooped in defeat. "Well, if you hear anything…"

"Put your name down in the central database." The woman patted her hand. "There now, things will get better. Least that's what my boy says."

Anyara thanked her and walked off, browsing more stalls and choosing a few more vegetables, bargaining as hard each time. They all started out suspicious of her accent, but either her sharp skills or her sad story won them over. One even claimed he'd heard an accent like hers, but couldn't remember where.

At the end, they took a seat at an outside bar, ordering a measure of the local rough beer. He laughed at her wrinkled nose after her first cautious sip.

She poked her tongue back at him and chuckled. Then grew serious again. "Life is tough here. I thought this continent was supposed to be too lightly populated to show environmental effects."

He'd thought the same. "Feel like exploring Deuteron without interference, my lady partner?"

"How?" she said, eyes narrowing at him. "As soon as you use any credits, your security will be down on us. Even out of uniform, they look scary. No one will answer our questions with them around, but we need them."

"Maybe, but I have more than one separate credit fund." The marshals had demanded details of the one he'd used off world, but he'd seen no reason to tell them all his secrets. Nor, so far, had they seen any sign of their off-world enemies following them to Arcadia.

Unfortunately, the predators didn't need to come on-world. Arcadia was a ganda ripe for the greedy, and the names of the corporations starting to echo in his head were well versed in the hunting paths of the Alliance Council.

He leaned towards her, playing with her hair and looking like any fond partner with his very beautiful lady. "You need evidence of environmental decay; I need proof of copyright fraud and smuggling. Deuteron can give us both, but only if we're free to operate on our own. I'll have to let the marshals track us, but they'll interfere only if we need it. Otherwise, they are tragging good at staying out of sight. My security will have to stew until we've finished." He took a breath. "I wish I didn't have to ask this of you. I wish I could keep you locked up safe in my room at Manascraoch and never risk any harm coming to you…"

"Except boredom and frustration." She tapped him on the arm. "Will you stop trying to talk me out of this and tell me your plan. You always have one." She gave an exaggerated sigh. "Just one request. Can it please include the occasional civilised sleeper room and cleansing unit?"

"Hopefully, but I can't promise."

She groaned.

He didn't remove his block on the marshals' tracker until they were well out of town and heading east on a meandering passage through the remote rural hinterland. Their flyer was barely adequate, but the seller had promised it was airworthy. It did come with camping equipment and, most importantly of all, a fake registration the seller assured him would fool any Protos bureaucrat. The dry way the woman said it made it clear that this was normal for everyday

Deuteronians. He wasn't sure which they wanted to avoid more: the registration tax or interference by Protos regulators. Both sounded equally hated.

It was Marcus an Fallon himself who came online when he restarted the marshals' link. "Ser den Coille. Nice of you to call in. Having a pleasant trip?"

Rumour said an Fallon could tear the skin off a recruit with just one look. He'd never realised how true it was before. "Marshal," he said carefully, linking Anyara in … in case he needed a witness.

"Your permit to return to Arcadia was conditional on certain terms."

"I'm meeting them."

"Not from where I sit." The man's voice was flat and controlled, too controlled. The respected marshal had a temper it seemed. "Explain."

At the end, the marshal's face looked no different than at the beginning. "Messera Esteemed Scholar, is this detour necessary?"

"Conditions here are not quite as I expected."

"You can confirm you are unhurt and safe?"

Anyara reached for his hand openly, holding it as she said calmly," I am."

"She will come to no harm with me," said Seolta hotly.

"No, but will she survive the experience unchanged?" An Fallon eyed him coldly. "As should be obvious to you, Arcadia cannot afford anything happening to the Sera. I have ordered increased surveillance."

"Just make sure it's discreet," said Seolta, and for the first time got a response. The very slightest twitch of the man's mouth.

"I think my people can manage that."

"And Seolta? Will you keep him safe too?" said Anyara.

The marshal's head jerked up. "That was never in our brief, Messera Esteemed Scholar."

"It is in mine," she said.

"Anyara, *mo Graidh,* it's all right…"

She glared at him, then at the marshal. "You will give me your word you will come to Ser Seolta's assistance if he is in trouble, exactly as you would for me. I need his help to do my work."

A frown crossed the marshal's face, but Anyara didn't back down. A quick one of those looks of the marshal's, leaving Seolta wishing he dared pull his collar up to hide behind, then a brusque nod.

"Agreed, Sera." Then a tight smile stretched the ascetic face. "Ser Seolta, our systems department wants to talk to you when you get back. Specifically about that surprise package you added to your comlink."

"Have they deactivated it?" said Seolta, alarmed.

"No," said an Fallon, and Seolta relaxed again. "They haven't figured out how. I trust you can assist them with that when you get back to Urbis."

"For a fee," said Seolta, too relieved to be sensible.

An Fallon looked like he wanted to reach over the waves and grab him by the scruff of his neck. "It would have been helpful if you had used your skills to advance Arcadia earlier, young man." He scowled. "I will look into a consultancy," then abruptly signed off.

"You going to tell me what that was all about?" said Anyara with a matching frown on her face.

He squirmed inside. "I modified the marshal's tracking link to block it."

"And…"

He contemplated refusing telling her for exactly one microsecond. Lying to her was out of the question. "It sends an alarm to the marshals if your com is taken from you or you are separated from me without agreement."

"You've locked me to your side?"

"For your safety."

She pulled her hand out of his. "How far can I go? Can I use the cleansing unit in private?"

"Of course. The range is wide, and it has to be without permission."

"Without *your* permission. That doesn't sound a basis for a healthy relationship, Messer den Coille."

He'd mucked this up badly, but couldn't apologise. "I had to. You have to stay alive, and what if I can't ensure that?"

"I have been keeping myself alive for many years."

"From *your* enemies. Now you've acquired mine as well." Maybe he shouldn't have reminded her of that. She paled again, then shook her head.

"No, Seolta. You do not get to be in control of me, not like that. I will agree to your modifications on two conditions only. You grant me systems permission to stop the warning, and you set your com up with the same protections."

"The marshals won't come for me. You heard them."

"They will now. They promised it." She crossed her arms and stared fixedly out the front of the flyer.

He had no choice and felt the tug of amusement at his lips. His calm and even-tempered academic had just beaten him in a way only his mother had ever managed before, and he had no problem with it at all.

About time you grew up.

He didn't even snap back at his conscience. "Agreed, my heart." He checked the skies and their surrounds, set the controls to auto, then pulled up his com, making the screens transparent.

"You do know those graphics make no sense to me at all."

"But you can see what I'm doing." He highlighted the tracking system as he modified the warning mode. He knew what he was doing this time, and it took only moments. Then he closed down and turned to her. "Done. Open your com to me, please."

She watched his face, not his fingers, as she brought up the screen and held it out for him.

"Here," he said. "All you have to do is switch off this link and the alarm is disengaged."

Only then did she drop her eyes, to follow where his finger pointed. She nodded and looked back to him as she shut down her screen.

"But … please don't." he said.

"Only if necessary to save your life," she said, "and you must promise the same."

His head was still trying to get around that last comment. "And to save yours." That was what mattered.

"Not if it puts you at risk," she said stubbornly, reaching out and pulling him close. Her lips sought his. "I need you."

CHAPTER THIRTY

Anyara looked out the side window at the view opening up below. They were flying over farmland, a charming mix of grazing grasslands, tree-filled hollows and multicoloured patches of croplands, the bare soil showing up in all colours from rich black to red-brown. Machines busily sowed this year's crop, watched over in places by humans seemingly frightened to leave the machines to do their job. She'd feel the same if her whole livelihood depended on getting this right, had done it on the station with new or delicate crops.

"I like this continent. They understand farming."

Seolta glanced out his window. "I guess so," he said, before going back to studying the holomap and plotting out their route. She'd learned he had little interest in the details of growing plants, despite his inborn need to feel trees under him, but he still listened to her as she rambled on for hours. He said he enjoyed watching her come to life in front of him, whatever that meant. On the other hand, he understood systems and business in a way she never would, and sometimes he'd pick up a pattern in her thoughts, putting her ideas into firm economic reality. Showing her how to win in ways she'd never imagined.

Together they could be formidable, she suspected—if they lived long enough.

He let out another curse, fingers flying and brows creasing. Then shoved back in disgust.

"We're going to have to put down at the next settlement. The fuel supply ducts are blocking up again."

Their decrepit old flyer had hiccupped repeatedly since leaving Mangolon. So far, Seolta had managed to nurse it along, but it had finally beaten him.

She looked at the holomaps. "There's a farmhouse just over that hill."

They set down in front of the collection of sheds and barns. A planting machine was parked outside the largest building and a man emerged from it, glaring suspiciously at their flyer as it parked beside the dusty yards.

Seolta climbed out first. He'd tried telling her to stay inside, but she pointed out that a stranded couple was less threatening than a lone man in a disreputable flyer. Especially one who knew nothing about farming.

"Morning, Ser," the farmer said.

He was young but had the look of someone who spent most of his time outdoors. She recognised that weather-beaten and sun-worn face with a thrill. Only an EA-worlder had such a face.

"Our flyer's playing up. Can anyone here do repairs?" said Seolta.

The man stared sullenly back, the pole in his hand held tightly as if ready to use it against them.

She put on her most conciliating voice. "We'll pay for your time, or we can give you a hand with the sowing. That field we flew over looks ripe for planting." She put up a hand to shade her eyes as she studied the fields. "What crops do you grow around these parts?"

"Sorflex and costa mostly." The farmer held tight to the pole.

"The season here is long enough for costa?" she said in surprise. The giant grass had a notoriously long ripening period, but was an excellent source of readily digestible carbohydrates.

"Just." The man's grip on the pole slackened a touch. "You know about cropping?"

She smiled, holding her hands up. "A little. I'm more familiar with simulated environment cropping, though. I'd love to see how you do it here."

"City farming," said the man, letting the pole relax completely. "Not the same."

"No, but it feeds my clients. Our nutrient quotient figures are excellent."

This time the farmer took a step forward, the pole forgotten. "NQs don't tell everything. Eat that SE stuff too long and you'll end up synthesised yourself."

She put her hands on her hips, and discreetly jostled Seolta as she saw him open his mouth. "Our grains are the equal of anything you produce and we get an excellent return."

"Yeah, I'll bet," said the man sourly. "Come on then, and I'll show you the work it takes to make proper food. Then maybe you city types will stop trying to rip off honest farmers like us."

He turned, gesturing abruptly for them to come with him.

There followed some of her most enjoyable times on this planet. The man explained everything he did, in what she was sure to Seolta must be exhaustive detail but to her was pure delight. She argued and he argued back, let her feel the seeds, showed her over his planter and watched as she proved to him that she'd controlled similar machines countless times before, although not on such a scale. Together they walked over the field, lifted the rich soil, rubbed it through their hands, sniffed it and talked of loam and organic matter, water retention and mineral composition.

She could only marvel at it.

"Mind you, it'd grow more if them regulators over in Protos would get their chains off us."

"Sales taxes?" guessed Seolta.

The man scowled, still not trusting the non-farmer. "That too." He turned to Anyara. "You seen them new irrigators and crop monitors? I could grow twice as much if they'd let us do the things those Urbis Basin farmers take for granted."

"In what way?" said Anyara, hoping she sounded as naïve as she tried. It was as she'd guessed though, when she'd first heard of the development halt on Deuteron. The man couldn't break in any more land, wasn't allowed to apply the synthetic additives or use the engineered cropping types taken for granted on Protos.

She had to get a good look at those Protos farms. She murmured sympathetically, then at the end suggested a few ways the man could maximise his farm within the current constraints.

"You really think we could do that here?" They were checking out the plantings in a rough hollow in the middle of his cropping lands.

She nodded. "A few bushes interspersed with your scrub types down there should yield enough berries to give you a ten percent increase in profit for the year without compromising your other income streams. And charge a premium for being a modified and integrated enterprise. I've heard that's going to become more important."

"So I've been told," he muttered.

"Oh? Where?" she asked casually.

The man shrugged, clearly reluctant.

"I heard a man talking at a meeting down in Mangolon. Interesting talk," she said. "Too many wanted to talk to him for me to get close, but someone in the crowd said he was heading up this way next. I'd like to have a chance to have a chat with him."

"An offworlder?"

"Yes, guess so. You seen him?"

The farmer shoved his hands into his coverall pockets. "He was at the last stock sale. Lot of folks keen to talk to him. They reckon he's got full pockets and wants product." Another shrug. "We'll see what the regulators think of him. So far their local office is staying out of it."

"Another path for you to sell through? Can't see why anyone would object to that," she said, still keeping her voice casual.

"No? You ain't from round here then," said the farmer with a half chuckle.

They carried on with the tour of the farm, and Anyara was thrilled to see the way it mixed in cropping, rough ground, and grazing.

At the end of the farm tour, Seolta had to remind the farmer of the repairs needed for the flyer. By this stage, he and Anyara were long past any suspicions, and the man fixed it in no time, accompanied by a scathing dismissal of big-city types who ventured out into the country in a useless flyer without any knowledge of how to service it. Then he gave them a full rundown on how to keep the battered heap going.

"The salesman saw you two coming," pronounced the farmer.

As he finished, he stepped back. "That should keep you going for a spell. Stop in at the service hub in Mander. Jab there will set it right for the rest of your trip and sell you a decent tool kit. That one of yours is a joke."

With that, he gave them a curt nod. "Got to get back to work. Can't spend all day jawing." And he disappeared back into the shed. She and Seolta grinned at each other.

"Guess that means it's time for us to go," he said.

She held her breath as they lifted off, but the farmer knew what he was doing. Not that she was surprised. The farm had been a well run operation, everything in its place and the man's figures a rare treat. He was as good as his word about the service hub too. The grizzled old mechanic there promised to have their flyer working a treat by the next morning.

The mystery of the offworlder buyer remained though.

"One of Hilmar's agents?" she'd asked as they left the farm.

"It's a possibility, or Malgrave's, or one of the other corporations. We need more information."

"You also need the intermediaries."

"Like the Falasches?"

"Them, and others," she said.

"Hopefully those Restin samples will help. Now to find out who's supplying it and where it's made."

"And my audit?" Should she stop while he sorted out this latest threat?

He gave her a one of those 'what are you talking about' looks. "Is as important as ever, *mo Graidh*. We need to know if the environmental issue is just a conspiracy against Arcadia by greedy fools, or are we really in trouble. A Restin trademark dispute will give us names; your audit gives us the wider crime."

"Even if it's true that Arcadia is out of balance," and from what she'd seen so far, she was becoming convinced of it, "that doesn't mean there aren't those plotting to use that to grab a piece of the planet."

"No, it doesn't." His face looked every bit as grim as she felt. That evening, they stayed in Mander while their flyer was being serviced, and he put a call through to Marcus an Fallon, who looked equally grim by the end of their report.

"We've ignored Deuteron too long. When do you get back to Urbis?"

"In a couple of weeks, as scheduled. Cutting our trip short would only raise questions, and Anyara needs to finish her work."

"And you have to stay with her. Sending in a full squad of marshals would look too suspicious." An Fallon tapped a finger on the table, mouth set as he tapped that finger again and again. "We need your brother. I'll suggest he comes up to Urbis."

"Cumchdach isn't easily fooled. He'll smell trouble," said Seolta.

"He needs to," was the marshal's answer.

They set off the next morning with the memory of that call still fresh. Anyara still looked out the window, still took delight in the opening views below, the mix of balanced farms and ever more natural habitat as they moved farther away from settlement and closer to the central plateau; but she took less time to enjoy it, focussing grimly on taking her readings and demanding Seolta land for sampling whenever her scans showed a transition in ecotypes or change in the dominant species.

They headed up the escarpment, and now the change was dramatic. Down below lay fertility, order, habitations, no matter how rare; up here was a vast spread of tough shrubs, bogs and rocks, the land apparently empty. But nature didn't work like that— the greatest delight of her discoveries here—and she was soon busy scanning and identifying whole new networks of species.

"You've never been here before?" she said to him in amazement.

He was staring out the windows, as transfixed as she by this empty, harsh, and stunning land. "No trees," he pointed out.

"Yes, there are." She brought up holos of the stunted shrubs lining a bog just below them.

He laughed. "Those aren't trees.

"They are, you know. They're a close relative of those trees we saw by the lake down west."

"In name only," said Seolta as adamantly, dismissing the scrawny dwarves with a wave of his hand.

She wasn't about to let him denigrate her current heroes so readily. "Those graceful giants wouldn't last a cycle up here, even if they could grow. Now these beauties…"

"I will concede much to you, my heart, but there is nothing beautiful about those *weeds*."

She huffed and shut off the holo and he let out a loud guffaw. "All right. Not weeds. But not beautiful either, though I will agree there is something about this land."

They both continued to stare out the window as the vast uplands scrolled in front of them. "Does no one live here?" she asked. There was the occasional water meadow and softer lumps that might have attracted a settler.

"No return in it," said Seolta. "Mining's out, for a start. There are good mineral deposits here, and the odd small-scale outfit working them, according to the files. But EA mines can't hope to compete commercially with habitat ones like you have on Surned. Too many environmental constraints on EA worlds."

"I'm beginning to see why environmental rules are resented here."

"Doesn't mean we can ignore them," he said dryly, though she doubted he felt it, not in his heart. Seolta den Coille had once done his very best to subvert them, after all. "Farming's not an option either. Why try to farm this when there's much better land elsewhere. We are well off saturation density on this world."

Unlike many habitat worlds, she couldn't help thinking. Sometimes, she was still shocked at how Seolta took for granted the bounty of his home world. He stood up then, setting the flyer to auto and went back to the prepper, bringing back drinks and snacks. "I do know how lucky we are," he murmured as he passed them over with a teasing glint in his eye.

She blushed. "I didn't say anything."

"You're good at hiding your thoughts, but there is a tiny crease that forms just there," he touched her forehead gently. He sat down again and took a sip of his drink. "Find us a set-down place for the night, will you? One with good rocky surrounds that I can use to bounce our security screen off."

It wasn't until she'd found a place and they had settled in for the night that he came back to the subject. They slept inside the flyer in these parts, safe from the large predators and tiny blood-seeking creatures that plagued anything slightly tasty.

"Habitat worlds are bound by economics of supply; we are too, but the environment is our biggest constraint. We have what the planet gives. On a habitat, you have what you can buy."

She stared at him in astonishment. "Any higher school child knows that. It's biome basics."

"Maybe, but I didn't understand it properly, not in my bones, until I left here." He touched the hair clasp. "You still need this some days, and you monitor the flyer's atmosphere usage data. Why it's even present on an Arcadian flyer has always been a puzzle to me."

"They're mandated by Alliance law," she replied automatically, putting down the scanner she'd just picked up and trying not to check its readings.

"For us, their only use is as a fire or fuel leak back-up alarm."

"What about at high altitude?" she said. "You've taken us above the cloud layer many times." And wasn't that a wonder. She never tired of looking at the fluffy piles of puffed up magic, so bright on the upper side regardless of how dark or threatening they looked below.

"That's a different monitoring system," he told her firmly. "Now, please stop niggling at me, my heart. It's been a whole day since I last held you, and I have missed you badly."

She couldn't resist that particular gleam in his eye. She made a show of reluctance but they both knew it was only that and, with a sigh of contentment, she let him pull her into his arms. Later, she sat on the open hatch and just looked, absorbing the place and the evening.

Seolta came and sat beside her, touching shoulders. "What's caught your attention this time, my heart."

"This." She swept out her hand. "I'd never been in a place not made for people."

"The surface of Surned," he reminded her, clearly thinking of his own nearly lethal encounter with her home planet.

"Yes, but we never go out there without protection and backups, suited, in a vehicle. On Surned, you take your habitat with you." She'd told him this before, but in this isolated place where no humans had ever lived, it took on a new importance. "Here, we can breathe the air, drink the water, walk freely, but *we* are not the purpose of this world. I don't know what is, or even if there is one. Maybe it just exists and we are irrelevant. We matter here only if we support the whole, or if we harm it. None of this is made for us. It's quite humbling," she added with a laugh.

All too soon, they had to say goodbye to Deuteron. She had come to like this forgotten continent and its people. After the empty wastes of its central plateau they headed east to the tortured rocks of the far eastern coastal lands. No wonder Protos had never thought the continent worth bothering with, she thought, staring down at wind-wracked outcrops twisted and torn by the storms that lashed this harsh landscape from time to time. From there, it was north and a return to warmer lands. Spring was coming, and as they neared the tropics, the precious sunlight became a menace.

"This place is worse than Sarwenna Beren's desert," said Seolta with loathing as they lifted off for the last time, heading up into the huge mountain ranges separating this region from the dense jungles of the northern coastal swamps. She gasped when they reached the high peaks, avoiding lightning storms and lashings of rain and hail to break out over a misty, humid and bustling world filled with a biota that sent her scanner into overdrive.

"So much life."

"And most of it trying to kill you," warned Seolta. "Do not ask me to set down anywhere here. Underneath all those trees is nothing but bogs and watercourses. We'll head out to the north coast. The odd offshore islands there give some safety."

The rest of the trip was a series of mad swoops down into the jungle followed by overnight retreats to hot sandy beaches or bare shelves of rock. An amazing place, but even she was glad to farewell the continent and head back to the civilisation of the northern Protos regions. They flew in over a broad river valley, one of the few flowing towards the western coast. Most of the large and fertile band at the north of the main continent was a giant catchment area for the mega estuarine zone surrounding the capital city.

"Why ever would they site a city on the shifting substrate of an estuary?" she asked, staring at the holo-map.

"Ask my little sister that one day, if you dare. Making the trainee eco-engineers come up with a new way to help the city adapt to its placement is a standard torture handed out to final-year students. Mostly, from what I can gather, it's where the settlers first arrived and they just stayed there."

"An accident?"

He grinned. "More of our settlements are than you would believe."

"But … there are rules."

"The Fourth Declaration on the Protocols of Colonisation for Earth Analogue Worlds," he declaimed pompously, then smiled ruefully. "They sell copies of it in the Urbis marketplace as souvenirs. They're popular with young boys for target practice."

What could she say to that?

He took pity on her. "We weren't the first world settled. The authorities watched that one zealously. In our case, economics took over, and the merchants and agriculturists made it here first. The Alliance was short of food at the time." He grimaced. "My ancestors were not a worthy bunch by all accounts."

Flying up the long, flat valley, she could believe it. Seolta had told her this was the most fertile, the heaviest settled, the jewel of the planet. She'd liked the regular patchwork and orderliness when they'd first flown over it, reminding her of the controlled biomes of her home station, but that was before she'd seen how they farmed on Deuteron. Now she loathed this region. Their visits to the farms and businesses she pointed out to him didn't help one bit.

"That pompous, patronising *worm*," she seethed after a visit to a farm right in the prosperous heart of the delta country. Rich black loam, perfectly groomed fields, grazing animals all in their place. One output only allowed on this farm, and any hint of an alternative approach was met with the kind of small-minded hubris she'd faced off against far too often. "You heard him. 'Young lady, when you've been in farming as long as we have…' I'm an Esteemed Scholar of the premier academic institute in the Alliance, and he talks to me like I'm some simple-minded first schooler."

Seolta said nothing, looking like he was trying to strangle a smile.

"Do not laugh at me," she said. "I was trying to help him. He could improve the sustainability and his bank balance with a few tweaks, and he wouldn't listen to one suggestion. He'll have to when the Council comes calling. That farm of his will be run into the ground in a few years if he keeps overexploiting its resources the way he's doing."

"Put it in your report," said Seolta with a mostly straight face. "That will make sure the Council takes action. Name, address and all relevant details, right down to the smallest bit of data you scanned."

She'd been recording, but hadn't told the man, and that brought her down to ground. "I stole that data," she suddenly realised, appalled. "I didn't give him a chance."

"You think he deserves one, or that it would make any difference? The only thing it might have done is make him threaten to harm you, and that is not allowed." He lost the smirk. "We're working undercover," he reminded her.

They were, spying on his own people and his planet, and she could give him no guarantee that her findings would help it. "You don't need to be involved in this," she whispered and slumped back.

"Yes, I do, and you are going to present an accurate and *honest* report to my Council and to the Alliance bodies. It's the only way to solve this nightmare."

He had to be right. It was all that gave her hope. At last, she came to the end of the audit. She was glad to leave the delta country behind. Too much of this area was everything she'd worked so hard against. Pristine fields, razed of undergrowth, tree cover, anything not immediately profitable. Change was beginning, but most had little understanding that there was a problem, let alone how to change. It reminded her too depressingly of all those isolated and stratified biome rooms, with living organisms kept carefully under control and well away from *contamination* by the people dependent on them. It didn't work. She'd proved there was an alternative on Kevand Station, and had begun to believe that others might come to see it too. The Academy had recognised her, for stars' sake.

She was still to meet with Survey head office and found herself dreading it. They'd given the Alliance the first warnings, but harsh reality was too often another matter. Luckily, protocol demanded she submit her results to the Alliance first. "Can we visit your family before I make my report," she said to him in their hotel room in Urbis. In case it's not possible afterwards, was her thought, but she didn't put it into words. He took one look at her face and kissed her long and hard.

"Thank you. Yes."

"You should never have met me," she said unhappily.

"It's as the Survey reports said?"

"Worse, if anything. Oh, change is under way. Your family is one of the more cooperative companies, but what's being done is too little. They're all so scared of the new, yet if they'd just try it, just give up a little, the long term potential is stunning."

He reached for her, kissed her slow and deep. "Whatever the outcome, I am glad I met you, my heart. We will go home, we will visit my family, you can badger my mother for all her stories of my worst childhood pranks, and then, if you still love me…"

"Still…" She looked up at him in alarm. "Of course. And you?" she asked, suddenly terrified of the answer.

The kiss was enough, but his soft voice was better. "I love you, my Anyara. Now, after you deliver your dreaded report, and will love you still when we are sitting on the ship taking us away from my world. I have only one request."

His kiss was taking away all ability to think straight. "What?" she murmured.

"Marry me, *mo Graidh*. In my home, with my family, before we leave."

"Marry?" Her voice squeaked on the word. It still gave her goosebumps, this word out of myth. "Aren't we near enough now?"

"Not … quite. Arcadian marriage is a deeper commitment than an Alliance Life Partnership. It's harder to break if children are involved, and…"

She swallowed. "It's important to you."

"I need to say you are mine and I am yours. This is how we do it here." He dropped his hands and stood back. "But not if you don't want it. Give me an answer in an hour. I'm transmitting the full marriage contract to you. I'll take a walk and you can give me your answer when I come back."

"No," she said. "I'm the one who will go for a walk." She lifted her com and disengaged his alarm signal to let her separate from him safely.

"It's too dangerous."

"With the marshals and your security covering me? I'm safer walking in Urbis than in the heart of the Academy."

He went to protest.

"No, I need this. Please."

He had to let her go, but she could see how he hated it, and nearly turned back and told him her answer immediately. But she needed space, needed to decide whether she could do this to him. She quickly read through the marriage contract as she walked down the first street. She'd had an idea of it for long enough and little in it surprised her. He was right, it bound both of them more than a life partnership, but that wasn't the crux of it.

By marrying her, he gave up all hope of a future on Arcadia. Once she presented her report, she'd have so many enemies here it would never be safe for them to return.

Misery bound her. She walked along, blind to her surrounds. On her station, everything had been orderly and simple. Cherish her biomes, avoid her uncle's notice, stay alive.

Only the last one remained a constant.

And would you really prefer to have never met Seolta den Coille. Never fallen in love?

If there was no risk to him, she'd marry him in an instant, but she was still her uncle's niece, still an offworlder.

She had fallen in love with not just him in these last weeks but also with the marvels and exuberant life of his world, with its proof over and over again of all her theories. Complexity and integration were what gave stability to ecosystems. Biomes worked best with intricate networks of influence, interdependent species together making a stronger whole. Abrupt margins, artificial limitations, heavy-handed interventions: none of them survived long term, nor did they make a place where people could live. Not well.

Lost in thought, she headed down a path in a small park, drawn by the scents of living plants and animals. Wind rippled through the small shrubs lining the path and sent the trees above her into a rustling chorus of rattling branches and whispering leaves. She let her hand trail along the tall grasses, felt the sting of their rough edges, heard the crunch of her feet on the fine gravel of the pathway and smelled the rich burn of newly turned earth, the soft fragrance of new blossoms, the tang of freshly crushed ground cover.

Crushed ground cover? She suddenly stopped. The trees kept up their chorus, but no animal sounds filled the air.

A hand grabbed her. "Well met, Messera Esteemed Scholar," said a gruff voice. "Come with us, please."

Where were her guards? The marshals? "Let me go."

A woman seized hold of her other side. "You're safe back with your own again, Messera. Please come this way."

That accent. "You're from my uncle."

"Yes, Messera. He's very worried about you," said the first man.

"About how many credits my absence is costing him, you mean. Let me go."

"We have a flyer waiting," the man said.

"You can't kidnap an Esteemed Scholar of the Academy." The pair were marching her straight for the exit. A skimmer stood outside. She mustn't get on board.

"The Academy is the one who asked for Surned's assistance," lied the woman, grunting at Anyara's repeated struggles.

"I'll bet they did. What have you done with my security troops and the Arcadian marshals? How did you even get groundside here? You can't invade a planet and attack its enforcement patrols."

"They are safe and we'll be well gone before they recover." They bundled her into the skimmer despite all her attempts to stop them, then snatched at her com and stripped it off, flinging it out the door of the skimmer before zooming down the street. She couldn't even call for help and had disengaged Seolta's alarm.

He'd never know she didn't want to leave him. Not until it was too late.

Seolta paced the hotel room. She'd needed time and he'd given it to her. But letting her roam free in a cesspit like Urbis hadn't been in his plans. Nor had disengaging the alarm on her com to let her go.

Fortunately, she'd asked to disengage it only to let them separate without setting off an alarm. It would still warn him if she lost her com for any reason. Hopefully, the marshals' tracker still worked.

Nothing will happen to her.

Suddenly, chaos erupted in his room and he discovered how badly he'd miscalculated. The raucous screech of his com's alarm filled the air. Two marshals barged into his room and a ping came through on his com, one demanding an immediate answer.

"Where is she?" said the senior marshal.

"Commander Talav, of the Fleet cruiser *Best Order*," said a voice as the holo vision of a man materialised in his room. "The Messera Anyara has been taken by Surned security," the commander said.

The marshals pointed their weapons straight at Seolta and the holo image showed the red surge of an armed magno pulse. Seolta thrust up his hand.

"Stop," he shouted. "Marshal, she's lost her com. And what in tragging roots is a Fleet commander doing here?" He hauled in a breath. "I've no time for this. Get out of my way. She's in trouble."

He charged for the door, and fought hard as the marshals brought him down. He'd had fight training but mostly for self-defence and to keep fit. He had some nasty tricks up his sleeve, but they weren't a match for the best enforcement troops on his planet. In a disgustingly short time, the pair had him locked on the floor and trussed up. An Fallon walked in straight afterwards.

He had to get to her. They wrestled him into a chair and one of them sprayed him with a restraining field. He couldn't even fight now.

"You have to let me go. They've got her."

"It's Surned forces. They are her own kind."

He growled in frustration. "Her uncle had a contract out on her." Didn't they understand. "She could be dead."

The Fleet commander moved to stand with the marshals. "You're not even here," Seolta reminded him.

"My troops are on their way down to the surface and we have put out a full search for the Surned vessel."

"Why are you even here?"

"We had a watching brief," said the commander.

"Watching… You've been up there all this time, a fully armed and capable Fleet cruiser. You could have rescued us from that volcano or when we nearly drowned at sea," he suddenly realised.

The commander looked stony-faced back, but there was the slightest flush on his face. "The files on the western continent are inadequate. No one had warned us of the signal interference in that region."

Nice to hear they weren't perfect. "So what are you doing now? Do you even know where she is?"

"We have a tracking field on her. She is in a skimmer heading for a shielded shuttle sitting on an outer suburb transport hub. It's masquerading as an intercontinental private shuttle."

He strained, trying to make his muscles answer him. "Get after her. You have to stop them. If they get her off the planet, I'll never get her back."

"Our brief does not extend to kidnapping private citizens from their sovereign entities," said the commander. "That vessel is registered to the Surned Consular Office and their Arcadian entry permit claims they have the Academy's sanction. The Messera is going to her own kind. We have no reason to believe she is not free or is at risk."

"If Hilmar doesn't kill her for her inheritance, then he and the Academy are going to keep her locked down for the rest of her life so they can profit from her work. That's not freedom, not in my book." He squirmed, and got a twitch from his leg muscles. "Check out her earnings profile. The woman is worth zillions in income, not to mention her power as an influencer."

"You are well informed of her value," said an Fallon coldly. He may have lowered his own weapon, but he still held it ready, and the other marshals kept theirs pointed at him, armed and ready to fire. "Up to your usual games, Ser den Coille? The cleverest brain in the mountains in action?"

All the old rage came churning up. He had to get free. Anyara was in danger. "You know me better than that, an Fallon. You were in the squad rescuing Ethan and Sarwenna Beren. I draw the line at killing."

The man looked as cold as ever, but did nod. "You did. Then. It was the only reason I didn't oppose the decision to ship you out. Generally I'm not a fan of political decisions. They have a bad habit of coming back to bite."

Seolta tried to flex his hands, straining against the field.

"The question is," continued an Fallon, "do you draw a line when it comes to acquiring power or influence."

"Not generally," admitted Seolta. An Fallon was another of the small group he didn't lie to unless he had to, mostly because it was a wasted exercise. "When it comes to Anyara a Prithand2, I draw the line at anything that will harm one hair on her head. You can believe that or not, but *let me go*." He made another futile attempt to get free but only succeeded in making the field clamp down harder. "Aargh. She did not go with those wernets of her own free will." He fought for sanity, fought to think, talk, to not scream in fury. He'd managed it before, months of lying, coverups, plotting with dregs, all in pursuit of a hollow revenge. He could certainly do it now for the woman who lay at the very core of his life.

"Stop her getting on that shuttle, take her to a place where she can feel safe, then ask her what she wants to do. It's the least you owe her. After that, you can take her anywhere she chooses. I won't interfere."

"Not the labs at Manascraoch?"

"Only if she wants," he repeated, wishing he knew how to make the marshal believe him.

He switched to the holo of the commander. "As a free citizen of the Alliance, she has a right to protection by the Fleet." There was a law covering that. He wracked his brains. Did he have the numbering right? His tutors at higher school had drilled it into them, but that was many years ago. He took a breath. "Commander, I call on you under Alliance Treaty Agreement, section 1, part 33, to take all means required to ensure that the rights of Messera Anyara a Prithand2 are being upheld, by confirming that she is going on board that shuttle of her own free will."

If he'd been in a better frame of mind, he'd have laughed at the shock on an Fallon's face.

CHAPTER THIRTY-ONE

Anyara peered blearily at the hatch. It began to open and someone voiced orders but she couldn't make them out. A blur of words, sharp voices and hard surfaces battered against her. She tried to put up her hands to block it all out, then discovered they were locked to her sides.

A dread sense of terror spread a dark shadow over her.

Whoever these people were, they were not friends. Not like her students. Not like … Seolta. She clung to his name as if to a sheltering pod in an asteroid storm. The haze blurred everything else.

Hands tugged at her, rough paws pulling her out of this vessel and towards one that loomed above her. She mustn't board that ship.

They dragged at her, and she dug her heels in, fear lending her strength.

"We're wasting time," said a rough voice. "Get her on that shuttle before anyone comes."

Mustn't let them.

She opened her mouth to scream. A hand clapped over her mouth, and another one slapped the back of her head. Then a mask dropped over her. She tried to wriggle free.

It was so dark under the mask.

A sound, a thump behind her.

What was happening?

More thumps. A whoosh, a brush of air and someone touching her. Then a voice, a new one, and the mask was gone.

She blinked. A new face. "I know you." She peered closer. "You're Arcadian. You know Seolta."

A cold grunt. "You might say that. Are you all right, Sera?"

"I'm not really sure." She went to stand, then stumbled, and a new face intruded. "I don't know you."

The woman pulled out a scanner and waved it over her. "She's been drugged, sir."

A grunt. "Maybe the man was speaking the truth for a change."

Hands pulled at her again, and she tugged back, wishing she didn't feel so weak. "It's all right, Sera," said the older man.

"Messera. Please come with us. You need help," said the woman in a soothing voice

"Where's Seolta?" She had to get back to him. "He'll think I left him."

"You can see him soon. Come, Messera. I'm a medic. You're safe now."

It was all confusing after that. She was put on a stretcher and taken onto another vessel. This one smelled of disinfectant and medicines and something inside her relaxed. The woman had said she was a medic.

More people in uniform arrived and this uniform she knew. "You're Fleet," she said in surprise then peered at the face bending over her. "I've met you before."

"First Troop Officer Waldex, Messera." He produced his ID then saluted her, smartly and exactly on point. The kind of salute given only by someone who'd done it many times before and had it engrained in his muscles.

"Please, take me to Seolta. He's my life partner." This soldier would understand. "He'll make this all right again."

Closed faces and no replies.

She tried to sit up. "You have to."

"Messera, you'll hurt yourself."

Then it all went blank again.

She came to in a room smelling even more strongly of the paraphernalia of medics. At least this time, her head was clear and the fuzzy distance was gone. She struggled to sit up. A woman hurried to help her.

"How are you feeling, Messera?"

"You're Fleet too."

The woman nodded. "You're safe on board the *Best Order*."

"This isn't your sector."

"We've been stationed above Arcadia since your arrival here, Messera. The Council thought it best to have an independent ship monitoring your visit and chose us as you had already been on board. In case of misadventure," she added in explanation.

"Such as being kidnapped?"

The woman took on that bland face they must teach in military school. "I am only a medic," she said.

Anyara didn't believe that for a moment, but let it lie. "And my life partner? Where is Seolta?"

"He's safe, Messera. The marshals are looking after him."

"Now you're frightening me. Please, I want him here, now."

The woman didn't listen to her any more than the other blank-faced officers she pleaded with. "I need him. Please, bring him to me."

"We have not yet cleared the Messer den Coille for boarding. We will let you know as soon as the process is completed."

"Then he can come aboard?"

The woman patted her hand. "I'll let you know." Then she left her alone. They'd found and returned her com, but when she tried to contact Seolta, all she got was a maddening blocked signal.

Much later, a man came into her room with a posse of medics and security around him. This one she remembered clearly.

"Commander Talav. It's about time. Where is my life partner and when can I get back to my work?"

If she'd disconcerted him, he made no show of it. "All in good time, Messera. When you have recovered from your ordeal."

She doubted they had the same understanding of which particular 'ordeal' she'd suffered "Have you charged my kidnappers yet?"

"It's in process, Messera. I merely came to enquire whether you are comfortable and assure you that the *Best Order* and its crew will do everything possible to ensure your wellbeing and safety."

She'd been handling officials since she was a teenager. She gave him a stare she'd learned from Seolta, one that said she wanted an answer. All he gave her was a formal half bow and told her to call on his staff for anything she needed.

"Can you at least tell me where we are? Are we still in orbit around Arcadia?"

"For now," he said, and there was no amusement in his face at all.

"I have a report to deliver and a wedding to attend," she yelled after his departing back. "Let me go."

Seolta paced the floors of the spartan room they'd left him in. A waiting room, they'd called it, but it was too like a cell for that. He'd bet on it being an interrogation room, spiked with hidden sensors and with walls steeped in the memories of too many others left 'waiting' here. Just when he thought he might lose it with worry, the door opened and an Fallon himself walked in.

"Have they got her?" Seolta demanded.

"The Sera is safely aboard the *Best Order* under guard by Alliance special forces.

"And the kidnappers?"

"The Surned ship is under surveillance and the matter of charges is in process."

"And…"

The man clasped his hands behind his back. "She was drugged. She is recovering now in the *Best Order*'s medic ward."

Seolta sealed shut his overcoat. "Take me up there."

"Not possible, Ser den Coille."

"I can call up a Den Coille shuttle if yours are busy."

"That is not the issue."

Just once, he'd wished he could read this man. "What is?"

"The Sera is the subject of a Section 1 Treaty query. Until her status is clarified, she is staying on board the Fleet cruiser."

"I filed that query."

An Fallon allowed himself the very slightest of smirks. "Yes, Ser, you did, and until it is resolved, she must stay under Fleet protection. There are a number of matters clouding the issue."

Seolta had heard statements like that too often. "I'm calling my lawyers."

"That would be wise," said Marcus an Fallon, and that terrified Seolta more than anything. Nor were the lawyers reassuring.

They sat in the firm's main office, a place Seolta had sat in many times before, sealing deals and manipulating firms and credits. Today, the stakes at risk were the very core of his life.

"As we understand it, Ser Seolta, there is a dispute over who kidnapped the Sera: her uncle, allegedly with the Academy's support, or you."

"What?" Seolta shot up. "They drugged her."

"They claim they did so for her own welfare. Have you heard of the Dissociative Anomalous Bonding syndrome."

"I'm a businessman. That sounds like psychobabble."

"Don't call it that in the hearings."

He was about to sit down again, but that had him pacing madly. "Hearings? Who's on trial."

"Please sit down, Ser den Coille. They are preliminary hearings only, to clarify the facts."

Seolta did as ordered, feeling sick. "Give it to me straight."

By the end of the lawyer's spiel, he didn't know whether to be angry, horrified, or scared silly. Hilmar and his Surned underlings were alleging he'd fed Anyara false information to scare her into leaving her home and then used that fear to kidnap her.

"They claim Sera Anyara is suffering from DAB syndrome and is therefore mentally impaired, making anything she says invalid. You allegedly frightened her by feeding her a pack of lies then manipulated her into believing she was safe only with you. It's why she let you take her from her home, a place she had previously appeared to be happy and fulfilled, then later from the Academy. She came with you because she is under your psychological control. Her actions were not voluntary, so it can be said you kidnapped her."

"Anyara a Prithand2 is as sound of mind as any person I know. They can't be seriously considering this." Seolta half rose.

"The charge has been made and therefore must be considered. Sit *down*, Ser."

Seolta grudgingly took his seat again. "What evidence do they have?"

"Against you, plenty. Any number of witnesses from Kevand Station will attest to her contentment there. You were later discovered on a pirate vessel and rescued by the Fleet. Then, thanks to you, she left the Academy and was held in the Arcadian embassy. She is an Esteemed Scholar with a lab of her own and a team of eager students, all of whom are ready to swear to her passion for her work. Furthermore…"

"Yes?"

"There is your prior history," said the man reluctantly. "You have a long record of manipulating dealings with other companies to enhance the profitability of Den Coille, and there are the actions that led to your exile. It will not be hard for a court panel to conclude that you are quite capable of the manipulation of Sera Anyara."

"Is there anything that proves my version?"

"Not definitely. Not yet. Do you have anything?"

"Maybe." He laid out the evidence he had so far of Hilmar's possible involvement in fraudulently selling Festin under a false label and the assassination contract he'd signed with Hilmar. He'd kept a file copy of it. Then there were the records of Anyara's earnings over the years, credits that never made it into her personal accounts and about which she'd known nothing.

The lawyers looked them over, talked among themselves, then brought down a privacy screen and he knew only from the mad flicking of fingers that they were checking out something on their com screens.

After a very long time, they raised the privacy screen again. "It may help, but none of it can be proven in the short term. Hilmar a Kevand3 is too wily to have left a copy of the assassination contract filed anywhere it could be found by enforcement officials. Yours would be the only surviving one and, with your history, it means little. The commercial fraud may be useful, but is only evidence of a company dispute, and both it and the embezzlement claim will take a long time to investigate and consider. All they do now is raise doubt."

"Will they keep Sera Anyara out of Hilmar's and the Academy's control?"

"Hilmar, certainly, while the embezzlement question is pending. As for the Academy…. There is nothing in this evidence to suggest that she is not an honoured member of the Academy and free to do as she pleases.

"Not even Anyara's word that she had to use subterfuge to escape the Academy?"

The lawyer lifted a hand to wave it away. "You've already claimed they had good reason to up her security, given her uncle's threats. You can't have it both ways, Ser."

"They want to control her and her earnings. That's what she believes too."

"Then prove it. More importantly, you, Ser den Coille, are likely to spend many years in Alliance custody waiting for the matter to be resolved. Are you sure you wouldn't rather sue for a resolution, and accept a financial penalty instead? We understand from the Fleet commander that the other side are prepared to accept this as long as you agree to never contact Sera Anyara again."

He gulped. He'd been in prison enough times in his life. "What would happen to her?"

"Since there is no proven risk to her safety, I daresay she would return to her work at the Academy."

"Can the Fleet guarantee that whatever happens will be as she wishes?"

"Oh, I'm sure they can, once they have finished any psych counselling and de-conditioning."

That word, 'deconditioning'… "She'll be left wide open to whatever her uncle or those leeches in the Academy want to do to her."

This time, he ignored the lawyers when they told him to sit down. He paced furiously across the room, blind to the tasteful legal office and seeing only the rough stone walls, the grey windows of his first prison. He'd survived it once.

"File the counterclaim. We fight."

The lawyers talked, argued, yelled at him to make him change his mind. In the end, he marched out of the room, and was taken back to the Marshals' Headquarters, with guards either side of him and restraints snapped tight on his wrists.

Anyara took one look at the latest medic hovering at her door before slamming it in his face. Then she called up the commander.

"I don't care if he is in a meeting. Get him on line, now," she snapped at her com when the standard file message came back. She also logged in a call to the Alliance office in Urbis, and filed a request for assistance. Then she set it to go public within the hour, unless she commed otherwise.

The Fleet Commander's holo snapped into view a bare moment later. "You have a problem, Messera?"

Luckily, she'd thought to get dressed before calling him. The man was in full formal uniform and looked seriously peeved.

"Am I being charged with a crime, Commander?"

That set him back. "Of course not, Messera."

"Actions against the stability of the Alliance?"

"Not as far as can be ascertained."

"Any other legislated reason for detaining a free citizen of the Alliance?"

"No, Messera." The first hint of caution touched his voice.

"Then please accept my thanks for your ship's excellent care and arrange for me to be transferred back down to Urbis and to my legally filed life partner."

"I understand that the Messer is currently not free for you to join him."

"Not free? What have you done?"

"Charges have been laid. The exact nature of your association with your life partner is in question."

It was worse than she thought. "Don't tell me he's locked up again."

The man simply stared.

"Commander, we have a life partnership filed on Alliance Central. Any doubt about whether either of us was fit to agree to the contract needed to have been filed on Central at the time. It's too late now."

"Perhaps," said the commander.

"No *perhaps* about it. Are you going to take me down to Urbis, or do I let the public complaint proceed?" The vidcasters routinely monitored such complaints. They were juicy sources of headline-making gossip.

He tried to stare her down. She'd lived with her uncle's threats too many years to be frightened by a Fleet commander with an engrained moral backbone. The man would not harm her if doing so broke a law. Not knowingly.

He did insist on having her transported to Alliance Headquarters, rather than back to her hotel room. She was nearly free, but staring out the window at the grey rain lashing the buildings opposite, it felt like prison bars slamming shut.

She'd had enough of people doing that to her. She called up the service directory and entered a search.

Moments later, she had an appointment with the most respected psych med in Urbis. A woman with no association with Den Coille, the Alliance embassy or the Arcadian government. A woman as straight to the bone as Commander Talav.

"I am going out, she said to the Fleet guards at her door. They protested of course, but Anyara kept walking, refusing to listen to anything they said. Short of physically manhandling her or drugging her again, legally they could do nothing. It didn't stop them talking, commanding, giving her order after order as they tried every argument against her. She kept forgetting to breathe until she reached the outside streets and sat in the skimmer cab she'd ordered.

They'd actually let her go.

A squad of marshals appeared as soon as she exited the cab at the medic's clinic. She glared at the woman in front. "I am not breaking any planetary laws. You have no right to hinder me."

The woman looked no happier than Anyara. "We are here for your protection, Sera, not to stop you going about your legitimate business. We have been ordered to accompany you."

She could either retreat back to the Alliance buildings and lose any hope of freeing Seolta from whatever they'd done to him, or put up with the forbidding squad. "Come on, then," she said, ungraciously, "and you can also tell me exactly what you've done to my life partner."

"Who?" asked the woman, as if startled.

She throttled down her temper. She hadn't thought she had one, but right now it was a fraction short of a boil over. "Seolta mar Bram an Scathach den Coille. My legally registered life partner."

"Aah. Do you mean he's your fiancé, Sera?"

Another strange term. She took a punt. "Yes," she said as forcefully as possible. "We are to be married shortly.

"That … is interesting. You are not yet married, then?"

"No, but as good as. A life partnership is recognised on all Alliance planets."

One of the other squad members was hastily checking his com. "She's right, Sera." The trooper moved his wrist and she had to guess he was sharing a screen with his squad leader. "It's not quite the same as marriage, but it does give her legal rights concerning Ser den Coille."

The squad leader glanced down the file. "Hmmph," she said in a cross voice then glared at Anyara as if at an annoying bug. "Ser den Coille has been detained pending the outcome of a hearing into his role in your current status."

"Where?" That was the most important question. But … no, it wasn't. "How do I get him released?"

"You will have to discuss that with the Ser's lawyers," the leader said stiffly.

She stood, thinking furiously. This was to do with her own 'current status'. They couldn't think… She swung around. The psych meeting was more urgent than ever.

She entered the clinic with more than a little trepidation. It didn't matter. She shoved back her head and straightened her back with all the strength she could muster. Seolta was depending on her.

The psych med turned out to be a woman in middle years and easy to talk to. At the end, the woman leaned back in her chair. "Sera, it is my considered opinion that you are most definitely sound in mind and fully in control of your own decisions. There is no evidence that you are affected by any manipulation or coercion. Quite the contrary. You are a remarkably strong-minded woman, Sera. I'm not sure it would be possible to coerce you." She snapped off her file. "I will send my findings to the marshals, your lawyer, and the Alliance council, but you have nothing to worry about regarding your mental state. It has been a pleasure to meet with you."

Anyara received her copy of the file with relief.

She marched out, the squad of marshals dogging her footsteps, and put a call through to Seolta's lawyers. By the afternoon, she was firmly ensconced in an apartment owned by the Den Coille corporation in the best part of Urbis, had met with the lawyers, and filed her own complaint with the marshals and with the Alliance Central legal authorities. If her uncle wanted to throw around his contacts and influence, she'd throw hers right back at him.

She had also deferred any meeting with Arcadia's Ecological Survey, in light of her changed circumstances, and submitted the report she'd been sent to Arcadia to prepare to the Alliance Council, notifying all the applicable departments and the Arcadian Survey. She'd leave it up to the Survey what they told their planetary council. They'd have to ask for a copy along with everyone else. Right now, she saw no reason she owed them any warning. Not until she had Seolta safely back and they were off this wonderful and terrifying world. She didn't know whether to weep or cheer for that. She'd fallen in love with Seolta's world and knew it was his heart.

More than you are?

No. She had to believe that. She was betting her life on it.

What if she was wrong? Then he walked in the door and she hurled herself at him.

She was safe. That was his first thought. She was patting him down madly, his usually calm and intelligent partner gabbling a stream of mangled words and clinging tightly as her hands searched frantically to see whether he'd been hurt. He took hold of her hands, kissed her with all his pent-up need, then pulled her close.

"I'm fine, *mo Graidh*. I've been detained, not tortured," he said, trying for levity, then wished he hadn't at the horror on her face. He tucked a hand under her chin. "The Fleet held me, not your uncle's thugs."

"And now?"

"Back to Alliance Central. You have a report to defend, I have a fraud charge to file, and there is to be a hearing. Your psych med is good, but she can't wipe out a complaint filed in Central, not with the kind of politics involved."

"You're safe?"

"I will be," he tried. "With your help," he amended. "This is what I do, my heart. Talk through the evidence and make sure it comes out on my side's favour."

She gave a half chuckle. Not fully convinced, he'd guess, but his Anyara was a fighter.

"First, though, I asked you a question. Have you had enough time to give me an answer?" He studied her face, as puzzlement, then understanding, then exasperation washed over her face in quick succession.

"Are you asking me to marry you when I've spent the last hours terrified I'd never see you again?"

"Aahhh … yes."

"You sure you still want to? Having me for a marriage partner isn't a wise move for you at present."

He knew what she meant, what she thought, but she was wrong. "You are all I need, all I want."

"I'm not, you know." She said it with a smile and a laugh of sheer glee. "Your head is too busy. But," and her face became very serious, "can you promise me that I am at the heart of you, as you are of me?"

For once, words deserted him. How could she still doubt that? There was only one way to convince her. He kissed her, uncaring who watched, putting everything he felt, all his worry, his hopes and his passion in it. She drew back at the end, studying his face, her gaze resting on his lips in a way that had him wishing all the security around them banished to the depths of Sarwenna Beren's desert. Then she held his eyes. "Yes, I will marry you, Seolta den Coille, and will love you all the rest of my days."

He had to kiss her again. The rest would work itself out. She had given him all that mattered.

They were married in his home, in front of his family. Anyara felt guilty that so few could attend, having seen the holos of his brother Cumchdach's wedding.

"That was a political marriage," said Seolta, laughing at her worries. "Both of them are envious as all roots of us."

He looked stunning. His tunic and trousers were of the finest fabric, made by a southern Mountainer group from yet another of the miraculous trees that cloaked these forbidding slopes. Traced with an interlocking pattern of vines and leaves, it matched the ivory gown his sisters had presented to her.

"I saw this on a trip to Urbis not long after he left the planet, and something made me buy it," said his sister Samhchair. "Now I know why. It was waiting for you."

"Hah," said his irreverent younger sister, the one she'd been relieved let her call her Fee instead of her full Mountainer name. "I can't believe anyone wants to marry Seolta. Are you sure you know what you're doing, Sera?"

If she hadn't seen this woman's frequent playful verbal sparring with her brother, she might have been insulted. They are too alike, was the general family adage, and they were, in some ways, but Fee had a cool band of rationality hidden beneath that volatile exterior, whereas Seolta's outer façade of cold-blooded business savvy hid a streak of hot fury. Fee had fought back when their enemies threatened them; Seolta had buried his rage and turned it against himself and his world, a mistake for which he'd be paying for the rest of his life.

"I know exactly what I am doing and whom I am marrying," Anyara responded proudly. "He is already my chosen life partner." She was not Arcadian and it was time they got used to it.

Then she walked into the spacious hall that was the main public room of the sprawling den Coille family complex where he waited for her, and nothing else mattered.

They had only two more days before they must leave, and Seolta seized hold of them. Tension stalked his family, but they plastered on smiles and buried all talk of the future, until he broke the unwritten ban on the last evening.

The whole family were gathered in their favourite room, a large lounging room close to the trunk of the house tree filled with an assortment of mismatched but much loved seats and the casual oddments of a busy family's life. Anyara had missed out on her meeting with the Survey after the turmoil in Urbis, but had made up for it with vid links and was now deep in habitat discussion with Fioruisghe. Words he still didn't understand and had no intention of learning littered their talk, and he touched her cheek and moved over to join his father and older brother in their contemplation of a fine bottle of salaschar. He took a sip, and raised his glass to his father.

"As good as promised. I'm going to miss this. Alliance Central is home to many wonders, but they have yet to develop an appreciation for salaschar."

A shadow passed over his father's face and he glanced over at Anyara. "You sure about this, son?"

He knew what his father meant. "It keeps her safe, whatever the outcome, and gives her a choice."

"You think that's possible? She was born in a habitat. You're asking her to sit in the middle, caught on the knife edge between habitat and EA."

There was too much truth in that. "At least in the middle, Hilmar can't claim her. This way, she's *safe.*"

"And you?" His father had a reputation for going for the heart of a problem.

"Hopefully, if they accept the evidence."

"If they don't? Where does that leave her?" said Cumchdach. His brother wasn't the kind to let him get away with anything either.

"Safer than *not* married to me."

His father took another sip, eyeing him over the rim of his glass, then gave a nod and his arguments were at an end. "Trials are expensive. Do you need any funds?"

"I'm not destitute yet, Da. I think I can manage."

His father chuckled. "I assumed as much." He lifted a glass to Anyara. "Does she know that if anything happens to you, she will be left a very wealthy woman?"

It was his turn to laugh. "You should see what Hilmar was taking for her consultation fees. She doesn't need any credits from me."

His father gave his rare grin. "You're going for a charge of embezzlement as well?"

"Embezzlement and abuse of guardianship."

"Good," said his father.

Then came the last morning and the time for them to leave. Anyara tried standing off to one side as his family hugged him and whispered last minute instructions, but he pulled her back into his side. She was part of him now. His wife.

The word still left him stunned with pleasure.

Last was his mother. She held his face in both her hands, the same hands that had soothed him, protected him, loved him since babyhood. She glanced at the ring shining on his finger, and then at Anyara.

"All your life you have been hungry. For what, I don't think you knew, but a company can't give it to you."

Seolta squirmed inside. "You like Ethan Winter," he said, "and he's in love with Solaris."

"Ethan always understood that a company is more than credit balances. He always knew it was the people, though it took a while for him to put it into words. For you, though… You were searching for so long. Now, my son, I think you've found it. There is a contentment in you."

His mother looked at his wife. "Thank you, Sera."

More last hugs, and they were lifting off. This time, he held hard to his wife's hand and watched out the window as his home disappeared. This time, he knew to the full what he was losing. He was on a Fleet ship heading back into exile and to a possible prison sentence. Anyara clung tight to his arm and held him as his world dwindled from sight, held him as the tears froze inside him.

She was safe. He had won.

CHAPTER THIRTY-TWO

They returned to the Arcadian embassy on Central and, to Anyara, it was as if their trip had never happened. The same staff, the same ambassador, the exact same conflicts. The trip back had been slick and swift. A Fleet cruiser like the *Best Order* used routes banned to commercial ships. They were even in the same luxurious suite as last time.

"This is the first place I made love to you," said Seolta the first morning in the sleeper together.

"But not the last," she said with a grin and he laughed, that free and open laugh he released only when they were alone.

She hung on to the memory as they met with the ambassador on arrival in Central.

"Messera the Esteemed Scholar doesn't need to be here, surely," said the ambassador.

"My wife certainly does."

That strange word still gave her a tingle of goosebumps, or maybe it was the way he said it, that hint of disbelief and satisfaction.

The ambassador sat with a thump. "You're married? Where?"

Seolta put on his most malicious smile and she could have kicked him. "In the great room of my family home in Manascraoch. It was witnessed and sealed by the Arcadian authorities."

"Do you have any idea what you've done?"

"Oh, yes," he said.

Anyara looked at both in puzzlement. "What does she mean? What has our marriage got to do with any of this?"

The ambassador clenched her fists, then slowly opened them and laid her palms flat on the table. "Everything, Sera. Welcome to Arcadia."

"We're not on Arcadia."

Seolta put an arm around her. "What the ambassador is trying to say, my darling heart, is that you are now a citizen of Arcadia with full rights to the protection and care of the Arcadian authorities. You are also free to return there at any time."

Anyara's mouth dropped open.

"Surned is going to lay a complaint," said the ambassador. "They're already claiming you kidnapped her."

Anyara ignored her, turning to thump him square in the chest with all she had. "I *thought* you wanted to marry me because you loved me and marriage is how your planet shows that."

She couldn't believe the pain knifing through her, and rubbed angrily at the tears staining her cheeks.

"I did. I do. I also need to keep you safe, whatever happens to me. You will always have a home there now, a sanctuary if you need it."

"If anything happens to you? What do you think I am? I've had a lifetime of being locked away and 'protected for my own good'."

He didn't make the mistake of touching her. She couldn't take that, not after this.

"I'm sorry. I should have told you."

"Yes, you should. We are a *partnership*. If anything happens to you, it happens to me too."

"No." The denial was automatic. "You have to be safe. I'm worthless, a slug who nearly destroyed his home. You…"

How was it possible to be so angry with someone while also terrified for them? "What do you expect to happen to you?"

"Prison, to start with," said the ambassador dryly. "After that, it depends on who wins the fight to lay charges against him. The Alliance for spying and kidnapping, or Surned for espionage and kidnapping. If Surned wins, at least the prison sentence will be short."

"My uncle wouldn't let him live," said Anyara horrified.

"Exactly," said the ambassador. She leaned back and set her hands out of sight again. "Time to call in the lawyers, Ser den Coille."

At the end of it, the lawyers exchanged one of those looks unique to the legal fraternity. She never knew whether it meant they'd been handed all their dreams in one case or wanted to fly a galaxy away from the fiasco. She'd caught it too many times when dealing with the Kevand Station's legal team. There, it had been a squirm of terrified delight as they worked out how to keep themselves alive while double-crossing her uncle.

This time, the mess was a whole lot bigger.

"To summarise the various cases," said the lead lawyer. "First, the Restin fraud charge. The defendants in this case to be the companies named on the label of Restin as manufacturers and packers, with a subsidiary case of breach of contract against the Falasch corporation as distributors of Restin and Hilmar a Kevand3 as interplanetary agent. Do you have any evidence to prove this Restin is actually Festin, sold contrary to Den Coille's agreed contracts, apart from the packet details on the sample you bought on Deuteron and the recorded gossip and vid-ads?"

"The Den Coille labs are analysing the Restin now, comparing it with Festin. We own the manufacturing process and the collecting rights for all festia on Arcadia. If it contains festia pollen, it's ours and they stole it."

"You'll have to submit the two products for analysis by the Commerce Ministry's labs here on Central as well. I'd get an independent one done too, just in case."

Bribery and pressure on the lab by outside forces, that meant. By people like her uncle and his allies, none of whom played nice. The lawyer went on as if accusing an Alliance agency of being corrupt was nothing. Anyara gulped and curled her fists in her lap.

"Next, the personal threats to you, Ser den Coille." said the man. "You claim that various 'accidents' you have recently suffered were deliberate, and that Hilmar a Kevand3 and associates are implicated. Specifically: a crash on Surned during a storm, an attempted poisoning on a Fleet ship, targeting either you or your wife, and a crash during the pre-Games race on Central. Specifically, you accuse the Meth Varkan and Jongma corporations of engineering the race crash. Do you have any evidence?"

"Not … yet," said Seolta. "Only circumstantial. I am waiting for the official investigations to be completed."

"They'll take too long to be of any use to us," said the woman lawyer sitting next to the lead. "Given the parties involved, I can guarantee they will take many cycles to complete."

"File it anyway," said Seolta. "It puts them on notice and strengthens the other charges."

"And may slow the other charges against you," said the third lawyer, a grey-haired, crumpled man slouching in his chair. The criminal trial expert, according to his dossier, his record belied the unprofessional air of the man. She might have been worried by his appearance if she hadn't met those acute eyes when being introduced. This was a man who hid a keen brain behind a disarming exterior. Or she hoped he did. Seolta's life and hers depended on it.

Seolta lifted a hand, tilting it sideways in sparse agreement. "Hopefully enough to persuade a judge to let me stay out of prison till the charges can be heard."

A "hmmph" from the man gave his opinion of that.

"Next we come to the charge that the Messera's uncle made a contract with you to assassinate her," said the woman.

"I have a copy on file."

He sent it over to the lawyers, who duly read it but none seemed excited.

"It's not likely to help much," said the woman. "Messer Hilmar will deny it, and no other similar contract will be found. Assassins aren't in the habit of publicly advertising their occupation. Also, your marriage makes it worse."

Surely not. That was so wrong. "How?" Anyara wanted to know.

Seolta turned to her. "If anything happens to you, *mo Graidh*, as your husband and under Arcadian law, I inherit everything you own."

"By laying the embezzlement charge, Messera, you've made it public that what you own is considerable."

"My uncle has been stealing from me for years. He owes me."

"Yes, and that charge can be proved. Our forensic accountants are rubbing their hands in glee as we speak. We will win the case against your uncle, although I would recommend not including the Academy. We can imply that they may have been aware of the situation, but the Academy will claim that they were working to free you and reclaim your rights.

"There's enough truth in that to be credible," said Seolta.

"They were working to get all my earnings for themselves. I doubt I'd have seen much of it," she said huffily.

"Exactly, Messera," said the woman, "which is what the defendants will say about your husband. You're now married, free of your uncle, and you sadly suffer an accident. As you've seen, they are easily organised. Leaving the Ser Seolta den Coille in full control of your fortune.

"Not forgetting he is an exile from his home planet due to his arguably criminal activities there and has admitted accepting an assassination contract from your uncle," said the lead.

"We should drop the embezzlement charge," suddenly said the oldest lawyer.

"Except you can't. Not if you want any hope of defeating the charges against Seolta. They have a good case there."

"His chances?" said Anyara fearfully.

The older man waggled his hand. Then he leaned forward. "If you support him in this, Messera, you risk losing your reputation and your work, with all the hope it brings to the Alliance worlds. Do you want to do that?"

"He is my husband," she said staunchly, "and if he goes to prison, neither of us will survive the next yearly cycle. My uncle and his cohorts will see to it."

Seolta took her hand. "Not necessarily, my heart. You need to listen to them. Go back to the Academy. They'll keep you safe. You will have a good life there."

She wrenched her hand out of his. "You want rid of me."

"No!" he said as if torn from the very core of him. "You are my heart. If anything happens to you…" He sat rigidly. "I would like nothing better than to spend the rest of my worthless life with you, and that it be long and peaceful."

"You aren't made for peaceful," she said, nearly choking on her tears.

"No," he said, his broken smile matching her heart, "but you will be *alive*."

"No!" she said as forcefully. "Not without you." She turned to the lawyer. "File the assassination charges against my uncle. We will find evidence. Can you force Alliance Security to release what they have?"

The older man's smile matched the images of a hunting foxllar. "No, but filing a request for it will scare the darks out of them. It won't stop the assassination charge and any other charges they bring against Ser Seolta for plotting against you, Messera Anyara, but there's a good chance they'll drop the kidnapping one."

"So they should," said Seolta. "Either I kidnapped Anyara, or her uncle was wrongfully detaining her. If they can't prove he's innocent, he can't claim he's taking her to protect her. Stopping him taking her is the most important thing here."

"He can't anyway, not now you married me and made me a citizen of Arcadia," she said, realising for the first time exactly why he'd done that. Horror filled her. "They can lock you up forever, or until you have an *accident*, while I escape to Arcadia and stay out of his reach. Was that your plan?" She could have thumped him again. "You think I'll let you buy my freedom with your life?"

"You won't be fully safe, not until all the conspirators have been exposed, and I can't do that for the ones on Arcadia. Not from here. I can only feed information back. Uncovering them is for the marshals and Cumchdach, but it's safer than Surned."

"So you'd give up your life for a *chance* for me. It seems a poor reward."

"It's better than no chance," he said, and she heard the frustration in his voice. "Don't ask me to settle for that."

A cough. "So I'd better make sure you win your case, Ser den Coille," said the rumpled lawyer, a glint in his eye. "I'll notify you as soon as they lay charges."

All three lawyers leaned back, very suspect smiles on their faces, as if contemplating nirvana. "Is there anything else?" said the lead lawyer, beginning to shut down his files.

She clenched her hands together. "There is also the matter of my report."

"What report?" said the lead sharply, sitting back down again.

"An audit of the environmental status of the planet Arcadia, with an evaluation of the effect of settlement."

All three lawyers sat up. "You mean that demand to fix Arcadia or everyone will be kicked off and a new population of settlers granted residency? You're involved in that?"

She could only nod sheepishly. "That's why we were sent there. I have the required biome expertise and am considered an independent specialist."

"When does it come out?"

"I sent it off before we left Arcadia."

"To?"

"The Alliance Council. They will have forwarded a copy to the Biota and Exoplanetary Research Ministries and to the Arcadian Council."

"We'll need a copy."

"It's embargoed until the Council releases it."

The lead considered that for a split instant. "If it's material to a client's security, his legal counsel has rights of access to any but files rated Top Security Risk. Is it so rated, Messera?"

She shook her head wordlessly, feeling a gulf opening under her.

"Then forward it, please. You can trust us not to disseminate it until the Council releases it."

Shaking, she activated her com and sent it. "I haven't shown it to anyone else yet, not even Seolta."

The lead took one look at the file, swore, and scrolled through the body of the report at maniacal speed. At the end, he slumped back. "Stars alive. This is political dynamite. Let your husband read your file copy, but *do not* forward it to him. However," he glanced again at the report with loathing, "I suggest you also send a copy directly to each Council member, EA and habitat, and ensure they read it."

She nodded. "And the ambassador?"

"Will be provided a copy by the Arcadian Representative, you can be certain of that."

The lead glared at her and all three lawyers stood to leave. "We will be in touch, Messers. In the meantime, I strongly suggest you confine yourselves to the embassy and its grounds. Good day."

"Wait. What are our chances?"

The lead lawyer looked down his nose. "Drop all the charges, Messera."

The woman said nothing, her mouth pinched closed.

She turned to the last, the older, rumpled figure slouching at the back. "Messer?"

He looked at her, then at Seolta, as if assessing them. "You'll win the Restin fraud case but make enemies. Dangerous ones. As for the rest … It's like a minefield with interconnecting strands. Each charge sets off another. You're best to drop them all, except the Restin case. Or just the embezzlement one, but confine it to your uncle. That makes it a purely family matter rather than one with wider implications."

"And if we go for the full barrage. What's the most likely outcome?"

This time his eyes rested on her. "A win in them all gives you the most but… It's the Messer's history that's the problem. Even the attacks against him can be seen as justified attempts to control a dangerous wildcard. Business and politics don't like uncontrolled elements."

"Prison?" said Seolta.

"Yes, Messer. It won't be a sympathetic sentence either."

Seolta nodded as if he'd expected that. "What happens to Arcadia?"

"The Restin case raises serious trade questions. Whether it's enough is uncertain but the rest is up to your home world.

"And the Messera?"

"Could go to Arcadia, but the Academy's the safest option."

"Safe, and a prisoner," said Anyara with loathing.

Seolta turned to her, and wouldn't let her back down from the truth in his eyes. "You will be alive."

The battle began later that day. First, her report went out to all the individual members of the Alliance Council, as recommended by the lawyers. She also gave it to Seolta to read. At the end, he lifted his head. She usually knew exactly what he was thinking. This time, he tapped a finger against the chair.

"You agree with the Survey?"

"Mostly," she said carefully.

The tapping increased. "Fioruisghe will be pleased with this."

"It's what I found," she said. "I can't help it if you don't like it."

His fingers paused. "That's not what I said." He glanced at the report again. "This won't make things easy. No wonder the lawyers were disturbed. What you found about settlement? Can you prove it?"

"It's obvious if you compare the Deuteron farmlands with the Urbis delta lands, which are near to farmed out thanks to treating the land as a factory floor rather than a living biome. Likewise, most habitat settlers treat their biota as a system tool, one that stays tidily locked away in a biome room. If you look at the past changes to your Mountainer and Plains regions, and the newly starting repairs, that balance is still fragile." She saw him flinch, and took a breath before ploughing on. "Our Deuteron farmer proved that swapping settlers who understand their land with ones new to planetary life, let alone the individual Arcadian regions, will only hinder the repair of the planet."

His finger tapped again, once, twice. He had opposed any changes in his home region, trying to stop them by working with a corrupt Alliance official to warn off his family. His sister was as stubborn as he, though, and his father too shrewd a judge of changing times to be stopped. Now, she had said his sister was the one in the right and that more change was needed.

"You're correct in saying the political pressure for replacing Arcadians with outsiders is coming from habitat worlds." Tap, tap on the table. He looked down, as if he suddenly realised what he was doing, and his fingers froze. Then he glanced up at her fingers clutching the hair clip he'd given her on Arcadia. "They haven't thought it through, though. How many habitat dwellers would stay after that first shock of landing on a domeless world?"

She gave a ghost of a laugh. "Some would. Have you seen our backstreets?"

"Oh, yes, they'd make great farmers," he said caustically.

She gathered up her courage. "Enough would make it to allow the replacement of part of the population."

"The troublesome part. That gives the Alliance Council unquestioned control of Arcadia. Do as we say or lose your home."

"Yes." It's all she could say. His face said he understood everything that went with it. Losing control of your home was bad enough under a fair ruling body. With a Council divided by economic and power struggles between habitat and EA, driven on by a growing mass of lower-tier habitat dwellers hungry for space, food and opportunity but with no idea of the skills needed on an EA world, and a planet seemingly empty to any habitat dweller, it was a recipe for disaster for Arcadia.

"Will my recommendations be enough?"

"No," he said, as bald and honest as she'd been. "All the parties will pick out the parts that suit them. For now, the EA worlds have the upper hand in Council with their higher population figures. It should give us time to sort out the problems back home." He took a breath. "We have to force a full Council vote."

"Can we do that?" she asked.

"We can hope," he said as that finger tapped out its song of dread. "We can hope," he said again, as if defying the fates.

The Academy arrived the next morning. She received them in the embassy's formal sitting room, decorated with vids and fabrics from Arcadia, flowers picked from the embassy's garden, and living plants twining up the window frames and sideboards. It reminded her enough of Seolta's home city to keep her back straight, but it was his presence in the next room, linked to her com with a full privacy lock that gave her the courage to stare the dean in the face and lift a startled brow when he began his speech with a rebuke at her sudden departure.

"I wasn't aware that I was under bondage to the Academy."

The dean spluttered, then caught himself and sat back in his chair, one ankle crossed over the other.

"Of course not, Esteemed Scholar. The Academy only wishes to do all it cán to enable your work to continue, and ensure you are free of those who wish to suborn you to their own goals."

The man was from a habitat world and well connected. He also needed her.

"You have read my report, Dean?"

"Oh, yes," he said with a wide, gushing smile. "First rate. A fine piece of work."

"Thank you," she said, feeling like a small creature eyed by an oversized predator.

He had brought along a colleague, one she didn't recognise, though there was something familiar about her. She looked pointedly at the woman now, sitting beside the dean with hands folded tidily in her lap. Older than the dean by a few years, she would guess, and by his flustered spluttering, his superior as well. The woman had skin a shade darker than Seolta's, though more washed out in the way of someone who had spent a long time in an artificial habitat. If she belonged to the Academy, that was to be expected. She'd let her hair go grey, but the styling of it came from a top-tier grooming unit, and something about her looked familiar. It was the eyes, though, that made Anyara wary: alert, watchful, and a colour that was hard to define. A mix of grey, green and deepest brown, flecked with specks of gold. It was an unusual combination and gave her no clue about the woman's origin.

"I have been wanting to make your acquaintance for some time, Messera," said the woman.

"Oh?" Anyara said, feeling like a cornered creature.

The woman put out hand. "Messera Esteemed Scholar Tularin Nanko."

"Ooohh," said Anyara. The woman's work was famous. "I've followed your work since my first cycle at the Academy." Tularin

Nanko had been the first to discuss strategies for mixing species of different planetary origin. Why was she here now? "It's an honour to meet you."

"Thank you. These days, I sadly don't get enough time for research, but your report interests me."

"It does?" Anyara hid her hands in the folds of her tunic to stop wringing them together.

"A fine piece of work, as the dean says. Exactly what we expect from our Esteemed Scholars. You bring credit to the Academy."

"Thank you."

The woman smiled, and it did nothing to reassure Anyara.

"I need to explain," she said. "These days, I am the Academy's liaison officer, and your work has useful implications for the whole of the Alliance. I understand you had never visited an EA world before."

"That's right."

"Yet your review of the Arcadian biome is excellent. Your audit provides a useful summary of plant interactions and the effects of disrupting them, and the Academy is keen to see that work taken further."

Anyara crossed her arms, discreetly touching her com. "In what way, Messera Esteemed Scholar?"

"The Academy would like you to return to work with us. Your unique take on bio-systems would enhance a number of projects we have under way on habitat and engineered worlds."

The door opened and Seolta walked in. She had to work hard to hide her look of relief. "Let me make known to you my husband, Messer Seolta den Coille. Any commitments I make will, of course, need to be discussed with him. In a new relationship like ours, we are reluctant to take on any work requiring separation."

Seolta was wearing that smile she hated, the one he used with competitors and enemies. She gave him a quick glance and he moderated it slightly. She wasn't convinced it was any better. This was the schmoozing, seductive one used when he had a prey in sight and a plan for them to follow.

The Esteemed Scholar Nenko wasn't fooled, though. She graciously bowed her head. "A pleasure to meet you, Messer den Coille. I have heard a great deal about your extraordinary adventures and your worthy family. I would very much like to see one of your famous tree cities one day."

Anyara could have told the woman to drop the condescending voice. According to his elder sister, Seolta had been dealing with unfriendly competitors since he was a child. He took the chair beside Anyara, lifted her hand and very openly held it close. "Perhaps you can send us the details of what you propose, Messera Esteemed Scholar. My wife is always happy to consider any project which enhances the wellbeing of the ordinary citizens of the Alliance."

The woman didn't bat an eye. "Happy to hear it, Messer."

The dean nearly choked. Anyara didn't blame him. She seriously doubted that helping out ordinary, *poor* people was ever in the Esteemed Scholar's sights.

The woman rose soon after, with a promise to forward the details to Anyara as soon as she returned to her office.

"What was that about?" said Anyara as soon as they had left.

"The first volley, at a guess," said Seolta with a narrow-eyed look at the door the pair had exited. "Bring up her com files and show me her background."

She brought up the scholar's record, slowing down to show him the research section. "Her work's amazing."

He scanned through it. "Was amazing. Look at her family section. Born on a habitat world, and connected by partnership to another. Her eldest daughter is currently an advisor in the office of a habitat Councillor. There's nothing neutral about Messera Esteemed Scholar Tularin Nanko."

"I'm from a habitat world, and I'm certainly not about to do anything against the *ordinary* people of those worlds." Her arms locked around her body, and a shiver tore through her. One that wouldn't stop. Seolta swore and pulled her into his body, swearing harder as the shiver went on. She locked her arms tight until the shaking stopped.

"I'm calling back the lawyers." His voice rumbled through her head, edged with steel. "Time for the battering ram. We're going for the ballistic option."

She couldn't speak but her head gave one hard nod. Yes.

The next day, they released the first barrage. Seolta had spent the night on his com, and by morning they had the results of the lab's analysis on the fake Restin, confirming it was indistinguishable from Festin and derived from Den Coille festia pollen; a promise for an initial report on the forensic accountancy review of her uncle's guardianship and handling of her earnings; and an appointment with the security committee of the Council regarding the poisoning on a Fleet ship and associated matters. They posted it on the public schedule.

"Otherwise, they'll bury anything you say," said the ambassador, looking cycles older with each new attack pouring out of the embassy. It didn't help that Seolta sent off each legal bombshell with a flourish of his wrist and a kiss goodbye.

"They want to bury us. Let them dig themselves out from under this lot first." He grinned madly as the last one disappeared over the com links and the answering ping came back from the receiving court. By mid-morning, all the charges had been filed and a Central enforcement officer had arrived at the embassy gate to serve Seolta the expected summons to answer a charge of kidnapping and attempted murder of Anyara.

"Don't worry," said the still crumpled defence lawyer. "This is a retaliatory volley, no more. They can't force the embassy to expel you."

"What about when we go to our appointment with the Council?" asked Seolta

"Haven't they've given us a guarantee of safe passage?" said Anyara. Seolta appeared to thrive on the tensions buffeting the room; she just wanted to slip back into her beautiful lab at the Academy and bury her hands in dirt and biota.

"Best make your visits by holo-vid.," said the lawyer. "Not as effective as in person, but safer."

"For Anyara, yes," said Seolta.

Anyara stood up and walked out. She marched into the garden, bolting towards the quiet grove of trees at the far end. There, she sank to the ground, burying her fingers into the dark soil and breathed in, desperate for the smell of leaf and mould to drive out the noise of words and com messages.

Seolta found her there. When she didn't return, he'd gone looking, checking the cleansing suites and kitchen. Next their room, but that was untouched. He looked out the window and saw a stirring in the trees and a flash of colour that didn't belong. His heart suddenly beating hard, he ran to the shaft and hurtled down headfirst with body arrowed to increase the power of the downwards airflow, swinging up to slow the flow in time to land on the lower floor and race out the garden doors. Feet pumping, he ran down the white stone pathways, ignoring the flowers, the complicated interwoven patterns of the famous knot garden, intent only on the place he'd seen that patch of colour.

He slowed as he came to the shrubbery, suddenly afraid. He nearly didn't enter but had to.

She was crouched down, hands clinging to the soil, her face whiter than ever with those precious freckles standing out against the stark pallor of her skin. He knelt beside her and his arms pulled her into his body. His breath whooshed out when she let him and he heard her breathe, in and out, and felt the pounding of her heart in her chest.

"What is it, my heart? What has frightened you?"

She heard him. The jerk of her head betrayed her, but she kept staring firmly at the ground.

"Do you want me to stop?"

That brought her head up. "You can't. They'll kill you."

"Possibly." As so many times before, he wished he could lie to her, but she'd pick it up before the first word left his mouth.

She sat back, easing herself against the nearest bush and flattening her hands on the rough bark. "When you go to that committee appointment, I'm going with you."

Now she'd frightened him. "It's too dangerous."

"Then why are you going?"

He hadn't yet fully decided to go in person.

If you can't lie to her, then don't lie to yourself.

He sat beside her on the dirt, breathing in the familiar scent of leaves and listened to their rustling above him. He took a deep breath and reached for her hand. "All the court cases are only means to ends. They won't achieve anything, even in the unlikely event we win them all. What we need is the Council." Her face told him to get on with it. She knew all this. "A face-to-face meeting works better. In a vidcast, you miss too many signals. Even in the best full sensory surround 'cast. It's just … not the same." He glanced at her, but she still stared at the ground and he could see little. "It also tells them too much. Tells them I'm afraid to risk the streets."

That brought her head up. "With good reason. They'll arrest you as soon as you step foot outside the embassy."

"They can try, but I'm covered by the ambassador's diplomatic privilege."

"I'm going with you."

He tried to talk her out of it, but she was stubborn, his Anyara.

They set out with a fully armed escort and a diplomatic shield surrounding them, also fully armed. He didn't care how many Alliance rules it broke. He wasn't letting Anyara risk the streets without protection.

The Security Committee building was set in the heart of the capital. They arrived after a tense drive through the streets, followed by enforcement officers and a persistent court official zipping from street corner to ramp and sending out a continuous whine that he hadn't responded to the court summons. Seolta gave him a cheery wave after the third time the man's skimmer tried to jump in front of their convoy and was shoved back by their guards. Anyara jolted him with her elbow and he sent the man a grin of thanks. He'd not only reduced the dangerous trip to farce; he'd brought Anyara out of her fears.

The Committee building and home of the Security branch was a nondescript pile of plascrete, reminding him strongly of the Survey's building where he'd been imprisoned along with his brothers and Ethan. He had to touch Anyara's shoulder as they passed through the outer screens. He was here on business. Those corrupt Survey guards were all securely locked away on a remote Arcadian prison island.

You're not safe.

No, he wasn't, not to any smug bureaucrat thinking to push him around.

"Ready, *mo Graidh?*"

"I do wish you would stop wearing that particular smile. It makes me more scared than ever."

"It has a purpose," he murmured back.

"That's what worries me."

The Committee waited for them in an innocuous receiving room, complete with comfortable chairs. They sat at the large table in the centre of the room. At the head of the table sat an older woman flanked by the rest of the committee on both sides. Councillor Kamesh, the powerful senior councillor in charge of both the Security and Inter-Alliance Cooperation agencies.

"Messer den Coille, Messera Anyara a Prithand2. Thank you for coming."

They both bowed their heads.

She opened the files on her com, as did the rest of the Committee. He and Anyara were granted the summary only. Their lead lawyer also sat with them. He coughed delicately. "Committee rules require full sharing of any applicable files with all persons present likely to be affected by the contents."

A slight tightening around the woman's eyes was the only sign she gave. Kamesh was a veteran of the Council. She was also of habitat origin. Regardless, their own coms now showed an expanded version of the files in question. He doubted they were the full one available to the Committee, but from his lawyers' acquiescence, they were the best they were going to get.

"You have been creating quite a furore," she said now, eyes scrolling through the files. "You have evidence to support these claims?"

"In the files forwarded to you," said the lawyer.

Kamesh never gave a hint of annoyance, but she also took her time pulling up the accessory files and reviewing them. They had been sent to the Committee yesterday, ample time for all of them to be fully familiar with the contents.

Seolta ignored the playacting and watched the rest of the Committee. They had discussed the make-up of the panel long into the night. Evenly split between EA and habitat worlds, he still didn't know how they'd vote. Like Den Coille, all EA and habitat businesses had many interlocking connections across the divide. EA and habitat needed each other. What he didn't know was the strength of the habitats' hunger for new ground. He'd seen enough on Surned to show him the potential among the lower streets, but what about the other levels, the ones most likely to select the representatives on the Alliance Council ?

He wasn't the only one worried. The Councillor from the EA planet Hansur leaned forward. "I don't like this talk of outside parties working deceitfully to acquire Arcadian companies and land. That's what we should really be discussing. You deserved worse than exile, young man." he glared at Seolta, "but Arcadia should have brought the matter before the full Council."

Then he eyed Anyara. "And you, young lady. Your uncle was involved in these schemes. How do we know this whole spectacle isn't designed to hide more of the same?"

Their lawyer highlighted the file of Anyara's claim against her uncle. "As you can see, the Messera is a victim here. She has no reason to support her uncle."

Seolta brought up the embezzlement file as well. He was still stunned at the final totals they'd unearthed. Anyara should have been a very wealthy woman in her own right, even without her stake in Surned.

"On the contrary," he said, "the Messera is opposed to her uncle and is seeking restitution for his mishandling of her financial affairs. Furthermore, if you see here," he highlighted another section, "he has previously blocked any attempt by the Messera to relocate to the Academy and further her work there, by which, he may have put back her research by many cycles, to the detriment of all the habitat worlds."

That tightening around Kamesh's eyes became more pronounced. "We have all heard of the Esteemed Scholar's work and the reports of the productivity and ease of living on her home station. However, the Esteemed Scholar is not currently working at her home station. Her return there seems to be blocked as effectively by her marriage to Messer Seolta as her movements were by Messer Hilmar."

Anyara sat up. "I can work best at the Academy, but it was their actions that drove me out, not Messer Seolta's. Once I am again satisfied that I will be free to move in or out of the Academy as I wish, I will be happy to return to my lab and my work there. I also need assurance of my husband's safety."

They were at an impasse. Seolta watched all the faces, seeking any chink to exploit. You could smell the suspicion in the air, an acrid mix of sweat, chemical sanitisers, and ozone. The panel put up a privacy screen, and he began to seriously worry. This had been their best chance.

He watched as mouths talked, screens scrolled, switched and scrambled into new configurations. He wished he could figure out what they were thinking. Their own security stood at the far wall, flanked by Alliance agents. Faces inscrutable, but their bodies told a different story. Tense, rigid, as if ready for action.

He caught the eye of their security chief, then glanced pointedly at Anyara. Whatever happened, she must be kept safe.

Then the privacy screen vanished.

"The matters here are beyond this committee's scope. Given the volume, complexity and counter charges of the legal matters set out by all the parties involved, the matter will be forwarded to the full Council at the earliest opportunity."

He breathed again. Impossible to believe, but they had won this round.

"In the meantime, for their own protection, the Messera will be escorted to the Academy and the Messer will be held here."

He leapt up and Anyara yelled out in protest. More security guards entered the room.

Too late. He reached out a hand, but Anyara was already being escorted out. "She is a citizen of Arcadia," he yelled. To no avail. He was grabbed by both arms and dragged out a door. Anyara was firmly marched out the opposite one.

"If you hurt her…"

The nearest agent slapped a restraint on his arms and feet and he was tugged along. "The Esteemed Scholar will come to no harm," said the leader. "She is too valuable."

The look on his face said very clearly that Seolta wasn't.

Seolta looked at his latest prison cell and paced from one side to the other. It was the usual size; too small for comfort and big enough to let him stand and take a few paces, with a hard sleeper that was like a plank of stone, and a cleansing unit that barely lived up to the name. The only positive he found in his new cell was that the food they brought him was palatable.

"What is it about me that makes people take one look and throw me in the nearest cell," he said, grumpily poking at the lumps of qatras fruit.

"Your free and frank manner or your beguiling face," said a voice from the doorway. The shield dropped momentarily and a woman walked in. Seolta didn't make the mistake of taking it as an invitation to escape, not with the posse of hulking guards standing outside the cell and watching his every movement. The woman looked like the cheerful and cuddly grandmother of a friend of his—short, stout and with a decided tilt to her lips—but those guards said she was important and her over tunic may be the ubiquitous pointed and cross-over style currently common on Central, but it had the unmistakable quality of cut that came only from a top couturier house. He bowed low.

"You have the advantage of me, Messera."

"I'm glad you realise it, young man." She settled onto the sleeper, making it look like she routinely sat on prison sleepers in cold cells. He doubted that very much, but he suspected this woman had a knack of making any place her own. He watched her, every sense alert and keeping all movements slow and obvious. Those guards carried weapons, all held ready.

The woman gave a short nod of her head, looking disarmingly like the small quanga that flitted through the branches of the baullnia outside his window at home every morning. He fought back the thought.

"You may call me Messera," she said.

"Messera who?"

Her smile widened. "You are a cautious young man."

"I'm locked in a prison cell with your guards blocking the door. I have reason to be."

She crossed her legs, setting her hands on her knees. "I had a feeling I was going to like you."

Her eyes weren't those of a kindly grandmother. He kept his hands firmly on the table, in clear sight of all the watchers.

"Are we even in the Security headquarters still?" They had dragged him through closed hallways, ones with the suffocating feeling of heading below ground.

"Oh, no, of course not. We're in the main Council building," she added, surprising him. "I wanted to talk to you, young man, without observers, and this was the easiest way."

A clattering of sound in the hallway interrupted her. "Ah, about time."

Then his breath stopped. Anyara walked into the room, escorted by more guards.

"She has nothing to do with this. Let her go."

"I think not, young man. Welcome, Messera Esteemed Scholar." A guard brought in another chair and Anyara sat quietly, her face white.

The older woman gestured to the guards and they left the room. "Now we can get on with it," she said, as if they were at a family gathering. "Let me introduce myself. Messera Yarma, Secretary-General of the Alliance Council Secretariat.

Seolta's gut plummeted. He'd heard of this woman. Who hadn't? She virtually ran the day-to-day work of the Council, but few had ever seen an image of her. For her security, was the official explanation, but Seolta suspected the woman had other reasons. This was a woman who understood the power of the streets, and few would look twice if she chose to wander through the shops and markets of any planet.

"What can we do for you, Messera?" he said deferentially.

"I hope we can help each other," she surprised him with. "I apologise for the setting. It seemed the best way to avoid scrutiny, and you have both created a great deal of consternation."

"We only reported facts," said Anyara, giving the woman that steady look of hers.

"That, Messera Esteemed Scholar, is the problem. Now it's for the Council to decide what to do about them."

"The tension between habitat and EA worlds?" Seolta asked.

"Exactly. Up till now, we'd managed to nicely restrain it. Then you two decided to make it public."

"Restrain!" He didn't care how important the woman was. "Hilmar a Kevand3 used an internal Arcadian stoush to try stealing two Arcadian corporations."

"With your help," said the woman curtly, no longer so genial.

"I'm well aware of what I did."

"You weren't thinking straight at the time," said Anyara as quickly, then turned to the older woman. "You know why he did it. So do the Arcadian Council. If they'd been better at controlling their departments, Seolta wouldn't have been in that prison or falsely threatened with execution. He wasn't responsible for what he did."

He put a hand on her. "Yes, I was, *mo Graidh*. It doesn't matter why or how angry I was. I knew exactly what I was doing when I conspired with your uncle and Malgrave. I fooled myself that I could manage them, thinking they wouldn't hurt my family or their business, that I only did it to keep the business safe. The reality is, I did it for revenge, pure and simple, and there's nothing praiseworthy in that."

Messera Yarma clapped slowly. "Well done, young man. There's hope for you yet."

"Thank you," he said dryly, "but it wasn't said for your benefit."

"Oh, I'm aware of that." A disconcerting twinkle lit those acute eyes. "Now, if you've finished your overdue apology to your wife, can we get back to business?"

Seolta was in no mood to pander to anyone. "You want us to rescind our court filings and disappear quietly into some obscure backwater? Not possible."

She broke into laughter.

"No, young man, I want you to tell the Council what's going on and bring the whole festering sore to a head. Given the charges you've laid and Messera Anyara's report, they have no choice but to listen, and that is long overdue."

"Open Council?" said Anyara.

"You're your father's daughter, right enough. I met him once. A fine man, but too knowing for his own good. He spoke out against his brother-in-law's growing domination of all the Surned habitats. I wouldn't have expected him to be so naïve."

"That's why they died?" Shock struck her face.

The older woman leaned forward and patted her hand. "It's unprovable, my dear. That's all that matters. But you two have produced evidence. Now it's for the Secretariat and the Council to use it without getting you both killed."

"Deputy Malgrave? No one mentions her," Seolta said.

"With good reason." Messera Yarma's voice had gone suddenly icy. "If you are wise, you will forget that name, Messers."

"She gets off free and gratis. She did more to manipulate the Arcadian companies than ever Hilmar did. The only reason I went after Hilmar was I couldn't find Malgrave," said Seolta.

"Malgrave has been dealt with," said Yarma. "She will not be bothering you again."

Seolta studied her then lifted his hands in surrender. He'd always suspected more lay behind Malgrave. The woman was the front of a larger conspiracy, but one day, there would be restitution. If not by him, and it seemed increasingly unlikely, that glitter in the older woman's eyes gave him some reassurance.

"And Hilmar a Kevand3?" asked Seolta.

The ice sharpened in the woman's eyes. "Still after revenge, Messer den Coille?"

He thought of lying, then quickly discarded it. "To a degree," he admitted, "but Surned is my wife's home world and the people of its streets deserve better."

The ice retreated. "It's in progress. That's the best I can offer at this time, Messers. This case will ensure that Surned comes under scrutiny from both habitat and EA factions. That will constrain his actions in the meantime."

Then the woman turned to face Anyara. "The one thing I can promise, Messera, is that Kevand Station will be protected and your safe access will be guaranteed, even if we have to station a Fleet vessel permanently there. Nothing will be allowed to impede your research.

Anyara's face went white and her hand reached for his. A tear touched her cheek.

"Thank you," she said. "I never expected…"

He'd stolen her home and she'd never once complained. Never let him see what it cost her. "We'll go there as soon as we're free," he promised her and hoped she knew it for an apology.

She lifted her head, eyes meeting his and gave a firm nod. "Yes, we will."

The Secretary-General coughed. "If there's nothing else, I have work to do." Yarma reached for her com as if closing them off, like a finished file.

"You can start by releasing Seolta back to the embassy," said Anyara, and Yarma's hand snapped back.

She shook her head. "He wouldn't survive the trip."

"So I am to stay here, dependent on the loyalty of your guards for my safety? And Anyara?"

"You can count on them, young man, despite your previous experiences, and you're lucky to be held here. The state prison is far less accommodating; and there is yet no certainty you won't end up there." Seolta had known that, but her blunt statement left him hollow. He glanced at Anyara, and the woman's eyes followed. "Your wife will return to the Academy. My guards will go with her, and the Academy has been reminded who is the principal source of its funds. You may be a potential high earner, Messera, but you cannot compete with the Council."

She stood, smoothing down her tunic. "I will see you again in three standard days. You will be brought to the Secretariat building and from there can pass by our secured passages into the Council building. It will not be an open session. None of the real work of Council is, but the results will be openly published."

All trace of geniality suddenly vanished from the woman, and if Seolta had any doubt, it confirmed she was exactly who she said. "The Alliance will not survive this nonsense and it is going to stop. Habitats and EA worlds need each other, and it's time they were reminded of it."

Anyara didn't see Seolta again until she arrived at the Secretariat building, on the morning of the third day as promised. She'd spent those days working in her lab, staying until late at night and feverishly setting down all the strands of thought she had picked up on her visit to Arcadia. Whatever Messera Yarma might suggest to the contrary, Anyara had lived with the threat of death too long. This might be her only chance to set down what she'd learned. She lingered till late each night, telling her plants and microbes what she had found on Arcadia and all about her adventures there. Of the small pond in the high plateau regions where no one lived and the biome continued in ignorance of people.

Busyness put off the moment when she must retreat to her lonely room and toss fruitlessly for the rest of the sleep period, trying not to worry about Seolta. He had to be safe.

When she saw him again, he was untouched and whole. She still had to pat him down, touch her hands all over him, caress his face where the grey shadows clung under those beautiful eyes. He hadn't slept well either. He seized hold of her hands, clutching them tight.

"You're safe, my heart. The Academy…"

"Treated me with all honour. My lab was untouched, and my work still there. Messera Yarma has a powerful arm."

"Pleased to hear it," said the deceptively gentle voice of the older lady. "Come along to my office and we can sort through your presentation."

Any illusion she'd had about the older woman disappeared in that office. Waiting for them was a team of lawyers, public speech writers, political advisors, specialists from the biome and bio-engineering sections of the Secretariat and a bunch of economists and business experts that managed to silence even Seolta with their insights. At the end of the session, she may have been properly armed to appear before the Council, but she fully intended to collapse on a sleeper afterwards and vanish into sleep for a standard day. The woman even remembered to feed them and afterwards offered a range of stimulants from the mild and innocuous to the scarily heavy-duty, all monitored by a doctor.

Anyara shook her head. If they were going to face the full Alliance Council, she wanted her brain fully in charge, not muted by chemical props. Seolta also refused, but did look longingly at a bottle of salaschar. "Later," she heard him murmur as he touched the bottle reverently and she had to hide her smile.

An aide entered. "It's time, Messera," he said to the Secretary-General.

Anyara swallowed. She could do this. Then they were all walking towards the main Council chamber.

CHAPTER THIRTY-THREE

She wished there were decorations to relieve the blank nothingness of the walls surrounding them. Would they become the same, become nothing too? Seolta's fingers touched hers and he leaned closer.

"Once this is all over, *mo Graidh*, I'm taking you somewhere private—very private—and after that… I have very specific plans for that gorgeous body of yours."

Her spluttered laughter had a tinge of hysteria, but it banished the threat of the walls and she threw him a look of thanks.

The main Council chamber was no less intimidating. Circular in shape and built to hold an audience of thousands, the planetary representatives sat in the largest seats on the front tier. Each EA world had a single desk, and the habitat worlds were arranged by population size. Surned warranted one full representative, but most other habitats were organised in blocks with joint representation. Regardless, voting was by number of citizens, with the EA worlds outvoting the habitats by sheer population size. Or usually they did. Messera Yarma had warned against relying on it.

Walking the streets of her station, Anyara had always felt it unfair that the habitats could never win, but today she belonged on the EA side.

Behind the circle of Councillors sat the advisors, the Councillors' own experts and political officers, with the Secretariat proper in a further circle at the back. None were allowed to speak unless invited to do so by a Councillor. They must not be forgotten, though. All were in constant com communication with their own Councillor.

Anyara and Seolta were escorted to a podium at the centre of the chamber, with the Secretary-General and her main advisors seated at desks below them. Anyara kept her eyes to the floor as they walked in, but standing at the podium, she had no choice but to look up. Her hand clenched hard on Seolta's. Every single front row desk was occupied, as well as the ranged tiers above. A full panel of representatives scrutinised them today.

"You wanted their attention," she said to Seolta. His eyes were moving around the circle, pausing momentarily on each face. They'd agreed that he was to start the talking as she had little experience of speaking to crowds, but she had warned him not to treat the representatives as competing businesses. He'd laughed, but she wasn't convinced he'd heed her warning. Now she watched as he assessed each person seated in judgement of them.

"We've got it," he said quietly to her. "They're all here, from the remotest station collective to the most complacent EA world."

The questioning began. The Secretariat officials had warned they would start with inconsequential ones, innocuous enough to not scare off any of the Council members. "But don't treat them as unimportant," the political advisor had said. "Nothing said in that chamber is unimportant, and it is all recorded for later dissection."

Breathing was as much as Anyara could manage at the moment, but she straightened her back and listened hard.

Then came a question for her. "You have produced a fine-sounding report, Messera Anyara."

"Thank you, Councillor." It was the representative from one of the EA worlds, one with considerable off-world trading interests.

"However, I understand this was your first visit to an EA world. We acknowledge your considerable expertise in habitat biome management, but how does that make you any kind of expert on what makes a whole planet work. You could be making the Arcadian situation look bad to ease your uncle's plans to expand into an EA world."

She shoved up her chin. "The principles are the same for a habitat and an EA world, though an EA world operates at a level of complexity not available to a habitat world. In regard to working for my uncle, please look at the information on the charges I have laid against my uncle. It is not likely that I would be working with him."

"Yes, yes, but you are his heir. There's no other family member. Any increase in his holdings will eventually profit you."

"If I survive long enough," she said, surprising herself at the amount of rancour she managed to inject into her voice.

Seolta put a hand on the podium. "As my wife, under Arcadian law the Messera is also my heir. Any action she takes against Arcadia will diminish my own holdings considerably. It's a fine balance, isn't it. Whether the gain in her uncle's estate can offset the losses in our joint estate."

"My report is generally in accord with the findings of Arcadia's own Ecological Survey Department and has been accepted by the Academy," said Anyara. "They have agreed to fund my ongoing research project into the application of the observed changes on Arcadia to habitat biome management."

A habitat councillor spoke up next. "On balance, you recommend retaining the existing settlers, despite their failings. Surely those failings suggest a dangerous arrogance in too many of them, leading to significant damage to Arcadia. The kind of damage to an EA world the Alliance cannot afford."

"Agreed," said another. "There are many from other habitat worlds only too ready to take their places on an EA world. Surely it's better to replace the current careless inhabitants with others only too willing to make a good home on such a world and treat it with the respect it deserves."

Anyara kept her face as unemotional as possible and spoke in the even voice of the expert, letting none of her terror show through. "Perhaps, but it is unlikely that habitat citizens would have the necessary skills or understanding of the way an EA world operates. I know I found it a shock, and part of my early training was with EA world bioengineers. As I said in my report, the sheer ignorance of habitat colonisers makes them more likely to be detrimental to Arcadia than beneficial."

The councillors looked like they wanted to argue the point, but the president refused, saying that the matter needed further consideration by a full Council and putting it down for the next routine session.

"The consequences of any decision on this are too far-reaching to be decided today. The Arcadian Council and the appropriate Alliance ministries may put their cases at that session. I hope that Messera Anyara will be available to explain any points at that time."

Anyara nodded agreement, thoroughly relieved at the temporary reprieve.

The president instructed the record to note it for the next session and went on to the next questioner in the list. Anyara didn't fool herself that the matter was settled, but she turned towards the man talking. Another habitat councillor, this one was thankfully more interested in her integration theories. A traditionalist focussed on his own habitats, a squabble about control of a fairytale EA world held little interest for him. Her studies, on the other hand, had strong implications for his world now. This was reality, for him and for the other habitats. She could see them all perking up and waiting to hear the outcome as he harrumphed at her theories and called her biome systems 'chaotic nonsense'.

"The councillor may wish to review the performance parameters of Kevand Station since the Messera took control of its biome," said Seolta. He had raised his voice slightly, and a number of previously scowling habitat councillors suddenly brought up their com files. Her work might be lauded by the Academy but that was no guarantee of its dissemination to the non-academic world.

One of them signalled a question. "Are these figures correct?"

"The files are fully verified by the Secretariat and the Academy," she said.

A summons came through on the main board and the head of the Academy stood. "The Esteemed Scholar's work has been reviewed and accepted," said the man. "Her current work project is aimed at exploring the kind of integrations she had introduced on her home station to create templates for use in other habitat types. The Academy has set up a team to work under the direction of the Messera. The councillor is free to review any of the publicly available research results at any time he wishes."

"And if the Council finds against both interviewees today and takes action to restrain them?"

"The team would have to be disbanded. The Esteemed Scholar's input is critical to its work."

"And improvements to biome management?"

"Would be seriously impacted, Councillor."

That set off a series of mutterings and com link exchanges going well up into the second row of advisors.

They tried a few more meaningless questions, designed primarily to trip her up and easy enough to deflect. Soon afterwards, they switched the attack back to Seolta. She saw his jaw relax and the most pernicious of smiles bloom on his face. She moved a fraction closer to him. She may be safe enough for now, but he wasn't, and he must remember that.

Seolta felt the brush of her hand against his thigh and interpreted it easily. She wanted him to be careful. But his future mattered to him only as it affected her, and the Councillors had already confirmed her importance. She was safe. Priority one achieved; now to make this bunch of self-seeking antiques do their job and keep Arcadia safe. The darts flowed ever quicker and more pointed in his direction. It was like a boardroom at full blast. He grinned inside.

A new councillor entered the fray, a man from a habitat world with trade links to Hilmar of Surned. "You ask us to believe this offworlder, this dubious outcast from Arcadia is innocent of any crime. He claims he didn't kidnap the Esteemed Scholar, yet by his own admission he is fully aware of the Messera's wealth and potential. She may be his heir under Arcadian law; equally, their law rules that the Messera's wealth becomes the joint property of both partners. This disgraced exile has managed to secure himself both a profitable income and a source of real power in the Alliance. All of which he is well aware of, by his own admission."

Seolta put on his serious face. "Did I know of the Messera's wealth and potential power—certainly. Is that the reason I married her? Not at all," he said more quickly than he wanted, but beside him he could see Anyara starting to open her mouth. He jostled her slightly, and she glared, then shut her mouth and her eyes widened.

"If you will refer to the files now being forwarded to you," he said after a glance at the benches. "It is a report from the Central Psych Unit." He thanked the roots Messera Yarma had insisted on this. He'd hated it, and Anyara had locked up tight afterwards. What lay between them was their own business. Except it wasn't, not here.

"Is the psych med available for interview?" said the suspicious councillor.

"She is outside," said the Secretary-General, voice unruffled. "I will have her called in."

Moments later, the tall, serene woman who had interviewed them walked onto the floor of the chamber. The councillor let her stand there as he slowly read through the details on her findings. No one else in the room seemed inclined to hurry it along, and too many eyes glinted as they trawled through this window into the precious gift Anyara had given him. The councillor lifted his head, putting a sneer on his mouth.

"A nice piece of work. Who paid for this, Messera?"

"The report was requested by and billed to the Council Secretariat," said the psych med.

Messera Yarma fixed what Seolta had come to think of as her 'stern mama' look on the councillor. "The Messera is routinely employed by the Secretariat for evaluations such as this. She is a fully qualified and eminent member of her profession and her reports have been used by the Council for many cycles. Does the Councillor wish to re-visit those evaluations also?"

"No, of course not, Messera Secretary, but in this case, we are dealing with a man skilled in deception. Messer den Coille managed to fool his own family."

"I can assure the councillor that I have dealt with similar individuals in the past," the psych med said, as serene as ever.

Another councillor signalled an interruption. "The Messera has been used frequently before and is well known. This delay is wasting time."

No one rose to support the first councillor, and Seolta began to breathe easier.

The habitat councillor scowled. "So did Messer den Coille kidnap Messera the Esteemed Scholar or not?"

"I am not a legal practitioner," the psych med stated. "However, there is no evidence of any captive syndrome in the Esteemed Scholar, or any other sign of coercion. The partnership was freely entered by both. There were outside influences, but the decision of each party was made primarily to protect the other. The relationship between the couple appears genuine. I see no reason for concern that there has been any abuse of power or manipulation by Messer den Coille. I concur that he is capable of doing so but has not in this case."

'I am not a good man,' he'd told Anyara, and the psych med had just agreed. He didn't know whether to be pleased or insulted. He risked a glance at Anyara, and caught the slight twitch of laughter at the corner of her mouth.

"I love you," she mouthed at him.

They were going to stay in that private place a very long time after this was over.

"Thank you," the Secretary-General was saying to the psych med, and the woman left.

Hilmar's stooge made some more comments and asked a few more questions, all of which left a nasty taste in Seolta's mouth and had Anyara blushing bright scarlet, her pale skin suffused with colour. The last one had Messera Yarma rising and calling a point of order.

"I would remind members that this is the floor of the Council, not a cheap streetside vidcast."

The councillor muttered something that could be mistaken for an apology, if you were generous, and subsided back into his seat. Seolta saw little sign of any sympathy among the other councillors, even the Surned one. The man had become clumsy in his attacks, the one crime Council members did not forgive. There were no more questions on their relationship.

That settled the kidnapping charge and counter charge. He ticked them off his list. Anyara's report was accepted and under consideration, with her position assured. Hilmar's embezzlement tacitly accepted, the charges of kidnappings to be left as unprovable and removed from Council consideration. Now for the real point of contention. The attacks by habitat corporate raiders on an EA world. He looked at the Arcadian Councillor and the man hit his speaker's signal in response.

"You have the reports of the earlier infractions which resulted in Messer den Coille's exile. Now we have the fraud case against the sellers of Restin. You all have a copy of the lab analysis and the evidential statement from Messer Bram den Coille, head of Den Coille, the makers of Festin. The so-called Restin samples, collected from various worlds, is indistinguishable from, and can therefore be presumed to be illegally acquired and on-sold Festin. You will also see the accompanying file showing that the collection of festia pollen, as well as the manufacture and distribution of Festin, are all recognised by Alliance law as being under the sole ownership of the

Den Coille company. The government of Arcadia is currently looking further into the matter of any internal infractions of Den Coille's commercial rights."

That would hurt Cumchdach and Anna. She was born den Falasch and her father was knee deep in this mess. Seolta always seemed to be hurting his older brother and wished he could do something about it. Cumchdach had stood by him so often in the past, the staunch and solid defender of his childhood, but Seolta had no illusions. Anna came first for Cumchdach and had done so since they had first met as teenagers. Anna might not know that, but Seolta and his family certainly did.

Cumchdach would have to sort out the Arcadian side. He'd have Marshal an Fallon to help, but sort it out he would.

As for the off-planet parties…

Another councillor had signalled to speak, representing one of the station conglomerates. "The companies reported as being involved are significant Alliance actors. This is a serious allegation with far-reaching consequences." Unspoken was the other investigation underway, the one into the Seolta's poisoning onboard the Fleet vessel and the attack on him in the race, all possibly involving the same companies. Seolta studied the faces on the benches, and saw only a tight-lipped hostility. To each other and to himself.

"It can't be that hard to duplicate a simple food ingredient," the station councillor added.

"As with any natural ingredient, it is neither simple nor readily duplicated without leaving unique tracers," said Seolta. "We have since collected Restin samples from many parts of the Alliance, all sold at cheaper rates than Festin by using local companies as the claimed supplier to avoid import taxes. Then we had them verified by those unique tracers. All the Restin found was derived from

Arcadian Mountainer region festia pollen, using Den Coille manufacturing processes and in Den Coille factories. We keep those very secure and the company has found no evidence of any commercial theft. This is Festin, bought at wholesale and distributed through usual channels, but later re-packaged and on-sold as Restin."

The councillor waved a hand in dismissal. "You're telling me your *secure* systems didn't pick up any inventory discrepancies between what you sold and what left your stores?"

"Not before this," he said grimly. "We have now. It was done by a company we trusted and which had access to our systems for normal commercial reasons. They abused that trust and Den Coille will deal with that. The fraud complaint was filed to halt the market demand for the fake product. We can stop this distributor, but we need to make sure no one else thinks to replace them."

The Arcadian Councillor broke in. "Festin is a major export earner for Arcadia. Any fraudulent abuse of that hurts my home world and my government takes it seriously. Fair trade rules are the basis of the Alliance. It cannot function if those rules are discarded."

Muttering filled the room, none of it happy. Seolta's mention of import taxes had clinched it. All of them were affected by that. Messera Yarma stood. "The Council will go into private session. All non-members are dismissed."

Before he had a chance to argue, Alliance troops escorted them both out of the chamber, followed by all the advisors and other hangers-on in the galleries. Only the members remained.

They were escorted to a side room and left to stew.

"What's happening," he tried to ask the Arcadian representative's advisor. The woman shook her head. She lifted her com and swiped her hand sideways. She was shut out from com communications too. She gestured to the troopers collected at the outer sides of the hall just before another squad came up.

"You will accompany us, Messers den Coille and Prithand2," said the leader.

He held frantically onto Anyara's hand as they were both taken to a side room and the door locked. For their protection, or to detain them? He wished he knew.

The waiting time stretched on. Plenty long enough to review every word said, and every possible nuance. His confidence sank with each reviewed phrase.

"What do you think?" she said.

"You're safe," he assured her.

"That wasn't what I was asking."

He stared at the floor. How could he tell her the truth?

She shot up. "I am not agreeing to anything that leaves you in prison or worse."

"You have to, my heart. I wish I could change the past, but I can't. I did betray my family and my planet. I did let anger make me stupid and work with your uncle and Alliance Deputy Malgrave to undermine the changes Arcadia needs, and I did go after your uncle for revenge. You mustn't pay the price." He reached for her. "What they said out there—all of it's true, and I can't truly claim to have changed. Not deep down."

"You wouldn't do any of that now."

"No, but only because I have a different set of facts to work on. If it meant protecting you, I would lie, grovel and twist the truth as much as ever. Those councillors can't be fooled. You heard them."

"I'm still not accepting any deal that doesn't protect you too."

She was so stubborn, his Anyara. She stood, hands clenched by her side, defying his words, reality and all those lauded councillors and administrators out there. "Who says they'll find against you? They believed you in the kidnapping case."

"They let it drop for reasons of political expediency."

"You're wrong," she said, before choking and burrowing hard into his shoulder. "Hold me please."

His arms locked around her. "Whatever you need, my heart. Forever."

After a long while, he persuaded her to sit with him. There was nothing in the small room, so they had to make do with curling together in a corner. The room would be packed with sensors, but he no longer cared. This could be their last time together. He held her tightly and told her tales: stories of childhood, memories of deals he'd won and deals he shouldn't have but for the short-sighted greed of his opponents.

When the door opened, he'd finally managed to make her laugh. A small, watery chuckle, but he felt as if he'd won a brilliant coup.

"Messers, the Council is ready for you again." The trooper looked too young for his role, heels clicking as he stared down at them, but he'd mastered the cold mask of the enforcement officer that gave nothing away. They scrambled up, pulling hair and clothes straight.

In the chamber, the representatives sat in their seats, faces still, while behind them the advisors, clerics, experts, hangers-on and other paraphernalia stared down at them, looking important and off-putting. Or that was the impression he gathered they were trying to send. Whether they achieved it depended on the state of the intended victim, and he was not about to cede them anything. Neither was Anyara by the jut of her chin.

He straightened his back. Whatever the outcome, he would go out as the husband of Messera Esteemed Scholar Anyara a

Prithand2. He lifted up his head and stared right back at them all as he marched in to take his place.

Anyara could smell the tension in the room. That indefinable mix of stale sweat too rapidly cooled by an over-efficient ventilation system and the sanitising filters used in crowded places. There had been a lot of talking and shouting in this room. At one end, the EA world representatives sat cold-faced while the habitat worlds clustered at the other. None seemed happy, but she couldn't discern the outcome. The habitats might cluster together, but their faces and bodies showed the opposite. There was precious little trust on offer in the chamber.

Her uncle's influence spread into many worlds, but had he overreached this time? She reached for Seolta, just for a touch of his arm, and he moved closer. She doubted few could read him here, not in this mood, but to her he looked like a man heading for his execution. They reached the podium and she grabbed at his hand under cover of the surrounding rim. Whatever the outcome, it applied to both of them. If the men and women of the Council didn't realise that by now, it's time they found out.

In front of them, the Secretary-General took her seat, settled herself into place and glanced at her advisors. Then she leaned forward and touched her com to the link panel. "Has the Council come to a determination on the matters presented?"

A man stood. The Council didn't have a prescribed leader, but there were clearly recognised senior members, either from strategically important worlds or by dint of their own personality, but who spoke for the Council varied. This time, it was the representative for a conglomeration of station hubs, ones which sat at significant trade junctions. "We have, Messera."

The Secretary-General and her advisors stayed seated but all around, Anyara felt attention crystallise.

"The Council has made the following conclusions," the man said. "On a number of charges, there appears to be conflicting evidence and insufficient clarity for a ruling. The matter of the fraudulent sale of Festin is to be left to the courts, but the rest are to be withdrawn."

Much as Seolta had predicted and as she'd expected. Bury the ones threatening inter-Alliance stability, but the fraud one was too contentious. Leave it for a court ruling, likely to be in Den Coille's favour, as a warning to any other company or world thinking to try the same. Messera Yarma had said the EA block's population vote outweighed the habitat's and she was proven right.

"However," continued the man, "the Council does view with some concern the actions of the principal parties involved in these matters. The Esteemed Scholar's work is critical to the well being of many habitat worlds and any interference in that work for partisan reasons is cause for concern."

Seolta tensed and she felt his hand clasp hers tighter.

"While the Messera Esteemed Scholar's new status as a citizen of the planet Arcadia can be seen as having positive benefits, granting her access for research purposes as she deems necessary, her recent connection to a known conspirator and her familial relationship to a party involved in the fraud claim does create difficulties. The Council will require mitigation of these problems."

She thrust forward on the podium, ignoring Seolta's grab to hold her back. "I am married to Messer Seolta den Coille. That is non-negotiable." She glared at the room. "Messer Hilmar a Kevand3 is my uncle, my mother's brother by birth. I can't change that either, but I will not give up my shares in the Kevand corporation. To do so benefits no one but my uncle. Furthermore, those shares are the only protection I can provide to my home, Kevand Station."

"The Academy has placed your station under the Council's protection. It is integral to your research project. You have no cause for concern there. As for the rest...."

She'd fired all her shots. This couldn't be the end.

Seolta touched her arm. "I may have a solution," he said to the room. The Council representatives didn't look convinced but waited. "Our marriage stands, as you heard. I can't convince the Messera Esteemed Scholar to change that, for which I am everlastingly grateful. However, the point at issue appears to be my profiting from her work and prominence. I will therefore rescind all claim to our joint marital properties, with the exception of my stake in Den Coille industries. That I will sell to my family and put the proceeds into a trust to benefit my wife and ensure I do not become a burden on the Alliance's funds. That should surely remove all conflicts of interest. Furthermore, there is my current sentence of exile from Arcadia. The Alliance may interpret that as it wishes, and confine me in whatever manner it sees best to protect the Alliance's affairs."

"No." She swung on him. "You can't do this."

"I can, my heart," he said softly. "You keep the benefits of being married to me without any of the repercussions."

"You're offering to go to prison, forever if necessary. I lose *you*. That's the only benefit of being married to you that matters."

"I'm sorry. I wish I hadn't done it all, but you mustn't pay the price."

A blank silence fell on the room, and she suddenly realised they were under a privacy cone. By the looks of the activity outside, it was to prevent them interfering in the Council's deliberations, not to let them have a last moment together. The Arcadian representative looked furious, and the ambassador leaned down to have a word. The representative's face settled into terse lines. Then he gave a brusque nod.

"Can you lip read," she said hopefully to Seolta.

"Not at this distance."

Then the privacy cone lifted and the volume of noise shattered whatever remnants of peace she might have held.

The station representative rose again. "The representative from Arcadia has offered a compromise. The Council will go into secure session to discuss it. In the meantime, all others are required to withdraw."

Guards marched towards the podium and snapped out an order for them to follow. Anyara's heart jolted. "Where are you taking us?"

No answer, not until they'd been marched out of the chamber and back down the connecting tunnels to that small and confining room. A senior Alliance Patrol officer walked in.

Seolta moved to stand in front of her. She was tempted to shove her way forward, but he'd probably push her back to safety behind him again. The situation was bad enough already. She wasn't about to be caught in a tug of war with the superior-faced officer.

"What happens now?" demanded Seolta.

The guards lined up across the doorway. She had a bad feeling about this.

"For your own safety, you will be held under Council control until it completes its deliberations."

Seolta snapped rigid. "Held where?"

"The Messera Esteemed Scholar will be transferred to the Academy."

That bad feeling went up a whole level higher. "And Messer den Coille?" she asked.

"Will be transferred to the holding unit of the Central penitentiary."

"No," she shrieked. She'd never get him out again.

"It's only short term," said Seolta, but she saw how pale he'd gone. He didn't believe that either.

"Take him back to the Council holding cells."

"It's no longer safe, Messera. Not now he's appeared in public."

"It's all right, *mo Graidh*," Seolta began, but before he could say more, the guards had surrounded him and marched him away while others circled her. He threw her back a harassed look, as if memorising her face, then twisted his head around and marched stiffly away.

Would she ever see him again?

Another prison cell. But this one wasn't like the others. This one felt permanent. A sleeper, cleansing unit and table, like all the rest, but this cell was marginally bigger. He'd paced enough cells to automatically size them now, and the one window, high up and barred, gave a view of buildings and the sky dome.

"Dinner's at fourth hour and there's an hour recreation afterwards. Later, you can join the others in the common room for it, after your quarantine and initiation period are completed."

"I'm held here only temporarily," he tried. The man ignored him.

"Your work roster will be provided after the system completes your assessment. You will receive a com message tomorrow advising you of the time and documents required. Your lawyer can have input but the system will need to be notified a standard day before."

His flat-voiced delivery completed, the man began to shut the door.

Seolta started forward, and a light blazed between him and the door.

"Stop, there's been a mistake. I'm not meant to be in the permanent side of the prison."

"They all say that," said the man, and slammed shut the door of his cell with an ominous thud.

The night took forever. Again and again, he tossed on the hard sleeper. Marginally softer than previous sleepers it may be, but it was nothing like his one back home, and all through the night, a low glow shone from the top corner of his cell. He was under full surveillance.

This will be your life.

Forever.

He could be free. All he had to do was renounce his marriage, renounce Anyara, leave her to the Academy. She was safe from her uncle; he'd achieved that at least. The Academy had no intention of losing any more of their profit to Surned's corrupt ruler.

She'd be safe. The Academy would find some way of getting her access to Arcadia. Roots, the Council could order it if necessary.

But she'd lose her citizenship. Arcadia would be lost to her as a sanctuary, and Anyara would think he didn't love her.

The night dragged on.

A night in her old room in the Academy did nothing to restore her. Where had they taken Seolta and what were they doing to him? The same guards came the next morning and brought her to that claustrophobic Council room. This time it was empty. They left her alone there, until the Council was ready for her, said the lead guard with a smothered sneer. So much for her vaunted importance.

The room hadn't felt so small with Seolta in it. She huddled in the corner. She'd only once felt this lost before. The morning they told her about her parents. The room even had that same chill. Not a real one. The temperature in a building like this would be held at constant office standard, but shivers racked her body and icicles pierced her skin.

Alone. She was alone again.

A sound from outside. Boots tramping. She scuttled up to stand facing whatever was to come. The door opened.

Seolta stood there. Shadows smeared his eyes and he stood as if holding himself up by sheer force of will.

He had never looked more beautiful.

She stepped forward, then began to run. He beat her, his arms flinging around her and his lips taking hers before she'd taken another step. Then he held her, his hands cradling her face. "You're alive." Then, "I love you, *mo Graidh*."

She dropped her head to his shoulder and the tears wouldn't stop. His hands soothed her, down and down over her hair, but it was his taut strength that dried them and, slowly, she lifted her head. "And I, you. I love you, Seolta a Manascraoch, and will to the end of my days. Never, *never*, let them make you believe otherwise."

He laughed, stilted, half choking, but a chuckle. "No one could make me believe that, my heart."

A cough from the doorway. "The Council is waiting, Messers."

Seolta put his arm around her waist and turned them to face the guards. "With a verdict?"

"That is for the Council to say," said the man. No more would any tell them until they stood again at that podium, facing out to the Council chamber. It was as full as last time, with a fraught silence making the air thick with tension.

The station representative rose as spokesman. The habitat faction still held the chair, then. Anyara's heart faltered.

"The council has decided as follows," he said, then paused, stringing out her nerves to near breaking. He coughed, eyed the room to ensure he had its full attention, and finally continued. "In the matter of the commercial fraud case, this can only be furthered on Arcadia. Any wider implications will need ongoing discussion and monitoring, but that is best managed by agreement among the various ambassadors involved."

Cynically, she doubted that was possible, but Seolta followed the man's words intently as if listening to a secret message.

"To facilitate this, Arcadia has agreed to modify the current exile of Messer den Coille. Given his intimate knowledge of the products and markets involved, he is appointed to a consultancy role on inter-Alliance trade, reporting directly to the Senior Commerce Principal of the Secretariat in conjunction with the Security branch. Arcadia has agreed to allow the Messer limited access to Arcadia to assist with the Esteemed Scholar's work there, subject to prior arrangement with the Arcadian Council." The Arcadian representative looked like he'd swallowed a mudslug. Anyara was still trying to understand what she'd heard. They didn't mean… The station representative continued speaking as if he hadn't just rearranged her world, turning to her. "The Messera Anyara will of course, continue her valuable work and is invited to return to her position at the Academy."

Anyara's jaw had dropped and she hastily pulled it back under control. "Did they just say what I think they said?"

Seolta looked more stunned than she'd ever seen him. He shook his head, and looked at the station representative. Then brought up his com with a shared screen and pointed at the playback. He set the words in writing and they read through them together. For once, he appeared lost for words.

She looked up again, suddenly desperate to grab this lifeline before someone snatched it away again. "We accept, most gratefully, Messers, with conditions." She set her shoulders. "It must be understood that I take the Academy position freely, and can surrender it at any time if I consider there is any sign of failure of good will by the Academy. It is not to be used to coerce either myself or my husband into any given course of action."

She saw the Academy officials in an upper tier gesturing frantically and tapping open their com channels. The lead representative glared in their direction, then looked around the chamber to call for a vote on it. She waited as the final tallies were gathered. How badly did the other habitat worlds want her work and how scared were the EA worlds of habitat invasion?

Then the representative nodded once. "The conditions are accepted." He cleared his throat, and her heart sank. There was more?

"The last matter to be considered is the status of Arcadia in regard to its environmental compliance. The Esteemed Scholar's report raises new options. The target date for full compliance to be achieved is therefore suspended and the order for the expulsion of settlers if there is no significant environmental change is to be further considered.

The Arcadian representative rose and formally accepted.

Seolta had won after all. Arcadia had a chance.

Messera Yarma rose and gestured to their guards. "The parties are free to leave the chamber. The Secretariat will make all further arrangements as necessary."

Days later, she still found it hard to believe. A trip home to Kevand Station had been arranged for later in the year cycle, and they were offered and accepted an apartment in the grounds of the Academy.

Much better than her old rooms, although she missed the familiarity of the battered walls and scratchings of past occupants. This had been recently renovated and was linked to her lab by a hastily built, covered passageway. For security reasons, they were told.

Better then, but not perfect. She still took delight in showing Seolta over her lab. He made noises of praise, which had her laughing. "It works splendidly," she told him. He looked sceptical, and gagged when she lifted the lid of the microbe bath to show off the latest batch of algae for her new waste reducer. "Aren't you beautiful," she cooed to the squishy mess. "Now back to sleep and grow, grow, grow."

"Must you talk to the stuff?" he said, moving to stand beside the air inlet screens.

She grinned. "They grow much better when they know they are appreciated."

He was about to say something, then looked at her face and shut his mouth, moving discreetly to the door. "Fine. Well done."

He was much happier in his own office, tracking down the trade routes of the false Restin with the Secretariat's Commerce branch. "The woman is more devious than I am," he said one day with a grin on his face.

"That is not supposed to be a commendation."

His grin only widened and she had to laugh. That evening, they sent a com to his family and next morning she sat with him as the reply came back. They had set the recording from the moment they opened his message, and she and Seolta used a holo. It wasn't quite the same as being among them, but if they refused to notice the time lags, it was near enough to bring tears to Seolta's eyes. She touched his hand to let him know she was there.

The family had all gathered in the main room, including Fee's husband Caleb and Cumchdach's wife Anna, now very pregnant.

The baby had been only a dream when they were last there, the only obvious sign Anna's dreadful morning sickness, but now she sat awkwardly on the couch. She had to be near her time. Anyara had taken a liking to the botanist and was stunned at how much time had passed, studying Anna's face and pleased at the healthy colour of it. Seolta was telling his father and brothers about the Restin case. Anyara was only half listening, but was still watching Anna's face, trying to work out dates, when a name was mentioned and Anna's face blanched.

"Falasch. My family?"

"May be involved," said Cumchdach guardedly.

The normally calm and self-contained Anna shoved her hand back against the couch and began to lever herself up. "May? No, you know something." She was still trying to stand up. Cumchdach rushed to help her, but she thrust back his hand and accepted Samhchair's help instead. "You think he's guilty." Cumchdach tried to touch her again, but she threw off his hand and hurried out of the room as fast as her ungainly body would let her. "Do not follow me," she told him. Not today…" Then she was gone and his face was stricken.

"You didn't tell her?" said their mother.

Cumchdach looked miserable. "She's been so ill, and what with the baby and all…"

"Is there any chance Eolas den Falasch isn't involved?" asked Caleb.

Cumchdach shook his head and their father looked grim. "Thanks to your information, Seolta, we now have enough evidence. We're changing distributors," said Bram den Coille.

"Ah. That will ruin den Falasch," said Seolta.

Anyara watched the family. "Surely it's not all that bad. Anna will come around. She's upset now, but she's expecting

Cumchdach's child. That must mean something," she said on a private link to Seolta.

Seolta was watching his brother with a sad look on his face. "There was no good way to tell Anna this, but he should have done it earlier. I warned him when we were there."

"This will hurt them badly."

"Yes." Seolta had hunched his shoulders. "I always seem to do that to Cumchdach. He is a good man, truly is."

She knelt beside him and put her arms around him. "You can't do anything to make it right. That's up to them. All you can do is work to find out the truth at this end."

Then Cumchdach stared directly at them. "This is on me, brother. Not you. I will find out exactly how much and why the den Falaschs are involved. You do your work and look after your wife; I will look after mine." With that, he left the room and no one stopped him.

"He's right, son," said Bram. "You've been given a chance here. Seize it with both hands."

His mother was the last to speak. "We love you, Seolta mar Bram an Scathach den Coille, and we are proud of you. Never forget that. And Sera Anyara, look after my son. He needs you."

Then it was the end. Seolta put the recording on hold, leaving the family standing in cameo, every single one of them staring in their direction.

"Your mother was right," said Anyara finally. "Your family is a rare treasure. You are lucky."

"I am." He turned in her arms, setting his lips on hers. Long moments afterwards, she drew back, "And she was exactly right, my heart. I need you. Now, tomorrow, and forever. Thank you, my love.

EPILOGUE

A door opened and Anyara turned to watch Seolta walk in. He was thinking of something, but seeing her, the smile bloomed on his face.

"How was the meeting?" she asked.

"As expected. Lose some, win some. I know they're taking action against Hilmar but no one's talking publicly. I swear Alliance Central officials are worse than those on Arcadia." Then he grinned, "I finally got them to agree to investigate Meth Varkan. They're to start before the next round of the Restin court case. And you? How did the Council hearing go?"

Seolta had been banned from the Council hearing into Arcadia's environmental status.

"You've got time, another two years, and they've agreed to reconsider the full expulsion of Arcadian settlers."

"Subject to review by an independent panel of off-planet auditors. Are you one?"

She laughed. "You have the full findings already."

He grinned back. "Marcus an Fallon commed me as soon as it came through. I had finally managed to surprise him and do something good, he said. Then he told me to thank you for saving our world." He grinned again. "I didn't ask him what the good was I'd done, but I suspect it was marrying you."

She could never have achieved anything without him, but she didn't have to tell him that. He was carrying something, she realised. "We're celebrating?"

"Definitely we are, my heart." He pulled out a very rare bottle of salaschar and, better still, a box of her favourite chocotabs. She was addicted to the candies since she'd discovered them in a Central store. "What have you there?"

She waved her com at him. "The latest report from your sister-in-law." Anna den Coille may have a suspect father, but the woman was a skilled botanist and shared Anyara's own approach to biomes. She was close to the end of her pregnancy but it hadn't stopped her agreeing to further Anyara's work on the farms of Deuteron. "She's sent out a crew of cadets to that farm we visited and is champing to get there herself."

A gust of laughter. "That must have made Cumchdach happy."

"Not so you'd notice."

"You are going to cause as much strife in my family as Fioruisghe."

She might have been worried if she hadn't seen the sparkle in his eyes. She liked his younger sister, but couldn't feel at ease with her in the way she did with Anna. Fee may share her passion for living systems, but she was a child of the wilderness, unpredictable and driven. Anna was quieter, more contained. She didn't leave you gasping for breath.

And Anyara sensed that Anna had a history that echoed her own.

Then Seolta opened the bottle and passed her a plate of chocotabs, before lifting her up and carrying her to the large and comfortable couch in their new Academy apartment. In no time, Anyara forgot about Anna, family, and troublesome biomes.

Many years ago, her home and family had been brutally ripped away from her.

Now she had found both again.

Thank you for reading EXILED. I hope you enjoyed Seolta's adventures as much as I enjoyed writing them down. He took me to more places than I'd ever imagined or expected. Please consider posting a review on your favourite book site. I appreciate all honest reviews.

Look out for Cumchdach and Anna's story, coming next in the Arcadia series.

They've been friends since middle school, lovers since adulthood hit with a bang, so why is marriage so hard?

Cumchdach den Coille has loved Ann den Falasch since he first met her. He would lay down his life for her, give her anything she wants. She married him but she doesn't seem to want him, and now her father has done his usual expert job of messing up her life. This time, the man is cheating Cumchdach's company and family. Cumchdach had always thought the man stupid, but now he's destroyed Cumchdach's marriage, and that is one theft he can never forgive — even if Anna doesn't love him as much as he loves her.

Anna den Falasch has loved the eldest son of the powerful den Coille family since she first met him. He likes her, wants her badly, takes for granted that she will be his partner in his family and business, helping run them as well as she does her home city. But never once has he said he loves her.

For advance notice of new releases, including Cumchdach and Anna's story, and special subscriber extras, sign up for my newsletter at https://www.subscribepage.com/mbj-landing-page and I'll send you a bonus, subscriber exclusive short story.

And if you enjoyed the Arcadia series, try my Hathe series for more edgy science fiction with a touch of romance starting with TOIL and STRIFE, the first book in the pair

ACKNOWLEDGEMENTS

With thanks to all those who have helped me bring "EXILED" to reality. Firstly to my amazing and hugely knowledgeable editor, Laura Daniel—any remaining errors are due to my stubbornness—and to Louise for her very helpful insights. To Amygdala Designs for my lovely cover. To Victoria who first set me on the right path to formatting. And to my fellow writers at SpecFicNZ, RWNZ and RWA, particularly the Auckland specficers and RWNZers: thank you for your generosity, your never-ending support, the laughter and the mutual moans, but most of all for helping me to believe I can do this!

Biggest thanks of all go to my family. To my parents, for raising me in a house full of books, taking us to libraries and taking it for granted that we would all get an education and be able to think for ourselves; to my sons who are always proud of what I do even when it seems weird to them; and most of all to my husband who is always there for me, even though I'm far away in my own world more often than not. Thank you all for your acceptance, for everything you've taught me over the years, and for the smiles on your faces when I really need them.